THE INFERNAL QUIXOTE

Frontispiece from volume 1 of the 1801 London edition. It depicts the scene in volume 3, chapter 17 (rather uncharacteristic of the novel as a whole) when Mr. Rattle and Mr. Harrety espy Emily and Nancy Evans on a Welsh mountainside: "Most sure they are Goddesses, or rather Angels." (By permission of the British Library: 12614.aa.22)

THE INFERNAL QUIXOTE
A Tale of the Day

Charles Lucas

edited by M.O. Grenby

broadview editions

National Library of Canada Cataloguing in Publication

Lucas, Charles, 1769–1854
    The infernal Quixote : a tale of the day / Charles Lucas ; edited by M.O. Grenby.

(Broadview editions)
Includes bibliographical references.
ISBN 1-55111-444-5

    1. Ireland—History—Rebellion of 1798—Fiction.   I. Grenby, M.O. (Matthew Orville), 1970–.   II. Title.   III. Series.

PR4894.L346I54 2004   823'.6   C2004-902688-7

Broadview Press Ltd. is an independent, international publishing house, incorporated in 1985. Broadview believes in shared ownership, both with its employees and with the general public; since the year 2000 Broadview shares have traded publicly on the Toronto Venture Exchange under the symbol BDP.

We welcome comments and suggestions regarding any aspect of our publications – please feel free to contact us at the addresses below or at broadview@broadviewpress.com.

North America
Post Office Box 1243, Peterborough, Ontario, Canada K9J 7H5
3576 California Road, Orchard Park, NY, USA 14127
Tel: (705) 743-8990; Fax: (705) 743-8353;
e-mail: customerservice@broadviewpress.com

UK, Ireland, and continental Europe
NBN Plymbridge, Estover Road, Plymouth PL6 7PY UK
Tel: 44 (0) 1752 202301   Fax: 44 (0) 1752 202331
Fax Order Line: 44 (0) 1752 202333
Customer Service: cservs@nbnplymbridge.com Orders: orders@nbnplymbridge.com

Australia and New Zealand
UNIREPS, University of New South Wales
Sydney, NSW, 2052
Tel: 61 2 9664 0999; Fax: 61 2 9664 5420
email: info.press@unsw.edu.au

www.broadviewpress.com

Series Editor: Professor L.W. Conolly
Advisory editor for this volume: Profesor Eugene Benson

Typesetting and assembly: True to Type Inc., Mississauga, Canada.

PRINTED IN CANADA

Contents

Acknowledgements

I am grateful to the British Library, whose copy of *The Infernal Quixote* was used to check the text. Above all, I would like to thank Jeanette Grenby, my mother, without whose patient and (surprisingly) uncomplaining transcription work this edition would not have seen the light of day.

M.O.G.
London

Introduction

For most of the two centuries since it was published in 1801, it has been easy to scoff at Charles Lucas's *The Infernal Quixote*. It has been dismissed as yet another production of the tawdry Minerva Press, the most notorious producer of popular, production-line novels in the late eighteenth and early nineteenth centuries. It has also been glibly categorized as a straightforward expression of reactionary political views, and, as a result, as uninteresting and unimportant. In recent times, however, both the popular novels of the Minerva Press and its competitors, and the conservative novels published in Britain during the French Revolution and its aftermath, have become the focus of an increasing degree of scholarly attention. *The Infernal Quixote*, as a splendid example of both these things, is well worthy of republication. But *The Infernal Quixote* is more than just a good example of a Minerva and an anti-Jacobin novel. It is also a "national tale," a novel of the Irish Rebellion of 1798, its narrative being as closely woven in with historical events as anything which Sir Walter Scott was to produce a dozen or so years later. And it might equally well be characterized as a "masculinist" novel, a religious novel, or a satire of contemporary society. Certainly, it is a novel of huge usefulness to students and scholars who wish to explore the values, prejudices and anxieties of a nation in the midst of a political and social crisis in the 1790s and early 1800s. Perhaps not the least of the reasons for reading *The Infernal Quixote*, though, is that, for whatever polemical purposes Lucas was writing, he managed to produce a genuinely entertaining novel.

Not a great deal is known about Charles Lucas. His entry in the *New Dictionary of National Biography* records little more than that he was born in 1769, that he died eighty-five years later, in 1854, that he was a minister of the Church of England, and that he published several novels and poems. His first work, *The Old Serpentine Temple of the Druids* (1795), a poem, sought to explain the huge neolithic-era stone circle, and the large complex of standing stones and artificial earthworks, in the midst of which Lucas lived as curate of Avebury. Following the pioneering investigations of the antiquarian William Stukeley, Lucas equated the religion of the "druids," for whom he thought the Avebury complex had been constructed, with a sort of primitive Christianity. His poem compared the lack of respect shown to modern-day clergymen with the reverence which, he inferred from the vast monuments at Avebury, had been accorded to the druids. The public's disdain of Church of England ministers was a theme Lucas returned to in his last publications, pamphlets on religious subjects published in the 1840s and early 1850s. In between, however, had come one much less cantankerous verse work, *Joseph: A Religious Poem*, and at least four novels. Other works have occasionally been attributed to Lucas, but in the preface to his final novel, *Gwelygordd; or, the Child of Sin*, Lucas stated unequivocally that he "has published [only] three novels before" (Appendix A).[1]

Two of Lucas's novels, *The Abissinian Reformer, or the Bible and Sabre* (1808) and *Gwelygordd* (1820), were published after the political crisis engendered by the French Revolution had passed. They satirized British society but were not so narrowly political that they could be considered a part of the "war of ideas" which raged in Britain in the 1790s and early 1800s. Lucas's first two novels, on the other hand, were deeply immersed in their political context. The first was *The Castle of St. Donats; or, the History of Jack Smith*, published in 1798. Like *The Infernal Quixote*, it combined an established fictional form—in this case, the gothic—with a blatant anti-Revolutionary and loyalist stance. This agenda was more explicitly spelled out by the title of the French translation of 1803: *Le Château de Saint-Donats, ou Histoire du fils d'un Emigré échappé aux massacres en France*. Having escaped the French Revolution while an infant, the novel's apparently orphaned protagonist underwent several adventures in foreign castles and amongst British political reformers until eventually ending up at the castle of St. Donats in Wales. There, he discovered his father, an émigré duke fled from Revolutionary France. Somewhat oddly, the duke is found living in a well, impersonating the castle ghost. Our hero's relationship to his father is proved not by a birthmark, nor by the sudden discovery of a long-lost letter—traditional literary techniques—but by the fact that father and son possess a pair of uniquely anti-Revolutionary artefacts: two crucifixes each containing a lock of the hair from every member of the deposed French royal family.

---

1 Peter Garside, with Jacqueline Belanger and Anthony Mandal, have suggested that Lucas wrote *The Faux Pas, or Fatal Attachment: A Novel [...] By C.L.* (1800) and *The Strolling Player; or, Life and Adventures of William Templeton* (1802). Robert Watt's *Bibliotheca Britannica* credits Lucas with having published *Free Thoughts on a General Reform in 1796* (R. Watt 2:620). This work does not appear to have survived.

It may well have been this combination of the fictionally conventional with an overt political loyalism which persuaded William Lane, the domineering proprietor of the Minerva Press, to publish the presumably unsolicited work of an obscure country curate. After all, Lane was well-known for both the conventionality of his publications and for his ardent political loyalism. He had, for instance, zealously supported Pitt the Younger's government against the reform-minded Foxites during the Regency Crisis of 1789-90 (Blakey 13). Moreover, he had advertised in 1794 that with the radical ideas encouraged by the French Revolution still spreading in Britain, he would be happy to publish works on "such subjects as tend to the public good" but that, he would "never convey to the happy subjects of this kingdom false founded doctrines or opinions" (Appendix B). This advertisement for suitable material, along with the fact that Lane had already published at least one ultra-conservative novel— Henry James Pye's *The Democrat* (1795)—was perhaps what encouraged Lucas to submit his manuscript to the Minerva.

Lucas further refined his method of fusing politics with fictional conventions in *The Infernal Quixote*, also published by Lane. What he produced was, in some respects, the classic anti-Jacobin novel. As many as fifty of this kind of politically and socially conservative novel were published in the five or so years on either side of 1800 (Grenby; Butler 88-123). Although their authors shared a broad agenda, they employed several different strategies to persuade their readers of the blessings of the *status quo* and to denounce the iniquity of the French Revolution and those who hoped to export it. Some anti-Jacobin novels concentrated on portraying the French Revolution, or revolution in another region or time period, and used fiction to dramatize the evils of such rebellions. Others sought to expose and ridicule the "new philosophy" of the French and British radicals, meaning everything from the scepticism of Hume, Voltaire, and Rousseau to the arguments for political and sexual equality of Tom Paine and Mary Wollstonecraft. Another group used the threat of revolution to argue against any change to the social hierarchy and, to justify this social immobility, demanded an immediate reform of the behaviour of the social élite. *The Infernal Quixote* did all of these things; Lucas was proud to admit it. *The Infernal Quixote* was "avowedly written against the modern principles of atheism and licentiousness, disguised as philosophy and liberty," he wrote in *Gwelygordd*. "The work was written," he added unequivocally, "to counteract the *revolutionary* mania among the community at large" (Appendix A).

That Lucas—a clergyman—thought that a novel was a fitting place to counteract the revolutionary mania is not, in itself, without significance. The novel—at least as it was discussed in moralizing sermons, contemptuous reviews, and angry letters to the editors of periodicals—was still regarded with suspicion in the late eighteenth century, something Lucas complained of in *Gwelygordd* (Appendix A; see also Heidler, Gallaway, and Taylor). Novels were widely seen as conduits for immorality and even sedition, especially because they were generally thought (however erroneously) to appeal exclusively to impressionable readers who were young, female, or lower class—or perhaps all three. Such readers would be unable, it was feared, to discriminate between fiction and real life, between good and bad books. The appearance in the early 1790s of a number of "Jacobin novels," most notably William Godwin's *Caleb Williams* (1794), increased anxiety about the dangerous effects of fiction on these new readers, even if the number and degree of radicalism of Jacobin novels was often exaggerated (Kelly). The result was a determination on the part of many conservatives to overcome their former disdain for the novel, and to produce fiction which furthered their own cause: "to parry the Enemy with their own weapons," as one anti-Jacobin novelist put it (Walker 1:6). In itself, *The Infernal Quixote* testifies that this was a conviction Lucas shared.

Many anti-Jacobin novelists, adding a more overtly political dimension to the format familiar from Jane Austen's *Northanger Abbey* (begun in 1798), delighted in dramatizing the dangerous effects of novels, and especially their propensity to seduce young women into sexual transgression and unorthodox political opinions.[1] Lucas also highlighted the political perils of reading, but chose to concentrate his fire not on novels, but on the radical political tracts which had begun to attract a wide audience in the 1790s, and which constituted one half of what is often referred to as the "war of ideas." *The Infernal Quixote* is littered with references to Tom Paine's *Rights of Man* (1791-92) and *Age of Reason* (1794-95), Mary Wollstonecraft's *Vindication of the Rights of Woman* (1792) and, above all, William Godwin's *Enquiry Concerning Political Justice* (1793-98), which Lucas evidently knew remarkably well.[2] The novel's eponymous anti-hero,

---

1   See for example the calamitous effect of novels on Bridgetina Botherim and Julia Delmond in Elizabeth Hamilton's *Memoirs of Modern Philosophers* (1800).

2   Godwin's *Enquiry Concerning Political Justice* originally appeared in 1793, and was heavily revised for a second edition which appeared in 1795 (although the title-page bears the date 1796), and again for a third edition

Lord James Marauder is depicted using these books to seduce the young Emily Bellaire. He employs Wollstonecraft's and Godwin's opinions on the independence of women, and on marriage (see Appendix C), to particular effect to persuade Emily to elope, marking sections of the text for her and leading a discussion of their meaning (83-85). Meanwhile, his rival and the hero of the novel, Wilson Wilson (so-named after a slip-up at his Christening reminiscent of Laurence Sterne's *Tristram Shandy*), sends other texts—by the politically conservative Hannah More for instance (77)—hoping to shore up her virtue. As well as dramatizing their effects on his characters, Lucas also cited, quoted from, and discussed the same texts in numerous footnotes. In doing so, he made the reader of his own novel the counterpart of Emily. Just as Marauder and Wilson had caught her up in this battle of the books, so Lucas envisaged his readers as being bombarded by dangerous texts, which it was his duty to warn against. His readers, he reasoned, must have been in need of books which could bolster their religion and loyalty. This is what provided the *raison d'être* for *The Infernal Quixote*. It is also what made the Minerva Press, supposedly patronized by the susceptible, new readers who were likely to be seduced by the "new philosophy," the perfect vehicle for Lucas's counter-offensive.

The "war of ideas" was being waged on many different fronts. Lucas chose to fight on just a few of them. His major accusation was that Godwin and Wollstonecraft taught sexual incontinence, something he dramatized in the seduction of Emily and in his depiction of the Cloudleys, who disguise their licentiousness behind a veneer of "new philosophy" (214-23 and 277-83). In fact, Book VIII of Godwin's *Enquiry*, in which he gave his views on marriage (an extract of which appears in Appendix C), quickly became one of the most controversial parts of the work, just as the moderate, reasoned arguments of Wollstonecraft's *Vindication* quickly became submerged in the general scorn for her perceived promiscuity as revealed in her

---

which appeared in 1797 (although the title-page is dated 1798). The page numbers Lucas cites in *The Infernal Quixote*, and textual variants in each edition, enable us to be sure that Lucas always quoted from the second edition. Since this second edition was reviewed only once (in the *English Review*, vols. 27-28), and since the passages from the *Enquiry* which Lucas quotes do not all feature in this review, we can be confident that Lucas was actually quoting from Godwin's book itself—presumably his own copy—and not from one of the lengthy digests which appeared in periodicals.

biography, written by Godwin in 1798. Godwin actually moderated his views on marriage in his revised editions of *Political Justice* (Philp 3:7-9), but by then the association between the 'new philosophy' centred on Godwin and the disruption of marital relations had become too firmly established, and too useful to the anti-Jacobins, to be dispensed with. After all, Godwin and Wollstonecraft were offending not only against the established laws and mores of society, but against the code of the novel too.

Godwin's suggestion that "The abolition of marriage in the form now practised, will be attended with no evils" (Appendix C) offended Lucas in two ways. On the one hand, Lucas took the paternalistic (he would have said chivalrous) position that were marriage to be abandoned, then just as surely as had happened in France after the Revolution (he thought), women would lose all their social status, even the "rights and privileges which the fair sex claim, as mothers, daughters, wives, sisters," and that they would be "no longer regarded, but as objects of sensual pleasure" (83). On the other hand, more generally, he understood the dissolution of the marriage bond as another example of a long-established pattern of behaviour being disregarded. Thus he has Wilson condemn Emily when, after she has eloped with Marauder, she leaves a note arguing that "If a person means to be happy, they must learn to think and act for themselves" and that "The prejudices of a misjudging world I despise" (89). It was this willingness to ignore convention, and to use reason, not tradition, to judge what was appropriate behaviour, that Lucas deplored above all else, wherever he found it. This is why he has one of his characters condemn the French Revolutionaries in the very same words Emily had used: "These fellows are determined to think and act for themselves, and are daily tumbling backward in every virtue and every science" (110). And thus, to take one further example, he condemns Methodists, for they ignore "the service of virtue matured by reflection"—that is to say, the Anglican religious rite, passed on through generations—preferring "the sanguine rhapsodies of an heated enthusiasm"—enthusiasm, in this case, being just as likely to lead to error as reason might (158). His position was deeply embedded in the "Revolution controversy" of the 1790s. Paine, in the political sphere, and Godwin, in the social sphere, had argued that each generation had a right, a duty even, rationally to redesign the laws and behavioural codes which governed their society, so as to accommodate their own needs. Edmund Burke, in his *Reflections of the Revolution in France* (1790), argued exactly the opposite. Each generation, he argued, received from its predecessors its laws and values as an *entailed* inheritance. No one, therefore, had the right to dismantle the constitution or social convention, and replace it with a system they had designed themselves. For Lucas, "new philosophy" did just this. He called it "A species of Wisdom, which man discovers by the aid of his own individual powers, corporeal and mental, without owning the aid of any superior Being" (174). In this respect, then, *The Infernal Quixote* was a thoroughly Burkean novel.

But Lucas's conservatism was not always as absolute as Burke's had become in the 1790s. The *Critical Review* professed itself puzzled that an ardent anti-Jacobin like Lucas could depict a humble carpenter's son—Wilson—becoming a model of virtue and valour, while showing Marauder—the son of an aristocrat and therefore the embodiment of the Burkean, hereditary social order—turn out a disgrace (Appendix D). Indeed, it comes as something of a surprise that, at the end of *The Infernal Quixote*, the hero is not revealed to be an aristocrat in disguise, as had happened in *The Castle of St. Donats* and as was so often the case with Minerva novels. As the *Critical Review* was hinting, though, Burke and his true disciples—anti-Jacobin novelists such as Sir Samuel Egerton Bridges and Robert Bisset—would never have countenanced such an infringement of the fundamental conservative conviction that the aristocracy deserved their place at the head of the social order. To say otherwise in such ticklish times, as Lucas was doing, could be regarded as an incitement to question the lack of flexibility in the hierarchy, which was precisely what the radicals were doing. One possible explanation of Lucas's lapse from conservative orthodoxy here is that he was influenced by the growing Evangelical movement. The Evangelicals, religious reformers working with the Church of England, contended that the best way to sustain the nation against the Jacobin threat was for individuals, and particularly the social élite, to reform their behaviour and rededicate themselves to their religion. Certainly Lucas has Wilson argue strongly against the latitudinarianism of Mr. Vantage, who contends that Christianity should be adhered to not because it is truer than other religions, or true at all, but because it has a pacifying effect on the population (163-65). Similarly, Lucas congratulates the (somewhat autobiographical) curate of Hazleton, Wilson's home village, for having prevented the Duke of Silsbury's gamekeeper from shooting on a Sunday: a favourite campaign of the Evangelicals (43). Whether tinged with Evangelicalism or not, *The Infernal Quixote* was unquestionably a religious novel. Lucas included elaborate set-piece debates in the novel to defend the importance of an established, state church (225-26) and to dramatize the gradual conversion of the sceptic,

Hambden Arnon, to Christianity (130-31 and 247-48). Tellingly, Lucas's most direct address to his readers, occurring almost at the close of the novel, did not warn of the danger of Jacobinism or "new philosophy." Rather, he preached a conventional religious sermon, reminding his readers to prepare for the hereafter (409-10).

Lucas preached this sermon just after his central character, Marauder, had thrown himself off a cliff to his death. It is a scene reminiscent of the close of *The Monk*, Matthew Lewis's notorious novel published just five years earlier. There, Ambrosio, an eminent leader of society turned to villainy, just like Marauder, had been flung into the abyss by the Devil. In *The Infernal Quixote* it is Marauder himself who personifies Satan. This has been clear even from the title-page: Marauder is, after all, the *infernal* quixote, and the novel's epigraph—"Better to reign in Hell than serve in Heaven," from John Milton's *Paradise Lost*—makes the correlation yet clearer. It is a quotation repeated at the crisis of the novel when Marauder finally determines that if he cannot gain a dukedom by legal means, he will switch to Jacobinism to advance his career: "since heaven was to him"—Satan—"a hell, I'll make the hell of democracy my heaven" (125).

The parallel between Marauder and Milton's Satan was, as Lucas was happy to admit, drawn from William Godwin's analysis of *Paradise Lost* in the *Enquiry Concerning Political Justice*, which Lucas quoted in an accompanying footnote. Godwin had sought to explain Satan's behaviour. Satan, he suggested, saw no reason for the unequal, unjust and unalterable hierarchy which existed in heaven, so he rebelled. Marauder, deprived of his expected dukedom, might well have done the same thing, Lucas tacitly asserted, but he subtly altered Marauder's reasons for rebelling. It was not the idea of hierarchy itself which Marauder disdained, but rather the lack of advancement which, in his precise circumstances, he was able to achieve. On the one hand, then, Lucas continued to insist on the parallel between Marauder and Satan. It was a comparison which formed the foundation for the entire novel and was designed to deepen the reader's contempt for Marauder and his Jacobinism. On the other hand, though, Lucas succeeded in presenting Marauder as acting not from the same noble motives for which Godwin had congratulated Milton's Satan, but out of pure selfishness and the desire for personal advancement. Marauder did not bridle at inequality, but rather revelled in it. He adopted "democracy" and "new philosophy" only when his other avenues of advancement were blocked, and to achieve the power (political and financial, as well as sexual) which he felt he had been denied. This being the case, the title's designation of Marauder as a "Quixote" becomes ironic. A quixote—from Cervantes' *Don Quixote* onwards—is defined by his or her naïve idealism. Accordingly, Milton's Satan, as read by Godwin, might conceivably be accounted quixotic. Marauder certainly was not, for his adoption of Jacobinism was deliberate, cynical, and misanthropic. The novel might, with less irony, have been called "The Infernal Machiavel."

The most memorable sections of *The Infernal Quixote* are the bravura set-piece exposés of Jacobinism and the half-comic, half-serious depictions of British radicals meeting in London. It is these which give us such an unusually transparent view of the way that ordinary conservatives regarded the French Revolution and British radicalism in the years around 1800. At one point, for instance, Lucas dramatizes the meeting of a reforming society, modelled on the London Corresponding Society (LCS), or perhaps one of the many other artisan and working-class groupings which flourished in the early 1790s (166-70). The LCS was founded to discuss and encourage constitutional reform. For a fee of a penny a week, its members could attend two sorts of meetings—administrative assemblies which debated the management of the Society, its correspondence, publications, and so on, and which appointed delegates to the central committee, and the Sunday night meetings at which political texts and ideas were discussed. It is presumably the second of these which Lucas represented in his novel. What limited evidence of LCS activity is available suggests that Lucas severely travestied their meetings. Most LCS members were politically moderate, and they aimed for political reform rather than religious upheaval, as their publications clearly show (see Appendix E). On the other hand, Lucas does give a flavour of the LCS meetings. A chairman, such as Lucas presents, was supposed to prevent interruptions and to limit speakers to one contribution on any given subject and to speeches of no more than ten minutes (Thrale xxv-xxvi). In any case, however accurate a description Lucas provides of the way such corresponding societies were actually run, he reveals a great deal more about how anti-Jacobins like Lucas imagined these groups to be. Apart from the fact that he represented them as discussing religious matters, Lucas characterized those who attended these meetings as hiding their treasonable intentions behind the "plea of a fair debate" (166) and as extremely worried about the infiltration of their society by government agents. The members worry that Lucas's protagonists are spies, and they fret about what they have said, hurriedly leaving, "lest some treason should have slipped out" (170).[1] Thus, subtly, does Lucas convey his opinion that the society's members know they are guilty of treason, only hiding behind the pretence of enlightened debate. In essence, what Lucas was providing with his description of the reforming society was a defence of the "Two Acts" of 1795 which, partly in response to the London Corresponding Society's mass meetings, had banned political meetings of fifty or more people and had made it treason even to suggest using force to change royal policy or to incite hatred of the King, the government or the constitution.

The second volume of *The Infernal Quixote* also contains Lucas's two celebrated set-pieces, both of which give the impression that they were written somewhat earlier and then shoe-horned into the narrative. The first is the "Double Oration" (162-63), purporting to be an agitator's speech, which, by substituting certain words as directed, could serve equally as a call to arms for Jacobins or a fiery sermon to religious "Enthusiasts" (that is to say, Methodists). Lucas doubtlessly intended the Oration to be humorous, but it also effectively makes several didactic points. The hero's friend, Rattle, uses it as his final proof that Enthusiasm and new philosophy were to all intents and purposes the same thing: nothing but vanity and empty rhetoric. The Oration's very existence, though, was also supposed to demonstrate that those who professed to be either Methodist preachers or radical democrats did not actually themselves believe in what they preached. The Oration only existed, Lucas implies, because its owner would use whichever version was most likely to hoodwink the audience.

The same point was made by Lucas's second elaborate set-piece, the vast taxonomy of British radicalism which takes up a substantial part of volume two (172-99). As with the Double Oration, this enumeration of all the varieties of Jacobinism was designed to be comic. It was also supposed to exhibit Lucas's learning, for he illustrated his various categories of radicalism with references to recent literary controversies and scientific developments, as well as to classical mythology, the Bible, and the writings of his more frequent targets: Godwin, Rousseau, Voltaire, Paine, and Hume. Moreover, Lucas must

---

1 It was with good reason that the LCS was worried about spies. The Society was infiltrated by government informers, and several of its leaders were charged with high treason in the notorious trials of 1794—they were acquitted—and again in 1798, when they were held without trial for, in some cases, several years.

surely have designed his investigation of the extent of radical thought simultaneously to worry readers—that Jacobinism was so prevalent and extensive—and to soothe them, for if the whole Jacobin matrix could be classified and explained, then it could be controlled and countered. Above all, though, what this taxonomy of Jacobinism was designed to reveal was that the radical critique of society, from whichever stable of radicalism it came, was not a cogent, coherent, rational political philosophy, but instead, simply a means of clothing vice. Lucas was endeavouring, he said, to "shew the *natural* (not acquired) class to which the numerous tribe of *Volunteer Philosophers*, male and female, belong" (173). He was convinced, in other words, that to be a member of the "Peripatetics," the "Reasoners," the "Nothingers," or any of the other categories into which he divided radicalism, was not an act of choice nor a reasoned response to the current state of the nation. Rather, new philosophers were born possessing the characteristics of one or other of the groups which Lucas described, just as surely as men and women were born wise or foolish, virtuous or vicious. That they later adopted highfalutin names and retrospective rationales for their behaviour did not alter the fact that they had merely found a congenial home for the foolishness or wickedness of which they had always been guilty.

Lucas's categorization of Jacobinism was idiosyncratic and perhaps rather facetious. On the other hand, it was not more far-fetched than the conspiracy theories widely circulating in the later 1790s which alleged that a secret society called the Illuminati had joined forces with Jesuits, free-masons, political philosophers, atheists, and others in an attempt to undermine religion and government throughout Europe. In fact, Lucas's taxonomy of Jacobinism uses many of the same terms as the Abbé Augstin Barruel's *Memoirs, Illustrating the History of Jacobinism*, his exposé of the grand conspiracy, and was almost certainly partially drawn from it (see Appendix F).[1] Indeed, much of Lucas's information on the United Irishmen might also have come from a fifty-page "Note" added to the fourth volume of the English translation of Barruel which strove to prove that the Irish Rebellion was merely another part of the great, international conspiracy. What is curious, then, given that Barruel seems to have been such a large

---

1   Besides Barruel's *Memoirs*, the well-known texts "exposing" the grand conspiracy were William Playfair's *The History of Jacobinism* (1795) and John Robison's *Proofs of a Conspiracy* (1797). Lucas was evidently familiar with at least Robison's book, for he quotes from it (101).

influence on Lucas, is that *The Infernal Quixote* treats the Illuminati-Freemasonry-Philosophes conspiracy so lightly. Lucas's tone is far lighter than Barruel's, and his taxonomy of Jacobinism has a certain whimsical quality. He seems also to dissent from Barruel, who insisted that the Jacobin activists did nothing which was not long premeditated (see Appendix F), by showing Marauder to have been nothing but an opportunist whose Jacobinism was a response to his particular changing circumstances. Moreover, Lucas seems deliberately to have undermined the nation's peril with his depiction of a meeting of an Illuminati-like secret society in London (208-11). During his initiation, Harrety is blind-folded, sworn-in by men in bizarre masks, menaced by daggers, and shown a skeleton and a rotting corpse: the fate, he is told, of any initiate who betrays the society. At first sight this seems to dramatize Barruel's warnings and to be designed to disquiet the reader. A few pages later, however, Lucas's revelations that the skeleton was purchased from a local surgeon, that the corpse was merely overstock from a famous museum of waxworks, and that the whole brotherhood could be broken up and scattered by a few officers of the law, makes the episode seem rather farcical.

What the men in masks, the daggers, and the waxwork corpse indubitably bring to mind is the paraphernalia of the gothic novel. Even the explanation that the rotting corpse is actually a waxwork is reminiscent of the "explained gothic" which Ann Radcliffe used to such acclaim in the 1790s, and in particular of the "rotting cadaver"—actually made of wax—in her *Mysteries of Udolpho* (1794). It has been suggested that there was a natural affinity between the anti-Jacobin and the gothic (J. Watt 42-69; and see also Clery 156-71). It might also have been the case that Radcliffe's explained gothic appealed to Lucas because it enabled him to solve the central dilemma of all anti-Jacobin propagandists, namely that they had to construct the Jacobin menace as worrying enough to persuade readers to be on their guard (and to take these anti-Jacobin novels seriously), while simultaneously scorning Jacobinism as incoherent and irresolute, led by incompetent and self-seeking rogues, and able to be dispelled with reassuring ease. Just as Radcliffe had done, Lucas scared the reader—with a wax effigy, with an armed, secret society meeting in the heart of the nation's capital—and then, once the effect was achieved, he explained that the spectre he had raised was not really so frightening as it had first appeared and could easily be explained away.

It also seems likely that with these ostentatiously gothic touches,

Lucas was deliberately trying to engage what he thought would be the typical Minerva Press readership, trying to maximize the appeal of his anti-Jacobin propaganda. The Minerva Press, after all, was notorious for the many supposedly imitative gothic productions which dominated the literary market-place in the late eighteenth and early nineteenth centuries (as the titles listed in Appendix B bear out; see also Blakey, and Clery 135-38). Readers of Minerva books were usually envisaged as women. Lucas himself apparently thought that the audience of his novels was "at least nine tenths" female (Lucas 1:xlvi). This makes the introduction of so much politics into the novel even more significant, for Lucas clearly had few qualms about politicizing what he took to be a largely female readership. It also makes the rather masculinist tenor of his novel somewhat surprising. This is not to say that Lucas was a "masculinist" in the same way that Mary Wollstonecraft, say, was a feminist. Rather, it might be said that *The Infernal Quixote* is a masculinist novel because throughout, Lucas might be considered to be writing largely for a male audience. This is manifested in several ways. Most novels of this period included a fairly standardized description of the physical appearance of the heroine and often emphasized her "inner" beauty. Fairly typical is Radcliffe's description of Emily in *Udolpho*: "lovely as was her person," the reader is told, it was often more "the varied expression of her countenance," that "threw such a grace around her" (Radcliffe 5). Lucas's descriptions of his heroines, particularly Fanny, are in the same mould, but are noticeably more salacious:

> Her clear complexion was animated with the glow of health, and here and there the transparent skin discovered the purple veins. Her countenance open and engaging, invited love; while her forehead, of a charming form, was the very emblem of dignity. Her hair, fine and dark, flowed down her polished neck and shoulders in beautiful ringlets; her nose was a model of the Grecian; her eyes black, with long lashes and arched brows, were mildly bright, yet they rolled not with a voluptuous round, but by their penetrating steadiness, commanded respect from every one. (364, and see 63-64)

This, it might be suggested, is a portrait rooted in concupiscence. Certainly, Lucas is inviting the reader, male or female, to objectify his heroine. Moreover, Lucas frequently describes—in rather lurid terms—the effect that the appearance of his female characters has on his male protagonists. Seeing "the opening beauties" of the fourteen-year-old Fanny, "suddenly raised [Marauder's] passions"; the reader is told: "the opportunity which offered, he could not resist, the temptation he could not withstand" (152). In fact, Marauder's attempted seductions of Emily and Fanny are viewed entirely from the male perspective—from the perspective of Marauder within the text, and from the perspective of a male reader outside it. More especially, the didacticism inherent in these episodes is directed wholly at male readers, who are urged not to use "new philosophy" to undermine the virtue of women. Emily, and to a lesser extent Fanny, are viewed as passive figures, for whom Lucas has no lesson. This contrasts markedly with female characters in many other contemporary anti-Jacobin novels (not all of them written by women). In Elizabeth Hamilton's *Memoirs of Modern Philosophers* (1800), for example, both Bridgetina Botherim and Julia Delmond are reprimanded for reading the novels and the "new philosophy" which will make them easy prey for villains like Marauder. In *The Infernal Quixote*, though, Lucas does not expend effort to teach female readers to avoid the fate of Emily, just as he does not actually directly attack the writing of Wollstonecraft, preferring to stigmatize her merely as an accessory— almost a dupe—of Godwin.

Lucas's inclusion of so much recent history in his novel—almost the whole of the third volume is taken up with a minute description of the Irish Rebellion of 1798—might also be taken to indicate an attempt to "masculinise" the novel. After all, Sir Walter Scott has frequently been seen as attempting to overcome the low status of the novel, and particularly its association with female readers, by appropriating what was probably the most respectable literary discourse of the Enlightenment: historiography. On the other hand, it might be argued that the obverse is true: that Lucas was not historicizing fiction so much as fictionalizing history. His description of events in Ireland is surprisingly accurate, but it is perhaps the greatest achievement of *The Infernal Quixote* that it is so well integrated into the novel's narrative. Certainly, Lucas's decision to set so much of his novel in Ireland enhanced the efficacy of his propaganda. As Nicola J. Watson has pointed out, "Ireland could be imagined [...] as a locus at once of foreign and domestic revolution," which was why "the struggle between Jacobin and anti-Jacobin narratives migrated rapidly and comfortably" across the Irish Sea (Watson 112). For Lucas, this meant that a Jacobin revolution could be presented as both near enough to be alarming, and distant enough to encourage his readers with the thought that Great Britain, with a loyal population, a good government and healthy institutions, could never be so frail and corrupt as to succumb to rebellion herself. To say otherwise would have been tantamount to admitting that the radicals had a point, and that major institutional changes needed to be made.

The Irish Rebellion broke out in 1798, but it had been brewing for several years. As in mainland Britain, long-standing grievances had been inflamed by the outbreak of the French Revolution. An alliance between newly confident political radicals, many of them influenced by Thomas Paine, and the historically oppressed and residually dis-contented sections of Irish society, mainly poor Catholics, resulted in the formation of a new political society: the United Irishmen (U.I.). As their early manifestos make clear (one of which is reprinted here as Appendix G.1), the U.I. aimed principally for a reform of the Irish Parliament.[1] Many of the U.I.'s supporters, though, had more local-ized, economic and sectarian objectives. By the mid-1790s, the U.I. leadership was looking to the French for the military support which would overthrow the established regime. This was almost forthcom-ing in December 1796 when a large invasion fleet was only prevent-ed from landing at Bantry Bay, in south-west Ireland, by severe storms. Threatened with internal sedition and foreign invasion, the Irish government responded with rigorous coercion. General Lake conducted a brutal campaign against the U.I. in 1797 and early 1798 which was partly successful and partly responsible for heightening the rebels' resolve (see Appendix G.2).

Although French military support was deemed by many of the U.I. leaders to be necessary if the regime was to be overthrown (and if the fury of the peasantry was to be controlled after a successful insurrection), the decision was finally taken to rise without external support. The rebels' action was disorganized and sporadic, partly because of the arrest of many of the Rebellion's leaders, including the charismatic Lord Edward Fitzgerald, before the day fixed for the uprising. The rebels won minor and short-lived victories in the counties to the north and west of Dublin, but it was only in Wexford, in south-east Ireland, that they made substantial progress. Several towns were taken by the rebels and government troops were held at bay for almost a month. However, the Wexford rebels were isolated from outside support and the rising was finally crushed on 21 June at Vinegar Hill. Two months later—two months too late—the French

---

1 Until 1801, Ireland had its own Parliament which operated under the sovereignty of George III, and also under the sway of British government, which appointed the Lord Lieutenant of Ireland. The Irish Parliament's members were drawn only from amongst Protestants and the wealthy.

landed, at Killala Bay in the north-west of the country. After an initial victory at Castlebar they were defeated on 8 September at Ballinamuck, few Irish rebels having joined them. The Rebellion had been defeated (for more on the Rebellion see Curtin, Dickson *et al.*; Eliot 1982 and 1989; Gahan, Keogh and Furlong; Pakenham, and Whelan).

Although these events had taken place two or three years before the publication of *The Infernal Quixote*, they would certainly have been fresh in Lucas's readers' minds. One of the major consequences of the failed Rebellion—the Act of Union which abolished the Irish Parliament and integrated Ireland into the United Kingdom—had come into effect only on 1 January 1801. The causes and course of the Rebellion were still matters of public debate, and Lucas would not have had difficulty finding material to draw on for the novel. He took "the political facts" of the Rebellion, he remembered in the preface to *Gwelygordd*, from "state-papers" (Appendix A). He was probably referring to the *Report of the Secret Committee of the House of Commons*, composed from the confessions, made before the Irish Parliament, of several of the Rebellion's leaders, to which was added a compendium of U.I. publications (two of which are reprinted in Appendix G). These reports were widely published in Ireland and Britain and Lucas would have had easy access to them.[1] Being confessions, made to save their authors from trial and execution, these documents were not wholly trustworthy, especially in their representation of the motives of the rebels. The deponents admitted that the U.I. leaders had merely used the campaign for political reform as a cover for their real, revolutionary aims, and that their main aim was to nationalize the property of all above a certain rank. Further, they revealed that it had been agreed as early as 1796 that physical force was the only way to achieve redress of their grievances, and that military training, and negotiations for a French invasion, had commenced in that year. They blamed the French for not having arrived on time, and the U.I. leadership for not having given the signal to rise in rebellion sooner (Packenham 290). Lucas swallowed these accounts whole, or at least affected to do so. They were incorporated wholesale into his novel, having been fused with the paranoid

---

1   He cites the *Report of the Secret Committee* documents in a note: 328n.
    Much of the information Lucas took from the *Report* was also reprinted
    in the concluding "Note" to vol.4 of Barruel's *Memoirs, Illustrating the History of Jacobinism*.

conspiracy theorizing of Barruel and transposed into Lucas's own idiosyncratic terms:

> The *real intentions* of the Union were only known to the leading members; and, *by their own confessions*, have at length appeared to be (what every rational man from the first supposed) the introduction of that no-principle of the French, which seeks the gratification of its own interest, without any regard to the laws of God or man, and which has already been so fully defined under the term DIABOLISM. (275-76)

Marauder—or McGinnis as he became in Ireland—slotted easily into a movement such as Lucas represented the U.I. to be. As soon as he renounced his aristocratic pretensions, he was recruited to the cause, his Irish friend Fahany enticing him with the news that the U.I. planned "to separate Ireland from this country" and particularizing "the glory, wealth, and power which must necessarily accrue to the daring leaders of the multitude" (141). To emphasize the personal profit which Marauder—and by extension all U.I. leaders—hoped to reap from the Rebellion, Lucas depicted Fahany and Marauder obtaining as many mortgages on their Irish property as they could, secure in the knowledge that once they had "freed St. Patrick's noble country," all debts would be wiped out (142).

Lucas was guilty of taking at face value a very prejudiced construction of the Irish Rebellion, and then warping it further to fit the aims of his novel. Yet otherwise, his treatment of the events, ideas and even the technicalities of the Rebellion was historically very well grounded. Lucas went to great pains to describe the U.I.'s "affiliating system," its political and military chain of command, from the Lower Baronial Committees to the General Executive Directory (274-75; it should be noted, however, that this hierarchical structure was cited by Barruel's translator as one proof of the U.I.'s affinity to the Illuminati and freemasons: Barruel, "Note"). Partly, no doubt, Lucas went into so much detail for purposes of verisimilitude, and to reinforce the reality of his characterization of the rebels. It must also be seen as an attempt to lay bare the danger of the Rebellion, but then to anatomize it, and thereby neutralize it, in just the same way that Lucas's taxonomy of Jacobinism had been designed both to alarm and reassure readers. This same intention simultaneously to frighten and comfort the reader explains what was perhaps the most surprising part of Lucas's description of the Rebellion: his apparent criticism of the U.I. leadership for not organizing the Rebellion as well as might have been expected. He has Marauder criticize the U.I. Directory's tactics on several occasions—when they use the newspapers to publicize their strength and intentions, and thereby warn the government; when their concern for their imprisoned comrades dissuades them from rising even though the nation is ripe for rebellion (271 and 312)—and he concludes that Marauder's ambitions "seemed to meet with no check but from the timidity of his own party" (301). One would have thought Lucas would have delighted in the failures of the rebels. Instead, he chose to show just how narrow an escape Ireland had had, and that it was in no way due to the efforts of the government or the army that the Rebellion had not succeeded.

Lucas's decision to locate his anti-hero's activities in County Tipperary is also rather curious, for historians agree that "no rebellion of serious proportions manifested itself there in 1798" (Power 302).[1] This is not to say that Tipperary contained no rebels. In fact, the U.I. had made substantial progress in spreading the affiliating system to the county. Full-scale rebellion was probably only prevented because insurgency became manifest there too soon—in 1797 and early 1798—and the county was consequently ruthlessly suppressed by the local sheriff, Thomas Judkin "Flogger" Fitzgerald (Hayes i).[2] These tactics were so successful that there was no full-scale rising when the Rebellion was finally declared nationally in May. Lucas's

---

1 It is possible that Lucas chose Tipperary because he considered the recent history of the main sites of rebel activity—Kildare and Wexford—too well known by his readers for him to be able convincingly to introduce Marauder as a fictional rebel general. Alternatively, it may have been that Lucas chose to set his fiction in Tipperary because he believed it to have been one of the hot-beds of revolt. This impression might have come from the testimony of Thomas Judkin Fitzgerald who was called on several times, during 1799, 1800, and 1801, to defend the extremely severe methods of suppression he had used there. As Thomas Power writes, Fitzgerald "found it necessary to construe retrospectively the existence of a rebellion in Tipperary in 1798 as a cover for his actions" (Power 318). Reading accounts of these trials in the newspapers while he was writing *The Infernal Quixote*, Lucas might have thought Tipperary the perfect setting for his depiction of U.I. activity at its most extreme.

2 Tipperary was "proclaimed" on 2 April 1798, making it subject to government legislation against insurrection (36 George III, c.20) which imposed a curfew and arms searches, and authorized the death penalty for administering illegal oaths. A further notice was issued on 6 April, requiring all stolen arms to be handed in within ten days, or troops would be quartered on the population. See Power 314.

version of Tipperary history accords with this very well. Although Lucas introduces Marauder into historical events from the attempted French landing at Bantry Bay in 1796, which he proposes to assist (268-69), to the actual landing, almost two years later, at Killala Bay in August 1798 (319), most of the outrages perpetrated by Marauder occur in the months before the outbreak of the Rebellion proper. Typical is the storming of the town of Cahir in southern Tipperary in March 1798. Lucas's description matches almost exactly those given by historians. Here, for instance, is Thomas Packenham's account:

> About one o'clock in the afternoon of March 28th, a body of nearly a thousand country people led by officers dressed in blue and scarlet regimentals, marched into the town of Cahir in Tipperary and, having posted guards at the avenues, proceeded from house to house disarming the inhabitants. They surrounded the house of the local magnate, Lord Cahir, and stripped this too of all its arms. And then, after an address by their commander, warning his men against any deeds of violence, they marched peacefully away again. (Packenham 56-57)

It matches in all important regards the description given by Lucas save only the number of rebels (and this is a matter which historians have disputed[1]):

> In a little time M'Ginnis [i.e. Marauder] had above a hundred horse under his command, and infantry to a very large amount, armed promiscuously. So strong did he consider himself, that, having arranged his plans with some of his neighbouring Officers, he joined them early in the month of March with a respectable body of cavalry, and invested the town of Cahir, in the county of Tipperary. This he boldly did in the open day; and, with the utmost order and discipline, searched every house for arms and ammunition, and carried the whole away with him. (301)

If the research which Lucas must have conducted to represent the Rebellion so accurately is impressive, so is the restraint he showed in

---

1   Power says that various contemporary estimates put the figure at between 300 and 800 (313). Hayes adds that the raid was organized by the Clonmel branch of the U.I., possibly led by one Philip Cunningham (36-37).

not making Marauder into a paramount leader of the rising, whose actions outstripped anything which actually took place in 1798.

Lucas's very firm contextualization of Marauder's activities in Tipperary also serves to distance the character of Marauder from the real-life U.I. leader, Lord Edward Fitzgerald. Why Lucas should have wished to do so is obscure. Perhaps he wished to prevent the admiration which many contemporaries felt for the gallant, charismatic and glamorous Fitzgerald from attaching itself to Marauder. Without Lucas distancing his anti-hero from Fitzgerald it would certainly have been natural for readers to associate the two. Fitzgerald was the son of the Duke of Leinster while Marauder was nephew to the Duke of Silsbury. Fitzgerald had fought as a loyalist during the American Revolution before being dismissed from the army in 1792 for his vocal support of the French Revolution and joining the U.I. in 1796 (Tillyard). Marauder had converted from the cause of "aristocracy" to "democracy" at about the same point in time. Long after publication, Lucas asserted that his characters in *The Infernal Quixote* "were almost all drawn from the etchings of real life" (Appendix A). He cannot have been unaware of the parallels between Marauder and Fitzgerald, and of the glamour which might attach itself to a novel which alluded to one of the most notorious characters of the age, but the care he took to distinguish between Fitzgerald in Dublin and Marauder in Tipperary might be taken to suggest that he had another real-life model for his character. If so, this is most likely to have been Hervey Montmorency Morres, or Morris (1767-1839), the U.I. representative for Tipperary from May 1796 and the commander of a group of rebels in Nenagh, a town in the north-west of the county—precisely where Marauder is reported to have had his estate (263). Morres had initially fought with the Austrian army against the French Revolution, but switched in 1796—like Fitzgerald and Marauder—to the rebel cause in Ireland. Like Marauder, he was attached to the U.I. general military committee and appointed adjutant-general for the Munster region, finally being put in charge of the U.I. assault on Dublin (O'Dwyer 276-77).

Whether or not Marauder was based on Morres or, in part at least, on Fitzgerald, Lucas can be congratulated for embedding his narrative so firmly in actual historical events. He can also be applauded for the panache with which, in certain sections of the novel, he fused history with fiction. The best example of this is the climactic meeting of Marauder and Wilson, the former at the head of a body of rebels, the latter commanding a troop of the Southford Fencibles (a fictional regiment of the British army), the episode which closes the third volume. Though the characters are fictional, and this specific skirmish never actually took place, Lucas's account is clearly based on other similar encounters. He sites it precisely in the history of the Rebellion, telling us that it took place just after the French had landed at Killala Bay—on 22 August 1798. Furthermore, the victory which Wilson wins in his personal duel with Marauder—against the odds—becomes emblematic of the turn of the tide in the war between the insurgents and the state. The episode plays a historiographical role then, the vanquishing of Marauder representing the final defeat of the Rebellion. It also works well as propaganda, the Rebellion being presented as a severe threat, so that, even if it had been defeated this time, the nation should still be on its guard against the Jacobin menace. But above all, the episode is tremendously satisfying in narrative terms. Wilson arrives to fight Marauder in the nick of time, after having been absent from the narrative for a volume and a half. Their destinies, Lucas suddenly reveals, were indeed entwined, just as Dr. Line, the astrologer who expatiated on their births at the beginning of the first volume, had forecast. It is Lucas's successful integration of both their careers with the fate of the state which is even more impressive, and inevitably brings to mind the novels of Scott, the first of which, *Waverley*, would be published thirteen years later in 1814.

The Infernal Quixote was not the only novel to fuse a fictional narrative with the social, economic, and political realities of late eighteenth- and early nineteenth-century Ireland. Maria Edgeworth's *Castle Rackrent, an Hibernian Tale* had appeared a year earlier, in 1800, and it has generally been regarded as inspiring a substantial vogue for Irish "national tales." As has recently been pointed out though, the trickle of Irish novels, of which *The Infernal Quixote* was a part, did not become a flood until 1808, which suggests that it was *The Wild Irish Girl; A National Tale* by Sydney Owenson, later Lady Morgan, published in 1806, which was more influential (Garside 51; and see Belanger, which updates Brown, and Brown and Clarke).[1] *The Infernal Quixote* was, however, certainly the first novel to be set amidst the Irish Rebellion, though many others soon followed. The next was probably the anonymous *The Soldier of Pennaflor: or, A Sea-*

---

1 Other important Irish "national tales" included *The Wild Irish Boy* (1808) and *The Milesian Chief* (1812) by Charles Robert Maturin, and further works by Maria Edgeworth, such as *Tales of Fashionable Life* (1809 and 1812), *Harrington, a Tale, and Ormond, a Tale* (published together in 1817).

son in Ireland (1810) which echoed *The Infernal Quixote* in many ways. The rebel leaders are presented as noblemen who had basely risen up against their king, country, and laws, and the U.I. are accused of having sent "agents through the country, who, inflaming the peasants by the specious pretences of Catholic emancipation and Parliamentary reform, sowed those seeds of animosity, gloom and discontent, which hapless circumstances have since matured into insurrection and rebellion."The hero went with General Lake to the Battle of Vinegar Hill and, like Wilson, is described leading government troops against the rebels (3:116, 124 and 151ff.). Also picking up on the literary potential of a disenchanted nobleman leading the Irish rebels were William Hamilton Maxwell's *O'Hara; or, 1798* (1825), whose epigraph quoted Byron opining that Lord Edward Fitzgerald's story "would make the finest subject in the world for an historical Novel," and Lady Caroline Lamb's *Glenarvon* (1816) which incorporated a thinly-veiled portrait of Byron himself playing the Marauder role.[1] Where *The Infernal Quixote* differs from many of the subsequent novels which were set during the Rebellion, is that Lucas certainly did not reduce "the 1798 uprising to mere background action, come and gone in the space between chapters," as Lamb can be said to have done in *Glenarvon* (Trumpener 333n.61; but compare Kelsall). His was a thoroughly political novel in which the Rebellion was never merely *scenic*. What *The Infernal Quixote* does have in common with all the novels of the Irish Rebellion which followed over the next generation was their militant loyalism. Only after several decades had passed did they begin to demur from the line Lucas had established, that the rebel leaders were opportunistic and self-seeking rabble-rousers who had hijacked what might have been a legitimate political cause, but which, under their command, quickly became a violent, vindictive, and depoliticized cover for their own megalomania.

---

1   Other novels dealing with the Irish Rebellion include the anonymous *The United Irishman, or the Fatal Effects of Credulity; a Tale Founded on Facts* (2 vols., Dublin, printed for the author, 1819), later republished as *The Cavern in the Wicklow Mountains, or Fate of the O'Brien Family; A Tale Founded on Facts* (1821); [Alexander Sutherland], *Redmond the Rebel; or, They Met at Waterloo. A Novel* (3 vols. London: A.K. Newman and Co., Leadenhall-Street, 1819); [James MacHenry], *The Insurgent Chief; or, O'Halloran. An Irish Historical Tale of 1798 [...] By Solomon Secondsight* (3 vols. Philadelphia: H.C. Carey and I. Lea, and London: reprinted for A.K. Newman and Co., 1824). See Belanger.

The *Infernal Quixote* may have anticipated in several important ways much later Irish fiction, as well as the novels of Scott, but it was probably not in itself a hugely influential novel. There was no second edition, although Lucas spoke warmly of an unauthorized translation of his novel into French published in 1801 (Appendix A). The stigma attached to Minerva Press novels also probably ensured that the novel did not become widely known in the higher reaches of "literary society." Lucas would not necessarily have been unhappy about this. His was a propaganda novel, written to expose the wiles of political and religious dissidents, to warn his readers of the dangers of Jacobinism, foreign and domestic, and, at the same time, to reassure them that if they were resolute, loyal, and pious, the threat could be overcome. A truly popular novel was the best way to accomplish this, which helps to explain why Lucas adopted the Minerva mode. What he achieved was one of the most readable of all the political novels which contributed to the "Revolution Controversy" of the 1790s and early 1800s. At its best *The Infernal Quixote* is sententious and polemical without being preachy; it is propaganda with panache. It is an enjoyable comic romp, but without ever losing sight of the serious danger which Lucas and so many of his contemporaries thought Britain was facing at the turn of the nineteenth century.

Charles Lucas: A Brief Chronology

1769   Charles Lucas born, son of William Lucas of Daventry. Educated at the school in the Cathedral Close at Salisbury and then at Harrow School.

1786   Admitted to Oriel College, Oxford, where he remained a student until 1790. The University does not recognize him as a graduate, but he styles himself Master of Arts on the titlepages of his publications.

1791   Appointed curate of Avebury, Wiltshire (a curate was technically an assistant to a parish priest, but he would often take full responsibility for the parish).

1795   Publication of *The Old Serpentine Temple of the Druids*, a poem (with a second edition 1801).

1796   *Free Thoughts on a General Reform* published in Bath (attributed to Lucas, but no edition survives).

1798   Publication of *The Castle of St. Donats; or, the History of Jack Smith* at the Minerva Press. American editions appear in 1800 and 1801.

1801   Publication of *The Infernal Quixote, A Tale of the Day*. A French translation, *L'infernal Don Quichotte*, appears in Paris in the same year.

1803   Marries Sarah Ann Williams, sister of the Rev. H. Williams, on 5 January. They have a large family. Lucas's first novel is published in France as *Le Château de Saint-Donats, ou Histoire du fils d'un Emigré échappé aux massacres en France*.

1808   *The Abissinian Reformer, or the Bible and Sabre*, a novel published by George Richards in London.

1810   Publication of *Joseph. A Religious Poem* by S. McDowall in London.

1816   Lucas moves to Devizes, Wiltshire, probably to take on a new curacy.

1820   Publication of *Gwelygordd; or, the Child of Sin. A Tale of Welsh Origin*.

c.1840   *Observations on the Modern Clergy and the Present State of the Church* published by Simpson in Devizes.

c.1850   Publication (by Randle of Devizes) of *An Epitome from the Chief Passages of Scripture: [...] as a Refutation of the Romish Doctrine of Transubstantiation, Which Heresy has been Lately Revived in the Church of England by Garbled Quotations, by*

Many Professed Ministers, by Omitting the Scriptural Context, by Bold Preaching, Where No Confutation can be Offered, and by the Countenance of Spiritual Authority in High Places.

1854   Lucas dies.

A Note on the Text

The text given here has been taken from the first (and only) English edition of *The Infernal Quixote*, published by William Lane's Minerva Press in London in 1801. Typographical errors have been silently corrected, and archaic or idiosyncratic spellings and punctuation have been modified where they might have led to confusion (for example "chuse" has been changed to "choose," and "your's" to "yours"). The long *s* has been modernized. Otherwise, original spellings have been left as they were found ("fox-chace" or "Bastile," for instance). Lucas's own footnotes are designated by asterisks (*) and daggers (†), as in the 1801 edition, and are further identified by Lucas's initials appearing in square brackets at the beginning of the note. Occasionally the positions of these notes have been slightly altered in the interests of clarity. All other annotations, designated by superscript numbers or appearing in square brackets after Lucas's notes, are my own.

THE

INFERNAL QUIXOTE.

A TALE OF THE DAY.

IN FOUR VOLUMES.

BY

CHARLES LUCAS, A.M.

AUTHOR OF THE CASTLE OF ST. DONATS, &c.

" Better to reign in Hell than ferve in Heaven."

MILTON'S SATAN.

VOL. I.

LONDON:

PRINTED AT THE

Minerva-Press,

FOR WILLIAM LANE, LEADENHALL-STREET.

1801.

DEDICATION

TO HIM,

Who, in the exalted station of a public life, steady to his friends and to his trust, finds his upright conduct sanctioned even by his opponents.—
Who, in his domestic circle meets from every beloved relative and social tie, the endearing smiles of affection.—

TO HIM,

Whose merits, while they claim the tribute of praise, mark by their genuine lustre, without the nominal adulation of Honours, Titles, Dignities, which is the man.—

TO HIM,

Whom, the universal voice hails as the next example to the virtue that shines from the throne, these pages are most humbly and most respectfully dedicated by

THE AUTHOR

THE PEERS OF HELL assembled;—by their ARCHLEADER summoned.

Up SATAN rose. Harrowed with doubt and soul-corroding thought—the PANDÆMONIUM attentive heard him speak.—

"My wiles and labours, restless subtleties, and never-ceasing pains, in aid of our untied cause 'gainst Heaven and Earth, well do you know, ye Chiefs.

"Success—so long wavering—smiles on our efforts. The reign of ANTICHRIST is begun.—Thanks to the daring, restless sons of France, inspired by me and mine!

"The seeds of HELL, so ably scattered through each Christian land, luxuriant yield their fruit, and choke the sober weak celestial plants.

"Yet still there is a spot resists my utmost efforts—too well ye know the place.

"In vain that imp Voltaire, and yonder miserable group—on earth conceited, prating, proud Philosophers—gifted with all our learning, tried; in vain Robespierre, with his more numerous gang, more wretched and contemptible—the DEMAGOGUES OF FRANCE, but now the lowest SLAVES OF HELL—armed with our powers, essayed to force success; in vain the chosen, favoured pupils of either school, or war and learning, still unceasing labour. Our Hell-born virtues nor art nor force can graft upon *their* tree of civil and religious LIBERTY.

"Oh! most ungrateful to recount how oft we've baffled been.— Confusion! when MY IDOLS fell before the simple, plain Augustine.—Then ARTHUR, inveterate assailed me.—Still from other shores I poured upon the Isle, armed with the conquering sword, my worshippers; till ALFRED, wondrous man! in peace, in war, with never-ceasing care opposed my reign, and firmly fixed the ADAMANTINE FOUNDATIONS OF CHRISTIAN TEMPLES!

"Thus failed my old decoy, Idolatry! No matter—I strived with other wiles. For some time Priestcraft, Superstition, and a specious assemblage of Christian virtues aided our cause. Horror! another Alfred reigns—the shield celestial from public and from private foe protects him—his tutelary genius, as yet triumphant, smiles at our toils;—but enough of this degrading subject.

"Hear, POTENTATES OF HELL, ARCHFOES OF HEAVEN, my Brethren united, free, equal participators of unconfined, indiscriminate, independent CHAOS,—hear what my labouring prescience, diving deep with every learned lore into the bowels of FUTURITY, has discovered.

"This auspicious day gives to the light in Albion's favoured Isle—"

The purport of this SATANIC SPEECH the following history will unfold; it is unnecessary, therefore, to detail it any further:—but leaving this fragment as—a prologue—a prelude—a flight of fancy—an enigma—a romantic effusion—a poetical licence—a momordian scrap for critics, a Zoilean sop—or, in short, what the reader pleases to think it—the tale commences.

CHAPTER I.

Merrily rang the bells in the village of Hazleton.

'Twas in the month of March, when hares run madly—when young maidens think of the coming spring, and old ones rejoice that, as the days are lengthened, the expense of fire and candle decreases—when tradesmen's wives dream of pleasure, and their husbands of long journeys, toil, trouble, and loss—when the country buck is about to patch up his old hunter, and the city beau to purchase him as a fresh ambling nag for his summer recreation—when old debauchers lament that the long nights are past, and every gaming house in St. James's droops its head—when the sons of Day look forward with joy, and Night's shamefaced crew backwards with remorse:—'twas on the 21st of the month of March, in the year 1773, after the birth of Christ, when Sol enters into the Ram, and the budding season commences, that the Rev. Mr. Lockeridge mounted his old grey hunter for the last time that season, and leisurely proceeded up the village in that motion, in which the true sportsman delights to go to cover.

A loud bawling from a cottage door arrested his progress, and the father of a new-born babe required of his Reverence to baptize the sickly infant.

The divine turned round. He did not ride home to divest himself of his present garb; he did not put on the gown, the cassock, and the band, nor did he put off his spurs, his spencer, or his belt; but giving his horse to a lad at the door, he entered the house, laid his hunting whip and cap upon the table, and demanded water and a prayer-book.

Dr. Line, the man-midwife, was in the room.

Now Dr. Line was not a little of the Methodist, and beheld these unsanctified emotions with no small portion of displeasure.

As the young pastor entered the cottage, the following conversation took place.

"Well, my friend, how is your wife and little one?"

"My wife, Sir, and thank God! is as well as can be expected;" the general favourable answer from the tip-top of Nobility to the very lowest of the mobility, and perhaps the only *general* sentence in use among all ranks and conditions; "but the child is sickly, and we'll thank your Reverence to give 'un a *neame*."

"A boy?"

"Yes, Sir."

"Come, give me the prayer-book. Good people, all kneel down."

The father brought the Curate a cushion.

"No," said he, "give it that gentleman," pointing to Dr. Line; "he has more need of it than me."

Then, kneeling down, in a solemn tone he read the proper prayers, till he came to name the child.

"What name do you give it?" said the Curate.

"My name, Sir," replied the father.

"Wilson!" exclaimed the Curate, "I baptize thee, &c. &c."

"Lord Sir" said the father, "that's my sirname!"

"Yes," replied the Curate, thoughtfully, "had I recollected myself sooner, I should have concluded you meant your Christian name; but you should have given me the name, for though I know your sirname, I am as yet ignorant of the other."

"William, Sir," said the man; "is it too late now?"

"I am not casuist enough to determine; some great man has said it is." He thought on the famous Mr. Tristram Shandy.[1]—"But why should you object to its being as it is? Wilson is a good name, you are a good man, and I hope your son will prove a Wilson Wilson in its best sense."

"This mistake, Sir," said Dr. Line, bowing very low, "I don't mean to affix any blame on your Reverence, may perhaps prove a lucky omen."

"I am very well satisfied, Sir," said the father.

The Curate concluded the service, took up his cap and whip, and, as he left the cottage, said to the owner—"If you'll send to my lodging, the old woman will let you have a bottle of wine for your wife and child, or any thing else that you may want, if I have it.—Good morning, Sir!" to the Doctor; "good morning, my friend!" to the other: "I hope the child will be well by Sunday, and that you will bring him to Church; and that you'll never have cause to repent that his Christian name is Wilson."

The pastor of the church departed.

"I'll go to *your* Church next Sunday," said Dr. Line, whose *own*, by the by, was a large barn, where he sometimes expounded himself; "and if you want a godfather, I'll willingly stand in for him myself."

With humble thanks the offer was accepted.

There was something so very unaffected, so serious, if not sanctified, in the manner of the Curate, that Dr. Line, in spite of

---

1 In Laurence Sterne's *The Life and Opinions of Tristram Shandy, Gent.* (1759-67), the hero is intended to be christened "Trismegistus." A maid charged with telling the clergyman this name forgets it, resulting in the child being given his father's least favourite name, Tristram (vol.4, ch.14).

his prepossessions, could not fail giving this indirect tribute to his praise.

"Yet," continued the Doctor, "what a pity 'tis your young pastor has not a little more—a little more—decency about him."

"Decency, Sir! there is not a more decent man in the parish, whether he be Methodist, or not."

"By decency, I mean propriety of behaviour, as it becomes a Minister of the Gospel of Christ!"

"Why as to his saying prayers without his gown or surplice, and just before he is going a hunting, though he had his spurs and other things on, I can't see much harm in that, Doctor; and I am sure he said it so devoutly from his heart, that it did me good to hear him—and a better heart no man in the kingdom has."

The Doctor, if not convinced, dropped his argument.

"How long has this gentleman been with you?"

"About three years; but he lived in t'other parish till lately, where the Duke's Castle is;—but I've known him from a child. Poor young gentleman! he was disappointed in love, they said, about four years ago, and so soon after he took orders, lives always in the country, never visits any of the neighbouring gentlefolks, but spends all his time in reading, hunting, writing, shooting, and preaching."

"What, does he never to my Lord's, here?"

"Oh, no! he affronted my Lord soon after he came to the Curacy."

"How so?"

"My Lord's gamekeeper used frequently to kill a bird or two on Sunday, and he wrote to my Lord about it, and so Lord James took huff; and our Parson said he did not care for my Lord more than he did for any of us, when he did not behave properly, and that the gamekeeper should not shoot on Sundays."

"Why, here have I lived all my life in this parish, and never knew till to day that this was the gentleman that prevented the gamekeeper from shooting. I never spoke to him before today."

"I don't much wonder at these things, Doctor; you be one of the Methodists, you know, and you kind of folk don't much love the parsons, though I believe that you be better than all the rest put together; but then you be always at your books, and looking at the stars: you do seldom speak to any of us, unless it is to do us some good, and give some Doctor's stuff."

"But how, neighbour Wilson, did your Curate prevent the man's shooting on Sundays?"

"Why, first, Sir, he told all the Justices of it at the Quarter Sessions, and informed against him; and then he took and wrote to the

Bishop about it; and so my Lord grew ashamed of the business, and gave it up."

While I am telling the behaviour and conversation of the Curate, of William Wilson the carpenter, and of Dr. Line the man-midwife of the parish, I have not yet explained the first line of this history, the harbinger of the momentous records about to ensue—

"Merrily rang the bells in the village of Hazleton."

CHAPTER II.

"Surely these bells will never have done ringing for this son and heir," said Dr. Line.

"Why, Doctor," replied the other, "I like to hear them; I fancy to myself it's for my own child, and Margery thinks it is a good omen to have a son born on the same day, and, for what I know, the same hour and minute that my Lady Marauder is brought to bed; and I fancy this bell-ringing, though we don't pay for it, will do our young one as much good as it does little Lord James."

"I want to calculate the nativity of a child on whom Fortune so auspiciously smiles, and this continual peal confuses and prevents me. No doubt he will prove a most wonderful man!—Heir to the Dukedom of Silsbury—born at the vernal equinox, when Nature, heavenly goddess, first begins the year.—Fine things, neighbour, to set off with!"

"Pray, Doctor, which do you think was born first—my child, or his Lordship's?"

"I really can't say; they came into the world so nearly together."

"Then pray, Doctor, where is the difference to the stars between the children?"

Now Dr. Line did not expect such a question as this: it was a direct attack upon his favourite hobby-horse. Like a man at a loss for an answer, he replied, as if it was very evident!—"Pshaw! a great deal, to be sure!"

"Sir! why?"

"How the—" Dr. Line never swore.—"How, I say, should I be able to explain to you the nature of these things—to you, who don't know Mars from Venus, who never saw the ring of Saturn, or the belt of Jove—to you, who are not even acquainted with Ursa Major, who know not a planet from a fixed star, or a comet from a meteor—to whom the moon is—"

How much further Dr. Line would have proceeded, and when he would have finished his rhapsody on his neighbour's ignorance it is impossible to say, as the other put a stop to it by pleading guilty to all.

"Well, well, Doctor, I beg pardon—I'm sure I didn't mean to offend; I thought there might be some notable difference that I might have understood, why my son and his Lordship's, both born at the same time, should have different fortunes. But if so be they be the same, I thank God for it; and if not, why I hope God will give him grace to behave like a good Christian; and then, whatever is the fortune of the young Duke that is to be, we shall have no great need to envy him."

A pure sentiment of religion, however awkwardly delivered, was enough at any time to disarm the displeasure of Dr. Line. He shook William Wilson cordially by the hand; and, the bells having ceased ringing, took up his hat, and hastened homeward.

Dr. Line lived the further side of the village from the Church, in a small cottage, neat and plain, and sheltered all around with a little coppice. The whole was his own, and that was about one acre.

In the midst of a rising spot (which, if I thought the majority of my readers were antiquarians, I would have said, with all due remarks, was an ancient tumulus, or burial-place of a British Druid some three thousand years ago), the Doctor had built his house; and about thirty years before the present period, planted the wood around it.

Exclusive of an annual income of forty pounds, which he had in the funds, this was his whole property. He practised indeed as surgeon, apothecary, and man-midwife; but as he kept no horse, and was most liberal in his terms, his gains were very small. His pleasure and his business, his labour and his recreation, his expenses and his studies, were all directed to objects above this earth. The knowledge of the heavenly bodies, their natures, powers, and influences employed his whole mind: yet this *astronomical knowledge* was only subservient to his *astrological fancies*. Dr. Sibley[1] was, in his opinion, the most learned man that ever lived; Nicholas Culpepper[2] was the next. Oh! what would he not have given (if he had had it) to have read in

---

1 Dr. Ebenezer Sibly (d.1800), author of several works of astrology, including *A New and Complete Illustration of the Celestial Science of Astrology* (1787), which included nativities and short memoirs of several remarkable people. Sibly was also a noted Whig, supporting radical political candidates.

2 Nicholas Culpeper (1616-54), another astrological writer and a noted Parliamentarian and radical dissenter during the Civil War.

English (for he knew no other language) the works of Bellantius, Pirovanus, Marascallerus, Goclenius, Caietanus, Paracelsus, Jovianus Pontanus, Michael Scott, Christopher Heydon, and other worthies of this kind without number, and now almost without name!

CHAPTER III.

The Doctor, arrived at home, set to his studies with a most hearty goodwill. He calculated the hour of the child's birth. He took a view of the heavens at the time, with the positions, influences, and aspects of the different planets; and, by the assistance of White's Ephemeris,[1] which the Doctor annually purchased, he was able to be very exact.

The horoscope proved to his satisfaction; he was perfectly satisfied with his labour, and cast the nativity to a nicety.—Whose nativity? the reader may be inclined to say.—The son of Lord James Marauder, Dr. Line undoubtedly meant; whether it will answer as well for the son of William Wilson, the carpenter of Hazleton, who was born at the same hour, the following history will exemplify.

But why was the Doctor more desirous of casting the nativity of Lord James Marauder's son, than he was of the carpenter's?—Did the Doctor expect any payment for it?

No: the Doctor was much too humble a subject to be known at the great house; and, in defiance of his poverty, he had too much decent pride to be a beggar: besides, a German professor of midwifery had been bespoke from the metropolis, for the purpose of delivering my Lady. A complete set of wonderful apparatus had assisted at the birth, and young master had arrived in this world with as much preparation and attendance, as if his mother had been an Eve, and the first of the human species that had procreated in this terrestrial globe.

Perhaps then it was the same motive that induced the good people that attended her Ladyship, also induced our Doctor to calculate her child's nativity—his ostensible consequence in the eyes of the world.

Lord James Marauder was the second son of the late Duke of Silsbury. His elder brother, the present Duke, was unmarried; and though he had arrived many years at the title, never went to court, or attempted to signalize himself in any respect as a Peer of the

---

1 Robert White's *Atlas Ouranios, the coelestial atlas; or, a new ephemeris* was published annually from 1750.

realm. In the early part of his life, indeed, he had run through the course of fashionable dissipation; but finding himself a man of but little consequence in the gay world, and fond of field sports, he had not even visited the metropolis for the last two years; for the Duke had been brought up in the Roman Catholic faith, in which he still tenaciously abided;—without, therefore, looking for other reasons, this will account for his continual residence in the country.[1]

As for Lord James, he had early changed to the side of Fortune, was elected a Member of Parliament, and became Colonel of the Militia: of course this conduct did not conciliate the affections of his brother. Lord James had before run away with Miss Marauder, the rich Irish heiress; and, according to the will of the lady's father, changed his family name of Kennet for that of Marauder. A treaty of marriage was on foot between the guardians of this lady and his Grace, who thus doubly felt the blow. Lord James had also clandestinely purchased a small estate and manor in the very neighbourhood of his noble brother. Most inveterate then was the hatred of the Duke against Lord James; he continually abused him in his words, and opposed him in his actions; yet as regularly four days in the week did he employ himself in a morning in a manner most agreeable to the expectant wishes of the other; that is,—He constantly ventured his neck in a fox-chace.

Lord James, therefore, every other day, at least, looked out for an express that his Grace had taken his last gallop; and generally on the evening of Monday, Wednesday, Friday and Saturday (the days the Duke hunted), Lord James took his walk up the hill that led to his brother's castle, in hopes of meeting the messenger with the mournful tidings.—But Lord James Marauder was no arithmetician, or he would have known that, after all the Duke's bold riding, the odds were most considerably against any serious accident; and here, for the sake of young hunters, that they may not be checked in their sport by the coward fears of one fall too many, I shall briefly state the odds.

In the *first* place, in the course of a long day's hunting, it is *ten to one* in favour of a bold and good rider, well mounted, that he has any accident at all.

---

1 Until 1828-29, Roman Catholics were barred in Britain from holding civil and military office. The Duke of Silsbury was therefore prohibited from sitting in the House of Lords, though his rank would have entitled him to it, and it was only his brother's conversion ("to the side of Fortune") which enabled him to hold a military rank and become a member of the House of Commons.

Secondly, supposing he falls, it is *eight to one* that neither he nor his horse are materially hurt.

Again, it is *six to one* the horse is hurt, and not the rider.

Next, if the rider is hurt, it is *twelve to one* that a bone is broken.

And, *lastly*, it is *twenty to one*, if a bone is broken, that the wound is mortal.

Ergo, 10 X 8 X 6 X 12 X 20 = 115200
     1 X 1 X 1 X 1 X 1 = 1

And 115200 = 1

Thus stated in details:

That he has any fall is 10-to-1

That himself or horse is hurt 80-to-1

That it is the horse, and not himself 480-to-1

That no bone is broken 5760-to-1

That the hurt is not mortal 115200-to-1

Therefore, out of 115200 persons who go a hunting in a morning, but one is supposed to end his course that way.

Fair ladies, to you must the compiler of these papers apologize for these last pages, so incongruous to the development of private history: yet among you are some of the bold daughters of Nimrod, votaries of Diana in the day-time, and far be it from me to suppose that ye are not equal votaries in the Even—you, perhaps, will need no apology; and also ye, who fear lest the winds of Heaven should visit your faces too roughly, who want not the course daubing of dame Nature, but delight in the soft touch of Art and Fancy, do not despise and condemn this calculation:—have ye not fathers, brothers, kinsmen, dear friends, or more, dear lovers who partake of this recreation? and is it not a satisfaction to you to know how little is the danger to those you love? But enough of this. I hasten back to my proper game, the nativity of young Marauder, eldest son of Lord James, grandson of the late Duke of Silsbury, and nephew of the present, besides a pedigree that might easily be traced to half the crowned heads in Europe.

The astrological data from which Dr. Line cast the nativity of the child, were—"On Monday, the 21st of March, between the hours of five and six, was born a male child, A.D. 1773."

As I have thus particularlized the year, month, day, and even the hour in which Lady James Marauder produced my young hero to the world; and as an astrologer, who wishes to have a concise view of his future history, may look back to the exact situation of the heavens at that time, I shall no further anticipate his life than with just mentioning the preamble to the worthy Doctor's statement.

"The face of Nature smiles on thee, my boy; the Planets are propitious; and Honours, Wealth, and Fame hover around thy cradle.

"The fates have decided thy line of life in *three* divisions, and have given to each full five-and-twenty revolutions of this earthly planet. The *first* is due to Love; the *second* Glory claims; and Power grasps the *third*."

Why I have been so minute in the birth of the sons of Lord James Marauder and William Wilson, will, in the course of the following pages, more fully appear. Henceforth the history demands a more rapid description.

CHAPTER IV.

I pass over the days of childhood of the two young men, whose births have been so fully described.

I am happy to inform the reader that the respectable Dean Bottom, Dean of the diocese, thought proper to recollect an old College acquaintance in the Curate of the parishes of Hazleton and Castleberry; and through his means Mr. Lockeridge received a living in the diocese, the valuable Rectory of Wheatland.

I could here spin out a fine episode, by following him to India, where he went in pursuit of his first love, who, I might almost say, had been kidnapped by her relations to that meretricious soil. As fire tries fine gold, so danger tries our virtues, whether they are real or not. He found his fair one, though compelled to accompany a stern father, had resolutely withheld from many a suitor her hand as well as her heart. Her parent was lately deceased, and almost the whole of a small property he had left to her stepmother. This young lady was preparing to return to England when Mr. Lockeridge arrived. They were immediately married; and the Rector of Wheatland, after a nine months' voyage, staid but six weeks before he prepared to return to his native country, bringing back with him to Europe a treasure more precious than all the riches of Nabobs, Nizims, and Rajahs.

The period of six years had elapsed from young Marauder's and Wilson's birth, when Mr. Lockeridge with his spouse returned from India.

As Rector of Wheatland, he had the appointment of a boy to a public grammar-school in his neighbourhood; and two years after, young Wilson Wilson was the lad chosen to be the object of his bounty.

Dr. Line lived in *statu quo* at his favourite spot, where, as he yearly noticed the growth of his circumambient plantation, did he perceive, at the same time, that his circle of the heavens decreased.— "An emblem," he would say, "of mortality;—we lose in one thing what we gain in another."

The preferment of Mr. Lockeridge had not diminished the civility and intimacy which had strengthened between the Curate and

Dr. Line, from the naming of young Wilson. It was by the Doctor's recommendation that the boy had been sent to the school. Dr. Line himself first taught his godson his A B C; and from the daily instruction which he gave him at the holidays, might be not improperly called his philosophical tutor. In truth, he learned no great deal at the school, not from any fault in the teachers, but in the scholar himself. Latin and Greek he would at any time resign for a lecture on the starry bodies, which concluded with a peep through the telescope; and he was much more conspicuous at boxing, wrestling, and cricketing, than at an oration, composition, or versification. His mind was too violent, perhaps too strong, to bear regular trammels.

When he arrived at his fifteenth year, Dr. Line and his clerical patron, by absolute dint of reasoning, prevailed upon him to be more attentive to his classical studies; and in the two last years he remained at the school, he learned more Greek and Latin than he had done in all the former seven.

I cannot help remarking that Dr. Line always concluded his arguments to him to learn Latin and Greek,—"And you will be able to read, not only Nicholas Culpepper and Dr. Sibley, but Bellantius, Pirovanus, Marascallerus, Goclenius, Caietanus, Paracelsus, Jovianus Pontanus, Michael Scott, &c. &c. &c. &c."

Far different, and with far greater *éclat* was the education of young Marauder conducted. Two private preceptors lived in the house. One taught the ancient languages, the other the modern; not forgetting (what is called) the use of the globes, the mathematics, and all its appurtenances. Daily did Lord James hear of the improvement of his son; and daily did he perceive specimens of that ready wit, bold remarks, and argumentative powers which so early distinguished the young man. Nor were the gymnastics and pugilistic sciences neglected. The names of Goddard and Angelo, of Medoza and Johnson, with many others of inferior note, were well known in his Lordship's mansion.[1]

Very early in life did young Marauder shew a bold, haughty, and commanding spirit; and though he wanted not for abilities, yet he

---

1 "Angelo" is presumably Domenico Angelo Malevolti Tremamondo (1716-1802) an equestrian and fencing master, the author of *L'École d'Armes avec l'Explication générale des Principales Attitudes et Positions concernant l'Escrime* (1763), translated as *The School of Fencing*. Daniel Mendoza (1764-1836) was the most celebrated boxer of his generation and the author of *The Modern Art of Boxing* (1789). Tom Johnson (1750-97), another boxer, was the unofficial "champion of England" from 1783 to 1791.

always chose his own time for learning, and his own subjects. Many boys in the neighbourhood were frequently sent for to Lord James's, to be his playfellows; but a lad in the village, who was articled to a petty attorney, that acted as his Lordship's steward, was his chief, though humble companion and favourite.

This youth was eight or nine years older than Marauder, was of a sly and subtle disposition, and soon gained the favour of the family at the great house.—He was not only the first to indulge the young heir in all his whims, freaks, and fancies, but was the first to invent new ones for him.

Young Marauder was very fond of trying experiments of some kind or other, which it is unnecessary to repeat, as, like most boyish sports, when left to themselves, they begin and end in cruelty.

Imphell, the attorney's clerk, never boggled at any thing the other required; he was the chief instrument of his wanton mischief, and the tyrant of those boys whose ages came between the future Duke's and his own.

As Marauder grew older, Imphell generally accompanied him on horseback, and was a ready nomenclator to tell him the history of the neighbourhood.

Among other of the young hero's amusements, experiments with gunpowder he particularly delighted in. He was not only a very good shot, but with a little mortar he would throw a bomb to such a nicety, that even that high military character, the Duke of Richmond himself, would have been pleased with his skill.

Once he laid a scheme to give a genteel jump to his French tutor, who had displeased him; but owing to a mistake, the train lighted on Imphell, who was tossed some six or eight yards into a pond of water, without receiving any other injury, so judiciously had his young pupil managed his work.

When Imphell came to the age of one-and-twenty, Lord James, by his son's particular desire, agreed with the attorney, for a small annuity, to give up the business to his clerk, the chief part of which was the management of his Lordship's estate. Yet this did not prevent Imphell's attendance on the son of his benefactor, till Marauder went abroad.

Young Wilson was most of his time at school; the summer holidays he generally spent with his clerical patron, and the winter ones with his parents, and astrological friend at home.

In their fifteenth year, by a circumstance I am about to relate, the young men first became acquainted; till that period Wilson was totally unknown to Mr. Marauder, though the former well knew the son of Lord James by sight.

Young Marauder had given five guineas to be played for at backsword,[1] in the Whitsun-Week. Wilson happened to be at home, and attended the revel as a spectator. A favourite groom of Mr. Marauder's was about to carry off the prize, when Wilson prevailed on a stout Irishman, who worked for his father, to mount the stage.

At the first blow the Irishman sent his opponent sprawling on the ground; a dispute instantly arose concerning fair play: Wilson was loud in defence of his friend, and leaped upon the stage.

Mr. Marauder, who was present, and whose word had as yet been law, ordered him off.

The son of the carpenter demurred.

The embryo Duke indignantly seized a stick, and with many abusive words threatened him with manual chastisement on the spot.

Wilson replied—"You are surrounded with dependants, Sir, or you should soon be convinced how little I fear you."

"If you suppose, Sirrah, I want any one to assist me in chastising your insolence, you are greatly mistaken. Defend yourself: I attack you but with your own low weapons."

"Come, then, and drive me down."

Wilson instantly seized a cudgel.

Mr. Marauder considered himself as an adept at the broadsword; and confident of his strength, was about to attempt to fulfil his words, when Imphell, the attorney, his Lordship's bailiff, and some other attendants interfered, and with difficulty restrained him.

"Sir, he's beneath your notice," exclaimed Imphell, as they all pushed forward between the combatants.

The bailiff, a stout man, was in a moment on the stage. He struck at Wilson with his fist; while Imphell was endeavouring to restrain his angry patron.

The youth turned the blow aside with his cudgel, as his smote the other with great violence on the arm. His father's workman, on whose account the quarrel had commenced, seeing the danger his young master was in, at this instant caught him in his arms, and, before the rest could make good their attack, leaped off the other side of the stage with him.

The bailiff, who was enraged at the blow he had received, was eager to be revenged. Marauder broke from Imphell, and sprung on the stage; but so many now interfered, and not a few friends of the carpenter placed themselves before his son, that the bailiff was oblig-

---

1 A sword made of a single wooden stick with a basket hilt.

ed to be satisfied as he was. The difference too between a raw lad of fifteen, and a robust man of forty, prevented the combat from proceeding any further.

Mr. Marauder himself was very violent, and was only prevented by the interference of some gentlemen, who were with him, from being the principal in the affray.

Wilson, nearly as haughty, walked off with the Irishman, remarking, in no low key, that it required more than high birth, education, or abilities to make a gentleman.

From this period Mr. Marauder never forgot Wilson, whom he called the carpenter's insolent son; and Wilson, who had before heard a great deal of the abilities and accomplishments of his Lordship's heir, was not much inclined, from this specimen, to believe the whole to be true.

The worthy Dr. Line, who, from the concomitant circumstances of their birth, had daily, for near fifteen years, expected to see them fly into one another's arms, and become a second Castor and Pollux, was most wonderfully astonished when he heard of the affray. Yet still he anticipated great things, and again and again reviewed, applauded, and confirmed his original calculations.

Happily for the Doctor, a new comet had lately been discovered; and from the inauspicious influence of this, he accounted for the retrograde motion of things.

CHAPTER V.

The malign mists, which the sudden affray, related in the last chapter, had raised, were by no means allayed by Lord James. Urged by his son, in whose temper forgiveness had neither a natural nor artificial growth, he exerted his influence to injure the father of young Wilson, and to drive him from the village.

But his Lordship had more of the will than the power, and, except in taking from the carpenter his own particular work, things remained in nearly the same state.

The greater part of the estates in the parish belonged to his brother the Duke, of which William Wilson's house, garden, and field made a part. The manor, and a small estate, indeed, belonged to Lord James; and it was the circumstance of his having purchased these privately (I before noticed) which increased the division between the brothers.

Many a scheme had Lord James devised when he should come to the title—many an alteration and improvement had he planned.

Among the first he had determined to turn out Wilson's family.—This was a point in which he had promised his son, whose haughty temper remembered, with increased acrimony, the affront which had been put upon him at the revel.

Young Marauder was in some respects like his father—in most superior. In abilities, education, and person he left Lord James far behind. Proud of the lineage from which he was descended, buoyed up with the great honours daily expected, he saw himself in the first situation in the kingdom, and in every other person, but the Majesty, fancied he beheld an inferior.

To recapitulate, in a few words, the chief motives which occasioned the animosity between the Duke and his brother, will account for the virulence with which it was continued.

Lord James Kennet married Elizabeth Marauder, a great heiress, and by her father's will was obliged to take the family name. Once possessed of the wealth for which he married, he changed his religion, and came into Parliament. He now also bought the manor of Hazleton, where the Duke had two thousand a year, and which his Grace had been trying to purchase from the time he came into the title;—and what heightened the whole, Lord James, by having embraced the established religion, became possessed of the national advantages and honours his brother, as a Catholic, could not hold. Exclusive of his seat in Parliament, he was Colonel of the Militia; and on the next vacancy, the Lord Lieutenancy of the Country was promised him: yet, after all, his Lordship was suspected to be not a whit better Protestant in his heart, though worldly motives had induced him to recant his errors.

But there was still a reason behind, not generally known, and more grating than all this: Lady James was of a Roman Catholic family; her father's will required that she should marry one of the same persuasion. Lord James obeyed, and changed after his marriage. The Duke himself had intended to solicit, and had spoken to her guardians; but while his Grace's counsel were examining if the property was so great as reported, Lord James, in his brother's name, called on the lawyers—was satisfied—flew to the lady, and ran off with her himself to Gretna Green.

What the principles of Mr. Marauder were, will most fully appear in the course of these pages. Whatever they were at present, his father seemed perfectly well satisfied with them. One thing was evident, that Lord James's recantation had not grievously offended any of his friends (besides the Duke) of the Roman persuasion. Generally a Priest or two of that communion resided in the house, and many of the latter, French emigrants. My Lady, too, still remained a good Catholic; and his Lordship kindly lent her the use of his chapel—a strong instance of the liberality of his notions, and that he was not prejudiced to his new faith.

In his sixteenth year young Marauder left England to visit France and Italy. Many reasons induced his father to permit his departure at so early an age. When his passions had interfered, Marauder had already shewn himself capable of such violent measures as had justly alarmed his friends. In some cases all Imphell's art and ingenuity had scarcely been able to defend his young patron. These acts had been attributed to high courage, and an undaunted boyish spirit; but a circumstance which happened in his own family, began to make his Lordship think more seriously of the matter.

Sir Gourdy Kirtle, a first cousin of my Lady, had in his sixtieth year broke his vows of bachelorship, and married for love. The blooming daughter of a tenant was the happy bride. They came in the third honey-moon on a visit to Lord James. Lady Kirtle soon considered her new cousin with no unfavourable eye; and in every moment of Sir Gourdy's absence, the youth was not idle in endeavouring to ingratiate himself into the fair lady's favour. A thousand little nameless attentions, which an elderly husband, from many a cause, will omit, Marauder was ever ready to perform. In walking, riding, fishing, on land or water, her kind cousin attended; yet with such art did he conduct himself, that Sir Gourdy had no idea of his danger from a youth of fifteen.

His Lordship's suspicions were first roused from a remark of Lady Marauder, that since the visit of their cousins, her son seemed to have dropped his boyish fancies; and she hoped the steady conduct and grave counsel of Sir Gourdy would work a perfect reformation. Lord James, by a little attention, soon found that his fears were true, and determined, at all events, to remove his son from the fascinating object directly. A plausible excuse for going to town separated them for some days; in the interim Lord James watched so narrowly, that he discovered a scheme for a private meeting during the winter, which both parties were to spend in town. The knowledge of this induced Lord James to send his son abroad immediately, to which the youth, in defiance of his new flame, joyfully consented.

Lord James gave him a commission in the Militia before his departure—a grateful feather in the cap of a youth just entering the paths of manhood. The allowance of his father was most liberal, and his establishment such as became the heir of one of the first Dukedoms in England.

His Lordship's prudence in sending away his son at so critical a time was soon justified by the event. In the meridian of St. James's a lover was not long wanting to Lady Kirtle, nor a kind friend to Sir Gourdy to remove the mist from his eyes; and in eleven months and a few odd days after the marriage-knot was tied, did the Baronet once more find himself at liberty.

CHAPTER VI.

Seventeen years had now passed by since the birth of the renowned youth, who will make the most conspicuous figure in these pages, and Lord James was as far from the Dukedom as at the first moment of his father's death; when on a Monday evening, as he took his usual walk up the hill, he perceived, at a great distance, a horseman riding towards him.

The morn had been frosty, the fields of course were hard and slippery, most congenial to fractures and broken bones, though by no means hard enough to prevent the sports of the field.

With redoubled eagerness then he viewed the rider.

Nearer and more near as he approached, was he certified in its being the family livery.

Lord James anxiously drew out his pocket-glass, and mounted upon a high stone to take a better view. Some frozen particles yet lay on the top of the stone;—my Lord was heavy; his feet glided from beneath him his nose saluted the moist earth; and his shins more hapless, encountered the hard and rugged edges of the stone.

The horseman, who indeed was a servant of the Duke's, but he had no message for him, laughed, and passed by without further notice.

His Lordship arose angry, fretted, disappointed, and hurt. A ragged bruise had torn the flesh; and by the time Lord James Marauder arrived at home his leg had put on so unfavourable an appearance, that it was thought necessary to send for the family surgeon.

What is the need of sending for a capital surgeon if he does not exhibit his superior skill, but acts according to the rules of the most common and illiterate? and in what respect is a great man a better patient than a poor one, if he does not employ the doctor for a greater length of time? Medical men should recommend one another, wherever there are *assets* enough for all. The surgeon, rightly considering these things, thought it advisable to call in the physician; the physician prescribed for the good of the apothecary; the apothecary recommended some excellent nurses, &c. &c. &c.

In short, what with the doctors, the physic, and the original malady, his Lordship was no longer able to wait for the death of his brother; but having taken five dozen drafts, aperients and astringents, diaphoretics and diuretics, febrifuges and anodynes, according as each became necessary, in eight weeks from the untoward accident, he himself took his departure to the other world!

Thus, in his forty-fifth year, did Lord James Marauder receive his summons to leave this earthly state by means of a grazed shin, at the very moment he expected to hear that his brother had departed by a broken neck.

CHAPTER VII.

Lady James Marauder was inconsolable: every prospect of being a Duchess was gone for ever. Mr. Marauder, who was summoned to England upon the occasion, bore his loss with more philosophy—an early prognostic of an elevated and superior mind, which had not in vain imbibed the stoical principle. Amid the infallible arguments by which he conquered his grief, it did not escape him that he was one step nearer the title.

The chief advantage that had accrued to Lord James from his renouncing his Catholic errors, may be reckoned his seat in the House of Commons; and this had helped him to some pretty places in his friend the Minster's gift.[1]

Mr. Marauder, since his travels, had put on the whole man; and to the former wit and learning of youth, he added reflection, penetration, and judgment.

As a minor, he was not yet able to be a candidate for the Borough his father's death had vacated, as wanting a seat, he wanted also the necessary qualifications to entitle him to his father's honours and advantages. Mr. Marauder, therefore, saw no reason to profess the same tenets or the same conduct; and very wisely considering that the purchase of his honoured uncle's, his Grace of Silsbury's, life was not worth four years, (young Marauder was a most excellent reckoner as well as reasoner), which period must elapse before he could take his seat; and recollecting also that he might, at any time, be as easily reconvinced of his errors, after the fall of the Dukedom, he, for the present, openly professed himself a Catholic as soon as

---

1 By supporting the Prime Minister, a Member of Parliament could expect substantial patronage, often in the form of lucrative sinecures, or "places."

the funeral of his father was over.—Lady James had never thought it worth her while to change; and being of Irish birth, and of an old rich Catholic family, had ever remained in the religion of her forefathers.

The son's religious principles, therefore, could not be otherwise than grateful to the mother; but Mr. Marauder looked further: he considered his profession of the same faith as preparatory to a reconciliation with his uncle.

All due respect had been paid at Lord James's decease, though the Duke hung back, and could not be said to make any approach on his part. But modesty, which many philosophers say is only a species of shame, (and Marauder early in life prided himself on his philosophy), was not one of the vices of this young heir.

"What is modesty?" he would say.—"It is a consciousness of some defect or weakness. It is not proverbial that a villain cannot look you in the face? and why are men ashamed or shy, but under the idea that the people they are addressing, are their betters—or that the actions they are performing, are not altogether right? The weakness of the mind I feel not; and what I know to be proper, I will act, with a total indifference concerning the opinion of others."

With these sentiments Mr. Marauder, about a month from the funeral, sent the Duke the following note:

"*My Lord Duke,*
"Your well-known virtues,"—[if his Grace had a virtue, it was certainly not a cardinal one]—"flatter me with the hope that your nephew will not petition for your pardon in vain. I renounce the errors of my unhappy father, and I entreat your Grace not to visit his offences on his innocent son.

"I humbly wait your Grace's permission to pay my respects in person to so near, so beloved a relation,"—[Mr. Marauder had never seen the Duke, but at a distance, in his life]—"and I ever shall remain,

"My Lord Duke,
"Your obedient and dutiful nephew,
"JAMES MARAUDER."

Mr. Marauder, in answer, received the following note, evidently written by another person, but signed by his Grace.

"*Young Man,*
"Your father thought proper, by unexampled baseness and treachery,

to tear asunder the link which once held us together. I see no purpose in uniting it again. You have already a large and splendid fortune, and can want nothing of me: I am getting old, and like not new faces.

"I thank you for your civility, and wish you well; but would advise you to pursue your intentions in life without regarding there is such a person as

"Your kinsman,
"SILSBURY."

Mr. Marauder, not discouraged, applied again by his friends; and what might have been the issue I cannot say, had it not been for an accident which happened soon after.

The Duke of Silsbury had for many years kept a woman, who had originally been one of his servants. By her he had had eight children. The eldest lad, two years younger than Wilson, went to the same school. The boys were frequently together. Wilson, at the holidays, had been often with him at the Castle; and the boy would come over and stay with him at his father's. Sometimes they were permitted to join his Grace in the chace, and sometimes they walked out with their guns.

Wilson going home for a few days, the other went with him; and in the latter amusement Mr. Marauder, who was likewise sporting, met them.

He instantly recollected Wilson, and, walking up, demanded their certificates.

In both it was found wanting.

The young men were summoned before a Justice of the Peace; and Mr. Marauder, far from thinking who the other was, compelled them both to pay the double penalty, as they were unqualified, and without a license.

How great was Mr. Marauder's surprise, when having laid the information, he triumphantly attended the Justice, and found the Duke's old steward there, who paid down the money for both,—and turning to the young heir, gave him a note.

"Whether or not you knew who Harry Overton was, I care not; your behaviour to young Wilson is enough to make me rejoice that *Mr. Marauder* never had, and never shall be noticed by

"*SILSBURY*"

This circumstance brought Wilson Wilson to his Grace's notice, who, with the true spirit of opposition, did many favours to him and his family, that it might reach his beloved nephew's ears.

The Duke pretended to be more and more pleased with the young man; and when Dr. Line and the worthy Clergyman were about to continue their patronage, by getting him an exhibition, and sending him to the University, his Grace offered to take him home to the Castle, and keep him as a companion and instructor for his children. This offer was much too liberal to be refused, as the Duke commenced his patronage by giving him a life-hold property of *one hundred and fifty pounds* a year—a sufficiency to qualify him for sporting; as much, perhaps, out of revenge against his nephew, as goodwill towards the other.

Here was a circumstance that particularly pleased Dr. Line, who prognosticated most wonderful things from hence, and took a journey to his friend Lockeridge's, on purpose to remark in what an astonishing way the fates of Marauder and Wilson were entwined.

"Though the advantages of birth, education, and connections have so eminently exalted the noble Marauder above his twin luminary, see, my friend, how in his eccentric course, like a comet, Wilson gradually approaches him. Even the sinister acts of the one turn to the benefit of the other; yet I do not believe before the age of one-and-twenty that any great friendship or intimacy will take place; then we shall see them, &c. &c. &c. &c. &c. &c."

The Doctor was got on his favourite nag, and, without any hindrance from the Rector, cantered away at a famous rate.

I shall not repeat his speech, as I dislike the method of the historian, who introduces a fortune-teller or a dream to anticipate the wonders of his story.

Perhaps I have been too guilty of the fault already, and the least I can do is to stop in time.

When the Doctor had finished, Mr. Lockeridge replied with a smile—"Do you suppose our young friend will be also a Duke?"

"I cannot positively say; but I wish Mr. Marauder had a sister, and I should have no doubts of Wilson Wilson's marrying her."

To clear up all these doubts, I shall now proceed rapidly with my history.

CHAPTER VIII.

After this unlucky mistake concerning the sporting, Mr. Marauder set off to London; but his stay there was very short: for, having looked over his father's affairs, and settled his correspondence, he thought proper to pay a second visit to the Continent.

In his situation at the Duke's, Wilson had continued three years, though without any particular occurrence; acquitting himself in other respects, as well as in his office of tutor, to the perfect satisfaction of his new patron.

Neither had these years been idly employed as to his own improvement. The Clergyman and Dr. Line saw with pleasure that the seeds of virtue and religion, which they had so sedulously planted in his mind, were now producing their true fruits. In defiance of the lowness of his origin, he was universally respected, and his society courted by the gentleman in the neighbourhood.

His dutiful behaviour to his parents, and his affectionate kindness to his younger brothers and sisters, was so very different from those of humble birth in general, who get forward in the world, that he was the praise and theme of every tongue. At no time did he conduct himself as if he was superior or better than any of them; he never denied or wished to conceal his origin; his father was an honest man, "the noblest work of God!" says Mr. Pope; and though only a carpenter, (now, indeed, by the assistance of his son and his own industry, a builder), he gloried in that he was his father.

These three years Mr. Marauder was absent from England on his travels. Tired of the restraint he found at home, and having lost all hopes of profiting by his attendance on the Duke, he did not wish to return to his native country till his minority was nearly passed.

After staying, at the beginning of his tour, a few months in France, he lounged at an easy rate through most parts of Italy, seeing every thing worthy his notice, and forming acquaintances among some of the first families.

Provided with proper letters of recommendation, he had been the first time introduced into all circles as the undoubted heir of the Dukedom of Silsbury. The great world was thus open before him, and the spirit and talents of the young Englishman soon distinguished him; his gallantry, courage, and conduct were frequently put to the trial, and crowned him with success and applause.

Unlike these men of fortune who have a conductor or leader, commonly called a tutor, to attend them, he in every case acted and judged for himself. A tenacious observer of his own consequence, he condescended sometimes to stoop to the level of an inferior, but never suffered a dependant to presume to exalt himself to his.

A Mr. Subtile, a Scotch gentleman of family, accompanied him from England, whom he always treated with a polite intimacy, but at no times with a grain of familiarity.

Mr. Subtile was a man of letters more than of native abilities, and his knowledge was rather useful than brilliant. His manners were mild and plausible, but his mind restless and schismatic. He had been a Fellow and Tutor at Cambridge; but had been obliged to resign his situation on account of an imprudent disclosure of notions, destructive in their effect, both to the established Church and State. He had ever preferred a wandering life, and necessity only constrained him to be occasionally at Cambridge; most parts of France and Italy he was very well acquainted with, and was well versed in their manners, language, and customs. His information was of great use to Mr. Marauder, whose guardians settled an annuity upon him for his attendance. He perfectly knew how to conduct himself towards the young heir, who, though he might require and listen to advice, would never bear the least remonstrance.

Marauder, at the commencement of his tour, was little better than a boy; but he threw the trammels of childhood aside, and soon evinced a knowledge of men and manners that astonished every one who became acquainted with him.

His father's death left him entirely at his own disposal; and while he shewed the abilities of youth, he discovered also the judgment of age.

Neither a dupe to the artifices of the Italian Syrens, nor caught in the specious snares of the titled gamester, he could play around the fire, yet escape from the blaze. The veterans of the gay world, and the ladies of the highest fashion beheld him with amazement. A fair and famous wit said of him, that he surpassed every European nation in their own characteristics.

"Young Marauder," exclaimed she at a large *conversazione*, "excels you all at your own weapons: he has the levity and gallantry of the French, the pride and *hauteur* of the Spaniard, the conviviality of the German, the craft of the Italian, the revenge of the Portuguese, the prudence of the Dutch, and the extravagance and courage of his own countrymen—he is beloved by our sex, and envied by yours!"

I shall not here relate the minute occurrences of his travels; many circumstances which took place at that period, will occur in the regular course of these memoirs;—neither is it necessary at present to introduce his more particular acquaintance—friends as the world calls them: they will soon introduce themselves.

Of these, a Mr. Arnon, a late acquaintance, he was become very intimate with; and a Mr. Fahany, a young Irishman, who for abilities, learning, family, and fortune, was inferior to none in that kingdom. This gentleman he had met in Italy, who had, with the highest politeness, noticed him, and with whom he was now on terms of the greatest confidence.

Upon Marauder's return to England, he spent great part of his time at a Mr. Cloudley's, who will be hereafter more regularly noticed—an acquaintance introduced to him by Mr. Arnon.

Mr. Cloudley, who always lived in the country, soon became very partial to him, and was never so happy as when Marauder favoured himself and family with his company.

In his twenty-first year he bade a farewell to the enchanting Italian dames, and came to take possession of that splendid fortune which he was already entitled to.

CHAPTER IX.

Let me again and again beg pardon of my fair readers for having so long neglected to introduce any of their own sex. I hope to make ample amends by a character or two I shall now offer to their notice.

In the beginning of the third year that Wilson was at the Castle, Mr. Vasaley (a gentleman who lived in the neighbourhood), brought to his house two young ladies, to whom he had been left guardian.

A handsome fortune of twenty thousand pounds devolved to each, when she came of age.

Emily, the eldest, was so perfectly fascinating, that the veriest misanthropist could not behold her with indifference. She was in her twentieth year. Her height was exactly that nice medium of female beauty, which forms a pleasing symmetry to the small and pointed features of the most lovely face. Her complexion was delicately fair; her eyes not large, but quick, with a languishing softness which caught the observer the moment he thought he had escaped the first penetrating glance. Her nose and forehead were models of the Circassian; her cheeks graced on each side with a captivating dimple, in which the little god of Love, with his whole artillery, seemed to lay reclined. Reader, didst thou ever see that enchanting picture of Mary Queen of Scots, painted by Zucchiro, in the possession of F. Timberman, Esq.?[1] If thou hast, thou mayst form some idea of the

---

1   Frederico Zuccari, or Zuccaro (1540-1609), was the foremost painter of his day. Many of the portraits attributed to him are of doubtful authenticity.

features of the more lovely Emily. Her hair, in native ringlets, luxuriously flowed around her bosom; and, to finish the portrait, the taper fingers, the round and polished arm, the small foot and finished ankle, in a moment reminded the enrapt admirer of the far-famed Medicean Venus.

I would next describe the person of her lovely sister, Fanny, in which a page would be well employed; but as her thirteenth year was but lately passed, I may very well defer it with saying, that, though in many respects different, there was a strong likeness between the sisters. At present, if Emily had sat for the picture of Flora, Fanny would have made no bad Hebe.[1]

Wilson, from whom the arrows of the sportive god had as yet recoiled unhurt, stood like a second Cymon when he beheld this Iphigenia.[2]

Cupid, who lay laughing among the auburn tresses in her neck, saw the opportunity; and before the poor youth could recover from his surprise, let fly his keenest arrow to the very bottom of his heart.

In vain the young man rallied, and endeavoured to extract the dart—every attempt only rankled the barb the deeper; and before he left Mr. Vasaley's house the soft smiles of the fair maiden, as she sung

"In the dead of the night when with labour oppress'd,
All mortals enjoy the sweet blessings of rest, &c. &c."[3]

completely subdued him.

The Duke's castle was not much more than a mile from Mr. Vasaley's house. Wilson, like most true lovers, first began to despair; yet, in defiance of his sense, his prudence, and almost of his will, did his feet, every evening lead him towards Mr. Vasaley's. Often has he walked to within a few yards of the dwelling, which contained his beloved object, and seeing no one, hastily turned back again;—still he took the same path, reasoning and debating with himself, and

---

1 Flora was the Roman goddess of flowering plants. Hebe, in Greek mythology, was the daughter of Zeus, a goddess of youth and cupbearer to the Gods (and hence was often associated with domesticity). She eventually became the wife of Hercules.

2 In the first story of the fifth day in Boccaccio's *Decameron*, the simple and innocent Cymon falls in love with Iphigenia at first sight.

3 A slight misquotation from John Hall-Stevenson's "Anacreon. Ode III," *The Works of John Hall-Stevenson, Esq.* (3 vols. London: J. Debrett and T. Beckett, 1795) 3:22-23.

frequently after four times walking it, has he at last summoned resolution to enter the house.

It cannot be supposed his passions long remained hid from his lovely mistress: every attempt at concealment only the more exposed him.

When he considered her beauty, her accomplishments, her handsome fortune—his own insignificance on the other side, he determined to conquer his fruitless, his presumptuous love.

Mr. and Mrs. Vasaley—people of the common fashionable character—soon rallied her upon her conquest; nor did the young lady despise it. The great respectability of his character, his connections, his own abilities, his person, his manners, were such as would never be injured by the lowness of his birth; but wherever Wilson was known, these soon affixed a proper consequence to him. And these too upon acquaintance increased, while the other was all but forgotten.

Besides, as his origin was a subject of which he was himself never ashamed, so in vain did others attempt to injure him there. In all companies he spoke (if the course of conversation led him, but never introduced the subject) of his parents with that humility, duty, and truth, that could never fail to leave an impression favourable to himself in the minds of his auditors.—As an instance.

Mr. and Mrs. Vasaley, and both the young ladies were present; Mr. Vasaley invited him to dinner the next day.

"I am obliged to you, Sir," replied Wilson, "and would with the greatest pleasure accept your invitation, but I have promised my mother to dine with the family, as it is my father's birth-day, which happens but once in four years."

"How can that be?" asked Miss Emily.

"He was born, Ma'am, on the 29th of February."

"Indeed!" said Mr. Vasaley; "it is a very remarkable circumstance."

"Your father, Sir," said Miss Emily, "I presume lives in this neighbourhood?"

"He is a carpenter, Ma'am, in the next village."

Miss Emily blushed; Mr. Wilson did not, but continued—"The kindness of my friends having brought me up in a different situation in life, has made me a very unprofitable son. My father has been a most kind parent; and had he not yielded up his interest for what he conceived my profit, I might long before this have been of considerable service to him in his business, and saved him much trouble in his old age."

"Truly, Sir," said Mr. Vasaley, "the satisfaction of seeing you—"

then pausing a little, "noticed by his Grace must overbalance every inconvenience."

"Why, Sir," replied Wilson, smiling "my father, I believe, would be as happy with me at home; my mother's vanity, I confess—Ladies, you will pardon one of your own sex;—but I must say no more, or you will accuse me of satirizing you."

"When we think," replied Mrs. Vasaley, "that you are satirizing us, we will chuse Miss Emily for our champion."

This was uttered with great affected archness: Wilson coloured not a little, but, recovering himself, replied—"Miss Emily, indeed, would turn my satire to praise at any time."

When Wilson had departed, Miss Emily, addressing herself to Mrs. Vasaley, said—"My dear Mrs. Vasaley, surely this Mr. Wilson can never be the son of a common carpenter?"

"'Tis even so, my dear;—I told you so before."

"Oh, I thought you were in joke. Well, whoever he is, he is a gentleman;—yet I can scarcely believe any of you."

But, among all Mr. Vasaley's household, Wilson had not a warmer defender than the beautiful little Fanny; and among the many admirers who already began to court the smiles of Miss Emily, Wilson was ever aided by the good word and kind wishes of the sister.

That urbanity of manners, which was so conspicuous in this young man, penetrated, like the genial warmth of the sun, into every breast; that steady uprightness of conduct, which ever applauded what was right in others, and condemned what was wrong, made him appear to all what he really was—the friend of humankind.— No poor man every thought him proud, no rich one mean. In whatever company he was present, he never affected to be superior to any one; and among the greatest men in the kingdom, not the smallest traces of an abject servility was to be perceived. In his friendships steady—in his love constant—in his whole deportment mild, resolute, and open to the truth. By nature he was warm and hasty; and though he laboured to divest himself of these angry ebullitions, yet the dignified glow of offended virtue would frequently burst forth in defiance of every exertion.

The rules by which he endeavoured to form his conduct, were the genuine principles of Christianity, which he would affirm were so plain and simple, that common reason alone was necessary to inform us what was right or wrong.

A man, such as I have described, whatever disadvantages of birth he might labour under, could not fail to be an interesting object to a woman of sense. No fair one could form an acquaintance without respecting him, and his addresses must at least appear in the light of a compliment.

But when the increasing notice which the Duke of Silsbury took of him, is considered, it even gave him a worldly consequence superior to most young men.

When he first became an inmate of the castle, he rarely saw his Grace. Sometimes, when he joined the hounds, the Duke would enter into conversation with him. Every conference satisfied him that Wilson was more worthy of his notice. The Duke made him a present of two hunters, and kept them entirely for his riding. If Wilson was absent from a day's sport, the Duke began to miss him. When any particular sport was expected, Wilson was ever informed; and perceiving it pleased his patron, he seldom failed to attend. By degrees his Grace saw more and more of him within the castle. He took pleasure in seeing and hearing the improvements of his children; and he soon found that Wilson was become a general favourite.

The house-steward was very old and infirm; Wilson frequently assisted him, and, on his demise (the beginning of the third year), his Grace offered the place to the other, which was with gratitude accepted.

Thus, by slow and regular gradations, did his Grace's favour increase; and by the time Wilson had entered his twenty-first year, it was generally known that this young man was left one of the trustees to his Grace's younger children.

I have related these things now that the reader may see why so beautiful, so accomplished, and rich a young lady as Miss Emily Bellaire, did not spurn at his addresses; as I wish not to have the *dernier* resort of the Novelist historian to the almighty power of Love.

The first critic of the Augustan age remarked upon poetry—*and Novels we know are a species of poetry.*—

"Nec Deus intersit nisi dignus vindice nodus
"Inciderit:"[1]

Which is as much as to say, never let young heroes and heroines play the fool, if they can possibly help it.

Therefore it is, that I wish *rationally* to account for the lovely Miss Emily permitting the devoirs of young Wilson; for, though the fair

---

1   "Nor let a god come in, unless the difficulty be worthy of such an intervention," from the *Epistularum Liber Secundus*, Epistula III (commonly known as *Ars Poetica*), by Quintus Horatius Flaccus (Horace).

lady fed her fond lover's flame with hopes, she could not be said absolutely to have accepted him.

To speak literally, Miss Emily certainly gave the young gentleman every encouragement to persevere in his suit; yet she had neither *bona fide* (in honour) entered into any positive engagement to marry him, nor had she dismissed all other pretenders. No, the fascinating smile was not yet confined, and daily almost, may I say, were human victims offered up at the shrine of her beauty.

CHAPTER X.

As Miss Emily Bellaire soon became the fashionable object of the men's admiration, and the ladies' envy, in this part of the country, it is no matter of wonder than the fame of her beauty should reach the ears of the gallant Marauder, who was just returned from his travels.

Mr. Marauder spent the greatest part of his time in town, on his first arrival from abroad, as Lady James was then in London, and afterwards he was at his friend Cloudley's. It was very late, therefore, in the summer before he made his appearance at Hazleton.

Mr. Marauder's acquaintance with the neighbouring gentry was very distant indeed; he considered them as beings of a lower order.

Immediately on his arrival in England he had been presented at Court by the Earl of Gayden, as the presumptive heir of the Dukedom of Silsbury; he had since been introduced to the first Nobility in the kingdom, and was now forming his establishment on the most fashionable scale, as became his splendid fortune and vast expectations.

Lady James was at this time in the country, and her dutiful son came down for two days to enquire after her health.

In the course of a morning's ride he met Miss Emily on horseback, attended by Wilson. A few paces behind were Mr. Vasaley, another gentleman, and the little Fanny.

Miss Emily's green blind did not hide her face. Marauder saw in a moment that her beauty had not been magnified.

He stopped his horse when he came to Mr. Vasaley, and politely bowed.

The bow was returned, as a bow generally is from a very great man to one who feels himself an inferior.

Farther than this their acquaintance had not yet commenced; but as Mr. Marauder stopped his horse, Mr. Vasaley said—"How long, Sir, have we had the honour of your company in the country?"

"A few days, Mr. Vasaley;—I purpose staying some weeks,"—an

hasty determination,—"and have stopped my horse to tell you I hope we shall be better neighbours than I have yet found it in my power to be."

"You do me great honour, Sir; I am extremely happy to hear it, and will have the pleasure of paying my respects to you tomorrow."

"I shall be at home all the morning. I hope Mrs. Vasaley is well; I beg my compliments. Good day, Sir."

Such was the origin of Mr. Marauder's introduction to the family of Mr. Vasaley.

The following day Mr. Vasaley's visit was returned. Miss Emily was visible, and her dimples played not in vain. Mr. Marauder smiled most graciously, and accepted an invitation of Mr. Vasaley to dine on the third day.

Here Wilson was, by Mr. Marauder's own desire, introduced to him.

Mr. Marauder said—(no one but their common friend, Mr. Vasaley, was present at the time)—"I should be sorry, Mr. Wilson, that any misunderstanding should take place between me and my neighbours. The impetuosity of boys is no excuse for the quarrels of men. I am happy to meet you at my friend, Mr. Vasaley's."

Wilson replied—"I with pleasure, Sir, accept your offers of civility, and assure you it is my wish to be on terms of friendship with every human creature on the face of the earth."

Perhaps this was not the kind of answer to gain the favour of rising greatness; but Wilson spoke it from his heart. Mr. Marauder politely bowed, and the gentleman walked into the other room to the ladies.

This beginning of civilities between two young men, born under the same planet, with the same influences, did not long escape the ears of Dr. Line. Now his predictions began to be fulfilled, and he looked forward with confidence to the completion of them.

He borrowed immediately the excise-man's horse, and took his usual journey to his clerical friend. Nay, so anxious was he to be the messenger of good tidings, that he is reported to have rode nearly five miles an hour—a speedy rate to which he had long been unused.

"Oh Mr. Lockeridge!" exclaimed he, "in these degenerate days, when the noble science of astrology is confounded with the juggles of the magician, rejoice with me that my plain and simple calculation has evinced that a knowledge of the heavenly bodies is a sure and certain rule to judge of the occurrences of this inferior, poor, dependant spot of earth."

He told his tale: Mr. Lockeridge congratulated him, with his usual good-nature, on the rising friendship of the young men.

"Yes, my dear friend, the hour of maturity is at hand; their fates reach their climax—their destinies, interwoven, verge to the same point—and peace, friendship, and unanimity entwine them together."

The warm heart of Dr. Line was never checked by his friend with any cynical remark.

CHAPTER XI.

A reconciliation having thus taken place between the young *gentlemen* (if by that universal term they may be linked together), they frequently met at Mr. Vasaley's.

The attractive magnet drew them with an irresistible impulse.

Wilson had been for some time a declared admirer.

Mr. Marauder did not appear in so ostensible a light. Yet not unmoved did Wilson perceive the attentions of the future Duke. The quick eye of love was alarmed; he fancied the lovely damsel too much encouraged his rival.

Perhaps the reader will be able to judge more of the feelings of the parties if I transcribe a love scene, than from a thousand remarks:—if they are themselves lovers, I am sure they will; if they know not how to love, they are every way uninterested.

One morning, in a delicious *tête-à-tête* with his fair mistress—many sweet and tender things had already passed—she said—"Well, Sir, how do you like Mr. Marauder? don't you think him very agreeable?"

"I am afraid lest Miss Emily should think him too agreeable."

"Oh, ridiculous! Come, don't pretend to be jealous. What, you suppose every well-dressed man to be a most formidable rival?"

"Ah! Emily, how can you accuse me of needless jealousy? Does Mr. Marauder attempt to conceal the passion you have inspired him with? Do I not know by my own feelings what is the object that brings him to Mr. Vasaley's?"

Emily smiled. Wilson continued.—

"Have I not, dearest Emily, reason to be alarmed when I consider the powerful recommendations with which my rival is armed—when I know my own insignificance?"

Miss Emily tried to look grave.

"I am sorry, Mr. Wilson, you should have so bad an opinion of me as to suppose the gifts of Fortune will affect my heart. But I believe you have no very favourable sentiments of women in general, and I see no reason why you should exempt me from the list."

"My dearest Emily," taking her hand, "how can you so cruelly torment me? On your favour have I built my fondest hopes, and I tremble when I see any one attempt to rob me of my treasure."

Emily's looks spoke encouragement; Wilson, with increasing ardour, proceeded.—"But will my lovely girl promise me her favour, will she sanction my love, will she consent to my wishes and kindly permit me to speak to her guardians, to say I have her approbation to address them—to hasten—"

"Oh dear me! what a hurry the good man is in! Indeed I can promise nothing. You know we are both children in the eyes of the law. You cannot tell what may happen. Wait patiently, my good friend," laying her hand familiarly on his.

Wilson kissing it in raptures—"Shall I call you cruel or kind? If you knew, my dearest Emily, how wretched this suspense makes me, surely you would bless me with a more determinate answer. Let me then speak to your trustees. Why should my beloved girl delay? I know I am unworthy such excellence; but if you could read my heart, where every motion, every thought—"

"I am not to be hurried, my good man: I insist upon it you say not a word to my guardians, unless you mean to forfeit my favour for ever. Is it necessary to have any other approbation than mine?"

"No, no, my charming Emily, it is you alone are the object of my pride and my ambition. I wish but to hasten over the tedious forms and ceremonies that prevent me from claiming you by a legal title. Oh glorious moment! when the holy bands of matrimony shall give you to these arms—when I am blessed with a right to protect and defend you! Say, my dearest, loveliest Emily, shall I sweep away the impediments?"

"Not a step further, as you value me. Good day! I must begone and dress me. We see you in the evening?"

"As true as the dial to the sun."

"Well, good bye!—spare your similes to another time."—So spoke the fair daughter of Eve, and was off in a moment.

Wilson had not been gone ten minutes before Marauder called. Emily ran down stairs immediately.

"Here comes my lovely murderess," exclaimed Mr. Marauder, meeting her at the door, and taking her not unwilling hand.—"Ah! Emily, how many poor hearts have you broken? What number do I stand in your list?"

"Oh!" replied Emily, with a killing smile, "I put you on the blank side, among the insensibles."

"No, Emily, if sensibility claims your love, you will put me first on the white side. Only feel my heart, my charming angel! how it beats to fly to you!"

With a little coyness on the part of the fair maiden, he pressed her hand to his breast; she, laughing, replied—"It's a wanderer, I believe, and seems ready to be off."

"Not so, dear Emily; like a poor ghost, you charm it within the circle of your attractions. It is vain for me that I think of returning to town—that I seat me calmly in my mother's parlour—that I attempt to read, write or otherwise employ me: I instantly find I have lost my better part, and as I know you to be the thief, I am come to reclaim it."

"Well, take it, and begone!"

"No, I lose it with such pleasure, I would rather make an exchange, if a certain sentimental young *gentleman* whom I saw at a distance striding over the fields, has not been beforehand with me."

"Ridiculous! Mr. Marauder."

"What, is the fluttering thing only bespoke, and not yet departed?"

Emily, whose expressive countenance had before given its zest to every word she uttered, answered but with *a look*—such a look!

Marauder, interpreting it in his own favour, continued—"Then let me catch it in my arms, and make sure of it ere it is too late."

As he spoke, he caught the tempting object in his arms, and hastily snatched a kiss.

"Upon my life, Mr. Marauder, I shall leave you!" pretending displeasure by an assumed gravity; "you are getting rude, Sir!"

"Can my lovely Emily be surprised I am not insensible when all the world adores her? She called me a stoic just now; I only wish to convince her I am not so to her charms."

"It is very fortunate we poor simple maidens do not give credit to every word you fine gentlemen utter."

"Is it necessary I should *speak* to declare the language of my soul? Do not *my looks* every moment betray me? If I called Emily ordinary—if I said her eyes wanted brightness, her features expression, her form the graces, who would know my picture? Is my language to be laconic, my manner torpid, as if I conversed with her grandmother?"

"Nonsense, Mr. Marauder! I shall fly if you do not talk more reasonably."

"Charming maid!" continued Marauder, dropping on one knee, and taking again her snowy hand; "no, it is not the enchanting face, the bewitching form that I adore—it is that heavenly soul, which every turn of the countenance shews, where the very angels themselves might look with pleasure, and see themselves outshone. 'Tis this I worship—this day and night employs my busy mind, and to make myself master of this beloved idol, I would, like the giants of old, shake the throne of Jove himself."

"Indeed, Mr. Marauder, you are getting very serious."

"Yes, my lovely friend—Oh! that I might call you by a dearer name!—I wish to be so. Thus on my knee let me entreat your love. Say, and ease my heart, that no cursed rival deprives me of it. Dearest Emily, dearest, most beloved maid, turn not away!—Oh say I am not indifferent to you!"

"Why should I *answer* this smart speech?" replied Emily, with an arch smile. "You told me before I was to read your looks;—can you not read mine?"

"Yes," retorted Marauder, springing up, "I will, at least, explain them in my own favour, and the sacred kiss of love shall seal my glowing hopes."

Mr. Marauder was as good as his word.

"Really, Sir," exclaimed Emily, trying to pout, "I shall be very angry; as you don't know how to behave, I must begone.—Good gracious!" continued she, looking at her watch, "it wants but half an hour of dinner-time.—Hark! there is the first bell!"

Emily tripped lightly away.

"She is and shall be mine!" said Marauder to himself, looking eagerly after her.

Nothing, perhaps, can be more dull and unmeaning than a love scene literally told:—it is the language of the eyes, the pathos of the acting, an indescribable *je ne sais quoi*, which cannot be translated into any one language, but is in reality that universal language of which so much has been said, so little understood. Every love-sick enamorato, from the clown that breaks the clods, to the smirking courtier that shivers at a breeze—from the dustman of St. Giles's, to the Grand Signior, or still grander Emperor of China, equally understand it.

It is not then for any information in that universal science of love that I have repeated the two last scenes; but that the reader may form in his own mind a clear opinion of each of the gentlemen in the eyes—I cannot say heart—of the beauteous Emily.

The advantages that both lovers had personally and mentally were by no means of a *par*. That they were in Mr. Marauder's favour was clearly evident. In manly beauty they might be equal; yet in a fashionable case, a suavity blended with a dignity of manners, a thoughtless gracefulness of action, not omitting the power of dress, Wilson could in no point compare with the other.

Again, in affairs of gallantry Marauder had been deeply versed, and ever successful. He might almost have said with Cæsar, upon another occasion—

"Veni, vidi, vici!"[1]

or more literally, in Marauder's case, it was—"I came, I *was seen*, I conquered;" but Wilson was a novice in these matters. Wilson too was only able to utter with confusion the dictates of the heart:—Mr. Marauder, perfectly collected, spoke from the reflection of the mind. Again, in the knowledge of these sweet things, Miss Emily was as much *superior* to Wilson, as she was *inferior* to Marauder.

Labouring under these disadvantages, it is no wonder Wilson made but a slow progress in his amorous siege, though in less than six weeks Marauder made sure of the citadel.

CHAPTER XII.

From Mr. Marauder's first acquaintance with Miss Emily, it had been an invariable rule with him to scoff and ridicule Wilson and his principles; but this was carried on by degrees, till in the end he had completely undermined him in the favour of Miss Emily.

Most cautious, indeed, was Marauder in Wilson's presence; and, in general, his satire was more in distant allusions than personal remarks. Among many of the topics was religion, which it was evident Wilson highly respected. This was a subject Marauder could treat a thousand ways; though when Wilson was in company, he took good care not to expose his own principles by giving his opinion too freely: not that he valued the pleasure or displeasure of the other, but the time was not come when he wished to take off the mask.

Marauder seemed to have imbibed an inveterate dislike against Ministers of religion.—"Canting hypocrites; sly Priests, who fancy every one to be such fools as to believe their nonsense; slaves of prejudice; fellows who wilfully shut their eyes, then say it is dark," and

---

1 "I came, I saw, I conquered": Julius Caesar, as recorded in Suetonius, *Lives of the Caesars,* "Divus Julius" section 37.

many such-like common-place terms were frequently uttered by him. He brought many books also to Miss Emily, particular passages of which he often marked, and sometimes pointedly read.

Among the first was Mrs. Wollstonecraft's Rights of Women.

One day having read some pages from it, he remarked—"Well, my dear Emily, what think you of this lady's notions?"

"I think she is very favourable to our sex."

"Not a whit too much so, my dear girl; why should there be any inferiority in the one sex than the other? In what are we superior to you? In beauty and wit you always excel us; and were your education not so confined, I doubt not you would equally rival us in the most learned studies. Yes, some of your sex have already done it. For classical learning and critical judgment, a Dacier has been most eminent;[1] and this ingenious and elegant authoress is herself a strong example."

Marauder ran on with such a string of female names, that even Emily began to fancy herself half a Grecian; so artfully did he mix the most pernicious doctrines with the most grateful flattery.

As Marauder did not openly profess himself the favoured lover of Emily Bellaire, Wilson was totally ignorant of the progress his rival had made; and though sometimes a little jealousy might ruffle his mind, Miss Emily was so guarded before company, that at the very moment when Marauder made sure of his conquest, Wilson also flattered himself with having more interest than ever.

The motives, as well as the means, of secrecy between the parties, will fully appear as the history continues. No one, indeed, was so ignorant of the progress Marauder had made as Wilson himself.

Mr. and Mrs. Vasaley in part knew it; but they were too much *people of the world* to think there was any harm in a little flirting.

Once Vasaley mentioned to his wife that he was afraid Emily Bellaire gave Wilson too much encouragement if she really meant to have Mr. Marauder.

But Mrs. Vasaley replied—"It would be a very hard thing if a beautiful young woman, before she tied herself for life, might not indulge in a little innocent coquetry. Besides, Miss Emily's choice might depend at last upon the *temper* of the person she chose; and how could she so well know the peculiarities of his temper, if she did not give him some encouragement to continue his suit?"

---

1 Anne Dacier, née Lefèbvre (1654-1720), a French translator of classical texts, most famously the *Iliad* (1699) and *Odyssey* (1708).

Many other arguments, equally cogent and reasonable, Mrs. Vasaley produced, and Mr. Vasaley allowed them to be so.

Little Fanny, though seven years younger than her sister, was a child of very promising abilities as well as person, and endowed with an excellent understanding, undebased by vanity, uncorrupted by flattery. Young as she was, she perceived the insincerity of her sister's behaviour; and being always most partial to Wilson, and no great admirer of Marauder, who sometimes treated her with great freedom, and sometimes great indifference, she frequently, in her artless way, mentioned it. She, of course, also had more opportunities of seeing her sister's behaviour than any one else.

Fanny was about thirteen—an age of childhood to a young female, but by no means an age of ignorance.

One day when Marauder had just left Emily, and Fanny had been present the latter part of the time, she said—"Dear me, sister, what would Mr. Wilson think, if he knew you heard so kindly all the fine things Mr. Marauder has been speaking?"

"I care very little, Fanny, what Mr. Wilson thinks."

"Why surely, Emily, you don't like Mr. Marauder better than Mr. Wilson? and before you know Mr. Marauder, I thought you was in love with Mr. Wilson: you used to say to me he was so sensible, and so handsome, and so good-natured, and so—"

"Pshaw! Fanny, you will be a child all your life. Can't you see a vast difference between the son of a carpenter, and a fine young man, that is to be Duke, and to have all these great estates round the country here?"

Mr. Vasaley's, among others, was rented of the Duke.

"I don't know, Emily, that he is a bit the better for that; and I am sure I think there is no more comparison between Mr. Wilson and this fine saucy gentleman, than—"

"I believe, Fanny, you are in love with Wilson yourself; you are always so praising him, and so pleased when you see him."

Fanny coloured. Emily continued.

"And, to do him justice, he praises you almost as much: you are so sweet a child, amiable a temper, excellent a disposition—and then he is always bringing you books to read. I declare, I think, when he comes here, he makes as much love to you as me."

"How can you talk so, Emily? You know it is all for love of you; and he always calls me his little sister."

"Yes, and kisses you for his love of me."

Poor Fanny coloured more than ever.

"Well, he has only to wait," said Emily, "six or eight years, and you'll make him a most excellent wife. Faith! he is too steady and precise for me."

"You didn't say so, sister," replied Fanny, recovering herself, "before you knew Mr. Marauder; and as for kissing, Mr. Marauder is always wanting to kiss me, but I hate him, and he never did and never shall kiss me; so you may say what you will about me and Mr. Wilson, but I am certain you don't treat him well."

"Indeed, Fanny, you give yourself great airs."

"No, sister, I don't mean to do so."

"Why do you pretend to judge of my conduct, and speak so contemptuously of Mr. Marauder, whom every body says is the most polite, well-bred, fashionable man? He is the nephew to the Duke of Silsbury, and will some day be Duke himself, whilst Wilson is no better than a head servant."

"Yet the Duke likes him better than his nephew, and treats him with more kindness."

"For all that, Mr. Marauder will be Duke at last, and have all the estates besides."

"Well, sister Emily, I only spoke as I thought best for you. Mr. Marauder is always so sly and cunning; and though he makes me such fine speeches when you are not by, I shall never like him the better for it."

"Why, what does he say to you, child?"

"He says how tall and genteel I am, and how much I am like you, and—"

"Oh he does! there is great harm in that, to be sure."

"And he tries to take hold of me—but he shall not touch me; and though Mr. Wilson did kiss me, it was when you was by, for he's not so artful and impudent; and I think you'll be much happier with him."

"I tell you what, Fanny," retorted Emily, very gravely, "you know nothing at all about these matters: remember, child, you are but just entered in your teens, and it's pretty, indeed, that you should pretend to question and instruct your eldest sister. There, go and read that fine book about the Bible—your favourite's present—Miss Moore's Sacred Dramas, as he calls them;[1] that's most proper for a child to do."

"It would do you no harm, Emily, to read them, although Mr. Marauder did abuse them, and laugh, and call them a pack of Parson's stuff: and I hate him for that too."

---

1 Hannah More's *Sacred Dramas, Chiefly intended for Young Persons, to which is added Sensibility, a Poem* (1782) cast episodes from the Bible in dramatic form.

"I tell you what, Fanny," continued Miss Emily, with the authority of an elder sister, "it's very wrong of you to talk in this way of Mr. Marauder, and pretend to judge of his conduct. Mind your dolls and your books, and don't trouble yourself with things you can't understand."

Such were the different opinions of the company at Mr. Vasaley's concerning the two gentlemen.

CHAPTER XIII.

In the short space of two months, after their first acquaintance, Mr. Marauder completely alienated the affections, or at least the inclinations, of Emily Bellaire from Wilson, and transferred them to his own proper person. His whole artillery of prayers, vows, compliments, and flattery had been levelled at a weak fortification, where Vanity commanded in chief, and Folly was Prime-Minister. The outworks were already won, and the citadel was ready to surrender at discretion; but Marauder, like a complete General, was not fond of giving too favourable terms.

To drop my military metaphor, Mr. Marauder, not doubting of his success, seriously reasoned with himself whether he should take Miss Emily for a *wife* or a *mistress*. *Many* were the arguments for the last opinion—*one* only for the first.

"Miss Emily Bellaire," he would say to himself, "is most lovely and beautiful—perfections as necessary, perhaps more so, in a mistress as a wife.—Yes; but she has twenty thousand pounds.

"Emily Bellaire is sharp, ingenious, and accomplished in the routine of fashion—giddy and thoughtless in the world. Qualities of very little use in a wife?—Yes; but she has twenty thousand pounds.

"Emily Bellaire has no great advantages in her birth, family, or connections; her expectations very few, her acquaintance neither possessed of interest nor consequence. These things are not wanted in a mistress?—No; but she has twenty thousand pounds.

"Do I want money?—No.

"If I marry her, can she be supported without it?—No.

"If she is my mistress, will not her own fortune be sufficient?— Yes, in a little time.

"And when I come to the Dukedom, will the interest of twenty thousand pounds support the Duchess of Silsbury?—No, no, no.

"What then shall I gain upon the whole by matrimony?—Nothing.

"What shall I lose by making her my mistress?—Nothing.

"By which shall I triumph most successfully over the carpenter's son?—Not by matrimony.

"By which shall I gain most *éclat* in the eyes of the world?—Not by matrimony.

"By which shall I be most free, most independent, and unencumbered?—Not by matrimony.

"Well, then, my lovely Emily, uncramped by foolish ties, thou shalt be mine. If I marry thee, I may repent, and cannot change my destiny. Without matrimony I shall have no need for repentance, and may change my mind whenever I think proper."

Mr. Marauder, having reasoned upon this business, was finally determined by reading the will of Mr. Bellaire, Miss Emily's father.

"I leave to my dear daughters, Emily and Fanny Bellaire, the whole of my property, which on account of my children being both females, I have invested in the public funds: namely, forty thousand pounds in the Three per Cent. Consols. That is, to each of my daughters twenty thousand pounds, &c. &c. &c. &c."

Mr. Marauder was satisfied; and duly considering that twenty thousand pounds Three per Cent. stock, greatly weakened the only argument for matrimony, drew his conclusion in a *negative* on the subject.

Neither was the young man ignorant of the wonderful arrangements of William Godwin; but Marauder, though, if it suited his purpose, he would make use of the conceit of folly of another, had too much sense to be led by them himself.

When he pointed out to Emily, Godwin's *wise* arguments, that "it is absurd to expect the inclinations and wishes of two human beings to coincide through any long period of time. To oblige them to act and to live together, is to subject them to some inevitable portion of thwarting, bickering, and unhappiness,"*—Marauder laughed at this

---

★ [CL] The words of this contemptible writer are here and in other places quoted word for word. See vol.ii. Political Justice, page 497. [As Lucas says, he quotes directly from William Godwin's *Enquiry Concerning Political Justice, and its Influence on Morals and Happiness.* The first edition was published in 1793, but Lucas cites the revised second edition of 1795/1796. See Introduction and Appendix C for more on Lucas's use of Godwin's text. Whenever Lucas quotes from *Political Justice* a page reference to what is probably the most available edition (edited by Isaac Krammick, first published by Penguin in 1976 and periodically reprinted) has been given here in the footnotes, thus: *Political Justice*, ed. Krammick, Penguin edn., 761. This Penguin edition uses Godwin's substantially revised edition, which often differs in detail from the second edition which Lucas was using.]

author; and when he afterwards read page 499, vol.2.—"So long as I seek by despotic and artificial means to engross a woman to myself, and to prohibit my neighbour from proving his superior claim, I am guilty of the most odious selfishness;" he would exclaim—"Dear Emily, I am the most selfish man breathing!" Yet still the poison, however loathsome it might appear, could not fail, in some degree, to contaminate so young and inexperienced a mind.

To Emily Bellaire, so lovely and so beautiful, it was of more consequence that her guardian and his wife were weak, silly, fashionable people, than if she had not possessed those personal attractions. What vanity and fashionable folly induced the credulous fair one to believe, Mrs. Vasaley, whose judgment was most light and trifling, countenanced and approved. As for Mr. Vasaley, he might have been a very worthy, good kind of a man, if he had never acted from his own judgment and abilities; and, instead of being the master of a family, had passed through life without ever possessing *a will of his own*.

CHAPTER XIV.

Marauder, having fully reasoned upon the point of matrimony, next laid out a regular plan to forward his views without it.

As he resolved these things in his ride to Mr. Vasaley's, he remarked—"I presume it will keep me a few weeks longer from possession. Matrimony I might have to-morrow."

According to the plan he had adopted, the moment he arrived at Mr. Vasaley's, Marauder looked unusually grave.

As soon as the lovers were alone, Miss Emily could not fail remarking it.

After many attempts at an evasion to make the lady more anxious, Marauder produced a letter, saying—"Last night I received this cursed epistle! If I thought Wilson had been advising his Grace, I would blow his brains out."

Miss Emily was alarmed, and read—

"SIR,
"I have undoubted intelligence that you are entering into a matrimonial engagement. Let me forewarn you—if you ally yourself to one, however beautiful and rich, that has not a family and alliance to boast such as the Duke of Silsbury might expect, you will *for ever* forfeit the favour of one already greatly displeased.

"SILSBURY"

"To shew," exclaimed Marauder, "my dearest Emily, how I despise the writer, how I love the subject, if she will deign to accept my hand, to-morrow, by the Parson's assistance, we will bid him defiance! Oh most lovely of your sex! there is nothing I would not sacrifice to gain your smiles and favour! Infamous scrawl!" seizing suddenly the paper, "thus, thus let me tear thee to atoms!"

Emily, flattered at his warmth, pleased with his ardour, strongly protested against so hasty a marriage. Her lover, on the other hand, as eagerly pressed for it, though in so general a manner, that had the fair-one unexpectedly consented, every arrangement still remained to be settled, and a thousand means were open to defer it.

Mr. Marauder now burst forth into a violent abuse against the Duke and Wilson; neither of whom I need not inform the reader, knew no more of the letter than Dr. Line's friend in the moon.

Turning the course of his oratory from satire to praise, Marauder declared, in the most solemn terms, that in every respect he considered a match with his beloved Emily beyond his expectations.

"Pardon me, lovely girl, if I seem to flatter you:—you know my sincerity. Such beauty alone deserves the first rank; but with the sense, the judgment, the abilities my dear girl possesses, the first Prince in Europe would be most highly honoured with her hand; and when to these is added a splendid fortune, such as falls to my Emily's lot, where is the parent who, even in cold, prudential reasons, would not rejoice in the alliance for his son? Believe me that the cursed writing was all malice and revenge. 'Tis true, for I will conceal nothing from my Emily, there are a few estates the Duke has promised to leave with the title, and which are in his own disposal; and, as the wretch cannot live long, it might, in a worldly light, be better—No, nothing can be better that would debar me for one moment of the possession of her who is more dear to me than all the titles, honours, or riches the whole world can ever give!"

With a deep sigh he pressed her to his bosom.

Emily was really affected; and the tempter perceived that opportunity only was wanting to make sure of his prey.

With well-dissembled sorrow, Mr. Marauder affectionately kissed the pearly drops from her lovely face, and they returned together into the drawing-room.

Mr. Marauder had dined at Mr. Vasaley's; much company was expected in the evening: he therefore seized on a few minutes for the foregoing scene, rightly judging that the confusion of a large assembly was best adapted to prevent any regular judgment in the mind of his fair mistress.

Mr. Marauder was indebted to Nature for a fine and handsome person, and to Art for a judicious display of it. He was tall in stature, and of a commanding aspect, aquiline nose, a bold and full eye, large mouth, strong and well limbed, haughty in his usual gait, and very erect. He spoke the living languages, particularly French and Italian, fluently; was well versed in modern literature, politics, history, and geography. A constant smile exhilarated his features, which varied to a contemptuous sneer, or an insinuating blandishment, as the different human passions affected him. Other particularities of his character have appeared before, and will more fully expand themselves in the continuation of this narrative. Mr. Marauder was nearly the same age as Emily; and in a knowledge of the female heart was a most wonderful adept. Nor is it a matter of any surprise, when we consider that his education had been among a series of gallantry.

From his youth too every thing had been subservient to him. His haughty, ambitious soul could never brook restraint from any one.

His tutors had not led his mind to what *they* thought most proper, but had improved it in those points in which he thought proper to be instructed.

Literature, as it is generally called, he despised. He chiefly prided himself upon that insight he had gained into the passions and foibles of mankind.

He never formed an acquaintance, but his first study was to discover his weakness and failings; and on these points he secretly, constantly attacked him.

To Mr. Vasaley he kept up his dignity; but with occasional condescensions, made him believe he greatly esteemed him.

To Wilson he assumed an air of openness and ease.

To Mrs. Vasaley, direct or indirect flattery was his sole conversation; but to little Fanny, whom, as a sweet bud of beauty, he could not fail of regarding, by all his wiles he could never make himself an object of favour. With a spirited modesty she damped his kindness, and checked his freedom; when, at last, finding all his arts baffled, he affected an indifference which was foreign to his real sentiments.

According to the plan Marauder had formed in his own mind, he took every opportunity of insinuating these principles he conceived necessary for his purpose into the mind of the too credulous Emily. Flattery ever took the lead in the conversation, and softened the heart for what was to follow.

One day, to a very strong and expressive panegyric on the *female* character, Miss Emily replied—"The ladies, I am sure, are very much obliged to you for being so able a defender."

"Not in the least, my dear girl; I speak but the simple truth. All men, if they would but confess it, know it so; therefore it is, they have made laws to give man the superiority, and pretend oftentimes to call these laws by the name of religion.—What is matrimony? But a catch to decoy the poor female to the obedience of an insolent man."

"Oh! if you talk in this way, you'll absolutely frighten me."

"No, my dearest Emily, it is only that I love you too well to deceive you. After all the abuse we have given our neighbours, the French, they have nobly broken through this foolish tie, and generously give to the female that freedom she so well knows how to use."

"I never was in France, yet I have always understood that they were the most polite and gallant nation in the world; but I thought now they had killed their king, they were no better than savages."

Marauder, in the most plausible terms, attributed this infamous act to a few individuals; and then, in terms the most glowing, pointed out the present method of contracting alliances in that kingdom.

He did not explain to the fair Emily to what an humiliating condition the female sex is now reduced in France—that there is not a single act of the Government in which they are considered as having any rights whatever.

He did not tell her that women were no longer regarded, but as objects of sensual pleasure.

He did not inform her that they had no voice, no authority, no vote in the meetings, the councils, or any part of the legislature.

He did not explain that the beloved rights and privileges which the fair sex claim, as mothers, daughters, wives, sisters, were perishing every day; that the virtuous woman and the prostitute, the wife of the Magistrate and the Opera girl were all ranked together in a pestilential den of degenerate equality.

No: he expatiated on the generous principle of the French, which made no distinction between the sexes, which gave equal liberty to both the parties to annul the marriage contract, and which left the fair-one to her own free-will, unshackled by the arbitrary restraints of a tyrannical husband.

All this was quite new to Miss Emily; the pleasing side was alone exhibited; and she admired the candour and generosity of the man who could tell her *bold truths*—a favourite explanatory term of Mr. Marauder.

The following sentiment—of that first of writers, that rational, philosophical, learned, modest, and ingenious of all human naturals, William Godwin—was most familiar to Mr. Marauder; but though Marauder knew better than to quote the sentiment in the *wise-man's own words*, I cannot refrain from gratifying the reader with them, literally taken from his scientific work—"The History of the Intrigues of his own Wife."[1]

"It is difficult," says Mr. Godwin, "to recommend any thing to indiscriminate adoption, contrary to the established rules and prejudices of mankind; but certainly nothing can be so ridiculous upon the face of it, or so contrary to the *genuine march of sentiment*, as to require the overflowings of the soul to wait upon a ceremony, and that which, wherever delicacy and imagination exist, is of all things most sacredly private, to blow a trumpet before it, and to record the moment when it is arrived to his climax."

When this sentiment, in a less philosophical form, came from the tongue of Mr. Marauder, whether there was (what Mr. Godwin just before calls) "a period of throes and resolute explanation attendant on the tale," in any of the love scenes between Miss Emily and the to-be Duke, I cannot say; for this simple reason, that I am not able, with the whole powers of *my* mind, to comprehend what the ingenious Philosopher Godwin means. Perhaps in a future edition of the memoirs of his wife, *ci-devant* mistress, he will favour the *anti-illuminati* with an explanation after each sentence—if it be possible.

With or without (whichever it was) "a period of throes and resolute explanation attendant on the tale," Mr. Marauder did more than his author; he made himself clearly understood by his fair hearer.

Miss Emily's learning was chiefly confined to a knowledge of the French language. Mr. Marauder frequently conversed with her in that tongue—the very language of deceit.

Among the many other writings which Marauder recommended and brought for Emily's perusal, were the celebrated works of Rousseau.[2] Miss Emily read them with a wonderful avidity and satisfaction, favoured by many marginal notes of her attentive lover.

Many other original French Novels, such as Voltaire's Tales, Diderot's Novels, he studiously selected; and where the sentiments appeared too strong, he would soften and explain them. The English writings, except a few chosen *morceaus*, were a fund of satire for

---

1   Godwin's *Memoirs of the Author of A Vindication of the Rights of Woman* (1798; rpt. Peterborough, ON: Broadview Press, 2001, ed. Pamela Clemit and Gina Luria Walker) was widely condemned for its ostentatiously honest account of Mary Wollstonecraft's life.

2   Probably Jean-Jacques Rousseau's *Julie, ou la Nouvelle Héloïse* (1761), which portrays the passionate love of the tutor, St. Preux, and Julie, his pupil, or his *Les Confessions* (1782 and 1789) which describe the author's own romantic adventures.

Marauder; he ridiculed their confined notions, their very dread of speaking the truth, their ignorance of the human heart, their prejudices in favour of their own country.

By conversing with Miss Emily in French, under the idea of improving her in that language, they were under less restraints in the company of the obliging Vasaley and his wife, who affected indeed not to be ignorant of so fashionable an accomplishment, but whose knowledge was only of the parrot-kind.

But lest any of these new notions should, in any degree, alarm his fair convert, he ever spoke in the most rapturous terms of that day when his beloved Emily should be advanced to a station in life she was born to adorn, and should shine in the first circles of fashion as the Duchess of Silsbury.

When Mr. Marauder first made love to Emily Bellaire, there was a boldness, a freedom, an ease in his manners, a self-conceit and *hauteur* which were stamped on his character; now he was all softness, diffidence, humility—his love was almost adoration;—he cautiously avoided what might be termed taking the smallest liberty; and by the time he had entangled the lovely maid most completely into his toil, did he appear to be the most humble of her captives.

When in company with Wilson, this behaviour had more the appearance of despondency than success, and proved the best means he could possibly have adapted to deceive all parties.

Miss Emily, of course, thought her ascendancy greater than ever. He easily made her believe that it was her interest that prevented his instantly and publicly marrying her. Again and again did he press her to consent—despise the anger of his uncle—swear, in the most sacred terms, that it was for her dear sake alone he did not openly claim her as his wife; and, generally, he finished a love-scene with the most insinuating, though respectful endearments, and with vows innumerable, and most solemnly uttered. For however he might think in religious matters, in this case he was by no means deficient in sacred vows and professions; and with the most enrapt enthusiasm did he call on every power above to attest his vows of everlasting love and constancy, while Miss Emily thought not of the poet's maxim—

"But if he swears, he'll certainly deceive you."[1]

---

1   Chamont in Thomas Otway's *The Orphan* (1680) says: "Trust not a man. We are by nature false, / Dissembling, subtle, cruel, and unconstant. / When a man talks of love, with caution trust him; / But, if he swears, he'll certainly deceive thee" (II, 286-89).

Thus did Marauder use every agency of heaven and earth that he was able to employ, to make the fair Emily believe that his love of her was the sole reason for delaying their nuptials: yet, at times, so anxious did he seem for an hasty marriage, in defiance of all obstacles, that he once waited upon her with a license in his pocket. Whether or not it was a real one is no matter, as it was never intended to be used.

Miss Emily, not to be outdone in generosity, strenuously insisted against such hasty proceedings; but it produced the proper effect which Mr. Marauder intended—of throwing Miss Emily more and more off her guard.

CHAPTER XV.

At last the period arrived when Marauder was to give the finishing blow to his ingenious stratagems, when the grand scheme he had so deeply planned was to be put in execution.

It was determined that he was to carry his beloved Emily to town, and there to be privately married; but to deceive the Duke and his party in the country, she was to elope from Mr. Vasaley's, and to live with Marauder as his mistress till after the death of his Grace.

Had Emily Bellaire been a poor, portionless girl, she probably might have had some doubt of the sincerity of her lover, in defiance of all his fine speeches; but so highly had she been buoyed up with her own consequence, her great riches, and so forth, that she entertained not the remotest idea that Marauder considered her in any respect as his inferior. The mean revenge and jealousy of Wilson, she conceived, had misled the Duke; and so well woven was the tale, that had she even had any person to apply to as a confidant, most probably she had never discovered the deceit.

Still it may be a matter of some surprise that Wilson came to be so easily deceived; but it was agreed to, between Mr. Marauder and his fair-one, that she should encourage Wilson's pretences, as a blind to deceive the Duke.

Not that the Duke of Silsbury knew or cared the least about it; but it answered his dutiful nephew's views to pretend that he *did*.

In deceiving Wilson they found little difficulty, as Marauder (it had been said) never carried himself as the favoured lover before company; and, from the very origin of their acquaintance, he always professed himself an admirer.

Marauder, too, generally contrived to visit Miss Emily in a morning—a time of the day when his rival was almost always engaged.

The Duke's children necessarily required part of his time, and he rarely failed, twice a week at least, attending his Grace on his hunting parties;—these avocations of business and pleasure fully occupied his mornings.

Mr. and Mrs. Vasaley, indeed, had some suspicion; yet Miss Emily discovered neither to them nor her sister more than she could possibly help.

Her guardian and his fashionable *cara sposa* perceived with pleasure the prospect of a connection with a man, who, in the course of a few years, would undoubtedly be a Duke; and, as they had before favoured Wilson's pretensions, they were not so anxious for any communications on the subject as they otherwise would have been. They stood in great awe of Wilson, and were fearful he might suspect them of double dealing.—So naturally does Virtue claim the command over low and cunning spirits.

With a secret joy, then, they saw the intimacy increase with a person of Mr. Marauder's family, without knowing to what height it was carried; and not a little did they pride themselves in that connection, which, by their beautiful ward's alliance with him, should so greatly *increase their own consequence.*—And this is the motive that induces parents and guardians, and they who are commonly called friends, so continually to prefer lucrative marriages in the persons of their children or wards, even when in their own individual cases they would act very differently. For as the love of self is, alas! the prevailing motive in all our actions, so it easily accounts for their conduct in this respect.

A parent, guardian, or friend *mentally* reasons in this way; and for the sake of the argument, we will suppose it is a father in the disposal of his daughter.

"What benefit," says he to himself, "accrues to me by marrying my child to a plain, honest, good-tempered man, with little consequence or fortune? To be sure, she will have every chance of common happiness; but it will be entirely confined to herself—it will not influence her family.

"Now if I marry her to a man of consequence and riches, however disagreeable in mind and person, yet the good things of this world that he is possessed of, I shall in some degree participate.

"Am I fond of riding in splendid carriages, of being seen in noble company, of receiving that notice which is ever paid to those allied to wealth and honours,—or am I fond of excellent dinners, of fine wine, of admiration, envy, superiority? Here I am gratified in some, or all of these; here then I gain a something directly or indirectly;

and then my child may not, after all, be unhappy; and I, at least, can say that I have done my part to provide her with these necessary comforts of life all mankind are seeking after.

"In a low and humble marriage I am degraded in the eyes of the world; by allying myself to greatness of any kind, I am exalted by it. The world will command my conduct—not for the man, but the things; and, in either case, the individual man does not affect me, and should he prove unpleasant, I can separate myself from him."

Such-like arguments, with a hundred other, all originating in self, pass through the mind of mankind, and are the great motives that influence them in those incongruous and preposterous matches which too frequently take place; and kinsfolk, friends, and acquaintance of the Vasaley-kind will most commonly be met with.

Without a judgment that looks forward to something better than the things of this world—unless the consideration of what is just and right, instead of what is self-agreeable and pleasant, first takes place, the duty of those who have the superintendence of young minds will be very badly performed.

In these and other cases I am not to think what the world concludes right but I am to promote those measures that will most conduce to virtue, religion, and happiness.

CHAPTER XVI.

The morning on which it was determined for Miss Emily to elope with Mr. Marauder to town, her lover called, as he frequently did, at Mr. Vasaley's, to ask the ladies to take a ride.

Wilson, they knew, was otherwise engaged with the Duke, in a part of the country far distant from their route.

Miss Fanny, who was not partial to Mr. Marauder's company, chose to stay at home, but Mr. and Mrs. Vasaley rode out with them.

Mrs. Vasaley was a very indifferent horsewoman, and rode slow; Mr. Marauder and the fair lady cantered on before.

A chaise and four was in waiting for them at the next market town, and they were off in it immediately they arrived there.

Mr. and Mrs. Vasaley, after riding a few miles, returned home, thinking Miss Emily and her beau would soon follow them. The young couple having often done so before, they had not the smallest apprehension from their absence; but when dinner-time arrived, and no Emily appeared, they began to be alarmed.

A note from the bold heroine to Mr. Vasaley soon explained the affair.

"MY DEAR SIR,

"I have thought proper at last to follow the dictates of my heart, and to accept the protection of the only man I ever truly loved. Time will explain my motives. If a person means to be happy, they must learn to think and act for themselves. The prejudices of a misjudging world I despise. Tell Fanny, as soon as I am settled in my own house, both my dear Mr. Marauder and myself hope she will make it her home, where we shall rejoice also to welcome our kind friends, Mr. and Mrs. Vasaley.

"The servant, who brings this, will take the care of my cloaths. Health and happiness to my dear sister, Mrs. Vasaley, and yourself!

From their beloved
EMILY."

Mr. and Mrs. Vasaley read the note with many expressions of sorrow, but, in truth, with great indifference; poor little Fanny scarcely said a word, yet felt more than can be described. She passed a restless night drowned in tears, inconsolable for the fate of her sister, fearing the worst, yet ignorant of the extent of her fears.

The next evening Wilson called. Fanny saw him coming, and, with her eyes streaming with the pearly dew, rushed out of the house to meet him.

Overcome with her sorrow, she dropped almost lifeless in his arms.

Greatly surprised and concerned at her grief, he, with the affection of a beloved brother, gently enquired the cause.

"Oh Mr. Wilson! that wicked—my poor sister. Yesterday they rode out, and she is gone away with him to London."

"Your sister, my dearest Fanny," guessing very easily the person, "carried off by Mr. Marauder?—Insolent rascal! but I will instantly pursue and retake her. Who had he to assist him in forcing her away?"

"Mr. Vasaley has received a letter from Emily. She does not appear to have been taken away against her will."

Wilson appeared thunderstruck. Pausing for a few moments, he exclaimed—"Not taken away against her will?—Impossible, Fanny! For what purpose could she elope? If she had thought proper to accept Mr. Marauder, who could prevent her?"

Mr. Vasaley now came up, and with very few words gave Wilson Emily's note.

Hastily he read it over.

Again and again he more clearly perused it.

"Yes, it is your sister's hand-writing; it does not seem forced, or even constrained. Are these her sentiments—'not happy unless we think and act for ourselves?'—Alas! I fear if she follows that maxim, she will never be happy. What," turning to Mr. Vasaley, "did none of you know of this?"

Mr. Vasaley made a lame speech professing his ignorance of her partiality for Mr. Marauder, but spoke boldly and clearly concerning his not knowing the intention of running away.

Wilson, being unable to get any insight into this mysterious affair, and extremely hurt at every part of Miss Emily's conduct, soon took his leave.

Fanny followed him to the door.—"I am afraid, Mr. Wilson, you are displeased with me. Indeed I knew nothing of it."

"My dear, my kind Fanny, you are the last person in the world I could blame. Do not distress yourself my lovely girl. To see you unhappy, will afflict me more than all the rest. I have lately suspected some mystery in your sister, and came this evening on purpose to gain a final answer. This unkind behaviour I cannot but feel; yet, believe me, dear Fanny, that Emily's conduct shall never alienate my love and affection for you. If my good girl at any time wants a friend or adviser, in me she shall find one that will never forsake her."

"Thank-you, dear Mr. Wilson; but when shall I see you again? I have got a great deal to say and to ask you."

"Tomorrow, in the afternoon, I will certainly be here; and hope my Fanny will dry up her tears, for I am afraid her sister does not deserve them."

CHAPTER XVII.

Return we to the lovers, who, borne on the soft winds which the sportive deity had raised, flew rapidly away.

Whether the rumbling of a four-wheeled carriage inspires the tender passion, I am not casuist enough to determine; but it certainly is most excellently adapted, in many respects, for that kind of oratory which the gay votaries of Cupid excel in.

Those breaks—pauses—unfinished sentences are wonderfully assisted by the irregular motion of the vehicle. The intervals of sighs, aspiration, respiration, consideration, dubitation, and all of this kind are extremely well filled up by the music of those quadruple spheres.

It may be called the *desideratum* of all languages—"A sound that is an echo to the sense."

While it aids so powerfully the speaker, it is equally efficacious to the hearer. It produces that state of inaction on the mind which is so necessary to attention. All which whether Mr. Marauder thought or understood is no matter, but he certainly made the very best use of it.

After violent profession of everlasting love and constancy, after a volubility of praises to his fair companion for that independency of mind which soars beyond the notions of the vulgar, and can break asunder the fetters of prejudice, he lamented the vast numbers of people who were still slaves to the idle opinion of the world.

"How few do I find like my beloved Emily, whose good sense and clear reason can so soon distinguish what is *right* in defiance of foolish customs, and whose minds are strong enough to perform it!"

"Among those who pretend to teach others scarcely do I know where to find one "black coat,"* Mr. Marauder's most moderate term for a Clergyman, "that I dare trust the secret of our marriage to. Of all bigoted wretches those are the worst.† If the Duke should hear we are privately married, it were as well that I publicly claimed, and that I should at once glory in my heavenly prize in the open face of the world."

★ [CL] How well does Miss Hannah Moore in her "Strictures on Female Education," describe this!—"That cold compound of irony, irreligion, selfishness, and sneer, which make up what the French, from whom we borrow the word, express by the term *persiflage*, has of late years made an incredible progress in blasting the opening buds of piety in young persons of fashion.

"A cold pleasantry, a temporary cant-word, the jargon of the day, for the *great vulgar have their jargon*, blights the first promise of seriousness. The ladies of *ton* have certain watch-words, which may be detected as indications of this spirit. The Clergy are spoken of under the ludicrous appellation of *the Parsons*. Some ludicrous association is infallibly combined with every idea of religion, &c. &c. &c."—*See vol. I. page 15.* [Hannah More's *Strictures on the Modern System of Female Education* was first published in 1799 (2 vols. London: T. Cadell and W. Davies). Lucas's quotation comes from this first edition (2:14-15) and is accurate save for one or two transcription errors.]

† [CL] As a specimen of the *jargon* of the *low vulgar*, hear Tom Pain in one of his civilest keys—*Age of Reason, part ii. page* 87.—"The sum total of a *parson's* learning, with a *few* exceptions, is a b, ab—and hic, hæc, hoc; and their knowledge of science is, three times three is one."—Mr. Pain has lately set up a new religion! [Lucas quotes from Thomas Paine's *The Age of Reason. Part the Second. Being an investigation of true and fabulous theology* (1795), although he mangles Paine's mockery of the trinity when reduced to mathematics: "three times one is three."]

At this moment smack went the postillion's whips, and away they rattled over some new-laid stones. The long pause was not lost on Miss Emily. Mr. Marauder proceeded—"Oh my dearest girl! it is on your strength of mind I rely. Blest man that I am to have met with such an angel!"

The carriage gave a spring.

"Perhaps there may be women in the world not inferior in the human face divine; it is possible there may be some who pretend to be your equal in form and grace; but I defy the whole world to produce one with so sublime a soul, who has sacrificed every thing to the man she thought worthy to be blessed with her affections."

The drivers came to the brow of a steep hill, and dashed down it with such spirit, that they seemed to fly over the soil.

Poor Emily believed herself a little deity; and was ready, with a complete stock of modern philosophy, to be the victim of any vice the sophistry of her lover might point out.

The horses pulling gently up, as they ascended the next rise, Mr. Marauder seized the opportunity, in the softest and kindest, most humble and affectionate terms, gradually to unfold his intentions, which, as they became more and more glaring, so was he himself more and more respectful in his manner and address. In short, the purport of Mr. Marauder's oratorical flattery was to persuade the fair Emily to live with him, without having recourse to a *sham* marriage, for a *real* one was totally out of the question.

Yet, with all Marauder's art, his impudence, and plausibility, he did not openly dare to propose a thing of this kind, much less did he venture the smallest hint of it before they set off. He wished the offer indirectly to come from Miss Emily herself, or, at least, to get her in that frame of mind which would preclude all danger of a repulse.

But, after all, in either case he ran no risk; for if the fair maid insisted on the ceremony of their marriage, the ceremony of their marriage was to take place the moment they came to town. If he could prevail on Miss Emily to suppose that there was great danger in trusting the secret of their marriage to any one, and to despise such unmeaning forms, which were of no real use, but only subjected themselves to discovery, he should then save himself the trouble of a deception, which might perhaps produce some unpleasant circumstances in the detection.

It was a long time before he could inspire such very noble and free sentiments in his fair-one's breast.

Skilled in the human passions, he assailed them in every shape, and at last succeeded.

But I verily believe if the fleeting thoughts that passed through the mind of the lovely victim, ere she resigned herself to the sacrifice, were to be clearly analyzed, that this consideration—"I have already gone too far to think of receding," was the one that finally influenced the decision.

In ancient times Necessity was a famous maker of virtues. Among the juggles of the modern Philosophers, and their new selection of virtues, I believe *Necessity* may again step forward, and put in a bold claim for the far greater number.

"Answer me," she may say, "ye spirits of independent heroes of France? Answer me, ye Philosophers, Legislators, and Warriors? Answer me, all ye who worship the GODDESS REASON *by name*, but spurn her *in spirit*? Say, what inspired that firmness of mind, that unconquerable greatness of soul, that desperate serenity, which poured out the poison, which grasped the danger, or which fired the annihilating pistol, and thus, rising above difficulties and sufferings, stamped on your carcasses the *all-conquering virtue of suicide?*—Was it not Necessity?

"Was it not that which makes the coward fight—which makes the thief honest—the murderer no assassin?

"Was it not Necessity, the softener and excuser of every vice?"

"Αναγχη φδε ζεοι μαχουται;"—says the old Greek proverb.[1]

I am not willing any further to particularize the fall of this beautiful young woman—the giddy, the incautious Emily Bellaire.

The machinations of the arch-fiend too well succeeded. As the poor victim gave a faint and tacit consent—"Dear Marauder, on you alone I trust; for you I give up all that the world holds dear!" the fell destroyer dropped upon his knee; and, in terms the most solemn and sacred his tongue could utter, he called on the Almighty Deity to witness his everlasting vows of truth and constancy; and imprecated every evil upon his own head, if he betrayed the trust she had so generously reposed in him——

The words passed away from his lips as the unsubstantial visions of the night; but they were recorded, with an iron pen, on that eternal tablet of brass, never to be erased or obliterated.

---

1 "Against necessity not even the gods fight." Attributed to Simonides of Ceos (c.556–c.468 BC).

CHAPTER XVIII.

Why should I describe the sensations of Emily upon the conduct she had pursued, or relate how little the cool moments of reflection applauded the sacrifices she had made to the gaudy phantom of a *generous disinterestedness*.

Soon, very soon, did she begin to try *not to perceive* that the fuel of flattery, which had so liberally supplied her romantic flame, was now more sparingly bestowed. Time for thought was not wanting.

Mr. Marauder, whose whole life was already become a bustle of political intrigue, was necessarily at times long absent from home: most irksome were such moments to the lovely enthusiast.

Mr. Marauder's connections, both by birth and fortune, were great and splendid; and, it may be said, by his talents were become much more so.

With great reason was he considered by the leading men in power, as a youth of most promising abilities. That commanding air, that undaunted address, and determined behaviour, which so eminently distinguished him, were, as it might be, the passport of his abilities.

Too wise to shew himself as yet of any party, before he had the means of adding weight to his opinions, he privately and alternately seemed to favour each.

The Roman Catholic interest was totally out of the question, as he had professed to embrace these principles for no other reason than to gain the favour of the Duke; and his motives in this case had been at once perceived by the politicians of both sides.

His acquaintance, therefore, was not confined to any party or set of men. Ministerialists and Anti-ministerialists, Aristocrats, Free-thinkers, and Sectaries of all denominations, occasionally frequented his table; and the gentlemen, who had more particularly the honour of knowing him, were soon convinced that neither religious nor political bigotry would ever balk his preferment.

Though his watchful prudence had thus prevented his enslaving himself to a party, before he had the power of full means to be a principal, yet he could not hide that *hauteur* and pride, which his high birth, his daily expectations, flattered him should soon see gratified.

Arrived at the end of his twenty-first year, he took upon himself the sole command of his own fortunes.

The parsimony of his father, and the excellent management of his trustees, had increased the sum total to twenty thousand a year.

Lady James Marauder departed this life soon after he had run away with Emily to town, and thus left him in full possession of the whole. To a man like Marauder, who had studied in the stoical school with such success, needless lamentations and sorrow were not even affected. A splendid burial and a superb monument were the testimonials to the world both of his sorrow and his greatness.

Most of his time he spent in London; and his house, his establishments, and his table were among the first at the west end of town.

At first he was somewhat at a loss how to introduce Emily to his acquaintance; but when he considered upon the subject, he saw advantages accruing to himself even from the unpleasantness of her situation.

Among the French Emigrants who flocked to this country, Marauder had thought proper to notice some, the most conspicuous for their consequence and abilities.[1]

Dukes and Nobles of the first rank thought themselves honoured by his invitations; and *Madame le Duchesse* without any squeamishness, never refused the company of *la belle Emily*. That there were many of the *ci-devant* inferior Nobility, and even *pauvre Madames refugees*, who would have refused his favours, is most true; but they were not the people Mr. Marauder thought worthy his acquaintance.

Emily, who was much better read in French than English writers, found the society of the lively *émigrés* much to her taste; and she very soon became an adept in the Voltairian philosophy, which a charming Marchioness assisted in explaining to her.

Exclusive of the Marchioness and her husband, I shall here mention a few other persons whom, at this period, Miss Emily got acquainted with.

And first, a Mr. Rattle, a young man of about one-and-twenty. He was in possession of a handsome independent fortune, by the death of an elder brother; was intended by his friends, for the law, and had been some years an inhabitant of the Temple. Yet, of all studies, this he most neglected and detested; and, from the moment he came of age, vowed he would resign his chambers, and no longer keep up the appearance of it.

---

1 Refugees from the Revolution in France (the "*émigrés*"), particularly Catholic clergy and *ci-devant* (i.e. former) aristocrats, began to arrive in substantial numbers in Britain in 1790 and 1791. Those who did not return to France by January 1792 were condemned as traitors by the new French government, and their property was confiscated.

Like Mr. Shandy's creaking door, that he had determined to oil for the last ten years of his life, were Mr. Rattle's apartments;[1] and, day after day succeeded—Mr. Rattle vowed—tomorrow never came, and he was still an inhabitant of the Temple. So great was his antipathy to men of law, that he frequently made himself ridiculous, for fear of being taken for one; yet the moment he recollected himself, he was the first to ridicule his own prejudices.

This prejudice, indeed, was the weaker side of his character, which was most strange and eccentric. In abilities by no means deficient; in learning too inconstant to be deep; quick, hasty, and sanguine, his thoughts and determinations upon a subject came all together. His mind seemed to be an alembic,[2] in which every thing came out ready analyzed. Never prejudiced on any other subject, as before said, but the law, he spoke exactly as he thought at the moment, never forming his opinion by others, ancient or modern.

Vulgar errors, like Sir Thomas Brown, M.D. he exploded.[3] Whether of men or things, he judged for himself. From the smallest niceties of a person's conduct would he in a moment give the most decided opinion of him. He would positively pronounce an unknown lady to be a fool, because he had seen a laced frill on her son's shirt; and he has been known to call a man the most cruel wretch on the face of the earth, from the first view of his horse or his dog. His likes or dislikes were as quickly formed; and often, as soon as a stranger's name was mentioned, he acted concerning the person, and spoke of him as if he had been acquainted with him for years.

As an instance—Mr. Marauder one day asked him if he knew a Mr. Callis.

"Who is he?" said Rattle.

"The gentleman that seconded Dirk, the bruiser, on a sudden quarrel at Margate."

"No; is he a *very* young man?"

"I believe not."

"Then," concluded Rattle, "he must be both a fool and a blackguard."

---

1 The creaking hinge of the parlour door is a running joke in Sterne's *Tristram Shandy*. See especially vol.3, ch.21-22.

2 A distilling apparatus sometimes used by chemists.

3 *Pseudodoxia Epidemica, or Enquiries into very many received tenets and commonly presumed truths, which examined prove but Vulgar and Common Errors* by Sir Thomas Browne (1605-82) first appeared in 1646.

Another time Rattle was desirous of being introduced to Sir Gravely Sapient, the great Naturalist. Unluckily at the time Sir Gravely was *peeling* a nectarine. Rattle made a most low bow, looked very solemn, and was off before the Baronet could finish his fruit. He told the friend who introduced him, that he was sufficiently satisfied of Sir Gravely Sapient's abilities, and he has never visited the Naturalist since.

When Rattle first came to town, he was to write in the office of an eminent solicitor. Rattle went but once. His guardian called upon him at his chambers, and enquired the reasons he did not continue his attendance; he answered—"He had no opinion of the man; he did not like his character; he had every reason to doubt his principles."

To his guardian's assertions, that the lawyer was a man of respectability, honesty, and so forth, Rattle shook his head.—"I never knew an honest lawyer that abused my Lord Kenyon."[1]

His guardian was obliged to give up the point.

Rattle was once in the company of the learned Dr. Lexicon.[2] The Doctor spoke of a superb edition of Aristophanes, that was soon to be published with notes, &c. &c &c.

"Pray, Doctor," said Rattle, "can you inform me of any modern author that equals Aristophanes in these three points,"—The Doctor was all attention.—"for impertinence, indecency, and blasphemy?"

Dr. Lexicon said not another word concerning that work.

In politics Rattle was of no party, indiscriminately attacking them all; rarely a defender of any one, and more rarely of the great. He spoke with a volubility that nothing could stop, and in a tone nervous and animating. He never took offence at any severe reply that was made him, and therefore in a great degree precluded others from being offended with him. Other particulars of this eccentric genius will more clearly open themselves in the following pages.

Two other gentlemen, whom Emily met at Mr. Marauder's table, were a Mr. Arnon and his son.

The father about fifty—the son six-and-twenty. The son was lately arrived from America, therefore Mr. Marauder had not, personally known him long; but with the father he was very intimate.

The free and liberal notions, as he had always called them, which Mr. Marauder entertained, he was generally indebted to Mr. Arnon for maturing and giving form to.

---

1 Lord Lloyd Kenyon (1732-1802), Lord Chief Justice from 1788.
2 Presumably Dr. Samuel Johnson (1709-84), famous for his lexicographical work on his *Dictionary* as well as for his literary output.

Mr. Arnon had some knowledge of most of the sciences, was a cool and wary politician, having been in many of the Courts of Europe; and he was deeply read in metaphysical writings, and perfectly conversant in the works of Spinoza, Hobbs, Shaftesbury, Hume, Voltaire, Diderot, Alembert, and the whole gang of modern sceptics in the English, French, and German languages.

He had brought up his son according to their principles; and at twelve years of age would frequently produce him among his acquaintance as a young philosopher, (a very clever boy he certainly was), and boasted that the child had never looked in a Bible in his life. At this age he was sent to a public school, where he remained between three and four years, and then accompanied his father to France, and was present with him at most of the principal scenes at the commencement of the Revolution.

Some dreadful circumstances, which particularly came under their own notice, so shocked the son, that he hastily left France, and the father soon after followed him.

The young man had then shewn such promising abilities, joined with such good sense and judgment, that Mr. Arnon immediately entrusted him with a mercantile commission of very considerable consequence. This the son had executed greatly to the satisfaction of his father, and was lately returned to England.

The elder Mr. Arnon was shrewd, artful, and enterprising; bold, though considerate; mild, though determined; rarely affected by his passions, never swayed against his interest. The younger, whose other name was Hambden, was more learned, but far less scheming and enterprising; open, brave, undesigning, friendly, generous. In short, it was not the least of the merits of the father that the other was his son.

At the commencement of the American war, Mr. Arnon and a particular friend of his, a gentleman of large property in this country, had been suspected of holding secret correspondence with the enemy. They had before signalised themselves in their writings, and declared their principles.

Having received timely notice that Government intended to arrest them, they destroyed all their papers, and left the country. After many hardships they were wrecked on a distant coast. Mr. Arnon's friend died there; and having lost his only child by fever in their passage, he left his whole property in America and England to Mr. Arnon, and entailed it on the little Hambden.

The suspicions against the gentlemen Government was not able to prove. Mr Arnon remained abroad in different countries till the war was ended, and then returned home, and took possession of his property without any opposition; and it was to look after the American estates that his son had lately been abroad.

The junior Mr. Arnon, who was most generally known under the name of Hambden, and whom, to distinguish from his father, we shall so call, was named in compliment to the deceased friend, in whose company he had left the kingdom, Mr. John Hambden, who boasted himself a regular descendant of the celebrated patriot of that name.[1]

CHAPTER XIX.

Mr. Arnon rarely gave vent to those strong democratical principles for which he was famous, at Mr. Marauder's table, as he knew his young friend to be so decidedly in the aristocratical interest; yet they frequently disputed with great civility on the use and abuse of titles, and so forth.

In deference, too, to the *ci-devant* Nobility, Mr. Arnon often avoided the subject, though, it must be confessed, they cared very little about the matter; and, from the conversation of many of them, a stranger might suppose they were of the democratical party.

On anti-religious subjects Mr. Arnon was not so choice. Mr. Marauder listened and joined in the discourse, in defiance of his having renounced his Protestant errors, and embraced the Roman Catholic faith.

Hambden was not fond of that continual satire his father indulged in; and Rattle, who dashed at every subject, was sure to oppose them all.

It may be proper to remark that Mr. Marauder affected in his house more of the French than the English customs; the ladies, therefore, were partakers of their debates, and put in their claim of petticoat philosophers.

Mr. Arnon was one day describing the attack of the Bastile, at which, with his son, he was present.

---

1 A cousin of Oliver Cromwell, John Hampden (1594-1643) opposed the ship money tax which Charles I attempted to collect in 1635 and thereby helped to precipitate a final breach between King and Parliament. Hampden subsequently served as a republican leader during the Long Parliament of 1640 and as a colonel in the Parliamentary army during the Civil War.

"There fell," cried he, "the mighty bulwark of tyranny and superstition!"

"Mighty! indeed!" exclaimed Rattle; "there was not a priest or a prisoner within the walls. Mr. Arnon, you was never in a greater error in your life. The French Government, unlike the Spanish, instead of being superstitious, had long before this not a grain or religion left; and so far from being tyrannous, it was the *want* of what you call *tyranny* that overthrew the State."

"What, Sir, do you call *lettres de cachet*?[1] What, Sir, will you say concerning the exorbitant power of the *Noblesse*?"

"*Exorbitant* power! Where the devil was it? Yes, they made a most glorious struggle! You either must allow that the French Nobles were greater fools than all the scum of the country, which, considering they were all Voltairian philosophers, you'll not very readily grant, or that they had no power at all. As for the *lettres de cachet*, how many prisoners did you find in durance by them?"

Mr. Arnon, not being able to enumerate many, replied concerning the *Noblesse*—"That many of the very first abilities joined the popular cause."

"Fine abilities! through greater cowardice!"

The Marquis grinned applause.

"What say you," retorted Mr. Arnon, "concerning Fayette?"[2]

"That all *his* abilities consisted in twice playing the rogue, and once the fool. The greatest bungler in your whole set! A private in Cromwell's crew would have made a better hero. He hadn't sense even to be consistent; and I firmly believe, the only reason the

---

1 During the *ancien régime* in France, a *lettre de cachet* signed by the King and a secretary of state could be used to order the imprisonment without trial or appeal of any individual. The arbitrary nature of these *lettres* formed one of the chief complaints of the Estates General at the commencement of the Revolution, and they were abolished in 1790, but recent historians have suggested that only a small number were ever actually issued and their use was strictly regulated.

2 Marie-Joseph-Paul-Yves-Roch-Gilbert du Motier, marquis de Lafayette (1757-1834) served successfully as a commander of anti-British forces during the War of American Independence and became the leader of the liberal aristocrats on his return to France. After the storming of the Bastille in 1789 he was appointed to head the Parisian National Guard, which he led to protect the King and Queen at the storming of the palace of Versailles. After he ordered his troops to open fire on demonstrators at the Champ de Mars in 1791, he lost popularity with the Revolutionary leaders and he defected to the Austrians in 1792.

French rulers admire him, is out of their enthusiastic love of opposition. Dumourier did what Fayette ought to have done.[1] Enough of this fellow. But, Mr. Arnon, is it true that the French dressed up a pretty girl as the Goddess of Reason, and deified her?"

"Most assuredly! and what more worthy of our adoration than a beautiful woman?"—Mr. Arnon, looking at the ladies, who began to be interested in the conversation, and attentively listened, continued—"Madame Montmoro was the charming representative.[*] Nature pointed out to her disciples how best to worship her. Here was no vague, wandering, uncertain, blind enthusiasm; no inanimate idol was presented us, but a masterpiece of Nature, a sacred image, enough to inflame all hearts. Where Philosophy had first informed us, our senses soon convinced us we acted right. We saw, we were convinced, and we adored."

"Did you ever see," said Rattle, "Dr. Graham's Hygeia, or Goddess of Health?"[2]

"Where?" asked Mr. Arnon.

"In this noble metropolis. I have not the smallest doubt that the French borrowed their idea from an English Quack Doctor."

The ladies looked displeased. Rattle, not observing them, continued—"By the by, Mr. Arnon, the speech the Doctor used to make,

---

[*] [CL] Madame Barlier was exhibited in the same manner, says Professor Robinson, page 252. [Lucas is citing John Robison's *Proofs of a Conspiracy against all the Religions and Governments of Europe, carried on in the secret meetings of Free Masons, Illuminati, and Reading Societies* (London: T. Cadell and W. Davies, 1797) which describes "the present humiliating condition of woman in France" (251-52). Madame Momoro, the wife of the Revolutionary printer, was said to have represented Reason at the fête at Notre Dame in November 1793. See Thomas Carlyle, *The French Revolution* (2 vols. London: Macmillan, 1900) 2:342.]

---

1 Leading the Revolutionary army, Charles-François de Périer Dumouriez (1739-1823) defeated an invading Prussian army at the Battle of Valmy and later, in 1792, crushed the Austrians at Jermappes. Disapproving of the increasing militancy of the Revolution, Dumouriez went over to the Austrians in 1793.

2 From 1775, Dr. James Graham (1745-94) offered a variety of bizarre medical treatments, including an "electrical throne" and the famous "celestial bed" (to promote fertility), at his "Temple of Health" in London. A woman impersonating the "Goddess of Health"—Lady Emma Hamilton is said to have once taken the part—was generally on hand as he administered his cures or delivered his lectures.

was very like your rhapsody, which I also remember was similar to the one used at Paris. Whether the Doctor's regimen and medicine destroyed *his* Goddess of Health, I can't say. Your worthies, I know, in spite of all their love and adoration, chopped off the head of *their rational Divinity*, poor Madame Montmoro!"

The ladies shuddered.

Said Hambden—"You must not confound, Rattle, the infamous factions of France with the first noble emancipators of their country."

"*Ex pede Herculem.*[1] Do you, Hambden, defend the Goddess of Reason?"

"No," replied Hambden, with a smile, "unless we take one of the present company for a representative."

"And then," said Rattle, "even I shall become an idolater."

The conversation would have turned to other subjects, had not certain ideas met the mind of Emily, which she could not so easily dismiss.

Mr. Marauder had often told his fair victim this pretty story of the Goddess of Reason. He had dressed the tale up well. He had called Emily *his* Goddess of Reason, but the catastrophe he had ever omitted.

He perceived, therefore, that she looked very grave; and he was unwilling to give up the Goddess of Reason so easily as Hambden had.

"The improbable stories which were told afterwards," said Mr. Marauder, "whether true or false, can never invalidate the liberal actions of those who profess to worship no other deity than *their reason*. Instead of unmeaning ceremonies, and needless prayers to a being they neither see nor know any thing about, these men, who took *Nature* for their guide, paid their obeisance to *that* which must delight every man, and warm the breast of the coldest and veriest cynic—the most perfect of *Nature's* works, *a woman in the prime of beauty*. They worshipped *her* as *Reason exemplified*, not as the gaudy image of an imaginary being."

Rattle replied, endeavouring to look grave, and to argue coolly on the subject; but in a moment or two he flew off in the same manner as usual.—"I must spare half my arguments, Mr. Marauder, when

---

1 "From the foot (we recognise) Hercules"—i.e. one may judge the whole from the specimen. Lucas himself translates this as "A statue of Hercules is known by a foot" in his *The Abissinian Reformer* (1808) 3:21n.

I consider that you are not, like me, a plain Protestant, an abominator of image and figure-worship altogether. But if the French worshipped their idol as the representative of a certain set of ideas, if they only personified their thoughts, and put them into a practical outside, there was something more than knavery in the case—complete *Folly*. That *latter Goddess*, too, I believe they have already got with her cap and bells, endeavouring to assume the appearance, as well as the name, of *Liberty*. But since they are so fond of dressing up their fancies into a real form, I recommend to their study an author they don't yet very well understand—*Shakespeare*.

"Observe his *Midsummer's Night's Dream.*—The Grecian Clowns; Bottom, the Weaver; Quince, the Carpenter; Snug, the Joiner; Flute, the Bellows-mender; Snout, the Tinker; and Starveling, the Tailor, would make, I find, excellent French Philosophers. Their personification of a *wall*, or *moonshine*, equals at least our Gallic neighbours' reason.—'Some man or other,' says Philosopher Bottom, 'must present Wall, and let him have some plaster, or some lime, or some rough-cast about him to signify *Wall*;—and again, 'one must come in with a bush of thorns and a lanthorn, and say he comes to disfigure, or to present the person of *Moonshine*.' You see, Mr. Marauder, how pat my simile is?"[1]

"No doubt, Mr. Rattle, you think so; but I can inform you the *French* borrowed *theirs* from the Ancients."

"You mean, my dear Sir, as to that notable exhibition of theirs, the deification of Monsieur Voltaire.[2] These fellows, at the moment they affect to despise religion, are guilty of the grossest idolatry; and unenlightened set of savages would have been ashamed of it. After having collected together the wisdom of I know not how many centuries, they glory in a species of knowledge that an heathen three thousand years ago had considered beneath his notice. That deification, which the degeneracy of Rome, under the infatuated tyranny of its Emperors, yielded to, and which they copied from the primitive customs of man ere yet he was civilized, have these pretended sons of Freedom voluntarily bestowed on a *conceited poet*, well known as a *rank poltroon*, a *false historian*, and an *ignorant sceptic*."

"You are so violent, Rattle," said Mr. Marauder, having got off from the *Goddess of Reason*, and wishing to conclude the argument, "so very violent in your opinions, that I cannot possibly dispute with

---

1   See William Shakespeare's *A Midsummer-Night's Dream*, III, i.
2   Voltaire's remains were disinterred and, with much ceremony, moved to the Panthéon in Paris in July 1791.

you. Yet this merit you cannot deny the French, of overturning with complete success the old superstition."

"Does *Mr. Marauder* call it *superstition?*"

"I speak," replied Mr. Marauder, affecting indifference, "not as a religious party, but as an impartial observer."

"If the highwaymen of this country," continued Rattle, "were to get the upper hand, I presume they would pull down the gibbets, and most probably celebrate a *fête* on Hounslow Heath."[1]

"I find, Rattle, I must give up the Herculean task of convincing you. As this argument cannot be very entertaining to the ladies, give us your opinion of the new play we have all been to see."

CHAPTER XX.

The conversation now took a turn more adapted to the fair Emily and her female friends, till from having thoroughly canvassed the new play, the old ones came upon the *tapis*. Shakespeare of course was mentioned, and universally applauded. Here Mr. Marauder made sure that Rattle would join in his praise, as he had often heard him speak of that great genius in the highest turns of rapture.

"It's all very true," said Rattle, with a bit of a sigh, "but he spoils all for want of feeling."

Every gentleman and every lady in the company attacked Mr. Rattle most severely. He stood the storm very patiently: when it had a little subsided, he continued—

"Ah, poor Falstaff! Harry of Monmouth would never have treated thee as the Prince of the Drama has made him."

"No, Rattle," said Hambden, taking up the defence of his favourite, "this old cavil shall not avail you. A writer you greatly admire, the ingenious author of an Essay on the Dramatic Character of Sir John, confesses that the punishment of Falstaff is but poetical justice."[2]

"Morgan spake not from his heart:* he tells us *not to complain*; that Sir John is finally given up to shame and dishonour. A very clear rea-

---

* [CL] See an Essay on the Dramatic Character of Sir John Falstaff, page 179.

---

1 An area of open land to the west of London notorious for the attacks of robbers and highwaymen.

2 Maurice Morgann (1726-1802) published *An essay on the dramatic character of Sir John Falstaff* in 1777.

son this, that there was a cause for complaint. Shakespeare seems to have perceived it himself, when he makes Fluellen, the Welchman, compare the Prince's conduct to Falstaff, to Alexander's to Clitus; the excuse afterwards is evidently very bad. But allowing this cursed poetical justice, why was Bardolf to be hanged for stealing a pix?"[1]

"Can the punishment of such a fellow be an excuse for condemning Shakespeare for want of feeling?"

"Yes; after all their jokes on his fiery nose—after making him a companion with the Prince, and an object for his wit and ridicule—after confessing him by the voices of all the gang to be the best of the three worthies—poor Bardolf! for the sake of the old joke, Fluellen says—'One Bardolf, if your Majesty knows the man; his face is all bubukles and whelks, and knobs, and flames of fire, and his lips blow at his nose, and it is like a coal of fire, sometimes blue, and sometimes red; but his nose is executed, and his fire's out.'—On this account the poor fellow is with great indifference fixed upon, in allusion to an old legend, as the most proper person to be hanged for stealing a pix.[2]

"Shakespeare draws Bardolf himself, with much more feeling than the Prince when he hears of Falstaff's death.—'I would I were with him, wherever he is, either in Heaven or in Hell!'[3]—Had Shakespeare felt this sentiment so well as he has placed it in the mouth of a reprobate, I am well assured he would never have hanged the poor devil at last. If these will not satisfy you, I have at least a half a hundred others. There's little poetical justice, I believe, in the deaths of Ophelia, or her poor father; but as for the murder of the dutiful, lively and innocent Cordelia—let Shakespeare answer for it."[4]

Hambden, finding it in vain to argue with so determined an adversary, thought he had better turn the virulence of his friend Rattle's satire to some other subject.

They canvassed, therefore, the merits of the other dramatic favourites, whom Rattle praised or condemned with equal intemperance.

"One of the best things in the English language," said Rattle, "is

---

1 Alexander the Great murdered Clitus even though they had formerly been friends and Clitus had saved his life. Rattle is referring to Shakespeare's *Henry V*, IV, vii, 5-12.
2 *Henry V*, III, vi, 48.
3 *Henry V*, II, iii, 8.
4 See Shakespeare's *Hamlet*, IV, vii and III, iv, and *King Lear*, V, iii.

Steele's Conscious Lovers; every sentiment is interesting, and pregnant with religion, honour, and virtue."[1]

"All borrowed!" replied Hambden, who was determined to attack him in his own way. "I mean to say it is no better than a decent translation of Terence's Andrian: but what think you of Sheridan's School for Scandal?[2] There's originality for you, with genuine wit and humour."

"Positively," exclaimed Rattle, "the very worst thing in the English language—a disgrace to the nation to have had it acted."

Every one of the company laughed most heartily at Mr. Rattle for his violent abuse of so famous a work, each striving who should most commend it.

"But," concluded Mr. Arnon, "the astonishing run it has had is a sufficient instance of its merit."

"Pshaw! you may as well argue that way in defence of half the trash upon the town. I say the principle of the School for Scandal is an artful attack against all religion and morality. The chief characters, the Brothers, are borrowed from Tom Jones and Blifield; and its plot is taken from an excellent old Novel called Sidney Biddulph, where a rich old codger, Mr. Warner, comes from abroad, and disguises himself as a poor man, to make trial of his relations, Sir George and Mrs. Arnold. The success is the same as in the play.[3]

"The generosity of the hero Charles, is at the expense of his justice—a virtue that seems despised by the author. In short, all that can be said in favour of it is—that open vice is better—"

"Mr. Rattle," said Emily, "I can bear it no longer—you are too bad; I don't know when I shall forgive you for abusing my favourite play."

"If Mrs. Marauder is against me," said Rattle, (For though it was totally contrary to the principle by which Mr. Marauder deceived Emily, she was always called by his name)—"if Mrs. Marauder is against me, I give up the argument; and as the School for Scandal is so far honoured as to be her favourite, I henceforth declare, against all opposers, that it is possessed of wit, honour, and originality."

Rattle was one of the warmest admirers of the fair sex, and Emily's bright eyes had shot him through and through. In truth, the

---

1 Sir Richard Steele's The Conscious Lovers. A comedy, first performed and printed in 1722.

2 Richard Brinsley Sheridan's School for Scandal, first produced 1777.

3 Henry Fielding's Tom Jones was first published in 1749; Frances Sheridan's Memoirs of Miss Sidney Bidulph was first published in 1761-67.

pleasure of seeing her was the great inducement that now brought him frequently to Mr. Marauder's table—a man he was far from feeling any particular friendship for.

From *plays* the subject descended to *players*.

Mrs. Siddons met with universal approbation.[1] Emily spoke of her in the highest terms; and perceiving Rattle was silent, she required his opinion.

Rattle hummed and hawed;—"Undoubtedly she was most excellent; her voice clear; her expression just; her manners easy and noble; her shriek most inimitable; and what is superior to every thing, if you see her in one character, you see her in all. Upon my honour, Ma'am, she is a most capital actress."

"Of her elder brother no doubt you have full food for satire?" said Mr. Marauder.[2]

"He's, without exception, the best improvement on harsh nature I ever met with in my life."

"And what of her younger?"

"A wonderful instance of the *influence* of family."

"What think you of Mrs. Jordan?"[3]

"Any thing but majesty."

"Bannister?"[4]

"Two very great faults—modesty and good-nature."

"How so?"

"Both together induce him to act low parts, beneath the scope of his abilities."

"Quick?"[5]

---

1 Sarah Siddons (1755-1831), née Kemble, was the foremost actress of her day.

2 Of Sarah Siddon's brothers (all younger than herself), John Philip Kemble (1757-1823) was the most successful, though he was much lampooned for his statuesque style of acting, which had just begun to fall out of fashion. His younger brothers, George Stephen (1758-1822) and Charles (1775-1854), were less talented actors, and in their early careers relied on the fame of their celebrated sister to find engagements.

3 Dorothea Jordan (1762-1816) made her debut on the London stage in 1785 and quickly became one of the most popular actresses of the age. From 1790, she was widely known to be the mistress of the Duke of Clarence, later William IV.

4 John Bannister (1760-1836), a leading comic actor in the 1780s and 1790s.

5 According to some contemporary reports, the comic actor John Quick (1748-1831) had a voice which squeaked like a fiddle.

"His squeak is most excellent; but we've rather too much of it."

"Mr. Rattle," said Emily, "not a word more, if such are your remarks on the first comic actors that ever trod the stage."

"I differ from you, Rattle," said Mr. Marauder, "in almost every remark you have made."

Marauder, who knew Emily's taste, began to canvass their merits in a very different manner, and, with great judgment, gave them that praise so well known, so deservedly their due.

The ladies retired.

Mr. Arnon entered upon more learned subjects; and, from a neat discourse upon the improvement in the arts and sciences, he soon came round to his favourite subject—the praise of the French.

"One of their Generals reconnoitred the enemy's camp in an air-balloon?" asked Rattle.

"A ridiculous story!" said Mr. Arnon, conceiving Rattle was ready to laugh at it; "I doubt if it ever happened."[1]

"I have heard from a very good authority that it is true," replied the other, "and I think greatly to his credit. It has been the fashion of this country for every fool to laugh at the air-balloon; but I conceive it to be the best practical exhibition of a bold and useful theory which the age can produce."

The rest of the company knew not whether Rattle was in jest or earnest. He continued—"James Sadler, a pastry cook at Oxford, had the spirit himself to make the bold experiment in the midst of that learned seminary.[2] For an act which reflected honour on his abilities, as well as his courage, what reward did the sons of Apollo bestow?—A few shillings to gratify their curiosity! Had the circumstance took place at Cambridge, probably he had made his fortune; had it happened in former days, we should have had him among the stars."

---

1 The French army first employed hot air balloons for reconnaissance at the Battle of Fleuris, in Belgium, on 26 June 1794, but the equipment of the "First Brigade of Aeronautics" was destroyed when the French fleet was devastated at the Battle of the Nile in 1798 and the brigade was disbanded the following year.

2 James Sadler (1753-1828) became the first Briton to ascend in a balloon on 4 October 1784 at Christ-Church Meadows, Oxford. Sadler worked as assistant to the scientist Thomas Beddoes and later became an engineer and a professional balloonist.

"And you really mean to commend it?" said Marauder, sneeringly.

"If science is none the worse for courage to put it in practice."

"Surely," said Mr. Arnon, "the French have the first merit in this, as well as in the telegraph."—Mr. Arnon began to exult.—"Their superior genius still takes the lead; but the most noble, most glorious thing this age has produced, is the emendation and perfection, I may say, of the calendar by these sons of Freedom."[1]

"The offspring of Folly!" exclaimed Rattle, with an air of triumph, "the poorest astronomers in the Julian period would have called them. Mr Arnon, I beg of you to point out in what the excellence consists."

Mr. Arnon's praise had transcended his reason; but he replied—"In the more equal division of the months, and the more equal distribution of time."

"When I understood," said Rattle, trying to speak deliberately, "that these Philosophers had altered the calendar, I naturally presumed that, without regarding party distinctions, accidental circumstances, or their own prejudices, they had accommodated it to the seasons of the year, as the different constellations point them out to us; but to my extreme surprise, and what gives me the most contemptible opinion of the *learned Nation*, all their philosophy, mathematical knowledge, astronomical wisdom is contained in this grand point—that Royalty was abolished on the 21st of September, therefore their year is to begin on the next day, the 22d. Again, instead of dividing the months as near as possible according to the moons, their months consist of 30 days each, 10 days to a week, and 3 weeks to a month: now 30 times 12 being only 360, *five days* still remain, and these (which I have no doubt is a very good joke in France) are called *the days without breeches*! and so there is an end of the Frenchman's year. If a revolution should ever take place in Ireland, they may make as great a blunder; but it is impossible for them to evince greater conceit and folly."

"What can be more imperfect and irregular than our own year?" asked Mr. Arnon, who, though he know himself in the wrong, was not willing to resign the point.

"No alteration," replied Rattle, "I should have supposed, had not the French convinced me otherwise. As yet every emendation had been an improvement upon the wisdom of the former ages, till a

---

1 In 1793, the French Revolutionary Convention attempted to introduce the more rational and less Christian calendar described here. It lasted until 1806, when the Gregorian calendar was re-introduced.

French astronomer[*] came, P.F.N. Fabre d'Eglantine, a player and poet.[1] To this man was the task assigned of altering the calendar—to a wretch whose character has been thus ably defined—'A weak critic, a trifling writer, an ignorant Philosopher, and an irresolute Atheist.'—These fellows are determined to think and act for themselves, and are daily tumbling backward in every virtue and every science. Hambden," continued Rattle, "You understand these things; am I not right in the calendar?"

"It is so seldom you are, I will not deny it at present. Now, in return, let me ask you what you think of their new law?"

"D—n their law!" exclaimed Rattle.

The company enjoyed his momentary confusion, and the laugh went completely against him.

Marauder particularly enjoyed it, and continued the blow.— "Nay, nay, Rattle, don't be ashamed of your profession. What, in France, can equal the glorious uncertainty of the English law? And then, for our venerable Court of Chancery, cool and deliberate reasoning supplies the place of hasty decision. Shall I recall to your recollection your favourite subject—Mr. Hastings's trial;[2] or does the elegant, ingenious, learned, and intelligible manner in which the Chancery suits are conducted, meet your approbation better?"

---

[*] [CL] But it is unjust and invidious to judge of the literary sapience of the Great Nation under the despotism of Robespierre, &c. &c. &c. &c. Monthly Magazine for April 1800, page 276—"At the death of Voltaire, the apothecary, charged with embalming him, had permission to retain that part of his brain which the French call cervolet, (cerebellum). It was preserved by him in spirits of wine, with a sort of religious care, from that time till the death of the possessor, the son of whom has just made an offer of it to Government, who has accepted it. This interesting remain of the Patriarch of Ferney is to be included in a monument, and conveniently placed in the midst of the chefs d'œuvres of his works, with which the Public Library is enriched."—See the end of the last chapter.

---

1 Although he had no knowledge of astronomy, and was chiefly known as a satirical writer and deputy to the National Convention, Philippe Fabre d'Églantine (1750-94) was appointed to chair the committee which drew up the French republican calendar. He was later guillotined for his moderate views.

2 Warren Hastings (1732-1818) was impeached for what Edmund Burke amongst others perceived as his misconduct during his term as governor-general of India. After a trial which lasted from 1788 to 1795, Hastings was finally acquitted.

"I love my country," replied Rattle warmly, "and therefore I feel for her faults. I'll give you for answer, Sir, a scrap of paper I tore from a new portmanteau which came home this morning."—He read the paper.—"Behold, ye Englishman, the blessing of an hasty reformation! See! how *private* villains undertake to manage the *public* good. See! and learn.—The French have, in truth, destroyed the old rusty fetters which had long ceased to gall; but have they substituted none in their stead? Yes, new and gilded, which rankle to the very bone! They have in a moment destroyed the tedious formalities of the law; and now suspicion, apprehension, and death follow *without a word*. Slow Justice is gone, and hasty Murder has taken her place. The long catalogue of useless prayers, unmeaning ceremonies, and days of fasting, are gone by; and, in their place, a still longer catalogue of recorded perjuries, ceremonies—would I could say *unmeaning*—and days, not of *voluntary* fasting, indeed, but of want and misery.'—I have sent to the trunk-maker's, and hope some day or other to favour you with the remainder."

"It is a favour I will very willingly dispense with," said Marauder.

"Well, Rattle," said Hambden, laughing, "I think, indeed, our English laws shine best by comparison; and if ever I see you my Lord Chancellor, I shall hope to have our suit determined."

A small estate, which came to Mr. Arnon from his late friend, was still disputed in the Court of Chancery, and to which Hambden referred.

"I confess," exclaimed Mr. Arnon, with a sneer, "after all Mr. Rattle's arguments, I should prefer justice without law, to law without justice; for, as Mr. Pain says—"

"Do you really mean, my dear Sir," asked Rattle, hastily, "to quote that worthy, respectable writer *in earnest?*"

Mr. Arnon was ashamed of his intended authority. He know in what a contemptible light his son always considered this *great man*, and he replied—"There is no need of any quotation to strengthen what I have advanced—it is an axiom of itself."

"How quickly you resign that man of *modesty* and *veracity!*" replied Rattle, recovering his usual flow of spirits; "but let me introduce him to your notice in an epigram from Martial, which my younger brother sent me from Cambridge the other day, and which, in my opinion, is very comprehensive and conclusive.

"Est *niger* et *nequam*, cum sis cognomine *nequam*;
"*Nigrior* esse potes, *nequior* esse nequis."

To Thomas Pain.
Both *Vice* and *Pain* art thou—for *Pain's* thy name;
Thy vice increases,—Pain is still the same."

CHAPTER XXI.

Since Emily's elopement, Mr. and Mrs. Vaseley's family was in no respects a desirable situation for a young girl at the very age of improvement.

Fanny, who had never felt any partiality for Mr. Vasaley or his spouse, could not but determine it in her own mind that they had acted very improperly in their conduct concerning Mr. Marauder and her sister: for, although neither the guardian nor his lady ever suspected that Mr. Marauder would carry their fair ward away, yet they privately encouraged his addresses when they know she was in a manner engaged to Wilson.

Mr. Townsend, an elderly man, and an old bachelor, their other guardian, was, of course, informed of the elopement of Miss Emily. He came to Mr. Vasaley's immediately.

Fanny, who had before mentioned it to her friend Wilson, signified her wish to Mr. Townsend to be in a situation where she might improve herself in those accomplishments she had superficially learned at school, and which she had left, at the death of her mother, to be a companion for her sister Emily, who, in return, used frequently to talk of instructing her younger sister herself.

Mr. Townsend, before his departure, promised to look out for an eligible situation; and in a few weeks wrote word that he had prevailed upon a widow lady, near his own residence, to take his young ward as one of her family.

When Lady Berwick accompanied her husband to his command in the East Indies, she left her three young daughters under the care of her friend, Mrs. Mountford, a Clergyman's widow, and the half-sister of Lady Berwick's mother.

This lady had two daughters and a son of her own, which, with the three Miss Berwicks, composed the society into which Fanny Bellaire was to be admitted.

When the time approached for her departure, Fanny, not without many a tear, prepared to leave the spot. It has been before said how little she liked or respected the Vasaleys; and had the cause of her tears been nicely investigated, she would have scarcely been able to have give a good reason even to herself.

The truth was, she was unwilling to leave Wilson—a person she had once expected to be her brother, one who had warmly professed and shewed himself to be her friend—who had directed that excellent genius, for which she had been early conspicuous, to proper objects—who, so far from treating her like an ignorant young female, with unmeaning praises and destructive flattery, had assisted her opening mind in the attainment of true excellence, a knowledge of virtue, morality, and religion.

Fanny, considering Wilson in this light, and knowing also that he practised himself those duties he recommended to others, could not part with such a *friend*, without feeling a sensation much more interesting that usually accompanies the term.

She had no relations nearer allied to her than the Vasaleys and Mr. Townsend. Mrs. Vasaley was her father's first cousin; and Mr. Townsend stood in the same degree of kindred to her mother. Wilson therefore had been as father, guardian, kinsman, friend, every thing dear that her young mind had yet felt the want of.

Mr. Townsend came to Mr. Vasaley's house the day before Fanny was to leave it. Wilson called in the evening to wish her a good journey.

Mr. and Mrs. Vasaley were in the room when he entered. Mr. Townsend was acquainted with him, and well knew his character; and the Vasaleys, to make up for their former conduct and partiality towards Marauder, had been most profuse in his praise.

After the usual compliments had passed, and he had been seated a few minutes, he asked for Miss Fanny.

"The poor girl," said Mr. Townsend, "is very sorrowful at leaving her good friends here; and she was afraid of not seeing you before she departed."

Fanny entered.

Wilson had determined to ask her permission, in the presence of her guardians, occasionally to write to her, and to beg the favour of her answer; yet a delicacy of feeling, he could not account for, a long time prevented him. In vain he reasoned with himself on the subject; he felt an interest in her fate more than a mere friend can feel, and feared, as if it was a thing of the greatest moment, the possibility of a refusal.

That he loved her otherwise than as a sister he had not the remotest idea, though Emily herself had always perceived their great partiality for each other. There was a delicacy, a tenderness, a chasteness, an anxiety that daily increased upon him whenever he addressed Fanny, and now was more conspicuous than every it had been before.

With Emily, beautiful and fascinating, his passions had been interested, and he thought himself deeply in love; but with Fanny his heart was caught, and he was ignorant it was even in danger.

That a young Philosopher of one-and-twenty should be in love with a pretty child of fourteen, was a paradox he could not conceive possible; yet Emily, in her giddy laughing way, had often told him so, and Wilson had as often turned it to a compliment upon herself. The gay Marauder also had been equally affected by the fascinating graces of the mind and person which adorned Fanny Bellaire, but not with equal ignorance upon the occasion. From hence a *corollary* may be drawn, more correct than any from the long-shaken brain of the author of Political Justice—that *the purity of love is in proportion to its ignorance.*

After many a *hem!* and many an *ah!* Wilson found courage to take the opportunity of Fanny's calling him her *friend* Mr. Wilson, to propose the correspondence.—"You have kindly, Miss Fanny, thought proper to honour me with the name of *friend*; may I, under that name, hope to have the liberty of writing to you, and will you sometimes favour me with your answer?"

Fanny, artless and innocent, had not yet learned to conceal her feelings. She was hurt at the cold and formal manner in which, in her opinion, so simply a favour had been asked. The tears stood in her eyes as she answered—"I fear, Mr. Wilson, you must think me very ungrateful not to be always happy to hear from you. I am greatly indebted to you for the kindness and friendship you have shewn me every since I have been here; and the treatment you have had from our family, has been very unkind in return. I am sure you have been as a brother to me; and one time I was in hopes I might have really called you so."

"I am afraid I shall lose my other ward if this is the case," said Mr. Townsend, laughingly. "But, my dear little girl," continued he, taking Fanny by the hand, "though we have not the happiness to be allied to Mr. Wilson, I hope you will always consider him as a brother, as I shall a friend of the family; and, whoever is the happy man that one day or other is to be blessed with my Fanny, he will have reason to thank Mr. Wilson for the care he has taken of you."

Wilson therefore frequently received a letter from his young pupil; and while he admired the expanding beauties of her mind, he soon began to remark that she grew more and more cautious and reserved in her expressions towards him. Had he read over his own letters with the like attention, he could not have failed to make a similar remark in them.

CHAPTER XXII.

The summer after Marauder came of age, Emily passed at Brighton; and, amid the splendour of beauty and fashion which adorned its shores, shone forth avowedly as the first constellation in every eye.

In taste, in style, in elegance, in the richness of equipages and dress, the *chere amies* of Princes, Dukes, and Lords were left far behind.

The admiration she excited could not but gratify her vanity in the highest degree; yet, strange as it may appear, she felt sensations which already told her that all was *vexation of spirit*. The pride of Marauder joyfully received the incense—that pride which waited but for one event to be at its full powers.

Early in the winter they returned to town. Marauder was more immersed in a continual bustle than ever; the whole of his affairs was to Emily a secret.

As he often came home in the middle of the night, their apartments, though adjoining, were now separate; and she never saw him at his own table, but with a crowd of company.

So passed the early part of the winter, Emily drooping and pining very fast away; her health, though visibly impaired, was scarcely noticed by the busy eye of Marauder.

The new year began with better auspices.

Our earth has once perfected its annual orb, and thrice, besides, had her sister planet, the pallid Goddess of the Chace, completed her attractive course around the sal-impregnated fluids of this globe, since the delicious attachment of congenial minds had commenced between Emily Bellaire and the gallant Marauder, when the GRAND EVENT, the great hinge, as it were, upon which these volumes turn, so long expected, so ardently desired, took place.

The DUKE OF SILSBURY, without a fall from his horse, was, to the surprise of every body, carried off in the midst of a long frost by an apoplectic fit, which the Physicians agreed was occasioned by the want of his necessary exercise.

An Irish servant, who waited upon Wilson, made a very judicious remark upon this occasion of the learned Doctors.—"They may talk what they will, Master, upon we Irish blunderers, but, by Jasus! this is the most complete thing I every heard in my born days—that his Grace should have ventured his neck to have insured his life. Faith! a pretty way of living to run the risk of dying."

No sooner was the Duke's death known, than the baliff of steward of Mr. Marauder set off post to town.

Without ceremony he rushed into the room, where his master sat with a few French nobility, some English gentry, and the adored Emily.

The host turned his head round, surprised at the rudeness of his servant, who, walking boldly to the table, poured out a glass of wine, and drank—"*Long life to the Duke of Silsbury!*"

The young heir, with a joy that burst even the fetters of his pride, caught his meaning, and applauded the insolent hint.

He immediately rang the bell violently.—"Order my carriage and horses this moment!" said he. "Mr. Grinder, you'll follow me as quick as possible. No, you shall accompany me."—Recollecting himself, he politely apologized to the company;—nay, a very nice observer might have thought that he seemed to be a little ashamed of his own intemperate behaviour; and the gross exultation of his servant; but his gratified pride soon smothered it all, and he hastily took his leave, and departed.

Poor Emily was like one thunderstruck.—"Good night, and sweet dreams to my lovely girl!" was the *great man's* address as he left the room.

Instead of hailing her as his lovely Duchess, a term he was formerly very fond of using, he had departed with a familiar nod, such as a superior, highly gratified, bestows on an inferior.—"My lovely girl" left a shuddering at her breast that crushed in a moment the airy palaces she had so arduously reared, and scattered the whole fabric at the instant it seemed to be realized.

At the first place where they changed horses, the new Duke thought proper to send Emily a note by the post, more for the sake of giving some vent to his exulting pride, than from any particular love, though he certainly meant it as a hint to check any fond hopes she might have still entertained of participating in the title. The following is the letter:

"For one moment, my charming Emily, ambition took place of love, when I flew this night from your bewitching arms to invest myself with the family honours.

"I shall be at the Castle early in the morning. Ere you receive this, a certain pretender will have lost his little consequence, and may provide himself with a situation far more fit as a journeyman carpenter.

"I will try to bring our Fanny back with me to the land of Love, where with my Emily she shall enjoy its delights. We must make your lovely sister a convert to the religion of Reason and

Truth!—Ye Gods! what a glorious idea to be the Priest of such Goddesses!

"Blest, ever blest, ye free enchantments of the mind! Curse, Oh! curse again and again the rankling fetters, which foolish Parsons and Politicians rivet upon slaves ten times more foolish than themselves!

"So contrary to nature is compulsion, that were I compelled to love even my Emily, I fear I should be disobedient.

"Health, love, and freedom ever attend on the Goddess of my vows! From her constant adorer,

"SILSBURY"

Emily read the note with somewhat more than surprise. She perused it again and again. Something new, something more and more unpleasant alarmed her spirits, and chilled her trembling heart.

A little recovered, she called her new philosophy to her aid, and attempted to reason with herself upon the subject. Could she doubt the honour of the man to whom she had sacrificed every thing?—Ah! no.

She read the letter once more. Yes, she did doubt it.

Long had Emily felt the irksomeness of her situation; and the *hope* that she should soon be instated in her proper sphere alone supported her spirits. This letter seemed to destroy it all; and for the first time the mental vision began to open upon the dreary prospect around her.

When once secrecy supplies the place of candour in the female breast, the approach of Vice is made easy;—the words of Deceit prevail—"She forsaketh the guide of her youth, and forgetteth the covenant of God;" and ruin, remorse, and repentance range successively through the soul.

Let me hasten to the castle to introduce the new Duke.

Volume II

CHAPTER I.

The illness of the late possessor of the family honours and titles was but a few days. His Grace was insensible after the attack.

The moment his death was announced to the family, Wilson sent off an express to Sir Avebury Hinton, who he knew was left one of the guardians and trustees for the children.

Sir Avebury left home immediately, but deviated a few miles from the road, to bring along with him a Mr. Kennet, a distant relation of the family, an eminent Counsellor, but who had long retired from pleading at the Bar.

When the Duke's nephew, who arrived first, came to the Castle gates, he smothered his joy a little, put on a grave countenance, as the case required, and assumed his usual *hauteur* and self-consequence.

The porter enquiring the gentleman's name, one of the servants that attended him, for there were three besides the steward, informed him—"*The Duke of Silsbury!*"

The sound quickly re-echoed through the Castle. Wilson was roused at the bustle and noise in the outward court, and went out.

The chariot, with four post-horses, foaming with sweat and dirt, drove up.

The young hero stalked out, and, slightly noticing Wilson, was walking into the hall; the steward, with some books under his arm, following him, when Wilson thought proper to accost the man of honours.

"Mr. Marauder, may I beg the honour of a few words?"

"Sir!!!" repeated the other, in a mixed note of surprise, *hauteur*, reprehension, contempt and anger.

"Young man," said the steward, "his Grace desired me to say he had no occasion for your services, but you might remain at the Castle till it was convenient for you to depart. If you have any accounts to settle, you are to bring them to me."

"I neither have, nor wish to have any concerns, any accounts with you or Mr. Marauder," replied Wilson, in a firm voice.

The servant, who had come to the vestibule as the carriage drove up, stopped, and looked at Mr. Wilson, as waiting for his orders.

"What does the fool stop for?" said his late Grace's nephew. "You seem none of you to know who is your master."

As the glance which accompanied these words included Mr. Wilson, he thought proper to answer—

"I believe no one here is ignorant that it is the present Duke, Sir."

"Well, Sir, and who is the present Duke?"

Wilson did not answer him as Nathan did David, and say, "Thou art the man!" but "The late Duke's eldest son."

"Damnation! this insolence is not to be borne. 'Tis well, Sir, for you that my respect for the dead saves you from instant chastisement."

Wilson, who had as yet choked the rising passion which the remembrance of his infamous conduct towards Emily did, at his first appearance, inspire—who had still restrained the swelling anger in defiance of his insolent pride, and had determined to wait the arrival of Sir Avebury for a full explanation, was thrown at once from his guard by the word *chastisement!*

"*Chastisement!*" repeated he, in his sternest, though not loudest key; "yes, my respect," softening his voice, "for the dead—my love for the living, tie my hands. I say no more to you, Mr. Marauder. Sir Avebury Hinton, and your relation, the Honourable Mr. Kennet will soon be here, and they will declare to you the particulars."

"Thus ever insolent," retorted the other, "you shall rue the day you first insulted me. Think you, Sir, that I am to be deceived by the stale story that the late Duke was married to his strumpet? Think you, Sir, I have never heard this before—that I did not hear, and despise it? But I waste words upon you!" Turning to a servant, "Shew me to a room!"

"Mr. Marauder," replied Wilson, with a manly firmness and indignation, "you shall have proof, and damning proof! For myself, I neither respect your consequence, nor dread your anger."

Mr. Marauder seemed willing to answer; but Wilson, fearful he should no longer command his temper, hastily withdrew; and the servant shewed his late Grace's indignant nephew into the library.

Far different sensations than those with which he entered the court-yard, occupied Mr. Marauder's mind.

The great respectability of Sir Avebury Hinton's and his relation's character he well knew; yet, judging of the rest of mankind by his own heart, he looked upon the tale of the Duke's marriage to be a despairing effort of Wilson, to keep possession of his situation at the Castle. Again, he supposed that in the latter part of his life the Duke might have been privately married, and that Wilson might have had the art and address to affix a prior date to the licence. In either case, he made no doubt of detecting and exposing his old rival; and he gloried in the revenge, which he was resolved the utmost rigour of the law should inflict upon him.

So full was he of this idea, that he reached down a law book from the shelf, to review the cases of perjury, forgery, and such-like. Mr. Marauder was rarely inclined to consult any one. Bold and daring, he was always the principal, and acted for himself; yet he once or twice wavered concerning sending for his attorney, Imphell, who now resided at the next market town. But, determined not to shew the least doubt of his right, he declined, and waiting with tolerable patience, considering Wilson's case, for the arrival of Sir Avebury and Counsellor Kennet.

In less than an hour they were ushered into the room where the would-be Duke was.

The gentlemen were personally known to each other. Wilson was with them.

Sir Avebury began.—"We are informed, Mr. Marauder, that you doubt the legality of the late Duke's marriage."

Mr. Marauder.—"I am extremely sorry to see so respectable a gentleman become the dupe of so palpable an artifice."

Counsellor.—"There is not even the appearance of artifice in this case. The legality of the marriage of his Grace, Samuel Duke of Silsbury, with Elizabeth Overton, can be no subject for doubt. His Grace, Sir, was twice married on the same day, about a month before the birth of his eldest son. The Priests, who married him, are yet living:—the Rev. Mr. Lockeridge, now Rector of Wheatland, but who then lived at Hazleton, and did the duty of Castleberry—"

Mr. Marauder, hastily.—"The very man, whose name I expected would be used as a cloke in this affair. Is his patronage of the grand instrument of all this," pointing to Wilson, "unknown to you? Are ye not acquainted with the birth, parentage, education, and dependence of this *gentleman* upon *that very Parson.* Perhaps the carpenter of Hazleton and his son are witnesses; though he might be young at the time, no doubt he was then a promising boy."

"I should wish," replied Sir Avebury, with great steadiness and bowing politely to Wilson, "for no better a witness than this young man's father; but him we do not want. I was present at the one, the Roman Catholic ceremony; and, among many proofs, the register of the Church of Castleberry, which you may instantly see by applying at the Vicar's house at Hazleton, will convince you of the other."

"It will not convince me!" retorted Mr. Marauder, evidently troubled in his mind at what he had heard, but endeavouring to conceal it under the mask of anger; "it will not convince me! I know how easy it is to insert a thing of that kind. When I discover a plot, I naturally expect the perpetrators will try to make it as complete as possible. Gentlemen, you ought to have known better: as for that man, he is beneath my personal notice; but not that punishment his folly deserves, and I swear most solemnly shall have!"

Wilson spoke.—"Happy might I have been, had the name of Marauder never offered itself to my notice. His revenge I despise as much as I abhor his person."

"Insolent fellow, beware! Even the giant crushes the gnat that stings him."

"The imaginary greatness of Mr. Marauder is crumbled to pieces. I am satisfied."

Wilson withdrew to the other end of the library, and, taking down a book, seated himself in a chair.

The other two gentlemen spoke not a word.

Mr. Marauder paused a few moments, at first in suspense, whether he should attempt to take forcible possession of the Castle; but considering the smallness of his retinue, he thought proper to adopt other methods.

"So, gentlemen, you still continue to countenance this deceit, and, presuming on your being the executors of the late Duke of Silsbury, deny me my lawful rights. I shall be sorry to involve you in the disgrace, which must necessarily attach to the exposure of this damned piece of villainy."

"On this subject," said Sir Avebury, "we have neither fears nor doubts."

"We hold," continued the Barrister, "the property of the late Duke in trust; for Samuel, his eldest son, a minor, now Duke of Silsbury. The testator has thought proper to join Mr. Wilson Wilson with us in the trust, and we applaud his discernment and choice."

"By G-d!" exclaimed Marauder, no longer preserving even the appearance of decency, but swearing in the grossest terms, "you are all alike! You shall quickly hear from me again, gentlemen. I did expect your grey hairs had covered sense and honour; at present I know not whether ye are the dupes or the humble assistants in this infamous plot. Remember I have forewarned you; let the exposure fall on your own heads. Drive up, my carriage; I'll stay here no longer!"

Mr. Marauder flew out of the room, and, in the height of his rage, departed alone, leaving his worthy coadjutor, who had not spoken all the time, but stood humbly behind his master, to follow him as he could. This worthy gentleman would have stopped one of the outriders, but he pretended not to hear him; and he was therefore compelled, amid the mocks and laughter of the servants, to trudge it on foot.

As there is no character more deserving contempt than the base and sycophantic tool of villainy, so there seems to be none who more frequently meet with it.

CHAPTER II.

When Mr. Marauder came a little to himself, he began to be staggered at the proofs which he had just heard of his uncle's marriage.

Though alone in the chariot, he vented, so profusely and so virulently, his curses against the Duke, Wilson, Sir Avebury, the Barrister, his kinsman, the Clergyman, and every one concerned in the business, that the postboys stopped, thinking he spoke to them.

He had ordered them to drive to the market town where the attorney lived; but, on second thoughts, he now countermanded them to the village of Hazleton.

When there, he drove to the Vicarage, and desired to examine the register of the marriages for the Church at Castleberry.

The Vicar, who had resided there ever since Mr. Lockeridge had gone to Wheatland, told him that it was not permitted, unless by authority, but he would give him a copy of any thing he desired.

Accordingly he departed, not without again testifying his anger, with a copy of the Duke's marriage.

To his great surprise and confusion, he perceived the names of two gentlemen of unsullied fame and character, whom he knew the Duke highly respected. Dean Bottom, a well-known dignitary of the Church of England, and Pookham Bottom, Esq. his elder brother, and Member of Parliament for the county.

Mr. Marauder, not yet satisfied, sent to Imphell, the attorney, and desired him to thoroughly sift the affair, and to let him know the result as soon as possible.

The true statement of which was to this purpose:—

Samuel, Duke of Silsbury, as soon as he was satisfied that his mistress was in the family way, determined to be privately married to her, and to have the marriage witnessed in the most regular manner.

The Church at Castleberry was his own parish Church, though it made part of the living at Hazleton. Mr. Lockeridge, as the livings were consolidated, was the Curate of both.

The Duke, in his common sporting garb, and his spouse in her usual attire, one very wet morning, met at the Church, and were united together. The Dean and his brother were present.

It is of no use to dwell upon the reasons his Grace always assigned for not discovering his marriage during his life. To Wilson he had, some years before his death, revealed it, under promise of secrecy; and Wilson had endeavoured to persuade his Grace to make it public. But the Duke always positively refused with many specious pretences.

He said his children might be educated with less extravagance and more humility: that their mother was perfectly well satisfied in the present respect shewed her, and was easy in her own mind, without publishing it to the world: that if his marriage was made public, he should, in a great degree, be obliged to change his mode of life; that his own relations would think it necessary to visit his Duchess; that her's would not be contented with the present civilities shewn them; with many other excuses, equally cogent.

But, after all, his marriage was solely performed to gratify his hatred against his brother; and the motives for concealing it, to indulge his own pride. The report of the marriage indeed, from the very first, had spread about the country; but as in so many years it had not met with any confirmation, it soon became totally discredited.

Lord James and his family had quickly heard the report, and gave but little credit to it; but when they afterwards understood that the supposed Duchess was delivered of a *boy*, and that his Grace did not hail him as his heir, they totally disbelieved it. Every succeeding birth weakened, in their mind, the probability of the story being true; and the gentlemen, who were present at the double ceremony, were of tried honour; therefore any circumstances to corroborate the report, were not likely to transpire.

Marauder's consultation with the attorney was to very little purpose, who gave him not the smallest hopes of setting aside his uncle's marriage.

Again and again did Marauder give the other to understand (for they had not been so long acquainted, without perfectly knowing each other), that if it were possible, by any means whatever, to succeed, he would not relinquish his claim.

The subject was examined in every point of view. The double marriage, the number of witnesses, the respectability of their characters, and the large family left by the Duke, the whole of which were born in wedlock, were subjects all duly considered.

The attorney, who was equal to any thing of the chicane kind, remarked, that the only possible means was, by one bold stroke, to invalidate the whole.

"Is it possible, Imphell?" asked Mr. Marauder.

"I think it is, Sir," replied the other.

"One hundred thousand pounds are ready for the purpose; and an ample compensation shall be made you, if you succeed in this business. But what are your means?"

"To prove a former marriage of the Duchess. I will be bound to find a husband, priest, and witnesses."

Mr. Marauder was for some time thoughtful; at last, striking his forehead, he exclaimed—"Oh! Imphell, thou art indeed a most noble fellow, but it will not do. This woman lived always with her parents in the same parish, till she came to the Duke's; and, what is worse for our cause, she was under age when she first came to live with him."

"Then, Sir," said Mr. Imphell, "I have no hopes to give you; unless we could furnish the Duke with a former wife."

"The regular and retired life which the old wretch lived, again totally prevents us," replied Mr. Marauder; "yet, my good friend, investigate each particular; let nothing escape you, and, if you see the smallest opening, let me know immediately. Here, take these notes for five hundred pounds; if you can use them for my purpose, they shall be repaid you tenfold; if not, keep them yourself: your ardour in my service entitles you to them: I know, at all times, I may depend on you."

With assertions unbounded, the most profuse thanks, and everlasting gratitude, Mr. Imphell pocketed the notes, and took his leave.

Thus, in a moment, were all those bold and splendid visions of the proud young man dissolved as a dream, and Marauder awoke to individual insignificance. Deeply did he review in his mind the pageantry that was passed by, till disappointed possession turned his foolish idolatry into rank hatred.

"Cursed Aristocracy!" said he, "thou art but the semblance of greatness: I'll no longer pursue the gaudy shadow! Could I have found thy ascent ready prepared for glory, I would have mounted to the top. I will not servilely follow behind, but I'll hew me out another path.

'Better to reign in hell than serve in heaven,'[1]

said the arch-fiend; and since heaven was to him a hell, I'll make the hell of democracy my heaven.

'Great talents and great virtues,' says the ingenious Godwin, 'are

---

1   John Milton, *Paradise Lost* (1667), bk. I, l.263.

ever united.'*—A man of uncommon genius is a man of high passions and lofty designs; and our passions will be found in the last analysis, to have their surest foundation in a sense of justice. If a man be of an aspiring, ambitious temper, it is because, at present, he finds himself out of his place, and wishes to be in it. I have this temper—I feel these great talents and great virtues within, and I will mark out a road that shall put me in my proper place.[1]

"Forms and ceremonies, titles and names, distinctions and parties, even opinions and principles are but the tools with which a wise man will cut his way through the world.

"Why was Cromwell a fanatic? 'Twas his interest.

"Why was Luther a reformer? 'Twas his interest.

---

* [CL] "This quotation is verbatim, page 327. In the page before Godwin says, from which Marauder seems to argue—

"It has no doubt resulted from a train of speculations similar to this," (that eminent talents are connected with eminent virtues), "that poetical readers have commonly remarked Milton's devil to be a being of considerable virtue. It must be admitted that his energies centered too much in personal regards. But why did he rebel against his Maker? It was, as he himself informs us, because he saw no sufficient reason for that extreme inequality of rank and power which the Creator assumed: it was because prescription and precedent form no adequate ground for implicit faith. After his fall, why did he still cherish the spirit of opposition? From a persuasion that he was hardly and injuriously treated. He was not discouraged by the inequality of the contest; because a sense of reason and justice was stronger in his mind than a sense of brute force; because *he had much of the feelings of an Epictetus or a Cato, and little of those of a slave.* He bore his torments with fortitude, because he disdained to be subdued by despotic power. He sought revenge, because he could not think with tameness of the unexpostulating authority that assumed to dispose of him. How beneficial and illustrious might the temper, from which these qualities flowed, have proved *with a small diversity of situation!*"

In this extract we see not only the morality and principles of Godwin, but the art and sophistry with which he introduces them. Beginning to speak in the words and sentiments of others; he slily introduces his own detestable dogmas.

---

1 Marauder's speech, as Lucas acknowledges, is in large part quoted directly from the second edition of Godwin's *Political Justice*, 1:327. The passage musing on Milton's Satan which appears in Lucas's note comes from the same source, 1:326 (*Political Justice*, ed. Kramnick, Penguin edn., 309).

"Did not Buonaparte offer his services to *Royalty?* Yes. He was unsuccessful in his application; he tried Democracy, and thrives better.

"From this moment, then, I despise thee, Aristocracy, unless I can bend thee to *my* purpose: I will not be *thy* slave; but now I'll try with *other* weapons, and with more glorious hopes. Money, the sinews of success in every point, is not wanting; 'tis mine to employ it with skill."

Marauder at no time doubted his own abilities; and as for prejudices to particular tenets and principles, any further than they suited his interest, the young philosopher had long shewn himself superior.

His two most intimate acquaintances were avowed democrats; and, when it had answered his purpose, he had frequently shewn temporary conversions; particularly in his visits to Mr. Cloudley, who practised in his household the purest species of democracy.

Leaving Marauder for a short time to his new cogitations, let us see how *la belle Emily* does.

CHAPTER III.

The second morning after the supposed Duke had departed to take possession of the family honours, her dear friend, the Marchioness, called upon his Emily. She had oftentimes shewn herself *this dear friend*, by amusing Emily with the gossiping tales of the day.

After mutual salutations—"My amiable creature," cried the Marchioness, "the Chevalier Touard has told me another curious tale concerning your dear man."

"Well," said Emily, affecting a lightness of spirits, which had long been genuine from her heart, "by all means let me hear it."

"My beautiful young friend," said the other, "I am assured of your incredulity for the trifles, or, on my life, I am eternally silent."

Emily.—"You know my contempt for the stuff, my dear Marchioness."

Marchioness.—"So the old Alderman has told his spruce young cousin, that his daughter might be a Duchess as soon she pleased."

Emily.—"What! does Alderman Barrow know of the Duke's death?"

Marchioness.—"Mr. Marauder—I mean his Grace—wrote to the lovely damsel herself the night he departed. Touard says he was of the party and saw the letter."

Emily asked no more questions—she had the utmost difficulty to conceal her feelings. The Marchioness soon departed, and a plentiful flow of tears gave her a momentary relief.

I shall here briefly explain the reason of the Marchioness's tale. Alderman Barrow, supposed to be the richest commoner in the kingdom, had an only daughter. Nor beauty, grace, nor sense, nor any accomplishment, mental or personal, had the young lady; but she was the sole heiress of all her father's wealth, who publicly said, if she married with his consent, the happy bridegroom should receive, on the wedding day, one hundred thousand pounds in ready money.

Nothing under Nobility dared aspire; yet Marauder had so plausibly explained his situation to the old man, he had so amorously ogled the young maiden, that the Alderman had already entered into a contract with him; and had not Mr. Marauder been so hastily called away by his uncle's death, the marriage was, in a few weeks, to have been solemnized.

Alderman Barrow had a nephew, his sister's son, young, rich, and most dashing. Bond Street, St. James's, and the Park, every fine day, from three to five, were honoured with his phaeton, chariot, or curricle, according to the fashionable taste.

The rage was now four different coloured horses; as such, a black and white, a strawberry and roan, were his favourites.

The young man, before the Revolution, had been twice or thrice in France, making in the whole some weeks. He played with a grace, and paid his money to people of the first fashion.

His name was Toward.

He was become particularly fond of foreigners, who, unlike his countrymen, seemed to pay him great notice. The Marquis and the Marchioness were his most intimate friends. He had assisted the Marquis in some embarrassments; he had lost a few hundreds to the lovely Marchioness; she had, in return, lost to him—What? Nothing. Yet Toward thought he had gained a great prize; grinned horribly *a la François*; spoke broken French; the Marquis called him *friend,* the Marchioness *Chevalier,* and they, moreover, softened his name to Touard. Surely he was a happy man!

So came the intelligence to Emily of Alderman Barrow and his daughter—a tale she had heard of before, but totally disbelieved till this morning.

It may not be amiss to remark that, by the *voluntary* resignation of Mr. Marauder, Le Chevalier Touard came into the Marchioness's favour.

Toward was introduced by Marauder himself a few weeks before Emily came to town; for Marauder, though resident in the country, had made occasional visits to the metropolis, to prepare (as he said) the house for his dear Emily, and to settle a few other matters.

Before Marauder left London on account of the Duke's death, he had, while the horses were getting ready, gone into his study alone, and written a letter. This Emily, flying into the study the moment he was gone, perceived.

The letter was to Miss Barrow, and to this purpose.

"*My dearest Clarinda,*

"My uncle, the Duke, died this morning. I fly on the wings of love to take possession of the family honours and property; which, immediately on my return, I shall rejoice to lay at the feet of the lovely mistress of my heart. With respectful remembrance to the worthy Alderman, most faithfully and eternally

"I remain your devoted servant,
"SILSBURY."

That a Duke proud, haughty, and rich, should so earnestly seek an alliance with a commoner, is something strange. Nor was it his vast concerns in the East Indies, nor his astonishing estates in the West, that humbled the spirit of Marauder to the match; but when he heard the Alderman had purchased a fourth borough, then the point was determined in his own mind.

Enraged was the no-Duke that he had not before concluded the match; but he had other thoughts of far more moment at present to trouble him.

CHAPTER IV.

Marauder, perceiving every contest concerning the title must be in vain, and burning with an inveterate hatred against Wilson, was determined to wreak his revenge on him.

Mr. Arnon, the younger, he knew was in the neighbourhood, on a tour through the west of England. Marauder informed him he was in the country, and hoped the other would oblige him with his company in his way. About three days after the Duke's funeral, Hambden Arnon arrived at Marauder's house.

Marauder embraced the opportunity of unfolding, according to his own notions, Wilson's conduct; and begged the favour of Hambden to call on Wilson, and fix a time and place that he might receive satisfaction.

Hambden, to whose education this species of manslaughter was familiar, though the urbanity of his own disposition had ever prevented his being a principal, did not refuse the request of his father's friend, but, with full powers to arrange the work of death, went to the Castle.

On enquiring for Mr. Wilson, he was shewn by a servant to his apartments.

Hambden began.—"I come, Sir, with an unpleasant message from my friend, Mr. Marauder. You have grossly affronted him. He has long been convinced that you are his *private* enemy, and he demands you, by me, to be his *public.* Your time and place I am to require."

Wilson.—"Sir, I wish to inform you, I have never been Mr. Marauder's private enemy, whatever cause I might have had to be so. The affront you allude to I did not give; my conduct in that affair was but a species of *self-defence,* and in no other manner can I *hostilely* meet your friend."

Hambden.—"Do I rightly understand you, Sir? Do you refuse that satisfaction my friend requires? Will you not fix a time and place?"

Wilson paused a moment for an answer. He evidently laboured to conquer his feelings.

"Sir, I never will name a time and place to attempt the death of any man, not even *my* greatest enemy; and that I believe is Mr. Marauder."

Hambden.—"Will you meet Mr. Marauder by his own appointment?"

Again the other paused.—The man, the injured man, struggled for revenge; at last, he but faintly and irresolutely answered—"No!"

Hambden.—"This, Sir, is most strange! Violent as Mr. Marauder's anger was against you, he did not, I am sure, doubt your courage. Do you think proper to give me any reason for your conduct?"

Wilson.—"You may tell Mr. Marauder, Sir, that it is not fear prevents my meeting him; that, on the principle of self-defence, I shall, as I have before, oppose him. My principles teach me forgiveness; I endeavour to practise them."

Hambden.—"What principle, may I ask, can possibly induce a man of honour, and a gentleman, to refuse his enemy an opportunity of receiving satisfaction?"

Wilson.—"The Christian, Sir."

Hambden.—"Of Christianity I have never made profession, nor been educated in its doctrines; yet it is evident that principle must be wrong, which denies to a person justice, where a fault has been committed against him."

Wilson.—"Yes; but the Christian does not. It is ever ready to pardon, to atone, to reconcile. If a man, Sir, who acts up to the principles of Christianity, is injured, he forgives; if he offends another, it is required of him, not to give his adversary an opportunity of revenge, but of reconcilement."

Hambden.—"Is a Christian a judge in his own cause?"

Wilson.—"Yes, in cases that reach not the common law, because he is answerable to God for his conduct more than to man. If I have injured Mr. Marauder, which I deny, the laws are open."

Hambden.—"The laws cannot reach every point. A man of honour carries in his own breast something superior, which makes that perfect, human ordinances have left imperfect."

Wilson.—"In that sentiment I agree with you, but this love of justice is not influenced by the prejudices or customs of individuals; as I said before, it goes to a higher tribunal."

Mr. Hambden Arnon paused, and seemed thoughtful.

"There is much truth, Sir, in what you say. Yet what reparation has Mr. Marauder for the insult he conceives you have given him?"

This question produced an explanation of Wilson's quarrel with Mr. Marauder. He told Mr. Hambden the whole. He began from their first quarrel, their acquaintance, their jealousies of each other, to the arrival of Mr. Marauder after the death of the Duke. In clear and impartial language Wilson narrated the facts which had come to his own knowledge, and concluded by saying—

"If Mr. Marauder can confute what I have mentioned, then, Sir, you may have reason to suppose that *fear*, not *principle*, prevents my meeting him in a hostile manner."

Mr. Hambden Arnon was so well pleased with the whole of Wilson's conversation, that he determined, if the circumstances he had heard, appeared to be true, (which, from Wilson's open honesty, he had no reason to doubt), to call on him in a day or two, apologize for his former visit, and beg the honour of his acquaintance; and, as he took his leave, he made a civil speech to that purpose.

When Mr. Hambden Arnon returned to Marauder, he fully related his interview with Wilson, and his refusal to meet him a hostile manner.

Mr. Marauder said but little. Having given vent to his passions, he had reflected on the consequences of a duel: not through personal fear, or the smallest diminution of his hatred to Wilson, but the troublesome consequences it might, at the present time, be of to himself. Mr. Hambden was thoroughly satisfied that Wilson's conduct was perfectly correct; and as Mr. Marauder's surmises, that Wilson had prejudiced the Duke against him, were denied by the other, Hambden gave it as his opinion that Mr. Marauder could no longer, with any propriety, insist upon Wilson's meeting him in the field.

With a tolerable good grace, Marauder acquiesced in the opinion of his friend, and dissembled a satisfaction he was very far from feeling.

So the affair rested.

CHAPTER V.

While things were thus going forward in the country, the conduct of Marauder, and the suspicious circumstances which had come to Emily's knowledge, at first made her very ill, and she was obliged to send for a physician.

In a few days her fever abated; her spirits, naturally good, supported her, and pride and anger came to her assistance.

Marauder, in the confusion of his own affairs, and irresolute how to act, was both unwilling and ashamed to write to Emily. This confirmed her suspicions; and, a week having passed since his departure, she indignantly left the house, and took lodgings a few miles from town.

About this time a letter was brought to her, which had been two days coming by the post.

"Dear Emily,

"I am damnably harassed by a pack of designing villains, and your enamorato at their head. 'Tis a deep-laid, and, I fear, a too successful scheme to deprive me of the title and estates. I have no thoughts of coming to town. I wish I could ask my dear Emily to come to me into the country; but you know the prejudices and nonsense of the neighbourhood. In truth I am most cursedly sick of this country, where tyranny, villany, and folly, in the persons of magistrates, parsons, and laws, reign triumphant. What says my Emily to a trip to the land of reason, virtue, and equality, with her constant adorer!"

This hasty note, partly through shame, and partly disappointed pride, Marauder purposely omitted to affix a name to.

Emily, having once learned to act and think for herself, the day she left Marauder's house, before she had as yet positively resolved to go, upon the receipt of this note, ordered her chariot, and drove to Alderman Barrow's.

She desired to speak to the Alderman.

She was shewn into a superb room—the Alderman attended.

Now the Alderman was a great admirer of beauty, and, most profoundly bowing, begged the honour of her name and commands.

Emily.—"Before I fully answer you, Sir, let me ask you one question—has Mr. Marauder made a matrimonial offer to your daughter?"

"*Mr. Marauder,*" replied the Alderman, smirking—"it never was a secret, Ma'am—made an offer some months ago; and the young Duke of Silsbury is shortly to be married to her. May I repeat—the favour of your name, Ma'am?"

"My name, *I am happy* to inform you, Sir, is Emily Bellaire," replied Miss Emily, trying to assume a conscious dignity. "I can also inform you that Mr. Marauder will never be a Duke. You are at liberty, Sir, to read this letter, which will save me any further explanation."

Mr. Barrow, having read the letter, returned it; and, though he seemed inclined to detain the fair heroine, she slightly bowed, and with the grace and *hauteur* of a Duchess, withdrew to her carriage: not that the Alderman was so deficient in politeness, or daunted by her manner, to neglect handing her into it, which he did with a tender squeeze.

Mr. Barrow had frequently heard that Marauder kept a very pretty girl; but the Alderman was too much a man of taste to make that an exception to his alliance, more particularly as one of the marriage conditions was, that he should give up his Miss. The thoughtful old gentleman also intended secretly in his own mind, if she suited his fancy, to take her to himself.

The letter, which Miss Emily had shewn him, put a complete stop to all thoughts of the marriage; but, as to the lady, it gave him a great many more on her account. He sent a trusty servant immediately to follow the carriage, and find her address, suspecting a *fracas* would take place with her former lover, and hoping to profit by it.

The man executed his commission most fully. He could, therefore, inform his master on his return, that the lady called at Mr. Marauder's, took up her maid and some trunks, and drove to a handsome lodging near Islington.

The Alderman was in raptures; he liberally rewarded the man, and sent him back to Emily with a very amorous epistle: most splendid were his offers, most fulsome his praise, and most glaring his expressions.

Emily was at first inclined to laugh heartily when she read his note; but, in a moment, recollecting the infamous light in which she had placed herself, she as suddenly gave full vent to her tears.

She answered the Alderman's letters most haughtily, to put a stop to any further application; but felt herself completely humbled by its contents. Finding her retreat discovered, she dismissed her chariot and men-servants, and the next morning, with only one maid, changed her residence.

Now had she time and leisure to reflect upon her former behaviour, and now did she begin to perceive the destructive tendency of that sophistry, which had blinded her understanding.

The hour of trial was come;—what new rules had she learned in the school of philosophy to support her? Alas! here she could the least bear reflection. This had been her greatest enemy—this had taken away that soother of the heaviest afflictions, CONSCIOUS INNOCENCE, and to this she owed her ruin.

Marauder was much too agitated with his own immediate concern, to make it a cause of alarm that he did not hear from Emily Bellaire; his vanity totally excluded the idea from his mind that *she* could possibly leave *him*.

Though dissatisfied with the termination of his quarrel with Wilson, and displeased with Hambden Arnon for some praises he had bestowed on his adversary, particularly when he understood that Hambden intended to call at the Castle again, yet he did his utmost to restrain his violent temper; and however he meant to act in future, he was very careful to deceive. After a little reasoning with himself, he so completely succeeded, that Hambden believed him to be perfectly satisfied that the affair had ended as it did.

On the third day, amid a profusion of friendly expressions, Arnon took his leave; and immediately, according to his intentions, waited on Wilson at the Castle.

CHAPTER VI.

After the common civilities had passed, and Hambden had mentioned that Marauder had dropped the intention of calling him to an account, to which Wilson made no reply, Hambden said—

"The more I reflect, Sir, upon your conduct the other day, the more am I satisfied that the principle of philanthropy, which influenced your behaviour, *in that instance*, is right; yet, as the preserver of the private peace of many families—as the refiner of men and manners—as an instrument of politeness and civility, I may almost call it the preventer of quarrels, and the destroyer of animosities, surely in many cases DUELLING is to be defended."

Wilson replied—"'Tis a greater evil which swallows up the lesser ones. Your argument is the best in its favour: you mean that the fear of being called to an account *in this way*, prevents the greater part of mankind from being guilty of incivilities and abusive language towards one another, and many other private injuries, which the laws of this country do not reach."

"I do," answered Hambden.

Wilson.—"But there are other means of preventing these evils."

Hambden remarked by saying—"Look at the Roman and the rest of the nations, where duelling, *as it is among us*, was unknown—what virulence of language, what quarrels, which frequently ended in murder!"

Wilson continued—"Among such people, where single combat and human slaughter was but an amusement, our refinement might have been of service. But we, of this kingdom, profess a superior principle, which takes away the necessity of duelling."

"You mean Christianity," replied Hambden. "But from the conduct of my countrymen who profess it, I have every reason to suppose that a stronger motive than their religion preserves the private peace of society, though you may be an exception."

"My own behaviour," said Wilson, "whether right or wrong, is out of the question. I now speak of Christianity in general; and the behaviour of one particular sect, who are the strongest examples of the outward actions of the religion, will suffice to shew that Christianity, while it *forbids all duelling*, will, of itself, insure civility of speech and of manners, and inoffensive conduct. I mean the Quakers, who never fight; but who do not, on that account, indulge in intemperate language or behaviour. Every true Christian is in this respect a Quaker."

Mr. Hambden attentively revolved in his mind what Wilson had said, and then replied—"You have convinced me that there is a principle more cogent than DUELLING to preserve order and rectitude of conduct in society: but that eager search after wealth, for which the sect you have mentioned is remarkable, is, in my mind, totally contrary to the love of God and love of our neighbour, which all religions profess."

"Sectaries may be right in particular tenets, though not in the whole," replied Wilson. "*In judging of the principles of Christianity, you are not to take the conduct of any man, or set of men: search for the pure spirit of the religion itself.* Covetousness is most forcibly forbidden by the Christian law. Remember, Sir, the religion itself is still the same, though its professors should grossly pervert it, or even if the guardian of the realm should be the first to slight and insult it. If the most conspicuous man in this kingdom, the man of all others his country looks up to as an example, was not only to signalise himself as a duellist, but add to it the profanation of the Sabbath, by chusing that day to break the laws of God and man, the disgrace and the infamy would fall *on his own head*: Christianity would be equally pure and free from stain."

"Since you would not have me judge *by the name* of Christianity," said Hambden "how do you reconcile to the virtues of this religion what Tacitus says of the primitive Christians? Tacitus, a fair and impartial historian, certainly but little prejudiced in religious matters, for he has been accused of having none at all, has in his book to this purpose:—'They (the Christians) were so abhorred *for their detestable crimes*, that Nero accused them of setting fire to Rome, and, in that plea, subjected them to the most exquisite tortures.'"

Wilson replied—"Yes, Tacitus has said so. But, at the same time, he has clearly vindicated them *from the only crime mentioned*, Nero's accusation of firing the city; which he has declared was, in defiance of all Nero's power and craft, universally believed to be authorized by himself.

"This severe accusation of the primitive Christians, by so candid an historian as Tacitus, may indeed, at first view, appear strange to the Christians of the present day, and very different from our ideas of the first fathers of the Church. But, luckily, to clear up this subject, Tacitus has mentioned *what those detestable crimes were*, namely—'For their hate and enmity of human-kind.'

"Now if we recollect the *worldly* greatness of Rome—that even among *their virtues* were ranked *pride, ambition, a spirit of revenge, a love of war, unbounded extravagance, and dissipation*—that the wilful and wanton murder of the human race was in the highest degree commended and applauded (as in their *public shews of gladiators*—masters, on the most trifling occasions, killing their servants, &c. &c.), and that, in the hour of danger and difficulty, *suicide* was applauded and encouraged: if we consider, on the other hand, the doctrines of the Christians, *meekness, mildness, patience, forgiveness, suffering without revenge*, &c. &c. &c. a contempt of all *shew* and *exterior greatness*, an abhorrence of all *sanguinary practices*, and lastly, a conscious knowledge of the natural depravity of the human-kind, and a dread of that false courage that can *wilfully rush into the presence of its Creator*; if, I say, Sir, we consider all these things (and every page in Tacitus will shew us that, whether he had a religion or not, he was a *true Roman*), we shall no longer be surprised, that what he calls 'an hate and enmity to human kind,' (i.e. *a disregard of the things of this world, and love only of a future one*), should be taken by him in the list of detestable crimes."

When Wilson had spoken, he reached for the shelf a Tacitus, and pointed out to Hambden Arnon the passages he had alluded to.

Hambden bowed assent.

Wilson continued.—"Tacitus also calls the worship of the Jews 'profane rites and superstition.' But what was the religion of the Romans? It was a worship paid to Deities altogether frantic and impure, by sacrifices and follies ridiculous and vain. It consisted in no purification of heart, nor amendment of morals—the things which men and societies require; but in sounds, gesticulations, and the blood of beasts: not in truth and sense, in benevolence and rectitude of mind, but in lying oracles, unaccountable mysteries, and a raving imagination; sometimes in professed acts of lewdness, often in those of fury and madness—"

"However, Sir," replied Arnon, interrupting him, "you may describe the superstitious fears and follies of the Greeks, Romans, and other nations we have any account of, you cannot exceed *my* ideas of their unaccountable ignorance and depravity. I fully agree with you that they were grossly wrong themselves, and that they could scarce help mistaking the principles of Christianity. Neither am I ignorant, that though Trajan at first prosecuted the Christians, yet he desisted upon the representation of Pliny, Proconsul of Bithynia, who described them to the Emperor as innocent and simple, a harmless, inoffensive kind of people.

"You have induced me to consider the Christian religion in another light, and it shall be my first business to investigate their original writings."

Wilson.—"I have every hope that the *wonderful spirit of virtue and morality* which pervades the whole, will convince you that it is the true and only religion."

"You speak," replied Arnon, "*of the spirit of religion.* Do you mean by it any other than the *literal words* of the books called the Old and New Testament?"

Wilson.—"Yes. The *Old* and *New Testament* have been so frequently transcribed and translated, that many errors, many mistakes, many omissions and additions, must necessarily occur, particularly in the former, which may easily afford an opportunity to the sceptic to cavil at and condemn; but it is the tenor of the whole a fair judge would consider."

Hambden asked—"Do you not call the whole inspired?"

Wilson replied—"Certainly not in *the letter*, as that is in the power of any individual to alter. Many copies of the sacred writings are different; both cannot be right. But it is from the *New* Testament the

Christian draws his rule of life and belief; for Christ made that perfect which was before imperfect, and gave us more pure, certain, and infallible laws. These, after his death, many of his followers committed to writing, with some account of his life and morals."

Hambden.—"I am obliged to you for this remark. I believe a person may be prejudiced against a thing as well as partial to it. As preparatory to my reading the religious books of the Jews and Christians," (Wilson smiled at the term), "can you recommend me any small tract that you think may facilitate the understanding them?"

Wilson.—"Here is a book written by a layman—you may have perhaps heard of it, as he was at one time no Christian—'Soame Jenyn's View of the Internal Evidence of the Christian Religion.'[1]— Till you can furnish yourself with books which enter more fully into the subject, this, I think, will answer the purpose, and I beg you'll accept of it."

The conversation now took a general turn. The gentlemen became very much pleased with one another. Wilson found little difficulty in prevailing with his new acquaintance to spend the day with him.

In a few weeks Wilson was to be in town, to meet, on business, the other executors of the Duke; and so earnestly did Hambden Arnon press him to make his house his home, that he promised to do so; and they parted in the evening with the warmest wishes on both sides to continue the acquaintance.

CHAPTER VII.

A week had passed since the funeral of his Grace, in which Marauder had had many closetings with his attorney; but the prospects concerning the title were further removed than ever.

In the meantime he had heard of the fair Emily's departure, of which he affected great indifference, as he had no doubt of recovering her whenever he might chuse to take the trouble. He therefore penned a kind note, begging her to return to his house; assuring her, whatever was the cause of her taking offence, it was without inten-

---

1 Soame Jenyns (1704-87) published *A View of the Internal Evidence of the Christian Religion* in 1776. It was immediately popular, but controversial, many commentators arguing that it was too ingenious in its proofs of Christianity. Others praised the book's efficacy in converting the irreligious.

tion on his part; and he concluded, as usual, with everlasting vows of love and constancy.

It might have been supposed that Marauder would have embraced the opportunity of getting rid of Emily.

Gratified in his passion, and cloyed with possession, perhaps he would have done so, but he had reasons most forcible and persuasive still to keep in good terms with the lady: of these we shall presently more fully speak.

His intended bride he gave up all thoughts of, by no means desirous of running off with Clarinda without a certainty of the cash, and well knowing that the prospects of the Dukedom, while it was the cause of the large dowry, was also the bait to the Alderman, whose vast wealth and borough interest were in too tenacious hands—only to be opened by the law. Yet Marauder, ever cautious and artful, resigned the fair one of his own accord, with a good grace; and with well-affected *nonchalance* told the Alderman that, since he was disappointed in that consequence he had flattered himself he should have raised Miss Barrow to, he should never think, by prosecuting his claim, of preventing the prospects of a more splendid alliance with another.

Old Barrow declared to every one that, though Mr. Marauder had lost the title, he was quite a gentleman; and, if he could be sure of his vote, he should have the next vacancy in his Boroughs.

While Marauder was thus preparing the ground, that he might more easily prosecute any schemes of ambition he thought worthy his notice, a gentleman he had been intimately acquainted with in Italy, and whose sword had been more than once drawn with Marauder's for their mutual assistance, came from Ireland.

This gentleman had a very considerable property in the county of Fermanagh, in the province of Ulster, and had spent the latter part of the year 1794, and beginning of 1795, in making himself better acquainted with it; a thing he had ever before neglected, and which the mother of prudence, necessity, had at length constrained him to.

Mr. Fahany was about four-and-thirty, and had been possessed of every worldly endowment at the age of one-and-twenty, to make a man happy.

He had had a splendid fortune, a lovely, beautiful wife, fine children, and respectable connections. His person was then favourable; and in polished manners, and classical abilities he was inferior to few men. With these advantages, natural and acquired, he was restless, discontented, and most miserable. Totally devoid of every religious and moral principle, his wit and learning were employed to make others like himself. Without attempting the least command over his passions, he was cloyed with every vice; and now, in the prime of manhood, a primitive old age had already seized his frame, weakened by constant debaucheries. His personal affairs were involved and confused by extravagance and continual losses at the gaming-table, among the lowest of the human race. His wife, injured, disgusted, and disgraced, fled from his arms, and by no entreaties could be prevailed upon to return. His three children, neglected by their father, were scattered at different schools, far inferior to their abilities or rank in life.

Such had been, and such was now Fahany.

Personal distress had at length compelled him to look into his concerns, and he had departed to Ireland for that purpose about the time Emily came to town. Fahany left England for three months, and had been absent above fourteen; he had not visited his estates before, since his twenty-first year; and novelty, in any form, had irresistible charms for him.

When he arrived in London, and found Marauder was at his seat in the country, he lost no time in following him; and he now came full of schemes and inventions, to retrieve his shattered fortune, and found his friend very well disposed to listen to, and partake of them.

Marauder had troubled Fahany with a few commissions concerning his own estate in Ireland; but many other reasons had he for so hastily calling on the other.

Among the first, an affair which had happened at Turin, seemed likely to be revived.

"Geutespiere," said Fahany, "I understand from my Italian correspondent, is by this time in England."

"For what purpose?" asked Marauder.

"Solely to call us out. My friend writes me word that he publicly gave this as his motive."

"Indeed! the French Captain is somewhat hot. I shall let his blood with great pleasure. What is become of the credulous Leonora?"

"The Captain, having proved his honour, reproached her with her infidelity; and the fair damsel, in despair, has thrown herself into a Convent."

"Foolish girl! she had charms yet remaining enough for any honest *bourgeois*. Have you any other intelligence of this Hotspur's arrival?"

"None."

"Probably the young hero has thought better of the business."

"Very likely."

The affair to which this conversation alluded, was not very honourable either to Marauder or his friend. It was of the love-kind.

Leonora Contelli, a young lady, native of Turin, who had been
educated in France, had fixed her affections on a French Officer,
afterwards in the emigrant service, of the name of Geutespiere.
At the commencement of the Revolution this lady returned
home.

Marauder, who was intimate with her uncle, having tried for
some time in vain to ingratiate himself into her favour, by the assistance of Fahany adopted the following stratagem.

Fahany had been acquainted with Captain Geutespiere, and was
just arrived from the Allied Army, where the Captain was with his
regiment of Emigrants. They easily, therefore, got possession of some
of the young Officer's writing, and, by the assistance of this, forged
a note of hand from Geutespiere to Fahany, payable out of the fortune of Leonora the moment he was married to her.

This Fahany pretended to have won at the gaming-table; and a
third person, who was made a dupe in the affair, told the story to the
uncle. He, of course, informed his niece, wishing her to break off the
connection. The young lady, doubting the truth of the story,
enquired of Marauder, who professed a total ignorance of the trans-
action: he could only inform her that his countryman, Fahany, with
whom he was but little acquainted, was devoted to gaming.

By the young lady's desire, he enquired into the circumstance;
and, at last, was able to satisfy herself and uncle with a sight of the
note.

The young lady's temper Marauder had studied. It was warm, mer-
cenary, and revengeful. He had laid his schemes accordingly; and, having once removed the object which obstructed his wishes, he, with
redoubled ardour, renewed his suit, and in the end was victorious.

The incredulous fair one was soon forsaken; the gentlemen left
Turin, and thought no more of the business, till the letter from
Fahany's correspondent revived it.

Greatly was Fahany rejoiced to find that his young friend was in
the way to relinquish his aristocratical prejudices—prejudices that
could no longer be of service to either of them. He unfolded to him
the plan in agitation to separate Ireland from this country; he par-
ticularized the case with which it might be achieved, and the glory,
wealth, and power which must necessarily accrue to the daring leaders of the multitude.

Marauder was fired at the idea, and in the warmth of his heart
cried—"And *I* am a Roman Catholic!"

Marauder now minutely enquired into the situation of Ireland, and the methods of conducting the enterprise. Mr. Fahany confessed to his friend that he was himself a Defender, and had taken the oaths;[1] but that they had no idea yet of acting in an hostile manner, but were in hopes that the Parliament would grant certain indulgences to the Roman Catholics (the great body of the commonalty), which would strengthen the means, and insure their success.

Marauder, no longer surprised at his friend's story, wondered he should leave the country at so critical a time. The other told him he had particular engagements in London, but that he should return in a few months.

A thought now struck the quick mind of Marauder, which he instantly communicated to his friend.

"I know your business, Fahany; you want some ready cash."

"That I confess is one of the motives for my journey. I mean to sell my estate near Cork. It will fetch me about ten thousand."

"Sell nothing, my friend in *that* country; but dispose of every thing *here*."

"That I have done long ago."

"With our present plans then, if we want money, *mortgage is the order of the day.* Take up in London what money you may want on your Irish estates. The money is easy enough to be got by giving a small premium; and, when we have freed St. Patrick's noble country, we'll wipe out the mortgage, both interest and principal, at the same time."

"You are a devilish clever fellow, Marauder. I am obliged to you for the hint, which I'll most assuredly put in practice. My dear fellow, you shall have my vote to be *Minister of Finance* the moment we have drove out the English."

CHAPTER VIII.

Marauder proposed to Fahany to return with him to Ireland, and view the state of affairs there; but first of all he wished to see Emily and her sister Fanny, whose young beauties were not easily eradicated from his mind. The chief motive which induced Marauder to

---

1 Although they later merged with the United Irishmen, the Defenders began as a purely Catholic underground group organized to combat the Protestant "Peep O'Day Boys" in the 1780s. Both sides used violence as they attempted to redress perceived social, economic and political grievances.

wish to be on good terms with Emily, was the remembrance of the lovely Fanny, as by Emily's assistance he intended to get the other into his power.

Before Fahany's departure, in the course of conversation, he had told him that he should pay a visit to the prettiest girl in the universe, whom he hoped, some day or other, to get into his power.

"I have no doubt you'll succeed, as I never knew you fail in an affair of this sort."

"When the time comes," replied Marauder, with an expressive look, "I shall be able also to help my friend. You have no objection, I know, to a transfer."

"None in the least; any thing but the drudgery of making love."—And he quoted Quin's reply to a certain lady, and a maxim from Petronius.[1]

Marauder smiled, but it was a smile that applauded himself; and, taking Emily's picture from his pocket, he shewed it to Fahany.

The other was all in raptures; he could not sufficiently praise the beauty, grace, and symmetry of the fair unknown.

"This lovely warbler," continued Marauder, "I left encaged when I came from town; but a little unwillingness to marry her upon the death of the Duke, which was the lure by which I caught her, has, at present, frightened her away. Here, keep the picture, and if you find the truant, let me know; and your reward in the end shall be her fair self, for I only need her as a decoy to ensnare her fellow-bird."

Fahany was so anxious to put in practice the money-scheme (without which he could carry on no other), which Marauder had pointed out to him, that he did not wait for his friend's return to town; but, after a visit of a few days, took his leave. It may be necessary to remark that their correspondence had long been conducted by a cipher.

Upon Marauder's enquiries after Fanny, he found she had left Mr. Vasaley's, or he would have made little difficulty in calling there.

He soon discovered she was at Richmond, and he resolved to call on her in his way to town, and to say her sister Emily had particularly requested him so to do.

When he had settled, therefore, a few concerns with his worthy attorney, without loss of time he set forward on his journey.

---

1 Possibly James Quin (1693-1766), famous actor and celebrated wit. Gaius Petronius Arbiter (d. AD 66) was the reputed author of the *Satyricon*, (c. AD 61), a ribald and hedonistic satire.

He easily found her residence, and, without discovering his name, was shewn into a parlour.

Fanny came tripping into the room, anxiously hoping the gentleman might be her friend Wilson.

So great was her disappointment, so strong her disgust, that she was about to leave the room immediately, but Marauder prevented her by saying—

"Your sister, Miss Bellaire, desired me to call upon you."

Fanny stopped. Marauder pretended many anxious enquiries from her sister concerning her health, and the situation she was in, and professed how desirous they both were to be favoured with her company. Fanny was very cold, very reserved, and desirous to be gone; but could not refuse her tears when she mentioned and enquired for her sister.

Marauder quickly perceived that the idea of Emily's *not being married* hindered her from accepting his proposals of living with her sister; he therefore thought it best to make her believe that he was married to Emily the moment they came to town, but that it had been necessary to keep it a secret.

With this intention he said—"I am sorry, my dear Miss Fanny, to perceive you treat me with such reserve. Am I never to hope that you will consider me as a brother?"

"Sir!!!" replied Fanny, not a little surprised.

"It was neither my intention nor my dear Mrs. Marauder's," continued the would-be kinsman, "to deceive our *friends*. But I thought it then necessary for your dear sister's sake, that the marriage should not transpire till after the death of the Duke."

"Am I to conclude, then, Mr. Marauder," said Fanny, steadily, "that you were married to my sister the moment you arrived in town?"

"Certainly: I hope my dear Miss Fanny never doubted it. His Grace, I presume, you have heard is dead. By a successful plot I am for the present deprived of the title and estates. I have no longer any wish to conceal my marriage; and the moment I discovered the retreat of my dear sister, Mrs. Marauder was wretched till I called on you, to press you to take up your abode with us: and indeed I never executed a commission with more pleasure in my life."

"I am rather surprised my sister did not accompany you."

"For that," replied Mr. Marauder, "I am solely to blame."—(A falsehood once invented, requires many a one to support it, but in this he was by no means at a loss.)—"I flatter myself, before we return, your dear sister will have presented me with the blessed name of a father. You will not, I hope, disappoint her in refusing to accompany me. Your presence, at this crisis, will be most soothing and obliging."

When Marauder first called on Fanny, he had no intention of carrying her off with him. The most he expected from his visit was, that she would be prepared to accompany himself and Emily at another time, and he had no doubt of exerting his usual influence over Emily to make her act and say just what he pleased. He could easily, he was assured, make her believe, that whatever he had said to Fanny, was on her account; and he had specious pretences not only to delay their marriage, but to make Emily join in the deceit on Fanny that they were already united, and to countenance what ever else he might think it necessary to advance.

But the questions of Fanny had carried things farther than he at first intended; and now, by a happy invention, (one of those lucky hits he prided himself upon), he could not fail getting her immediately into his power: and so highly was the beautiful girl improved within the last fifteen months, from the daily conversation of women of sense and fashion, that Marauder lost the child in the more mature graces of person and stature, and was resolved to profit by his present success, and make sure of his lovely prize.

To the last wish of her pretended brother, Fanny replied by asking—How far her sister's residence was from where they were?

Marauder was rather at a loss to answer, for he purposed carrying Fanny at least fifty miles, to a lone house he had on the Berkshire Downs, of which more will be said hereafter; and he thought if he mentioned so far, it might prevent her accompanying him; he therefore said—"No great distance."

On Fanny's repeating the question, he replied—"My house near London is about twenty miles from town."

"Well, I will certainly accompany you."

Marauder, with his utmost endeavours, could not wholly conceal his joy, but rung the bell for his carriage to draw up directly.

"Yet," continued Fanny, "it is necessary, Sir, I should send to Mr. Townsend before I leave this house. My guardian lives within a few doors."

Marauder was too anxious to admit any delay.

"Certainly, my dear Miss Fanny; but as the business is rather urgent, if you leave a note, I think it will be as well as speaking to your worthy guardian. My servant shall take it directly, and he will soon overtake the carriage."

Nothing could suit Marauder better; his servant understood each look of his master. The note, he knew, would never reach Mr.

Townsend, and, as he had before cautioned his servant not to discover who he was, he now concluded he should be able to carry off Fanny, and no one be acquainted with whom she departed.

But Fanny's reply checked these hopes. "No, Sir, it will not take up much time, and it is necessary I should speak to my guardian, as well as the lady who has been so obliging as to admit me one of her family here."

Marauder, as I have said, had a lone house most peculiarly situated on the Berkshire Downs.

This house was called uninhabited, and was a late purchase of Marauder's, merely for the situation. To this he had resolved to take Fanny, the moment he had supposed her so completely in his power. The mention of Mr. Townsend, whose steadiness of character he had heard of, changed his thoughts; and, reverting to his original intentions, that another time would be more favourable for his plan, he considered in his mind how to act; while Fanny was sending a servant, by whom she requested to speak to Mr. Townsend.

Revolving over his conduct, Marauder perceived that he had been much too anxious; and fearful of raising suspicions in her breast, which indeed was not entirely free from them, and somewhat alarmed at meeting with, and answering the questions of, Mr. Townsend, he said—"On second thoughts, my dear sister, I think it will be better for you not to hurry yourself in this business; for though, when I left my Emily the other day, she was so desirous that I should bring you back with me, yet considering the distance of thirty miles or more—"

"Thirty miles, Mr. Marauder, does my sister live from hence, and the other day did you leave her? I understood you said it was but eight or ten from here, and twenty from town, and that you were just arrived from the place."

"The small seat I have a little beyond Epping is full twenty miles the other side of London; and I thought I had mentioned to you, Miss Fanny, the very urgent business which compelled me to leave your sister at so critical a time."

"The death of the Duke of Silsbury you mentioned, Sir, and I had heard of it before; but I supposed you were now come from my sister."

Marauder most readily adapted a story to his purpose, and concluded with telling Fanny that he would fly post haste to his dear wife, and send her an express to-morrow how Emily was.

Fanny consented.

Marauder took his leave before Mr. Townsend came, rejoicing at the success of his conduct, and certain of Fanny as soon as his schemes were ripe.

"Sweet Fanny!" cried he to himself, the moment the chariot drove off, "you shall be mine. In defiance of these bewitching eyes, which pierce my very soul, I'll soon have the little Gipsy in my power. Then the pouting lip and scornful brown shall soften to the voice of love, then—"

Marauder, for some miles, was lost in these pleasing fancies; and, recollecting himself, he revolved the means of realizing his hopes. To find Emily, and make her unknowingly an assistant in his intentions, was his first resolution; and by the time he arrived in town, he had thoroughly arranged the affair to his own satisfaction.

Without loss of time he drove to his town-house; (is it necessary to mention that the one twenty miles farther, beyond Epping, was but an ideal one?) and quickly became acquainted with Emily's address.

He prepared directly to follow her; and, not doubting in the remotest manner his success, he, at the same instant, dictated a letter to Fanny.

In this he said that his beloved Emily was perfectly safe and out of danger, though he had to lament his disappointment of a son and heir; that in a day or two, if Mrs. Marauder was sufficiently received, they would together call for their dear sister, and hoped she would be prepared to take up her abode with them. He mentioned also that Mrs. Marauder was so earnestly wishing to see her, that in case his beloved wife was not able to undertake the journey, he should himself come and conduct her to his house. The letter was written in the language of the most affectionate of husbands and brothers, and was dispatched by a special messenger.

With eagerness he hastened to Emily's lodgings. So resolved was he in this point of getting Fanny into his clutches, that it lulled for a time his darling thoughts of ambition. Full of the successful projects before him, he arrived at Islington.

Emily had left her lodgings, and the people of the house could give him no intelligence of her present abode. He searched for the people who were acquainted with her footman and coachman; these servants he found were discharged. The relations of her maid had not heard from her for some time. This somewhat checked his intended plan; but he never gave up a point, and commenced a most diligent search to find her retreat.

Perceiving his labours, at the end of the second day, to be employed to no purpose, he was resolved to return to Fanny, and, in defiance of the consequences, to embrace the opportunity which his former story offered, to gain possession of her person.

Though bold and daring was Marauder, yet he was crafty and most vigilant. His grand scheme, he perceived, was arrived at its climax before the period he intended; but he was determined not to lose the auspicious moment which Fortune had presented him, even if he should be compelled in the end to leave his country.

A restless and enterprising mind, a fierce and undaunted spirit were the outlines of Marauder's character; youth spurred him on, and success had buoyed him up.

Few were the scenes of life he had not experienced, and none that his vanity did not think him equal to.

He looked on no man as his superior, and rarely beheld any one as his equal; yet experience and a knowledge of mankind put a gloss upon him, by which he shewed a specious outside impenetrable to almost every gaze.

CHAPTER IX.

To get Fanny Bellaire safe into his hands was, at present, the first object to Marauder; and of this he did not doubt.

Willing to ensure success, he, for that purpose, forged a letter, as from Emily, pressing Fanny most earnestly to accompany her husband; and, as he had many letters of Emily's by him, he had not the smallest fear of detection.

Fanny, in the meantime, had been favoured with the company of another visitor. A few hours after Marauder had left her, a stranger called at the house, and enquiring if Miss Fanny Bellaire lived there, desired to see her alone.

When Fanny came into the room, she perceived a lady, with a long thick veil over her face, dressed in deep mourning.

The lady arose at her entrance, threw up the veil, and the features of the once beautiful Emily appeared to her view.

Fanny was riveted to the spot. Emily she believed at that moment on the bed of sickness, perhaps of death; and the idea for an instant flashed on her alarmed mind, that the figure, now before her, was the departed spirit of her sister. The roses had fled the cheeks, and disappointment and remorse had emaciated the countenance; melancholy had usurped the place of mirth, and the dimpling smiles of pleasure were obliterated by the furrows of care.

"Does my Fanny wish to forget her sister?" said Emily in a faint voice.

Fanny could make no answer, but threw herself into her arms, and sobbed aloud.

When the sisters had a little recovered from the agitation their first meeting had occasioned, Fanny, whose young mind was filled with doubts and alarms, expressed her surprise at seeing her, and faintly mentioned that her husband, Mr. Marauder, had not long been gone.

Emily trembled, and, with downcast eyes, endeavoured with firmness to say, what her heart felt was true, that she rejoiced he was not her *husband*.—"But, dear Fanny, what brings him here? Will he return? If you ever loved me, do not say you have seen me. Let me be gone directly, and—never see you more."

"Dearest sister Emily," replied Fanny, "do not be alarmed. You are safe from every intruder here. No one knows you; those friends of mine, you may think proper to trust, you may rely on. I will immediately give orders that Mr. Marauder shall not be admitted beyond the parlour below. Mrs. Mountford, who lives in this house, is the most kind and affectionate of women. Our guardian, Mr. Townsend, lives near, and has not been gone from the house half an hour. I will send for him again; you may rely on his goodness."

Fanny entered into the particulars of Mr. Marauder's calling on her, and quickly found from Emily that the whole he had recounted to her was a falsity. They mutually testified their surprise to each other, for what purpose he could think of calling on Fanny, and wishing to take her away with him. Fanny attributed it to a wish to be reconciled to Emily by her intercession; but her sister, who knew mankind better, without mentioning her suspicions, was much nearer the mark.

I pass over their conversation with Mr. Townsend, who soon came to them, and his kind behaviour to the truly penitent Emily; as also the prudent and friendly conduct of the worthy Mrs. Mountford. This lady and their guardian were the only persons to whom Emily was discovered, as it was thought needless as well as improper to disclose her to the Miss Berricks.

Emily declared to Mr. Townsend and her sister that no consideration whatever should induce her to marry Marauder. She further informed them that her mind was fixed, as soon as her affairs were arranged with her guardian, to retire alone to a distant part of the kingdom, where she might live retired, unknowing and unknown.

They endeavoured to prevail on her to depart from her intentions, but she replied—"No, my dear sister, my own vanity and folly have deservedly brought their punishment along with them; and I am resolved to suffer alone. I very well know how great the disgrace would be to all my acquaintance, were I to live among you. I have neither the wish nor the will. I rejoice to find my dear sister in an agreeable and worthy family, and I hope occasionally to hear of her happiness, as my friends assuredly in return shall hear from me."

Finding Emily had made up her mind, and that all their arguments and entreaties to the contrary were of no avail, Mr. Townsend and Fanny were necessitated to acquiesce in her determination. Though Emily's new philosophy had proved a treacherous friend in the hour of need, yet it was not an easy thing to explode it entirely from her mind; among other traces a kind of positiveness remained, which she vainly mistook for a firm and resigned spirit.

In the human soul, when a reformation takes place, we bravely tear up our hated vices by the roots; yet the fibres, spreading far and deep, will make frequent attempts to spring forth, and, by degrees will succeed, unless we complete the noble work by exterminating them as fast as they make their approaches.

"No man," says the old proverb, "can all at once be a villain;" neither is any man in an instant all virtue and goodness. The greatest villain on the face of the earth has his moments of compunction, and what is often taken for hypocrisy, is often temporary repentance; but it is a regular course of good action that purifies the soul, and virtue, as it was yesterday, must be the same to-day, and for ever;—temptation must be overcome, evil must be avoided, again and again, ere a man can lay his hand on his heart, and say—"I have kept the commandments of my God."

CHAPTER X.

Emily agreed to remain a few weeks with her sister, at the earnest entreaty of the ladies and her guardian; while she prepared herself a residence to her taste, arranged her establishment, correspondence, and so forth.

The next day the messenger came from Marauder, whom they dismissed without any answer.

It was about the hour of noon on the third day, that Marauder himself, high in hopes, came to fetch Fanny away. Conscious that he was now known to her guardian and the family she lived with, and determined in his intention, he put a bold face on the matter.

He drove up to the door in his own chariot and four, with two servants on horseback, and, alighting, was shewn into a parlour.

Upon asking for Miss Fanny Bellaire, and giving his name to a servant who required it, he was informed that Miss Fanny had ordered herself to be denied to him, and that she had changed her mind.

Marauder, in no way daunted, but supposing it some prudent whim of her guardian's, which he doubted not the forged letter from Emily would dissipate, smiled at the message as conscious of his success, and desired the servant to deliver her the letter.

The sister read—

"*My dearest, beloved Fanny,*
"The affectionate kindness of my dear husband, who could not be prevailed on to leave me, prevented his coming for you before. The doctors will not permit me to travel so far this week; but so anxious am I to see my dear sister, that I have insisted on Marauder's coming for you to-day, and I will meet you this evening at my town-house, where, at a gentle rate, and in a very easy carriage, I shall arrive to receive you. I have written this scrawl to assure my dear Fanny how unhappy I shall be till I once more press her in the arms of
"Her loving and affectionate sister,
"Emily Marauder."

A sensation of horror struck them both as they read the letter. The depravity of the writer was so apparent, they felt alarmed that he had been admitted into the parlour below, though the possibility of his carrying off Fanny by violence was sufficiently guarded against.

Fanny, somewhat recovered from her alarm, with a trembling hand wrote—

"*Sir,*
"My sister has been here.
"Fanny Bellaire."

Marauder, with indifference, opened the note, as he supposed it to be some trifling excuse for delaying him. He glanced his eyes over it, and started from his seat. Not otherwise did the Arch-fiend start up when the celestial spear of Ithuriel touched him.

So completely was Marauder daunted, that, without knowing what he did, he obeyed the motion of the servant, who held the door open for him, walked immediately out of the house, and leaped into his chariot.

In a moment recovering himself, he would have returned. The servant had shut to the door.

A dreadful oath burst from his lips, and he ordered his servants to drive to the first inn.

From hence, after writing a dozen notes to Fanny, none of which even satisfied himself, he sent the following.

"*My dearest Miss Fanny,*

"Believe me, from the very best of motives, have I been tempted to use deceit. Without it I feared you would never have been prevailed upon to assist me in the search after your sister, and to intercede for my pardon. May I beg you'll inform me where my Emily is? and you shall soon be convinced of my sincerity, my constancy, and my gratitude.

"Ever yours, most faithfully and affectionately,

"J. MARAUDER."

Fanny, in a few words, replied that her sister was concealed from his search, and had resolved never to see him again.

Marauder made repeated trials to get an interview with Fanny; but, finding it in vain, he for the present relinquished his intentions, firmly resolved, the moment it was convenient to his other plans, to carry her off by force.

As soon as Marauder's anger at his disappointment was in some measure subsided, and his passions cooled by reflection, he began to think it was better for him that he had not at that time succeeded. An amour, which was likely to afford him some trouble, would greatly interfere with his ambitious plans; and he had many necessary steps to take before he could arrive at that eminence, which his daring prospects aimed at.

The youth of Fanny was another argument to make his wait with more patience for the possession of those beauties, which, ripening every day, became more worthy his notice.

At the time he first intended calling on Fanny, we have seen that he had not the most distant idea of getting her into his power. He went, as it were, to review a beautiful object, which, at a future day, he intended to be master of. But the opening beauties of the lovely girl, and the wonderful improvements in her person since he had last seen her, had suddenly raised his passions; and the opportunity which offered, he could not resist, the temptation he could not withstand.

Now again he coolly reviewed his situation, his ambitious hopes and prospects; and his soul was fired with flashes of aggrandizement, which consumed the lighter sparks of love,—Love! So Marauder called it; but the touchstone of truth proves it to be a passion created by the powers of darkness, not of light.

As there are few virtues for which *a general rule* cannot be given to try them by, so *true love* may easily be distinguished from every spurious kind, by observing whether the passion, which assumes its name, benefits the object beloved or not; for *Love*, whatever form he may appear in, *ever seeks the good of the beloved*.

And this is the grand touchstone, more infallible than all the rules of ancient and modern writers on the art of love. Not Anacreon, at the head of the old Grecians, nor Ovid of the Romans; not Petrarch, with the whole tribe of the Italians, French, and Spaniards; nor, among others at home, the venerable Chaucer, the incomparable Spenser, and well-known Cowley and Waller, not forgetting Dr. Darwin, can produce a more clear and simple rule to define true love.

Plato says there are two Cupids, as different as day and night—one endowed with every virtue, the other with every vice; the one rules and softens the passions of the soul, the other is a mean and grovelling slave to them; the one is mild, pure, and constant to its object—the other, headstrong and violent, varies with every wind.

Marauder knew nothing of the former of these, yet Marauder swore he was in love; the God of his idolatry, then, was that other Cupid, offspring of Hell.

Perhaps, then, that which conduced more than even ambition itself to allay, for a time, the passion the lovely Fanny had kindled in the breast of Marauder, was another object—an object of glory as well as desire.

Lady Cassel, the gay wife of Sir Thomas—a Baronet, of every bloody hand the most fashion-formed in the kingdom—for the first winter now sparkled in the meridian of St. James's.

Sir Thomas's mistresses, horses, and carriages had long been the rage. When *such* a man sacrificed all for *one* woman, what must his wife be?

In short, so well pleased was the Baronet with his lot, that it was a difficult point to say which was most gratified, himself or the lady, in hearing the daily panegyrics, which, from the Court to the Playhouse, re-echoed in praise of his choice.

The beaux soon settled Lady Cassel's character—"Ever tempting, never attainable;"—not so Marauder; he allowed the first, and determined to try the second.

The lady's failings (alas! even beauties have them!) he first made himself master of. The *love of fame* was the most conspicuous:—"If she loves the passion itself," said he, "she'll soon love the possessor."

Marauder quickly made himself of notice in Lady Cassel's eyes; her Abigail was his own; the morning paper, which graced her toilet, told of his renown—now the friend of a Prince—now the attendance of a Duchess:—so that when Marauder opened his attack on the citadel, his *good name* had already made a wonderful interest in the garrison.

Yet not in the manner of a conqueror did he assail the fair Lady, but as a captive.

The game he had already so successfully played with Emily, he again began with a like prospect of success; though his manner of conducting it was somewhat different.

Admiration and respect threw the object of adoration off her guard; and the first assault carried the place.

A private masquerade favoured his views, and in the habit of a slave he triumphed over the glories of a Queen of the East.

Too proud was Marauder of his success to conceal it; every eye but the Baronet's saw it, every ear but his heard it, every tongue but his told it. In this case, the dashing Sir Thomas wilfully lost the use of his senses; nor did he think proper to recover them, till his Lady some time afterwards eloped with a young Irishman, who was about to join his regiment in that kingdom.

In the foregoing summer at Brighton, Marauder's first acquaintance had commenced with Lady Cassel; nor did he omit any opportunity of offering up incense at the shrine of her vanity. He soon perceived that the flowery wreaths, which entwined the marriage knot, were too green and flourishing to be easily unloosed; he therefore put not forth his strength in vain, but prepared himself for a more convenient season. The winter seemed more propitious to his hopes; till the death of the Duke for some time deferred, and the beauties of Fanny almost made him forget, his purpose.

Checked in the one attempt, he renewed the other with redoubled vigour; and success made him for a while forget that he had ever met with disappointment.

CHAPTER XI.

At the commencement of this amour of Marauder's, Wilson arrived in town. He called on Fanny in the way, but not a word transpired concerning Marauder; neither did he see Emily.

Instead of that innocent vivacity with which it had been usual for Fanny to accost her friend, he perceived a restraint, which lessened the pleasure he took in observing her mental and personal improvements. A somewhat similar observation as to his address and manner, Fanny could not fail to notice, though far from attributing it to the right motive.

In the noon of the day Wilson came to Richmond; he walked with Mrs. Mountford, Mr. Townsend, and Fanny upon the hill. They passed an elegant young man, well dressed, of an open countenance, and of a pleasing person; but with a wildness in his look, that interested, while it could not fail to strike, an attentive observer.

On their return they observed him nearly on the same spot noticing the company. Observing Fanny attentively, he clasped his hands together, and spoke in a mild, though expressive manner, loud enough to be heard by the company passing—"Amid the follies and depravity of my countrywomen, your appearance, young lady, revives the philanthropic principle within me, and flatters me that virtue is still an inhabitant of our isle. When I perceive the most beautiful of Nature's works has the sense to discriminate—"

Fanny and the rest had stopped at his first address, but blushing deeply, she drew her veil over her face, and they continued their walk; though they plainly heard the stranger asking her pardon for his abruptness.

The day was remarkably fine, and many well-dressed people were taking the same walk. Wilson, struck with the eccentricity of his character, and interested with his appearance, by the desire of the ladies, left them under Mr. Townsend's protection, and joined a group who had collected round the stranger, who, as Wilson came up, was speaking to this effect:—

"Let the years 1794 and 1795 for ever declare to what licentious caprices and disgraceful examples women may be subject. When the fashion of the day, (from France the deadly poison came), induced females of all ranks, conditions, and ages to seem to be with child— when different sized bundles, called pads, were *publicly* exposed, and *publicly* sold to suit the capricious or wanton whims of the dissipated purchaser, and offered to her notice by a contemptible man-milliner—then did the young girl, yet in the bud, cheapen, even by her mother's side, that article which was to feign her in a condition the profligate female would attempt to conceal; then did the ancient mother, in defiance of every good principle, virtue, morality, piety, not only countenance, but join herself in the same, hobbling with her sham burden! In vain did the father, husband, brother, or friend exclaim! Supreme fashion could overturn in the female mind every barrier of chaste love, decency, and sense, and at once rend the veil, already too thin, between modesty and depravity. Behold, then, the self-degrading female, the mother, the daughter, the ancient unmarried aunt, or still more ancient grandmother, bearing their infamous burdens!!! the size of which indicated the seeming number of months the whim of the bearer chose. See, the sash! ah, how unlike the zone of Venus! tightly braced close beneath the shoulders, supporting where the chaste delicate fair needs no support. Observe the walk, the gait, the air! and, lastly, mind the disgusting, though studied, seat! then candidly say is not the common prostitute the more decent of the two, and less danger to be apprehended from her to the morals of the rising generation, than the modish fair?[1]

"Blessed! doubly blessed! the chaste maid, who bravely spurns the base example—who, in defiance of the taste of Princes, the fashion of Nobility, knows her own worth, preserves her good sense, and keeps herself uncontaminated by actions so scandalous, depraved, debasing, infamous!!!!!!"

The ladies, who at the beginning of his speech surrounded him in no small number, had, one by one, gradually taken themselves away; a few tight-laced females alone remained, who seemed wonderfully pleased with the last compliment, which they took to themselves. The stranger, turning towards Wilson, whom he observed particularly noticing him, in a lower tone continued—"How, in a future day, will the almost incredulous philosopher account for this shameful fashion? He will probably call it, and I believe with truth, a bold, cunning, and successful invention of the deformed and ugly to make the more beautiful, and, in this evidently, the more foolish part of the female race like themselves."

Wilson could not fail giving a slight assent with his head; and the stranger taking the arm of a gentleman, who came up at the latter part of his speech, and who attempted in vain to move him before, walked coolly away as if nothing at all had happened.

The spectators, of course, with one accord, concluded him to be mad; but Wilson could not help owning that, like Hamlet's, there was method in it:

"For what he spoke, tho' it lack'd form a little,
"Was not like madness."[2]

---

1 A desire to emulate the new Princess of Wales, Caroline of Brunswick, was probably behind this fashion of 1795-96. The Princess gave birth to a daughter, Charlotte, on 7 January 1796.
2 Shakespeare, *Hamlet*, III, i, 164-65.

Wilson now saw the meaning of his address to Fanny, whose dress, though perfectly easy and genteel, was, in the strictest sense of the word, decent; he endeavoured to discover who the youth was, and his motives for thus haranguing in public, but without success.

As Wilson had no excuse for staying at Richmond, he took leave of Fanny the next day, yet promised to call again on his return from town.

This was the first time Wilson ever was in London; and he drove immediately, according to his promise, to the house of his new acquaintance, Hambden Arnon, whose establishment was separate from his father.

Hambden received his visitor with the utmost satisfaction and pleasure; and as he shook him cordially by the hand, he said—"My dear Sir, I am most happy to see you. The book you were so obliging as to give me, induces me more deeply to study a subject I am conscious I have too much neglected, and which I feel myself highly interested in."

In his society, Wilson met his father and Rattle, with many other gentlemen, most of whom were of the same principles as Mr. Arnon the elder.

It may be necessary to mention that one of the reasons why Mr. Arnon and his son had separate establishments was, Mr. Arnon had a female friend, who lived with him, and whose temper and manners were very uncongenial to Hambden, though the lady was rarely visible to any of his acquaintance.

CHAPTER XII.

Wilson one day met at Mr. Arnon's house some of the modern philosophers. This was the fist time he had been in company with a party of this kind; and he was as much entertained with the violent inconsistencies they advanced for the doctrines of wisdom, as he was disgusted with their self-conceit and affectation of knowledge.

Mr. Hermaph, a person well known in the schismatic world, made a violent invective against Bishops, Deans, &c. &c. &c ridiculing, with great success, as he supposed, an established form of worship. Rattle, whom in argument difficulties seldom daunted, replied—"And pray, Sir, amid the plenitude of your arguments, what may be your objection to the Liturgy of the Church of England?"

"Because, Sir, it is *a Liturgy*, a regular form of prayer. The service of the Deity is at the best but a *lip-service*—the heart is uninterested."

"Your arguments," replied Rattle, "are trite, and purely methodistical, and that of the most fanatical kind. The more regular Methodists, the followers of Wesley, use the prayers of the Church. You suppose, then, Sir, that the preacher should be inspired, and wait for the operation of the Spirit?"

"Ridiculous!" replied Mr. Hermaph. "You know, Mr. Rattle, such foolish suppositions are none of mine."

"What then, do you think that extempore harangues are more pure and perfect than a regular composition, revised, corrected, and generally approved?"

"I say it has more to do with the heart."

"If it has, it must be only with the heart of the person who prays. The rest of the congregation, who are ignorant of what is to be uttered, who perhaps have sentiments totally different from those he feels, cannot be said to be interested, or mentally affected."

"Well, well," said Mr. Hermaph, "I am no advocate for praying of any kind."

"Yet, Sir," said Wilson, taking up the argument, "you condemned the Church of England because it was a regular form. This, I think, Mr. Rattle has very ably defended; for when a prayer is repeated to the ears of the people, who already know what is to be uttered, their thoughts are prepared, their minds are ready, they join in the same ideas; and as the language is already chosen and correct, no gross expressions, no fulsome terms, no disgusting familiarity of words, no needless repetitions damp that ardour the heart feels. Reason approves what the tongue speaks; and what *you* and *the Methodists* call lip-service, is the service of virtue matured by reflection, in opposition to the sanguine rhapsodies of an heated enthusiasm, which, like watery bubbles, will not bear the touch of thought."

"What would you say," exclaimed another gentleman of the name of Subtile, "of an orator in the House of Commons, who learned his speech by heart before he went to the House?"

"A wonderful deal better," exclaimed Rattle hastily, "than making an oration to please the gallery. The gallery of the House of Commons is one of the chief means of corrupting the nation; our legislators are orators; fine words supply the place of good sense; the grand qualification is, that of an actor to entertain the gallery, and supply the newsmonger; men of learning and knowledge are abashed and ridiculed, every chattering fool, impudent coxcomb—"

"Stop, stop, my good friend," said the younger Arnon, interrupting him, "you are flying from the subject; we shall hear you talk treason next."

"This gentleman," said Wilson, alluding to Rattle, to whom he had been first introduced that day, "is rather hasty; but I believe not many of the declamations we have, would be the worse for a few hours' calm reflection in the closet. But Mr. Subtile's remark of comparing the orations of the House of Commons to the prayers of the Church, has no analogy to the subject, which was a form of prayer, and not a speech."

"Since you won't allow," replied Mr. Subtile, "my arguments concerning prayer, but, as all are equally interested, require every one to know what is about to be uttered, what will you say concerning the custom of the Church of England in reading a dull, unmeaning, written discourse by way of sermon?"

"That a *written* discourse," replied Wilson, "is more dull or unmeaning than an extempore one, even you, Sir, I believe will not affirm. I shall not repeat to you the same arguments which have been mentioned for the prayers; but only say that, in my opinion, oratory in the pulpit ought to yield to plain reading."

"You will make a schoolboy our reader and instructor next," said the elder Arnon.

"No. I only mean that the passions ought not to be roused or affected—that argument without the glow of language—that common sense and natural expression should be pronounced without the aid of the actor—that the people should be permitted to judge from the sense of what they hear, and not have their passions inflamed by well-turned periods, affecting language, soothing or inflaming terms. If these auxiliary helps are brought in to aid the sense, they are equally as improper whether they are written down, or uttered extempore. In short, gentlemen, plain and simple doctrine, uninfluenced by passion, whether affected or not, is the most likely way to arrive at the truth."

Said Mr. Subtile—"You think, Sir, by a regular service the people are interested. How are they interested in the lessons of the day?"

Wilson replied.—"Certain portions of the holy Scriptures being regularly read over in the service of the Church, at the same time they remind the learned Christian of what he has before read, instruct the uninformed, and give those, who cannot read, an opportunity of hearing the sacred Scriptures. Were the parts to be read left to the discretion of the Minister, he would of course read those only he himself chiefly approved of, or preferred; he would most probably be repeating the same; and if the Minister of the place changes, the portion of Scripture might not: but by the present regular custom, there is continual variety, and each in its turn is noticed and read."

"Right or wrong, Sir," said Mr. Hermaph, "it is a farce I shall not very soon join in. But I am sorry, Sir, *you also* should rank our opinions with those of the mad-headed enthusiasts of the day."

"Nay, nay, Sir," replied Rattle warmly, "I defy any rational man to see very little difference between you."

"Infidelity," replied the enlightened gentleman, "is as far removed from enthusiasm as the east is from the west."

"True," said Rattle, "yet the travellers, who take the opposite paths, will meet together at last."

"Sir, we are the *head* of the human species; enthusiasm is the *tail* grovelling in the mire," spoke Mr. Subtile warmly.

"Ah!" said Rattle, "I thank you for the thought. The serpent is no bad emblem of Infidelity and Enthusiasm. Which is the head, and which the tail, I leave to others to determine—you are generally depictured together; but, upon my honour, *I* think *you* the tail."

"We despise the bigoted wretches," exclaimed Mr. Subtile; "not fire and water are more opposite."

"Raving and melancholy madness," replied Rattle, laughing at the passion in which he had put men who openly professed themselves philosophers, "are both confined in Bedlam."

"On these subjects," said Mr. Arnon, "you known, Rattle, I have long given up the Herculean task of opening your eyes; you are so violent, fanciful, and headstrong, 'tis in vain to dispute with you."

"Now, gentlemen," continued Rattle, determined not to give up his point, "in the midst of all my fancies, let me see if I cannot make the comparison good. What says the Methodist? 'The blacker the sinner, the brighter the saint!' The modern Philosopher will tell you 'The greater the villain, the better the citizen.'

"To this purpose your friend Godwin argues.— 'It may be questioned whether an honest lawyer is not a more pernicious member of society than the dishonest lawyer.'*

"Again the Methodist says—'The more wicked and abandoned you have been, the more likely you are to be convinced of sin.'—So the Philosopher—'The more ignorant and depraved you are, the less likely you are to be prejudiced by the laws of morality and religion, and the more likely to become an independent freethinker and actor.' Witness the leaders in France. Thus Godwin, again abusing all national education, from the University down to the poor Sunday

---

* [CL] Political Justice, vol. ii. p. 399, Godwin concludes an honest lawyer most mischievous. [*Political Justice*, ed. Kramnick, Penguin edn., 690-91.]

Schools, says—'All this is directly contrary to the true interest of the mind; all this must be unlearned, before we can begin to be wise.'"*

"You strain the point to make your argument good," said Mr. Arnon.

"Yet I quote your scribe, Goldwin, *verbatim*," replied he, "and I have other proofs."†

"The author of the Spiritual Quixote, speaking of the *religious* enthusiasm, ere the irreligious was yet matured, said—'Enthusiasm is deaf to the calls of nature—nay esteems it meritorious to trample upon all the *relative* duties of life.'[1]

"Did not the wretches in France boast the murders of fathers, brothers, sons, &c. &c.? Does not Godwin also renounce these ties?

"Vanity and self-love are other traits of both religious and irreligious enthusiasm. Was not your grand apostle Voltaire so conceited as to dine in public with his niece, till some Englishmen, who were not sufficiently illuminated with this new philosophy to be spectators of their pride without disgust, said '..................'—Voltaire and the lady, who knew enough of English to understand them, overheard the remark, and it put a stop to this parade for the future."[2]

Rattle now opened his pocket-book, and took out a paper.— "Here is one proof you must all allow. This is a written—now what to call it I don't know—but it is either, or perhaps both, a *Methodist's sermon*, or the rant of a Democratical Enthusiast. Faith, Grace, Hope, and Charity make it the one; Liberty, Reason, Equality, and Justice

---

* [CL] Political Justice, vol. ii. p. 295. [*Political Justice*, ed. Kramnick, Penguin edn., 615.]

† [CL] Mr. R. might have produced the renowned Wm. Godwin himself as a proof of the near alliance between enthusiasm and infidelity. That wonderful, capacious, expansive mind, which can grasp at the highest objects, or minutely investigate the lowest, was once (we are told by his friends) enchained in the narrowest fetters of prejudice. Mr. Godwin was a preacher, and a very rigid dissenter of the Calvinist persuasion. [Like his grandfather, uncle and father, Godwin was a dissenting minister; preaching at Ware, in Hertfordshire, from 1778 until his growing scepticism overturned his Calvinist faith in 1783.]

---

1 Richard Graves published *The Spiritual Quixote: or, the Summer's Ramble of Mr. Geoffry Wildgoose. A Comic Romance* in 1773.

2 While at Ferney, towards the end of his life, Voltaire lived with his niece, Marie-Louis Mignot, Madame Denis, as if, to all appearances, they were a married couple.

make it the other. Call Saints Democrats; Sinners Aristocrats; for Satan, read Tyrants; and for more sacred names, take Nature and so forth.

RATTLE'S DOUBLE ORATION.

"Satan and his imps of darkness
"Tyrants and their ministers of tyranny are on the watch, my

beloved Brethren, to fasten you in the eternal chains of *Hell.* Rouse,
fellow Citizens, *Slavery.*

be vigilant; put on the *garments of Hope,* seize on the shield of *Grace,*
cap of Liberty, *Equality,*

and grasp the *sword of Faith.* The *glorious prospects* of *Paradise*
dagger of Justice. *injured rights* *Citizenship*

demand *your struggles* and the *joys* of *Heaven* shall be yours.
vengeance, *honours* *Victory*

This alone can save you—this will overturn the wiles of the

deadly Fiends. Listen to me, my *Brethren,* I bring to you the
haughty Tyrants. *fellow-Citizens;*

words of wisdom; I speak to you the language of truth; I'll teach you

how to overcome the *ghostly* enemy; I'll unite you all together in
cowardly

the bond of *Charity,* I'll plant for you the tree of *Life,*
Fraternization; *Liberty,*

and you shall *eat the fruit and live for ever.* Down with the
water it with the blood of your tyrants.

Temples of Satan and his Gang— throw their haughty turrets level
Mansions of Kings and Nobles—

with the ground; here let us lay the foundation of a glorious *Hope—*
Equality—

here let us build up an universal *Faith,* then, my fellow-men, the
Liberty;

Kingdom of all-sufficient *Grace* shall insure your happiness. We are
Power *Reason*

the *true Elect,*   *the precious Stones of the Temple;* and the *flaming*
    sovereign People, *Friends of Liberty;*   *glorious*

fires of Hell   *consume the reprobated outcasts,*
                   shall   those
virtues of the Guillotine   *cut down the haughty Aristocrats—*

base *slaves*   of *Satan,* from the face of the earth.
      instruments   *Tyranny*

"This was given me," concluded Rattle, "as a precious *morceau;*— *which* of these famous rhapsodies was the *original,* I leave to the superior judgement of you and your friends, Mr. Arnon, to find out."

There was a gentleman in the company, of whom Wilson could not be totally ignorant, as he was a M.P. and remarkable for his staunch support of the Government; yet in a late instance he had acted, in the steady administration of justice, as a county magistrate, directly contrary to the interest of his ministerial friends. Though his *political* opinions by no means agreed with many of the present company, his private sentiments were more congenial.

Mr. Vantage was intimately connected with Rattle, having for many years had the charge of his person and property, though it was not till after the death of his elder brother, that he took much notice of him. By this gentleman Rattle had been first introduced to Mr. Arnon's acquaintance; for Mr. Vantage and Mr. Arnon were successfully concerned in a commercial speculation.

Though Mr. Vantage was rarely a speaker in the House, yet his consummate prudence was ever considered as a sufficient proof of his wisdom and ability; and his opinions were always heard with attention, as the sure result of judgement and reflection. His known honesty, credit, and wealth were favourite themes among his commercial intimates, and his liberality and munificence were not forgotten by his domestic friends.

He had by no means failed in his earnest endeavours to deserve the good opinion of the world; and, with an undaunted spirit, he had, at an early age, shewn that his honour was as dear to him as his life.

In Mr. Vantage's opinion, the highest perfection of morality was to be found in the elegant and ingenious writings of the philosophical Earl of Shaftesbury;[1] every thing beyond was priestcraft, enthusiasm, or conceit.

---

1 Anthony Ashley Cooper, third Earl of Shaftesbury (1671-1713), a politician and philosopher, author of a number of neo-Platonist works and most famous for his deism.

This gentleman frequently smiled at the arguments and replies which had been advanced on both sides; with Rattle he had long given up the Herculean task of arguing, but Wilson he heard with a look of pity at the confined notions of so promising a young man; and observing, at this time, a favourable opportunity, thus delivered his own opinions:—

"While I fervently admire and applaud the establishment of a regular form of religious worship, instituted by the wisdom of the Government, I am astonished that any reasonable man should require an indiscriminate approbation of it.

"I may say not only the use, but the necessity of Government, demands order, regularity, and method in every part; and that which in the abstract cannot be defended, may in the whole be of the highest benefit. 'Tis thus I consider established laws, established religion; though the tedious formalities both of the one and of the other, may be unworthy the assent of a rational, reflective mind. Were I in Turkey, I should not be content to be *negatively* obedient to the laws of Mahomet: in China—Confucius or Fohi—the religion of the country would be mine. In this, in that, in every case, superstitions and priestcraft would be equally the object of my inward contempt, but peace and harmony would, in all, be my motive.

"In Church, in State, I fear schisms and oppositions as the harbingers of confusion, and from them I dread the introduction of every species of evil.

"Our virtues unite us together; let us encourage every thing that promotes virtue: and the man who cleaves to the social system, cannot be guilty of any actual vice."

Wilson, perceiving these sentiments congenial to the greater part of the company, and particularly addressed to him, replied—

"I cannot believe but that there is as great an individual distinction between good and evil, virtue and vice, as between light and darkness. If truth is different from falsehood, professions will follow principles, and conduct resulting from the same, will sanction the whole. If any man is willing to appear otherwise than what he really is, is he not guilty of deceit? If tests are no more than cloaks to conceal, can that which is right require concealment? If honour and honesty are any thing better than specious names to advance self-pride, self-interest— where is the honour of that man, who professes an outward assent to what his heart condemns? Where is his honesty, who embraces an opinion that he despises, because it may promote his interest? There is honour and honesty in the conduct of that Jew, Turk, or any professed infidel, who, living in a Christian country, will neither conform to professions they believe not, nor insidiously impose on the establishment, by accepting such stations and situations as are incompatible to any but the real professors; but where is the honour and honesty of those who either verbally affirm what they are not, or impose upon the received opinion of mankind by appearing to be so, without which falsehood they could not enjoy their present advantages? A man of pure honour and honesty will neither directly nor indirectly impose on any one; he will no more sanction a falsehood by his conduct, than by his word or his oath:—but the man, who accepts any station, civil, ecclesiastical, or military, under a Government, as a supposed professor of its established religion—which office, if he were not of the establishment, he could not hold—every time he speaks against that religion, is perjured either in his words or actions.

"The act of wearing the very dress of an Officer in the English Army or Navy, or of the different gowns of Law and Divinity, is to a man of genuine honour a direct pledge that he is a Christian; and every word that he utters to the contrary, is but so much satire against himself.

"Of oaths, of conforming to the most sacred rite of the established worship, though still more heinous in my mind, I shall not speak; as the man, who has not religion, owns no other tie than the vague names of honour and honesty."

Mr. Vantage's morality was too firmly fixed, too convenient to listen to arguments.

With a smile of self-knowledge and consequence, he said—"Young man, I admire the ingenuity of your arguments; but before you come to my age, you'll see these things in another light. The intricate wheels by which society is managed, the motives, the passions, the innumerable affections of mankind are things not to be learned in a day. Good and evil are so far from mere names, that the knowledge of them must be the study of years."*

---

* [CL] If peace, quietness, and a love of the social system are the harbingers of virtue, a certain character, which has borne the lash of many a pen, may step forward, and say—"Though I am notorious for the want of every moral principle, and particularly for my unwearied assiduity in seducing the innocent and helpless—though I laugh at the laws of God, and despise those of man, yet firmly do I cleave to the social system. I suffer reproofs and contumely rather than be guilty of any kind of warfare. Whenever I meet with opposition in my pursuits, I leave my prey; and though, from my youth, to extreme old age, I have been daily versed in the gratification of my desires, yet peaceably and quietly have I proceeded in my career: and though rank and wealth are mine, yet such is my innate love of society, that rarely am I to be found out of the crowded and convivial scenes of the metropolis." [Quotation untraced.]

To this Wilson made no reply, but Rattle quickly remarked—"If, my good Sir, the length of years gives a truer knowledge of good and evil, 'tis in vain to argue with you, as you have got so great a start of us."

When Wilson was alone with his friend Hambden, he could not fail testifying his surprise that there should be a set of men in this kingdom, who call themselves philosophers, and think they prove themselves to be such by a regular course of principles and practice contrary to the morality, laws, and religion of their country.

"You may gain the fullest information on this point," replied Hambden, "by attending some evening the harangues of a public and well-known Society, where, under the plea of a fair debate, every kind of opinion finds a vent."[1]

Wilson told him that he should be highly obliged if he would accompany him to the same.

CHAPTER XIII.

At a public meeting where, under the mask of discussing liberal opinions, the partisans of the French endeavoured to propagate their principles, Wilson, who had accompanied his friend Hambden, recognized the young man whose rhapsody had so astonished him at Richmond.

The stranger appeared perfectly calm, sedate, and attentive, while many of the company delivered their sentiments.

"Unhappy is the country," said an orator, finishing an harangue against Christianity, "where, under the mask of religion, the mind is shackled and restrained, and the property of individuals encroached upon by the sons of idleness and pleasure;—unhappy is the country where laws defend these things—*laws*, which should protect to every one their property, justify the theft—*laws*, which should assist in expanding the human mind, are the first to confine and depress it.

---

1 Probably meant to stand for the London Corresponding Society (LCS), the largest and most influential of the reforming societies which were active in the 1790s. The LCS was founded in 1792 with the aim of pressing for Parliamentary reform. It was quickly infiltrated by government spies and some of its leaders were arrested and charged with treason. Mass meetings organized by the LCS helped to provoke the Two Acts of 1795 which stiffened the treason laws and limited the right to hold public political meetings. The LCS was declared illegal in 1799. See Appendix E.

"When I look back upon the glorious commonwealths of Greece—when I reflect what Rome *once* was, what France *now* is, again and again I exclaim— 'Oh unhappy country! unhappy people! where law and religion go hand in hand, in opposition to reason, liberty and truth!' That pure and famous morality, which was known to the early ages, and which France again begins to sanction—that stern virtue which has made a Cato and a Brutus immortal,[1] was a far better lesson, and of far more benefit to mankind, than the cold, phlegmatic virtue of boasted Christianity. Where is the champion so bold as to deny these things?"

The stranger started up.—"Behold him here. Christianity needs not my weak voice, yet impiety shall have my scourge. Grant me patience, just Heaven! Are these new philosophers most knaves or fools? Philosophers indeed! who quote the nations where the life of the slave not only depended on the will of the master, but where the laws even forced poor wretches, bought, educated and fed for the purpose, to murder one another for his caprice and pleasure—as an example of Liberty!—and again he quotes the men, one of whom prostituted his wife for the service of his friend, and the other, who slew his greatest benefactor—as instances of virtue and morality! But in what did their virtue consist? Did they persevere, in defiance of troubles and misfortunes, in defending their country? Did they patiently follow the conqueror's chariot in chains and disgrace, that at a future period they might serve the cause of Liberty? No. When the day of disappointment came, they fled from these things—by their own murder!

"But surely these great men had virtue, and morality, and reason, and liberty, and truth, and equality, and all the wondrous catalogue *somewhere*? Yes. So have these modern worthies, and in the same place—*in their tongue;*—in their heads and their pens—not in their hearts and their actions.

"Shall I compare the Christian virtues to theirs? or shall I defend its rites, its ceremonies, its Ministers to the honourable judges before me?—whose applause has already told me—"

---

1 Marcus Porcius Cato ("Cato the Elder," 234-149 BC) and his great-grandson, also called Marcus Porcius Cato ("Cato the Younger," 95-46 BC) were both staunch conservatives, seeking to defend Rome against moral decadence and individuals seeking personal power, like Julius Caesar, whom Cato the Younger opposed. Marcus Junius Brutus (85-42 BC) also opposed the autocracy of Julius Caesar and became the leader of the conspirators who assassinated him.

The close of this quotation—if such it is—is not signalled.

At this part of his speech almost the whole of the company seemed inclined to interrupt him;—all speaking at once, and calling him—"Enthusiast, Methodist, Madman, Aristocrat, &c. &c. &c." and again and again crying out—"They can't be defended! Down with him, down with him!"

The young stranger stood still—smiled—put his arms across— and waited patiently the issue.

Rattle was in the house, and most violent on his side, vociferating among the first—"Let him proceed—let him proceed—no interruption!"

The Chairman, having quieted the storm, desired him to finish his speech, saying he could not allow him above three minutes more.

"Then let them choose their point;" said he, looking at the most clamorous, who were the former speakers—"what shall I defend?"

The last orator cried out—"Tithes, tithes!" and the others echoed it.

The stranger continued in a very different tone of voice, mild, though firm. "Am I to talk to *you* of the *origin* of tithes—that the Levites were left out of the division of the inheritance with the rest of the children of Israel; or to argue, why the tenth part was allotted to them free from trouble, labour, and care—that the Priesthood might be at leisure for the services of God, and not distracted with the cares of this world—that they might have the means to entertain strangers, relieve the poor, comfort the sick? Shall I defend tithes because Priests are forbid employments, trades, avocations, and so forth? No. Sooner let me talk to a thief of the necessity of justice—to a debauchee of the beauty of virtue—to a drunkard of the comforts of sobriety, than to— but enough. In *this* place I shall not make a religious question of it. My indignation I have warmly expressed; you have called me an enthusiast and madman. Now hear a few plain facts.

"The outcry concerning tithes is in every respect unjust and illiberal. The greater part of the tithes of this country are in the hands of *the Laity*; and those, which are held by the regular Clergy, are no hardship to the people. An estate is bought, or rented according to the different incumbrances it is burdened with. If it pays tithes—the occupier has bought it, or rents it *for that reason* so much the cheaper. The man, who has an estate, that is liable to pay tithes, and wishes to avoid them, equally injures the person whose right they are, as if he refused to pay a legacy or annuity settled on the estate.

"It is no *new* claim—the demand is undoubtedly older than his right to the property; and therefore may be called a prior claim. But all these demands, however they may have originally belonged to the Ministers of religion, are now become the property of all kinds and degrees of people. The greater part of the tithes belong to them, and the rest they have the power to purchase and to sell. Even the smallest livings, perpetual Curacies, distant reversions and presentations, are publicly bought and sold by the Laity; and *being a Clergyman* is now *not possessing a right to purchase*, but *doing the duty* for part of the profits. And has not every trade, every profession its exclusive rights? The real wages of the Clergy are small, very small—not more than 40 l. a year throughout the kingdom.

"The Clergy *seldom* take their tithes in kind; the Laity almost always: but I'll say no more. It cannot be unknown to you, gentlemen, that the most infamous Priest has virtues enough to be a first rate modern Philosopher—that the outcasts of Christianity, the very dregs—"

His oration was here stopped by the Chairman, who told him he had already spoken the allotted time.

An antagonist started up immediately, and liberally bestowed the epithets of madman, Aristocrat, &c. &c. on the young stranger, who calmly heard his abuse without moving a muscle.

To the surprise of Wilson and Hambden Arnon, Rattle next arose.—"I think, gentlemen," said he, very drily, "you have had a fair specimen this evening which has most sense in it, the *reason* of one party, or the *madness* of another. Sir," continued he, turning to the stranger, "I agree with your arguments, I venerate your principles, and I adore your contempt; and shall think myself particularly fortunate to be better acquainted with you." Handing his card to the stranger, he immediately walked out, and the other followed him.

The Chairman was about to stop Rattle for not speaking to the subject; but he did not stay long enough to give him the trouble.

The company who had been treated so cavalierly, were inclined to have hooted them as they left the place; but they did not recover from the consternation their strange behaviour had occasioned before the gentlemen were departed.

It was very amusing to Wilson and Hambden, who knew one of the parties, to hear the remarks of the company, which put a stop to the harangues for that evening. They found that neither of the new orators were known, or had been seen there before.

Some supposed them to be purposely sent by Mr. Pitt to insult them; others swore they were two madmen escaped from Bedlam; a third party believed them to be Priests in disguise. One man said, he fancied they were two emigrant Officers, they had so much the appearance of gentlemen; but this was objected to on account of their speaking English so fluently. The grand orator himself was of the opinion of those that gave the Prime Minister the credit of sending them there, which, as every one agreed they came there on purpose, seemed to be the most general opinion.

Every specifier now began to recollect his own discourse; and an alarming spasm, lest some treason should have slipped out, turned many a face pale: some idea of this kind diminished the company very fast.

Wilson and Hambden were themselves astonished at the enthusiastic ardour of Rattle, who seemed as mad as his new companion; and they knew not which to admire most, the cool indifference, undaunted boldness, and contemptuous conduct of two such young men, or the surprising success with which it had been crowned.

So far was this from a premeditated attack, that the young stranger had never been in London before that day; and walking the streets, had read the advertisement which brought him to the spot: and Rattle had this evening for the first time attended these debates.

CHAPTER XIV.

Hambden, who so well knew the animosity that subsisted between Marauder and Wilson, was now as careful to prevent any meeting taking place between them, as he had once been instrumental in endeavouring to promote it.

Marauder was indefatigable in putting his political schemes into a favourable way before he proceeded to Ireland with Fahany; and by the assistance of this friend, and the great influence of Mr. Arnon, he was appointed by the grand Society to an office of great trust and confidence.

Marauder's acquaintance in London had ever been very extensive, but had been rather confined to the higher rank. He was a member of a great many different Societies, and his abilities were not of that confined kind as to leave him long unknown in any of them. He became a partner in a faro-bank soon after he arrived in England; and was considered as an experienced veteran at every gaming-house in the purlieus of St. James's. For many years also he had been a member of the Jockey Club, had been elected one of the Whig Club before he went abroad the last time, and joined the Society of Free-Masons as soon as he was of sufficient age.

This promising young hero exhibited a strong instance of his natural character when the solemn and tremendous oath was administered to him.

Young men in general cannot help feeling a secret and unknown alarm while the horrid deprecation is uttered. Not so Marauder. He smiled with the utmost indifference, and turning to Arnon the elder, who was near him at the time, softly said—"Pretty mummery!"

This insatiable curiosity of being initiated into every Society had manifested itself abroad, and seemed a prelude to his ambition. But in most of these Societies Marauder had associated with men of rank and consequence—till disappointment came, and he forswore Aristocracy;—now he was as anxious to be acquainted with the lower orders, and very soon became one of the most active members of those secret Societies, who, by some general name and open profession of constitutional principles, concealed their attempts to overthrow both Church and State.

The accession of a man of his fortune and well-known consequence was highly gratifying to these parties. Many of the elder members, whose cold hearts prevented their aiming at popular notice, but whose warm purses chiefly kept the cause alive, seriously considered Marauder as their active head. They dreaded too the control of a low and needy Democrat, and were always ready to extol his abilities, and bring him into notice. In him too the speculating Philosophists saw a bold and able instrument to put their theories in practice.

Marauder, ever quicksighted, at once perceived their object, and, humouring them accordingly, was in a short time admitted to a knowledge of their most mysterious intentions.

Fahany was at times as sanguine as Marauder, but not so indefatigable; and the abilities and learning of the former were, by the art of the latter, constantly turned to his purpose. Hambden Arnon, indeed, Marauder had begun to consider with the jealous eye of a rival; but he had lately absented himself frequently from their meetings. It must be remembered that the wonderful change in Marauder's situation in life had not so much changed his *views* as his *means*.

Power, dominion, superiority he aimed at; and whether he mounted on the shoulders of Aristocrats or Democrats he cared not. Establishments of every kind he always considered as the checks of a bold and daring spirit, and to overturn these was his determined aim, whether his station had been such as the Prince of ...... the Duke of ...... or Lord ...., or that of a Robespierre, Danton, or Marat; in either case there was a power and authority above *him*, and upon the fall of *this* his ambitions were built.

This genuine spirit is that natural Reason, Equality, and Liberty which, under the name of modern PHILOSOPHY (though certainly PHILOSOPHISM, or more properly Diabolism) dazzles the eyes of the present generation of men.

Marauder could not fail noticing that this new kind of wise men were divided and subdivided into an astonishing number of sects; he therefore wisely assented with them all in their anti-principle principles, and unconfined himself, ranked, as it suited him, among them all.

I cannot help remarking here what a hard case it is for some of our young PHILOSOPHERS and PHILOSOPHESSES, who, puzzled by the multiplicity of sects, are at a loss to know to which they belong.

"O fortunatos nimium, sua si bona nôrint!"

VIRG.

"Oh happy they if their own sect they knew!"[1]

For the advantage of such innocent sufferers, with great study and labour a scale has been composed, by which the modern Philosopher may clearly know of which sect he is a member.

If a son of Crispin, who abominates all sole-menders beyond the service of the foot,[2]—if any high-minded tailor, who believes in no hell but his own, and considers that also as the best receptacle for the things of this world, should read this book, they may meet with a philosophical sect, that will suit them to a needle's point. Neither let the highest or lowest despair, for even a poor nightman may perhaps find himself to be a stoic.

CHAPTER XV.

The greater number of MODERN PHILOSOPHERS do not indeed confine themselves to one sect, but, with a more capacious mind, embrace the principles of many: others again are so delighted with that native wisdom which enlightened the earlier ages of the world, that they cannot properly be called MODERN PHILOSOPHERS, but ANCIENT PHILOSOPHERS MODERNIZED: and some there are, whose minds, confined by no object, no principle, and no rule, expand themselves over the divisions and subdivisions of every party, and nobly grasp at once the whole.

I shall not dispute THEIR RIGHTS to the term PHILOSOPHERS, and join the *hue-and-cry* that they are but PHILOSOPHISTS; let them have their favourite title by all means.

As the Lacedæmonians said to Alexander the Great, when he desired to be ranked among the Gods—

"*Ει Αλεξανδροϛ βοληται ειναι Θεοϛ, Θεοϛ εϛτω.*"
"If Alexander wishes to be a God—let him be a God."[3]

---

1 Virgil, *The Georgics*, 2:458.
2 St. Crispin is the patron saint of cobblers. British Jacobins were often characterized as shoe-makers.
3 Unattributed edict of the Lacedœmonians on Alexander the Great's claim to divinity.

So say I—"If these worthies wish to be PHILOSOPHERS, let them be PHILOSOPHERS."

Why should I maliciously deprive a child of its plaything? So far then from denying their claim to the title, I am about to prove, by analyzing it, that (as I said before), each member may know his own class.

Let it be observed that I am not about to treat of those Secret Societies, Free-Masons, Illuminati, and such-like, so ably discussed by Professor Robison, Abbe Baruel, and others;[1] because these depend upon the *will*—in the same manner as a Lawyer may take his degrees in Divinity, a Divine in Law or Physic, and so forth:—I am endeavouring to shew the *natural* (not acquired) class to which the numerous tribe of *Volunteer Philosophers*, male and female, belong.

My barber now, I understand, thinks himself a *Philosopher*—harangues to his neighbours on *Religion and Politics*, but the devil-a-bit does he know to what sect he belongs. By my scale he will see that he has a claim both to the PERIPATETIC and the NATURAL.

Yonder Cobbler too—you cannot mistake the man, he is a hardy dog—is a Philosopher of another class. He might have lived and died in abject poverty, had he not contrived to clap his head into the lion's mouth, and draw it out in safety. Indeed he narrowly escaped; therefore, since this time he has been contented to let others try, and they, who get off with a slight squeeze (for few now escape), the least thing they can do is to buy their shoes of him.[2] In reviewing the PHILO-

---

1   Several attempts were made to trace the cause of the French Revolution to a secret, pan-European conspiracy involving French philosophers, the free-masons and the "Illuminati," a shadowy set of political philosophers bent on the destruction of religion and government. The most celebrated were William Playfair's *The History of Jacobinism, its crimes, cruelties and perfidies* (London: John Stockdale, 1795), John Robison's *Proofs of a conspiracy against all the religions and governments of Europe, carried on in the secret meetings of Free Masons, Illuminati, and reading societies* (Edinburgh: William Creech, and London: T. Cadell and W. Davies, 1797) and the Abbé Augustin Barruel's *Memoirs Illustrating the History of Jacobinism. A Translation from the French* (4 vols. London: printed for the author by T. Burton and Co., 1797-98). See Introduction and Appendix F.

2   The allusion is to Thomas Hardy (1752-1832), a boot-maker and founder of the London Corresponding Society, one of the principal radical groups active in the early 1790s. With John Horne Tooke, John Thelwall, Thomas Holcroft and others, Hardy was put on trial for high treason in 1794—putting his head in the lion's mouth, as it were. All the accused were acquitted.

SOPHICAL SCALE, it is evident, at the first glance, that this worthy is a REASONER.

As in my humble opinion this NEW PHILOSOPHY has never been clearly explained, or systematically defined, I shall, *first*, distinguish it from the common Philosophy.

It may be called—"*A species of Wisdom, which man discovers by the aid of his own individual powers, corporeal and mental, without owning the aid of any superior Being, directly or indirectly.*"

Religion, therefore, being totally out of the question, they, like the devils in Milton—

"Disband, and wand'ring, each his several way
"Pursues, as inclination or sad choice
"Lead him perplext."
"In thoughts more elevate, *some* reason'd high
"Of Providence, Foreknowledge, Will, and Fate,
"Fixt Fate, free Will, Foreknowledge absolute;
"And found no end in wand'ring mazes lost;
"Of good and evil much they argu'd then,
"Of happiness, and final misery,
"Passion, and apathy, and glory, and shame—
"*Vain* Wisdom all, and *false* Philosophy!"[1]

As the grand principle of the whole seems to be the same with the Infernal Spirits, the term DIABOLISTS* is peculiarly applicable to these would-be PHILOSOPHERS, and a general name for their wonderful science may be also termed DIABOLISM.

---

* [CL] Some people, without Judge or Jury, condemn them at once as CACODÆMONS; perhaps the salving term of INFERNAL QUIXOTES may suit them, as it seems the fashion of the present day to rank all our assassins and self-murderers under the general name of MADMEN. [Barruel used the term "Cacouac" to label Voltaire, Diderot, D'Alembert, Frederick the Great and other infidel conspirators in his *Memoirs Illustrating the History of Jacobinism, op.cit.*, 1:37.]

---

1 Very slightly misquoted from Milton's *Paradise Lost*, book II, lines 523–25 and 558–65.

Secondly. To define this DIABOLISM systematically, it may be divided into nine Sects, the number of the Muses.

They may be thus called:—

Stoics,	
Epicureans,	*Of ancient race, but modernized.*
Peripatetics,	
Virtuosos.	

The Illuminati,	
The Libertinians,	
The Naturals,	*Modern.*
The Reasoners,	
The Nothingers,	

I. The STOICS, or INSENSIBLES, are very proud, esteeming themselves far superior to the rest. Except upon critical occasions, they rarely condescend to exert themselves; and the moment the exertion is over, they are as torpid as ever. All the others outwardly pay great respect to these, but laugh at them in their sleeve. Like the owl, their gravity is so good an emblem of wisdom, that the STOIC is often exhibited for that purpose.

They are in general fat, pursy[1] fellows, whose chief indulgence is in the monotonous note of the silent pipe. With these a puff bespeaks—the nation is ruined;—a puff declares—all religion is a joke; the voice of joy and gladness with these is heard with a puff; and troubles, misfortunes, or death of the best friends and nearest relatives are mourned only by a puff; in short, with these—*'tis all a puff.*

The French Rulers easily cajoled them to their purpose, praised them to the stars, and pushed them forward on every occasion; but when the STOIC, swelling with his imaginary greatness, began at last to talk and look big, the guillotine silenced him in a moment.

In the first National Assembly there were many of these; and the Dutch, we know, are very partial to this sect.

The STOICS are often found among those CRITICS, whose wit consists in abuse, and whose wisdom in other's faults.

All learning in their opinion is Latin and Greek; *Stubbornness* the only *Virtue*, and *Good-nature* the only *Vice*.

---

1   Short-winded; puffy; corpulent.

Poets with them are called—the flimsy race, and hexameters alone they desire to look at.

So great is their hatred of every other species of poetry, that a certain famous STOIC has passed the last thirty years of his life in translating of Homer into *English* hexameters: of which wonderful work I am able to favour the reader with the beginning.

"Sing, Muse Celestial, how first that wrathful Achilles,
"With rage inveterate, sent Pluto many a victim,
"Where by the naked shore limbs lay, dogs hungry devouring,
"When Peleus' great son boldly strove with Agamemnon,
"And, to the will of Jove, the allotted destinies answer'd.
"O day ill-fated! which urg'd offended Apollo
"'Mong hosts of Grecians to let his contagious arrows
"Pierce their thick numbers, and &c. &c. &c."[1]

This author has been wonderfully hurt by a brother Stoic informing him (for they are horribly ill-natured), that let him produce as many lines as he will, he would be bound to point out *double* the number of false quantities. It is to be feared that this threat will spoil the work.

The arguments of the Stoic are always unanswerable,—for this simple reason, that though they are the mildest creatures breathing, they cannot bear contradiction. Therefore their friends and acquaintance never touch them in this tender point, and wisely keep such naughty things as replies, &c. &c. out of their sight.

The gentle and patient David Hume, we are informed, could not hear the name of a certain author without flying out into most virulent passions of rage and swearing;[2] and, that he had good reason to do so, any one, who has read his *philosophical* works, must allow. What man could bear to have such an argument as this disputed?

David Hume on Suicide, page 12.—"It would be no crime of me to divert the Nile or the Danube from its course; where then is the crime of turning a few ounces of blood from their natural chan-

---

1   The *Illiad* was frequently reworked into a variety of prose and verse forms in the later eighteenth century. Lucas may be pastiching all these texts here (and showing off his own ingenuity), rather than quoting a particular translation.

2   This might be a reference to Jean-Jacques Rousseau, with whom Hume had a very public quarrel in 1766-67 after Rousseau had accused Hume of plotting against him.

nel?"—Again, the same page—"A hair, a fly, an insect is able to destroy this mighty being, whose life is of such importance. Is it an absurdity to suppose that *human prudence* may lawfully dispose of what depends upon such insignificant causes?"[1] Certainly not, Mr. Hume; you might have set fire to your own, or your neighbour's house, if you like; for *so insignificant a thing as a straw* may be the cause of its destruction at last.

In truth, the Stoic* might make a tolerable good hero with his *negative* virtues, if he would but keep his tongue between his teeth, tie his hands behind him, and never attempt the *active* ones.

II. The EPICUREANS, or GRATIFIERS OF THE SENSES, are as contrary to the last, as the sect of the *Sadducees* to the *Pharisees*.†

These signalise themselves by eating, drinking, wenching, &c. &c. &c. never satisfied, ever cloyed—constantly seeking for novelty.

They prove the Government to be wrong, because they are always in want of something else—and religion false, because it forbids us to gratify those senses Nature has given us. *Enjoyment* is a

---

* [CL] Who has not heard of the wonderful Madame Rowland (who certainly died a STOIC, however she might have lived), possesses of every virtue and qualification MODERN PHILOSOPHY can boast. In her prison she wrote her life—what a subject of exultation for all the STOICS! Yet the *unlearned no-Philosopher* would be rather surprised to find in this "Appel d'impartiale Postérité, vol. ii, p.8, part 3d."—a *what-shall-I-say* story of Madame Rowland not being accustomed to, and therefore not knowing the use of—a common chamber-pot? or page 18—How her papa flogged her for not taking physic.

While every *feeling heart* must lament the melancholy fate of this Lady—what must the *head* think of the abilities of her who, in her last moments, (or at any time) could thus write? [Madame Jeanne-Marie Roland (de La Platière) (1754-93), by directing her husband's political career, was able to become a leading figure of the moderate Girondin party during the early stages of the French Revolution. During her imprisonment after the Jacobins' coup of 1793, Madame Roland wrote *Appel à l'impartiale postérité*, her memoir. Her last words before being guillotined were "O Liberty, what crimes are committed in thy name."]

† [CL] If the reader should happen himself to be either a PERIPATETIC or NATURAL PHILOSOPHER, he will *not* understand the force of the simile. [The Sadducees and the Pharisees were two Jewish sects active at the time of Christ. The former were drawn mostly from amongst the priesthood, while the Pharisees represented a more democratic tendency and believed much more firmly in the idea of resurrection. For accounts of their theological differences see Matthew, 22:23ff., and Acts, 23:6ff.]

---

1 Slightly misquoted from David Hume's essay "On Suicide," probably written in 1750 but suppressed by the author until publication in 1777.

word always in their mouths, but which their hearts never seem to own.

They are continually mistaking *abuse* for *use*—*possession* for *enjoyment*—men of *learning* for men of *sense*—men of *reading* for men of *knowledge*—men that understand *languages* for men that understand *mankind*—*orators* for *actors, words* for *things*—and so forth.

Their grand creed is—that the Philosopher's stone consists in the discovery of a *sixth* sense; and their emblem is *Tantalus*—yet, unlike him, they are disappointed by possession itself.[1]

The Epicurean* is chiefly to be found among young men, well born, and moderately taught.

The old French Army had great numbers of them.

There is scarcely a *female Philosopher* to be found that is not an Epicurean; and, as soon as the French Revolution commenced, the *filles-de-joie* were the first to distinguish themselves. At present, some of these Philosophesses are united in the spider-woven bonds of the Gallic-Hymen with the most famous of their legislators and warriors.

In these kingdoms about a dozen famous names might be produced that indubitably belong to the Epicurean System; but, to the honour of my fair countrywomen, it has been clearly proved that ten times greater is the number, and far superior in learning, talents, and ability, who have signalised themselves in that old-fashioned wisdom of virtue and religion.

The Epicurean Philosophy is also very fashionable among the higher ranks. That venerable and dignified character the Duke of——, Lord D—l—r—n, Sir Thomas———, Sir William———, Sir John———, and a personage greater than all in birth, titles, and expectations may be said to spin in the very centre of the vortex.[2]

---

* [CL] Think not, my learned reader, that the MODERNIZED PLATONISTS are forgotten. They are to be found among the worn-out EPICUREANS, or most simple of the STOICS.

---

1 In Greek mythology, Tantalus was punished by the gods by the provision of food and drink which always remained just out of reach.

2 Many members of the aristocracy were satirized, their names lightly disguised with hyphens—as here—by Charles Pigott in his *The Jockey Club, or a Sketch of the Manners of the Age*, published in three parts in 1792. Although Lucas would have deplored Piggot's radical politics, he might well have been influenced by his allegations of upper-class licentiousness and drawn his information from *The Jockey Club*. However, Pigott names so many aristocratic epicureans that it is almost impossible to determine precisely who Lucas meant here, save only for the "personage [...] in the very centre of the vortex," who must be George, Prince of Wales.

It is evident that Fahany greatly participated of their opinions; and we shall by and by introduce a fair lady of this sect.

III. The PERIPATETICS or BUSY BODIES, are more conspicuous for their number than consequence. These are the echoes of all the others—the newsmongers, loungers; and being of themselves too ignorant to arrange, too idle to act, they become of use to their party by being ever in motion; and, day after day, run their usual round with the news of the moment, from the Coffee-house to the Library, to the Park, to Bond Street, St. James's, the Playhouse, and the Opera. At first view the reader may suppose that the MODERN PERIPATETICS have nothing to do with antiquity; but I must beg his pardon.—Demosthenes, the famous Grecian orator, in one of his Philippics makes particular mention of them, *as they are now*, "running about the streets, flying to the public places, every where crying out—What news? what news?"—Juvenal, the Roman satirist, also speaks of them, and so does Horace—again and again.

"Ibam fortè via sacra, &c. &c."[1]

In short, the learned reader may find passages in almost every ancient Greek and Roman author, that put their claim to antiquity out of doubt. I feel a delicacy in quoting the 17th chapter of the Acts of the Apostles, the 18th, and particularly, the 21st verse, as it is an authority they are not fond of;[2] yet it may be some satisfaction for them to know where they may find their claim to antiquity in a plain English (perhaps intelligible) form.

The learning, abilities, wit, and knowledge of these modernized Philosophers are (like the magpies) concentrated in one point, memory; some of them indeed participate of the ape, in mimicry.

When new blasphemy runs scarce, and conversation flags, the talents of these come into action. Texts of Scripture are generally familiar to them (chiefly, I suppose, for the reason that they were obliged to read the Bible at school, and have never read any book since); a word recalls a sentence to their remembrance; and sometimes the

---

1 This is the beginning of one of Horace's *Satires* (Book I, no.9) which represents the activities of a crashing bore who attaches himself to the poet, retailing all manner of tittle-tattle.

2 The Acts of the Apostles 17:17-21, describe Paul's encounters with "certain philosophers of the Epicureans, and of the Stoicks" and of the propensity of the Athenians to spend "their time in nothing else, but either to tell, or to hear some new thing."

application, by perverted indecency or coarse blasphemy, raises a laugh.

This they rarely venture at in a mixed company, unless in the repetition of one that has succeeded before; as it may happen to prove *mal-a-propos*.

The Devil, we are told, can quote Scripture—so can some of these; but the difference is, it is an even chance to the PERIPATETIC whether it answers *his* purpose, or not.

Young Chatter, of the Temple, is one of this sect. When St. André, the Jacobin, came over to England to give the chosen Brethren the fraternal embrace, poor Chatter, by a misapplication of Judas's kiss, is even said to have raised the colour in the tawny cheek of the Frenchman.

At a public meeting, crowded with Philosophers, the Duke of Wouldbe's modesty was rather squeamish in taking the chair.—"The old Christian proverb is in your Grace's favour," said Chatter.—"The first shall be last, and the last first."—His Grace was wonderfully down in the mouth, and never spoke on *Reform, Liberty, and Equality* with a worse air in his life.

The Peripatetics have a mortal antipathy to a Clergyman, or to any person, whom they have once heard utter a serious religious sentiment.

The reason is—their early pertness and folly have generally subjected them to severe reprimands and chastisement from friends and masters; and the very appearance of religion or gravity makes their shoulders smart, and ears tingle.

When they are in a troublesome talking mood, the simple monosyllable "Why?" will silence them at any time. To relate is their only fort, to argue is quite out of their way.

They have ambition without ability—information without knowledge—a cocked hat without manners—and a scarlet coat without courage. Their sole reading is the newspaper and review, and their best writing in the ability of the hand.

Never burdened with too much thought, nor fatigued with too much study and care, they, like the butterfly, flutter through the summer, but, after the first sharp frost, are heard of no more. The fleet, or a condemned regiment is their state of *oblivium*; sometimes indeed they linger upon an annuity, and degenerate into NATURALS (another sect I shall soon treat of); though, like forced converts, they are seldom of much eminence in their second state.

The PERIPATETIC PHILOSOPHER is frequently to be found among the spruce bucks of the city, that are very desirous of being seen at the west end of the town: Attorney's clerks, who, ambitious of being Barristers, will never be good for any thing; young Physicians with a little money and less learning, who ought to have been journeymen Apothecaries; young Parsons, more fit for any thing else, yet with too little courage for soldiers, too little sense for lawyers, and too little industry for tradesmen, ordained by influence, supported by interest, and ever on the watch for preferment; their whole conduct a continual theme against the religion they profess, and themselves the most infamous and contemptible of the Diabolistical Philosophers.

I remember a PERIPATETIC, who set up for a Philosopher, solely upon the merit of *not* having been in a Church for five years; another from the notable discovery that Samuel *did not write* the *second* book that bears his name, because the Prophet is dead in the first. He might hazard a similar critique on Moore's Almanack, and many other *modern* publications.

Some of these also establish themselves to be Philosophers, by adopting a practical joke, or taking up a piece of witticism that is lasting. Thus a PERIPATETIC, (well-known in their usual circle), by naming four young puppies that he had, after the four Evangelists, became a self-dubbed Philosopher instantly. Poor fellow! He unluckily lost his consequence by attempting to put his wit in a *legible garb* to an embryo-Parson, a Cambridge friend. This latter was not idle in exhibiting his old school-fellow's specimen of Philosophy—Matthew, Mark, Luke, and John, were never so *mispelt* in their lives! And our wise-man must now be contented to be a NATURAL for life.—But enough of these gentry. You meet with the Peripatetic so common in all public places, it is not necessary to say any more.

IV. The VIRTUOSOS, or LOVERS of WONDER, are certainly *not ancient Philosophers modernized*, but more properly *modern Philosophers antiquated*. These are continually telling what has been. In their opinion the less they know of a thing, the more wonderful it is, and therefore the more valuable.

All *modern* laws and customs they abominate. Lycurgus, Solon, and Numa are their models; and if they are ever inclined to believe a Deity, they are determined his name shall be Jupiter. They rake up old doctrines long ago confuted and exploded, and attempt to palm them on the world for the very acmè of what is right.

Their chief objection to the Bible is, that it is not sufficiently ancient; and, if happily they can detect a modern word which has crept into the text, it is a conclusive argument with them that the whole must be wrong.

By such ingenious criticisms as these, one of this sect has determined that the writings of Homer, Horace, and Virgil, and other supposed Grecians and Romans, are nothing more than *the forgeries* of a Monk of the twelfth century, as well as every passage where they are mentioned by other authors before that period;[1] in the same manner as the well known PROBATIONARY ODES, and numbers of ORIGINAL LETTERS.

In truth, their learning is too much for their brain, and their judgement too little for their learning, which their self-conceit, endeavouring to supply the place of judgement, overturns and confuses the whole; hence the term *addled* is peculiarly applicable to them.

A certain VIRTUOSO was about to leave this country, and live in China, as he understood *that* was the most ancient kingdom on the face of the earth. His plan was laid; he was resolved to be of the primitive religion, and to despise the innovation of Confucius. He never opened his lips without expressing his hatred of the tyranny of the Tartars; and he began to hold up his head, put his hands behind him, and turn out his toes—as a prelude to the military art—that he might head the natives, and enable them to recover their liberties. But the good old gentleman's schemes were all crushed by the information of a friend—that he would not be permitted to land.

The VIRTUOSOS hate the Government because it is a *modern* fabric; and use all their might to overturn the State, that they may revive the blessings of primeval times. All their writings in Divinity, Science, or Politics, are in praise of the GOLDEN AGE.

One thing they believe to be as true as Chinese chronology, that the seasons of the year in England have ever been in confusion since the style was altered.[2]

The sons of Hippocrates and Galen were *formerly* much devoted to the VIRTUOSEAN PHILOSOPHY; at the *present day* the merit of many a M.D. classes him among the Illuminati.

Philosophers, as they increase in years, get more and more partial to this sect. Numbers have been found among the lawgivers and

---

1 This appears to be a reference to Jean Hardouin (1646-1729), who, in 1697, in his *Chronologia veteris testamenti*, argued that almost all classical texts were composed by thirteenth-century monks under the direction of one Severus Archontius. See Anthony Grafton, *Forgers and Critics: Creativity and Duplicity in Western Scholarship* (Princeton: Princeton University Press, 1990) 72-73.

2 The Julian calendar was replaced in England by the Gregorian system in 1752.

political writers in France; in Germany they have particularly distinguished themselves, and a great many in this country—not omitting to notice the superintendents of some monthly writings of acknowledged celebrity.*

V. Of the same diabolitical party, though of the extreme from the Virtuosos, are the ILLUMINATI, or WISEACRES. These despise the knowledge of what is *past*, but are quite at home in what is *to come*. Their belief is—that all the world were fools till the present generation, and that they themselves are the wisest of this.

Their heads are so full of schemes, and their means so few to realize them, that they have been not inaptly compared to young ducks in a thunder storm, delighted with the water, yet confused with the jarring of the elements.

Their oratory, unlike the VIRTUOSOS, is for ever extempore; and sometimes the second argument cuts up the first with wonderful eclat. Thus—they will doubt the existence of a DEITY, because they never *saw* him; and argue against the DIVINITY of Jesus Christ, because he was a *visible* personage. In short, as they never know what they mean to do, so they seldom remember what they have already done.

Most true is the remark—that the understanding of these gentry is ever suffering the fate of Semele, Jupiter's mistress[1]—lost and confused in their own splendid speculations. The fair dame indeed left a young divinity behind her; but the gratification of their ideas is ever sure to prove an abortion.

---

* [CL] As for the LITERATI (properly Illiterati) or BOOKWORMS—the VIRTUOSOS and ILLUMINATI divide that famous sect among them, as it now stands. [The editors of all the main monthly literary periodicals were accused at one time or another of reformist or radical leanings. Ralph Griffiths, and his son George, editors of the *Monthly Review*, were moderate whigs, though during the Revolutionary wars they became more politically quiescent. The *Critical Review* was largely edited by Samuel Hamilton during the 1790s, and disappointed many of its readers by taking up an anti-government position after the outbreak of Revolution. The relatively liberal *English Review* was edited by William Thomson from 1794 and, in 1796, was absorbed by the *Analytical Review*, renowned as being the most liberal periodical of all. The *Analytical* was edited by Thomas Christie, but the radical Joseph Johnson took on many of the editorial duties until his imprisonment for publishing a seditious book in 1798. The *Analytical* went out of business in 1799.]

---

1   In Greek mythology, Semele demanded that her lover, Jupiter (i.e., Zeus), appear to her in his proper form. When he did so she was consumed by lightning. Semele gave birth to the god Dionysus.

The famous Anacharsis Cloots, who elegantly called himself the orator of the human race, was of this sect, which is evident by that most excellent advice he gave the French how to subjugate England—by taking possession of Scotland—which he called—the granary of England.[1]

Another clever fellow, whose name I forget, was a conspicuous member. He advised his brethren, the French, to avoid the English fleet by means of balloons, to land at once in the midst of Salisbury Plain, and march directly to London.

The ingenious inventors of the flat-bottomed boats may rank the foremost among the ILLUMINATI.

In this country we have a great many among our financiers, political schemers, and H.C. orators;[2] though, happily for the nation, they have not been able to put their ideas into practical form.

Nor must the wonderful abilities of some modern M.D.'s. be forgotten;—and already the *regulars* begin to foil the *irregulars* at their own weapons. Thus, Dr. B's. vivifying spirit, the gaceous oxid of azote, like the MEDEAN KETTLE of old, or the MOTTLED HERO'S astonishing Mill,[3] makes us all young again, and keeps alive too the profound notions of that able *Reasoner*, Mr Godwin;* while the

---

* [CL] Political Justice, vol. ii p. 517.—"If an unintermitted vivacity, and attention to the animal economy be necessary, then, before this omnipotence can be realized in its utmost severity of meaning, we must all be able to supersede the phenomenon of sleep. Sleep is one of the most conspicuous infirmities of the human frame."

   Page 519. "It would, no doubt, be of extreme moment to us, to be thoroughly acquainted with the power of motives, perseverance, and what is called resolution in this respect. We are sick, and we die, because in a certain sense we consent to suffer these accidents. This consent in the present state of mankind is unavoidable. We must have stronger motives, and clearer ways, before we can uniformly refuse it."—See Dr. Beddoes' Experiments, who (to speak in plain English), by certain fumes, produced a temporary inebriation. [*Political Justice*, ed. Kramnick, Penguin edn., 770-77.]

---

1 Jean Baptiste du val de Grace, Baron Von Cloots (1755-94) became known as the "Orator of the Human Race" after he proclaimed the adherence of all humanity to the Declaration of the Rights of Man in Paris in 1790.
2 Perhaps House of Commons orators.
3 Medea, the sorceress in Greek legend, was able to restore youth by chopping up an old animal or human and placing the parts in her kettle, or cauldron. The mill of youth, which minced old people into young, was a favourite theme for popular literature and song.

ANIMAL-MAGNETIZERS, the PERKINEAN TRACTATORS, with the VACCINEAN PREVENTATIVE, the GUESTONEAN MEDICINES, and I know not how many German mysteries, prove the far superior wisdom of the present day.[1]

If it is too *early* yet to speak more fully of the Vaccinean and other inventions, it is ever too *late* of the wonderful medicinal discoveries of our Gallic neighbours; but the literary and philosophical intelligence of the magazine of the month will always shew in this and other subjects the newest fashion of French Philosophy.

There are not many of THIS ILLUMINATED SECT in Scotland—not even among those who have the gift of the *second sight*; but there are a vast many very clever gentlemen of the Irish nation, whose claims are indubitable.

A Wiseacre if he knows (*o*) from (*ω*) instantly concludes himself a master of all ancient languages, and argues accordingly. He writes—and down tumbles the fame of Grecian and Roman worthies without mercy. He sets up an idol of his own, to whom he not only eagerly offers incense, but compels both ancients and moderns to bow before it. Touch him in this point, and he raves. Such a one will tell you that the single line—

---

1 Lucas here satirizes recent medical advances, most of which were, even as he was writing, being dismissed as forms of quackery. The "Dr. B" mentioned here is Dr. Thomas Beddoes (1760-1808), a physician of radical social and political opinions, married to Anna Edgeworth, sister of the novelist Maria. In 1798 he established a clinic for the treatment of illness by the inhalation of gases, including nitrous oxide, or laughing gas ("azote" is an archaic term for nitrogen), which he has been credited with discovering. Elisha Perkins developed a treatment for chronic pain involving the stroking of the affected parts of the body with metal pins, or "tractors" as he called them. His treatments, which he claimed were a sort of electrical galvanism, were sought after in Britain and America throughout the 1790s and into the nineteenth century. The theory of animal magnetism, developed by Dr. Franz Anton Mesmer (1734-1815), held that an invisible fluid flowed through healthy bodies, and that blockages of this fluid caused illness. Mesmer claimed to be able to alleviate these blockages by the use of magnets. Edward Jenner (1749-1823) published his findings on the efficacy of vaccination (a word he coined) against cowpox and smallpox in 1798, having first successfully inoculated a child in 1796. Byron also lampooned these medical developments in *English Bards and Scotch Reviewers* (1809): "What varied wonders tempt us as they pass! / The cow-pox, tractors, galvanism and gas, / In turns appear to make the vulgar stare, / Till the swoln bubble bursts—and all is air!" (ll.131-34)

"Ruin seize thee, ruthless King!"[1]

is infinitely superior to every thing in VIRGIL:—but when you come to—

"Uprose the king of men with speed,
"And saddles *strait* his coal-black steed;"[2]

HOMER, at the head of the Grecians, yields the palm, and *his* king of men, AGAMEMNON, sinks into nothing. See Letters on Literature, by Robert Heron.[3]

VI. The next are the LIBERTINIANS, or CHAMPIONS of LIBERTY. These are known by their haughty and tyrannical spirit; vociferators for *Equality*, they would lower all their superiors to their own situation in life; and so fond are they of *peace*, that they would murder half the world to gain it.

Their language and their conduct are in continual opposition. Their *ambitious views* they call EQUALITY; their *love of power*—LIBERTY; *depopulation* is with them CIVILIZATION; and *forced subsidies* a VOLUNTARY LOAN; the *sword* and the *pistol* are ARGUMENT and REASON; and *death*—CONVICTION.

One of these published a dictionary of this kind;[4] but unluckily the Government mistook it for treason, and prosecuted the printer and publisher, and some of the parties.

If the LIBERTINIAN calls you *friend*, depend upon it he means to make you of use to him; and the greatest favour you can receive from him is—not to be noticed.

---

1 The first line of "The Bard: A Pindaric Ode" by Thomas Gray (1716-71) which first appeared in *Odes by Mr. Gray* in 1757.
2 The first lines of Thomas Gray's "The Descent of Odin: An Ode," first published 1768.
3 John Pinkerton, using the pseudonym Robert Heron, published *Letters of Literature* in 1785.
4 Probably a reference to Charles Pigott (d.1794) whose *Political Dictionary: explaining the True Meaning of Words* was published posthumously in 1795. This was a radical and ironic text, defining a "Regicide," for instance, as "any brave fellow who dares consign an anointed despot to his native regions below." Pigott spent some of his last years in gaol, having been prosecuted in connection with his scandalous exposés of fashionable society, *The Jockey Club* (1792) and *The Female Jockey Club* (1794).

*He has little hypocrisy about him, for he is always a falsehood; and you may in general form a true opinion of what he says by supposing the contrary. Yet he is no common babbler or liar, nor deals in the marvellous, unless it will answer his purpose.

A successful villain is the object of his serious praise and imitation, and the length of the catalogue of crimes is the surest test of his greatness; therefore Sylla and Marius he prefers before Pompey and Caesar—Richard III before Cromwell—and for the same reason, Alfred of England, and Henry IV of France, were no heroes.[1]

The whole stock of a LIBERTINIAN often consists in impudence; and he is out of any thing sooner than countenance.

There are in this country a number of men of this sect, who having tried some profession or other, and their ability not equalling their ambition, they have eagerly embraced the first favourable opportunity of giving up their choice. Of these—some, by the death of elder brothers, slide into independence—others, by interest, get presented to places of profit, &c. &c. and throw off the red coat, or Doctor's wig, or unprofitable Lawyer's gown; these, in their metamorphosed state, generally expand their powers of capability, and adopt the notions of the NOTHINGERS.

The Libertinians, at one time, were almost universal in France; and the greater numbers are to be found in most countries among the dissatisfied in the Army and Navy.

They are frequent in these kingdoms among the higher orders, particularly among those out of place, out of power or out of pocket.

This sect is very well known, and almost all the others partake of it.

VII. The NATURALS are the sect most easily satisfied, as they mean

---

* [CL] Some of these remarks upon the character of the LIBERTINIAN, are borrowed from an *old* author; but, as 'tis said—'The Devil cannot get rid of his cloven foot.'—A very few others are taken that are not particularly mentioned.

---

1 Gaius Marius (c.157-86 BC) and Lucius Cornelius Sulla (or Sylla; 138-78 BC) were rival Roman politicians and generals. Both in their turn violently imposed harsh regimes on Rome. Pompey the Great (106-48 BC) and Julius Caesar (100-44 BC) were Roman generals and statesmen, enemies of one another in the civil wars. Richard III (1452-85) plotted successfully to become King of England. Oliver Cromwell (1599-1658) was a soldier who led the Parliamentary forces to victory in the English Civil War before becoming Lord Protector of England, Scotland and Ireland. Alfred the Great (849–899) was King of Wessex and prevented England from being entirely conquered by the Danes. Henri IV (1553-1610) was the first Bourbon king of France and established religious toleration with the Edict of Nantes in 1598.

to gain every thing by taking every thing away. They are often known by their appearance, which is not unlike that of those quiet lunatics, who are permitted to rove about the country, and who are in many places called "CRAZY BETTIES." They are very quiet and easy unless they are offended, and then they can fight and claw as well as the best.

As PETER deceived his brothers MARTIN and JACK, so are the NATURALS continually taken in by the REASONERS; with this difference—that as PETER made his brothers believe *one thing* was *every thing*, the loaf of bread was fish, flesh, and fowl;[1] so do the REASONERS persuade the NATURALS that *every thing* is *one thing*, that all their (the Reasoners) whims, fancies, tricks, and nonsense are the genuine offspring of NATURE.

The NATURALS have more thought than sense—more strength than courage—more haste than speed—and more fat than flesh. In short, somewhat like the Quakers, they are more admired by the rest, than imitated.

We shall soon come to the history of a very rigid one of this kind.

VIII. The REASONERS are the formers of the last mentioned sect, though they take good care never to be of it themselves.

They have the advantage of making whatever they like to be right, and, as we hear, there is *reason* in roasting of eggs, so they will say there is *reason* in every thing they do.* They can prove it is rea-

---

★ [CL] According to this principle Hume argues.—Dialogues concerning Natural Religion, page 263.—"To be a *Philosophical Sceptic* is, in a man of letters, the first and most essential step to be a *sound believing Christian.*"—Will anyone be so hardy as to deny that Mr. Hume was the *first*, or so impudent as to say he was the second?

Godwin, vol. ii. Political Justice, p. 511.—"In whatever sense he (Dr. Franklin) understood this expression, we are certainly at liberty to apply it *in the sense we shall think proper.*" Thus, *Gratitude*, when Godwin reasons, is a *dreadful vice*; and *Clemency*—"nothing but the *pitiable egotism* of him, who imagines he can do something better than Justice."—Political Justice, vol. ii. page 407.

See all the writings of these DIABOLISTS. [Hume's famous aphorism comes from the close of pt. 12 of his *Dialogue Concerning Natural Religion* (not published until 1779, after Hume's death). See *Essays and Treatises on Several Subjects. By David Hume … Containing Essays, Moral, Political, and Literary. A New Edition. To which are added, Dialogues Concerning Natural Religion* (2 vols. Edinburgh: Bell and Bradfute, and T. Duncan, and London: T. Cadell, 1793), 2: 597. Lucas's quotations of Godwin come from bk.VIII, ch.ix and bk.VII, ch.ix of the second edition of *Political Justice*, ed. Kramnick, Penguin edn., 696. "There is reason in roasting egg," according to *Brewer's Dictionary of Phrase and Fable*, is a common phrase signifying that "Even the most trivial thing has a reason for being done in one way rather than some other.

---

1 Peter, Martin, and Jack, symbolizing respectively the Roman Catholic, Anglican, and Dissenting churches, appear in Jonathan Swift's prose satire, *A Tale of the Tub* (1704).

sonable for others to fast, and they to feast. Why? Because fasting and feasting make things even; and whatever is even, is right.

The REASONERS will tell you that they are never deceived, because, like other frail mortals, they do not trust either to the legends of antiquity, the opinion of the wisest men, or even to *their senses,* but to a far superior principle—THEIR REASON.

One of this sect will thus argue—"Common prejudices, customs, and opinions deceive our fellow-men every day. How ridiculous is it to assert, under the foolish proof of daily experience, that it is easier to walk *down* hill than walk *up* hill! When a man walks *down* hill, every step is beyond the common level; the whole body receives a jar, and the foot is forced below that point, where it ought to have stopped. But when a man walks *up* hill, the ground, as it were, rises to meet his foot, he does not need the exertion of putting it down, he has nothing to do but to lift up his leg—the ground is ready to receive it; and, were it not for that prejudice we imbibe in our infancy, when we come to a steep hill, we might be over it in a moment."*

A learned gentleman of this section invented a scheme to prevent that blindness so incident to old age, by never using but one eye at a time.

His argument was unanswerable.

"*Two* threads, proceeding from one point, can never reach farther than *one;* therefore *one* eye sees as far as two. By using *both* eyes at a time, we see *double;* an inconvenience so great, that infants are a long time before they can bring their sight to focus. By using *both* eyes too, we do not look straight, but from that corner of each which is next the nose; if we used only *one* eye at a time, by carrying *that* side of the face rather forwarder than the other, the sight would come straight from the eye, and of course we should see objects much better, and thus keep the other eye for a future occasion."—A person talked of the advantage of seeing sideways; the REASONER cut him up in a moment.—"To see sideways is to see imperfectly; imperfection is ever to be avoided: and, for this cause, some one wisely invented blinkers for horses. Much better indeed would it be to blind one eye of the horse, keeping the nose a little to that side by a

---

* [CL] The learned reader may perhaps think the modern Reasoners not very unlike "the *Pyrrhonians,* or grosser sort of Sceptics (mentioned by Dryden in his Life of Plutarch), who bring all certainty into question, and startle even at the notions of common sense." [The Pyrrhonians were followers of Pyrrho (c.360-c.270 BC), a Greek philosopher, who maintained that since certainty was impossible, it was necessary to renounce all claims to knowledge.]

string on purpose, that the sight might come in a right line from the other eye."

Again, in eating of soup, this gentleman attacked with wonderful spirit, the ridiculous custom of stirring it.—"Motion begets heat; stirring is motion; therefore stirring of soups and so forth, continues and increases the heat."

Did these REASONERS put into practice their wonderful discoveries themselves? Oh no! Their pupils, the NATURALS, tried the experiments for them; and one poor gentleman spoiled a good set of teeth by eating hasty-pudding for a wager, without using a spoon, while his opponent was to swallow the same quantity in less time, in defiance of the violent motion the stirring of a spoon would give it. The NATURAL not only lost his wager, spoiled his teeth, scalded his throat, and burnt his stomach; but his friend, the REASONER, declared it was his own fault for shaking it too much and called him a fool into the bargain.*

By one short argument they prove all history to be false.—"We know," say they, "that historians make men *speak* otherwise than they really did;—*ergo*—they make them *act* otherwise too."

They prove the Jewish Religion is not the word of God, because the virtues there described did not arrive to that excellence since known in the world—*i.e.* which Christianity has made perfect; and judging the Christian Religion by the standard of ancient virtues—so far superior to the modern ones—they in like manner condemn that. Again they argue—"Virtue in the extreme is Vice. Christianity is Virtue in the extreme. Therefore Christianity is Vice."—Thus more than fulfilling the proverb of borrowing of PETER to pay PAUL, they also borrow again of PAUL to pay PETER.

A certain REASONER was resolved to prove that ST. MARK'S GOSPEL was not written by *him*, but long after his time.

One opponent alleged—"The original Greek copy is extant at Venice, in St. Mark's own hand."

"That is impossible," says the Reasoner; "because, according to the common nature of reason, time must have destroyed the materials on which it was written long ago."

But says another opponent, who had never heard of the original

---

* [CL] May not the gentleman, who, we are told, inhaled *two gallons each of Dr. Beddoe's Gas of the oxid of azote*, rank among the NATURALS?—"The pulse of the third gentleman," says the account, "gradually diminished in strength, and increased in frequency during the inhalation; at last his vision and hearing became indistinct and confused, and *a syncope was with difficulty prevented*."

being at Venice—"Eusebius speaks of St. Mark and other primitive Christians make mention of a Gospel written by him."

"Can you produce it, or have you ever seen it?"

"No."

"Then I won't believe a word of the matter."

The REASONERS have also made some wonderful discoveries, of which I shall concisely mention a few.

They have endeavoured to improve our language and expressions, our thoughts and ideas.

The common method of speaking—when the animal juices have imbibed any impure air, and insensible perspiration is checked—is "I have caught cold." This expression most grievously offends them.

"It is the very acme of folly and prejudice," says a noble REASONER;—"one grain of reason is enough to tell us that it is the very contrary. It should be—I *have caught a heat.* Large meetings, public assemblies, warm rooms, and the frequenting of all hot places will generally be *the cause.* What is *the effect?* A fever. What is a fever? An inward fire. What is the remedy? Universally, warmth—whether in physic, meat, drink, or cloathing. Achilles' spear is an emblem of medicine—that which gives the disease, will administer the cure. Poison expels poison, cold expels cold, and fire fire."

When Mr. Horne Took first published his—"Diversions of Purley,"[1]—a certain REASONER was in a most violent rage, and swore Mr. H.T. had a masterkey, and robbed the storehouse of his brain. But the *ci-divant Parson* having made good his ground, the REASONER is now determined to out-rival him. We may, therefore, shortly expect a very learned treatise to prove, that there is no other part of speech than a *substantive, simple or compound*; though I will not be certain whether this gentleman has yielded to the remonstrances of his friends, and may not return to his *original* intention of proving that it is an *adjective*.

His argumentative proofs he keeps to himself till the publication, though he has favoured his more intimate acquaintance with a few specimens of the work.

Vulgar—"Tom runs faster than any body else."

Rationally—"Tom superiority-speed."

The whole sentence *rationally* in two words, *one simple* and *one compound* substantive.

---

1 John Horne Tooke (1736–1812) was a radical politician, tried and acquitted in the Treason Trials of 1794, but also known as the father of modern philology. His principal work was *Epea Pteroenta, or the Diversions of Purley* (1786–1805), an early attempt to analyse language scientifically.

The two first lines from Homer.

Mr. Pope— "Achilles' wrath to Greece, the direful spring
"Of woes unnumber'd, heav'nly Goddess, sing!"

Rationally—"Achilles-rage Greece-woes-infinity-cause,
"Song, Goddess-Heaven!"

One *simple substantive*, and *three compounds* complete, what has taken Mr. Pope no less than thirteen words. How incomparably beautiful too the last line

"Song, Goddess-Heaven!"

Again, a specimen of familiar conversation.

Vulgarly—"How do you do, Dick?"
Rationally—"Health-possession, Dick?"
Vulgarly—"Very well I thank you, Tom."
Rationally—"Health-Dick, thanks-Tom."

What can be more simple, plain and beautiful?—Health and Dick, are *compounded* together, and thanks and Tom; the whole makes the answer in only *two compound substantives*.

If this rage continues, I know what will become of our Grammarians.

But the *argumentum invectum*[1] of the REASONER I must not omit, when, at his first onset, he disarms his adversary, and then—cut and slash without mercy. Thus—The REASONER contends that the HOTTENTOTS, or THE MEN IN THE MOON (no matter which), have the truest notions of religion.

The simple Christian denies the assertion.

The Reasoner begins,—declares the religion of the Men of the Moon, or the Cape—and one by one picks out the most prominent virtues of Christianity, which, with a long feather, naked feet, and plenty of Nature, becomes a very pretty picture, and assumes a most pleasing appearance.

The *Logician of Christianity* is non-plused; *his* virtues are already taken from him, and he cuts but a pitiful figure.

---

1 The case brought to bear.

But the most common method of the REASONER is to write a dialogue upon the subject between himself and the savage. He, very kindly, for Christianity; the Savage for himself. Oh! how the Savage cuts him up!

See the Travels of the Baron de Hontan,[1] and a few others of the *Voltairean* school, with *his* Huron, as a model for them.[2]

It would take me a volume alone to describe in a decently fair way this most superlatively *rational philosophical sect*; I shall give the *amende honorable*[3] to the whole with one specimen of their physiological knowledge.

An erudite and most able REASONER has discovered *point-blank*, that all that has been said for ages and ages concerning *solids and liquids*, is a mere hum,—that, in truth, every thing is A LIQUID, and only requires its proper degree of heat to become so.

Says he—"Iron, silver, gold, and all metals are easily brought to their primitive state of liquids. Flint makes glass—glass is easily melted, therefore flint is a liquid:—all kinds of earth are but soft stone, and flint is stone. Wood increases from moisture, and may be brought back to its pristine state by boiling, distilling, and so forth, if you do it long enough. Animals of every species may easily be melted, stewed, sweated, made spermaceti of, &c. &c. &c. *Probat exemplum*."[4]

This learned REASONER has not a doubt that the inhabitants of the planet MERCURY, from their proximity to the sun, are LIVING LIQUIDS, exactly like large globules of quicksilver, from whence, by some very wise men (nearly equal to himself) the metal was first called MERCURY.

The real, veritable, pure state of Cosmopolitism flourishes in its utmost perfection in this planet. Here, when two citizens meet, the very act of shaking hands unites them in indissoluble bonds of brotherly love; and thus the whole human race in MERCURY have only to meet, and the affiliating system of the country unites them in one great and happy society.

How they get separated again, he has not quite determined. One

---

1 Louis-Armand de Lom d'Arce, Baron de Lahontan (1666–1715), a French soldier who explored and described parts of what are now Canada and the United States in, amongst other works, *New Voyages to North-America* (1703).

2 Voltaire's *L'Ingenu; or, the sincere Huron: a true story* was first published in English in London in 1768.

3 Due apology.

4 The example proves it.

moment he fancied the setting of the sun did it; again, by a sudden concussion of the planet, the cause of which he means to discover; or by a cold comet, or snowy meteor. Of this he is certain, that if we (all the whole world) would unite together, and, at one moment, all pushing and pulling, impel *our planet* a little nearer the sun,—war, and all its train of horrors, envy, hatred, malice, revenge, and the rest of the black catalogue would be instantly annihilated, and universal philanthropy, though far inferior to a general cosmopolitical happiness, would fraternize mankind.

The heads of this sect are so very well known in this and other countries, it would be envious to particularize.* The leaders of the mob are very partial to them.

IX. The ninth, and last, sect is that of the NOTHINGERS. Of great and general import, of wonderful note, power, influence, and consequence.

This, being so far superior to the rest, requires a nice discrimination and description.

Their general rule is—"*There is nothing but what they know.*"—Of course it follows, that they know every thing.

The ties, the obligations, the duties which religion imposes upon us, they are free from: from hence they gain most amazing advantages, which every other poor mortal wants.

First. They are never guilty of any vice. For every action depends on the circumstances belonging to it: and if a man is beat, has his money, his wife, or any thing else taken from him, or is even killed, *according to law,* they who punish him, Judge, Jury, or Executioner, are not guilty of murder, nor of any other crime—but of Justice. So THESE WORTHIES, *who carry every law, divine and human, within*

---

* [CL] Rousseau was so strange a compound between a NATURAL and a REASONER (which rarely happens) that his brethren never knew what to make of him. When they treated him as a NATURAL, the indignant REASONER appeared; when they earnestly expected the bold sophistry of the REASONER, the irresolute NATURAL came forth. In lieu of a volume, take the following quotation from "The Translation of his Confessions," vol. ii. page 32.—"Instead of listening to her heart, which led her right, she listened to her reason that led her wrong."—Page 33—"M. de Travel, her first lover, was her teacher *in Philosophy*, and the principles he instilled into her, were those that were necessary to seduce her."

Quotations of Rousseau's *rationality* are not necessary. [Jean-Jacques Rousseau, *The Confessions of J.J. Rousseau: with the Reveries of the Solitary Walker. Translated from the French* (2 vols. London: J. Bew, 1783), bk.V, 2:32-33.]

their own breasts, can never be guilty of any *crime*; for, whatever their conduct is, they can justify it to themselves: they never act without a reason, and that reason is law.

Secondly. Whenever it suits their convenience, they can easily swear that *they do not believe* in any of the old exploded Christian doctrines; because they do not believe in any thing.

Thirdly. They can also swear that *they do believe* in whatever is necessary for their advantage that they should believe; because nothing is binding or sacred to them, therefore an oath cannot be so.

N.B. These two last advantages are made good use of by Placemen, Governors, Magistrates, Officers, and all of this sect (who generously sacrifice principle to the good of their country), and to whom an oath is necessary before they can hold any post or situation under the Government. Justices of the Peace and others, who take the sacrament solely to be qualified to act,[1] and ever before and after neglect it, exemplify my meaning, and may advance their claim to this sect of Diabolism.

Fourthly. The incredible advantage that the Nothinger has in conversation; which being restrained by no tie of decency or sanctity, the wit or satire is never confined. In argument, it is both an invincible shield and keen sword; for, having no principle of their own to defend, they may safely attack others, but are themselves invulnerable.*

---

* [CL] Yet with all these advantages, the wit and satire of Dr. W. alias Peter Pindar, have completely failed. Witness his illiberal and malicious attack on Miss A. Moore and her friends. Not one of his most sanguine admirers, not the most egregious NATURAL, can in this case defend the vice and weakness of the affected satirist. Poor *Peter Pindar* is no more, though the froth of the old venom of ribaldry and blasphemy still drivels from the toothless gums of Dr. W.

This note was written before the complete mental and corporeal chastisement of the Doctor by Mr. Giffard. ["Peter Pindar" was the pen-name taken by John Wolcot (1738-1819), author of numerous satires, many of which were directed against George III. Wolcot was himself satirized by William Gifford (1756-1826) in his *Epistle to Peter Pindar* (1800). Shortly after its publication the two met in Wright's shop in Piccadilly: Wolcot physically attacked Gifford, but Gifford came off victorious. The affray was commemorated in Alexander Geddes, *Bardomachia, or the Battle of the Bards* (1800).]

---

1 The 1673 Test Act (in force until 1828) required office-holders under the Crown—including Members of Parliament and magistrates—to swear an oath affirming their loyalty to the monarch and to receive communion within the Church of England at least once every year. Catholics and Dissenters were thus barred from holding office.

Fifthly. When every other argument for what *we* call Vice, fails, they use the following:—but I will quote Godwin's own words.

Political Justice, vol. i. page 389, &c.—"A candlestick has the power or capacity of retaining a candle in a perpendicular direction. A knife has a capacity of cutting. In the same manner a human being has the capacity of walking: *though it may be no more true of him than of the inanimate substance, that he has an option to exercise, or not to exercise, that capacity*. A knife is as capable as a man in being employed in purposes of utility, *and the one is no more free than the other as to its employment*. Both are equally the affair of necessity, &c. &c. &c.— The man differs from the knife, as the iron candlestick differs from the brass one; he has one more way of being acted upon. This additional way with man is motive—with the candlestick is magnetism. But if the doctrine of Necessity does not annihilate Virtue, it tends to introduce a great change in our ideas respecting it. According to this doctrine, it will be absurd for a man to say—"I will exert myself."—"I will take care to remember," or even, "I will do this."— All these expressions imply as if man were or could be something else than what motives made him. *Man is in reality a passive, not an active being.*"[1]

So speaks *verbatim* the supereminent Godwin; and, therefore, when any man pretends to condemn the actions of a NOTHINGER, the PHILOSOPHER exclaims—"I can't help it, and there's an end of the business."

The French rulers, wisely seeing these advantages, have endeavoured to choose their whole *diplomatique corps* from this sect; as is evident in their political Ministers, Ambassadors, Envoys, Generals, Negotiators for Peace, &c. &c. by whatever name they may be called. They have indeed employed this *no-principle* with great success, both at home and abroad. By this they cajoled the people; by this they overran the Italian States; by this they took the Isle of Malta, and landed in Egypt; whether this will fail them at last, time must determine.

Every Jacobin is of this sect, and they generally also embrace most of the others, except the NATURALS, and that they endeavour to make *le Souverain Peuple*.

In former times it required learning and virtue to make a Philosopher; now-a-days, so far from being of service, they chiefly

---

1 Lucas omits several lines from his quotation from the second edition of *Political Justice*, 2: 389-91.

act as a clog or hindrance; and *virtue of any kind* is sure to do the owner a mischief.

IGNORANCE, particularly where it is joined with IMPUDENCE and OBSTINACY, is of the highest service;* and *Vice of every species* cannot fail to make a MODERN PHILOSOPHER of one sect or the other.

Thus the Parricides in France, who boasted themselves the destroyers of a father, child, near kinsman, or beloved friend, were undoubtedly STOICS and LIBERTINIANS.

The amiable spectators, who enjoyed the executions, who went with a double goût[1] *a la guillotine* instead of *a la comediè* (and whom we ignoramuses should call accomplices in the crime), were EPICUREANS; while those men of learning, who quoted a Brutus and a Nero to encourage them to the noble act, were excellent VIRTUOSOS and REASONERS.

The tale-bearers, liars, and common perjurers, thieves, and petty rogues may range among the PERIPATETICS, ILLUMINATI, and NATURALS. But it required a mixture of vices to make a NOTHINGER.

Of which of all these was OUR GALLANT HERO, MARAUDER?— The answer is short—*Of all.* It may be said—*Above them all.* For

---

★ [CL] So Tom Pain claimed the title of PHILOSOPHER, for writing against the Bible before he had read it.

So that ingenious Philosopher, *Mr A Walker, Lecturer in Experimental Philosophy*, in his very learned remarks upon his excursion through Flanders, Germany, France, and Italy, thus talks of an oratorio he saw at Venice in 1787. The subject is the story of Susanna and the Elders.— "What should be the first scene in the second act, but the simple woman telling her husband how the naughty Elders intended to honour him at the bath? To be sure, the husband was very angry; and by the by, *I did not before know Susanna had a husband."* Page 162. Published 1790. Vide History of Susanna, *first* verse.

"1. There dwelt a man in Babylon, called *Joacim*;

"2. And *he took a wife*, whose name was *Susanna*, the daughter, &c. &c. &c." What a *well-read, modest,* and diffident man must this *Mr. A. Walker, Lecturer in Experimental Philosophy,* be! [Thomas Paine (1737-1809) published *The Age of Reason*, an attack on Christianity and Bible, in 1794-95. Adam Walker (c.1731-1821), author of *Analysis of a course of lectures on natural and experimental philosophy* (1766), published *Ideas suggested on the spot in a late excursion through Flanders, Germany, France and Italy*, from which Lucas quotes, in 1790.]

---

1 Taste (French).

though, like a Cromwell, he could talk to each in the peculiar cant of his party, he could also, like him, laugh at them all in his sleeve. In one thing he was superior to this great man;—for Cromwell indeed was somewhat tainted, even to the end of his life, with the same prejudices; and the excellent Tillotson[1] has sanctioned the general opinion—that his enthusiasm at last got the better of his hypocrisy;—but Marauder had none of those narrow notions to sway him, and when he had used his tool, he threw it by at pleasure.

The *Initiated*, or the persons who, like Marauder, are most deeply versed in the mysteries of these Sects, have a general rule, by which they judge every other person, and govern themselves; no general rule of antiquity—not that ever blessed one of Christianity will they allow to be more infallible.[*] It was by this the noble youth early in life began to guide himself, and this he invariably kept to, amid the sunshines or storms of his journey.

This key of his breast he suffered no one to possess but himself. He considered it as a NEPENTHE—as a PHILOSOPHER'S STONE—the GRAND DESIDERATUM OF A WISE MAN—NATURE'S BEST SECRET—AN UNIVERSAL BIAS—THE TOUCHSTONE of every one's real worth—a LOADSTONE repulsive or attractive at the owner's choice; it was a guide by which he steered to *the longitude of his wishes;* [2] it was the *mystic number* by which *he squared the circle of his actions;*—this golden rule was—

ALL PRINCIPLE IS FOLLY.

No tie of love, friendship, or affection, natural or acquired, held

---

[*] [CL] Godwin's Political Justice, vol. i. page 127.—"A comprehensive maxim which has been laid down on the subject (justice), is—that we should love our neighbours as ourselves. But this maxim, though possessing considerable merit as a popular principle, *is not modelled with the strictness of philosophical accuracy.*"—Excellent reasoner! [*Political Justice*, ed. Kramnick, Penguin edn., 169.]

---

1 John Tillotson (1630-94), Archbishop of Canterbury from 1691, who married Oliver Cromwell's niece.
2 Nepenthe: a legendary drug causing forgetfulness of grief and sorrow; Philosopher's Stone: the substance thought by alchemists to turn base metals into gold; Touchstone: a type of rock used to determine the purity of gold; Loadstone: magnetic oxide of iron used in compasses.

him. He could snap asunder the sacred chain of an oath, and burst the close bands of Gratitude.*

Every *mental* power was subservient to our hero; his words and actions were his ready tools; and with the failings, the weaknesses, the follies, and even vices of mankind, he continued to build that mighty bulwark (which, like the tower of Babel, never could be raised equal to the labourer's wishes), HIS OWN INTEREST.

CHAPTER XVI.

It was a great amusement to Wilson, while he was in town, to frequent the public places in company with Rattle. Hambden Arnon, from his long residence abroad, was not so capable of *shewing the town*, and Rattle had kindly volunteered his services for that purpose.

Wilson quickly found that his entertaining companion knew the characters and persons of all the *men of renown*, in whatever station of life they excelled, and seemed himself to have an acquaintance with the greater part of them.

Methodist Preachers and Freethinkers, Dukes and Jockies, Men of learning and Men of words, and Rogues high and low—in short, the *more knowing ones* of every denomination came under his ken.

The morning after the debate, somewhat early in the routine of fashion, ere the mall had begun, as they were entering the Park together, Rattle stopped short.

"Now, Wilson, I'll introduce you to the greatest rogue in Europe."

"I return you my sincerest thanks for the intended favour, but must decline your kindness."

"No; on my life you shall not. If I conjure up a devil, I'll teach you how to charm him. As Hotspur says—tell truth, and shame the devil.[1]—Hush! *Ecce signum!*[2]—Mr. Cowspring, this is Mr. Wilson, a very worthy man, my friend, and who is not ashamed of being the son of a carpenter."

The person to whom Wilson was thus strangely introduced,

---

* [CL] Godwin says, Political Justice, vol.i page 130.—"Gratitude, therefore, if by gratitude we understand a sentiment of preference which I entertain towards another, upon the ground of my having been the subject of his benefits, *is no part of justice or virtue.*" [*Political Justice*, ed. Kramnick, Penguin edn., 171.]

---

1 Shakespeare, *Henry IV, Part 1*, III, i, 61.
2 Behold the sign.

extended both his hands, as if he would have taken hold of Wilson's; but he, thinking upon what Rattle had said, made not the smallest advance on his part.

"What brings you out so early?" said Rattle.

"The cause of truth, which is triumphing over the whole world."

"How? I have heard nothing."

"Five millions more of the inhabitants of this earth now glow with the rays of Reason! Superstition and Tyranny hide their heads!"

"Where? In the basket of the guillotine?"

"Ah! Rattle, are you still wavering? If you and your friend will take your dinner to-day at my table, you shall hear the particulars. You know it is my public day."

Wilson was about to excuse himself, but Rattle jogged him, and said—"We'll endeavour to wait on you.—How have you succeeded lately in your converts?"

"I make converts! Sometimes, indeed, the force of reason shews the pure truth."

"What think you of the force of gold?"

"I assure you, on my word and honour, I never in my life attempted to induce any one to be of my opinions, but by clear and open arguments."

"The young Ensign, whom I sat next to, the last time I was at your house, told me that you had entreated him *to become a member of a Society upon the pure principles of Philanthropy*; and that, in that case you could furnish him with the cash to purchase his Lieutenancy— as you were sworn to assist none out of your own Society. He asked me if I were a member. I told him not yet."

"Upon my word and honour, Mr. Rattle, this must be some mistake. I—I shall be most happy to see you and your friend to-day. I must leave you at present, as I am in great haste."—And the gentleman, in a quick slouching pace, continued his walk.

"Certainly you have no intention of accepting his offer?" said Wilson.

"Indeed but I have. You see his character already. There will be some twenty or thirty people there. We may leave the place as soon as we like; for I wish you to go, that you may see with your own eyes the respect which is paid to wealth in the—But I will not anticipate your entertainment. Of this you may be assured, that he is an acquaintance you may drop with the same ease you would a buffoon or mimic that you were in company with for the moment. What is commonly called—*to be cut*—is so common a thing with this man, that he never regards it."

Wilson was persuaded, and consented to accompany Rattle.

The person so strangely introduced to Wilson, he had supposed, at a little distance, to be a very elderly man; but a nearer view of him shewed his age to be scarce fifty. His dress was common, loose, and slovenly; his hair, uncombed, hung down his face over his eyes, of the same length before and behind; his hat had a large brim, and slouched. As he spoke, he neither looked at Wilson nor Rattle, but his eyes were fixed on the ground; and, though he had spoken only a few words, and those of no consequence, he had uttered them with a steady and reflective air, as if they had been of the greatest moment.

As soon as Wilson had consented to dine at his house, Rattle said—"Whom should you suppose this man to be?"

"I give up the enigma. I beg you'll explain it."

"This is General Cowspring."

"A General!"

"Attend.—At seventeen his parents purchased him a commission in the Guards. He spent twenty thousand pounds before he was twenty. Thoroughly acquainted with the tricks of the town, from a *Pigeon* he became a *Rook*—in other words—from having been cheated, he began to cheat. In the next ten years his fortune was considerably increased, but his character was entirely gone. Now broke out the American war; he had changed his regiment, and was ordered abroad; and, at the very time his acquaintance thought that he would be dismissed the service for bribery and extortion, and a gross want of courage, he came home a Lieutenant Colonel.

"Having learned experience, he added another vice to his list, *Hypocrisy*; and began again to make a figure in London. For many years he played the sycophant in all courtly places, in hopes of a regiment: he soon became a full Colonel and General without one. He had just begun to plume himself upon his new title, when the disgrace, which had been so long smothered, on a sudden burst forth, and stifled in a moment his full-blown honours. *General* Cowspring was concealed for some months, at the end of which period he again appeared, stripped of his well-bought rank, though with a fresh stock of assurance to begin the world again, as Mr. Cowspring.

"About this time died his elder brother. Cowspring, who had not spoken to him for years, flew instantly to the spot. He was heir at law—no will was to be found, though an attorney and three tenants swore to the making and signing one; his brother, therefore, must have destroyed it in his illness, and the *ci-devant* General became possessed of an unincumbered estate of twenty thousand a year.

"The person, in whose favour the will had been made, commenced a law-suit; though, it is supposed, with very little hope of success.

"He now ranged himself in the files of Opposition; but, as they seemed rather ashamed of their new member, and by no means gave him what he wished for, a leading part, he quickly left them, and commenced *Democrat professed*.

"Here he was received with open arms, and every guinea he gave to aid the glorious cause of FRATERNIZATION, was repaid him ten-fold *in praises*.

"He is at present entered so deep into the schemes of the party, that it is impossible for him to go back; and three-fourths of his income, I have been credibly informed, is absolutely given up to the cause, with very little controul on his part.

"His sole employment is making converts; for this reason he courts the company of all young men, particularly those in the Army, Navy, and Public Offices. Occasionally too, he lends a sum of money, or makes a small present, ever accompanied with *Tom Pain's Age of Reason*.

"His library in the country is notorious as the largest collection of infamous books that was ever known in the world, with every tract that has been written against Christianity.

"If this man is at any time in company with young people, his conversation instantly turns to his beloved subject; he has always a book ready in his pocket, and, when he calls at a house, as soon as the master of the family can come into the room, he finds his young son or daughter reading a chosen passage against the very vitals of religion and virtue. Once or twice he has been disgracefully turned out of doors; and, not long since, a lad of sixteen, who had just left Westminster, and got a cockade in his hat, read one sentence of Cowspring's book, and, with all the ardour of a schoolboy, spit plump in his face. Yet still he goes on; his known wealth gains him fresh respect and notice, all his own party countenance him, and I have met him at Marauder's and Arnon's.

"The whole party have been long trying to catch me; and Cowspring, I know, has great hopes, as I occasionally visit at his pub-lic dinners; but I believe he would dispense with my attendance if he knew my motive, which is to caution any strangers I see there from getting into his clutches; and among others I have succeeded with the young Ensign that I mentioned.

"I have now given you Cowspring's *public* character; his *private* I will not touch upon, but solely say—conceive it as bad as possible, you cannot equal report."

"But, Rattle, I do not chuse to dine at this fellow's house."

"I tell you it is a public exhibition. How many people go to Lady———'s, Mrs.———'s, and other gaming-houses, and never speak to the owners at any other time! I have never visited him but at his public table; and as for his house in the country—I should not even speak to him in that neighbourhood if I met him a thousand times; but it is different in London."

"I think it a shocking thing it should be so, and much to be lamented that men, who profess to have good characters, should give any countenance to the riches of a villain. My curiosity, I confess, is much raised to go to Cowspring's, but I assure you I will not, and my introductory bow shall be my last."

Wilson had scarcely made this determination before they perceived Cowspring returning.

"'Tis true!" exclaimed the latter, with great exultation. "The French have beat the *Despots of Tyranny*. To you, Sir," said he, turning to Wilson, "whose innate reason and contempt of servile prejudices make you glory in the name of Citizen, uninfluenced by the name of aristocratical distinctions, this success must be glorious tidings."

"You allude to what Mr. Rattle said, that I am the son of a carpenter?" replied Wilson gravely.

"I honour you that you glory in the term," said the other.

"Then you mistake," continued Wilson. "My father's humble situation in life has at no time been a subject of glory to me, yet I shall never be ashamed of it, since his conduct and character have made it respectable."—Mr. Cowspring looked strangely disappointed.

"But what is the news?" said Rattle.

"The whole Austrian army is completely annihilated; and the man, who calls himself the Emperor of Germany, will soon be hurled from his throne."

Wilson spoke warmly, and in evident anger.—"And so, Sir, the success of our common enemy, and the misfortunes of our Ally, are the causes of your exultation. Sir, I care not who or what you are, but this you have now proved to me, that you are directly or indirectly a traitor *to your King and Country*."

Mr. Wilson, with contempt, turned from him; Rattle laughed heartily; and the wretch, without the least reply, slouched off even faster than he did the first time.

"These smart rubs," said Rattle, "this worthy fellow continually meets with. His natural cowardice humbles him for the moment, but he soon again begins the old trade of trying to make converts. I presume you now know the gang, who act upon the principle of *recruit-*

ing Serjeants—of swearing their recruits in as soon as possible. This old dog, I told you, had been pressing me to enter into their Society with every plausible argument he can use; and if I find any thing amiss (he says) it will then be time enough to secede; but I have been told that if you are once sworn, you can never retreat."

Wilson professed his ignorance of the whole any further than their principles, which, both in private and public, he had heard without any very thick disguise. Rattle, who seemed full of his subject, and very inclinable to be communicative, continued—

"They swear you, in the most solemn and sacred, the most horrid and shocking terms, *to be true to the Brotherhood.* What this Brotherhood is they unfold by degrees, and having once caught you, they entangle you still more and more by fresh oaths; and you curse yourself in every term the most subtile art can invent, if you ever betray them. The oath of the Free-masons is bad enough; but they tell me it is nothing to this."

"You seem to speak methodically. How do these things transpire?"

"Partly by treachery, partly by remorse, and sometimes inadvertently," continued Rattle, in a serious and reflective tone, very unusual with him.

"Poor Looder, who shot himself last autumn, was inveigled among them. I was then half persuaded to become a member. I spoke to Looder.—'I'll not advise you,' said he, and trembled as he spoke. 'Rattle, I have been miserable ever since! I had many things to vex me, and I thought to have found help here. You cannot conceive how I am entangled. I have a great mind to tell you every thing, in defiance of all the oaths and daggers in the world.'—The conversation was here interrupted, and I never saw Looder afterwards. The horrid catastrophe took place the next day."

Rattle did not wait for any reflections from Wilson, but continued—"Did you observe that handsome man, who left Cowspring the last time he came up to us, and who bowed to me as he passed?"

"I could not remove my eyes from him. So noble a countenance, so undaunted a look;—but that brow of care, Rattle?"

"Entangled by their wiles, and harassed by domestic troubles, poor fellow! I fear he thinks all mankind his foe. But his spirit will not sink like Looder's; desperate, he has rashly devoted himself to the party, and is about to play a bold stroke in that clime, where his birth, his misfortunes, his injuries first commenced—the West Indies."

"You make me anxious to know more. Proceed."

"At the early age of five years, young Santhorpe lost his parents.

With a narrow prudence, the will of his father appointed a capital Banking House in London the executors.

"Royston Santhorpe comes over to England, heir to six thousand a year, with the small debt of ten thousand pounds. What might not a sixteen years' minority accomplish?

"The *prudent* guardians sent him to one of those trumpery schools, which affectation and pomposity, impudence and ignorance form from the follies and vices of the metropolis.

"The master of the school had been under clerk, and confidential servant to the active partner of this Banking House, and married the *endowed* trull of his principal. Such the connection for young Santhorpe! For whose board and education was paid one hundred guineas a year.

"The native abilities of the boy's mind, his energetic soul met with no liberal and genial spirit to aid its struggles. Torpid dullness depressed him, conceit disgusted him, and hypocrisy corrupted him. His friends, relations, connections, every dear tie were swallowed up in the name of *guardian*; and this guardian only visible in the form of clerks and money-servants.

"For twelve years Santhorpe remained at this school, without leaving its baneful, cold, unfriendly atmosphere.

"The man began to exert himself—for four long years did he struggle ere he could break his trammels.

"At one-and-twenty he left his school. His accounts were produced. His estate was in want of every thing, and the debt was twice doubled. Large interest, with great premiums had been for sixteen years paid for every sum wanted. His income remained for sixteen years without interest, but with great care, in his guardian Bankers hands.

"He now took possession of an exhausted, impoverished estate, with a debt of forty thousand pounds!

"What must Royston Santhorpe think of mankind, when every connection had proved the villain? What must Royston Santhorpe think of Religion, Laws, and Government, when nothing but infamy, open, public, unpunished, existed to him?

"The specious principle of Democracy tempted the injured youth. 'Twas the form of revenge as well as the form of friendship.

"It was not long before one of the prowling sons of the *new Philosophy* caught the unwary prey, and he entered into the system with the highest ardour. Bold and undaunted in mind, strong and vigorous in body, he is restless to be distinguished in a conspicuous manner.

"Under the auspices of these worthies, Royston Santhorpe is going over to the West Indies, to endeavour to recover the property almost alienated by his guardians. What interest, what powers he may bear with him, I cannot know, though I can easily conceive;—and since the English laws have been so long against him, I most readily conclude that he will be against them.

"If the French party succeed in the island to which he is going, and if he joins them, the large debts in England are wiped out in a moment; but if they do not succeed, and Santhorpe keeps with his countrymen, his estate must at last be sold; and what will remain, from the mortgages and expences, to him?"

"And can nothing be done for his affairs, and to extricate him from the clutches of this accursed party?"

"What reason has he to trust to the friendly professions of others? His means for some years have existed from the party. He is no longer a child; and, perhaps, when he gets into another country, he may see and renounce his errors.

"Exclusive of the entanglement of his private property, there are two prosecutions at the present time against him, which also induce him to leave England. His late schoolmaster called on him some time since, to pay (every thing being removed from the Banker's hands) some arrears due for his schooling. Words arose; and he disciplined his master most severely with a horsewhip: and, in the midst of the Public Change, when he found no redress from the law, he spit in the face of his acting guardian.

"He has also already been noticed by the Government for his public harangues.

"His able and enterprising mind has thus begun to distinguish itself; and some late writings in a famous anti-ministerial paper are said to come from his pen. Yet such has been his conduct both in private and public, so nice is his innate sense of honour, so pleasing his manners, that no one, who has the least acquaintance with him, can be his enemy; and though his departure from this country is pretty well known, no means are likely to be taken to prevent it."

"How came you so well acquainted with his history and character, Rattle?"

"I have often heard Arnon, Marauder, and my late guardian, Vantage, speak of him; and Santhorpe has mentioned, when I have been present, many particulars of his Banking guardian's conduct. I became acquainted with him at the time he entered the Society, and I hinted to him my opinion of the party he was connected with. He looked at me with a calm, though determined air, and said—"Sir, *I am sworn*. My life has been a sea of troubles. Here I first began to swim, and here, if it is necessary, I am resolved to sink."

CHAPTER XVII.

Mr. Cowspring usually breakfasted every morning at some one of the largest London coffee-houses; from whence, among the number of individuals passing and repassing, he had been able to introduce many a member to his GRAND SOCIETY.

At one of these he met with the young man, whose wild, though virtuous, oratory had so astonished Wilson, and introduced him to the acquaintance of Rattle.

This youth was under age, heir to a small fortune; and having lost his father early in life, was by a fond mother educated in a private though excellent manner.

His last tutor was a most accomplished man, a French emigrant of high rank. He had painted to his pupil, in glowing colours, the horrors of Anarchy, Irreligion, and Democracy. The youth had caught the mental infection, and upon the death of his friend—who had been treacherously inveigled over to France, and there basely murdered by the guillotine—a deep melancholy had at first seized the young man; and while his sorrow kept him at home, he had deeply studied the sacred writings; and now, indignant against the impiety and immorality of the age, he boldly rushed out in opposition to vice wherever he should meet with it. In this alone his mania consisted, that in defiance of the common forms of the world, he would frequently speak his mind with a courage and want of diffidence, that would oftentimes surprise the very boldest of the sons of impudence, who had been long hacknied in the more bustling scenes of life.

The youth had been intended for the Church, was of a respectable family in Norfolk, and his name was Philip Harrety.

Mr. Cowspring, having noticed him for a few mornings, contrived to take his breakfast in part of the same box.

The strong natural abilities, the ingenuous character, and wild manners of the young man, induced the Philosopher to be very anxious to gain him to their Society.

The subject of the conversation turned upon universal Philanthropy.

"This, Sir," said Harrety, with the ardour of enthusiasm, "is the grand *arcana* of virtue, morality, and religion."

Mr. Cowspring thought that he was already a disciple, but as he did not answer the *secret signal*, he extolled the purity and perfection of his ideas, and said—"I am a member, Sir, of a band of United Brethren, whose sole aim is to propagate this cosmopolitical principle, and whose sublime mystery is the all-perfect knowledge of promoting the happiness of the human race, uninfluenced by religious prejudices, narrow-minded patriotism, and supercilious pride."

Cowspring spoke with caution. 'Twas but the day before that Wilson had so severely lectured him.

Harrety replied in rapture—condemned the *prejudices* of religion—owned the narrow and selfish views of the greater number of patriots—severely reprobated every species of pride—and praised, in the most sanguine terms, so excellent an institution.

Mr. Cowspring told him that he purposed going to their meeting that evening; and, if he would favour him with his company, he should be most happy to introduce him.

Harrety with ardour thanked him, and the gentlemen exchanged addresses.

The missionary of Philosophy further informed his embryo convert, that the meeting would not be over till a late hour; and he invited the youth to call at his house, and take an early refreshment.

To this Harrety consented, and, with mutual professions of esteem, they for the present separated.

"Now," thought Harrety, as soon as Cowspring had left him, "is the moment I have so long wished for arrived, when I shall be able to unite my weak abilities in the glorious task of reviving our primitive faith. How happy am I to find the world is not so wicked as I at first supposed it to be! This, no doubt, is one of the religious Societies I have heard of, and this night shall I see Christianity in the mild and heavenly garb the Saviour originally gave it. To the other side of the globe will I willingly go a missionary, if I can promote the cause of our blessed religion!"

Young Harrety elevated his mind to the highest pitch, and in the evening went to sup at Mr. Cowspring's.

Here the largeness of the house, the elegancy of the furniture, the fashionable style in which Mr. Cowspring seemed to live, gave him a high opinion of the owner, whose manners, in the midst of his wealth, were simple, his dress plain.

They waited not long after supper before Cowspring's carriage drove to the door, and they set off together to the place where the Society met, of which Harrety was so eager to become a member.

When they came to the house, an old and large ruinous building, through many windings and turnings, they were shewn at first into an ante-room.

Here were many other people; and what much surprised Harrety, every one but himself and friend wore a mask.

The youth had no time to make any remark, before a voice, which proceeded from a large STATUE in the room, said—"Let Cato and his pupil approach to the initiating chamber, that the blindness of ignorance may be illuminated by the first sparks of light."

Harrety was lost in astonishment. Cowspring came, and softly whispered him—"It is necessary you should be blinded a few minutes. Don't be alarmed—'tis but a form."

The pupil was not over pleased at this commencement of his initiation; yet he said not a word, but suffered a large hood to be placed over his head by a man in a strange mask.

Some one took him by the hand, whom he supposed to be Cowspring; and after many turnings, and the frequent noise of opening of doors, he stopped in a room, where, even through the thickness of his hood, he could perceive a blaze of light.

As soon as he was entered, the utmost silence prevailed, and the following was spoken in a voice firm and strong:—

"To emancipate the intellectual system from legal and superstitious servitude, to root out prejudices, to pull down despotic influences, ALMIGHTY REASON mounts her throne, *the human heart.*

"Man, as an intelligent being, wants not the moral freedom to will, nor the physical power to act: united together, our victory is sure; and the REIGN OF REASON shall commence with the *millennium* of Liberty and Equality."

Instantly a buzz of approbation went through the room.

Some one now cried out—"Name this infant!" and a person, touching Harrety, said—"Name thyself!"

The pupil answered—"Philip Harrety."

"Wouldst thou not chuse another name?"

"That is my real name."

"We know it, and applaud thy courage (though contrary to the general wisdom), which still would retain it. But in this Society be thou henceforth ALCIBIADES.[1] Hear then, Oh Alcibiades! *our golden rule.*—'Learn to discover others, but conceal thyself to all but the Brethren, and thou wilt be wise.'"

---

1 Alcibiades (c.450-404 BC): orphan and pupil of Socrates in Athens, who came to be known as a brave but unscrupulous politician and military commander.

Another voice said—"Produce the test."

A third voice said—"Alcibiades, repeat after me:

"May the eternal hatred and revenge of my brethren pursue me, if ever I disclose—"

"Swear not at all," exclaimed Harrety, throwing up the hood, "neither by heaven, for it is God's throne, nor by the earth, for it is his footstool! Are secrecy, disguise, and oaths to be the test of wisdom? Does universal philanthropy require concealment? Virtue binds good men together; oaths villains. An honest man takes no oath, but what the laws of his country demand of him. I expected to have found a society of Christian Philosophers, and not of trifling Sophists. I thought to have heard the dictates of pure wisdom, and not the sentimental slang of scepticism; and I looked for the gravity of men, and not the mummery of players."

So far, in defiance of all obstacles, did Harrety proceed in expressing his abhorrence of the *grand Society*. The spectacle before him was enough to have daunted the boldest heart; but his zeal for religion and virtue took away all personal fear.

The President, with a mask on like a lion's head, sat on the uppermost seat, in the midst of a blaze of light. On one side of him was a *skeleton*; on the other a man's dead body, with his clothes on. Over the latter was written—"*The reward of perjury!*" and over the skeleton—"*Who fears?*"

All was now in an uproar. Harrety, with a firm countenance, beheld the scene.

When the noise had a little subsided, the President said something to him in a threatening voice, unless he instantly took the test, and pointed to the dead body. Harrety vociferated—"Your oaths I abominate—yourselves I despise—your proceedings I detest!"

One man, who sat on the other side of the dead body, started up, and drew from under his cloak a dagger; and turning to the President, said—"Our eternal unchangeable laws demand the sacrifice. I am willing to be the minister of justice."

Instantly some of the persons near him seized him by the arms. Harrety struggled.—"Mr. Cowspring," exclaimed he, "will be answerable for my appearance. His life and yours all hang on mine. You dare not hurt me!"

He looked round for his new acquaintance, but could not distinguish him, as all were masked; but some one went and whispered to the President and would-be minister of justice. The former said—"Cato saves thy life; but if ever thou discoverest to any mortal the occurrences of this evening, nor heaven, nor earth, nor hell shall preserve thee from our vengeance."

As the President spoke, each man threw open his cloak, and producing a dagger, said—"I swear! I swear! I swear!"

The President again spoke—"Madman, thou hast heard our decree. Blind him again, and lead him out as he came in."

He was now forcibly blinded, and conducted out of the house.

After being led through many streets, Harrety declared to his conductors he would go no further; and if he was not released, he would immediately cry out.

A voice said to him, which he knew to be the volunteer minister of justice—"Remember, ten thousand daggers are at thy heart the moment thy lips betray thee!"—This man was no other than Marauder.

He was now uncovered, and his conductors disappeared. Harrety looked around for some object to certify him of the spot; and, being assured he should know the place again, he proceeded leisurely along the middle of the way. The shops were at this time all shut up; but as he turned into a larger street, he perceived a watchman. From this man he gained the name of the street where he had been left, and who also directed him to the nearest stand of coaches.

Without any accident he arrived safe at his lodgings.

CHAPTER XVIII.

The next morning Harrety called on Rattle, with whom an acquaintance had commenced from the time they left the debate together.

In defiance of all the threats of the former night, Harrety fully mentioned the whole occurrence.

Rattle told him he knew very well who Cowspring was, and he believed many other of his acquaintance were of the grand Society; and having related to him the history of Cowspring, and object of the party, asked him if he intended to proceed any further in the business.

"Without doubt," replied Harrety warmly.

"Are you not afraid of their daggers and their oaths? You had better let the affair rest. The secret shall not escape me."

"Do you not think," asked Harrety, "it may benefit my fellow-creatures to detect and expose this Society?"

"Certainly I do," replied Rattle; "but the danger to yourself——
——"

"I hold no compact with villains. Let the law protect *me*;—and if I *do* fall, my last breath shall thank my God that I left this life in the discharge of that great duty incumbent on every Christian—*a contempt of vice while in the service of virtue.*"

"However *I* may act, I cannot but applaud *your* determination," said Rattle candidly; "and as the best means for your safety and their apprehension, advise you, without loss of time, to apply to the Bow-street Magistrates."

To this Harrety consented.

That no spy might discover their intentions, Rattle alone waited upon one of the Justices as soon as it was dark. He informed the worthy Magistrate that Harrety had numbered his steps from the time he left the house, and noticed the different turnings; he was therefore certain he could conduct any person very near the spot, but that he was quite ignorant of the way he went in Mr. Cowspring's carriage.

The Magistrate told Rattle if his friend could point out within a few streets, he was well assured the Police Officers could tell the house, as they had a list of every private meeting of any size and consequence in the kingdom. The arrest of Mr. Cowspring alone would be of very little service, he said, as nothing could be alleged against him, and that they had no powers to compel him to discover his associates; but by seizing on the whole gang, they should get possessed of their papers, and any improper instruments they might have in their possession.

That day week, on which Harrety accompanied Cowspring to the meeting, was fixed on for the purpose.

It is not to be supposed that Mr. Cowspring frequented the Coffee-house where young Harrety lodged in the interim. He thought proper, the morning after his disappointment, to go to his country seat for a little time.

When the evening came, in which the Magistrates purposed to apprehend the Society, Harrety conducted the Bow-street officers, as near as he was able, to the spot. Rattle in high spirits accompanied them. As Harrety stopped, one of the officers instantly said—"You have mistaken your last turning, Sir; the next street will clear up the business."

They went, therefore, into the next street, and came to an old building, which Harrety instantly recognized.

The lower part of the house was a thoroughfare to the habitations of different poor families. They proceeded up two pair of stairs, and, listening, found there were voices within.

Two raps at the door produced the watch-word from within; but as they could not answer, they instantly began bursting open the doors. This took up some few minutes; and when they entered the inner apartment, the large blaze in the chimney shewed that every paper of consequence was destroyed. Neither Harrety nor Rattle assisted in the apprehension of the parties.

Eight persons were seized on. Their masks, as well as papers, had been burnt. Their daggers were thrown out of the window, and picked up the next day in an adjoining court.

Mr. Arnon was one of the persons apprehended, so were Fahany and Santhorpe. Marauder had, at the first alarm, climbed up the chimney, from whence to the top of the house, he knew was no great distance; for, with his usual caution, he had before examined the place.

The Officers of Justice, when they left the house, fastened the doors, purposing to make a search under the floors and around the wainscots in the morning, in hopes of gaining further discoveries; but when Marauder, late in the night, came down from his retreat, he carried about him tools sufficient to get the doors from their hinges, and complete his escape. Thus he narrowly evaded being taken.

The persons apprehended were immediately conducted before a Magistrate; but as nothing was alleged except Harrety's testimony that his life was threatened, and as these were only suspected to be the people, they were permitted to give bail for their appearance next day.

A messenger had been sent after Mr. Cowspring, whom the Magistrates knew to be in the country, and he was expected in the morning.

When all parties were on the next day assembled, Harrety made oath that his life was in danger from the threats of a set of people to which Mr. Cowspring had introduced him, though he could not specify their persons. As there was great reason to suppose these were the same, the Magistrates required them to find bail for their peaceable behaviour towards Harrety; and Mr. Cowspring's sureties were bound for double the sum of any of the rest.

This arrest, though it had failed in a great degree, was not without its use. The Justices gained possession of the names of the leading members, and Harrety was protected from any sinister attempts of the party against his life; for, in case of any thing happening to him, the character of Mr. Arnon, Fahany, Cowspring, and the rest would be called into question, and the affair, without doubt, minutely investigated.

Before the Magistrates the party apprehended did not *deny* that they were of the same Society, but endeavoured to make a joke of what Harrety both saw and heard; and though it in some degree took away from the horror of the appearance of what Harrety had seen, yet it added to the proofs that they were the same people. The dead body was found, though not of human substance; for as the skeleton was legally bought of a surgeon, so had the *body without life* been purchased from the refuse of the ingenious Mrs. Salmon, in Fleet-street, who had insured it to keep for any length of time.[1]

The discovery of the daggers too was a suspicious circumstance, though it could not be positively attached to the persons apprehended.

The whole conduct of Harrety, so dauntless and noble, was highly applauded by the Magistrates, who desired him, upon the smallest suspicion of any assault, to apply to them; and that a guard was ready, at a moment's notice, to attend him at any time.

Rattle did not appear publicly in this business, on account of his acquaintance with many of the parties; but more so, his intimacy with Hambden Arnon prevented his wish of taking an active and open part.

By the friendship of Wilson, Hambden was introduced to the other executors of the Duke, and to many respectable acquaintance, whose manners and stations were very different from those he had been usually in the habit of associating with.

CHAPTER XIX.

Among the persons of note in their grand Society, with whom Marauder was in the highest repute, was a Mr. Cloudley. This gentleman was a very staunch Philosopher, but more of the sect of the Naturals than any other.

Marauder wished for his assistance in some particular scheme he had in hand; but as it was inconvenient for himself to leave London at this time, Mr. Arnon undertook the commission.

His son Hambden was engaged; and wishing for a companion, he prevailed on Rattle to accompany him. Mr. Arnon, finding himself unable by arguments to convert Rattle to this new system, promised to give him ocular demonstration in a particular friend of his own.

Mr. Cloudley was a country gentleman, with a good estate in Kent, and a pretty wife, who brought him (what is called) a very decent fortune.

---

1 Mrs. Salmon's exhibition of waxworks, set out in historical tableaux, was open to the public in Fleet Street, London, from 1711 until the early nineteenth century.

Mr. Cloudley met with this fair lady at Bath, where she lived with her aunt. Conformity of ideas soon united in indissoluble bonds the happy pair.

A few years after their marriage, our Gallic neighbours having destroyed with complete success, their own *individual* happiness, adopted in its place a wonderful and most comprehensive scheme of *universal* felicity.

Our new couple were already filled with the eggs of novelty, scepticism, and reformation; the spreading mania therefore soon settled upon them, and the marks burst forth with astonishing fury.

When Mr. Arnon, a warm disciple himself, was about to go to France, his friends, the Cloudleys, determined to realize their wonder-pregnant schemes in the country.

Cloudley Hall underwent a thorough metamorphosis. Every individual and selfish consideration was nobly sacrificed to the general good of the family; master and mistress, man-servant and maid-servant, were scarcely to be distinguished from each other. Mr. Cloudley employed himself in agriculture; Mrs. Cloudley read and wrote morning, noon, and night; though sometimes, by way of relaxation, she fed the pigs, milked the cows, made hay, and did other little jobs.

It must not be omitted that Mrs. Cloudley boasted the largest library in the kingdom of female authors.

A promising young family came very fast. Misses and masters, as soon as they were able to run, were consigned to the direction of the all-instructing goddess, Nature. Clad in a check-shirt, and a pair of trowsers each (other covering they had none), boys and girls, barefooted and bareheaded, in all seasons and all weathers, ranged, uncontrolled, about the premises.

How did Mr. and Mrs. Cloudley, and their *philosophical* visitors, admire that wonderful natural *instinct* (as we call it, though Godwin says there is no such thing[*]) that guided them of their own accord, like pigs, geese, and turkeys, to return to the house whenever they wanted meat, drink, warmth, or rest.[1] The latter indeed was, in the

---

[*] [CL] Political Justice, Vol. i. p. 84.—"If it be meant that we should follow instinct, *it has been proved* that we have no instincts."—If the reader wishes to have it proved, I must refer him to *Political Justice*. [*Political Justice*, ed. Kramnick, Penguin edn., 138.]

---

1 The Cloudleys' belief in natural education is drawn loosely from Jean-Jacques Rousseau's *Émile* (1762): see for example bk. I, section 157, bk. II, section 421, or bk. III, section 636.

summer time, more frequently taken in the stable, the straw-house, or the barn, as in these places they could meet with a more comfortable bed; clean straw being allowed, in the place of repose where they all herded together, but once a month.

This excellent system had already succeeded in an astonishing degree; for speed, strength, and hardiness, they surpassed every child in the village.

Lucretia, the eldest daughter, was twelve years of age, and for kicking and cuffing was the terror of the stoutest plow-boys.

Amazonia, the second daughter, was eleven. Nature, indeed, had not done her duty here, as she never had properly set to rights a trifling accident that happened in her sixth year, from an encounter with a young ram. This young lady limped a little, stopped short in her growth—I mean as to height; for the deficiency was amply supplied by a full share of human substance behind. If the agility of the body was thus unluckily checked, that of the mind was not; for this young maiden shewed a wonderful propensity to mischief.

Four sons, aged six, seven, eight, and nine, completed the family.

At the age of ten, Mrs. Cloudley began to teach them their A. B. C. and to write, as she doubted whether dame Nature was able to initiate them in these points. The four-and-twenty letters, and their alliances, once become known, opportunities for further acquaintance were left to themselves.

"Subjects of study," said Mrs. and Mr. Cloudley, "we force not on them. In these they can exercise their *own will*; here they have *a choice, a right*;"—and Mrs. Cloudley, as well as her husband, was too true a Philosophess to prejudice their *wills*, or debar them of a *choice* or *right*.

Lucretia, with one lesson a day, knew, in less than two years, all her letters, and could make pot-hooks and sheep-crooks with great *éclat*.

Amazonia, the genius, already rivalled her.

"Such are the innate powers with which Nature has furnished the mind and how great and glorious must their strength be when left to themselves, unwarped by the follies, the prejudices, and the fashions of what is called civilized life and education!" said Mr. Cloudley.

It may be a matter of surprise how two people, endowed with such liberal and congenial minds, ever came to marry—to indulge in such a ridiculous, superfluous, unmeaning ceremony. To this I answer—that if William Godwin himself, *the Author of Political Justice*; and Mary Wollstonecraft, *the Authoress of the Rights of Woman*, saw cause "to subject themselves to those consequences which the laws of England annex to husband and wife,"* how many and more forcible reasons must a simple country gentleman and his fair one have, whose estate needed a wife's fortune to wipe away the life-mortgages, and whose son wanted legitimacy to entitle him to an entailed property.[1]

One fine morning Mr. Arnon introduced Rattle to this family mansion of a new system of morality realized.

I find the utmost difficulty in proceeding any further in this part of my tale. Unluckily for the reader, I am not myself an *Illuminati* or *Peripatetic* of this sect; or, without a blush, a pause, or an excuse, could I detail the particulars of the scene which met Rattle's eyes on his entering the courtyard.

The presence of the strangers, added to the ringing of the bell at the gate, alarmed the young *Naturals*. The fair Lucretia leaped from the back of a donkey, and, followed by Amazonia, ran giggling into the stable. Brutus, Voltaire, Hercules, Tom Pain—what a happy combination of names!—for so the four sons were called, from early traits in their character, which the philosophic eyes of their parents perceived, fled with *yoyou* notes towards the barn.

Enter into the court-yard from the house, Mr. Cloudley, with long matted locks uncombed, with an Oliverian[2] covering on his head, sandals on his feet, short coat or tunic, and belt around his waist.

Having given his friend Arnon the fraternal embrace, which, with great adroitness, under the pretence of a fit of sneezing, Rattle evaded, he welcomed them to Cloudley Hall. After a few common civilities and enquiries had passed between them, Cloudley said—"You see me a citizen of nature; my garb is solely for use."

"The belt, Sir?" said Rattle.

"Here I stick a sword, or pistol, or knife; or, in short, any thing."

"I see nothing there at present."

"Mr Rattle," said Arnon, "is the slave of custom—one of the prejudiced. I am in hopes your good example will convert him."

Mr. Cloudley looked at Rattle in such a manner while Mr. Arnon spoke, that a physiognomist would have supposed *he was the man of*

---

* [CL] Godwin's own words.

---

1 Lucas quotes from Godwin's *Memoirs of the Author of The Rights of Woman, op. cit.*, 106.
2 In the style of Oliver Cromwell.

prejudice; but, at the last sentence, the supercilious brow of *conceit* was much more evident.

"Well, Mr. Cloudley," said Rattle, rightly guessing the sensations of his mind, "do you think you shall succeed?"

"If, young man, the force of truth is not buried in your intellectual system by fashion and superstition."

The gentlemen all enter the house.

Mrs. Cloudley approaches in a riding jacket, with a short thin petticoat, striped drawers visible, sandals on her feet, and a man's hat on her head.

Introductions and civilities pass of course.

"To you, Sir," said Mrs. Cloudley, addressing Rattle, "this life that we lead here, though unperverted by art or custom, must at first appear strange."

The lady, I have said, had been a very pretty woman; she was still so. Though in her thirty-second year, and the mother of six children, Lady Jersey herself had not a younger look at that age.[1] There was something in her dress and manner too that was pleasingly striking; and the contrast with the fashionable dress of the day was considerably in her favour for grace, shape, and beauty. Her voice was melodious, her teeth exquisitely white, and her air, though free, was feminine.

Rattle, ever susceptible of beauty, was highly surprised at the one now present, and began to think the scene before him not so very ridiculous.—"My dear Madam," said he, "'tis new indeed, yet by no means unpleasant. I am only a learner, but shall be most happy to be your pupil."

Thus him, whom the writings and arguments of scores of *modern Philosophers* had been unable to subdue, *one kind glance* completely conquered.

Mrs. Cloudley's fascinating dimple, the omen of success, was immediately visible. Mr. Cloudley's looks evidently evinced another passion, *jealousy*. Rattle observed it, and could scarce refrain his laughter when he perceived the husband affecting a philosophical indifference. From this defeat in the combined forces opposed against him, were there any hopes that Rattle could escape the snare into which Arnon had drawn him. Turning to Mr. Cloudley, he said—"The ancient Philosophers considered a conquest over the

---

1 Frances, Lady Jersey (1753-1821), a renowned beauty and was for some time in the 1790s the mistress of the Prince of Wales.

passions of the soul as their first object; without this they argued that wisdom was not to be obtained. What are your first principles, Mr. Cloudley?"

"The *general welfare; individuals* will come of course."

Rattle had said—"Pshaw!" and was proceeding in his speech, when a horrid yell from without doors prevented any further reply.

Mr. Cloudley now put on the active Philosopher, reached down a large horsewhip that hung in the hall, and with great indifference proceeded to the sound.

"Come," said Mr. Cloudley to Rattle, who would willingly have stayed behind, "come and see how easy is the sway of reason and nature."

Rattle and Mr. Arnon followed him.

Mrs. Cloudley, with equal apathy as her husband concerning the noise, but with a kind glance towards her younger guest, walked up stairs, remarking as she left them, that "crying was a wonderful effort of nature to draw the moist vapours, the aqueous particles, from the brain, thereby clearing the understanding, and improving the mind."

The gentlemen now proceeded to the outward court, where they discovered the cause of the alarm.

Temperance is one of the first qualifications of a Philosopher, especially if you mean to bring up your children to this *new trade*. Wisely, therefore, were the young scientific spirits of the Cloudley family fed but *twice* a day, morning and evening.

A sharp stomach makes a sharp wit; and both being thus sharp, the latter, as in duty bound, returns the favour by providing for the former.

Among the alimentary inventions of the young Cloudleys, egg-hunting employed the day. Their preceptress, Nature, had gifted her favourite Brutus with a continual titillation on the saporific nerves—I presume meaning him for an EPICUREAN PHILOSOPHER. Amazonia knew this, and brought to her dear brother an egg, plump and fair.

Brutus made no bones of the matter; but, according to his method, clapped the whole into his mouth, cracking it nut-fashion.

Now Brutus's olfactory nerves were not such faithful guardians as they ought to have been; for they had not forewarned him that the ovarious contents had undergone many a metamorphosis since they had been grateful to the palate; as first, in taking the form of a young chick, which, not being ready to come forth with its other brothers and sisters, and been neglected, and left by the mother. Failing of success in this form, the chick began to change, and a colony of I know not what species of vermicular animals now inhabited the shell.

To make my story short.—Pop, full into the midst of these, whatever they were, at a venture, Brutus's two rows of masticators, like a Sampson, began slaying their thousands, when the confined effluvia burst forth.

Is it necessary to particularize any further?

Amazonia, giggling, stood near her brother. He instantly seized her by the matted locks, and pulled her to the ground. Lucretia heard, and knew her squall: she flew upon Brutus; and as fast as the one pulled, the other cuffed away. Voltaire, Hercules, and Tom Pain hastened from the top of a dung-cart to the scene of action, and with kicks and squalls endeavoured to rescue the unhappy Brutus. Lucretia scattered them all, gave Voltaire a bloody nose, knocked down Hercules, and kicked Tom Pain to the other end of the court.

Such was the scene of action as Cloudley, Arnon, and Rattle approached.

CHAPTER XX.

Gentle reader, didst thou ever read the first book of Virgil's Æneis, where, in a thunder-storm, while the sons of Eolus are kicking up a dust, up pops Neptune with a trident in his hand, which shaking at the Eolean fry, off they are in a tangent. Not otherwise was the appearance of the father of the Cloudley family; his weapon of authority was the large horse-whip before mentioned, with which he gave such a crack, that the walls of the court and the old building re-echoed with the sound.

Up jumped Lucretia; Brutus was not long after, roaring, sputtering, open-mouthed, with the slimy inexpressible, of a dingy yellow, streaming from each corner of his chops. Amazonia followed them with unusual nimbleness, as if conscious of the peace-working effects of her parent's sceptre. The younger ones had fled at the first crack; a second routed the whole.

Peace being so easily restored, Cloudley looked around for the applause of his companions.

Arnon did not disappoint him; but Rattle, who never dealt in flattery but with a lady, replied—"Where was Nature, my good Sir? In your horse-whip, or in the manner of using it?"

This was a question Cloudley was not ready for; he therefore paused a moment for an answer. He then logically replied—"*Nature is simple*—most *simple* was *my method*; therefore, *my method* is *Nature*."

"I deny the whole, Sir," said Rattle. "Thus I argue: your children have been *accustomed* to the horsewhip—custom is art; therefore—"

Arnon, who knew his friend Cloudley very well, as most unfit to bear a joke, stopped the further progress of Rattle's syllogism by some remark concerning Mrs. Cloudley, who was approaching towards them.

The gentlemen returned to the house with her, and soon after sat down to dinner.

The dinner, bad in quality, dressing, and accompaniments, was not worth the mentioning; and nothing deserving of notice passed till it was over. The company then walked into another room, where were some fruit and wine, of which the former was too sour, and the latter too sweet.

The moment after they left the dining-room, and were out of sight, Rattle heard a strange clatter, which he afterwards understood was occasioned by the young *yoyous* rushing in, and scrambling for the fragments.

In the course of the evening, Arnon attempted many times to leave his friend Rattle alone with Mrs. Cloudley, by drawing the husband aside; but the jealous watchfulness of Mr. Cloudley was roused by the evident attention of Rattle, who was seldom on his guard, and this always prevented him.

Arnon had no doubt of better success the next day; and already in his mind triumphed in the proselyte he had gained by the charms of Mrs. Cloudley. Rattle, at length, retired to his couch without the *téte-à-téte* with his kind hostess, which his friend seemed so desirous to get for him.

In spite of the wildness and eccentricity of his character, Rattle was far from wanting a virtuous principle. When alone in his chamber, he reviewed the occurrences of the day; he saw the easy character of the lady, his friend's officiousness, and his own danger; and he determined the next day he would conquer, by flying from the temptation. He began also to suspect that there was some trick in the case; for he knew Arnon well, that he was sly and subtle, full of schemes and contrivances, indifferent in obliging another, unless he had some object of his own in view; so that he was resolved to be doubly on his guard. Had he sooner known of the fascinating evil, he had not risked the temptation; but he had been surprised unawares, and happily a moment's reflection was spared him, and he summoned reason, principle, virtue, and religion to his aid.

Thus armed, in the morning, not early, he came down to

breakfast. Greatly indeed was he surprised to find Marauder was below.

As he entered the breakfast-room, and deep in thought, slowly opened the door, he had just time enough to see the bewitching Mrs. Cloudley sitting on Marauder's knee: she sprung up immediately. Marauder was coolly talking to the husband, who was busily writing in a closet adjoining.

Rattle testified his amazement at seeing Marauder, but took not the slightest notice of the familiar situation of the lady, to whom he made his obeisance with his accustomed courtesy. Cloudley, hearing his voice, quickly joined them.

Marauder, he found, was to leave them soon after breakfast, and to proceed immediately to Dover.

Rattle therefore broke the ice of his departure by offering to accompany him, alleging that he had a relation in that neighbourhood, whom he wished to visit while he was in this part of the country. Mr. Arnon and Mrs. Cloudley's disappointment was evident: Mr. Cloudley said nothing, and Marauder could not, as he was alone, refuse him a place in his chaise.

During the time of breakfast, many things became very evident to Rattle, whose suspicions were already raised; and who, affecting indifference, and not having yet declared his intentions of leaving them, was all the time on the watch.

He perceived the intimacy of Marauder with the lady, by their attempting so anxiously to conceal it; and he was astonished at the partiality the husband shewed for Marauder, considering him as an oracle of wisdom.

Arnon too was very thoughtful and silent. Rattle soon discovered that the other had noticed his suspicions; and a most curious group they formed, each endeavouring to hide his own thoughts, and watchful of those of his neighbour.

In defiance of the kind hints of Mrs. Cloudley, and persuasions of Mr. Arnon, Rattle had resolution to keep to the good plan he had adopted, and to leave Cloudley Hall at the same time with Marauder.

Rattle, by this prudent conduct, escaped a deep-laid snare. Arnon and Marauder had long wished to entangle him in their schemes; and had settled their plan that he should accompany the former to Cloudley Hall, little doubting but that, in a few days, the fair Maria Cloudley would make a convert of him. Marauder knew the Cytheræan powers of the lady full well, and also the weak side of Rattle, who had more than once been the dupe of a pretty woman;[1] and, in his sneering way, he had said to Arnon, before he left town—"Our friend Rattle has once honoured my choice with his approbation," (alluding to Emily), "and been ambitious to be my rival, though with little success, or he would not be so anxious to discover the retreat of the fair fugitive. I now generously give him an opportunity of supplanting me, and most heartily wish he may succeed. My dear friend, this Rattle has long been a spy upon us. Involve him in this intrigue, and we will soon turn him to our purpose, either by the almighty power of love, or by the *Hydra-fears* of a *crim-con* business.[2] Oh! how I shall laugh to see his honour, his character, his conscience, all that the world holds dear, in the hands of my dear little enchantress, Maria Cloudley!"

Before Marauder and Rattle left the house, Rattle had in part discovered the charm by which Marauder possessed such astonishing influence over Cloudley. "My dearest friend," said Marauder to him, "nothing but the very urgent business which compels me to leave you so abruptly, could force me so soon from a society I so highly value and admire. I know not which most to commend—the manly strength of your mind, which burst the fetters of art and custom, or the wonderful success which has followed it. Ever-blooming youth and health are among the most conspicuous of your blessings; and in your rising progeny, I expect to see the golden age revive. It is the pride of my life to call you my friend; and *your simple promise once given me*, I more rely on than the multiplied oaths of all the Potentates upon earth. Nature, the goddess you adore, crowns your offerings with success;—a wife most lovely, faithful, and sensible; children, the wonders of the world; while, with a mind strong and vigorous, a soul calm and determined, you revive the dignity of human nature, and participate, with a liberal hand, your blessings to your friends. We live not for ourselves alone; human nature claims us, or never would I leave this beloved society."

Such was the parting speech of Marauder, as he threw his arms around the credulous NATURAL; then, with his handkerchief to his face, he slowly ascended his chariot, and set off with Rattle.

From the two speeches of Marauder just mentioned, some idea may be formed, not only of the versatility of his character, but of his prudence and judgment in acting. Rattle's admiration of Emily had

---

1 Cytheria is another name for Venus, the goddess of love. Cytheræans were votaries, or sometimes prostitutes, at the temples of Venus.

2 An abbreviation for "Criminal conversation," the legal term for adultery.

not escaped the ready ken of Marauder, nor the diligent enquiries since her departure, his watchful intelligence; but as they did not interfere with his interest or his passions, he forbore to notice them.

CHAPTER XXI.

Rattle accompanied Marauder to Dover—a very silent ride on both sides. Here they separated; Rattle went to his relation's, dined with him, and set off in the evening to town.

The specimen of *modern Philosophy realized*, which Rattle had seen at the Cloudley's, and the snare which he had so happily evaded, more firmly rooted him in his dislike against Marauder and his associates.

The charm which had chiefly drawn him to Marauder's table, was fled; the lovely Emily was no where to be found; for Rattle had been indeed far more anxious to find the place of her abode than Marauder.

As Rattle journeyed to London, he had sufficient leisure fully to revolve in his mind the consequences which might have attended the vicious connection that was prepared for him; and many serious thoughts, he was little accustomed to, arose to his review. The state of the Cloudley family clearly shewed him the weakness of human nature when left to its own guidance; and Mrs. Cloudley herself was a melancholy instance how degrading every female excellence is without virtue.

To leave young minds to the care of Nature, is a principle not confined only to this family.

Many well-meaning parents are not willing to give their children early information in life, particularly in religious matters, under the idea that they will not prejudice them, but give their reason full scope, that their young minds may have the liberty of judging for themselves, and not become slaves to the errors of custom, or to the false opinion of others. But these conscientious people forget that *human nature* is ever imperfect of itself; that the mind, from its earliest infancy, will warp one way or other, and therefore it is necessary to turn it towards those principles that seem best. The human mind, without very early culture (what a modern Philosopher will call prejudice) will soon go to waste;—to speak without a metaphor, unless we instil some notions of right and wrong, of virtue and vice, idiotism or absolute madness will undoubtedly be the consequence.

This was the case of the wild man, Peter, who never, after he came to full age, could be reclaimed from his ignorant and savage nature; and many Cloudley families exhibit the same in a partial degree.[1]

The wisdom of man, unlike all other animals, seems to be the collection of former ages; in early youth is the mind to be stored with knowledge; and it is the duty of a parent to instil that which he thinks best, and not, through a foolish fear of doing too much, leave the whole undone.

The argument of these Sophists plays against all subjects, but strikes its venom at *Religion*—with this then I shall conclude the digression.

If Religion were left entirely to herself, if every one were to propose articles for his own faith, and if these strange medleys were to be tolerated by the legislature, few vestiges would remain of the original institution of Christ. The majority of the world are composed of the ignorant, the designing, the indolent, and the open reprobate; and these would easily make *that* their principles which suited themselves and their circumstances best. What then would be the situation of the rising generation? And what would they naturally think of a Religion and Government, where the different opinions of the wise-man and the fool, the learned and the unlearned, the good and the bad, were equally countenanced, and openly approved? How dark and gloomy is the prospect of the human mind left to itself! It is absolutely necessary, for the safety of each other, that our *unruly minds*, as well as *persons*, should have some law; and if *good principles* and *learning*, as well as *good conduct*, were not in some respect forced upon the mind, ignorance and wickedness would soon overpower learning and virtue.

These remarks do not confine *what is good* to the narrow principles of any class, but to that doctrine the whole life of Christ taught, and *the spirit of which* cannot be mistaken by those who mean well— whether it is called *Universal Philanthropy, Love, Good-will* or *Charity*.

---

1 Peter the Wild Boy was found living wild in woods near Hamelin, Hanover, in 1725. He was brought to Britain by order of George I and he quickly became a curiosity (the excessive interest being satirized in *The Most Wonderful Wonder that ever appeared to the Wonder of the British Nation* [1726], possibly by Jonathan Swift and John Arbuthnot). Peter died in 1785, still unable to talk well, although some contemporaries claimed he was an "imbecile" (with severe learning difficulties) rather than that his lack of childhood education had prevented him ever acquiring the trappings of civilization.

One famous explanation of it, under the last term (lately translated)
this chapter shall finish with.

1st Corinthians, Chapter xiii.

I.

Tho' praises with an angel's voice I sung,
Or all the sweetness of the human tongue,
And have not Charity—I am no more
Than sounding brass, or cymbals were before.

II.

And tho' the gift of prophecy were mine,
And ev'ry mystery and sense divine;
Tho' I had Faith e'en mountains to remove,
And have no Charity—I nothing prove.

III.

Tho' all my goods to feed the poor were giv'n,
My body burnt in earnest zeal for Heav'n,
And still the sacred attribute unsought
Of Godlike Charity—I am as nought.

IV.

Charity long suffereth, and is kind—
And Charity hath not an envious mind:
Nor vaunteth Charity her praises forth,
Nor, puff'd with pride, boasteth her fancied worth.

V.

Not greedy she, nor anxious for her own,
Not easily provok'd, nor judging wrong;
Rejoiceth not when others go astray;
But all her glory's in the righteous way.

VI.

In sufferings, trust, and hope, and patience, she
Is still the same,—nor faileth Charity;
But gifts prophetic shall in time decay,
Tongues they shall cease, and knowledge pass away.

VII.

For all our knowledge is in part confin'd,
And prophecies themselves have bounds consign'd:
But when a perfect spirit rules the heart,
No more instruction we shall need *in part*.

VIII.

When I was young, then childish was my word;
Childish I thought, and as a child I heard;
But when the age of manhood once began,
I left off childish things, and thought as man.

IX.

For now imperfect through a glass we see;
But face to face then open we shall be:
Now all my knowledge is but party shewn;
Then shall I know, as also I am known.

X.

FAITH, HOPE, and CHARITY are now—these three;
but the greatest of these is CHARITY.

CHAPTER XXII.

So much was Rattle disgusted at the scenes he had witnessed at the Cloudleys, that, before he arrived in town, he had resolved some most wonderful schemes of education in his head:—whether or not he was ever able to put them into execution, a future day may declare.

It will be needless to particularize that they were directly contrary to these he had so lately witnessed, as the very first part of Rattle's plan was, to teach his young ones to read before they were to speak; by this means furnishing their young minds with a proper idea and notion of things.

But leaving Rattle to his wonderful cogitations, the progress of Marauder in the road to glory proceeds.

The business which had hurried Marauder from town was of no common kind. He had received private intelligence that a Commissioner was coming over from France, under pretence of settling the terms for an exchange of prisoners; but that his real motives were to prepare the way for a peace.[1]

To counteract this, it was determined that some intelligent person should give him the meeting as soon as he was landed; and Marauder was fixed upon for that purpose.

M. M——, who was chosen to execute this commission, arrived at Dover the third day, and Marauder waited upon him with private, as well as his public letters of introduction. The Frenchman received him most favourably; and the other, with no small satisfaction, soon discovered from his conversation that he came to this country more in the character of a spy than in those of a Commissioner for an exchange of prisoners, or a negotiator for a peace.

Marauder, in his conversation, was all openness, confidence, and candour, trusting such would be the most sure means of making M. M—— the same.

In the most forcible language he represented to the Frenchman the weak and distressed situation of this country; he enlarged upon the national debt, and the want of future resources. He boldly declared to him that Ireland, Scotland, and England, one after the other, were ready to burst into open rebellion.

Of the Irish affairs he spoke with decision, as of a work already done, unless crushed in its birth of liberty by a premature peace. No arguments he could conceive were omitted, that he thought might influence the mind of the Frenchman.

Among other things, he artfully mentioned the natural situation of Ireland, from whence many Politicians had concluded that she never could exist as a civilized and mercantile state without a dependence on some other nation. This, with great affected candour, he pretended to believe.—"Yet, Sir," continued he to the Commissioner, "there is not a man in Ireland, uninfluenced by Ministerial pay, that does not look up to the GREAT NATION as the people with whom they wish to unite and fraternize. Commanded by French Officers, where is the power of England? The vast Navy of Britain will insensibly crumble to pieces. The Irish ports, crowded with

---

1 Citizen Niou, representing the French government, visited Britain in September 1798 to negotiate an exchange of prisoners of war. The terms of the exchange were complex and the exchange very protracted. By 1801, Monsieur Otto, Napoleon's agent, was residing in London as the commissioner supervising the exchange. He was also engaged in preparing the way for the peace negotiations which were to culminate in the Treaty of Amiens of 1801.

small frigates and privateers, will attack this unwieldy monster. Its trade, which has been centuries in collecting, will soon be torn from it, and participated among the different States of Europe. Its sinews, strength, and vigour already begin to fail; and the shilalah[1] of Ireland shall complete what the sword of France has begun.

The Frenchman heard him with pleasure, the discourse was so congenial to his own ideas; and enquired what were their means to shake off the English yoke, and what progress was made in the affiliating system.

Marauder minutely answered him, and declared himself personally versed in the situation of England, Scotland, and Ireland, though neither of the two last he had at that time ever set his foot on. He unfolded to the Commissioner the chain of connection by which the people in each country were linked together, in opposition to the established laws and Government. He dwelt upon the abilities, the power, the popularity of their leaders. He produced instances of disaffection in the Army and the Navy, and found no difficulty in making the Frenchman believe that it was general throughout the whole kingdom. In terms most hyperbolical did he praise the GREAT NATION (particularly in the cant of that party to which he knew the Commissioner belonged), and declared that every enlightened people on the face of the earth would follow the glorious example set them by France. He positively asserted that many of the ostensible agents of the Government in England were secretly adverse to the present situation of affairs, and that an immediate peace was the only measure to prop the falling Ministry, of which Mr. A——— and his agents were so well assured, that they would purchase it on any terms.

The arguments and bold assertions of Marauder completely succeeded; and every thing became perverted in the eyes of the Commissioner. The pacific endeavours of the Ministry he took for fear, and their civilities as a bait to deceive him. His conduct in settling an exchange of prisoners was so suspicious, and his demands were so exorbitant, that all hopes of a negotiation for a peace were soon lost.

By Marauder's advice also it was that the pretended object of his commission was not put in execution; as he argued that, in case of a sudden insurrection among the people, the French prisoners would be of the utmost service—not so much from their numbers, as their knowledge in military affairs.

---

1 More usually "shillelagh," a thick cudgel, originally from County Wicklow in Ireland.

The issue of this business is very well known. The method which had been originally adopted, as a prelude to allay the strife between the nations, became the means of irritating both parties. Measures for carrying on the war were renewed with redoubled virulence and vigour, and public and private enemies loudly prophesied that England was ruined.

Arnon joined his friend at Dover, and corroborated every thing which the other had advanced; and when Marauder returned to town, he left Arnon with the Frenchman, who had not received permission to come to London. Many other well-known characters waited upon him here; and Marauder, who knew all this from his correspondence with Arnon, gave indirect information to the Government, that the French Commissioner was privately intriguing with the disaffected in this country: the same was afterwards strengthened by the report of the messenger, who was sent in answer to the Commissioner's credentials.

Thus Marauder, who had been the chief agent in influencing M. M——, not only escaped suspicion himself, but dextrously fixed it on those whom curiosity had chiefly induced to visit him.

Volume III

CHAPTER I.

Scarcely had Marauder settled this business to the satisfaction of the leaders of his party, and his own renown, before he was earnestly pressed to go over to Ireland, and inspect into the state of affairs there. This he had for some time before determined upon, and Fahany, who had partly settled his Irish mortgages, prepared to accompany him. They left town together.

As they were walking through the town of Holyhead, a gentleman in a foreign military uniform came up to Fahany, and, in bad English said—

"Luckily met, Sir; I have been seeking you in Ireland, and am just landed in England, very ready to pay my draft. Where is your banker Marauder, for whose service it was drawn?"

Marauder, instantly guessing at the man, who was no other than Geutespiere, answered in French—"My name is Marauder; and if you have any thing to say to me, I can speak to you in your native language, and—"

"My name is Geutespiere; if you are the man who was with Mr. Fahany at Turin, you cannot be ignorant *who I am.*"

"Well, Sir," replied Marauder, with equal *hauteur*, "I am the person you mean. What are your commands?"

"Proceed, Sir," said Fahany, recovering from a conscious confusion he affected to hide under a contemptuous brow.

"I will, if possible with patience too," said the injured emigrant, "lest *my anger*, in this public place, *should disappoint my revenge.* Mr. Fahany, you produced my name to a note of hand for a large amount, which you pretended to have won of me."

"'Tis false," replied Fahany.

Geutespiere clapped his hand to his sword; but restraining himself, continued—"No matter—it is enough!—Mr. Marauder, you made the use intended by the forgery, and debauched the foolish, the inconstant, the perjured Leonora."

"In much stronger language, and not with language alone, would I answer your base implication," retorted Marauder, adding with a sneer, "but that I am not willing to let *your anger disappoint your revenge.* 'Tis true I have enjoyed Leonora; nor, till I was satiated with her charms, did she express any regret that she had sacrificed *for me* an *honourable* connection with a Captain Geutespiere."

With difficulty the irritated and injured Frenchman could

restrain his passion.—"Let me not again speak but act," said he; "where are you to be found?"

"Half an hour hence, had we not met you, we had been on the sea towards Ireland," said Fahany; "we shall now wait your commands at yonder hotel."

Geutespiere passed them, and they returned back to their inn.

In a short time a regular challenge came, brought by a young gentleman in the same uniform. Time and weapons were mentioned. Early the next morning with sword and pistols, *at the most retired spot*.—"We call on you at five," said the young solider, "and expect you will be ready to attend us, and point out *where that spot is*."

To this they assented.

Before six in the morning, the four gentlemen arrived at a wood a few miles from the town, and, without loss of time, prepared immediately for combat.

Marauder and Fahany expected that each of them was to take an opponent; but Geutespiere, in defiance of the most earnest entreaties of his companion, was resolved it should be otherwise.

"The battle is *mine*," said he; "the firing of a pistol will not fatigue me. If I fall, then, my friend, I cannot prevent your noble courage from revenging my death."

Marauder and Fahany tossed up who should be the first opponent to Geutespiere. The lot fell on Fahany.

The combatants fired together.

Fahany fell.

Marauder, without a word, took his place.

For the second time the pistols were discharged.

Marauder's aim was deadly. The ball passed into the heart of the brave emigrant; he bounded from the ground, and dropped dead on the spot.

Marauder was slightly wounded. Geutespiere's ball had passed through the fleshy part of his left arm; and Marauder mentally admired his own prudence, which had induced him, as he fired, to step his right foot forward, and thus probably prevented the ball from taking the same direction as his own had done.

A common duellist would not have perceived this masterstroke of Marauder's, much less did the young soldier; it was only known to, and worthy of, an adept and veteran in the art. Marauder had before practised it in Italy, when he avoided the shot of a famous Irishman, who had been in the service of France. This man, a professed duellist, had noticed the finesse; but Marauder's pistol stopped the remark which was about to issue from his lips, and buried his knowledge in eternal silence.

The young emigrant, perceiving the fate of his friend, hastened to reload the pistols, when the report of some guns at no great distance roused his attention.

"There is no time to be lost," said he, as he threw down the present implements of death, and drew his sword. He rushed upon his antagonist, crying—"Revenge! revenge! revenge!"

Marauder was prepared for him.

The fight lasted for some minutes. They were both pretty equally skilled in the sword; but Marauder had every other advantage. It required some skill indeed to avoid the first thrusts of the young Officer; but when once his exertions began to relax, the contest was no longer equal.

The Frenchman was wounded, fatigued, and faint. Marauder pressed upon him, became master of his sword-arm, closed, and threw him on the ground.

At this moment, while Marauder's hand was lifted up to put a finish to the bloody work, a rustling among the leaves caught his ear, and stopped the blow.

Two gentlemen, with fowling-pieces and spaniels, came out of the wood very near them.

Marauder spoke loud enough to be heard by them.—"Your life is in my power; I give it you, though your friend's rashness and your own compelled me to meet you in this manner."

These were the first words of English Marauder had spoken to either of the emigrant Officers.

The words indeed were not understood by him to whom they were addressed, but clearly heard by those he most wished to hear them.

"Your compassion, Sir," said one of the sportsmen, as they both came forward, "shews you a man of true honour. It may be necessary for you to leave this spot. Our servants are at hand, and will give every assistance that is necessary."

Marauder thanked them for their civility; but declined departing. He ran up to Fahany, and perceived, with great demonstrations of joy, that his friend was not mortally wounded;—the ball had passed through the upper part of his thigh.

The young emigrant, by loss of blood, was extremely faint. The gentlemen stanched it as well as they were able; and while one of them sent a servant for chaises and a surgeon, the other produced a present support, the brandy bottle. A moderate application of this revived the two wounded gentlemen; and Marauder was at last prevailed upon, by the persuasions of his friend Fahany, to continue his route to Ireland without him. But this he did not consent to till after the arrival of the surgeon and the carriages, and the medical gentleman had assured him his friend was out of danger.

It was the present policy of Marauder to make his conduct seem as humane as possible.

The character of Marauder was become very high in the estimation of the strangers; they provided him with a horse to carry him as far as the first post-town, from whence he could get into Scotland; and, as he was unencumbered with any other baggage than a portmanteau, and attended by his valet (who was sent for from Holyhead), he understood that it would be a pleasant journey to the Mull of Galloway in Scotland, and a short passage of twenty miles to the Irish coast.

His wound, which was trifling, was bound up by the surgeon before he left the field.

Marauder therefore took the advice of the strangers; and, proceeding towards Scotland, gave up the idea of going from Holyhead, lest the report of the duel might have been heard of there. His clothes he knew would reach Dublin before him, as they had been sent in the vessel in which Fahany and himself were to have sailed.

Fahany's wound, though by no means mortal, would not permit his accompanying him; and as to the event of a trial, they were both of them very indifferent, as they were able to prove that the challenge originated from the deceased.

Before he departed, Marauder was careful to whisper a few *data* in Fahany's ear.

The strangers also were so willing to come forward as witnesses of the generosity of humanity of Marauder, that their acquittal was certain.

The young Frenchman knew no otherwise of the affair, then as his deceased friend Geutespiere had told him; both Marauder and Fahany had denied the charge, and he soon began to think that his friend might been imposed on.

Duchesne (the other emigrant Officer's name) and Fahany were both carried to the house of one of the strangers, whose name was Forrester, and the dead body of Geutespiere was conveyed to Holyhead.

Duchesne sent to some of his countrymen of known respectability, to consult how it was best for him to act. They very properly took the opinion of some of the first lawyers, whose advice was that he should leave the kingdom as soon as possible; informing him also, that as the bearer of a challenge, and second of a challenger, besides being a principal, he was in danger of forfeiting his life to the laws of this country. Accordingly, he was conveyed on board a ship bound to Hamburgh, as soon as his wounds would permit, from which place he could easily join the Emigrant Army that was under the command of the Duke de Condé.

CHAPTER II.

In the meantime, with prosperous breezes, Marauder arrives at Dublin, and is introduced to the first company in that capital.

Marauder, whose ever active mind was in search after information, did not confine himself to one party, but gleaned his knowledge from both.

The particulars of his duel soon reached the sister kingdom, and was the means of making his name very generally known throughout the country.

The report came from the strangers, and was adorned, as it passed through various hands, with many heroical ornaments. The gallant gay Marauder found his company courted by every one; he was almost idolized by the women, respected and envied by the men.

When spoken to upon the late affair, a subject he was far from disliking, he would laughingly tell a fair lady, it was the fatal effects of beauty. Among the men, who thought so successful a rencounter added to his credit, he remarked that his passage back to England would be without cost, as he expected daily a King's Officer to conduct him over, that he might attend to take his trial. Sometimes he seriously spoke of the affair, and affected to lament the intemperate rashness and revengeful jealousy of Geutespiere, and the fatal effects which his own injured honour demanded.

Thus could he treat the most serious concerns as it suited the whim of the moment, though in reality every thing was subservient to his interest. Yet, in the midst of that easy and gay deportment he every where exhibited, was he seriously plotting some of the deepest and most subtle schemes.

It was near the latter end of the summer of 1795, when Marauder made his appearance in Dublin. The disturbances, which had alarmed the public ear, in the North, seemed to have subsided. A temporary explosion indeed was gone by; but slowly and insidiously did the spreading train creep throughout the kingdom. The latent seeds of rebellion were taking the deepest root in the province of

Ulster, and the old name of DEFENDER began to be swallowed up in the more general one of UNITED IRISHMEN.[1] The poison had crept into the southern parts of the nation; and Munster soon after rapidly swallowed the *organizing system.*

The more civilized parts around the metropolis were by no means backward; but the powers which were ready to oppose them, were better known here, and kept the disaffected somewhat in awe.

But the officinal forge, from when the whole mass of treason issued, was in the capital itself. Here were the secret and ingenious springs tempered, which were to influence the great machine. No mean geniuses directed the work; the very first political artists gave their aid, and the *Machiavellian* schemes of ancient and modern times were fully investigated to perfect the bold design.

Marauder beheld with redoubled pleasure the progress of the work, and, from his late conference with the French Commissioner, was able to give great information on the subject. About this time it was that Edward John Lewins was sent by the party over to France, to act as circumstances might require, in the capacity of *their accredited resident ambassador.*[2]

In the most fertile part of the county of Tipperary, in the province of Munster, Marauder's chief property lay—a county by no means behind the rest of the province in that licentious insolence, and artful hypocrisy, the very parents of sedition.

Having informed himself in Dublin with a perfect knowledge of the means at present in agitation to perfect the great undertaking, he set out immediately for his country seat, as he concluded he should very soon be summoned over to England.

---

1   The Catholic secret society known as the "Defenders" provided much of the support for the Society of United Irishmen once it had been formed, nominally on a non-sectarian basis, in Belfast on 18 October 1791. See Appendix G.1.

2   Edward John Lewins, or Lewens (1756-1828), was sent as the envoy of the Dublin committee of United Irishman to Hamburg in April 1797. He was charged with renewing negotiations with the French Revolutionary government for an invasion of Ireland to accompany an internal rebellion, this plan having originally been mooted in the previous year by the United Irishmen leaders, Lord Edward Fitzgerald and Arthur O'Connor. Lewins arrived in Paris in July 1797 and until just before the Rebellion broke out, he was still attempting to persuade the French to launch an immediate invasion. After the Rising, Lewins was banished from Great Britain and spent the remainder of his life in France.

Marauder's *personal appearance* at this time it will be proper to remark; the reason will be most evident in the progress of these pages.

Marauder was always well dressed; his clothes in the highest fashion; his hair long, and constantly powdered; his beard close shaved, and not the smallest appearance of a whisker.

Though he was by nature rather of a dark complexion, he did not appear so now: some of the most fashionable cosmetics he used in great quantities, and with great success. But though his exterior deportment was so very aristocratical, his conduct was adapted to conciliate the favour of his dependants.

He listened to all their complaints with the greatest patience, and redressed most of them. He regularly attended mass, confessed frequently, and ordered prayers to be said in his own chapel for the soul of his father, who had died a heretic. He was very liberal to the Priests, and gave away considerable sums to poor families recommended by them; though his gifts were of more ostentation than real value. One hundred guineas, divided among twenty or thirty families, made an astonishing noise in the country.

As in a morning he walked out with his gun, he never failed to converse with, and sound the sentiments of every farmer and labourer he could find at all communicative.

His present steward was an honest, industrious man, a Protestant; yet, perceiving that he was disliked, because he was violent against the DEFENDERS, and endeavoured to arm the neighbourhood in defence of the Government, Marauder privately promised his principal tenants that he should soon be removed. He hinted to them that there was a relation of his own, and an Irishman, whom he would send in his place; he told every one also, that he himself was obliged to go over to the West Indies, to look after some property he had got there; that he purposed to dispose of the same, and lay out the money in Ireland for the benefit of his tenants; and that on his return he should make that country his future residence.

While Marauder remained in Ireland, he did not spend, in his own estimation, an idle hour, personally investigating every thing that was going forward. He was all things to all men, and put on an assumed character throughout his stay in that kingdom.

Soon after he landed, he enrolled his name among the UNITED IRISH, and took the usual oaths—oaths, the purport of which he had sworn to again and again in England. Yet, at this very time, to his aristocratical acquaintance he lamented the evils which had so lately harassed Ireland, and even pretended, when he returned from the country, to give some information which he had received from his tenants; all of which was only calculated to mislead and deceive them.

In a private conversation which he had with a gentleman of considerable consequence in the Government, he spoke, among many other things, to this effect:—

"On this, Sir, you may rely, that the people of this country will never be so foolish as to think of satisfying their wants by force.

"The pernicious doctrines of the French, indeed, have made some little progress in Dublin; but the vast numbers of the commonalty, *who are of my persuasion*, above all others, reprobate their principles. We see, Sir, our holy religion overturned by the villains in France, and we are on our guard. My worldly prospects I have already sacrificed to the faith my forefathers professed, or I should at this time be a Member of the British Parliament. We, the Catholics I mean, are, I may say, the native friends of Ireland; and the emancipating of us will be the surest guard to the Crown, the liberties of the people, and the safety of the country."

The great man was struck with what Marauder said, and owned there was much reason in his remarks.

When Marauder returned to Dublin, he found a King's messenger in waiting for him, who had heard the affair of the duel in so favourable a light, and his intended prisoner's conduct so highly extolled, that, understanding he was expected from the country in a few days, he politely awaited his arrival.

Marauder returned with him to England. He was immediately put upon his trial for the death of Captain Geutespiere. Not a witness appeared against him; and with the usual form on such occasions, he was most honourably acquitted.

He found his friend Fahany perfectly recovered of his wound, and as able and as willing as before to participate *in any honourable piece of iniquity* he chose to point out to him.

There was a scheme or two, indeed, in which the assistance of a friend, who was so little scrupulous as Fahany, would be of great service to him; but his measures were not yet ripe.

When Marauder had intended, by the assistance of Emily, to get the lovely Fanny into his power, he knew Fahany would be at any time willing to take the first off his hands. Now Emily was no where to be found, and Fanny was too much upon her guard to put herself easily into his power. He doubted not that at any time he would be able to carry her off by violence, but this force would not answer his other purposes at present.

The intentions of Marauder upon Fanny, at every moment of leisure, occurred to his mind; but the continual hurry of affairs in which he had so deeply involved himself, totally prevented his putting them in practice. This beautiful subject staggered his philosophy more than any other; as yet he had never openly declared his pretensions to her favour, and he was resolved to make sure of his prize as soon as ever he avowed himself.

The natural pride and turbulence of Marauder's temper was heightened by his late disappointment; his activity was roused, his exertions were required, and a restlessness pervaded his whole conduct, that kept his mind or his body continually in motion.

CHAPTER III.

Most of the circumstances which had come under the notice of Marauder in Ireland, he discovered to his political friends here; but his mind was pregnant with some plans, that he was afraid to trust even to the dearest of them.

Immersed in political wiles, he observed, with the highest exultation, the prospects which were open to him. He saw no competitor that had any chance of succeeding against him; and the greatest men in abilities and resolution, were either removed out of his way, or were already under his direction.

The dauntless and desperate mind of Santhorpe had already hurried him to the active scenes which were raised in the West Indies. Injuries had roused him, revenge had called him, and he was now upon the seas; his expectations and high rights were in those countries, and no fear was left that he would soon return.

Hambden Arnon, whom once Marauder had considered with a jealous eye, had of late totally withdrawn himself from their society.

Fahany, bewildered in a maze of idleness, dissipation, and debauchery, never came forward but at the instigation of his friend; and Arnon, the Lycurgus of the party, looked upon Marauder as the hero who should establish his laws.[1]

As for the orators, the men of title, of wealth, and present name, he knew human nature too well to fear that such would be the active chiefs of a mob when real danger appeared.

In spite of the sanguine temperature of the young Chief, he could

---

1 Lycurgus (fl. seventh century BC?) is the traditional founder of the Spartan constitution, and therefore associated with lawyers.

not fail observing that *the human mind in England was, as yet, by no means ripe for an universal affiliating system.* Since his return from Ireland he saw the contrast, and concluded it might take some years to enlighten this country sufficiently for the purpose; and, as he was not ignorant of the wavering gale of popularity when it wants the support of the strong blasts of power, he determined to absent himself for a while, and voluntarily undergo a temporary *ostracism,* that he might return at the critical period mature in honours.

That the long medium of absence magnifies our virtues, and diminishes our vices, the quick mind of Marauder had often remarked, and of which he was now resolved to make a proper use.

His ambitious, restless soul longed for employment. The meeting of scribes and secretaries, trifling declaimers, and harebrained enthusiasts, he already began to loath.

Marauder was not accustomed to plot and to scheme, and then to doubt of the means of execution; his undertakings, although personal, had been most bold and daring; and his high spirit, his artful temper, had conducted him through them with success.

In his late rencounter with the emigrant Officers Geutespiere and Duchesne, his name had become public in the most favourable point of view; and he had been by no means sparing of his puffs in the public papers, in one of which he had a share. Now then, by a temporary retirement from the scene of glory, did he design that his fame should take root.

Had Marauder been portionless, he would long before this have entered into the French service, to join which, even when he was in Italy, he evinced the strongest desire; but the rumours of a war with England checked him: and when it broke out with this country, his interest, as well as prudence restrained him.

To enter into the English Army for a time, was a subject Marauder was fond of broaching, solely that he might gratify himself in the pleasure he took in ridiculing it. He would ironically talk of his own services (as his father had given him a commission in the Militia before he went abroad, though he had never but once joined the Regiment), and compare his experimental knowledge with many of our English Generals.

I shall not recapitulate any of the common-place sneers he threw out on a corps, who, however little they may affect the experienced language of warriors, or pompous braggadocios, have taught their enemies that genuine courage is ever ready to meet them in the open field.

So great was Marauder's hatred become to *all our established professions* that he had a set of phrases and cant terms for each of them.

A commission in the Army he called—purchased honour;[1] the Officer was called—a red-coated trader; physicians were—regulated murderers; lawyers—licensed pickpockets, and such-like names.

But his grand virulence was directed against the Clergy, of whom many of his epithets have already appeared in this history; and the writings of any modern philosopher will present innumerable others, from the respectable Voltaire, down, down, down to the almost equally respectable Thomas Pain, Thomas Holcroft, or Thomas Dutton.*

To retire from this cold country, whose rocky soil refuses to admit the roots of the most flourishing scion from the Gallic tree of liberty, was indeed no mighty secret; yet concerning this removal *there was a secret* Marauder dared not trust to any one.

Mr. Arnon and Fahany were his confidential friends; but to be a great man, he knew that a person should only tell enough of his own secrets to get the whole of others. This Marauder practised with every success.

He had lately conceived a most bold and noble scheme; and he had soon resolved in his own mind, without communicating his thoughts to any living creature, to put it into execution. If he had a confidant in this affair, he knew he could carry it on with much more ease; but he was very unwilling to risk his secret with any one. For many weeks after his return to England did he revolve within himself whether or not he should impart it to Fahany, and again he thought that Arnon would be the best confidant.

While he was thus unresolved, he perceived Fahany, replenished

---

* [CL] The *candid* and *liberal-minded* Godwin says, in his second volume of Political Justice, page 235, after a long abuse of the Clergy: The people "are bid to look for instruction and morality to a denomination of men, *formal, embarrassed, and hypocritical, in whom the main spring of intellect is unbent, and incapable of action."*—How well-informed, how just, how profound is this wight!!! Addison, in one of his Spectators, says—"There is not any instance of weakness in the free-thinkers that raises my indignation more, than their pretending to ridicule the Christians as men of narrow understandings, and *to pass themselves upon the world for persons of superior sense, and more enlarged views."* [*Political Justice*, ed. Kramnick, Penguin edn., 572. The quotation, ostensibly from *The Spectator*, has not been traced.]

---

1 Until 1871 it was standard practice for officers to buy their commissions (i.e., warrants conferring rank) in the army.

with money, give himself up, as usual, to all manner of dissipation. In vain Marauder talked of the noble enterprise in hand, of the great benefit his money would be to him in their expected struggles in Ireland, of the folly of throwing away large sums at the gaming-table, and tried every inducement and persuasion to check his extravagance.

Fahany heard, assented, and swore he would restrain. The next night the wine entered his head, and folly his heart.

Arnon of late was become gloomy. To Marauder's enquiries he ever endeavoured to laugh it off; and, from being one of the most abstemious of men, he began to court the jolly god.

Ever fond of his son, he had been accustomed to delight in his company; now, if possible, he seemed more fond of him than ever, yet strange, avoided as much as possible his company.

This the wary, watchful Marauder soon noticed. He perceived the younger Arnon was totally lost to their cause, which, in some degree, accounted for the father's conduct; yet that his son's character was not diminished in his esteem was equally apparent, by Mr. Arnon's transferring some property to him at this time, and by frequently making him the most handsome presents.

When, therefore, Marauder had thoroughly investigated in his mind the situation of these friends, he gave up the idea of disclosing his secret to either of them, and set about arranging his affairs, that he might be able to act without the aid of any one.

For the first time he now opened his intention to Arnon and Fahany, that he was obliged to go over to the West Indies, to see about a property he had there, and which had been greatly neglected. He informed them that he purposed selling it as soon as possible after his arrival, and returning to England directly.

They pressed him earnestly, *for the public good*, to dispose of it here, and, if it was absolutely necessary, to send over an agent.

He answered it could not well be done; that he should not be absent, he hoped, in the whole, above twelve months; and that a relation of his own, whom he could in all cases rely upon as himself, would superintend his Irish concerns, and in every respect act as if he was present.—"You, perhaps, have seen," said he, "my friend and kinsman, Captain M'Ginnis?"

"Never, never," replied both; they had not even heard of his name.

"Indeed!" exclaimed Marauder; "but I am not surprised at it; 'tis to the aristocratical prejudices of my education you must ascribe the omission; no longer will a false notion of things hide from my dearest friends the most trifling of my thoughts. M'Ginnis, though the most worthy of men, is by principle a staunch Republican, from the noble examples he has witnessed in the French nation. This has induced him to throw up his commission in the Emperor's service. He writes me word that his conscience will no longer suffer him to defend the usurped power of despots, against the rites of the whole human race besides. You know in what strong aristocratical notions I was educated; these prevented my publicly noticing my kinsman, M'Ginnis; but now I see my error, I glory in my relation, and wait with impatience for his arrival from the Continent. I expect him soon in England, and I should wish to introduce him to two men I so highly esteem. He is reckoned not unlike me. He has much of the Irishman in his appearance and speech, though he has been many years in foreign service."

They both said they should be very happy to be acquainted with him.

"In case I fail," continued Marauder, "he is my heir-at-law by my mother's side, from whence my property comes. I think you will like him. I have often tried him, and can depend upon his honour. It is my intention, for the sake of concentrating my affairs, to have every kind of concern sent to me through his hands while I am absent; and as I shall write to him by each opportunity that offers, any letters or papers directed to him will be the best means to reach me. Before I depart to the West Indies, I mean to arrange with him a regular plan of correspondence; and any communication you can favour me with, I hope you will transmit immediately to him, and I'll answer for his preserving his trust inviolate."

This was the first intimation the dearest friends of Marauder received of Captain M'Ginnis, a personage who will make no little figure in the remainder of these memoirs.

CHAPTER IV.

After the conference mentioned in the last chapter, Marauder talked frequently to his acquaintance of his cousin, Captain M'Ginnis, and Arnon and Fahany were favoured with the hearing of many letters he had received from him.

For a long time he expected M'Ginnis in town every week; by and by he received a letter that he was obliged to go to Ireland; thus, by some circumstance or other, he was still disappointed.

At last he received a letter from Holyhead, that he was just landed in the packet, and would be with him on the next Monday.

Marauder invited a large party, Arnon and his son, Fahany, and above a dozen of their mutual friends, to meet him.

The dinner waited till nine o'clock; no Captain M'Ginnis came.

Very much disappointed, the company sat down. A most excellent dinner was totally spoiled;—the fish boiled to a powder—the venison roasted to a rag—the turtle soup alone passable. All the company were unhinged; the Epicurean philosophers pouted; and Marauder himself could not conceal that he was unusually alarmed.

In the midst of the second course, a loud rapping induced them to suppose that the captain was arrived. The servant entered the room with a letter for Marauder.

Bowing to his guests, he anxiously opened and read it. He rose from table, begged the company to keep their seats, and, handing the letter to Arnon, who sat next to him, immediately, without further apology, left the room.

The letter ran thus:—

"SIR,

"A gentleman, who has just strength enough to inform me that he is a relation of yours, and his name M'Ginnis, has, by the unskilfulness of a driver, been overturned in this town, and taken up for dead. I happened to be upon the spot, and am of the Faculty. It was some time before he recovered his senses sufficiently to inform me of the above. I am afraid now to give you any hopes; but, if you wish to see him alive, I earnestly entreat you to come immediately.

"I am, Sir, most respectfully,

"Your obedient, humble servant,

"J. SMITH."

Maidenhead, Monday, 5 o'clock.

Arnon read the letter aloud, and gave it to a servant, who stood in waiting, to carry it to his master.

The company saw no more of Marauder that evening.

In the morning, Arnon heard from him, that his kinsman was yet alive, but pronounced by the surgeons to be in very imminent danger.

By degrees Captain M'Ginnis got better; but not time enough for Arnon to see him before he was obliged to leave town, and to go into Yorkshire.

Fahany too was so engaged with women, wine and dice, that Captain M'Ginnis returned to Ireland without being introduced to either of these particular friends of Marauder.

Indeed at one time Marauder had half a mind to have so contrived it, that the Captain should have been personally introduced to them before he left England; but prudence advised him not.

"What then," the reader perhaps may say, "did not Marauder, after all, wish to introduce his kinsman?"

"He had no such intention from the first."

"Why not?"

"Because Captain M'Ginnis was at present but an imaginary being, whom, by and by, Marauder meant to personate himself."

Marauder, it is true, had some intention of introducing himself in masquerade to Fahany, as his cousin, the Captain; but, for once in his life, he doubted his own command over his risible faculties; and had he *entrusted his secret* to either of his worthy friends, Arnon would have the preference.

Fahany every night was at some gaming-table, and frequently at the very lowest of the kind. His money too, for he had taken up no less than £20,000 on his Irish estates, was going at a great rate. His wife's jointure, which he had not only neglected, but disputed the payment of, had lately been recovered by her trustees, and he had the pleasure of paying the gentlemen of the long robe[1] into the bargain.

Marauder did his utmost to wean him of his horrid connections, by forcing him upon some kind of employment. One while he prevailed on him to answer a ministerial pamphlet, and occasionally to write for the Reviews and Newspapers. But in vain was every argument of Marauder used to induce him to go over to Ireland, and settle upon his estate there; in this case he would probably have made a discovery to him of his own intentions. Fahany's excuse was his unsettled affairs in England; though it was evident that the lust of dissipation enslaved him.

Marauder, therefore, was obliged to be contented with his promise of coming over as soon as possible; and, wishing to get him some regular employment, which might make his abilities of use, he, at last, by dint of much entreaty, induced him to purchase a share in an anti-ministerial paper. In this he soon became a constant writer; the novelty of the thing pleased him much, the party applauded his remarks, and vanity for a time continued him in this pursuit, which generally took up those hours which otherwise were allotted to the gaming-house.

Marauder now began to prepare the means to introduce himself in his new character, with full powers and consequence; well knowing that he could neither give his kinsman too much authority, or that it would be used against his own interest. For this purpose he

---

1 Lawyers.

not only wrote frequently to his steward in Ireland upon the occasion; but to every person the least worthy of attention on his estate, he sent a formal notice, that till his return from the West Indies, they were to consider Captain M'Ginnis as himself; nor did he omit the reason—on account of his near kindred, and long-tried honour and friendship.

That there had been such a person as M'Ginnis, of his mother's side, was well known in Ireland, who, at a very early age, went into the sea-service, and the vessel was said to have been lost. This person's *name* Marauder fished up from the bottom of the ocean—got him a commission in the Imperial service—supported him on a liberal allowance while he remained there—now generously owned him as his heir—and, with the utmost liberality and confidence, gave him the management of his whole property while he himself was absent from Europe.

These particulars of his imaginary kinsman, Marauder at times gave forth.

In the course of a few months, having familiarized his friends to the name of M'Ginnis, he was very sedulous that his cousin should be known by the confidential members of the GRAND DIABOLISM, and other societies to which he belonged.

This was no difficult matter for him to do. When he informed them of the absolute necessity of his going to the West Indies, he mentioned Captain M'Ginnis as a man devoted to their cause, whom principle had driven from a chief command, and the expectations of the highest preferment in the Imperial service, and who now could give them the best information, concerning the general state of Ireland, and more particularly of those parts where his own property was situated. Whenever, too, he was able to produce early information of the plans and designs of either party in that kingdom, his truly worthy and respectable kinsman, Captain Patrick M'Ginnis, was sure to be the person from whom he received the intelligence.

CHAPTER V.

It may not be amiss to remark, that the chief circumstance which occasioned that depression of spirits in Mr. Arnon, originally arose from perceiving his son totally lost to that party, of which he had ever flattered himself Hambden would have been the principal leader.

What Marauder was so likely to be, he doubted not his own interest and connections, his son's abilities and knowledge, would easily have made him.

When first the father perceived that spirit of religious enquiry, which Wilson had raised, began to exert itself more and more in his son, he endeavoured, by the most plausible arguments of which he was master, by reasoning, and by ridicule, to check it entirely.

To one of these discourses of his father, Hambden replied—

"If they (the Christians) are wrong, Sir, are we right?"

"So far right," replied Mr. Arnon, "as not to be prejudiced to their opinions."

"Of their mysterious opinions," continued Hambden, "I am not yet competent to judge; but it is that wonderful system of morality, which the Christian religion has opened to mankind, that makes me fear I have been all my life in an error."

"How is it superior to the general class, which you and I, and every good man observe?"

"I mean not to condemn your conduct, Sir; I am too well satisfied my own has not been right. Christianity, Sir, is that purity of principle, which will not, by any mental persuasion, commit that which is wrong, even if it is to produce the greatest benefit."

The father seemed affected.—

"Surely, if the good which follows outweighs the evil, the latter becomes a virtue."

"Christianity says otherwise, and I am firmly convinced."

"But wrong, or evil, depends upon the situation of the person, or circumstances, at the time."

"To an heathen, Sir, it did; but never to a Christian. He is ever to do that which may conduce to the benefit of his fellow-creatures, and to rely upon God for the issue. One grand rule—to do unto others as he would be done unto—is, at all seasons, in prosperity and adversity, to be the bias of his actions."

"I see men act otherwise, and even among the Ministers of religion themselves."

"That, Sir, is the common argument against Christianity; but it certainly is none at all: for any law may be good, although the persons who have promised to keep it, break it."

"Christianity affects a perfection human nature is incapable of."

"True, Sir; but it is the duty of each member to approach as near as possible to this superior excellence; and therefore it is a duty incumbent on the very best of men, to endeavour to be better."

"Such great perfection I cannot think the Deity either expects or requires."

"God, who is all perfection himself, must necessarily rejoice to see others approach to the same. Our earthly wisdom is solely of use to us, as it makes us more honest, virtuous, and good—more fit for another world; for, whatever may be our endowments of mind or body, *here we cannot stay!* Petty faults or crimes may be forgiven in the ignorant and uninstructed; but in your case or mind, Sir, even in a moral sense alone, how severely would the world condemn us, were *we* to be guilty of a breach of any trust, or of *private* or *public* dishonesty!"

Oftentimes, when his son Hambden talked in this way, would Mr. Arnon start from his seat, and walk about with a confusion he could not conceal. At other times he would hastily leave the room. Hambden could by no means explain the cause. Mr. Arnon did not, on that account, yield to his son's arguments, and Hambden would often fancy his father was displeased; yet his conduct towards him always shewed the contrary. In short, it clearly appeared that, by conversations similar to these, the son raised certain sensations in his father's mind, that evidently made him uneasy.

In other conversations, Hambden expounded more at length, wishing his father to study those truths which he himself had so lately begun to be acquainted with; but he ever spoke with that modesty and affection, that Mr. Arnon had not the smallest reason to be displeased. Neither was he so in any respect, was apparent by the property which (as was before said) he about that time transferred to his son.

There certainly was much liberality of sentiment, as well as generosity of conduct, in Mr. Arnon's thus acting; because he had every reason to suppose that his son was likely to form a connection in a family, which, however respectable it might be, was of totally different principles from those that Mr. Arnon supported.

The worthy Dean, who had been the patron of Mr. Lockeridge, and one of the executors of the Duke of Silsbury, had, from the introduction of Wilson, greatly noticed Mr. Hambden Arnon. Happily for Hambden, he had become a convert to the principles of Christianity ere he had yet seen the pretty Anna, the amiable daughter of this dignified churchman; or it is not to be doubted, that his forsaken party would have given all the merit of the conversion to the bewitching eyes of the fair Christian.

When Hambden first became acquainted with the Dean, his family was in the country; and it was not till many months after that he became convinced how superior the female character shines, when clothed in the pure garb of religion.

From this period, indeed, his intimacy with the Dean's family had been most sedulously cultivated; and it was generally supposed that

Mr. Arnon's consent was the only thing wanting to his son, that he might publicly declare the wish of his heart to be, by the hand of the lovely Anna, favoured with so respectable an alliance.

Wilson was well acquainted with the sentiments of Hambden on this subject, but which, knowing how contrary it would be to his father's principles, he had not yet mentioned to him.

Mr. Arnon had not been thrice in the company of Wilson before he perceived not only how destructive to his own ideas were that young man's sentiments, but also, from his son's partiality to his new acquaintance, how great was his influence over him; and with pleasure he heard that his stay was to be so short in town.

None of the conversations I have alluded to between the father and son, took place till long after Wilson left London, but chiefly while Marauder was in Ireland.

These conversations had invariably recoiled on Mr. Arnon himself; and he now resolved to try more publicly, if he could, by argument, shame, or ridicule, to turn Hambden aside from his present notions, so hostile to his birth, education, and connections.

CHAPTER VI.

For this purpose Mr. Arnon invited Marauder and Fahany to meet Hambden, and purposely omitted asking any other company; he told them the object he had in view, and earnestly requested them to lend their assistance.

Of the abilities of both he knew his son had a very high opinion; and of Fahany he had lately remarked to his father, that he was astonished a man so well read, and of such high literary abilities, should consume his time, his health, and property among the most depraved of both sexes.

The gross conduct of a certain Clergyman in a very conspicuous situation, which at that time was talked of in every company, easily led to the subject Mr. Arnon was so desirous to introduce.[1]

---

1   There was no shortage of clerical scandals in the years leading up to the publication of *The Infernal Quixote*. In 1793, for instance, the Rev. Richard Burgh was found guilty of attempting to set fire to the King's Bench Prison where he had been imprisoned for debt, and in 1797 the Rev. Henry Bate disqualified himself from continuing as the minister of Bradwell-juxta-Mare because of his notorious hunting activities, which included killing a fox on the roof of his own church. See Andrew Barrow, *The Flesh is Weak. An Intimate History of the Church of England* (London: Hamish Hamilton, 1980).

"I think," said Fahany, "he was a sensible man; though I should have liked him better if he had had less hypocrisy."

"Hypocrisy," replied Arnon, "is every thing to a priest. 'Tis not only his garb, but his very subsistence."

"It is truly astonishing to me," continued Fahany, "that enlightened as this nation is, and with the glorious example of the French before them, the farce of religion is not entirely given up. If I still wanted an argument to convince me, it is the conduct of the very teachers themselves."

"That argument, I think, is against you," said Hambden.

"How so?" asked Fahany.

"If the Christian religion flourishes without any assistance—if they, whose duty it is to instruct others, neglect their trust—if the leading men in the kingdom, who profess these principles, are the first to violate them? I think all this is an argument of the truth of the religion: it cannot be the contrary."

"Good arguments!" said Fahany, ironically. "My modest friend Boccace has something like it in his first tale.[1] What that witty writer mentioned in jest, I had no idea, Hambden, you would dress up in earnest. Am I to think you so?"

"Boccace's hatred of priests, or his loose morals, cannot affect his arguments; but I had not *your friend* in my thoughts. As for *the Ministers of religion*, I do not believe them worse than other people."

"In Italy," said Marauder, "they were one *half* pimps, and the rest knaves."*

"*My* short acquaintance in Italy," replied Hambden, "found them too austere for the one, and too simple for the other. In France, I

---

* [CL] I presume Marauder spoke with the same latitude as the renowned Rowland Hill, when he said—"The poor man who roasts or broils his meat, loses HALF in the fire; the poor man who boils his meat, loses HALF in the water," &c. &c. *Vide* R.H's. Advice to the Poor, in all newspapers. [Rowland Hill (1744-1833), minister of the Evangelical Surrey Chapel in London, and a controversial preacher and writer.]

---

1 The first tale in the *Decameron* of Giovanni Boccaccio (1313-75) tells of a debauched man who, finding himself on his death-bed a long way away from home, passes himself off to his confessor as a man of great piety and comes to be venerated as a saint. The story ends with the narrator's satirical speculation as to whether those who pray for intercession to this "saint," who is actually surely in Hell, will be any the worse off as a result, and, by extension, whether the Church will suffer by the deception.

know, the parish Priests, the great body of regular Clergy, were the first patterns of piety and morality; in England, I am intimately acquainted but with one, and he, though a Dignitary in the Church, is an honour to his profession."

"I understand," said Marauder, with an arch look, "that the Dean of Winterbourn has a very pretty daughter."

Hambden coloured, but said—"Of the daughter, Sir, I was not speaking; the father's excellent character, I believe, no one will deny. But all this is nothing to the purpose; for, whatever may be the conduct of the Ministers of religion, the doctrine cannot alter or change."

"I suppose," said Marauder, laughing, "you have been reading the Bible lately?"

"I have," replied Hambden, gravely.

"And did you ever meet before such incoherent tales, such improbable, such strange things?" remarked Fahany.

"As what?" asked Hambden.

"These miracles," replied Fahany.

"They do not pretend to be otherwise," replied Hambden.

"And you believe them?" cried Marauder.

"Yes, in part, at least, I do. I begin to think them not so unworthy of credit as I once did."

"Pshaw! you cannot be in earnest," exclaimed Marauder.

"I hope also," said Fahany, "you believe those which Vespasian, the Roman Emperor, did. You cannot be ignorant that he also performed miracles."[1]

Hambden Arnon, with great steadiness, replied—"I have heard many Deists quote the passage you allude to from Tacitus; but it is strange they are not candid enough to tell the particulars. It has not, Mr. Fahany, I presume, escaped your memory, that in the cases of the two persons reputed to be cured by the Emperor, one of whom Vespasian restored to sight, and the other from lameness—that the physicians examined them, and said—'In this man the power of sight *was not wholly extinct*, and would return were the obstacles removed; the other man's joints were distorted, and might be restored by regular propping and straining.'—To a man just coming to the Empire, do you think the physicians were disposed to be flatterers? I need not repeat to you that these were the only two miracles Vespasian was ever said to have performed."

---

1   See Cornelius Tacitus, *The Histories* (c. AD 109), bk. IV, section 81.

"You cannot suppose I believe them more than yourself," replied Fahany. "Now give me your opinion of these;" and with great exactness he immediately quoted some of the most remarkable passages from the Old Testament, which have been again and again mentioned by the adversaries of Christianity for these last two hundred years.—"All these do you believe?" said he.

Hambden replied—"What tells me they were not so?"

"Reason," answered Fahany.

"How is human reason to judge of any thing out of the common course of nature?" Hambden continued; "yet there are so many passages, I candidly confess, that I do not comprehend; and considering the language in which they were originally written, and which is now almost lost—the vast number of years ago—how often they have been translated and transcribed, and most probably altered, I shall never attempt to defend a *verbal* criticism, which perhaps was originally occasioned by the folly, error, or mistake of some one long since."

"How can the word of God err?" said Marauder, with a contemptuous sneer.

"The word of God cannot err," replied Hambden, calmly; "but the history of that word, written or copied by a human being, liable to error, may. Some time ago the eighth commandment was printed wrong. Was the real commandment false on that account? As such, some parts of the Holy Scripture may have been injured."

"If the Scriptures were the word of God," said Mr. Arnon, "they must necessarily be the word of truth. But in every passage where the sun, moon, and stars are mentioned, they are spoken of as subservient to this world, and according to the notions of the vulgar and illiterate. Is this, Hambden, reconcilable to truth?"

"Certainly, Sir," replied his son. "We speak the same language now, though we pretend to know otherwise. When I say—the sun rises—there is a new moon—the earth is immoveable—the stars do not shine in the day-time—and many other expressions in daily use, I speak to the common ideas and understanding of mankind; I do not deceive, and no one would think of calling my words a falsity. So also did Moses, Joshua, David, Solomon, and the rest who assisted in writing the Bible, speak according to their own comprehension, and the people's received opinion. It was the word of God, his command, that was revealed to us; and his wisdom and knowledge, these were left to future ages, by degrees, in part to discover."

"I presume," said Marauder, "these *prophets*, in the present day, would be called *fools*."

"Very likely. They never used religion as a worldly wisdom, that is, for worldly purposes."

Marauder did not notice the application, but proceeded with that plausible and reflective manner he could at pleasure assume.—"Few men, I presume, Mr. Hambden, have more fully considered this subject than myself; few, I believe, have been more severe victims in the cause of religion that I have. Educated, after the strictest manner, in the principles of those dissentient from the Church of Rome, my early reason and watchful conscience shewed me they were wrong, and I adopted the original customs of the primitive Christians; but when my mind was expanded—to your most excellent father, and my worthy friend, Fahany, I gratefully acknowledge the force of truth and learning—I began to think for myself. No more shall the tricks of priestcraft deceive me; no more will I give credit to improbable, imperfect fictions; the mask of antiquity no longer shall appear to my view as reason, truth, and virtue. I have before laughed at your arguments, as I could not conceive it possible that you, brought up in none of my prejudices, could be in earnest; that you, with such an education, and such a father, could listen to the tales of men notorious for their ignorance and illiterateness. I need not recapitulate Mr. Arnon's arguments, concerning their total want of common philosophy, and all human learning; nor need I point out how spurious and doubtful most of the supposed writers are."

Even Hambden, who so well knew the man, was astonished at the specious art of the conscientious Marauder; but, with a smile, he replied—"As the conduct you have thought proper to adopt, Sir, must be left out of *the question*, I cannot fully *answer* you; but thus it appears to me, that there was no necessity for the peculiar servants of the Deity to be SCHOLARS and ASTRONOMERS, because they were PROPHETS. Neither does it lessen the Holy Scriptures, whether certain parts were written by those whose names they bear. It is from that excellent spirit which every where shines out in them—it is from the general temper of the whole, and particularly the prophecies, that I believe them to be true."

"And do you think the person called Jesus Christ was a Messiah, Saviour, and all that?" said Fahany.

"I am more and more induced to be of that opinion," replied Hambden.

"Mr. Hambden," exclaimed Fahany, "what can have possessed you? Will you sacrifice your reason and your judgement to the stale poetical fictions of a disgraced, an infamous, a vagabond people? Knaves invented the tale, and fools believed it."

"Were Grotius, Bacon, Milton, Newton, Locke, Hale, Addison, Lyttleton, Blackstone, Sir William Jones, without referring to other great names, or mentioning any of the Ministers of Christianity, FOOLS? Or were illiterate fishermen, born in ignorance, brought up in poverty, who suffered disgrace and punishment while living, and died as ignominious malefactors, KNAVES?* By whom were they led astray? By a poor and peaceable man like themselves, who neither aimed at, nor would accept power, riches, honours, pleasure, or any of the good things of this world, and patiently suffered ignominy, tortures, and death. Many have been the enthusiasts and impostors, who have endeavoured to deceive mankind, and to impose on the world pretended revelations; and some of them, from pride, obstinacy, or perhaps principle, have gone so far as to lay down their lives rather than retract; *but where can history shew one who ever made his own sufferings and death a necessary part of his original plan, and essential to his mission? This Jesus Christ actually did; he foresaw, foretold, declared their necessity, and patiently endured them.* When I contemplate the divine lessons, the perfect precepts, the beautiful discourses, and the consistent conduct of this person, I cannot but think *he was more than a man.*"

Fahany, who, at all times irritable, and without any command of his passions, now felt himself assailed in his tenderest point, burst at once from that coolness with which he had before heard Hambden, and exclaimed—

"Where was this wonderful man born? In Bethlehem of Judea, they say, a contemptible town of a more contemptible province of the Romans. From what people did he come? A slavish, base, and conquered nation, the outcasts of the earth. What man of note, fame, or consequence ever saw or heard of him? A few years were these great things, in which all the world were to be concerned, acting! in the same low, mean, despicable country! How do I know they were ever performed? How can I tell he ever existed?"

"Though you insult me, Sir, by your warmth," said Hambden, rather sharply, but with a determined steadiness, "you, without meaning it, honour my subject. If, by this intemperate conduct, the truth is to be investigated—if reason and argument are thus—"

---

* [CL] Part of this reply is, I believe *verbatim* from Soame Jenyn's Evidences of the Christian Religion. Any other *plagiarisms* of this kind, the *candid* reader will excuse; the diabolistical critic, of whatever philosophical sect he may be, may make the most of them, with the full contempt of the writer.

Fahany had recovered himself, and saw his hasty behaviour in its proper light. Interrupting Hambden, therefore, he, with that politeness he could with pleasure adopt, apologized for his warmth; and then, with the most studied calmness, proposed the same questions in a very different manner.

"On this part of the subject, Sir," replied Hambden, "I am thoroughly persuaded that you are *as well* informed, if not *far better*, than myself. I shall beg leave to answer your question with a few others; and, with your permission we will then drop the subject, as I am sure conviction will not follow on either side."

"I beg, Sir, you'll propose what you think proper, and I'll give you as direct an answer as is in my power."

"It is all that I require. Do you, Sir, from the books you have read, and the information you have by that means received, think there ever was such a person as the Christians call Jesus Christ?"

Fahany paused a little—"Why, yes."

"Do you suppose he was born at Bethlehem of Judæa?"

"Most likely."

"Did he derive his pedigree from David and from Judah?"

"That I know nothing about."

"Has any one of the least authority denied it?"

"I don't know that they have."

"According to the writings of the Jews, was it from among their own countrymen, the tribe of Judah, the lineage of David, that the Messiah was to come?"

"I believe it was."

"Have you reason to suppose that this Jesus, the reputed son of Joseph and Mary, of the lineage of David and Judah, was a good or bad man?"

"It is a thing I care not about."

"The accounts you have read of him in sacred and profane writers, must induce you to think one or the other."

"I never heard any thing against his moral character, but his setting himself up to be better and greater than others."

"Can you prove he was not?"

"I have nothing to say against him as a man.—Go on."

"Were there in those days at which he was said to be born, such men as Herod the Tetrarch, and afterwards Pontius Pilate, and many others mentioned in the books called the New Testament?"

"The Roman History acknowledges there were."

"Did the historical circumstances, mentioned throughout the New Testament, happen in the time, place, and manner there recorded?"

"Of all these things I have no doubt. The writer, whoever he was, would probably take care not to err in this respect. But I do not believe that he was born of a virgin—that he performed miracles—that he rose from the dead—and all the rest of the wonderful tales mentioned."

"You cannot prove *it was not so*; nor have I any proof but the assertion of his friends that *it was*. But it is from their assertion, from his own words, conduct, and doctrines, that I have lately begun to believe the whole to be true. Since, then, Sir, so much must necessarily depend upon *faith*, I will say no more, but that I shall be happy to see the day when we shall be all of the same opinion."

The conversation now took a different turn; Marauder was completely tired of the former subject—a subject to him most unmeaning and uninteresting.

Marauder could be religious, or the contrary, when the argument suited his purpose; but to dispute for what he called principle, was in his opinion the height of folly.—"How could you gratify the fool," said he to Fahany, when they had departed, "by talking of such nonsense?"

"More madman than fool, I believe," said the other. "Who would have supposed from him such notions, so contrary to his birth, his education, and connections?"

"You, I think, were almost as mad. I am astonished you should think such trifles worth a serious dispute; for my part, I am no more inclined to be a Vanini, than a Peter or a Paul."[1]

Marauder ever felt himself elevated when he reviewed his *own philosophy*; he continued his remarks with no small portion of blasphemy, and at last—"Yes, indeed, religion is a good thing if a man knows how to use it. It is a chain upon the hands of a fool, but a man of sense will use it as a scourge. When I was in Ireland—" Marauder perceived he was going too far in his concerns—"But enough, and too much of this. Come, Fahany, I'll go with you this evening to her Grace's faro-bank. I have a cool hundred in my pocket, which, as a country-woman, I can spare the dear creature. Remember, tomorrow you promised to finish for me that parody from Aristophanes. I must see it in our Saturday's paper."

Fahany assented; and they proceeded to the house of the illustri-

---

1   Lucilio Vanini (c.1585-1619), an Italian free-thinker, condemned to be burned at the stake in Toulouse for atheism and witchcraft.

ous dame, widow of a Prince, sister of a King, and head-proprietor of a gaming-table.[1]

CHAPTER VII.

From the conversation that had passed at Mr. Arnon's, he saw how little hopes he had of realizing his ambitious prospects in the person of his son Hambden; and from this time he ever avoided any discourse with his son that could lead to the subject.

A few mornings after he remarked to Marauder that he greatly feared his son was lost to their party.

Marauder, ever wary and thoughtful, replied—"I trust the loss of Mr. Hambden Arnon will not prove the cause of weakening your means."

After a little more conversation, and Marauder had remarked upon his generosity towards Hambden, he insidiously hinted that, as a citizen of the world—as the friend of human nature—as a lover of political justice, more glorious cares demanded his attention, than weak filial considerations. And before Marauder left him, he spoke in plainer language, and told him that his son had deserted the cause of *reason* and *truth*; and it required him to be very cautious that the property he possessed, did not fall into those hands that would employ it against the glorious cause in which himself and friends were together engaged.

Marauder, in thus advising Arnon to leave his property from his son, not only gratified his own dislike against Hambden, but gained for himself the next best chance of possessing it.

Most highly, indeed, did Arnon think of Marauder; he knew his abilities to be great, his ambition greater; his courage and his prudence he had often seen tried; and in every trait of his character, that heroic DIABOLISM shone forth, that shewed the greatness, the boldness, the unrestrained freedom of his soul:—therefore, when Arnon

---

1 This is probably Anne, Duchess of Cumberland (1743-1808), daughter of the first Earl of Carlhampton and wife (from 1771, after her first husband had died) of Henry Frederick, Duke of Cumberland, brother of George III. Since the Duke of Cumberland had died in 1790, Anne was certainly the widow of a prince, but Lucas's claim that she was the sister of a king might derive either from the fact that her brother-in-law was George III (who disapproved of her) or from the arrest of her own brother, Temple Simon Luttrell, in France during the Revolution and his captors' public exhibition of him as "the brother of the King of England."

expected his son from America, he was in hopes the similarity of their studies would unite them together, and that they would become a second Pylades and Orestes.[1] Neither did he apprehend that their prospects would interfere. Marauder then seemed to follow the high road of Aristocracy; Hambden he hoped would rise through the rugged track of Democracy.

All these fond expectations were now vanished, and even to himself his son began to be lost; for every interview alone with Hambden had lately brought to his mind reflection and remembrance, which, in defiance of his frequent boasts, told him that there was such a thing as conscience.

As the principal hero of this history is about to leave England, it may not be amiss to see in what situation he leaves the other characters, who have been presented to our notice.

Emily Bellaire, retired from the gay world, was become an inmate in the house of a country Clergyman, from whose example and her own dear-bought experience, she soon became as sedulous to improve the beauties of her *mind*, as she had formerly been of those of her *person*.

Fanny resided at Richmond with the same friends, not more lovely than beloved, not more beloved than worthy to be so. Already the fluttering beaux began to buzz around her; already the flattery of love and admiration stole into her ears, and proved her understanding was as excellent, and her mind as pure as the beautiful case that enclosed them.

Wilson, still at the Castle, was entered into a corps of which the young Duke of Silsbury was the Colonel; whose high rank in life had neither removed his friendship from Wilson, nor bore him away from the humble virtues of mildness and urbanity, which had ever adorned his character.

The military garb which Wilson sometimes wore, had not yet infused into him any bolder or more daring hopes when in the presence of Fanny. Some slight unintended remark of Mr. Townsend's had put a stop to their correspondence; and the number of fashionable youths, who assiduously courted her favour, some of whom had already declared their pretensions, began to make him more clearly understand those sensations, which had been gaining ground so fast in his heart.

---

1 In Euripides' (480-406 BC) play, *Iphigenia in Tauris*, Pylandes accompanied his friend Orestes, Prince of Mycenae, to Tauris, to take back to Athens a statue of Artemis.

Rattle, with young Harrety, in the autumn travelled through a great part of Scotland; the latter was now at the University, and Rattle had not yet been able to get rid of his chambers in the Temple. In the following spring they have agreed to make a tour through Wales; and Rattle is positively fixed, that he will then give up every thing of and belonging to the law.

The Reverend Mr Lockeridge, in the true enjoyment of his connubial lot, sees his eldest son, as a reward for his attention to this studies, ride by his side at the head of the foremost hounds; and 'Squire Thickset, who keeps the hounds, and has ten thousand a year, declares he shall marry his only daughter, Bet, who is already in her tenth year, and young Lockeridge two years older.

Dr. Line was at one time somewhat affronted by the astrological system; but, by a lucky turn in his calculation, every thing goes on more favourably than ever. Expounding on other celestial subjects, he has entirely resigned to his friend Lockeridge, whose virtues he thinks are not much inferior to those of Nicholas Culpepper, Dr. Sibley, &c. &c. &c.

Such was the situation of the more principal characters recorded in this history, when, in the beginning of the year 1796, Marauder prepared to go to Ireland, and assume the person of Captain M'Ginnis.

He settled with the most trusty of his friends a cipher correspondence, which he was to give to his cousin M'Ginnis: for he told them that he should first go to Ireland, and, having settled every thing with his kinsman, embark from thence for the West Indies.

The day at length arrived, when Marauder, having arranged every thing to his satisfaction, and having received accounts that affairs in the sister kingdom were hastening, with rapid steps, to a crisis, took a farewell of his acquaintance on this side of the water, and, high in hopes, deep in projects, prepared to execute his plan.

Before he embarked, he could not fail to congratulate himself on his prudent foresight, which had prevented his entrusting Fahany with his secret; who, was so far from preparing to return to Ireland, where he had been chosen to a high commission among the United Brethren, that he was again trying to raise more money on his property.

He had met with some difficulties in raising further mortgages on his Irish estates, and was endeavouring to make a title to sell some property in England; for this reason, he wanted his wife to live with him for a season, till, by her assistance, he had succeeded. This her friends violently opposed; nor was the lady, who had had too fatal an experience of her husband's reformation, again inclined to risk her health and happiness with a dissipated, unprincipled man.

Marauder had foreseen, from the first, that if he came into military service with Fahany, he could not fail being known to him, and this had almost induced him to discover his intentions. But now things appeared very different; and he had no idea that Fahany would be able to join him for some months, and most probably that he would never have resolution to break from his old haunts, and come over at all.

In the midst of his higher views, Marauder had not neglected his more trifling affairs.

He did not sell his landed property in England, lest it should lead to any suspicions; but he mortgaged the whole for as much as it would fetch. The house itself, at Hazleton, had been let some months; and a little before he left London, he let also his town-house for a year, under the care of his steward, Imphell, not choosing to dispose of it for a longer period, at a time, as he said, it was uncertain how soon he might return from the West Indies.

The small house he had on the Downs, he kept in his own hands. The *grand Society* had their private committee meetings here, and kept many papers of considerable consequence, the place of which was only known to Marauder and Arnon.

Neither did he think it prudent to take any servant with him; his haughty, absolute, and determined temper had ever prevented any one from being attached to him, and therefore, in this case, he more easily dispensed with any attendance.

CHAPTER VIII.

Marauder is for a while off the stage, and Patrick M'Ginnis, Esq., lately a Captain in the Imperial service, appears in his room, and makes his entrance in Dublin.

A complete metamorphosis in dress and person had now taken place.

The long well-powdered hair of Marauder, had yielded to a close curly crop, which Captain M'Ginnis daily rubbed with a liquid to make it still blacker. M'Ginnis's whiskers were long, and nearly met round this chin; some hair appeared upon his upper lip—his eyebrows were died black—his complexion was frequently washed with a docoction of walnuts—he wore the undress of the Imperial service—and a large cocked hat with a cockade in it.

M'Ginnis, unlike his cousin Marauder, spoke with the Irish twang (which a few months' practice, when he was alone, had made perfect), and seemed to take large quantities of snuff, a thing Marauder had never been seen to do.

It will not be amiss to remark, that while Marauder was on his travels, he had often been for weeks together with the Imperial troops; ever partial to a military life, he had with avidity noticed their discipline, manners, &c. &c. and this first gave him the idea of making M'Ginnis a Captain in the Imperial service.

From any ignorance in military matters he had not the smallest fears of detection; and the only thing he required to complete the deception, was the name of a regiment, if by accident he should meet with an Imperial Officer, that he might not be in danger of exposing himself. After a little time he satisfied his mind in this also; but he had never occasion to use it, so as to be in the remotest degree liable to detection.

It is necessary to mention these minutiæ, to shew the great art and circumspection of the hero of this tale; who, with cool and deliberate reasoning, and swayed by no other passion than uncertain ambition, boldly dared the most adventurous schemes.

Captain M'Ginnis purposed to make but a short stay, for the present, in Dublin.

He delivered a great many recommendatory letters from his kinsman Marauder; but as he had not yet assumed his character long enough to have a perfect command of his features, he was not over anxious to see the persons to whom they were addressed.

The day before he left Dublin, he had the resolution to dine with a large party of gentlemen and ladies, to whom he was well known before; and with high satisfaction perceived that no one had the most distant supposition of his being the same person.

His likeness to Mr. Marauder was of course remarked, but by no means universally assented to. The ladies thought him much handsomer, the men older in his look, but not so haughty and formal in his address. The first he was not supposed to hear; but to the second he replied that he was four years older than his cousin.

Marauder had not staid any where long enough to be seen in his real colours; M'Ginnis therefore was in less danger of being discovered.

Marauder had affected unusual reserve; M'Ginnis put on the utmost ease and familiarity.

Marauder had spoken in the highest terms of his cousin; and the other now, with interest, returned the compliment.

In short, never did two of the most finished gamesters play with better success into one another's hands, than did the conduct of Marauder prepare the way for M'Ginnis.

The first news M'Ginnis received from England was the marriage of Hambden Arnon, which took place in less than a week after he had taken his leave of his English friends.

Marauder's manners were so authoritative, that he had obtained an influence over Mr. Arnon the elder, he could not easily shake off. This had restrained him from speaking to his son concerning the connection he well knew Hambden had formed with the family of the Dean. The very day on which Marauder left England, Arnon wrote the following letter to his son, who was at that time on a visit to the Priest.

"To influence by the arbitrary ties of kindred when the argumentative power of reason fails, is contrary, my dear son, to the principles of your father. Though I lament the change of your mental opinions, I cannot but applaud your excellent conduct towards me; I wish to assure you, by my actions as well as words, that I do not behold it with indifference; and, as I have heard by many a tongue where your future hopes of domiciliary happiness are fixed, I give you the full consent, and fond wishes of a father that you may succeed in your choice. Your silence, my dear Hambden, I know proceeded from affection towards me; let me shew you I am not wanting. I beg, therefore, as a pledge of my love, that you will accept, for a wedding present, the house you are so partial to in Wales, with the small property adjoining; and believe me that the moment I hear of your marriage, I shall participate in your happiness.

"THOMAS ARNON."

This was the only thing wanting to complete the felicity of Hambden. He waited on his father immediately, to thank him for his kindness. The Dean and his fair daughter lent a willing ear to his suit; and he was married to the lovely Anna the day after he returned from his father.

The house in Wales was in a few weeks handsomely furnished, and prepared for their reception.

The account of this marriage was enclosed to M'Ginnis in a letter from Fahany, to be forwarded to Marauder. Arnon also wrote to his friend by the same post; but, without entering into any particulars, he solely mentioned that his son was married. The beginning of their correspondence *to M'Ginnis* was short, formal, and uninteresting; and thus early a difficulty arose that could not easily be obviated; as M'Ginnis could not answer, reason, remark, or in any respect notice the letters written to Marauder, without the discovery of the original plan, or the appearance of a breach of trust.

Often was M'Ginnis, at the commencement of his career, tempted to disclose the whole, that he might at once sweep away the petty obstacles to a more easy correspondence; but so self-opiniative was he, that he could rarely be persuaded he had acted unwisely; and, though he had confidence in no man, he was not willing his friends should perceive how little he trusted them.

Marauder's letters introduced M'Ginnis also to some leading members of the Society of United Irishmen, and again, in due form and order, he took the necessary oaths, which he had before sworn to as Marauder.

His plans thus arranged, without loss of time he went down to his seat in the country.

CHAPTER IX.

Marauder had received from his late steward, when he was in Ireland, every book and paper that was of the least consequence. Captain M'Ginnis, therefore, had very little trouble in taking possession of the accounts, and in settling the other affairs, which, as steward to his cousin, it was necessary for him to do.

M'Ginnis's first case, after he came down to the estate, was to make himself familiar among the tenants, and with the situation of the property, that a prior knowledge might not appear, and give the remotest suspicion of his ever having been there before.

He was, for this purpose, up very early, riding all the day about the farms and grounds, and enquiring the name of every person he met. He had not resided in the country a week, before he had been within every farmhouse; and he got a list of the names of each tenant who rented any part of the property, even to the smallest cottage.

The whole of Marauder's property was in the Province of Munster, and most of it in the county of Tipperary, on the north-west side.

The family mansion, where M'Ginnis first took up his residence, was pleasantly situated;—but, further into the wild part of the country, where its face is more mountainous, and the soil rocky, there is an old house, that has for ages stood, a monument to the savage life, which could prefer so dreary a spot, solely as a place of strength, and as being most difficult of access.

When Cromwell conquered the kingdom, and liberally bestowed some of the first estates on his followers, did the family of Marauder come into possession. This house was then considerably enlarged and fortified; and for years they lived in a continual kind of petty and private warfare with their neighbours. When James II came to the throne, the old soldier was dead; and his son, more polite, embraced the religious forms of those around him, and built the new mansion; but the flattering hopes of the family were all blown away with the flight of James, and the opinions of the Marauders had ever since continued inveterate to the Protestant establishment.

Some distance below the wild spot, where the ruins of the old residence, in tolerable repair, yet stand, runs the famous river Shannon, which boasts itself far larger than the Thames, but here about sixty miles from its source.

The trees which surrounded the house on the eastern side, wherever the soil would admit their growth, were chiefly remarkable for their wild and rugged appearance, but greatly added to the strength of the place; and M'Ginnis, at his first visit, observed that very strong forces, ignorant of the country, would with difficulty be able to attack a few resolute natives.

Under the pretence of shooting, he considerably amended the condition of the building; and put some servants into it, that he might sleep there whenever he thought proper.

The walls of the court-yard were repaired—a deep ditch, which surround the old building, was cleaned out—and the drawbridge, which had for years been down, was provided with a chain, and made to answer its original intention.

All this M'Ginnis did under pretence of protecting himself from the different parties that molested the country, when he made the house his shooting residence.

Early in the month of May, of the year 1796, M'Ginnis left his country residence, where he had remained not inactive the whole winter, and went to Dublin, on purpose to investigate the present intentions of the leaders of the Union.

A few particular acquaintance of Marauder's he was not sorry to find were absent, which made him attend the debates with less apprehensions of being known. He soon discovered his friends were employed in a mission to their French allies; and in the course of the year, he understood that L—d E—w—d F—tz—d and Art. O'C——r, Esq. had had an interview with the renowned General Hoche, in Switzerland that summer.[1] This Officer, he knew, was of the same party as the Commissioner whom Marauder had met in England; and he was certain the General had been informed of the state of affairs in both countries according to his representation: every reason therefore did he entertain that the mission of his friends would be successful.

He now became a most regular attendant of the private meetings of the grand Committee of United Irishmen, of which he had been chosen a member; nor was it long before his zeal and abilities, exclusive of the warm recommendatory letters of his kinsman, pointed him out to his associates as a sensible man, and a most able Officer. But very soon he found many difficulties arise, and obstacles he had in the beginning no thought of; and these were all from his own party.

He had come over to Ireland under the idea of an immediate rising of the people; but he found the leaders unprepared, the people unarmed. Yet, in defiance of these obstacles, he gave it as his opinion that there should be a general rising all over the kingdom, without loss of time.

"What are not the leaders ready?" said he; "a brave man always is. As for the people, are they to be taught the refinements of discipline, or how are they to learn the use of the gun or of the pike, under the eye of a watchful and suspicious Government? Stir up the people;— *Furor arma ministrat*[2]—*Rage* will soon furnish them with arms, and *vengeance* and *necessity* will soon teach them the use. The lordly English have as yet but few troops in Ireland; among the Irish soldiery,

---

1 Lord Edward Fitzgerald (1763-98), son of the duke of Leinster, spent his early life as a British soldier and adventurer. By the early 1790s he had taken up radical politics, joining the United Irishmen in 1796. In May of that year he joined Arthur O'Connor (1763-1852) in negotiating with Admiral Hoche for a French invasion of Ireland. Fitzgerald returned to Ireland to head the military committee of the United Irishmen. He was betrayed to the Irish authorities and, after a violent struggle, was arrested on 19 May 1798, dying of his wounds several days later. O'Connor, also a Protestant and very affluent, being heir to his uncle Lord Longueville, joined the United Irishmen in 1796. After a brief imprisonment after his return from France, he became editor of the "Press," the United Irishmen newspaper, and was rearrested and put on trial for high treason in 1798. He was acquitted, but nevertheless spent several years in gaol before emigrating to France.
2 "Rage provides arms." From Virgil, *Æneid*, bk. I, l.150.

numbers are already on our side—and the rest will soon follow if we can but put on the appearance of success. From every part of the kingdom let the multitude rush to the capital; there we shall find a supply of arms, provisions, and friends; there we shall meet our enemies—senators and lawyers I mean, not soldiers; surprised with the report from all parts, for a while, at least, they must be confused, distracted, and uncertain. Let us seize this moment, and Ireland is free!"

This was the doctrine M'Ginnis held out to his associates, but he could not prevail; delays increased delays; and many a time, with a curse, had he half resolved to leave them for ever.

Finding the leading members were of so contrary an opinion to his own, he grew disgusted with their debates, and with redoubled ardour pursued the object at home. He found the greater part of his tenants and labourers were all of the same cause; and from among the more respectable and opulent farmers, he determined to raise a troop of horse, and discipline them himself.

At the next meeting of the higher Committee he proposed his schemes, expecting to meet with unbounded applause; but even to this he found opposition, and one man had the rashness to say, that it was hostile to that principle of equality which was the basis of their freedom; that, by such an offer, he shewed himself ignorant of the nature of the people of Ireland, unworthy of his trust, and an enemy to those measures by which her real friends laboured to preserve her.

The gentleman who made these remarks, was considered, by the party, as a man of superior consequence. He was not only possessed of a title, but of a large landed property, part of it, indeed, entailed, and the rest burthened with annuities and mortgages; so that he was encumbered with debts, and found the greatest difficulty in raising a present supply. What had chiefly impoverished him, was the enormous debt he had incurred by contested elections; and in the opening of the Parliament then sitting, he had expended every farthing he could raise, without success, to put his friend in for the county. Disappointed in serving the people in one way, he was now determined to serve them and himself in another, and was received by *the Union* with open arms.

M'Ginnis, who could not fail to perceive his own consequence, as Lord of a large property, lost in that of steward, and had been at times induced to lament the deception he practised, which thus turned out to his cost, had been on the watch for an opportunity to signalize himself in his true character. His passions were before inflamed, and now, irritated to a particular object, who had often before opposed him, burst out.

As soon, then, as the other had spoken, he rushed up to him resolutely, without concealing his design, and, in defiance of the interference of one or two who were near, felled him with his fist, in a moment, on the ground—"Infamous scoundrel! presumptuous, cowardly villain!" and he swore deliberately and dreadfully, "may I have silenced thy blasphemous tongue for ever!"

Surprise, and no small portion of horror, had seized the spectators; but it was not M'Ginnis's intention to make enemies of these: instantly, therefore, softening his tone, and assuming those easy manners he could so well assume, he said—"Pardon me, gentlemen, my indignation has exceeded my discretion. Yet I have a double stake in this glorious cause—in my own person, and as the representative of my kinsman. Do you suppose, gentlemen, my worthy relation, Marauder, whose next heir I am, would have, without the smallest restraint or tie, given unlimited command and power to me, even to the disposal of his whole property,"—and he opened a letter, and threw it on the table—"had he conceived such a wretch as this would have dared to breathe with impunity the most distant reflection. Do you suppose, gentlemen, I would have thrown up my commission in the Imperial service—that I would have come to Ireland, where few smiles wait a Catholic, had I not looked forward to a glorious change?—and is this reptile to doubt my principles, or to drop the most distant insinuations against me?—For the general cause, I pardon all that is past; but if ever again such cursed reflections fall from his lips, I here swear most solemnly," and again he swore, "the last drop of his blood shall wipe them out."

The person who had so grievously offended him, heard the latter part of his speech, and was led out without any answer; he was much hurt in the head, had been stunned for some moments, and bled profusely.

M'Ginnis had rightly conjectured that his enemy had not spirit enough to take up the affair as a man of honour; in which case M'Ginnis was resolved to have shewn that he had as few fears as Marauder himself.

The new Austrian Officer having thus exhibited his spirit, and given himself a consequence in the eyes of his co-partners, his next endeavour was to soften what had happened, by the extreme of politeness and civility to the rest. In the latter point he did not succeed quite so well as in the former, neither did he care so much about it; yet it answered in a great degree the object he intended, which was to give a lift to his consequence.

After this M'Ginnis was always heard with due attention; but he found himself as far from the purport of his oratory, in an immediate rising of the people, as ever. Concerning his troop, he succeeded.

With the approbation of the superior Committee, he soon enrolled about twenty of his tenants, and offered their services to the Government. They were accepted. M'Ginnis quickly raised and embodied a small troop; and afterwards many loyal neighbouring inhabitants joined his corps, without knowing the principles of their Captain and his dependants.

Marauder's hospitality, and convivial way of life, was very acceptable to the Irish; and his profession of attachment to the Government completely deceived all but the United Irish. He had no doubt that he should by degrees, win over the rest to his party, which induced him to encourage the entrance of strangers into his troop; and thus, ere the summer was passed, he was able to bring into the field sixty men, well mounted, apparelled, and accoutred.

CHAPTER X.

The beginning of the winter Marauder was in Dublin; and heard, with the greatest pleasure, the successful mission of the Delegates, and the promises of speedy assistance from France, under the command of an experienced General. Marauder, in raptures, hastened back into the country.

When, in December, the French armament appeared in Bantry Bay, M'Ginnis was constantly on the watch, expecting every instant to hear that they were landed.[1] He assembled his troop; he gave them orders to be ready at a moment's warning to hasten to the spot, under the pretence of opposing the enemy.

The United Irishmen in his troop were so anxious, with difficulty he restrained them to keep the important secret. Once in the power of the French, he knew they must all act for the same cause,

---

1   A French invasion fleet—fifty ships carrying 15,000 troops—arrived in
    Bantry Bay, south-west Ireland, in December 1796. Adverse weather conditions meant that the troops were never able to land, and the fleet,
    much battered by storms, returned to France in January 1797.

or be treated as prisoners; and if any refused to join, their horses and accoutrements would aid the cause.

These great hopes soon passed away. The French departed; and the English fleets appeared along the coast.

Now again M'Ginnis frequented their private meetings. He was a Delegate to the Upper Baronial Committee, and of course, had received the rank of Colonel of a battalion of 600 men.

The first months of the year 1797 he employed in making his personal observations throughout the kingdom; and in the spring he joined a great meeting of the Ulster and Leinster Delegates, and a few from the other provinces.

At this meeting, which was of the first consequence, the parties became very violent.

The Ulster delegates were for an immediate rising; the Leinster were as violent for the contrary. The former accused the latter of want of ardour; they retorted on the other for haste, violence, and abuse of the principle of fraternization. The delegated Colonels from Munster, and a few from Connaught, seemed to wait for the determination of the superior powers of Ulster and Leinster; all but M'Ginnis—he decidedly gave his opinion for open and instant war.

The *leading men* of the kingdom were of the Leinster party; and one of their most famous orators gave the opinion of the rest in nearly the following words.

"The affiliating system of organization has enlarged itself beyond our most sanguine hopes. All ranks, orders, degrees of citizens emancipate themselves from the shackles of religious and political prejudices, and fraternize together in a Brotherhood of affection, a Communion of Rights, and an Union of Power. Daily does the philanthropic fervour expand. Every return of our forces brings in an increase of our numbers, an enlargement of our means, and the further perfection of their organized state.— While, then, we are in this flourishing and improving course, let us patiently wait the moment till our powers are arrived at their climax. This glorious Union is like a snow-ball, which acquires size as it is steadily rolled along; let it, therefore, continue its collective force, till it bursts of its own accord, and deluges the whole country."

To this M'Ginnis replied—"As yet the Union succeeds. Whilst its power and strength are at the full vigour, let us make the struggle for freedom. If we wait till we perceive this glorious Union begins to lose its *collective force*, depend upon it that the heart is become rotten. It will not diminish as it has increased. Like the stone of Tisyphus,[1] when it has once arisen to the top, it will suddenly fall headlong, and crush to pieces those who have laboured to raise it. But metaphorical language is the language of deceit; let me speak in a clearer tone, that every one of the Brotherhood may hear and understand me.

"Delegated Colonels of the Province of Ulster! have ye not been long waiting with impatience for the signal to assert your freedom?"

Twenty-two out of twenty-five answered—"Yes."

"Has not your revolutionary system been completed ever since the year 1795?"

"Yes."

"Are not your men organized, ready, and willing?"

"Yes."

"Will not the Province of Ulster alone bring into the field five times the number of forces that can at present be opposed to us?"

"Yes."

"Delegated Colonels of Leinster! can your organization be less forward?"

They answered—"No; but we wait a more favourable crisis—the aid of allies, bred up to war. Munster and Connaught will, in a few months, have double their present strength."

"Munster," replied M'Ginnis, "has been less daring than Leinster with the tongue; but we are not less bold. Connaught, with their present small numbers, are most arduous in the cause, and, weak as they are, propose no excuses to postpone the fight. Why should we wait the uncertain coming of the French? Delay cools our ardour—delay encourages the traitor—delay opens our intentions to the enemy—delay adds to the bulwark of tyranny—brings with every wind fresh troops from England, and raises more and more obstacles to our success. Last year I gave my voice for action: the same weak reasons opposed me. Now the number of our enemies is doubled, but not of ourselves; their vigilance is thoroughly awakened—our designs begin to be known; the English fleets guard the coasts, and the assistance of France is more doubtful than ever.

"The wary Leinster Delegates accuse the bold Ulster of violence and rapine;—caution and temperance are indeed most commend-

---

1 More usually "Sisyphus," King of Corinth, who, in Greek mythology, was punished in Hades by having repeatedly to push a stone up a hill only to have it roll down again as soon as the summit had been reached.

able; but I shall ever prefer the ebullitions of restrained courage, to the cold fears of a narrow prudence."

Another Colonel from Leinster said—"It would be madness to force the people to a premature rising. France promises us supplies. A trusty citizen," (Edward John Lewins was again sent in April, 1797) "who has already executed a commission with the highest credit, is about to be sent to France, to negotiate a second treaty, and hasten the promised succours. A little longer let us bear the yoke of tyranny, that we may throw it off for ever."

Another Delegate, on the same side, said—"The march of sentiment already pervades the minds of the sons of Erin. The night of tyranny is receding, and the day-star of liberty rises fast upon it. The philosophy that has enlightened the Continent, approaches to illumine our side. She rides upon the waves, and navies sink before her; she steps upon the shore, and armies disappear. Soon shall her virtue be your own; for philosophy is truth, and truth is success. Yet a little longer, ye children of Erin! bear with the yoke of the tyrant, and the embraces of fraternity shall unite the Brotherhood of this heterogeneous country in the organizing bond of unity. Soon, if we persevere in this affiliating system, shall the whole mass of an imperatorial people be regimented in unity; and a *representative legislature* shall insure to their rights an insulated independence."

This to-be-military orator now launched out in the same style, and in praises most strong of the *Union Star* and *The Press*—two notorious papers, which directly proscribed certain members of the Government as objects of assassination; and concluded with saying that those papers alone, without a sword being drawn, would in a short time undermine every enemy of the Union.

This citizen, who spoke last, had been concerned in writing for the *Union Star*, and was known to be chiefly instrumental in establishing *The Press*.

M'Ginnis was not ignorant of this, and with avidity seized the opportunity of venting his indignation.—"Curse on these papers! Curse on the conceit which planned them, and the strange jargon that forms them! They betray the public cause, by alarming the Government. They anticipate our measures, and put our adversaries on our guard. Is there an United Irishman that wants to be informed who his enemy is? Can any one, who is able to read that paper, be ignorant of the names of C. T. W. G. S.....? The present silence of the people is not the silence of fear and despondency, but of discretion; yes, and this noisy paper tells the Government so. If an assassin is necessary, who more proper than themselves, that dare not open war?

"For a long time have we been greatly formidable, and yet scarcely known. Favoured by the shade of night, we have successfully consulted together. Our decrees have been formed, published by word of mouth, and every vestige of writing has been destroyed. Silence has been our guard. Privately have we undermined the State; and we want but a steady hand to apply the match, and blow it into ruins.

"Now noise and tumult alarm the foe. Senseless clamour draws their attention; and still more senseless boasting betrays our purposes.

"The alarm once given, every instant we become weaker.

"Citizens, delegated Colonels, our cause has already taken up too many words; I vote for an immediate trial by the sword."

M'Ginnis voted in vain. The Leinster Colonels got the few that came from Connaught, and many of the Munster, of their side; and the Ulster departed, extremely incensed against their United Brethren; and many of them were never afterwards hearty in the affiliating system.

The foregoing debate may serve as a *literal* and *correct* specimen of the *language, sentiments,* and *conduct* of some of the more prominent characters from among the members of the Society of United Irishmen.

CHAPTER XI.

There was no subject M'Ginnis reprobated with so much violence as the different writings, by means of which the leading members endeavoured to inflame the minds of the people.

He was continually arguing that it was the ruin of the cause—that it only helped to betray their measures to the Ministry—that the common people did not understand any of them—the middle kind but very few—and that the better sort did not need them:—"Send emissaries, as many as you like, of their own rank and language among them, but no writing."

But the citizens of the quill would not yield up the point. Writings followed writings, till at last the lurking and inveterate spirit of rebellion seemed degenerated into bombast, impudence, abuse, and nonsense.

Some of the most devoted and obedient of the inferior Officers, by attempting to obey these rodomontade orders, were guilty of ludicrous absurdities. Among many others, there was a circumstance which M'Ginnis frequently quoted, that he might put the absurdity of the *Directorial jargon* in its proper light.

A famous writer, in an *official address* to the Brotherhood of United Irishmen, made use of the following words:—

"Let every member wear, day and night, an *amulet* round his neck, containing the great principle which unites the Brotherhood, in letters of gold, on a ribbon, striped with all the original colours, and enclosed in a sheath of white silk, to represent the pure Union of the mingled rays, and the abolition of all superficial distinctions, all colours and shades of difference, for the sake of an illustrious end. Let this *amulet* of Union, Faith, and Honour, depend from the neck, and be bound about the body, next to the skin, and close to the heart."*

It happened that M'Ginnis was on a certain day to have a private meeting of his Officers. After waiting a long time at the appointed spot, one after another, came a messenger from each, that he was not able to get the *amulet*. As M'Ginnis at last was leaving the place, one of his Captains rode up. He began apologies for his delay;—but his manner seemed so constrained, his articulation so uneasy, that M'Ginnis stopped him to know what was the matter with him.

"Nothing, but the *amulet*," he replied.

"The devil is in this *amulet*, whatever it is," exclaimed M'Ginnis, in his hasty way whenever any thing vexed him. "This is the excuse of all my Officers for their negligence in not attending to-day. Be so good, Captain, as to inform me what *the amulet* is?"

"Has not your Honour seen the last official address of the Directory?"

M'Ginnis scarcely restrained himself from saying, "D-mn the Directory!" he answered—"No."

The other, perhaps finding words not so pleasant at present, put his hand in his pocket, and produced the address which has just been quoted.

"Let every member wear, day and night, an *amulet* round his neck, &c. &c. &c. &c.

"I have done my best, Colonel, to fulfil the direction; but my brother Officers find great difficulty, and I know not how we shall be able to furnish the privates."

---

* [CL] This is no *imaginary sentimental slang*; the report of the Committee of the House of Commons in Ireland, published by authority, and from original papers, has the same words.—*Page 69, Appendix*. [The reference is to the *Report from the Committee of Secrecy, of the House of Commons in Ireland, as reported by the Right Honourable Lord Viscount Castlereagh, August 21, 1798* (London: J. Debrett and J. Wright, 1798) 67-72: see Appendix G.1. The same passage is also quoted in a "Note" appended to the English translation of the Abbé Barruel's *Memoirs, Illustrating the History of Jacobinism*: see Appendix F.]

M'Ginnis, not thinking it prudent to give verbal vent to the contemptuous anger which raged in his bosom, walked for a few seconds up and down the place. Recovering himself, he was more inclined to laugh at the ridiculous misinterpretation which had happened; and with a smiling face, said to the Officer—

"Well, Captain, how have you obeyed it?"

"I was obliged, Colonel, to get different colours;" and opening his shirt, he discovered a pretty tight binding of various coloured ribbons around his neck, about the body, next to the skin, and the two ends stuck with some cobbler's wax close to the region of the heart.

M'Ginnis, with as much gravity as he could assume, highly commended his zeal; but told him of his mistake, and released him from his unpleasant bondage.

"Every official order," continued he, "which is meant to be literally obeyed, I will, without fail, inform the Officers under my command of, that they may, in like manner, instruct the others; and I beg you'll remember, Captain, that there is no necessity for your obeying any notices from the Directory, that do not come immediately from me. I beg you'll inform your brother Officers of this; and I will be answerable for my trust, as, at every meeting of the Colonels before the superior Committee, we account for our conduct in the discharge of the duty reposed in us."

M'Ginnis in his own troop bore the rank of a regular Captain appointed by the Government; but the rank he held from his private connection with the *United Irishmen* was Colonel, or, as in his civil capacity he was called, a Delegate to the *Upper Baronial Committee*. As soon as open warfare commenced, he had no doubt his abilities would claim the station of a chief commander.

To point out systematically the relative degrees of the conspiracy, will not only elucidate what has been, and still will be noticed in these papers of this rebellion, but will also give the reader a correct and concise view of the grand machine that directed the whole.

The Society of United Irish began to be established as early as the year 1791.

The abolition of tithes, and, in short, a redress of all grievances, were the objects held out to the common people by the arch-promoters of the plan. Open hostility against the Government was artfully concealed.

As their numbers began to increase, their views became more open; they divided themselves into societies of twelve each, which twelve chose from among themselves their own secretary or treasurer. Five secretaries or treasurers united together, and elected one of their number to be a member of the *Lower Baronial Committee.* Every *Lower Baronial Committee* delegated one of their body; and ten of these formed an *Upper Baronial Committee,* which superintended the *Lower Baronials* in their respective counties.

Each *Upper Baronial* delegated one of their number to the next *Superior Committee,* called *District* in large towns, and *County Committee* in counties; and the *Districts,* or *Country Committee,* superintended the *Upper Baronial.*

These *Superior Committees* formed a *Subordinate Directory* in each of the four provinces, Leinster, Munster, Ulster, and Connaught.

The *Subordinate,* or *Provincial Directories* elected a *General Executive Directory* of five persons, *who governed the whole.*

But so judiciously was this last election managed, that the secretaries of the *Provincial Directories* alone knew on whom the election of CHIEF DIRECTORS fell.

Afterwards the Delegates to the *Lower* and *Upper Baronial Committees,* &c. &c. &c. had military rank attached to them, a scale of which may be given in this manner.

Twelve United Irishmen, or *Privates,* elect *one* of their number to be their *Secretary* or *Sergeant. Five Secretaries, or Sergeants,* elect *one* of their number to be a member of the *Lower Baronial,* or *Captain. Ten Lower Baronials,* or *Captains,* elect *one* of their number to be of the *Upper Baronial, or Colonel. One* from each *Upper Baronial* was sent to the *Provincial Directory.*

And the four *Provincial Directories* appointed *five Grand Directors,* which formed the EXECUTIVE DIRECTORY.

The Colonels of each county sent *three* names to the *Executive Directory,* who chose *one of the three* as ADJUTANT-GENERAL for that county.

Thus a *Colonel* commanded 600 men
   a Captain   60
   a Sergeant   12

The Adjutant-General according to the number in their respective counties.

Such was the *affiliating system* which united the Brethren together, and spread with astonishing rapidity over the whole soil. Each member as, with the most specious prospects, he was enticed by his neighbour to join them, was instantly, in the most sacred terms, sworn to secrecy and fidelity. The *real intentions* of the Union were only known to the leading members; and, *by their own confessions,* have at length appeared to be (what every rational man from the first supposed) the introduction of that no-principle of the French, which seeks the gratification of its own interest, without any regard to the laws of God or man, and which has already been so fully defined under the term DIABOLISM.

CHAPTER XII.

A letter from Fahany, which was enclosed for Marauder, M'Ginnis received in the beginning of the year 1797. As this letter will, in a great degree, shew the situation of his more particular friends in England (many, received before, but of no material moment, being omitted), it is here given.

Fahany's Letter to Marauder.

"My dearest friend, if one moment you can spare from the luscious banquet the new-world is ever courting you to partake—Ah Marauder! how I envy you the unrestrained indulgence of a western clime—

'Where, in the breast, resistless Venus reigns,
'And crimson currents fire the throbbing veins;
'Where the fine frenzy of the jetty eye,
'The raven ringlets, and the skin's dark die,
'The satin polish o'er the surface thrown,
'And motion's grace, that made Love's Goddess known!'*

"Curse on the confined customs, narrow notions, and religious prejudices of Europe! It is impossible for you to conceive with what anxiety I long for the full-ripe joys that eternally flourish beneath a *solar* reign. England was well defined by the ancients—

'Et penitus toto divisus orbe Britannos.'
VIRGIL.[1]

---

* [CL] A quotation somewhat (I believe) altered from the European Magazine. [This quotation has not been traced.]

---

1 "… and the British quite cut off from the whole world," Virgil, *Eclogues*, bk. 1, l.60.

'remotis
'Obstrepit occanis Britannis.'
HORACE.[1]

"Yet what is any part of the *old* world compared to the *new*? In works of nature and of art, America has ever been the theme of praise and wonder. In every thing she surpasses us; and equally excites the admiration of the philosopher, the naturalist, the historian, and the poet;—but I must break the enchantment which fascinates me to this delightful subject; away with the rapturous description—plain narrative must be the *order of the day*.

"If, my dearest fellow, from that soft couch of pleasure, thou wilt deign to cast a look towards us poor contemptible wights of this cold and barren region, I will a tale unfold, not to harrow up thy blood, but to set afloat in thy brain the titillations of the merry Euphrosyne.

"'Tis of the sapient Cloudley and *his* Maria, *thy* Maria, *my* Maria, the Maria of *every* votary of Cupid, that I am about to tell. Nor shall Lucretia, Amazonia, Brutus, Voltaire, Hercules, and Tom Pain, sweet little angels! be forgotten.—Now to proceed systematically in my story.

"In May last died old Rumble, whose heir-at-law our friend Cloudley is. But what of that?—Old Rumble left a will—his degenerate nephew disinherited—but one hundred a year settled upon each of the young Hopefuls.

"Cloudley put on his best garb of philosophy, through which his sweet resigned soul was most visible. He sent to me, as a bit of a cousin, and the trusty Arnon, upon the occasion.

"Arnon was too unwell to leave home (of him more hereafter); I therefore set off without him, to carry comfort to Cloudley Hall.

"At Rochester, where I stopped to change horses, who the devil should come up to my carriage but young Ivory!—Ivory is now a Captain in the —— regiment; and, having lately taken the initiated degree in our *Grand* Society, thinks himself a wondrous clever fellow. Instantly it struck me—what if I take Ivory down to comfort poor Maria!

"'Ivory,' said I, in a soft whisper, 'a beautiful woman—her husband a little jealous—you must be on your guard, my boy—your new

---

1 From Horace's *Odes*, bk. IV, Ode 14, which speaks of "… the monster-filled Britannic Ocean, which clamours against us, having been free from you" (ll.47–48).

uniform and curricle—not to mention how fascinating you have already been among the ladies—Hey! What say you?'

"Ivory was in raptures—embraced the proposal with joy.—'Horrid bore!—country town—damned quarters—wanted a lounge—just the thing!'

"The curricle was ready in a minute; I sent away my chaise, mounted with him, and away we bowled for Cloudley Hall, his valet and head-groom following.

"On the road I gave him his cue.

"Cloudley and his sweet creature were most happy with our company. Ivory played his cards admirably—profusely flattered and admired the husband—politely civil and distant to the wife. Cloudley's jealousy wore away by degrees, and all parties were happy.

"Never was a man in such raptures as Ivory.—'You told me,' said he, 'I should see a beautiful woman—by my soul, she's an angel! It is impossible she can be the mother of those children! Dear Fahany, I am eternally obliged to you!'

"Little did I dream of the conclusion to this business.

"In two days I went to town. Ivory, by Cloudley's earnest invitation, was to stay some time longer.—'What a promising youth,' said the well-judging philosopher to me, 'is this Captain Ivory! What a value to our Society! He reminds me of my absent friend Marauder.'

"Wishing to help the young dog, I enlarged upon his good qualities—the immense riches of his father, the Nabob—what a match for Lucretia!

"I had been returned to town about a week, when I received the following letter, express, from Cloudley:—

"Ruin and confusion overwhelm me. Maria's fled from my arms with the treacherous young Ivory. Lucretia and Amazonia are gone off with his two servants. Yesterday my daughters eloped towards Scotland—I hastened a few stages to overtake them—returned home this morning, and found the house forsaken. I can write no more. Come to the wretched

"J. CLOUDLEY."

"I was angry with the Captain for his monopoly, and flew to Cloudley immediately.

"Never was there such a scene of confusion. The two daughters have followed nature with Ivory's valet and groom to Scotland. This trick was not known to Maria and her paramour; but they embraced the opportunity of Cloudley's absence to be off likewise. Scarce had the mother departed, before Brutus and Voltaire mounted two young colts, which were breaking in, and scampered away, the devil knows where.

"The servants were running about the country in pursuit of them; and Hercules and Tom Pain fell to pillaging the house—eating, drinking, and breaking without mercy.—Such was the scene when Cloudley returned.

"The two boys were not, when I came, found; we heard they were at Dover, where they sold the horses. Cloudley speaks not a word, but sinks under his misfortunes; and from what little he does say, I firmly believe his intellects (never very good) have for ever taken their leave.

"He has frequently, at times, when touched with a fit of jealousy, evinced strong symptoms of the coming mania. As soon as I arrived, I endeavoured to rouse the stoic within him, by making light of the elopement of his spouse; as for the children, sons and daughters, I knew he was too much a citizen of the world to care about them.

"He replied to me—'I have a great mind to be Julius Caesar. Caesar's wife ought not to be suspected. No,' continued he, thinking deeply, 'that won't do; I shall be murdered by the Senate.'

"'Caesar,' said I, 'was a clever fellow. He wisely made his wife's suspicious conduct an excuse for getting rid of her. Possession had long banished passion.'

"'Ah!' said he, repeating my own words, 'possession had long banished passion! That's well said!'

"I could get very little more conversation with him that day. The next he seemed unusually busy about the house, and I fancied that his melancholy began to go off. Yet I saw him but seldom, and he did not join me at supper.

"The third morning from my arrival, we received tidings of Brutus and Voltaire; they had been traced from Dover along the coast to Portsmouth, and had entered on board a small vessel from Dover, which had departed instantly to sea, taking fresh sailors to join the fleet.

"I communicated this intelligence to Cloudley, and proposed to set off for Portsmouth directly, to learn the destination of the ship and so forth.

"'To sea,' said he, 'well, what of that? When Caesar conquered Rome, did not the son of Pompey the Great turn sailor? But I am not Pompey.—No.—Who am I?'

"'Cloudley, my friend, the friend of all mankind. Nature's citizen. The philosopher of the human race.'

"'Come nearer,' said he, in a soft tone. 'Hush! I'll tell you a secret. I always thought that I felt the soul of the immortal Cato, or else of the noble Cassius, I never could tell which, moving in my bosom. *Memini me esse Catonem, vel Cassium*.[1] Yet', continued he, loudly stalking about the room, 'I will remember the Senate House—'twas on the Ides of March. I plunged the dagger in the tyrant's breast.'

"He ran on with an unusual loquacity, relating the most memorable actions of both Cato and Cassius, as if he had himself performed them; suddenly stopping short, he came up to me.—'After all, this is nothing. I am a poor Roman Emperor I find. Here, here, here!' cried he, vociferating as loud as he could speak, and drawing a paper from his bosom, 'here is proof positive. My wife is Messalina,[2] and then who am I?—Who? I am the husband of Messalina. What is my name, what is my name, what is my name? Oh! What a wretch I am!' cried he, striking his forehead with both hands, 'I don't know my own name!'

"Mad as an heathen priest, in vain I tried to reason with him. He would not listen to a word, but every moment dignified me with some new title or other. I was a Catiline or Petronius,[3] as the whim suited him. Still he held the paper in his hand, which in vain I endeavoured to get from him. I enquired of the servants if they knew what it was. They could only inform me that he had been that morning searching his wife's room, and they concluded he found it there.

"In the evening he grew so bad, that the physician, whom I had sent for, thought it necessary to confine him. All his talk was about the new personification he had assumed, with lamentations truly ridiculous, that he knew not his own name.

"Thinking to make him easy, I mentioned to him *Claudius*, as the

---

1 "Remind me who is Cato, who is Cassius." Marcus Porcius Cato ("Cato the Younger," 95-46 BC) was an opponent of the tyrannical Julius Caesar; Gaius Cassius Longinus (d. 42 BC) was the original leader of the conspirators who assassinated him.

2 Messalina Vareria (AD 22-48), third wife of the Roman emperor Claudius, notorious for her licentiousness.

3 Lucius Sergius Catilina, or Cataline (c. 108-62 BC) and Petronius Maximus (AD 396-455) were both accused of attempting to seize power in the Roman Empire, by an insurrection and armed attack, and by assassination, respectively. Alternatively, Lucas may be referring to Gaius Arbiter Petronius, who was denounced as conspiring to assassinate the Emperor Nero.

husband of Messalina; but it was of no avail, though he had heard of the wanton dame. The name of her husband did not in the least strike his attention. He continued raving as they put the straight waistcoat on him, and forcibly bled him.—'Who am I? Oh! that I knew my name, then would I call my guards to my rescue! Beware how you touch me. I am a Roman Emperor, though I cannot tell my name. Here, here, here! Proof, proof, proof!'

"I now contrived to get the paper from him, and put another into his hand. His frantic demeanour had much torn and defaced it;[*] but such as I could make out, I send you a copy of, as a precious *morceau*. 'Twas a letter the fair *Maria* had left for him.

"*Mrs. Cloudley's Letter to her Husband*

"The history of the early ages of the world, ere mankind were constrained by custom, and perverted by art, tells me I act right; and the sacred love of truth constrains me to speak it.

"Cato, the wisest man in the Roman commonwealth, whose spirit you have so frequently told me you felt moving within your own breast, voluntarily gave up his beloved wife, Martia, to his friend, Hortensius, that her virtues might be increased, and more generally diffused through the commonwealth, and not narrowly confined to one object. For this glorious principle of the general good came the Queen of the South to the Jewish King, and the Amazonian Queen to the great Alexander. Lycurgus, the wisest of lawgivers, thought a man not to be blamed, who, having a young wife, should recommend some virtuous handsome young man, &c. &c.;[†] and a worthy man who was in love with a married woman, *upon the account of her modesty*, and the beauty of her children, would, among the *Spartans*, beg the favour of her for a season of her husband, that he might have a likely offspring. But these authorities, and thousands of others, you cannot, dear Cloudley, be ignorant of.

"*Lucretia*, let me inform you, is the offspring of the beautiful young coachman that drove my aunt at Bath. She was born, you must remember, eight months after the unmeaning ceremony passed between us.

"*Amazonia* is your own child; so, I believe, is *Brutus*.

---

* [CL] What was defaced from this letter when it came into Mr. Fahany's hands is not known; but many parts are now omitted, as well as Mr. Fahany's remarks upon it.

† [CL] Verbatim from Plutarch's Life of Lycurgus.

"*Voltaire* is the son of that charming youth, who from a neighbouring town came to cut my locks, ere we knew that nature would annually shed them herself.

"*Hercules* boasts for his sire your brawny ploughman; and Tom Pain is the son of that ingenious rat-catcher, who, in less than three weeks, routed those voracious animals from our house.

"Seriously reflect, Cloudley; living the recluse life that I have, whom could I find more worthy?

"The young creature that I prematurely lost, had it lived, might have claimed for its sire the dearest of your friends, the incomparable Marauder; him, whom your fond wishes look up to as the second Cromwell of England. Such has ever been my conduct to find the most noble of fathers for my children.

"Tomorrow I fly, not from *you*, but from *jealousy*, with the most charming youth Nature ever formed, and Truth and Virtue ever adopted.[*]

"Strange, dear Cloudley, that you, who would be the first of philosophers, should indulge the foolish prejudice of a slavish jealousy. This compels me to leave you; but whenever reason, virtue, sense, and political justice shall have cleared the mists which now obscure your understanding, will I return to Cloudley Hall with the generous Ivory;[†] then will we all live together in the primitive simplicity of love, freedom, and perfect morality, unfettered by foolish custom, and mental weakness.

"Health and wisdom to him who bears a name which confined

---

[*] [CL] This argument shews the lady's philosophy to be genuine.

[†] [CL] Mrs. C. perhaps alluded to some of this *new kind of morality*, out of Godwin's Political Justice, vol. ii. page 497.

"Add to this, that it is absurd to expect the inclinations and wishes of two human beings to coincide through any long period of time. To oblige them to act and to live together, is to subject them to some inevitable portion of thwarting, bickering, and unhappiness."

Page 499. "Add to this, that marriage, as now understood, is a monopoly, and the worst of monopolies. So long as two human beings are forbidden, by positive institution, to follow the dictates of their own mind, prejudice will ever be alive and vigorous. So long as I seek, by despotic and artificial means, to engross a woman to myself, and to prohibit my neighbour from proving his superior claim, I am guilty of the most odious selfishness."

Page 503. "In a state of equality it will be a question of no importance to know, who is the parent of each individual child." [*Political Justice*, ed. Kramnick, Penguin edn., 761-62. See Appendix C for the context of these quotations.]

law has given him, but which the rights of a woman and her will can bestow as she thinks most natural to the inward feelings of her mind; and this *Ivory* now bears by the spontaneous love of

"MARIA."

"Upon my life, Marauder, I know not what to think of the charming Maria; I must conclude her to be full as mad as her husband.

"From Cloudley Hall I hastened to Portsmouth, to search for my cousins, Brutus and Voltaire. I found they were entered on board a man of war. The fleet had just sailed; the town was quite deserted. I therefore set off immediately to London, bringing with me the finest girl from that renowned seaport. Now, as I know, Marauder, you laugh at my taste, I will not add a word more of my true-born Venus.

"Cloudley is sent to a private mad-house; the doctors despair of his recovery. The Court of Chancery are to have the management of his estate.

"I have now bad news to tell thee of Arnon. He has been ill some time; the physicians agree with his own opinion, that it is the dropsy. But, believe me, the cause of the disease is in his mind, Marauder. When I press him on the subject, he forces a laugh, and asks me if I wish to be his Father Confessor. The renegade Hambden I am sure has vexed him, though on that also he affects to talk with indifference. Yet the devil's surely in the man; he cannot be much displeased with his son, as he gave him, upon his marriage, the estate in Wales. There is an enigma in Arnon which thou must solve.

"Ah! Marauder, couldst thou not contrive to ship me over a dear, delicious, nice, beautiful black girl? By the time thou receivest this, I trust thou wilt be ready to return. Fail not to bring to this land of liberty one of those jetty angels with thee, or dread the reception thou wilt find from thy friend.

"H. FAHANY."

"This moment I flew down stairs to a noise at the door. I found my servant with a bloody nose, and a hackney coach driving furiously away. My *nymph of the flood* has thought proper to leave me for a jolly brisk Tar that she hailed in the street; *my gentleman*, like a fool, had tried to prevent her. I came down time enough for her blessing, which she liberally gave me from the coach window. Remember the sable beauty.

"Royston Santhorpe, we hear, is playing the devil in the West Indies. Thou oughtst to know most of him, write the particulars."

CHAPTER XIII.

Nightly attacks on the known friends of the Government had long been common. In many of these, M'Ginnis had exercised such of his troop as he could depend upon in a predatory kind of war.

The moment was now arrived when they were to act openly, and by day.

Of the threescore men, which was now the number M'Ginnis had raised for the pretended service of Government, two or three-and-thirty he knew were United Irishmen, and many of these domesticated in his house, as a superior kind of labourers on his estate.

M'Ginnis having assembled the whole troop, made them the following laconic speech:—

"Brave Irishmen and fellow-soldiers, what heart is there among you that does not bleed for the miseries that harass his beloved country? Who will not lift up his hand to protect—who will not strike down the enemy to defend her? For *this* are we armed, for *this* we draw the sword."—And to give due effect to his speech, he drew his sword. The United Irishmen did the same. The rest of the troop obeyed the signal. "And for *this* we swear not to sheath it till Ireland is free."—All who knew the purport of his speech, exclaimed,— "We swear!"

"Can there be one in this troop," continued M'Ginnis, "whose eyes are blinded, whose senses are confused, and who cannot distinguish his foe from his friend? Unjust landlords, who live on our labours, and consume them in a far country—cruel masters, who drain our strength with foreign laws—strangers to Ireland by birth, education, and principle. But the worst of our enemies are our degenerate countrymen, slaves to the English—tyrants to the men of Ireland. Who is ignorant of these? The unfavourable times, the enemy's suspicious treachery, the unarmed state of the afflicted peasantry, have yet constrained me to dissemble. But the iron laws, and the bloody execution of them by our tyrants, make a longer concealment of our principles a crime.

"If we join the foe, we remain the instruments of labour. Murder is our present employment, and slavery our reward. If we are in hand and heart *United Brethren*, war, revenge, and liberty await us.

"This coat, the badge of our servitude, as yet the base disguise of our virtue, now we need not; and thus I tear the scarlet trappings away! Henceforth, the evergreen of Ireland shall be openly displayed."—At this signal, without waiting for further orders, the

United Irishmen followed their Captain's example, and tore away the scarlet from their coats.—M'Ginnis continued. "Is there any one so base as to desert his countrymen, to fear the English Tyrant?" He had no need to proceed any further; all the rest set to work immediately.—"No, thanks to the Genius of Liberty! Not one."

M'Ginnis next enlarged upon the numbers which were in arms, their vast resources, the weakness and the fears of the enemy, &c. &c. &c. &c.

He particularly addressed himself to those who were not United Irishmen; told them they should be admitted that night into the same bond of Brotherhood and Unity; and, finally, he invited the whole company to his house among the rocks, to partake of a festive bowl, saying, that the following morning he had an object in view, when he purposed to prove their courage.

On the road to M'Ginnis's house, about ten of those who were not United Irishmen, suddenly turned round when they saw the advantage of the road, and galloped off. M'Ginnis did not attempt to pursue them, fearful of the rest.

M'Ginnis, from the beginning of his oration, had been on his guard, and had before fully arranged his plan. The number on both sides were nearly equal: but the pistols of the United Irishmen he had privately ordered to be loaded, and themselves to be provided with ammunition; while the rest of his troop were in every respect unprepared. Without any attempt on the part of the rest to leave their Captain, two-and-fifty men arrived at his house.

There was a gentleman who resided on the same rocky mountain on which M'Ginnis's mansion was situated, but somewhat below him on the other side. Mr. O'Connel had ever lived on the most neighbourly terms with Captain M'Ginnis, who frequently partook of his hospitality.

Not without the truest concern did this gentleman behold the misfortunes of his country, and lament the propagation of those accursed doctrines which were so sedulously planted in every mind.

Too mild and gentle in his nature to be offensive to either party, he had retired to these wilds, in hopes of being out of the reach of the rude hand of war. To him, who was too much a man of letters to be a man of the world, M'Ginnis had ever appeared what *he seemed to be*.

There were no other mansions but their own, except a few straggling huts, within many miles of the spot. The country, as was before said, was bare, rude, and uncultivated; and the whole property of Mr. O'Connel was but a life-residence from the family of Marauder.

The occasional near neighbourhood of M'Ginnis, a military man, was rather a pleasing circumstance to the other; and M'Ginnis had, in terms of friendship, offered his own services and those of his troop, if Mr. O'Connel should at any time entertain a fear of being attacked by the United Irishmen.

Yet the destruction of this harmless man and family, and the pillage of his property, was the first noble achievement M'Ginnis proposed. He knew there were some gentlemen at the house whom he chose to fancy were Government spies, because one of them had a brother who held an office under the Crown.

Mr. O'Connel's house was only one Irish mile from his own, but the worst road that can possibly be conceived. Though the country was so well known, it was necessary to proceed in the light of the sun; besides, Captain M'Ginnis wished to strike a decisive blow in the open face of day, both to encourage his troops, and to prevent the means of retracting from the undertaking that they had engaged in.

In the height of jollity, after supper, he declared his scheme.—"The number of the enemy," continued he, "in the whole cannot be above twenty, slaves and their servants! Well armed, doubtless, our tyrants always take care to be. So much the better; 'twill be part of our spoils. Ready cash, good store of wines, provisions of all kinds, are not wanting. Let the plunder be divided among you; I require but the glory of partaking in your danger."

Applause unbounded followed this speech. One of the company, not an United Irishman before that night (for the test had been given to the rest before supper), replied in a satirical speech, abusing Mr. O'Connel, and calling him a stupid, senseless, useless bookworm.—"I thought," continued he, "his fine-spun brain was the poet's only wealth: I am rejoiced to hear that he carries a *golden* bait. I've been told that the old fellow has a precious store of ancient coins: in the hands of United Irishmen they shall quickly become useful." The man concluded by praising the Brotherhood, of which he had just been made a member, and declaring his ignorance before of their number, strength, influence and intentions.

On account of their employment the next morning, which was to be as early as possible, M'Ginnis put an end to the meeting as soon as he decently could.

Carpets, mattresses, beds, couches, and every thing of the kind which the house afforded, were ordered to be brought into the large hall for the company; but the man who had spoken before, proposed that every one should sleep under his horse.

M'Ginnis had no suspicion that this person, who was the son of a surgeon at some distance, and was lately come from attending the Dublin hospitals to assist his father, was otherwise than hearty in the cause; as, in coming to the house, M'Ginnis remarked him at one time far behind the rest. He was then off his horse, (for this part of the road was impassable to man upon his horse), and so far from the troop, that M'Ginnis had no doubt he had turned his horse, and rode away, especially as he was very well mounted. But he had dissipated these suspicions, by calling out to them to stay for him.—"I don't know your crabbed road here; be so good, Captain, to wait a few seconds for me."

Marauder had a high opinion of the spirit and courage of young Moirane, (for that was his name), and saw with pleasure how readily he joined them.

Neither was Marauder deceived in his ideas of the other's bravery, but greatly so in the motive of his actions; for the whole behaviour of Moirane was founded on the deepest policy.

To fly alone, he knew he could at any time; but he wished to entice others away with him, and to be acquainted with the schemes and intentions of his Captain, that he might, if possible, counteract them.

The proposal of Moirane, that each man should sleep under his horse's manger, was approved of by the whole troop, and M'Ginnis himself set the example.

CHAPTER XIV.

Moirane was the first who roused in the morning, and began calling to the rest.

He had said to every one, whom he had observed sworn the over-night, before they went to rest,—"Assemble before the gates as early as possible."

As such, when he had led his horse out, most of the others were proceeding from their different stables, and but very few of the United Irish.

A sentinel stood by the gate, but he made no opposition, as Moirane, with great indifference, unlocked it, and let down the drawbridge. Many, leading their horses in their hands, went out. Moirane examined the door, spoke to the sentinel of its strength, took the key out of the lock, looked at it, tried it the other way, moving it backwards and forwards.

In the meantime many others came out, and M'Ginnis came forward from the stables: Moirane waited not a moment longer, but instantly shut the gate, and turned the key. His friends on the outside comprehended his meaning without a word, and drew their swords.

Five or six of the United Irishmen made no opposition.

Moirane sprung on his horse, and turning to the latter,—"Tell your Captain, when the riches, trade, and population of Ireland decrease by the ill management of the present Government, I will unite with M'Ginnis."

Turning to the rest, to the number of a dozen,—"Do any of you know the road to O'Connel's?"

One man replied in the affirmative.

"Then lead the way," said Moirane, "with all speed: I'll bring up the rear, and the first who follows, I'll blow his brains out." Looking at the United Irishmen,—"Gallop your horses to the right instantly!" The men obeyed, and Moirane, with the others, took the road to Mr. O'Connel's.

Before M'Ginnis burst open the door, he had been necessitated to assemble his men, lest he should be attacked at a disadvantage. When he had done this, he hastened on as quick as possible, that he might get to Mr. O'Connel's before the fugitives could have put the place in a state of defence.

He naturally suspected the other men who had taken the oath, and had not been able to depart with Moirane: he therefore separated them from his own party to the number of six, and ordered them to remain at some distance behind. He then sent one of them, whom he had detained for this purpose, to order them to come on directly, or to be gone the way they had come the day before. They every one took the opportunity, and made the best of their way from the place, under the direction of a guide he had before given them.

Had M'Ginnis been certain of their defection, he had probably destroyed the whole: but he buoyed himself up with the hopes that some of them might join him.

M'Ginnis did not venture to take them the nearest way to Mr. O'Connel's, as there was a small wooden bridge he concluded Moirane would break up, and a dangerous defile to go through; but made the utmost haste on the more open road.

When Moirane and his party arrived at Mr. O'Connel's house, and told them of their danger, he endeavoured to prevail on them instantly to prepare for resistance; but they were all in confusion— some were willing to stand the fight, but the greater part called for their horses immediately. Mr. O'Connel was the first to fly without loss of time, carrying with him nothing but his cash and valuable medals. He was an infirm and elderly man; and Moirane and his party, who saw it was in vain to resist, conducted him themselves to the nearest place of safety.

As soon as Mr. O'Connel was gone, his servants, whom he had ordered to take care of themselves, for he waited for no one, began to plunder before the enemy came. A few of the servants of his guests too, loitered behind under some pretence, but for the same purpose.

M'Ginnis and his troop came upon them in the midst of their new wealth, and not one escaped.

The scene of confusion and horror that now ensued is far too bad to be repeated. Five men and two women, who had all remained for the same greedy purpose, were killed without the slightest opposition, and entreating for mercy, with a thousand wounds; and M'Ginnis enjoyed the scene.

They next began pillaging the house; and so ravenous was each of them to seize upon the spoils, that their blows were turned against one and another, and their Captain was obliged to cut one of the most violent of them down before he could reduce them to any kind of order.

From among the good things in the eating way, M'Ginnis ordered a sumptuous dinner, and some of the troop officiated as cooks.

Drinking and carousing they staid a long time, and their Captain resolved to take up his abode there that night, and chose Mr. O'Connel's own apartment, which, by his absolute orders, had been protected from the general pillage.

In the morning, he had determined that the furniture should be carried away, and the house burnt down, lest the foe, at any future time, should get possession of it, and it might be put in a state of defence against himself.

There were only two ways of approach to this spot, which was placed in a lower situation than where M'Ginnis lived. One road they came in the morning, and the other, which was very steep and narrow, the fugitives had taken. Upon the brow of the last, M'Ginnis placed two sentinels, with orders to his Lieutenant, who was implicitly devoted to him to relieve them every three hours during the night.

M'Ginnis was wonderfully pleased with the occurrences of the day. The defection of part of his troop, indeed, gave him some trouble; but he was glad it had happened so early, before they were acquainted with his defiles, strong holds, intricate roads, and fastnesses. He had not the smallest fear of any attempt they would make against him, as he knew almost the whole of the peasantry were in his interest; and he resolved to increase the difficulties of the road to Mr. O'Connel's, and from thence to his own house, though the ascent made it sufficiently impregnable.

CHAPTER XV.

After carousing some hours with his gang, M'Ginnis retired to the room that he had reserved for himself, and which had been Mr. O'Connel's bedchamber.

This, though untouched by the troop of M'Ginnis, had nevertheless been attempted to be plundered by the servants, and many of the things had been scattered and thrown about.

The desk was open; M'Ginnis examined every drawer, but the valuables were all removed. There was plenty, indeed, of paper and writing, among which he perceived many letters, and some scraps of poetry.

Before he retired to rest, M'Ginnis amused himself with reading some of these over.

On one parcel was written *German Poetry*. M'Ginnis opened it.

A translation of the famous Leonora first struck his view.[1] This he had read in England; but as this translation was different, he perused a few lines, and put it in his pocket.

The next piece was called "SIR HILDEBRAND."

"This is a warlike Knight," said M'Ginnis; "I'll read his exploits."

SIR HILDEBRAND.
I.
Now the din of war's begun,
  Slaughter reeking o'er the plain,
See! the furies madd'ning run,
  And lust and rapine swell their train.
Sir Hildebrand amid the first,
Impetuous spurs his foaming horse.

"Come," said M'Ginnis, beginning his remarks, "this is not so bad—I did not think my neighbour had so much spirit in him; but I forget—it's only a translation from the German."

---

1 "Leonora," a German ballad by Gottfried August Bürger (1747-94), was first published in an English translation in 1796.

II.

To Walstein Castle speeds his way;
  Where, trembling at the raging storm,
Ellen, lovely mourner, lay,
  List'ning for a sire's return.
"He comes! he comes!" Ah! No, fair maid,
'Tis Hildebrand, with murd'rous blade.

"I should have no objection to be in Sir Hildebrand's place."

III.

Aghast th'affrighted menials fly,
  Or perish 'neath the conqueror's sword:
In vain, in vain, does Mercy cry;
  "No quarter!" was the Captain's word.

"This stanza will do for our exploits today."

Yet, when the Knight beheld her charms,
He dropp'd the goary blade, and clasp'd her in his arms.

"I wish I had been so fortunate as to have found an Ellen in this house."

IV.

Shrieks and prayers rend the air—
  Shrieks and prayers all must fail;
"Help me, O God!" implores the fair.
  "Nor man nor God shall now avail,"
Exclaims Sir Hildebrand, with lustful eyes,
"Nor man nor God shall rob me of my prize."

V.

"Time was when Walstein's haughty Lord
  "Refus'd with scorn my proffer'd vows,
"When *Ellen* spurn'd, and *I* implor'd;
  "'Tis *she* has rank'd me 'mong her foes.
"*Honour* and *love* the maid wou'd not unite;
"Then love and valour shall assert their right."

"Well done, Sir Hildebrand, you reason the point well, and I'll read your story through."

VI.

Strength exhausted, spirits fled,
  The virgin faints beneath his lust;
Like some poor victim, droops its head,
  And hides its sorrows in the dust.
Again Sir Hildebrand exulting cries,
"Nor man nor God shall rob me of my prize."

VII.

And is each guardian genius fled?
  Hark! hark! what sudden yells I hear!
See, see, the sparkling flames they spread,
  And e'en the victors quake for fear.
As rapid lightning, the flashes fly;
"Away! away! away!" the soldiers cry.

VIII.

Sir Hildebrand, with vengeful ire,
  Uprose, and seiz'd his bloody blade;
And then, with imprecations dire,
  He thus bespoke the trembling maid:—
"This instant swear to take me for thy Lord—
"This instant swear, or perish by my sword!"

IX.

A faint assent the virgin spoke,
  "Then follow me!" the monster cry'd.
Alas! th'obliterating stroke
  Was given! She cou'd no more, and dy'd.
The swelling fires surround the lovely clay;
The soul to heaven triumphant wings her way.

"So," continued M'Ginnis, "after this fine beginning, here's an end of this simple story. Your Poets always deceive: poetry is but the language of fiction. Your Poets and your Priests are all——But what's here? Some dull moral to conclude with! No. It's too much for that."

X.

Now comes the gloomy hour of night;
  Upon his couch the Knight he lay,
And still reviews with mental sight,
  The recent hours of the day.

"May every curse be heap'd upon my head,
"But I will find the maid, alive or dead!"

XI.

"She swore, and still shall be my bride!
  "Does Heaven above our vows record?"
"It does," a soft clear voice reply'd,
  "And Ellen comes to claim her Lord."
Up rose the Knight, and with a sudden bound
Rush'd from his tent, and hasten'd to the sound.

"Well, the fair damsel is come to life again; the story improves.
This, I suppose, is to be called Love and Honour: Love on the part
of the Knight, and Honour on that of the Lady."

XII.

The pallid moon, each twinkling star
  Without a veiling cloud, shone bright;
And, lo! he saw a glittering car,
  And Ellen seated, rob'd in white.
Four ebon coursers champ the foaming bit,
Four sable riders on their saddles sit.

XIII.

"Arise, Sir Knight, and mount my car!"
  In lively notes the virgin cry'd:
"From hostile tents of blood afar,
  "'Tis Ellen's choice to be a bride.
"Enough of war, enough of slaughter's past,
"Sir Hildebrand shall find repose at last."

XIV.

With nimble steps the warrior rose,
  And wou'd have clasp'd the beauteous maid;
But iron gratings interpos'd,
  And thrice in vain the Knight essay'd,
"Why do these envious bars," surpris'd he cry'd,
"From his lov'd spouse Sir Hildebrand divide?"

XV.

"Am I not a virgin pure?
  "Yes, Sir Knight, thou know'st it well.

"No mortal touch will I endure
  "Until I hear the wedding bell.
"Then fly, my speedy coursers—haste—away,
"And reach your destin'd mansion ere 'tis day."

XVI.

The snorting steeds obey the word;
  The riders crack the twanging thong;
The wheels scarce touch the crimson sword;
  The chariot seems to fly along!
Amaz'd, the Knight his wond'ring silence broke,
And thus unto the lovely maiden spoke:—

XVII.

"Whence come these noble steeds, my dear?
  "Sure, they were bred in regions far:
"By every Power above I swear,
  "That none so fleet yet drew a car."—
"Swear not, Sir Hildebrand; and, ere the morn,
"They'll bring thee to the clime where they were born."

XVIII.

With gathering speed the chariot springs,
  As from the hills the falling snow;
As light as on the breezy wings,
  Swift as the arrow from the bow.
Panting, the warrior gasps, and sucks the wind;
The vales, the plains, the mountains fly behind.

XIX.

So furious is the motion now,
  Scarcely the Knight retains his breath,
And cries—"Such rapid haste, I vow,
  "Might whirl one to the gates of Death!
"Speed so impetuous, how can Ellen bear?
"Can such rude motion suit a lovely fair?"

XX.

"Time was," the maiden answer gave,
  "When such rude haste might frighten me;
"But fears are fled beyond the grave,
  "There all is turn'd to certainty:

"And certainty, most valorous Knight,
"Shall be thy lot ere morning's light."

"So, after all, this is her ghost I see. Trash! Stuff! I'll have no more
of it!" and M'Ginnis threw the paper indignantly from him, and took
a turn up and down the room.—"Come, let us see how this goblin
story ends."

XXI.

"Why of the grave does Ellen speak?
"We live for happiness and love."—
"'Tis happiness and love I seek,"
Reply'd the maid, "and from above!"—
"Since," cry'd the Knight, "to me my Ellen's giv'n,
"I seek no other good, no other Heav'n."—

XXII.

Scarce had he spoke, when lo! a voice,
In deep and hollow accents, cry'd,—
"Sir Hildebrand, thou'st had thy choice,
"And death alone shall take thy bride.
"Death tears each bond, Death breaks each tie and vow;
"All yield to conq'ring Death, and so must *thou*!"

Again M'Ginnis threw down the paper, and spoke as if the words
had been addressed to himself.—"Well, then, let him meet me in
arms, and I'll not shrink from his blow! Now I have read so far, I'll
see the end of this pitiful story!"

XXIII.

"Who speaks?" impatient cry'd the Knight,
When, by the pallid moon, appear'd
An ancient man on steed milk-white,
With furrow'd cheek and hoary beard.
Bald was his head; one lock of hair alone
Hung down his face, suspended from his crown.

XXIV.

"Thy servant's come," exclaim'd the man;
"To bring thy marriage couch I haste.
"Behold this glass! The sand has ran."
He spoke, and swift the chariot past.

What means——? No more Sir Hildebrand cou'd say,
For Ellen loud exclaims in accents gay—

XXV.

"Stop, my good horses! well ye've sped—
    "Your work is done!"—Instant they stop.
"Behold, Sir Knight, your marriage bed!"
    He look'd, and wou'd have started up.
A cold strong hand upon his shoulder prest—
The cold strong hand his motion did arrest.

M'Ginnis started up, and sat down again. Without speaking a word, he read on.

XXVI.

Appall'd, he finds unusual fear
    Creep thro' each nerveless, trembling limb:
Aghast he looks, and sees a bier;
    These words declare it comes for him:——
"Here shall the flesh of Hildebrand decay;
But FIENDS OF DARKNESS bear his soul away!"

XXVII.

Scarce had he read—a loud-ton'd bell
    Tolls slowly out the note of death.
"Hark! hark! Sir Hildebrand, thy knell
    Is rung; thy body yields its breath!"
A voice exclaims: then, with a piercing howl,
"Fiends, seize your prey! your's is each villain's soul!"

"Confounded nonsense!" exclaimed M'Ginnis. "What a fool am I to spend my time in reading such trash! Here's not much more; let me see the ending of it."

XXVIII.

The wretch, despairing, turns his head—
    To Ellen strains his glaring eyes.
He sees, and sees indeed with dread,
    The maiden mounting t'wards the skies.
Seraphic guardians hail their lovely care,
And waft in safety through the yielding air.

XXIX.

In thund'ring notes an angel cries—
  "Behold, accurs'd! thy God's decree:
"He rescues from thy grasp the prize,
  "And dooms thee, wretch! to misery.
"Who dares his power, shall learn to fear his rod;
"Who spurns his word, shall tremble at his nod."

M'Ginnis exclaimed, not without a little of that sensation he
endeavoured to despise—"This, I suppose, would affect a superstitious fool. Pretty cant of words!"

XXX.

The ready fiends have got their prey;
  Struggling he writhes, he pants, he roars:
Then first his lips did "Mercy!" say,
  Then first confess'd the heavenly Pow'rs.
"When, wretch! to others hast thou mercy shown?
"Mercy condemns thee, and to Heav'n is flown."

M'Ginnis started up.—"I heard a groan! Pshaw! what is the matter with me? Is it possible this old woman's tale can—There! I heard
it again, by——Give me my sword!" and he snatched his sword
hastily off the table, and drawing it, flew with unusual agitation to
the spot. He listened, and now heard the groan distinctly repeated.
He looked around: under a large bureau he saw the legs of a man.
He pulled him from beneath.

A poor wounded fellow supplicated his mercy. M'Ginnis's heart
was a little softened. He seemed inclined to pity.

"Where are your wounds?"

"One on my side, Sir. I crept under this place, and am now
so weak with loss of blood, I could not stifle my groans any
longer."

"Can you walk?"

The man tried: he was too weak, and held by the furniture.

M'Ginnis stepped to the table, and gave him a glass of brandy. The
other drank it.

It revived him for a moment; he walked a few steps, and fell.

M'Ginnis had recovered that unfeeling tone of mind, in which he
laboured to excel. Smothering every sensation of human weakness,
he with affected apathy said, "We have no time to bestow upon the

sick." And as he spoke, with two blows of his sabre he finished the deed of blood!

He now called up one of his men, and ordered him to take away the dead body; and, with a sneering frown, worthy a modern Stoic, sat down at the table again.

The poem he had been reading still lay before him: it was not quite finished. He, with a philosophical calmness, continued.

XXXI.

The sun appears; the glorious morn
  Alike on rich and poor expands:
The thund'ring drum, the sounding horn
  Awake the drowsy martial bands.
They break the silken bonds of soft repose;
All but the Knight, Sir Hildebrand, arose.

XXXII.

Why does he sleep? His restless soul
  Ne'er yet indulg'd the weary head.
Why does he sleep? That restless soul
  Is far to distant regions fled!
The menials seek his tent: a ghastly sight
Arrests their steps, and fixes their affright.

XXXIII.

His grisly head all lifeless lies;
  His limbs distorted, stretch'd along;
Black is his face; his fiery eyes
  Have burst; suspended hung his tongue.
The carcase dark with livid spots appear,
And smells sulphureous taint the genial air.

XXXIV.

On every face sits pale alarm;
  A deathlike silence creeps around;
Each, shuddering, dreads some sudden harm,
  Till one, less conscious, utterance found.
"All power is thine, O God! Thy will is just.
"I own thy hand; on thee alone I trust!"

M'Ginnis was thoughtful for a few seconds. He put the paper

between his teeth, and tore it in halves. Recollecting himself, he said,—"Conscience! a pretty bugbear for grown-up children. Away with this trash—away with all the trumpery!" and he threw it into the fire.—"'Tis the work of some canting Parson. Would I had *him* here too! How willingly would I offer him up on this funeral pile!"

As he thus proceeded, muttering to himself, and in his hatred towards every thing virtuous and holy, venting, with his usual rancour, his invectives against the Ministers of religion, he continued throwing the rest of the papers before him upon the flames.

In a few minutes he was roused from his reverie by one of his men rushing into the room, and crying out—"A fire, Colonel—a fire!"

"Where?" exclaimed M'Ginnis.

"Your chimney, Colonel, is all in a blaze."

M'Ginnis seemed to recover himself as from a trance, when he observed the heap of papers he had piled upon the fire, and which in flames were flying up the chimney. Without a remark, he took the remainder off, and stifled the blaze under the grate.

But he could not so easily overcome the fire which raged in the chimney, and which rapidly began to spread.

For some time they endeavoured to smother it, but it proved in vain.

The building was old, and filled with large pieces of wood; and some, which crossed the chimney, quickly caught the fire.

M'Ginnis's men had drank hard; most of them at the commencement were fast asleep, and all ran about in hurry and confusion. The flames, too, were become powerful before any effectual measures could be taken to restrain them, and had blazed for some minutes before they had been discovered by the sentinel.

Greatly enraged was M'Ginnis with himself, for having been, in the most trifling degree, interested by the poem he had read.

At the very moment that he thought he shewed the highest contempt of conscience, by burying his sword in the breast of the wounded man, did he prove that it had in some degree affected him; for the deliberate act of his will was but an effort to stifle those feelings.

This bloody deed his inglorious mind had attributed in his own favour; but the inattention, that want of mental possession which followed, he could not so interpret even to himself.

M'Ginnis, finding it in vain to attempt a mastery over the flames, employed his troop in removing the most valuable of the furniture out of the house.

For this he had use; but, according to his promise, he gave his men a very liberal price for it, and, early in the morning, they assisted in bearing it to his own house.

CHAPTER XVI.

The gallant hero of these memoirs in having thus, in the open face of day, entered his men into the career of blood, and boldly thrown away the mask, no longer appears as a petty Captain of a provincial troop in his Majesty's service, but as a Colonel in *an United Body*, where there was a *Communion of Rights*, and an *Organized System* of *Fraternal Equality*. Fine things, as Dr. Line says, to begin with!

The sword thus unsheathed, M'Ginnis turned his thoughts to make his favourite habitation among the rocks still more inaccessible than Nature and the fears of two centuries had already done for him. Some parts of the old road he blew up. He made false roads to lead the unwary into his power, and dug subterranean passages.

His restless spirit was in its full glory, and the hours of repose were but the harbingers of his depredating activity; and day and night he had parties ranging about the country, and carrying off the goods and cattle of those whom he knew were hostile to his cause.

The whole country was all in a ferment: every man feared his neighbour as his foe; and resistance, unless where there were a few regular soldiers, was rarely attempted.

From the cultivated part of the land, which was covered with the cabins of the poor, did large parties of the natives sally forth at night, and plunder their helpless neighbours; and it was in these vast bodies of infantry that the strength of M'Ginnis consisted.

The houses of those who had been of his troop were the first destroyed: in some places he met with a temporary resistance, but in the end numbers succeeded.

In less than a month not a known enemy to the United Brethren resided within eight miles of M'Ginnis; and in a few weeks, for a great distance around him, the whole neighbourhood was in a state of successful rebellion; all of which he had the command of, and the success of which he attributed to his own decisive measures.

M'Ginnis did not confine himself to his rocky domain, but ranged over the whole country.

The Government forces, wherever he could find them in small bodies, he often attacked; and, favoured by the night, or by numbers, he succeeded, or made good his retreat.

His feats were not long in reaching the Directory, who rewarded his valour and conduct with the appointment of General of the District.

In a little time M'Ginnis had above a hundred horse under his command, and infantry to a very large amount, armed promiscuously. So strong did he consider himself, that, having arranged his plans with some of his neighbouring Officers, he joined them early in the month of March with a respectable body of cavalry, and invested the town of Cahir, in the county of Tipperary. This he boldly did in the open day; and, with the utmost order and discipline, searched every house for arms and ammunition, and carried the whole away with him.

In this expedition they mustered a thousand men, well armed, and chiefly horse.

They marched in exact order a chosen body of foot; the cavalry, divided in two parties, on the right and left, covered the infantry; and General M'Ginnis, upon as fine a horse as any in the King's service, rode in the front of the whole.

Yet, in defiance of all the exertions of M'Ginnis, the rising was not general: the more civilized parts hung back; the Executive Directory still delayed to give the word.

With what rage did our hero behold this delay: what curses did he not vent against their *babbling Chiefs*, as he always called them, in defiance of the honours they had invested him with.

To his most earnest remonstrances, the sole answer they deigned him was—that it was imprudent to rise before the arrival of the French, whom they daily expected.

Such was the state of M'Ginnis's affairs in Ireland at the commencement of the year 1798; and the ambitious prospects of the hero seemed to meet with no check but from the timidity of his own party. So general was the disaffection in that part of the country, that in the winter of 1797 he rarely inhabited his dwelling among the rocks, nor did he meet with any molestation within ten miles of his family residence. The robbery and murder of individuals had become so frequent, that it ceased to be a matter of surprise; and the uncivilized state, and natural wildness of that neighbourhood, made the depredations of M'Ginnis and his gang less an object of notice to the Government.

CHAPTER XVII.

From the scenes of blood and carnage which unhappy Ireland exhibits, let us turn our eyes towards England, where the *Phantom of licentious Liberty* has been offered up at the public altar of Peace and Security.

The letters of Fahany had informed M'Ginnis of the situation of *his* more intimate acquaintance;—but it will be necessary also to notice some occurrences which had happened to many other characters recorded in these volumes.

I shall omit a minute narration of young Harrety and Rattle's tour through the country, for many good and substantial reasons.— *Imprimis*, I have no time to spare from the main story, to enter into a long *episode*; and secondly, Mr. Rattle himself has some thoughts of favouring the world with the success of their joint mission, to oppose vice in every form.

They had travelled through the greater part of the West of England, and were proceeding northerly, when Harrety proposed that they should, without loss of time, turn into Wales.

In Wales Rattle called on his old friend Hambden Arnon, to whom, and his fair spouse, he introduced Harrety, with whose conversation, now a little modernized by being with Rattle, they were greatly amused. After staying here a few days, the two friends proceeded further into the country, till they arrived at the beautiful vale of Llandwillow. With what amazing rapidity runs the foaming Rockler adown the sides of the lofty Cloudwrapt! The summit of this wonderful hill, from whence this most impetuous of rivers derives its source, claimed their notice; and one fine summer evening, in the latter end of August, they rambled to the delightful spot.

Harrety was in raptures—Rattle not much less so. The former, glowing with the scene before him, burst forth—

"These are thy glorious works, Parent of Good,
"Almighty! Thine this universal frame,
"Thus wondrous, fair; thyself how wondrous then!
"Unspeakable!"[1]

Rattle at this instant clapped his hand on his friend's shoulder, with—"Hush! look on yonder brow," and pointed with his hand.

Harrety looked, and clasping his hands together—"Most sure they are Goddesses, or rather Angels. Nothing human have I seen so lovely. My dear fellow, let me address them."

"Soft! Harrety—they come this way. On my life 'tis—Confusion! they see us, and fly!"

---

1 John Milton, *Paradise Lost*, bk. V, l.153.

Harrety and Rattle flew up a winding path that led to an arbour, which Nature had formed on the top of a massy rock, from whose awful top rolled spontaneously a torrent, that would have sickened the sons of artificial cascades to have seen.

The travellers quickly gained the summit, but the Goddesses were vanished away.

Rattle flew one way, Harrety another; the pursuit was in vain. They returned to the grotto. For the first time since the commencement of their travels, they mutually accused one another.

"If you had suffered me to have addressed them," said Harrety.

"You alarmed them by your sudden harangue," said Rattle. "Goddesses, my dear friend, are always timorous."

"I'll live, I'll grow on this spot," continued Harrety, "but I will see them again! Marked you not that beautiful Nymph, more lovely than Poets feign Hebé[1] to have been? Did you observe the vest? Diana, the Goddess of Chastity, might have envied the foldings!—Ye pompous Drawing-rooms, Balls, Operas, and all ye Courts of Folly, hide your diminished heads! One child of Innocence, in the plain garb of Modesty, might shame ye all! I'll travel an hundred miles barefooted, to have one more view of the sweet maid!"

"Which of these wondrous beings, Harrety, is the object of your idolatry?"

"Both, upon my word."

"Nay, spare your friend one."

"Indeed, Rattle, though I had but a glimpse, yet I had a preference. That beauteous maid, whose snowy arms were not exposed to the rude rustic's gaze, demands my choice."

"My good fellow, you relieve me. I should have been sorry if you had chosen my Goddess; for, to let you into a secret, I firmly believe this is the charming fair-one I have been so long in pursuit of. You know her history. Since she fled from that villain, Marauder, in vain I have sought her; and 'tis but lately I heard that she was retired from all society, amid the mountains in Wales. This Hambden told me, but could not give me the least guess as to the spot. It is my firm belief I have now found her."

"Then let us away—fly from the dangerous spot! For your welfare, my friend, I resign my own hopes of again beholding the lovely maiden that was with her.—If this is the deceived, the penitent Emily, she is now in a new state of virtue and honour, and surely you would not again tempt her from their paths."

---

1 Daughter of Zeus and Hera in Greek mythology, and goddess of youth.

"Fear me not, Harrety; you have no reason to suppose me a villain."

"God forbid! my dear fellow; I wished only to lead you from *temptation*, that you might not fall into *evil*. Hymen frowns upon the unhappy connection with Marauder."

"Harrety, shall I quote your favourite book?—'There is more joy in heaven over one sinner that repenteth, than over ninety-and-nine just persons that need no repentance.'"[1]

"Enough—come on.—'*Meus dux est Crux*' is my family motto, and the rule of my actions."[2]

They descended the hill to a small village beneath; but not a being could they find that knew sufficient English to converse with them. It grew late; the sun was already set, and they were fain to take up their abode at a small ale-house, where cleanliness and civility sweetened their fare, and softened their couch.

CHAPTER XVIII.

In the morning they arose with the lark, and with the rising sun visited the grotto: from thence they crossed to the other side of the hill, from which they had ascended the evening before; but ere an hour had passed away, their steps irresistibly led them to the same spot.

Rattle's spirits were low; his love to Emily was true and constant, and he began to fancy that his warm imagination had deceived him.

Harrety was as usual; for, with all the wildness of his character, he was never subject to fits of despondency. Hope, smiling Hope, shined in his countenance.

As they came near the grotto, Harrety, remarking his friend's gravity, began—

"She disappear'd, and left me dark! I wak'd
"To find her, or for ever to deplore
"Her loss, and other pleasures all abjure."

Rattle, on a sudden, took up the quotation with his usual volubility—

"When out of hope, behold her not far off;
"Such as I saw her in my dream, adorn'd

---

1 Luke 15:7.
2 "My guide is the cross."

"With what all earth and heaven cou'd bestow
"To make her amiable."[1]

As he spoke, he sprung forward.

Emily (for it was no other) had started from her seat, and screamed as she flew out of the grotto.

Rattle was at her feet.

She instantly turned pale.

Rattle sprang up, and she fainted in his arms.

Harrety had scarcely time to make his obeisance to the other fair damsel; he flew, like a winged Mercury, to the torrent, for some water, and in a few seconds was sprinkling it in Emily's face.

Rattle, with one knee on the ground, was supporting his fair burden on the other, the young stranger untying her bonnet as Harrety returned with the water.

Emily soon opened her eyes, and stood up.

Rattle held her hand.

Harrety, whose feelings were solely occupied with the scene before him, instinctively took hold of the young stranger; yet in so mild and respectful a manner, that she had not the heart to withdraw her hand from him.

Emily turned from Rattle.—"Leave me, Mr. Rattle—leave me, I beseech you!"

"Never, dearest Emily, never—unless you say you hate me. Oh Emily! you are not ignorant how long I've loved you; though respect tied my tongue, my looks betrayed me. I never could, I never attempted to conceal my love,"—and he pressed her hand to his lips.

Harrety did the same to the young stranger, with an air and manner most soft and insinuating.

Emily could only repeat—"Leave me, Mr. Rattle!" and faintly tried to take away her hand.

Rattle continued—"Dearest Emily, I am not ignorant of any thing that has happened to you, and have long sought you in vain. Do not suppose, bad as you must think of mankind, that my intentions can be dishonourable. We are not all villains."

Emily sighed—her young friend did the same, and Harrety re-echoed *his* friend's words—"Indeed, fair Lady, we are not all villains," looking hard at Emily's young companion, who, as he spoke, mildly withdrew her hand from his.

---

1 John Milton, *Paradise Lost*, bk. VIII, ll. 478-84.

"No, Ma'am," continued Harrety, coming nearer to Emily, "with the most pure, the most disinterested love, does my friend seek your favour: your beauty first caught his eye, but your virtuous perseverance has won his heart. The noble conquest over yourself has doubly conquered him."

"This gentleman," said Rattle, introducing Harrety by name, "is no stranger to the sincerity of my affection. Permit me, ever-beloved Emily, to see you in the company of your friends."

"I have forfeited my own esteem," replied Emily, with a deep sigh, "and how can I think myself deserving of any one else's? When I fled from society into this wild country, you were the object I chiefly avoided."

"Me! dearest, sweetest Emily!"

"Your favourable opinion of me," continued Emily with a downcast look, "I was not ignorant of: I fear you guessed that you were not an object of dislike."

"This, dearest, dearest Emily!" exclaimed Rattle, as quick as thought, in raptures, "this open conduct is so like your true character, that candour I ever admired in you."

"Nay, Rattle," continued Emily, "I have learned sufficient caution in the world; but I wished to convince you of the trust I have in you, that you will not abuse my candour."

"If I do, then may—"

Harrety gave him a smart slap on the shoulders.

"My friend," said Rattle, "never swears; and he's checking me lest I should transgress. Yet, most adored Emily," dropping on one knee, and pressing her hand to his lips, "accept my vows of love and constancy—vows, sweet Emily, 'twill be the pride of my heart to publicly sanction, by the laws of my God and my country."

Rattle pleaded with the greatest success.

Emily, overpowered with her sensations, was nigh fainting a second time; but her lover's ready arms caught his lovely burden, and she turned not with coy disdain from his warm kiss of love.

In this respect young Harrety did not presume to follow his friend's example; but his looks clearly shewed that his inclination solely gave way to the propriety of his conduct.

The conversation became general, and the ladies permitted the attendance of their beaux towards their own habitation. Emily's residence was in another part of the village than that in which they had reposed the former night; and near to her house was another, which was the Parsonage, where the fair stranger lived.

The whole party went to the Parsonage. Emily introduced Rattle and his friend to the worthy Divine, his wife, and family.

They all breakfasted here; and Rattle was not sorry to find that Emily's former conduct seemed to be no secret to her friends, and that even *his* name was not before unknown to them.

Not less pleased were all the company with Harrety, who was in high raptures with every thing he saw and heard. Scarce was the breakfast over, as he was viewing from the window the beauties of nature, enriched and made useful by judgement and sense, but he exclaimed—"This surely was the blissful Paradise from whence Adam was driven. Such was the primeval state of innocency and peace in which our first parents lived; where, free from the vices and follies of man, free from the restless confusion and ever-bustling noise of the world—"

The lusty cryings of a young child, which rung again and again through the house, checked his rhapsody; and a little boy, about six years old, entered the room, blubbering most pitifully.

A new top, which Miss Emily had given him, had spun into the well; and to complete his troubles, his brother Dick had told him it served him right, for going so near to a forbidden spot.

"This is my youngest, Sir," said Mrs. Evans, addressing Harrety; "and I am sorry to say we rather make a pet of him. A certain lady in company I think I must blame for all this, who will absolutely spoil him. For shame, Tom! If I've any more of these airs, I'll put you in petticoats again, and send you into the nursery."

Tom's little Welch blood was by this time cooled: the vent was rapid, but soon over. Mrs. Evans sent him out for his brother.

"About six months ago," said she, "I punished him in the manner I mentioned, for he is a boy subject to violent passions—"

"Which he did not gain from me, my dear," said Mr. Evans, with a smile.

"Oh! certainly not—certainly not," said all the ladies at once; by which Rattle and Harrety easily understood that Mr. Evans was sometimes subject to these national paroxysms.

"I may as well plead guilty at once," said Mr. Evans; and turning to his wife—"Now, my dear, I hope before these strangers you will say something civil in return."

"I can only say," replied she, giving him her hand, "that I should almost be sorry to find you otherwise, for then I should lose one of a female's first privileges—the pleasure of finding fault. But I was telling Mr. Harrety of Tom, that the remembrance of his former punishment, in defiance of Miss Emily, is at present a sufficient check for these angry ebullitions."

In the course of conversation, Mrs. Evans informed her guests that she had seven children.

"My dearest Madam, it gives me the highest pleasure to hear it," exclaimed Harrety, in his warm way, though somewhat to the surprise of his hosts, who could little guess how the number of their family afforded satisfaction to the young stranger; "for, if the bold robbery my heart has already planned, should happily succeed, 'twill make the loss less severely felt."

The pretty Nancy Evans's deep blush reproved the hasty declaration of her admirer.

Harrety, whose eyes had sufficiently declared his meaning, felt the reproof.

"Pardon my abrupt method," continued he, "of expressing my feelings. Little hacknied in the ways of mankind, I have not learned to disguise them."

Harrety paused: Emily and Nancy walked out of the room.

Harrety continued.—"Yesterday I saw your lovely daughter for the first time; in a moment I was assured that she was not the offspring of a dissipated world: her dress, her air—I could not be mistaken!"

"Impossible!" exclaimed Rattle, warmly.

"This morning again I have seen her; I have conversed with her; my fancies of yesternight are realized; I find her beauties such as my warm wishes pointed them out to be. Is it necessary for me to plot and enquire further? No. I *despise* the heart that cannot act from its own feelings. Though I am quick in my resolves, I am not changeable—I act not from passion, but from feeling. Forms, customs, follies, and fashions of the world, I hate you! I aim but to be a Christian. Such as your daughter appears to me, innocent and lovely, I have long sought for—I require no more in a helpmate. My present means are liberal. Next year, by the blessing of God, I hope to enter into the sacred office. The Rectory of Groveley is in the presentation of my mother; my worthy uncle, Dr. Hearty, now holds it for me.—This is my history.—With the world I am no favourite; they call me enthusiast and madman. The world's opinion, given by the mouth of Vice and Folly, I despise. Whether I am any other than I now appear to you, my friend Rattle or any of my friends, for here I boast my greater riches, can inform you."

Harrety bowed with great ease to Mr. and Mrs. Evans, and joined the ladies whom he saw walking in the garden.

Rattle quickly corroborated every thing Harrety had said—spoke in the highest terms of him—sketched his birth, parentage and education—and, finally, gave Mr. Evans the address of his family and connection, that he might make any enquiries he thought necessary.

Not long was Rattle in adjusting this necessary business for his friend, before he made one of the party in the garden.

Which is most delicious, the renewal of a former passion, or the indulging in the first sensations of a new flame, may be a subject worthy the amplest discussion.

In the cases before us, doubtless each party thought their own *tête-à-tête* to be preferred.

Rattle, indeed, would have yielded the palm to no mortal breathing. He had not only found his long-lost Emily in equal grace and beauty, but her mind was cleared of those errors by which it had been before obscured; and she had not only seen, but amended her faults. To sum up his happiness, she approved and returned his love.

Young Harrety had at last realized the ideal perfection his sanguine thoughts had painted. Hope smiled upon him, but success was as yet at a distance.

While Rattle was haranguing, in favour of his young friend, to Mr. and Mrs. Evans, Harrety was not deficient in entertaining the ladies.

The pleasures of the country were his theme, where the beauties of Nature please the eye, uncrippled by the distortions of Art.

"But where Art embellishes and improves Nature, then, Mr. Harrety," said Emily, "you do not despise that genius which unites them together."

"No, Ma'am; Art ought to be to Nature, what proper learning is to the mind—what moderate exercise is to the body. Art should make Nature *useful*; but when it only tries to make it *beautiful*, it becomes a sweet that is grateful at first, soon cloys, and ever after disgusts. When, upon a *flat ground*, I proceed along a serpentine path, my reason condemns the winding of the way, though it may be the line of beauty; but, if the road winds up a hill, the small increase of distance is amply compensated, by making the ascent less steep, and use and beauty are united. I might carry my simile to the fair sex, in whom, in my humble opinion, one useful accomplishment outweighs a thousand of the tricks of fashion."

"The knowledge of a pudding or a pie—" said Emily.

"Is as much superior, Ma'am, to the whirling of a cymbal, or gabbling in a foreign tongue, as—"

"I am happy," replied Emily with a smile, "to hear you say so, for these former accomplishments I have lately learned, and the latter I have also lost; yet something I think may be said—"

The presence of Rattle stopped the defence Emily was about to make for those accomplishments in which she had once excelled; and in a few minutes the lovers mated together.

CHAPTER XIX.

Alone with the fair damsel, Harrety opened his pretensions.

"Have I your pardon, Miss Evans, for my presumptuous manner of addressing you?"

"Your sprightly sally more confused than offended me, Sir."

"Do not, my dear Miss Evans, for a moment believe that I was otherwise than in earnest. If you will permit me to offer my devoirs, it will be the glory of my life to be esteemed in your eyes, and to evince my truth and sincerity."

"So perfectly a stranger, Sir, as I am to you, my temper, mind, disposition so unknown, I cannot consider your behaviour otherwise than a joke."

"Upon my word, my pretensions are most real; every moment heightens my respect, my esteem, my love. Yet fixed as my hope is, I ask but to be permitted the honour of your acquaintance, that I may see and converse with you; and if on a further intimacy, you will sanction my choice, I have not the smallest fear that I shall ever repent the quick decision of my heart, which thus induces me to offer it to your notice."

Miss Nancy Evans did not refuse her lover's request.

Rattle and Harrety took up their residence in that neighbourhood for more than a month; at the end of which time, Rattle was united to Emily by the worthy Mr. Evans.

Fanny Bellaire came to the wedding, attended by their guardian, Mr. Townsend and Mrs Mountford's eldest daughter, a sensible young lady of about two-and-twenty.

Mr. Townsend left the young ladies with the new-married couple; and about a month after, Mr. and Mrs. Rattle returned with them to Richmond.

Harrety left his Welch friends a few days after the wedding, to wait on his mother, to gain her approbation of his choice.

Nancy Evans was every day more and more pleased with her admirer. Mr. and Mrs. Evans considered him almost as a superior being. His grammatical knowledge and manly mind astonished the worthy Vicar, and his mild and conciliating virtues were ever the theme of the mother: but, in the highest degree, were they pleased with the pure spirit of religion which influenced his whole conduct, and softened, with its benignant rays, his warm and susceptible heart.

Not less delighted with the object of his choice was Harrety; and while he poured the fond effusions of the purest love into her bosom, how often did his grateful soul offer up his silent thanks to that invisible hand, which had guided his steps to the mansion of peace and innocence!

From the period when Harrety first left his home to view the manners of the great world, he had at different periods often returned to his paternal mansion, where his mother resided: and, when he was absent, he regularly wrote to his beloved parent, though the uncertainty of his residence prevented his receiving a regular answer.

At the first commencement of his acquaintance with Mr. Evans and his family, he had informed his mother of the offer he had made to Nancy. His mother doted on her son; and so high was her opinion of his abilities, so well she knew the goodness of his heart, that, however strange his conduct might be, she never thought he acted wrong.

This over-fondness of his mother, happily the best of tutors had prevented from having any ill effects, while the youth became daily more deserving the universal favour he obtained. The education of Harrety, though irregularly conducted, had been most excellent; and since Mrs. Harrety had been unwilling to part with her son, Dr. Hearty himself, his mother's brother, who lived in the neighbourhood, superintended his instruction.

It had been for some time assented to by his mother that he should go to the University; but the death of his friend, the French Protestant, had so affected the youth, that it was for a time laid aside. His ramble to London had introduced him to Rattle, an acquaintance his friends saw with pleasure, whose lively manners and quick sense interested Harrety, and dissipated his former gloom.

His travels with Rattle still kept him from residing any time at College; and as he would now soon be of sufficient age to take holy orders, Dr. Hearty had no doubt that his superior abilities and learning would induce the Bishop of—to dispense with this part of his education.

This digression from the main incidents of the history of Marauder is somewhat necessary to the general tenor of my subject: but the more regular account of the conduct of M'Ginnis in Ireland is now resumed.

CHAPTER XX.

The arrests at Oliver Bond's the 12th of March, were a source of much exultation to General M'Ginnis, as he not only considered it in the light of removing his rivals, but now he trusted necessity would force out the rebellion.[1]

At this critical period, on the 31st of the month of March, 1798, was the GRAND PROCLAMATION issued by the Lord Lieutenant and Council.[2] In defiance of every exertion used by the leaders of the United Irish, it spread over the whole kingdom, like oil upon the turbulent waves; nor misrepresentation nor arguments availed. In the space of a few weeks its beneficial effects were perceived throughout the country.

Many parts of the Provinces were at the time in complete possession of the Rebels: on a sudden, the tide of popular frenzy began to subside. M'Ginnis, in spite of every exertion, was obliged to give way; and his depredations, day after day, were more and more confined. Quantities of arms, which had been for some months collecting and distributing among the lower classes of the people, were voluntarily given up to the Government, and the names of their leaders sealed their pardon.

No longer were the power and means of M'Ginnis concealed, no longer could he reign despotic over the country without opposition.

Troops began to assemble together with a determined spirit, to search the evil to the bottom; and the friends of the Government fled no more, but stood their ground.

Of all this—fatal change to the cause!—General M'Ginnis was writing to the new Executive Directory, and to the other leading members of the Union, who had been chosen in the place of those arrested; but he soon discovered that fears for the fate of their imprisoned friends prevented any bold stroke; and that, although an immediate insurrection was universally allowed necessary, they could by no means agree among themselves upon the manner of conducting it.

M'Ginnis now severely experienced the little power he had in the kingdom at large, and how confined his consequence was to his own neighbourhood. It was too late to repent his eagerness for a military

---

1   After a tip-off from the informer Thomas Reynolds, the entire executive of the Leinster province of the United Irishmen was arrested at the 12 March 1798 meeting at Oliver Bond's house in Dublin, save only three latecomers (including Lord Edward Fitzgerald).
2   Martial law was proclaimed on 30 March 1798, placing the yeomanry on permanent duty and allowing the "free quartering" of troops—that is to say, soldiers were able to extract supplies and demand accommodation from the people without recourse.

command—it was too late to press his ambition forward in the road of civil employments. Had he been among the Directory, he might have been the means of throwing down the gauntlet of war; but his present station was to obey: yet still his sanguine mind yielded not to the general weakness, but he encouraged his men, magnifying their hopes, and dwelling constantly upon the power, the numbers, and confidence of their Brethren, particularly in the Province of Ulster.

By these means, that part of the Province of Munster where M'Ginnis dwelt, still cleaved to the *affiliating system* with the warmest expectations, looking forward to the arrival of the French as a certain omen of success.

On the latter part of the month of May the exertions of the Government had been so vigorous, and the plans and intentions of the United Party been so ably investigated and laid open, that not the shadow of a hope any longer remained in secrecy. About the 23d of May an attempt was made for a general rising, which in some parts put on a formidable appearance.

The successes of the Rebels in the county of Dublin, in stopping of the mail-coaches, attacking small parties off their guard, and seizing on some few persons obnoxious to them, were re-echoed through the kingdom with so many exaggerations, that the more distant parts believed the work to be half done, and put on a new spirit upon the occasion.

General M'Ginnis was not behind hand in making the most of it, but embraced the opportunity to lead his men against some raw troops who had lately arrived in his neighbourhood.

He came upon them early in the morning, after a false alarm, in which he had harassed them all the night; and after a hard fought battle, succeeded by his numbers in destroying the whole.

This was in truth a great victory to him, as the first fruits of his success were the possession of some stores these troops had been appointed to guard. A large quantity of military accoutrements, with the baggage of most of the Officers of that regiment, fell also into his hands, and all of it was distributed among his men.

The account of this victory soon reached the ears of the Directory, and was by them, in the most pompous and self-sufficient terms, circulated through the kingdom. Specimens of their style have been given before.

Buoyed up with this great success, M'Ginnis began to find his ambitious hopes realized. Their late plunder had heightened the ardour of his troop, and totally dissipated the spirit of discontent and revolt which had begun to shew itself among the lower orders.

The General was resolved to improve their present advantage; and doubted not, in a very short time, to get the whole Province into a successful state of a rebellion, to make Munster the *rallying point of the Union*, and himself *the Generalissimo of the whole*.

CHAPTER XXI.

At this period he received another letter from Fahany, not, as usual, with a short address to M'Ginnis, but solely to Marauder.

M'Ginnis supposed that in his present character he had in some manner offended his old friend, and expected to meet with some disapprobation of his *new-self*, which in many letters had been the case. Some friends had informed him that his kinsman M'Ginnis took upon himself too much; others that he was haughty, proud, extravagant, &c. &c. &c.; and by these means he had a full opportunity of hearing what people thought and said of his conduct. Among the writers of this kind, Imphell had signalised himself in his duty to his patron, Marauder, though probably his real motive was envy of the trust and confidence which had been reposed in M'Ginnis.

The following was the letter he received from Fahany:—

"MARAUDER,
"Curse on all epithets, now there is no use in lying!"—

"What have we here?" thought M'Ginnis; "this is a curious beginning."

"Why I should write to you—why I should do any act but *one*, I can give no reason; yet write I will."—

"The enigma increases—no date to his letter: I presume my friend is in Bedlam."

"Perhaps if you were present, whose *head* I know to be pregnant with all that poets feign of art, craft, and invention—whose *heart*, unprejudiced with humanity, pity, or any mortal weakness, never checked what the other determined on—"

"Pretty indeed!—Compliments too!"

—"I might yet escape. Oh Marauder! if we were together in Italy—But I wish not to live—hear my story.

"At one of the most infamous (as the *world* chooses to bestow the term) gaming-houses in London—among the most infamous (but why are these *low* rogues more infamous than the *titled,* the *honourable* gamester?) of the fellows who frequent the same, I lost, three nights ago, five thousand guineas."—

"Fool! I thought so—I foresaw all this. But what does he mean by troubling me with the old tale of his folly? He cannot suppose that I'll advance the money?—Ah no! Marauder is too far off, and M'Ginnis must take care of his trust."

"Dreadfully enraged, I suspect foul play."——

"Dolt! there was no doubt of it."

"I got behind. I watched a man who had won part of my money—I fancied I detected him—I caught hold of his hand—I swore the dice were loaded—I insisted upon their being cut open; they were so, in my presence. I had been too hasty—the dice were fair. The man insisted upon my begging his pardon in the most abject terms. Still suspecting I had been wronged, I demurred. He abused me—I abused in return; the company interfered; I made some apology. Peace seemed to be restored. I played again. Luck went against me. Every fury in hell seized upon me. 'Twas my turn to throw.

"*There are* devils, Marauder! I felt them at that moment, and I feel them now! I caught one of the dice between my fingers—tried, as I had heard others did, to slide it *the number I wished* upon the table. I knew not what I did!

"The fellow I had insulted was on the watch—caught me in some bungling fact.

"The whole place was in an uproar.

"I abused and struck at my detector; he, with conscious strength, seized me violently by the nose. Hear me, Marauder! In vain I struggled with his Herculean grasp—he tore me along; and, amid the hisses of his associates, kicked me repeatedly, till I fell along in the street!

"Any means of revenge I would have employed—Means! I had none against a man the most conspicuous for bodily strength I ever met with."—

"Bad enough! But what of all this? Deny the fact of the cheating; prove your honesty by his blood!—Aye! Shoot him honourably the next day."

"You know, Marauder, I am no coward—you know my high sense of honour. Do you think I would suffer such a man to live?"—

"Most assuredly not. Of course he is no more. Why then this rodomontade tale?"

"I called next morning on one of the company present, desired him to be my second, and to bear my challenge to my enemy.

"'Challenge!' repeated he; 'are you ignorant who the fellow is?—Monkford, the fighting butcher! He uses his pistols another way. Nobody suspects him of cheating *with the rattlers*. He's a *Cully*.[1] We know *where* he picks up his cash. Leave him alone: the gentlemen of Bow-street will have him in a few days.'

"Such were my associates! What could I do, Marauder? The thing was become public. Sir Charles Tossup and Lord Jewson—*gentlemen, men of honour, respectable characters, like myself*, were present. All St. James's rung of it!

"I rushed into the country to hide my cursed head—to think—to plot—to fly the kingdom—any where—any where—any where—No where!!!—An execution at my house!—an arrest issued against me!—I am seized!—a prisoner in my own apartment. Marauder! you remember the beautiful spot, the avenues, the walks, the distant river winding among the trees. Every thing valuable and excellent is gone—the rest a chaos—a ruin; not the wreck of *Nature*, but of the infatuated villain, Fahany. No more!—The pistol is loaded by my side. I seal this; and then an abused wife is released—deserted children are provided for!

"Yet another dying word:—Twelve years am I your senior, Marauder. How far my *learning* and *abilities* are superior to yours, you, who have so oft employed them, cannot be ignorant."—

"The *book knowledge* I allow, friend; pardon me the rest."

"Yet, strange infatuation! I have ever been your dupe."—

Marauder smiled at what he conceived a strong proof of his own superiority, and read on.

---

1 Usually a slang term for a dupe, but "to cull" was to swindle someone else.

"When first I knew you, I might, in the cant of the sect, be called *a decent Deist*. Now what am I?—Ah! *would I were an Atheist!*—What do I believe? you may ask me—I cannot say; this alone I know, that I do not *disbelieve* any thing. I am bewildered in doubts and confusion, and every one seems right who *acts* not, who *reasons* not with Fahany. *You* were once a Roman Catholic; *your* people say prayers can atone for the dead. Be so again—remember *me*—pray for *me*—be any thing rather than like the self-murderer,

FAHANY."

M'Ginnis's first note of sorrow was a long whistle—"Whew!—a pretty reason for shooting himself, because a brother-gamester, who happened to be an odd compound of butcher, boxer, and highwayman, kicked him. What would I have done?—Met him in his own element, and, without asking any questions, have shot *him* instead of *myself*. But my poor friend, if he had purposed so to do, could not; for the naughty bailiffs had him in limbo. That was his own fault—another instance of his not knowing how to avoid *bad company*; yet, considering that he had no cash to pay—no means to get any, it is all very well as it is.—But this pretty epistle!—"

As M'Ginnis spoke with his accustomed manner of sneering at the fate of his friend, he held up the letter.

"Such is the last production of my most learned and able friend!—An excellent end for so fine a genius! Well, so much for Fahany. Fahany! one of the first scholars of the age. Fahany! the universal linguist—Fahany! who, at the age of one-and-twenty, had twelve thousand a year, without the smallest deduction—who married the prettiest woman in England, with a mind so pure, that even the husband could never find a blot: yet this Fahany, at the age of five-and-thirty, has ruined his fortune, health, and character, perverted his abilities, debased his learning, abused his own wife, tried to ruin his children, at last cheats for a few pounds, and suffering every indignity through his own baseness, blows his brains out to finish the scene!"

The jaundiced eye of M'Ginnis could view the wretched picture of his friend through the most sombre tint; but when he turned his looks inwardly to himself, how gaudy was the colouring, how highly was the painting varnished, how favourable was the light in which he placed it.

Lost in the pleasing contrast for some time, did M'Ginnis take a mental review of the occurrences of his own life; with the highest self-approbation did he consider the difference of his own conduct, and applaud that wary and prudent behaviour which he had no doubt would, long before he arrived at the age of the deceased Fahany, make him a man of the very first eminence.

The death of his companion in iniquity gave this *genuine modern philosopher* not a second moment of uneasiness. Certainly, in the whole, the circumstance was a satisfaction to him: Fahany had long been useless to him—a sufficient reason to make him indifferent about him. Fahany knew many a secret of villainy—they all perished with him.

There was a time indeed, in which Fahany was every thing to Marauder—when high in blood, the youth first travelled into Italy.

Young and inexperienced, with no particular acquaintance, Fahany was struck with his spirit—Fahany introduced him to all his friends—and Fahany soon became the tool of the crafty Marauder.

Not only in the infamous affair of Geutespiere had Fahany been at his service; but, ever ready to second him in his daring attempts, he had once condescended to play the part of a common assassin.

Marauder had taken a fancy to a pretty girl, not easily to be attained, before the affair of Leonora: a watchful brother, a low mechanic, was ever in his way.

Fahany advised a common bravo.

"No," said Marauder; "we may be betrayed—let us do the work ourselves."

The tradesman by the greatest luck escaped them, through the nimbleness of his heels.

His sister was the next day in a Convent. Marauder and Fahany thought it most prudent to leave the place, lest retaliation should follow suspicion; and Leonora, soon after falling in the way of Marauder, prevented any further attempt on their part.

By the same packet in which Fahany's letter was received, one also arrived from Arnon.

This letter was very short and gloomy. Arnon professed an earnest desire to see him, and seemed to allude to some secret which pressed upon his mind, and which he was anxious to communicate to his friend Marauder.

M'Ginnis read Arnon's letter with high glee.—"If I once again get to the speech of my old friend," cried he, "Hambden Arnon, beware!—Make the most of thy Welch property, for thy offended father will assuredly disinherit his renegade son."

CHAPTER XXII.

M'Ginnis remained no time idle and inactive; he soon after prepared to attack about *five hundred* men in the neighbourhood of Kilnclugh, before they could be joined by any other troops.

The body of horse, which he commanded in person, was about a hundred, well mounted and caparisoned; and the infantry which he could raise in the neighbourhood, to six or seven hundred men.

He considered his former action as having changed the fate of Ireland. The news of his victory he doubted not was spreading like wild-fire through the kingdom; and he was certain it would be a cordial to the spirits of those in arms, and a stimulus to the doubtful and the dilatory.

M'Ginnis was up early in the morning, vigorous with his former conquest, and alive with new hopes.

Scarcely had he reviewed his forces, and was giving to the Colonels and the Captains the necessary orders for the attack, when a messenger came up with a confirmation of the reports which were before in circulation, that a French force had actually landed, and had, with very little opposition, taken possession of the town of Killala.[1]

M'Ginnis's ambitious soul could in no wise restrain his joy: he read the note aloud to his army.—"Now, my brave fellows, Ireland is free; *our* deeds first checked the torrent; with arms unequal to the foe, *we* have already drove them before us. Now we are, all of us, provided with the same arms—ammunition in abundance, and resources without end. Unpractised in the art of war, the cannon has been of little use to you; now the first engineers in the world shall accompany your labours, and direct your attempts. The French will instantly proceed to the capital—there we will soon join them. This morning we must again signalise ourselves—your valour demands the plunder, but let it not restrain your pursuit; follow the foe, and take no prisoners."

M'Ginnis preceded his large body of infantry with his horse, and completely concealed their number. They came with the utmost silence upon the enemy, who were scattered through different parts of the neighbourhood: the horse wheeled to the right and left, and the foot, with guns, pikes, &c. &c. on a sudden rushed forward with violent noise and outcries, and got into their camp. The confusion was so great, that, instead of collecting together,

---

1 The French landed at Killala on 22 August 1798.

the enemy, in scattered parties, endeavoured to reach the neighbouring town, while M'Ginnis with his divided cavalry charged
them as they attempted to form without the trenches, or pursued
the fugitives.

The pursuit led M'Ginnis and his horse beyond his infantry; they,
contrary to strict orders, not only consumed their time in pillaging
the camp, and burdening themselves with useless plunder, but meeting with some tempting viands, began carousing.

M'Ginnis, pursuing the slaughter, was within sight of the town,
when he determined to follow up his success, to wait for his infantry,
and storm the place. The knowledge that there was a large party of
friends of the United Irish in the town, made him consider the event
as certain.

With some difficulty he called off his men, and formed them in
their ranks.

Every thing had smiled on the prospects of M'Ginnis. The path
which a Cæsar and a Cromwell trod with such success, seemed to
lay open to our hero; and, like them, he resolved that his own sword
should carve out as glorious a destiny.

He had just sent off a messenger to hasten the arrival of his
infantry, when, to his great joy, he saw a small body of cavalry coming out from the town.

M'Ginnis, his men, his horses, were upon their full mettle; he had
great trouble to restrain their ardour, and continue them in their present situation behind a wood, that the enemy might not be intimidat-
ed by knowing the number opposed to them. He waited till they had
crossed a small defile, very rugged, and dangerous from the unevenness
of the country, and the roads having been totally destroyed, before he
shewed his whole force. He charged them immediately.

M'Ginnis rode at the captain of the other troop, who did not
decline the combat; but owing to the ground, they passed one
another at some distance, exchanging their pistols. But who can
describe M'Ginnis's sensations when he recognized the well-known
face of Wilson? The other also was struck with the likeness to his old
enemy, but Marauder he had heard was gone to the West Indies; yet
the look of M'Ginnis, as he remembered Wilson, in defiance of the
difference between Marauder and the present person, dwelt forcibly
on his mind that this was the same.

Equally eager were both to meet in the next charge. The rough-
ness of the country prevented their acting in a body; and with their
ranks broken, each party attacked the other as they found it most to
their advantage.

Two men desirous of meeting, could not be long separated. After again passing each other within their swords' length, when Wilson was soon satisfied it was Marauder himself (for of his cousin he had never heard), they turned their horses short round, and slowly and determined came up to each other.

But now the noise of M'Ginnis's infantry approaching, checked the personal anger of Wilson, and induced him to provide for the safety of his men, instead of gratifying his own revenge.

He made a motion to them to retreat, and being well mounted, turned from M'Ginnis, and leaped over a wall into an adjacent field, across which he could more easily join his troop.

M'Ginnis had the first horses of any man in the kingdom, and instantly followed him; Wilson, finding himself pursued, could not decline the combat.

He wheeled his horse round as M'Ginnis came furiously up.

In a moment they were together. As they mutually struck, Wilson said—"Ah, Marauder!"

The other uttered only a curse.

M'Ginnis, considerate, crafty, and revengeful, thought only of making sure of his old enemy; the means he cared not about. Wilson, open and vindictive, fought with equal hatred.

After a few blows, M'Ginnis gave a fatal one to the horse of the other, and the ill-fated rider fell with the poor animal to the earth. M'Ginnis exulted, and, as Wilson sprung up, meditated a finishing blow, the full effect of which was turned aside by the other's sword; but the blood streamed in profusion down his face.

M'Ginnis again gave vent to his joy, and seconded his blow. Wilson, now more on his guard, sprung forward, avoided the cut, and seized the reins of the horse: at the same instant Wilson wounded him in the body.

The horse reared and plunged. A second blow from Wilson missed the body of his adversary, but alighted upon his thigh. M'Ginnis writhed with the pain, and losing his seat, the animal threw him.

Now had Wilson finished the crimes of the infamous Marauder, when the noise of the infantry, coming to the assistance of their Chief, induced him to leave his prey, and provide for his own safety. Without losing a moment, he sprung on M'Ginnis's horse, and hastening after his own troop, collected the stragglers, and made the best of their way to the town.

M'Ginnis's men, seeing the situation of their General, had no inclination to pursue them in their retreat.

The whole body were so panic-struck at the fate of their gallant leader, that they were not to be prevailed upon by any other of their Officers to make an attack upon the town.

Six of them carried M'Ginnis back in his military cloak, and a surgeon from among them soon examined his wound. Having stopped the blood, he pronounced, to the great joy of the men, that there was no danger if he was kept quiet.

M'Ginnis himself spoke not a word. Shame, passion, disappointed revenge harrowed his soul, and tied his tongue; and to the enquiries of his attendants where he chose to be taken, he solely answered—"To the rocks."

CHAPTER I.

The history of Wilson, not yet recorded, to the period when he encountered his twin luminary, under the auspices of the bloody planet Mars, though not pregnant with adventure, had nevertheless been highly interesting to himself.

The corps, in which Wilson had a command, thought proper to volunteer their services, in defence of their Protestant Brethren in Ireland, contrary to the opinion of some of their Officers, among whom was Wilson. Yet, when the Government accepted their offers, the virtuous principle of Wilson was not sufficiently strong to bear the opprobrium of cowardice, though in a right cause. This shews how weak is virtue when the temptation comes in the most trying point:

"Take any form but that, and my firm nerves
"Shall never tremble."[1]

Wilson had, what all the world are trying to get as an excuse for their own faults—EXAMPLE, to countenance him; and it was not till the rest of the Officers had agreed to go, that he also assented. Yet, by particularizing these circumstances, a defence for his conduct is not intended. He certainly acted wrong, and he himself was afterwards most ready to own it.

He had with difficulty prevented himself from accepting the challenge of Marauder; in *that* case a plea was wanting—in *this*, he fancied it was his duty to act as he did. Had he more narrowly asked his conscience, he would have found that there *was a duty* superior to the one he obeyed, and which he ought to have followed.—The stigma of a *public* coward is most hard to be borne!—True.—The trial it is confessed was difficult, and Wilson was conquered. Few people will condemn him for acting as he did; but it is to be considered that he was in a corps where the going was voluntary, and not according to any articles he had entered into.

He went over to Ireland, therefore, with the rest, in the beginning of the spring, and was for some time quartered in the neighbourhood of Dublin; but afterwards two troops were stationed in that part of Munster where M'Ginnis met with him.

---

1 Shakespeare, *Macbeth*, III, iv, 122-23.

Wilson could not leave England without visiting Fanny. He called; and, after common civilities, mentioned his intended departure.

Fanny, who was no casuist in these cases, whether or not he ought to go, considered only that he was really going. She burst into a flood of tears the moment he had spoken.

"Oh Mr Wilson! you know I consider you as a brother."—That unlucky word gave an electrical chill to the spirits of Wilson.—"I cannot hear of your going to that wretched country without shewing my sorrow. Let me entreat you not to go. I shall lose all my friends. My good guardian is going to Edinburgh, and will not be back for some months. If you, my brother, leave the kingdom—"

"My dear Miss Fanny, my promise is given to go with the regiment. Were it possible to be otherwise, one word from you would turn me at any time; or, could I be of the most trifling service—"

"You know, Mr. Wilson, how I am situated. Willingly would I live with my sister—she will not permit it."—(This conversation was long before the meeting with Rattle.)—"It is some consolation to me to hear how agreeable her retirement is become, by the friendship of the worthy Vicar and his family, whose residence is so close to her own. To my earnest entreaties to join her in Wales, she as constantly replies, that my affection shall never suffer by her follies and imprudence. Mr. Townsend and yourself are the only friends to whom I can unburthen my mind;—now you both leave me.—My acquaintance in this family are kind and amiable;—but, Oh how different from the friends of the heart—relations natural and adopted, in which last light, Mr. Wilson, I have long considered you."

"It is the pride of my life to be so highly favoured. Yet why, Miss Fanny, should you think yourself deserted when so many young men are ambitious of your notice."

In this awkward manner did poor Wilson commence a conversation, which Mr. Townsend desired him, that Fanny might choose one from the many beaux that surrounded her, before his journey to Scotland; for though she lived, by choice, in a very recluse manner, she had not escaped the notice and admiration of the other sex.

Many splendid offers had courted her favour, but all had been heard with the greatest coolness. Her guardian also had received overtures from many; but among others, he wished his ward to choose from two young men, whose birth, persons, fortunes, and accomplishments he considered as unexceptionable. Frequently he had spoken to her himself upon the subject, but he could never get a satisfactory answer. Upon this point he addressed Wilson, when the other informed him he was about to go to Ireland, and desired him to try to persuade Fanny to make a choice before they both left her.

"The friends I have," said Fanny, in reply to his last question, "I so severely feel the loss of, that I have no wish to entangle myself with new ones. It is better never to have, than to have and be forsaken."

"I did not think, Miss Fanny, I should ever accuse you of unkindness; but so far from forsaking you, indeed, if it would promote your happiness, I would suffer every ignominy sooner than leave you.— You frequently honour me with the title of brother,"—Wilson sighed; "may I not as such enquire if, among the gentlemen who court your favour, you do not approve of one more than the others."

"No; why should I?—I know very little, and wish not to know more, of any of the persons you mean."

"Mr. Wildermere," continued Wilson, with the greatest resolution, "you have been acquainted with some years, and Mr. Townsend informs me that he is a respectable young man of family and fortune;—the Honourable Mr. Leeson is the second son of a very worthy Nobleman, high in favour with the Minister. Both these, Miss Fanny, have long declared themselves your admirers."

"I have frequently answered them, Sir, that I have no wish to change my situation."

"When so valuable a prize is in view, young men are not so easily daunted."

"Mr. Wildermere I particularly dislike—he is so great a coxcomb. My acquaintance is less with Mr. Leeson, but I do not desire it to be greater."

"He bears a most excellent character; and his family—"

"Do you wish, Mr. Wilson, to recommend him to me?"

"My dear Miss Fanny, I cannot so far presume. *My* sole intention, as well as Mr. Townsend's, was—to see—we thought—if—I mean— had you chosen *one* protector before we departed, the rest would keep at a distance.—We should be happy to see you well allied."

"If it will make *you happy* to see me married," replied Fanny, with a little spirit, "I will endeavour to fix my affections, since a single life occasions so much trouble to my friends."

"No, Miss Fanny, do not, I beseech you, attribute my interference to so unkind a motive. Mr. Townsend wishes not to constrain nor to hasten your choice. The gentlemen I have mentioned, *he* considered as most eligible. I am but little acquainted with either of them. There are many others I know, who—"

"Well then, as my friends are so anxious I should be settled, I will endeavour to remove their suspense as soon as possible."

"You have then a preference, Miss Fanny?" exclaimed Wilson, in evident alarm; "may I presume to ask who is the man so highly blessed?"

"Surely, Mr. Wilson, it can be of no great concern to you. You are going to leave the kingdom long before it can take place. Perhaps it is neither of the gentlemen you have offered to my notice. It may be I have reason for concealment, even from you."

Fanny still spoke with some *asperity*, perhaps *coquetry*; if it were so, it was but a slight portion of that innate playfulness of the sex. Wilson, nevertheless, was extremely hurt; and tremblingly alive to his feelings, replied—

"I shall be most miserable, my dearest Miss Fanny, if what I have said has offended you."

"How can it, Sir?—You speak but as a brother, who finds the care of a sister somewhat troublesome to his feelings."

"No, Fanny, I speak *against* my feelings;—I speak what, I hope, may be for *your* benefit, but what ruins mine!—Yes, Fanny, 'tis the greatest happiness of my life to see you, to speak to you, to write to you;—but, when that day comes which gives you to another, I must write, speak, and see you *no more*."

Wilson was greatly affected. During the whole of the conversation did he try to over come his sensations; he trembled as he uttered the last words, and, as he finished, walked towards the window.

Fanny could not fail to notice the agitation of his mind; she walked up to him, and taking his hand, kindly said—

"My dear brother!"

Surely never did the note of affection come in so unseasonable a moment, or was so kind an epithet ever so ungrateful. Wilson could not stand it; hastily withdrawing his hand from hers, then again as eagerly catching it, and imprinting a kiss, he dropped it with a sigh, and said—

"Dear Fanny, God bless you!—I can no longer dissemble.—If I must be as a brother, never can I see you again; unless in the hour of difficulty and danger, which I trust will never be your lot;—should you need a protector, then, wherever he is, Wilson will leave the world to fly to you.—Yes, Fanny, my life, my fame, my fortune, I'll willingly devote to your service. But I cannot stand by, and give you into the arms of another.—Fond fool that I was! I have nourished the passion that consumes me!—Presuming on your friendship for me, I have sometimes fancied I might have another interest in your heart, very different from that of a brother. God bless you then, my dear *sister!*— Since it must be so, your *brother* will send his last farewell from Ireland."

Wilson was rushing hastily out of the room; Fanny spoke.

"Dear Wilson, stay—don't leave me in this hasty manner!—You shall be all that's dear to me;—but not my bro—"

The last word hung upon her lips as Wilson, having turned around, triumphantly clasped her in his arms, and stopped any further confession by the chaste kiss of love.

Fanny smiled upon him; the enraptured lover poured out the secrets of his whole soul to his mistress, and every fear fled away before a mutual eclaircissement.

Mr. Townsend was not long in knowing the effects of Wilson's oratory to induce Fanny to sanction the addresses of a more favoured lover, and he highly approved of her choice.

The Irish expedition was considered by the gentlemen as too far advanced to be now delayed, and Fanny silently acquiesced. Wilson, full of hopes, left England; enlivened with the promise of his Fanny, that her hand should be bestowed where her heart was already, as soon as he returned.

CHAPTER II.

When M'Ginnis was somewhat recovered from the faintness which the great loss of blood had occasioned, the agitation of his mind became so violent, that it was with difficulty the surgeon could restrain him from sallying forth in the evening, wounded as he was, in search of his adversary.

Exclusive of his original hatred against Wilson, revenge for his late miscarriage spurred him on; and, to complete his angry passions, he found that the other remembered him.

In the person of Wilson he saw his ancient enemy, his present foe, and the man who, at a future day, might be his utter ruin. Willingly would he have given half his property to accomplish the destruction of Wilson, which he was resolved should take place in a more sure, though less public manner than he had so lately attempted.

He spent a restless, sleepless night; full of plots, unresolved and confused.

The next day he was in a high fever; and being satisfied of the absolutely necessity of his own confinement and quiet for a time, he gave orders to the most trusty of his Officers, to take all but twenty chosen horse, and, with as many of the infantry as they could muster, to endeavour to join the French forces; he told them also, that he would himself follow as soon as his wounds would permit, which he hoped would be in a few days.

In the evening of the second day after his rencounter, M'Ginnis sent some trusty horsemen to the neighbourhood of Kilnclugh, to endeavour to bring off a few prisoners, that he might gain some information of the forces that remained in those parts, and if Wilson was still among them. He had reason to think that they had joined the troops of the Lord Lieutenant; though he was fearless of any attack in his present station.

They brought two men. By them he found that to prevent a junction of the rebel forces, they kept the same situation; and that Wilson, and part of the corps to which he belonged, were in barracks without the town, in an old Monastery.

One of the men was of the same troop, and for some time M'Ginnis questioned him, in hopes that he might prove equal to the task, which he at present intended. He found this man, as well as the other prisoner, totally unfit; and his mind now revolved among his own men, for one bold and resolute, whom he could trust.

After a little thought he fixed upon a fellow, of the name of O'Rourk, one who had repeatedly signalised himself for his intrepidity and spirit, and but the day preceding M'Ginnis's last attack, had been engaged in skirmishes in the same part of the country.

Often when M'Ginnis has viewed the bold, haughty, savage, and desperate conduct of this fellow, has he said within himself—

"Such a one should I have been, had I been born in his humble station."

When M'Ginnis first came to Ireland, this man was at sea, whither he had fled to avoid the stronger arm of the law. In a private quarrel with a countryman concerning a pretty girl, O'Rourk had left the other for dead, and fled the kingdom immediately. Hearing his rival was recovered, he left his ship, where he had also signalised himself in the mutiny, and returned home.[1] His mistress he found in the house of M'Ginnis, and much too high to listen to any overtures from him.

O'Rourk joined the United Irishmen; and having very soon brought himself into notice, M'Ginnis took him into his own corps, and in a little time he became a great favourite, and domesticated in the house. Here having frequent interviews with his mistress, it is likely his violent temper would have burst all bounds, had he not

---

1 The mutinies at Spithead, near Southampton, and the Nore, on the Thames estuary, in the spring and summer of 1797 immobilized the British navy. Although mostly caused by resentment at harsh conditions aboard ship, there were also political elements to the protests.

had sufficient employment to prevent brooding, mischief-making thought.

M'Ginnis had frequently noticed his behaviour to Nelly. Sometimes the damsel would condescend to trifle a little with her old lover, and the ruffian would catch a half-willing kiss. About a week before he had received his wound, M'Ginnis had discovered their former acquaintance, and he had wavered in his mind whether or not he should get rid at once of so dangerous a rival; but well knowing it was in his power at any time, by sending him on a dangerous adventure—or, if that should fail, by his own pistol in the confusion of an action, he spared him, at least for the present, while he had occasion for his services.

Concerning the fair Nelly, M'Ginnis cared but little, yet he was never inclined to resign any thing without an equivalent, or for his own peculiar advantage.

He now sent for O'Rourk into his chamber. The man came. The attendants were all dismissed out of the room.

"O'Rourk," said M'Ginnis, "I saw you kiss Nelly the other day as I crossed the court."

O'Rourk coloured with anger.

"Nay," continued M'Ginnis, "perhaps you can tell me you have a prior right—a better title than myself."

O'Rourk was silent, but his gloom gave way to his attention.

"O'Rourk," the other proceeded, "answer me with your usual candour—how do you like me as your Commander?"

"Well—very well," replied the other; "in action no man can excel you. You are haughty at home; but perhaps that is what they call discipline. I am satisfied."

"Of what use is my courage *now*?" said M'Ginnis, with a deep groan.

"I am sorry to see your Honour so grievously wounded," exclaimed the other, somewhat moved; "would I had been with you at the moment—my trusty shellala—"

"I marked my enemy on the left cheek," M'Ginnis continued, "but *my sword* failed me."—The nicety of truth he no more regarded than his kinsman, Marauder.—"Had you come up, O'Rourk, the villain would not have escaped."

"I hope we shall have him yet," replied O'Rourk, with glee, forgetting the beginning of the conversation.

"I know him well," said M'Ginnis; "had I not been in this stage, he should, ere now, have bit the dust. In England I have before seen the fellow. He is the rascal that ruined the fortune of my worthy relation, Marauder, your excellent landlord."—He indulged himself next in his invectives against Wilson, till he thought he had enough inflamed the passions of his vassal.

"Would I had him here by the throat!" exclaimed O'Rourk; "I'd bury my skean[1] in his heart's blood."

"With an enemy so infamous, treacherous, and unprincipled, any means are fair?" said his Officer to him, putting his words in the form of a question.

"Undoubtedly," replied the other.

"Never again will the wretch meet me face to face in battle. I hear he still survives, and I am cautioned to beware of treachery. It is my duty not only to guard against it, but to serve him in his own kind."

"If I should find him in his bed, your Honour, I'll not ask him to rise. If I can catch him in his cups, I will not wait till he has finished his draught."

"Yes, O'Rourk," said M'Ginnis, warmly, "that brave spirit of thine made me fix my eye upon thee, as one most trusty, and never to be daunted. But think not I mean to send thee on a hazardous attempt, and then talk of some petty reward. No; I'll furnish thee with the means of success. The danger shall not be great;—to a man of thy courage it shall be as nothing.—If then, O'Rourk, thou wilt undertake this work of friendship, not only will I give up to thee a comfortable farm, with ready money, and for ever make thee independent; but I will sacrifice my own desires to thine—thou shalt have Nelly too."

The joy of the savage forbade all utterance; the moist drops of gratitude glistened in his eyes; his rugged features softened with his silent thanks. But ardour in his generous patron's cause, revenge against *his* enemy quickly roused him.

"Where is the cursed villain to be found?—Tell me, your Honour, but *how* I am to know him, and the first day he ventures into the field, though the devil himself were by his side, I'll ride up to your enemy, and cleave him in his seat, or perish in the attempt!"

"His coming into the field," remarked M'Ginnis, sarcastically, "may be long, and uncertain at last. I'll shew you a nearer way. Get privately to his presence, shoot him, and make your escape."

"Sir!—murder him in cold blood!"

"Do you demur how you are to destroy such a wretch?—my

---

1   More usually "skene," an Irish dagger.

enemy—your enemy—the enemy of every United Irishman, every friend to his country?"

"General, have I ever been slack in the cause—when, in the day of battle, have I shrunk back?"

"What, then you require the noise and confusion of a common fight to rouse your courage.—Is it the brave O'Rourk that I am talking to?—Am I myself a coward who propose the deed?—Is the lovely reward of no value?"

"It is enough," he answered with firmness, "you are my Commander;—it shall be done. I would, indeed, rather have met hand to hand; but your reasons are sufficient—your cause, my country's cause make it right."

A satisfactory smile illumined the features of M'Ginnis;—he perceived O'Rourk had somewhat more to say.

"May I see Nelly before I go?—How am I to satisfy you the deed is done?"

"I'll take your word," replied M'Ginnis, with an affectation of candour. "See Nelly if you like: yet I think you had better not, till you return. Women—are women, O'Rourk; there is a kind of foolish pity they cannot overcome."

"I will not see her till I return with success. If I fail, you shall never behold me more."

"You cannot—you shall not fail," exclaimed M'Ginnis, with a dreadful oath.—"Now, O'Rourk, hear attentively the methods I have taken for your success.—Do you know my famous English stallion?"

"Do I know the first horse in the world, your Honour?—In speed, in strength he excels all I ever saw;—and in leaping, not even our famous Irish horses can beat him. On him I fear nothing."

"On him you shall ride.—Know you an old large building, once a Monastery, near the town of Kilnclagh?"

"Close to the left hand of the old gateway?"

"The same. In those apartments lodge my enemy and his comrades. Ride to the gates of the building, ring the bell, ask for their Captain Wilson. Take this parcel."—As M'Ginnis spoke, he opened a drawer, and holding it in his hand, continued—"Say you must deliver it to none but himself.—Mind me, O'Rourk;—examine this part which I now touch with my left hand—pull that piece which rises at top;—there, 'tis a pocket-pistol. Now 'tis cocked; see, the trigger is sprung from beneath. I have loaded it, and made it fast to the paper. Thus easily it uncocks, the trigger flies up. It goes with ease and safety in your pocket. Though small, I've proved 'tis sure."

O'Rourk expressed his surprise at the ingenuity of the contrivance.—"I could have sworn it had been a bundle of papers."

M'Ginnis, all animation, continued—"Have it ready in your hand; wait till this Wilson comes close to you; reach out your arm with the parcel—be steady—fire into the middle of his body. If it fails, blame me. I ask no more.—Then try the speed of my racer; and Nelly is for ever yours."

O'Rourk felt himself inspired with the ardour of his Commander.—"It cannot fail," said he; "if he will not come to the gate to me, I'll enter the court-yard. I know the low wall on the other side—'tis nothing of a leap."

"Be calm—be determined—and you are already successful."

O'Rourk seemed to reflect a moment. "Why his body?—Let me shoot him in the head?"

"No, it is possible to miss him there. Make sure of the body. I have prepared the balls. A touch is death."

It was early on the third morning that this conversation took place.—M'Ginnis proposed that he should set off immediately; O'Rourk assented. The distance was about eight Irish miles.

The horse was ordered.

Wary and thoughtful, M'Ginnis had revolved the whole plot in the preceding night; and such was his eagerness to complete the deadly deed, that, in defiance of his wounds, he sat up in his bed as soon as it was light, and prepared the fatal gift for one, to whom, from his youth, he had been an inveterate foe.

As O'Rourk was leaving the room, M'Ginnis again spoke.

"Stay one moment, my friend. Do you remember the name?—'Tis written on the parcel; but, to prevent a mistake, take this paper."

The fellow read—"Captain Wilson, of the Southford Fencibles.[1]—I cannot mistake my man."

"Mind also a fresh wound on the left cheek, or lower part of the temple."

"I shall know him in an instant," said O'Rourk.

"Hark!" exclaimed M'Ginnis, "the horse is ready—I hear him walking in the court-yard. How well I know his anxious step—so sharp and quick in all his paces! When I next hear him again, O'Rourk, I shall have lost my greatest enemy—and thou wilt have

---

1 Fencibles were regiments raised during the Revolutionary Wars and guaranteed only home service—i.e. defencibles. Several regiments were sent to Ireland to quell the Rebellion, mostly from Scotland, but the Southford Fencibles are a fiction.

gained thy dearest friend.—Come, one glass more to her health, and thy success."

O'Rourk tossed off his glass of brandy, and departed directly.

CHAPTER III.

Long did the time seem to M'Ginnis after O'Rourk was departed; he found himself in a state of dreadful suspense, such as he had never before so strongly experienced.

M'Ginnis was now weak with his wounds, and feverish with the agitation of his spirits; every thing affected him in a more powerful manner than when he was in health.

When two hours had passed, and O'Rourk was not returned, alarm, apprehension, suspicions of a thousand different kinds began to torment him. He could not bear any person in the room with him; yet every five minutes was he ringing his bell for the assistance of some one, that, together with the aid of his crutches, he might look out at the window.

The evening at last closed in, and O'Rourk returned not. Yet M'Ginnis was rather calmer than he was a few hours before, and tried to reason upon the subject.—Wilson might not be at home. O'Rourk was resolute and trusty, and waited, perhaps, for his coming.—He might have changed his quarters; O'Rourk would certainly go after him.

It was not quite dark. M'Ginnis lay upon his couch listening to every wind; the gnawing fangs of suspense, writhing him to and fro, no longer gave him a moment's ease.

He hears at a distance a horse coming;—he is all attention. Nearer and more near it approaches.

"It is—I'll swear it is my stallion!"

The horse *neighs*, and trots into the court-yard.

"Huzza!" cries M'Ginnis, "'tis the note of triumph."

He rings his bell violently. His servant comes. He hears a buzzing of voices in the yard. The name of O'Rourk is sounded.

"Fly!" cries M'Ginnis, "bring O'Rourk here immediately!"

The attendant disappears. No one for some minutes comes near him.—M'Ginnis rings and calls; he strikes his crutch against the ground, to bring up his servants.

The attendant comes up alone.

M'Ginnis exclaims—"Where is O'Rourk?—Is he wounded—is he hurt? No matter—he has succeeded in his business, and he shall have his reward."

Cautiously his servant answers him, knowing the violence of his master's temper—"The horse, Sir, is returned without O'Rourk."

"What?"

The man repeated the same words.

"Who rode him?"

"He came, Sir, without any rider."

M'Ginnis is thoughtful for a while.

"It must be so.—Yes, yes, he was thrown at the wall. I never had any great opinion of his horsemanship;—these sailors!—Go down," says he to the man, "examine the horse; see what trim he is in;—bring me, as quick as possible, the particulars."

The man was not long in returning. The horse, he said, was very dirty, the bridle torn to pieces, the saddle shewed he had been rolling in the high grass, where it was evident also the animal had filled his belly.

M'Ginnis heard all this with pleasure. The last remark convinced him that it was some time since the horse had thrown his rider, and where so likely as at his taking the leap.

Again he sent down the man to examine his legs, if any of the hair or skin was rubbed off.

The fellow reported that one of his hind-legs was grazed in the inside, as if he had come over a wall.

"Then I have no doubt.—Lead me down—I'll examine the marks myself."

The surgeon, who had been some time present, strongly objected against it; but so anxious was M'Ginnis, that he would not be satisfied unless the horse could be brought into the room he was in. As this was impracticable, M'Ginnis was carried by four people below, and the horse brought to him.

M'Ginnis narrowly examined his leg.—"It's as clear as the day," cried he; "on leaping he struck the wall, which threw O'Rourk, and occasioned this mark!"

With the greatest surprise the surgeon, and others who were present, saw his agitated behaviour, and heard his words; so very different from his usual conduct concerning himself, which had ever been cautious and reserved.

At first his surgeon thought that he was light-headed, and even now he began to apprehend that the fever was settled upon his brain. The purport of his words, and the whole of the circumstances to which he alluded, no person present had the most distant idea of. O'Rourk, they knew, went out in the morning, and the horse was returned without him; but why the latter should be a circumstance of joy, they could in no respect conceive.

M'Ginnis now began to recollect himself a little; and to the entreaties of his surgeon, who begged him to be more quiet, and wished to feel his pulse, he assented. The surgeon declared that he was in a high fever, and desired him to take some cooling draughts. To this M'Ginnis was necessitated to consent, and a strong opiate at last lulled him into a temporary slumber.

It is time to see with what success O'Rourk conducted himself.

CHAPTER IV.

O'Rourk was dressed in a plain garb, and a great-coat of M'Ginnis's; and furnished with an orange cockade, which he exchanged into the place of his own, as soon as he had proceeded a few miles on the road. He went at a pretty good rate, and did not attempt to indulge in any reflections upon the business he was about.

In little more than an hour he arrived there; for, as he intended to return with great speed, he purposely went the slower.

He rung at the bell.

A soldier appeared in the yard.

O'Rourk.—"Are the Southford Fencibles here?"

Soldier.—"Yes, some of them.—Whom do you want?"

O'Rourk.—"Captain Wilson."

Soldier.—"I am his servant, and have known him many a good year. You may send your business by me."

The man who spoke was evidently an Irishman.

"And you are an Irishman!" said O'Rourk, who forgot at the instant the colour of his own cockade.

"Well," replied the solider, "is there any thing surprising in that?—One would think *you* were of this united gang by your question. But what is your business with my master?"

O'Rourk.—"I have papers of great consequence, which I am to deliver unto his own person; so I beg you'll tell him that I wait here for the purpose, as I have a great way to go to-day."

"Well, come into the yard," said the other, opening the gate; "I'll call my master directly."

O'Rourk entered; the gate was again closed. The ruffian smiled at the needless precaution.

The soldier went in to call Captain Wilson.

O'Rourk recovered himself from the little confusion his first mistake had made, and walked his horse calmly up to the wall, to review the spot where he intended to take his leap.

He had just fixed it in his mind when Wilson, with his servant, came out.

With caution the messenger of death took out the fatal parcel. He deliberately placed his thumb on the cock.

Wilson approached him in a loose morning-gown, as from a sick chamber, with his handkerchief to his face.

"I am to deliver this to none but Captain Wilson, of the Southford Fencibles," said O'Rourk, in his rough tone.

"I am he," replied Wilson, with his voice rather muffled by his handkerchief.

"My master thought—heard," continued O'Rourk, upon his guard, and determined to make sure of his right prey, "that you were wounded, the other day, on the left cheek."

"Who is your master?" replied Wilson, and, as he spoke, he took his handkerchief from his face, to shew the cut near his left eye, which was covered with a black patch, and much swelled.

O'Rourk lifted up the fatal instrument, and pointed it with a certain aim.

Wilson's hand was stretched out to receive it.

The savage fixed his eyes, as he cocked the pistol, on his intended victim. In an instant he started in his seat, uttered the horrid yell so well known among the Irish, and dropped the fatal weapon.

"Gracious God!" exclaimed the fellow, lifting up his hands in an agony; "I have not murdered him!" and the big tears rolled down his brawny cheeks.

Wilson's servant sprung forward, and seized the reins of his horse.

Wilson cautiously picked up the parcel, and feeling it hard, tore open the paper, and found the pistol.

For some seconds O'Rourk sat on his horse, as one thunderstruck.

"Who sent you here?" said Wilson, speaking to him as if he recognized a person he had seen before, and guessed at his errand; "who employed you in this work of death?" looking at the pistol.

"*Your* life is safe," replied the other, in a kind of frenzy. "Though hell, I know, is open to receive me, I will not carry the murder of him who saved *my* life even there.—Come," continued he, looking wildly at Wilson's servant, who still held the horse, and who had drawn his sword, "dispatch me!" and he threw himself with violence off the horse, and laid on the ground.

Wilson desired his servant not to touch him, and ordered him to stand up.

The man obeyed.

"Give me then the pistol!"

Wilson held it from him.

"Oh wretch and villain that I am," exclaimed he, "it is fit I should be my own executioner!" and he looked wildly about him, as if for the means of destroying himself.

Wilson's servant let go the horse, and seized him by the arm. The fellow attempted not the least resistance.

"Well then lead me to the common death. I had rather die publicly on the scaffold, amid the shouts of the people, than live in peace and plenty by the murder of my preserver!"

"Your life is safe.—Answer what I have to say to you," said Wilson.

It has been mentioned that O'Rourk was not present at the engagement between M'Ginnis and Wilson; but had been out in a skirmish in the same part of the country, the very day before. Surprised in their plundering, many had been taken prisoners. O'Rourk having been disarmed by Wilson, was compelled to surrender.

Touched with compassion for the fate of a man, whose death he knew was inevitable, he gave credit to a pitiful story of O'Rourk's— that he had a wife and a large family, to save whom he had been obliged to join the United Irishmen; and Wilson, trusting to his promises, permitted his escape.

Though long had every virtuous glow been smothered in this man's breast, yet still a latent spark survived, which the strange occurrences of the day had suddenly excited.

O'Rourk's horse, the moment he was released, began galloping round the court. Captain Wilson ordered his servant to catch him; and thus addressed his late foe.

Wilson.—"Who set you on this attempt?"

O'Rourk.—"I must not tell."

Wilson.—"If you have, of your own accord, sworn otherwise, I will not require his name of you. Even to a villain an oath is sacred."

O'Rourk.—"I swore never to see his face again till I had murdered you; yet had I rather be ten times forsworn, than be guilty of your blood. My life is forfeited. Death I deserve. If you will not take it from me, I shall not long want the means of freeing myself. Why should I discover my employer? let the villainy die with me!"

Wilson.—"Cannot another attempt the same?—May not a timely discovery prevent it?—You but half save my life, if you will not forewarn me against whom I am to be upon my guard."

O'Rourk.—"Yes, yes, you are right. I'll sacrifice every tie to save you.—Beware of M'Ginnis."

Wilson.—"Of whom?"

O'Rourk.—"M'Ginnis, brave, haughty, and cruel!—M'Ginnis, sly, treacherous, and revengeful!—M'Ginnis, who fears not God nor man!—M'Ginnis, my employer, my Commander, a General of the United Irish—my patron, on whom all my hopes depended—who, as a reward, promised me wealth, independence, and the woman that I loved."

Wilson.—"Why against me does M'Ginnis send the assassin? I know not M'Ginnis."

O'Rourk.—"Not know M'Ginnis, who now lies on his couch with the wounds you inflicted; and the mark of whose sword you still bear on your left cheek."

Wilson.—"That came from another hand—Marauder's."

O'Rourk.—"No, no. M'Ginnis's, the kinsman—and, as they say, a strong likeness—of Marauder."

Wilson.—"I cannot be mistaken. The villain's looks recognized me. M'Ginnis's name I have never heard till I came into Ireland. M'Ginnis I have never seen. M'Ginnis I never offended. Marauder, from my youth, has been the first enemy—the most restless, the most inveterate I ever had. It must be Marauder."

While this conversation was taking place between Captain Wilson and O'Rourk, the servant of the young Officer was trying to catch the horse.

The noise brought a few men out of the building (for the rest of the troop were exercising in a field at no great distance), and, with their assistance, the horse was enclosed near the corner. When the animal found himself hard pressed, and as one of the men caught at the bridle, which had fallen down, he turned short round, reared on his hind-legs, and took the same wall O'Rourk had intended to ride him over; though not without striking one of his hind-legs, through the accident of the bridle being in the way. Now in the open country, he disregarded the trifling hurt, and galloped away with incredible speed, while Wilson's servant returned to his master.

Wilson clearly found from O'Rourk, that the person he had taken for Marauder, whoever he was, was the same that had plotted to assassinate him. Satisfied in this point, he turned his attention towards O'Rourk, and taking him up alone into his chamber, he at last, more by the force of entreaties than arguments, made the savage promise not to destroy himself.

O'Rourk declared every particular that he knew of M'Ginnis, as well as of himself.

Wilson, hearing that he had been in the sea service, and wishing to provide a safe situation for the man, gave him a passport to Dublin, with a letter to a friend of his, who was in the Navy, and whose ship he knew was at that time victualling.

The letter hinted at O'Rourk's former riotous conduct, and his leaving his ship (now in the East Indies); but Wilson dwelt at large upon his remorse and repentance; for he had no doubt that it was real, and had every reasonable hope that it was permanent, from the strong mind of the man.

Wilson knew that the gentleman to whom he recommended this man, was of a free and liberal disposition, uninfluenced by the selfish fears and illiberal suspicions which generally accompany those who are hacknied in the affairs of the world, and who, in their conduct with others, proceed with a caution, *misnamed prudence*, that damps every kind, generous, and virtuous emotion of the heart.— That merciless, that unforgiving temper, which so many possess whom the want of temptation, or the apathy of their passions, keeps virtuous, is indirectly the cause of as much vice in the world, as the uncurbed violence of indulged youth, whose wilful desires are their only law.

Who threw that poor girl on the town? the hapless victim of poverty, ignominy, disease, and death!!—Was it the unrestrained passion of the son in an unguarded moment; or the cool and deliberate judgement of his mother, that turned her penniless from her house, blasted her character, and took from her every friend?

The poor wretch that yesterday paid the forfeit of his crimes at the fatal tree, some years since committed a petty theft, was discovered, and properly punished. Shame drove him from home, repentance kept him honest.—Many years had passed by, and he had gained a new master, new friends, and a new name; when lo! a purse-proud man, who never felt temptation without the power of gratifying it, came to the spot. He recognized the poor sinner, he tore open the half-healed wound!—His master discards him—his friends forsake him;—again necessity and revenge supply him with the means of subsistence; he robs *him* whose excessive honesty had destroyed his daily bread—he is taken—and dies!

That these poor criminals neglected their duty to God, and to their neighbour, by yielding to temptation, is evident; but who was the tempter?—What then (a man in full possession of the good things of this world, may say) are the wicked to be treated like other men?—No; but the penitent are ever to be forgiven; not in *word* only, or in *deed*, but as far as we are able, in *thought*. The proverb says, "forget and forgive;"—which is, while you cease punishing the crime, let not your remembrance, directly or indirectly, revive the offence. The man who reminds the faults of another to that person's disadvantage, can never have forgiven the offence; because the very act of reminding, is indirectly punishing the offender. This is what makes scandal so hated of gods and men, as it is contrary to the first part of charity—*forgiveness*.

"Let him, who is without sin, throw the first stone." And the whole life of Jesus Christ was in direct opposition to this common conduct of mankind—oppressing the fallen. The rich, the great, the noble, the proud, the self-satisfied he avoided;—the man of fame, of honour, of renown, he noticed not. No; the wicked he exhorted, the penitent he sought for, the repentant sinner he cheered. What others, *who called themselves good*, would not do, he did—seek the society of those, whose noted crimes separated them from others, that, by his own conduct and doctrine, he might convince, reform, and save them; and this THE SAVIOUR continued to do, even in the agonies of death.

This want of *decent pride* his enemies objected against him. Yet which of all his followers proved an offender against human or divine laws? But one, and *he* was a man of wonderful honesty, who carried the bag, who boasted his good-will to the poor, who quickly saw a foible in another, and condemned the offender. In short, I firmly believe that as much goodness consists in turning another from vice, as in being virtuous ourselves.

To a man of this liberal turn of mind O'Rourk was sent.

When Wilson's letter was brought, he desired O'Rourk to come into the room.

"My friend Wilson has candidly told me your history, as well as character."

"I know it, your Honour."

"I am willing to try you."

"Your Honour shall never repent it."

"I hope not.—The secret shall never escape my lips to any one."—He put the letter into the fire.—"You have now the opportunity of beginning the world anew. You are safe with me; and, as you conduct yourself, so shall I trust you."

"I thank your Honour—I ask no other."

"I can get your pardon from the Government, as a repentant United Irishman. This will also exempt you from punishment for having left your ship, if by any accident you should hereafter be known. Consider me as your friend—behave accordingly—and you'll always find me so."

"God bless your Honour! If early in my life my masters had proved my friends, I had never, I think, turned out the rascal that I have."

"Well, all the ill, I trust, is now past.—If you require any money to rig yourself out, I will advance it you."

O'Rourk thanked him; but said the generosity of Captain Wilson had made it unnecessary. O'Rourk was sent on board the ship the next day; where we will leave him, and return to his employer.

CHAPTER V.

Though, on the over night, M'Ginnis considered the return of the horse without his rider as a favourable circumstance, yet with the morning, in spite of his confidence and self-deceit, his apprehensions returned, and he was restless and uneasy to know for certain whether the murderous business had been carried into effect. Concerning the fate of O'Rourk he was quite indifferent; and, provided he could hear that Wilson was no more, the death of his messenger would have afforded him rather joy than sorrow.

This perturbed and violent temper greatly delayed, from day to day, the recovery of M'Ginnis. Sometimes a messenger would reach him of the success of the French; and then his rage and indignation, to think that he was prevented from participating in their glory, could scarcely be restrained.

One day, about a week after O'Rourk's expedition, when he was somewhat in the mending order,—the wound in his side was closed, and he was able with one crutch to walk about the room,—his servant alarmed him with the news that one of the men, whose turn it was to keep guard at the entrance of the wood, had just arrived with the intelligence that the enemy were endeavouring to make their approaches through it.

M'Ginnis, convinced of the strength of the spot he had chosen, and well knowing the badness of the roads, the difficulties of the way, impervious to a stranger, could at first scarcely give credit to the man. He sent for him immediately into his chamber.

The fellow corroborated the story.

Orders were instantly issued to prepare for their defence, and to reconnoitre what forces were coming against them.

Cannon, M'Ginnis was certain, could not act; cavalry to a large amount, he knew, with his small and chosen troop, he could oppose with the greatest success; and infantry were so exposed to the fire of his men, that he had little apprehension, unless they were in great force. He was sorry, in his ardour for the general cause, that he had sent away any of his men before him; with the whole of his forces, in his present situation, he would have defied any numbers that the Government were at present able to send against him, so long as his provisions lasted.

Now he began to suspect that O'Rourk had betrayed him; yet, from the great promises he had made the man, it did not seem likely.

In a very little time another messenger came, who informed him that the enemy were proceeding with the greatest caution, and protecting themselves as they approached.

All hopes of ensnaring them he resigned, and determined to oppose every inch of ground; and, if he found the number too powerful, to cut his way through them towards the French, or retreat into the wild country behind him.

Now again did the Irish hero, in no very mild terms, lament his incapacity of heading his forces. With so choice a set of horses and men as he had remaining with him, and so well acquainted with the country, he would have had few apprehensions of joining the foreign supplies.

The advice of his surgeon could no longer prevent his going out on horseback, with a soft pad on his horse, instead of a saddle, on which he could rest his leg. He soon saw, from the number of his foes, that he could not withstand them for many days, when once they came to know the small number of his soldiers.

By making the most of his men, sometime shewing them on horseback, sometimes on foot, he kept the enemy at a distance, and made them proceed in the most regular manner.

He was now certified that O'Rourk had not betrayed his strength, and the best method of attacking him, from the systematic conduct of his enemy; and anxiously with his glass he looked among the foe, and rejoiced that he saw no one that bore the port of Wilson.

On the third day he discovered an opportunity of cutting off a small body of infantry; and he sent ten of his best horses down an intricate path for that purpose. Till this time he had ventured nothing in the open day, but made all his attacks at night.

His men sallied forth, and were proceeding to the charge, when some cavalry he had never seen before, rode up to support the pioneers.

Greatly superior in number to his horse, the latter turned round, and made all the haste back. The others pressed close upon them; but finding the pursuit in vain, retired slowly to their former station.

M'Ginnis fancied that the uniform of the cavalry was like that which Wilson had worn. When the pursuit was over, he was able to take a more distinct view of their leader, and, as the Officer occasionally turned his head towards them, he observed a patch on his left cheek.

Not another object human could have struck such terror into the soul of M'Ginnis!—Nay, I doubt if any of the victims of his infamy had, in the dead of night, appeared before him, that the horror of the spectacle would so strongly have affected his feelings, as the side-view of the face he now saw at a distance, in the full blaze of day.

When the horse of the enemy, in their return, came up to the pioneers, they fronted round, and stood still.

M'Ginnis's glass had dropped from his hand, and broke; he called for one more excellent, and recovering his presence of mind, dismounted from his horse, and leaned against the side of a tree.

With his telescope fixed, he had now a full view, though the distance was greater.

There more he looked, the more was he assured that the Officer was Wilson.

He saw him get off his horse, he saw him go towards the infantry. M'Ginnis directed his glass to the spot where the supposed Wilson stood. As he looked, he beheld a party directing a glass towards *him*. Wilson applied his eye to the instrument; M'Ginnis, for the first time in his life, felt the appalling stroke of shame; he went behind the tree.

From this moment a gloomy despondency, owing to the late virulence of his passions, his disappointment, his illness, his present debility, seized on the soul of M'Ginnis.

His former confidence failed him, and he instantly determined on flight, if a vigorous attack he meditated that night did not fully succeed.

The assault was returned with redoubled fury; M'Ginnis's men fled, and some few were taken prisoners.

Their Chief resolved to make his escape the following evening; and, having packed up every thing worth carrying off, he sent a few of his troop, with all his domestic servants, the wives of his men, and the whole of the baggage, down into the interior of the country, and, with the rest, prepared to join the French.

He arrived at a small town near the river Shannon, which he purposed to cross in the morning; but great was his surprise when he found his party opposed at the entrance into the place.

His men attempted to fight, but were soon surrounded. Four of them, with their General, whose wound had induced him to go in the rear, and who was mounted on his famous horse, alone got off.

Narrowly did M'Ginnis escape being taken. He received a shot from a carbine over the right temple, and another grazed his shoulder, in the pursuit. They were closely pressed for many miles, but the excellency of their horses saved them.

They got at last to a poor hovel, whose owner they knew had been a violent Defender, and here they left their Commander, who could not proceed any further.

What a change for the gallant, gay and haughty Marauder!—Disguised like a poor female, sore with his wounds, without necessary attendance, food, or clothing, he was left on a miserable couch, with the sole attendance of man, who seemed the legitimate child of rapine and hunger.

If Marauder (as a lady high in rank once said he did) bore the appearance of Milton's Satan, the Prince of Hell; one of the lowest of the fallen angels could not have been better personified than by the wretch, whose guest he now was.

This man might have lived in peace and plenty, with not only the necessaries, but the comforts of life, had not an envious and ambitious temper rankled in his bosom. Among the first to take the *Defender's oath*, he had rode nightly about the country, with a desperate gang, to plunder, lay waste, and sometimes murder: not that he was in want of any thing, for he lived as a gardener to a gentleman, who paid him most liberally.

One night, in an attack upon a house in the neighbourhood, he received a shot in his leg; this he endeavoured to conceal; neglect produced a mortification, and he was obliged to lose the limb. He had been before suspected; this corroborated the suspicions; he was of course discharged from his present service. His master's humanity did not attempt to get any proof against him, but generously gave him for life the house and garden in which he now lived.

One thing only works upon a mind like this—interest. This M'Ginnis knew, and as soon as he was alone with the man, he gave up to him the best part of the property he had visibly about him, and promised him without end at a future day. Nor did this man know the consequence of the person who was with him, M'Ginnis wearing the garb of a private man.

When the other four men departed, they promised to return with a proper conveyance. Their present object was to reach the French army as soon as possible, which they had no doubt, by this time, were got near the capital.

CHAPTER VI.

On the first evening that M'Ginnis occupied his forlorn habitation, he had to experience another mortification. His host, who had been out to get him some better refreshment, had heard a flying rumour, that the whole of the French army had surrendered prisoners of war to Marquis Cornwallis. This was certain, that the French forces had made no progress towards the capital, and few of the inhabitants, as they passed along, had joined them.[1]

If this news proved true, M'Ginnis saw that the great stake he now played for was *his own safety*, and he determined to leave the kingdom as privately as possible; and, as Marauder, arrive in England, and be the most inveterate against his rebel cousin, M'Ginnis.—His leisure time, and he had at present enough for reflections of all kinds, was chiefly occupied by schemes of English glory; yet, whenever he had moulded one to his purpose, the form of Wilson would start up, and haunt his prospects. The death of one so hated, so dreaded, he was resolved to perpetrate with his own hand; and the best method to put this in execution, was another amusement for him.

The wound in his face was not long in healing. The scar he would greatly have regarded, had it happened sooner, as it would have marked the person of M'Ginnis; at present he cared little about it. The large seam which remained, rather assisted to disguise him, than otherwise; and he knew he could easily invent a plausible story of his having received it in the West Indies.

As his health grew better, his views were more bold; and Fanny, whom he had almost forgotten, was no longer left out of the prospect.

In this concealment the Irish Chief remained a month; never went out in the daytime but as a poor, old, infirm, female; in the night he could prowl more leisurely about in his own garb.

A fifth week he staid at this hut to provide himself with a safe disguise, the search after the Rebel Chiefs being most diligent. Neither of his attendants ever returned, and the news of the defeat and surrender of their French Allies had been full surely confirmed.

---

1 The French had indeed been defeated, at Ballinamuck, about half-way to Dublin, on 8 September 1798, few Irish supporters having joined them.

When he at last left the hut, he had torn off the binding of his clothes, and fastened on a different colour, and otherwise altered his dress. His beard was grown, his hair long and matted, his whole appearance wretched, and the noble Marauder sallied forth from the cabin—A BEGGAR.

When he departed, he thought it prudent to give most of his remaining things of value to his host; and he endeavoured to make him believe that he purposed to destroy himself. He had still some money about him, and notes on England enough to pay his expenses there, as soon as he could get to a place where they might be turned into cash.

He had travelled a few miles, when a thought struck him to assume the person of a foreigner; and, as he was perfect master of the Italian language, he adopted that in preference to any other, as being less liable to be detected, and not subject to those suspicions the French would create.

When questioned by any one, or in want of necessaries, he made use of such phrases as these—"Me be une poor Italiene Jew; me va goine to Angle. Me lose ship—all go! Me swim—all die! Vat poor jew do?"—He forged also a name for the vessel.

By this disguise of an Italian Jew, he passed without the smallest suspicion.

At a gentleman's seat, where he was hospitably entertained, he met with an old acquaintance, who had full reason to remember him, as Marauder. This was no other than the young emigrant Officer, who came over to England with Captain Geutespiere, to call Marauder and Fahany to an account concerning the affair of Leonora. Captain Duchesne's regiment being disbanded, he was arrived in Ireland for an asylum, as he was rather fearful at present of going to England.

This Officer conversed with the Italian Jew for some time in the Italian language, and, among other things, told him how very like he was to a man, whom he should remember as long as he lived, though he never saw him but once. The Frenchman particularly noticed the sound of his voice, which Marauder had not thought it necessary to disguise, not at the first recollecting of the other. He left this place as soon as he decently could; the scrutinizing looks of the young Frenchman, and the officious manner so peculiar to that nation, teazed more than they alarmed him.

The late wound he had received on his right temple, the Officer enquired about; and the Jew gave him some plausible account of his receiving it at the time of his pretended shipwreck.

When Duchesne first addressed his old opponent, he asked if he understood French. The incautious Jew had just before conversed with the emigrant's servant in that language; and not immediately recognizing his former antagonist, replied, "A little." Instantly the other began with his accustomed volubility; Marauder, at the moment, remembered his features, and in his answer spoke so bad, that the emigrant was constrained to talk with the Italian Jew in his own language.

The subject for alarm here was not that he had the smallest idea of being taken for Marauder; but M'Ginnis, the rebel, was like Marauder, and if the young Frenchman's fancies became known to others, some one who had heard of the likeness between them, might conceive that he was M'Ginnis, after whom, at this very time, a diligent search was making. This circumstance made the Jew more careful than ever, and eager to get out of the country.

To prevent being traced, he furnished himself with other clothes, which he took care should assist the character that he had assumed; and by the time he got to Dublin, he totally relinquished the ship-wreck story, and had provided himself with a box and trinkets.

From Dublin he easily got a passage to Holyhead; and now Marauder felt himself a man again.

In the evening after he landed, he bought himself a large brown great-coat; scissors and razors he had in his box. In the street, before he went to any lodging for the night, he cut his beard off as close as he well could.

Muffled up in his great-coat, with his little box under his arm, the rest of his dress was not visible, and the swarthiness of his appearance was not easily noticed. In the morning early he set to work, shaved himself many times, cut his hair close to his head, plucked his eye-brows, put on again different clothes of a plain colour, but perfectly fashionable; a light coloured wig he had also provided, and he tied a silk handkerchief round his neck as if he had a violent cold, and wrapped himself up in his great-coat.

As soon as he had breakfasted, he ordered a chaise to the door, and set off.

After the first stage he took off the handkerchief, and by the time he arrived in town, was ready to appear in his proper person.

While Marauder was changing horses at a mean post-town in Wales, his curiosity was excited by a mob at some distance. He found the people had taken the law into their own hands, and were pun-ishing a thief caught in the fact. Being ever a warm admirer of pop-ular government, he soon became a near spectator. What was his astonishment!—the victim of the Welchmen's rage was his friend Cowspring!

He was too near the object to retreat, as he found himself recognized; therefore affecting compassion for the poor criminal, he gave some money among the most active demagogues, and, in a tone that told the other not to know him, ordered Cowspring to follow him.

When alone, of course, he gave vent to his surprise.

"I am eternally ruined!" exclaimed the *ci-devant* General, in the most doleful tone; "my law-suit is determined against me. A copy of the cursed will is found. I fled from London to save my life; and arrived so far on foot alone in a fruitless endeavour to fly the kingdom. Three months have I been wandering about this wild country. My fears so alarmed me, I fled without any means of support. Every thing of value sold, I was caught this morning borrowing that of my fellow-citizen, which *I* had most need of."

Marauder, finding how his affairs were, felt more contempt than pity for him; and giving him a *trifle*, under pretence of not having further means of assisting him, he took a direction to him under a fictitious name, and, with many promises, which he never meant to perform, left him.

So little more is to be said of this wretch, that I shall conclude his infamous story here.

After this meeting, the miserable Cowspring, finding his corporeal as well as mental troubles increasing upon him, and the promised succour from Marauder never arriving, with the last sum he was able to raise, purchased a deadly dose, and died as he had lived, with contempt and infamy.

The fact of wilful suicide was clearly proved, and the wretched body was condemned to that ignominious punishment, the whole of his life had before shewn that he deserved.

Marauder, as soon as he was alone in his chaise, turned his thoughts upon his dear self, as if nothing concerning one, with whom he had been in the highest intimacy, had happened, and began reasoning upon his own affairs.

Still totally irresolute how to act, one moment he had a mind to turn his chaise from the London road, and smuggle himself to the West Indies, and return immediately as Marauder; and this he was not so much deterred from through difficulty and danger, as through dislike to losing the time it would consume to put the scheme in execution.

Repeatedly did he revolve in his mind *the proofs of identity* that could be brought against him; and Wilson stood alone as the only person the least likely to offer any. The death of Wilson he was resolved to perpetrate as soon as his enemy returned to England, even if the act was accompanied by his own destruction; and so inveterate were his malice and his revenge towards him, that this also was an argument against his going to the West.

As for proofs that he had been there, he disregarded them; his care was that his enemies should not be able to prove the contrary.

Ever upon his guard, before he left England he had at no time told any one to what island he was going, or the business which carried him there. His friends *thought* it was to Jamaica, and that he had an estate there; but this was only conjecture, which he had never corroborated. In his new character of M'Ginnis, he was equally careful of what he said of Marauder; and their English acquaintance, who were most able to speak concerning his affairs, were now no more.

To clear himself from being an abettor of M'Ginnis's conduct he thought was of more consequence; and here too, whilst he knew there was no proof, no M'Ginnis to be brought against him, had he most craftily provided.

As M'Ginnis, he had written many letters to Marauder, in England, supposing in them that his kinsman was arrived from the West Indies. In some of these he professed great penitence for having abused the commission his generous kinsman had entrusted him with; and in his last letter, having declared that all hopes of establishing himself in Ireland were lost, he thus concludes:—

"My sole aim now is to get to France. In the disguise of a female emigrant (you know how well I understand their language and manners) I have no fear; and then, devoted to the French service, you shall never again hear of your ungrateful kinsman

"PATRICK M'GINNIS."

But then Marauder, as well as his cousin, had taken the oaths of the United Irishmen, when he was the first time in Dublin. Yes. Here was his answer.—He took them, as believing the cause to be for the general benefit of Ireland, in a peaceable way. To second this he had witnesses of power and consequence in that country; and his subsequent conduct in leaving the kingdom, when he perceived they were about to act in an hostile manner, was his proof that he entirely disapproved of their measures.

The corps that M'Ginnis had raised, was originally for the service of the Government;—this Marauder approved of; but the rebellious conduct of his cousin afterwards, he knew not for a long time, and was too far from the spot to be answerable for it.

All these thoughts, and many other to the same purpose, were again and again revolved in the mind of Marauder, as he travelled to town; and in his journey he amused himself with putting them upon paper, and forming a regular, systematic scheme.

Marauder, from the earliest age, had ever had the highest opinion of his own abilities; and many a pang did it cost him, when he was compelled to renounce the grand idea of being the Cromwell of Ireland.

All his subsequent misfortunes he attributed to the wounds he had received in his rencounter with Wilson, which prevented his acting in person; and the removal of him he considered as essentially necessary, not only to every worldly happiness, but to his very existence.

CHAPTER VII.

Marauder made immediate enquiries after his friend Arnon, and heard with pleasure that he was in town.

As he was fully prepared to appear in his own character, he drove to his house.

A whispering, and rather confusion among the servants surprised him as he got out; but the moment his name was announced, he was shewn into the room where his friend was.

There lay the philosopher, in a large sick chair, pale, emaciated in the face, his body puffed up, his legs enormously swelled.

Even Marauder started as he beheld him.

"Arnon, my friend," said he, assuming, as well as he was able, a mild note, "why do I see you thus—what is the matter?"

Arnon shook his head, and scarcely tried to smother a sigh.

"Marauder, welcome!—You arrive at the very crisis.—'Tis passed—I cannot keep up the ball any longer."

Mr. Arnon made a motion to a servant who attended him; the man, addressing himself to Marauder, informed him, in a few words, that his master's disorder was a dropsy, which the doctors had declared to be incurable.

Mr. Arnon rousing himself—"Now the hour is come," continued the man, from whose lips he had heard, and greedily imbibed the modern and ancient precepts of stoical sceptics,—"now the hour is come, I shudder at the thought of death!—Oh Marauder! what nonsense—would it were but nonsense!—what proud, vain-glorious doctrines have I talked to you!—Foolish wretch! to fancy that I knew every thing, when I know nothing."

Marauder looked disgusted; Arnon was too faint to regard his looks, and continued—

"My disorder, you've heard, is a dropsy. I know it is. My physicians tell me so—my apothecary—all of the same opinion.—I know full well the cause too—the deadly liquor I have lately so plentifully taken, to drown thought. Yet knowing all this, with all our knowledge we cannot find a remedy. I still linger and linger on. Even in this miserable state do I wish to live.—Oh Marauder! you are yet young. I liked your bold, aspiring temper—I wished Hambden to be like you."—Marauder's animation was revived, but was instantly depressed.—"Alas, I think otherwise *now*—I wish you to be like *him*.—Hear my dying words; for this purpose I have sent for my son, and he is expected every moment."

Marauder was restless, and very sorry that he had come to the house without proper enquiries.

"Nay, nay, my friend," said he, "drive away these weak thoughts;—be yourself again."

"Ah! young man, what for?—Again to vaunt myself in my weakness—again to impiously throw the bolts of the Deity, and talk what he can, and what he cannot do? This is all my knowledge—that I am a poor, miserable wretch!"

Marauder.—"Do not give way to the disorder—it overpowers your senses."

Arnon.—"Ah! there's the sting.—I *am* conquered indeed—my *fears* conquer me—they force me to speak—they make me, in spite of myself, own how wretched, helpless, and ignorant I am."

Marauder.—"But why *now* more than at *other* times. You always knew that you must die. You knew the uncertainty beyond—yet still how improbably—how—"

Arnon interrupted him.—"Ah Marauder! Marauder! it does not seem so improbable *now*. Is there any other animal, but man, that shews the least belief in a future state?—Saw you any of the savage nations, while you were in the West? Do not the most ignorant still look forward to an hereafter?"

The questions of Arnon staggered Marauder in more respects than one; and, even in the presence of a dying man, he could not entirely overcome his alarm.

"Savage nations!—Oh! yes—no; I have been chiefly in the civilized part;—but—" flying from a subject to himself most personal, Marauder continued—"Why should you credit now the tales of Priests, whose art, whose interest it is to raise these bug-bears?"

"With some it may be;—but even the worst still believe and

tremble.—Priests, Marauder, are men. What might the world have said of them, if you or I had been one of them?"

Marauder was rather offended; but this was no time to shew it. He muttered something about hypocrisy.

Arnon understood him.—"Of hypocrisy—I cannot say.—The weakness of human nature sways us all from our principles, without being hypocrites. Yet, Marauder, it is some merit to respect the virtue of others, though we are wanting ourselves."

"Come, come, my dear friend," said Marauder, affecting to be the philosopher, "rouse the wonted vigour of your mind. Let reason, which has ever enlightened you, shew you what is *truth*; your actions and your words have always yet agreed."

"Ah Marauder! there again you rack my inmost soul; would I *had* been an hypocrite! My words, I'm sure, were wrong—what then must have been my actions?—Others I have ruined as well as myself.—Poor Royston Santhorpe! There was a soul, Marauder,—alas! how debased—how perverted! Whatever wrongs we may suffer, that which is evil can never redress them. This truth I feel at last. Unhappy Santhorpe, thou hast made a dreadful expiation!"

As yet Marauder was not informed of the fatal catastrophe to which he alluded, but he embraced this opportunity to turn the subject of the conversation.

"I know nothing of Royston," said he; "I have not seen him since I left England. I heard, indeed, that he had espoused the cause of the French; and I made no doubt, with his ardour, resolution, and abilities—"

"Alas!" exclaimed the philosopher, "what are they all without virtue? He has yielded to ambition, to interest, and to revenge—he has fought against his country—he is taken—and dies the death of a traitor!—Oh Marauder, beware!—God, I thank thee! My son is safe!!!"

Marauder felt more indignant than affected;—he knew not what to say.

Arnon in a little time continued—"Is there another state, Marauder?—What must it be?—What a part here have I played!—and the end too!—I drank to drown thought;—and, as I laid me down at night, wished I might awake no more.—Suicide! what art thou?—Is there any other animal besides man that deliberately seeks thee?"

"Yes," said Marauder, eagerly, "'tis an innate principle planted in our nature.—'Tis a love of liberty!—Birds and beasts in confinement frequently perish by their own violence, and by voluntary hunger."

"'Tis specious, Marauder," replied Arnon, faintly smiling, yet with a vigour of mind the other did not think him capable of; "how often have I thought of it! Yet, when the savage beats himself to death in his toils, can you for a moment think he means to destroy himself?— No, no; he tries to escape. So, if he refuses his food, is it not through fear? Does not the alarm of *unknown* danger take away the sensation of hunger?—Do you think *they mean to die?*—Offer to destroy them, even in this state, will they not resist?"

"Oh my friend!" exclaimed Marauder, affecting a passion he did not feel, "how it grieves me to see *your noble mind become a prey to the weakness of your body!* This is not Arnon that speaks!—'tis sickness, a temporary debility; again, I trust, your native powers will be renewed—and again we'll laugh at these childish alarms, and listen to the dictates of Arnon."

"No, Marauder," Arnon spoke with a wonderful precision, "it is not with me as you think; never in my life did I feel my thoughts more clear. My mind nauseates its former food, and even the sweets of flattery have lost their relish. The head is right—but the heart is wrong. There is a weight upon my soul—a heavy secret rests there, which, as soon as Hambden arrives, must be dragged up; then, in defiance of this half-expired body, the nobler part, you will see, still lives."

Marauder was very restless. He was relieved from this conversation by the arrival of young Hambden. He waited to see the interview between the father and son, well knowing the dislike the father had to the company of Hambden before he had himself left England, and the uneasy sensations Arnon felt when in his son's company. From this the malicious temper of Marauder expected food, in the interview which was about to take place between them; and considered it as a pleasing revenge for the penance that he had suffered form the foregoing conversation.

The anxiety of Mr. Arnon, when he heard his son's voice, cannot be expressed.—"He comes! he comes!" he cried, and raising himself with an exertion in his chair, he fainted on Hambden's bosom.

A scene so moving Marauder little expected to be present at, but he attributed it to a wrong motive. He was quickly undeceived by what followed, and set right. Mr. Arnon soon recovered.

"Oh Hambden!" said he, "your presence gives me one moment of comfort before I die. Long you have been as an alien to me— rather *I* to *you.*—Say you will not leave me till I am gone.—Ah, my poor boy, happy had it been for you if I had gone sooner!"

Hambden said but little, yet that little was in the highest degree soothing to the heart of the father.

Marauder was heartily tired, and about to take his leave. Arnon stopped him.

"Stay a few moments. I have a heavy secret to disburden my mind of. The particulars will be found in my bureau when I am no more. Answer me, Hambden, one or two questions.—You know, my child, how I educated you in prejudice of those very principles which you have since adopted.—Alas! I fear you're right!—Do you forgive me?"

"Yes, my dear Sir, from my heart. You were prejudiced, as well as myself. Let me hope then, like me, you see your error, and—"

"Ah Hambden! talk not on that subject;—I am all wrong, I feel, I confess—but I dare not, I cannot think further. Answer me again—Have I, in other respects, acquitted myself to you as a father?"

"Some pitiful story," thought Marauder, "about the woman that he kept;—perhaps he has married the trull; or perhaps Mr. Hambden Arnon, after all, is a bastard; some such wonderful secret, I suppose. Would I were fairly out of the whining fellow's house!—the devil a bit would I enter again to hear *all* his secrets."

To Mr. Arnon's question, if he was satisfied with his conduct as a father, his son replied—

"Above my wishes, Sir; far above my deserts."

"No, Hambden, no.—Come a little nearer to me.—Hear, and forgive me. Every thing I have was always yours—*I am not your father!*"

"My dear Sir, speak again. To whom do I owe my being?"

Mr. Arnon was much distressed with the exertion he had undergone, and even wept. Hambden held him affectionately by the hand. A train of passions hovered on the brow of Marauder. In a few minutes Mr. Arnon proceeded.

"Will your kindness, my dear boy, and my weak deserts entitle me to your pardon?"

"Dear father, you have acquitted yourself to me as if I had been your son—do not for a moment doubt it.—Yet tell me, Sir, *who was my father?*"

"Hambden! whose name you bear. Hambden! the confidential friend that fled with me from England when you were but a little boy—my own son the same age. He died in the passage. We were driven on shore among a savage people. Your father soon died. I adopted you as mine; because by that means I possessed the property, which, in case of your death, was left to me and my son. Many years I lived among this people. The few of the sailors, if any ever returned to England, knew nothing of my affairs, or your father's. We fled the country with fictitious names. A discovery I never feared; yet something within me, I cannot account for, made me miserable, till I had discovered this secret to you, that I might die with your forgiveness."

Marauder could not refrain a taunting smile at his last words, as he contemptuously turned towards the window. Neither the sick man nor Hambden noticed it. The latter again expressed his gratitude to his foster father for the care that he had taken of him, and for his constant liberality; and, what was an additional consolation to Mr. Arnon, promised not to leave the house till the termination of his disorder.

Marauder, of late, had been in the habit of exercising himself in the stoical school of necessity, and in *practical* philosophy was become a most wonderful adept. A placid or angry brow he could assume at command; and by his looks, as well as his words, could he hide the purposes of his heart. With a well-studied compliment towards Mr. Arnon and Mr. Hambden, having removed a handkerchief from his eyes as he turned from the window, he prepared to take his leave; and, while he promised to be frequent in his visits to his sick friend, he mentally determined this should be his last, since he saw no prospect of ever getting any part of the property.

No conversation, except of the complimentary kind, had taken place between Hambden and Marauder; yet the latter, who was ever suspicious, remarked that Hambden seemed to regard him with scrutinizing eyes: and he began to fancy that Wilson might have written to his friend the particulars concerning *him*.

CHAPTER VIII.

Mr. Arnon was so weakened by the exertions he had made in the late discovery, that he was obliged, soon after the departure of Marauder, to be carried to his bed, which was in the same room. He did not recover sufficient strength to have any conversation with his reputed son that day.

Thinking as they did on religious subjects, when they conversed the next morning, the discourse insensibly turned that way.

Hambden was anxious that his foster father should profess the doctrines of Christianity, and adduced many arguments to the purpose.

"My dear boy," replied Arnon, "if I had any hope that my life might be spared, I would make it my study to understand those truths, which I own, for purity, morality, and every human virtue, surpass all others.—Your presence revives me—your forgiveness comforts me in the hour of death.—A knowledge of God's word, I fear, I have grossly neglected; and I have alarms and apprehensions of I know not what nature, which all my philosophy cannot subdue. I dare not say, I believe in the Christian religion, lest I should die with a falsehood in my mouth; for I cannot say what I believe. All I am conscious of is the wretchedness of my own nature, my own imperfections, and ignorance."

"My dear Sir, already are you half a Christian."

"Would to God I were!—I cannot deceive myself.—Oh Hambden! 'tis one happiness to me that my sophistry has not misled you. The whole course of my life has been against Christianity; yet, lost in doubts concerning its history—ignorant of its mysteries—neglecting its precepts—despising its tenets—I own, with my dying breath, that it is the only system of virtue. These, the thoughts of my death-bed, I care not how public they are made. I fear they have little effect on the ambitious soul of Marauder.—Oh Hambden, beware of him!—Like other rash young men, *he gratifies his passions*; but, unlike all others, *he commands them*."

Hambden informed the sick man that he was fully acquainted with the character of his former friend; and that Rattle had, many years ago, cautioned him against him.

The name of Rattle recalled many circumstances to Mr. Arnon's mind; he could not forget what labours he had taken to instil into him his own notions, and with what ease Rattle had baffled them.

"That wild young man," said he, "is another strong instance of the weakness of *my* philosophy. I could not repel *his* loose, irregular wit. Do you remember, Hambden, his reply to a full and systematic refutation which I thought I had made of the sacred books of the Jews and the Christians?"

"Very well, Sir;—it was soon after my return to England, when you had been reviewing the writings of some notorious characters, who then made a noise. You had given him, some time before, the works of that wretch, Thomas Pain, and you took, with the book in your hand, a complete review of the subject."

Arnon sighed—"'Twas so indeed. Go on."

"Rattle heard you out with unusual patience, and then, in his calmest manner, replied—'If, Mr. Arnon, your arguments were *unanswerable*, which I deny—if you could prove that the whole of the Bible was the work of priestcraft in the *present* century—if you could convince me that *Judaea was swallowed up by an earthquake* long before the circumstances happened recorded in the New Testament, and lately came up again; yet *I should continue to believe* that Jesus Christ was sent from the Almighty to give the world *a full light* of the *most perfect system* of all that is holy and good towards God and towards man. Believing *this*, no matter to me *when, where*, or *how* it happened."

"Yes, Hambden, you repeat *verbatim*. I laughed at his notions *then; now*—Oh Hambden! would I had followed *that* system."

At the words of comfort which flowed from the lips of Mr. Hambden, the despairing philosopher shook his head. He tried, for a few moments, to escape from such thoughts which pressed heavy on him; and, in the most affectionate manner, enquired after Hambden's wife and child.

The answers were such as he wished. He informed Mr. Arnon, also, that he expected them in town the next day, with the father of his wife, whom he had left at his house in Wales.

The respectable character of the Priest did not escape the notice of Arnon, though he was a man with whom he personally had not the least acquaintance.

If Mr. Arnon had lived, Hambden purposed introducing the Dean to him; but the present appearance of amendment was solely occasioned by the turn his spirits had taken on the arrival of his reputed son.

Mr. Arnon's weakness and faintness returned in the evening. Mr. Hambden was instantly summoned to his chamber. The agonies of death were upon him.

A servant remarked how ill he was.

The dying man heard him.—"My heart is broke!" exclaimed he.

Hambden held his hand;—the other, grasping it tight, turned his eyes upon him.

"*One* good lesson I give thee, child—*my death!*"

He spoke no more—convulsion succeeded convulsion; and, in the space of an hour, the dreadful scene was terminated.

Thus perished Arnon. A man, who for many years had carried a species of morality, independent of every religious principle, as far as most men of his day.

After living a plotting and abstemious life, from the twenty-fifth to the fiftieth year of his age—at the very time when he was in high reputation for converting others, both by his conversation and writings, to his own ideal plans, did he begin to doubt and waver upon what he had so often asserted to be clear and positive arguments. His alarms daily pressed in upon him. His reputed son—educated by himself, or under his own eye, who had from his earliest age learned his notions, and imbibed his prejudices—saw their falsity; the old arguments weakened of their effect at every attempt to recover him to his original principles; and soon young Hambden was lost to the cause.

Now his own philosophy began to be staggered, and he found himself bewildered in those paths he had all his life been treading in.

Insensibly he flew to the bottle. There for a time he found oblivion; novelty, for a little while, continued the deception. More and more frequent was the remedy applied—more and more weak were its effects. So unstable proved all his mental researches without the foundation of religion, that in a very few years he fell a victim to those intemperate habits, in opposing which he had, for a long space of time, considered his greatest virtue to consist.

Unhappy in the turn his son's abilities had taken, yet he could not blame him for his conduct; and though Hambden acted in opposition to those principles he himself professed, still he could not help confessing to himself that the young man's conduct was more and more worthy his notice.

The paper which Mr. Arnon left behind him, that contained the particulars of his flight from this country, when he adopted Hambden as his own son, it will not be necessary to trouble the reader with.

The method of their escape; the fictitious names they assumed; the difficulties of their voyage; the death of Mr. Arnon's own son; the notice he took of young Hambden; their shipwreck; their sufferings on shore; the suspicious conduct of the natives; the death of Mr. Hambden; the manner of Mr. Arnon's escape with young Hambden; his kindness and affection towards the boy, whose death he might easily have accomplished if he had been so disposed; their arrival in the civilized parts of America; and, finally, their return to Europe after the termination of the war;—all this was minutely recorded by Mr. Arnon, that his treatment of the youth might be some vindication for his having assumed the fortune during his life; but has nothing to do with the present story, and which I shall therefore willingly omit.

Neither did Mr. Arnon forget to leave satisfactory proofs that Hambden was really the son of his deceased friend. The great use of these was establishing Mr. Hambden's right to the property, then litigating in the Court of Chancery, as the heir at law; under which title it was disputed, in contradiction to Mr. Hambden the elder's bequest.

When Marauder heard that Arnon was no more, he determined to keep the specious form of civility by calling on Mr. Hambden; though his real motive was to endeavour to discover if he had received any suspicions from Wilson.

After enlarging on the virtues of the deceased, Marauder said—"Probably, among Mr. Arnon's papers, you will find some letters of mine from the West Indies. Of course, you will destroy them. But one that I wrote from St. Kits, which concerns some private business of my own, I will thank you to keep for me. In it there is an estimate of a small property of mine, which a friend of Mr. Arnon's had thoughts of purchasing; I brought a copy of the estimate with me, but have mislaid it among my papers."

"Certainly," replied Hambden, "*all* that came from you, I will keep, that there may be no mistake. You mentioned St. Kits. Was that your residence while you was abroad?"

"I was only there a few days—my business was very urgent."

"You were in many of the islands then?"

"Yes."

"How did you escape the yellow fever?"

"About a twelvemonth ago I had it dreadfully. My life was despaired of for some days. It carried off all my hair, as you see." And Marauder lifted up his perriwig, under which was not the smallest vestige of hair: an application of slack-lime, and other powerful destroyers, had unceasingly been applied since his return to England.

"It is astonishing to me that it has not grown again."

"The ravages of the fever were so dreadful. Dr. Balder assured me, among the thousands of patients he had attended, he never saw one so grievously afflicted, and survive it."

Marauder had seen in a morning-paper, that a physician, of the name he had mentioned, was lately dead in Jamaica. Hambden had observed it likewise.

"I see," said he, "by the papers, that the Doctor himself is dead. You were well acquainted with him, I presume."

Marauder testified his surprise at the account of his death, and answered—

"As much so as any person in the island."

"Was he a young or an old man?" Hambden asked this with great indifference, as is often the case in a forced conversation.

Marauder considered the question as ensnaring, and cautiously, with seeming ease, replied—

"Upon my honour I can't tell. Of a middle age, I should think. That climate is so prejudicial, there is no making any guess."

Marauder ran into a dissertation on the country, and the conversation concerning the Doctor ceased.

They now talked of the affairs of Ireland. Marauder was very indignant against his cousin, but he hoped the reports were not true that M'Ginnis was in arms against the Government.

"That I wished," continued Marauder, "for *Catholic emancipation*, and *Parliamentary reform*, I never denied;[1] they were the early principles of my soul, for which I have sacrificed the most splendid prospects; but my love of peace overcame these, and I earnestly desired my kinsman, when I saw him in England before my departure, on no account to oppose the Government, but, in case of emergency, to arm in its defence. How he has abused my confidence you must have heard. On my arrival in England I found this letter from him."

Hambden read the letter before mentioned.

Marauder continued—"I met with a gentleman, the other day, who was just arrived from France, and M'Ginnis, I find, is now in the French service."

"Your kinsman is quick in his motions," replied Hambden.

"You met him, I think, at my house in town?" said Marauder.

Of course Hambden replied in the negative; yet such was the language of deceit that he now held forth concerning himself and his cousin. He soon after concluded his visit.

CHAPTER IX.

Marauder was one morning passing, in his chariot, by the Admiralty, when, among some sailors, who were standing near the spot, he recognized the countenance of O'Rourk.

Instantly he threw himself back in his carriage, that the other might not notice him; but it was too late—the fellow he saw was struck with the likeness, and he observed him run forward some distance, that he might have another view of him.

Ever a master of dissimulation, Marauder was resolved to practise

---

1 Catholic emancipation, the abolition of the Test and Corporation Acts, enabling Roman Catholics to hold public office. It was not achieved until 1829. Parliamentary reform, in the 1790s, could mean anything from a limited redistribution of parliamentary seats to universal suffrage, but the term generally signified the extension of the franchise to a larger number of affluent males. Both were moderate measures of which even the Tory Prime Minister, William Pitt the Younger, had once approved.

it in its full extent. Late trials had made him a thorough adept in the art.

He stopped his carriage directly opposite to O'Rourk, told the footman he should get out, and walked up to a shop, near the door of which O'Rourk stood.

As he came up to him he turned round, looked at the concourse of people that were assembled, and, with a placid brow, a soft and polite tone, asked O'Rourk what the bustle meant.

O'Rourk for a moment could scarcely answer, but he soon replied —"The confirmation, your Honour, of Admiral Nelson's victory."[1]

"Oh!" said Marauder, with a smile, unlike any thing of the kind O'Rourk had ever seen before, "you were with him, I suppose."

The thing was impossible. O'Rourk was in the house of M'Ginnis on the very day of the victory.

"No, your Honour, I had not the good luck," he replied.

"I am sorry for it," continued Marauder. "Here is a trifle to drink the King and the Admiral's health;" and he put a shilling in his hand, and with great indifference walked into the shop.

O'Rourk looked at the shilling, and then at Marauder. It was impossible to be M'Ginnis—yet how wonderfully like him! O'Rourk civilly asked the servant his master's name.

"Marauder!" though O'Rourk to himself, "then it is no wonder Captain Wilson took M'Ginnis for him.—D-mn him! This may be all a sham—that devil M'Ginnis is up to any thing. Yet that scar in the temple M'Ginnis never had while I was with him.—How different he talks!—I scarce know what to think. Could Captain Wilson be mistaken?—No matter—M'Ginnis, or Marauder, he's the enemy of the Captain, and I'll have none of his money;" and, as he walked back to his comrades, he gave the shilling to a poor beggar woman.

"Lord bless you sailors!" said the woman, "you be the comfort of the nation. Come," continued she, to another beggar that came up, "I'll treat thee to a glass of gin. We've beat the French, and I've got some of their money."

"Hurrah!" said the other, "old England for ever!—Come along!"

Ye modern patriots of the French school is your love for your country less disinterested than that of these poor wretches?—Ye false Philosophers! true Diabolists! every comparison degrades you.

---

1 The Battle of the Nile took place on the night of 1 August 1798 in Aboukir Bay in the delta of the River Nile. The Royal Navy command-ed by Horatio Nelson succeeded in almost wholly destroying the French fleet.

Marauder had supposed, when he perceived that Wilson had escaped the intended assassination, that accident had prevented O'Rourk's attempt on horseback; and that fear, or remorse, had hindered his perpetrating it on foot, and returning to him: but Marauder's cogitations on the subject were not always the same, and the only thing he was certified of in his own mind, was, that O'Rourk had certainly not betrayed him to Wilson, because the troops which attacked him were ignorant of the best means of making their approach.

Had Marauder been told that there was a principle of virtue and honour in such a savage's breast, he would have most contemptuously despised the idea. Yet such had been the case, which, in the first instance, turned the hand of O'Rourk from the murder of Wilson; and, in the second, prevented him from making those discoveries, which it was in his power to have furnished Wilson with, to the ruin of Marauder.

Still the conduct of O'Rourk was to Marauder a mystery; willingly would he have had it unravelled, but he was not willing to risk his own personal safety. This grand secret of the identity of Marauder and M'Ginnis had never yet escaped him; even Imphell, devoted to his service, who fattened upon his smiles, had never been entrusted with it. The inconvenience *of being his own confidant* had at times indeed been very great; and though he might rejoice, in the instances of Fahany and Arnon, that he had made no discovery, still the want of a friend, in whom he could implicitly trust, was not less apparent.

As he was purchasing some trifles in the shop, his mind even wavered if he should not again trust and employ O'Rourk; attributing his first miscarriage entirely to accident. A second reflection was conclusive against it.

The interview with O'Rourk, though favourable to Marauder, had clearly shewn him that even this man was not without his suspicions; and the deeper he reviewed his past conduct and present situation, the more fully was he convinced that, in spite of all his exertions, his affairs were extremely critical.

The most trifling circumstances would continually bring such thoughts to his mind; and with a strange anxiety he waited for the moment when Wilson should arrive in England, resolved with his own hand to perpetrate the act that should for ever break the chain of knowledge which linked Marauder to M'Ginnis.

CHAPTER X.

Scarce a week had passed since the death of Arnon, when, as Marauder was leaving the Opera House, a young sprig of family, who was generally in London, for the same reason that some plants are never seen out of the hot-house, because they are fit for no other place, and just vegetate there, came tripping up to him.

"Are you going to leave us so soon?"

"I have an indispensable engagement."

"Ah! 'tis bad indeed here;—but you should stay and see the grand caper of the Olympia."

"I saw her six years ago, at Rome."

"Ah! you like not ancient beauties. What think you of the young damosel, who has fascinated all our glasses this evening?"

Marauder had not been long in the house. A foreign Nobleman, whom he expected to find there, did not come that evening, and he was going straight to a house, where he expected to meet him.

"Whom do you mean?—I saw no beauty worth a second view."

"Ah! you did not see her then, or you are impenetrable. I know all her history. She has twenty thousand pounds. She refused Wildermere two winters ago, and a dozen Lords, two dozen Baronets, and Squires innumerable since. She lives at Richmond, and her name is—"

"What?" said Marauder eagerly.

"Now, if you can tell me her name, I shall be eternally obliged to you. I am dying to be introduced to her—and as you—"

"What part of the house is she in?"

"She comes with Lady Modeley, and is in her box; opposite mine.—This is mine. *Entré*, and I will shew her to you in a minute.—Ah! here, take my glass. Look straight before you. Use your eyes, and bless me for shewing you such an object."

The hopes of Marauder were realized. It was indeed Fanny Bellaire.

"Butterfly," said Marauder, in an animated tone, to the other, "you are a devilish clever fellow. I had no idea you had so exquisite a taste. Do you know Lady Modeley?"

"Ah no."

"Or any person in the house that is at all acquainted with her?"

"No, upon my soul.—I thought you might introduce me."

Marauder could not well help muttering "Fool!" between his teeth. Butterfly did not take it to himself, but continued chattering.

Among the loveliest of women the beautiful Fanny might contend for the palm. She was now taller than Emily; and though she excelled not her sister in that fashionable *en bon point* the princely taste of the day so highly approves, yet the native symmetry of her shape, delicately true, would have claimed admiration from every clime.

Her clear complexion was animated with the glow of health, and here and there the transparent skin discovered the purple veins. Her countenance open and engaging, invited love; while her forehead, of a charming form, was the very emblem of dignity. Her hair, fine and dark, flowed down her polished neck and shoulders in beautiful ringlets; her nose was a model of the Grecian; her eyes black, with long lashes and arched brows, were mildly bright, yet they rolled not with a voluptuous round, but by their penetrating steadiness, commanded respect from every one.

Her smooth chin, when she smiled was ornamented on the rightside with a dimple, which seemed to point to the bewitching assemblage adjoining, where the whiteness of her teeth endeavoured in vain to rival the rubies of her lips.

Her arms were elegantly rounded; her hands and feet small, and every motion delighted with a graceful ease; and, when she spoke, the sweetness of her voice equally charmed, as the mildness of her manners was sure to interest.

The dress she wore was always—fashion improved by modesty; and every part of it seemed designed more for use than ornament.

The splendid trifles which, with an unmeaning shew, glitter upon the person, she needed not; and the costly dresses, in which Folly loves to vaunt its greatness, she neither required nor approved of. Elegantly neat, the diamond of her person shone through its simple encasement with an irresistible grace, while every motion shewed its beauties in a new light.

Such now was Fanny Bellaire, whose person and countenance truly beamed those virtues which reigned within; and if her form was fair, her soul was fairer.

With a mind firm and undaunted, she was never bigoted to her own opinion; and with a heart the most tender and friendly, she could pity and relieve the sorrows of others, without a foolish indulgence in the false luxury of grief. Her liveliness was tempered by prudence, and her wit by innocence.

An innate love of virtue, which the sad conduct of her sister had strengthened, kept, like a magic wand, the libertine in awe. Even Marauder's impudence felt abashed, and, in the midst of all his depravity and licentiousness, whenever he thought of Fanny, his amorous desires put on the form of marriage, though every obstacle was the same, as in the case of Emily.

The lovely object before him fascinated all the senses of Marauder; and the fashionable remarks of Butterfly evaporated, as fast as they came forth, in the vapid atmosphere which aided their birth.

For some time Marauder was lost in thought. Suddenly starting up—"I think I remember the young lady myself—some years ago, before I went to the West Indies. If I am right, I'll introduce you, Butterfly, *another time.*"

Without further ceremony Marauder left the *Peripatetic Philosopher*, and, determined in his own mind how to act, went at once into Lady Modeley's box. Walking up to Fanny, he accosted her in the easiest manner, though in most polite and respectful terms.

Fanny gave something like a scream; and, had it been possible, would probably have flown away.

He regarded it as the surprise of an old acquaintance, and addressing himself to her, said—"I presume you have not heard, Miss Bellaire, of my arrival in England. The moment I saw you, I could not resist the opportunity of paying my devoirs. I have been absent, indeed, longer than I intended, on very urgent business that called me to the West Indies. I am but lately arrived, and have ever since been making the most anxious enquiries after you. I was informed you had left England."

Whether a thing was true or not, Marauder never considered; whether it would answer his purpose or not, was the question. A lie, that could not be detected, stopped him not a moment. He had before enquired for Fanny, and heard she was with her sister; but knew she had not given up her residence at Richmond.

Fanny, overcoming her alarm, replied—"Why, Sir, should you wish to see me? When—"

"To entreat your pardon and forgiveness. That I offended you, though unwillingly, has made me most wretched and unhappy. Now I can fully explain my conduct; and I trust I shall be entitled to your favour, and the honour of your acquaintance. May I take the liberty of asking your address, that, with the sanction of your friends, I may—"

Marauder spoke in a soft and insinuating tone. Fanny knew him too well to be easily deceived, and interrupting him, with great firmness said—

"Mr. Marauder, I must beg to decline your acquaintance; the unhappy circumstance which happened in our family for ever precludes it. My forgiveness, Sir, if it is the least necessary, you have long had;—to forget is not in my power."

Not so easily daunted was Marauder; he kept his station to the end, made occasional remarks, and attempted to hand her to the carriage; but, perceiving she was resolute against it, he had the effrontery to conduct another of the party, who, perceiving him to be an acquaintance of Miss Bellaire's, permitted his civilities.

Mr. Townsend and some other gentlemen were of the company. As soon as Fanny arrived at Lady Modeley's, she spoke in private to her guardian, mentioned who the stranger was, and desired, if Marauder called, he would say that she had positively refused to have the least acquaintance with him.

He did call on Mr. Townsend the next morning; and, after a very plausible speech, that gentleman answered him, that Miss Fanny had particularly requested he might not be introduced to her.

"In a few weeks," continued Mr. Townsend, "she will be under the protection of another."

"Sir?" said Marauder, questionary, but checking his anxiety, "I presume you mean as to her leaving town."

"I allude, Sir, as to her settlement in life, which is no secret. I hope, in less than a month, to give her away to as worthy a man as ever breathed."

Mr. Townsend had mentioned this, thinking it would totally check any further enquiries.

"As you say, Sir, it is no secret, I may enquire who is the happy man?"

"Captain Wilson, Sir, whom you once knew. He is at present in Ireland, but expected home in a few days."

Mr. Townsend knew no particulars of any animosity between Marauder and him, except in the affair of Emily; and Marauder had just declared, in most solemn terms, his penitence and remorse for his former conduct to her, and his resolution to have married her.

In defiance of all Marauder's *philosophy*, his heart so vibrated when heard Fanny was to be married to Wilson, that, though he contained himself, he could not make an immediate reply. Such was his inward agitation that he bit his under-lip through with his teeth. Muttering something about how happy he should always be to hear of the welfare of one, whom he ever should consider as a dear relation, he finished by saying—"I suppose of course you remain in town till the ceremony is past?"

"No, Sir; my ward returns to Richmond to-morrow; and henceforth you may always consider her as Mrs. Wilson."

Marauder's rage was such, he could instantly have fired the house, and borne Fanny away in the midst of the flames; but, as things were, it was impossible: therefore all smiles and outward civility, through his heart rankled with revenge, malice, and disappointed passion, he took his leave.

The mind of Marauder was resolved how to act—to get possession of Fanny's person as soon as possible. To leave England he had before resolved for some time, till the present disturbances and suspicions concerning himself were blown away.

"Fanny shall accompany me," said he; "her haughty little spirit will, at the most, be tamed in a few weeks. I know what women are!—Mine she shall be. The house on the Downs will answer every purpose. I'll hasten to prepare the deaf man and his wife to receive her; and then, my sweet little devil, escape me if you can."

CHAPTER XI.

As preparatory to every thing else, enquiries were duly made concerning Fanny. She was at Richmond; and Marauder hastened instantly to the house on the Downs.

An old deaf man, and a woman had been left there when he went over to Ireland. The house stood alone, surrounded with a very high wall. The garden was small, and there was no other land belonging to this property; the house had been originally built as a hunting-seat.

Here Marauder had formerly had many private meetings with the self-elected friends of Freedom—here he had carried many a lady—here he had accommodated many a friend—and here were hidden some private papers, the place of which was known only to himself.

It has been mentioned before, that Marauder had first let, and afterwards mortgaged all his property in the parish where Wilson's parents lived. His house in town had only been let by the year; but he had also taken up money on this, to nearly its value.

His present residence in London was a ready-furnished mansion, by the month; and the small property on the Downs was all that he kept in his own hands, and which, under the care of Imphell, had occasionally been lent to some of his friends.

To this he could retire, at any time, in the most private manner; for not even the people who lived in it knew the real owner. It is not to be supposed that he had entirely neglected the house since his return to England; his attorney had been down, ordered some necessary repairs, and sent some furniture.

He was not sorry to find, at his arrival, that the old woman was dead; the extreme deafness of the man he had always considered as of the greatest convenience to him.

His next care was to send for his attorney, Imphell, across the country a few miles.

"Imphell," said he, "I want two trusty fellows, to assist me in a little job.—You can get me such?"

"Is it a business that requires resolution and spirit, Sir?"

"Yes; though nothing very particular. 'Tis to carry off a girl."

Imphell thought a little. "There are two to be tried next week at the Assizes. They applied to me to get them a Counsel; but the fools had been so improvident as not to have a farthing of cash, and I declined the affair."

"Are they deserving?" Marauder asked.

Imphell was inclined to be witty.—"Very deserving of the gallows, Sir."

"Ah my friend!" said Marauder, coolly, "little rogues swing, and great ones break the halter. But 'tis pity merit of any kind should fail for a trifle. Do you think they are to be got off with a little money?—And would they be *grateful* for my friendship?"

"Leave that to me, Sir. Ten guineas, I suppose, will save both their lives. It is a common burglary; but the chief witness is a man of great conscience—we must therefore puzzle and frighten him;—new dress and shave the delinquents, and then endeavour to set up an *alibi*. We'll do it, Sir, depend on it."

"Imphell, you are a worthy fellow. You are a man I can always depend on. Ingratitude is not my fort."

The other bowed to the ground, professed how handsomely his services had been rewarded, and how devoted he was to his commands.

The two men escaped; and on the fourth day after the conversation between Marauder and Imphell, decently dressed, waited on Marauder in town.

They brought a letter from the attorney.

"I understood from Imphell," said Marauder, "that you were two deserving men in distress, and I am happy to see you have escaped."

The men properly thanked his Honour.

"He tells me," continued Marauder, "you are not deficient in courage. I have a little business to employ you in, perhaps it may require a small portion.—How do you feel yourselves?"

Like the French at the renowned attack of the Bastile,[*] they both

---

[*] [CL] According to Miss Somebody's Letters, the gallant Parisians, as they advanced to the fortress, *all* cried out together—"We'll fill up the trenches with our dead bodies!" [It has proved impossible to trace this quotation or, as may very well be the case, mis-quotation. The Fall of the Bastille, which began the French Revolution on 14 July 1789, was described in published letters by several eye-witnesses, notably Helen Maria Williams, who is perhaps suggested here, and whose *Letters written in France* were first published in 1790.]

burst forth in the same sentiment—"We'll go to the devil to serve your Honour."

"A young girl has played me a confounded trick."

The fellows shook their head.

"And I wish to play her one in return."

The fellows grinned.

"This is the whole of the business."

"Any knocking on the head, your Honour, to gain the lady?"

Marauder paused; he thought of Wilson; but in that case he was resolved not to trust his revenge out of his own hands. He replied—

"I hope not.—Are you known in this part of the kingdom?"

"No, your Honour.—We ben't acquainted with the Bow Street gentlemen.[1] Our business has been generally in the West—in the horse line; but, being hard put to it, we opened the door of a dwelling-house, last spring. I've been an ostler, and a postboy, your Honour, and understand something about cattle; and Dick has good connections, to take them off our hands; and he's a man, though I say it before his face, that won't flinch to any man breathing."

Their noble friend was again thoughtful.

"A postboy you've been!—I'll alter my plan. You shall be postillion. My own horses will do. One pair shall be with us, another at a trusty house on the road. Get a hack-chaise to this side of Westminster Bridge, by five o'clock to-morrow morning.—You can read?"

"Dick can, your Honour."

"I'll write my orders on a card, then there can be no mistake. Beware of tippling;—you shall have time and means enough afterwards."

He wrote down the particulars, and with some money, gave them to the men.

They went to Richmond the next day.

Marauder took good care not to be visible in the daytime, but prowled about the house where Fanny resided, the greater part of the night.

He saw it was in vain to make any attempt upon the house.

Most careful was he in his conduct, most cautious in his enquiries; yet he discovered, the second day, that Wilson was not arrived.

---

1 The Bow Street Runners were a body of London constables constituted by the novelist and magistrate Henry Fielding in c.1748 to act as arresting officers, serve writs and undertake detective work. They were empowered to fight crime outside London in 1757.

Marauder bore about him constantly the fellow pistol to the one O'Rourk had been trusted with. He had steeped the balls in a deadly poison, and primed and loaded it himself. It was so small he carried it with ease in a side-pocket, and waited with increased anxiety for the return of Wilson, that he might make the intended use of it.

One or other of the men kept regular watch in the daytime, that notice might be given if Fanny went out.

The second day, which was a Sunday, she took an airing in her guardian's carriage. Marauder, without loss of time, followed it in his own. Dick behind, upon a saddle-horse. Tom drove.

They watched their opportunity. Marauder and Dick, with masks on their faces, stopped the other carriage.

They made Fanny and another lady get out. Marauder's chaise came up. He lifted Fanny into it, and seated himself. Dick cut the traces of Mr. Townsend's carriage, and, mounting his horse, they set off with great speed.

With difficulty Marauder had forced Fanny into the carriage. He spoke not a word; and finding she still cried out, and endeavoured to call for help, he drew up the blinds, and by main strength, tied a handkerchief over her mouth, to prevent her speaking. By this means he succeeded in avoiding all interruption, and arrived in safety at his house with his lovely prize.

During the journey, Fanny had been frequently offered refreshments, which she as often refused.

Fatigued and alarmed, she was carried up stairs; and Marauder, locking the door, left her.

Through the whole of the journey Marauder had been most completely disguised: a mask covered his face, and his apparel was such as to preclude all suspicion of his person.

CHAPTER XII.

Fanny had not been in the apartment above half an hour, before Marauder entered her room by another door. He was well dressed, his hair powdered, and his whole appearance such as if he had not been from home.

Fanny screamed the moment she saw him. With a smile, he begged her not to be alarmed, for that the making of any noise was as useless as it was unnecessary.

"Then restore me," exclaimed she, "to my friends again. For what purpose am I forced away hither, thus cruelly used and insulted?"

"What," said Marauder, "has either of the men I commissioned to bring you hither, dared to offer the least affront? I'll make an example of the wretch directly!"

This he spoke, that he might induce her to believe that he had not been himself actively concerned, lest the circumstance of the handkerchief being put round her mouth, might have created any personal dislike.

Fanny told him no particular affront had been offered her, except as before mentioned (for she was fearful that he would commit some violence on his instruments), but that she alluded to the general conduct of carrying her away; and she again demanded his reasons for his present behaviour.

Marauder, with the utmost shew of humility and softness, replied—"Dearest Fanny, hear me for one instant, that I may excuse this seeming rough conduct, which necessity has compelled me to adopt, and apologize for my whole behaviour."

"Return me to my friends, Sir;—then I'll hear and forgive every thing."

"That cannot be as yet. You are entirely in my power. None but my own servants are concerned. This house stands alone, surrounded by a bleak down; not a hut within five miles. No pursuit can trace you. Nay, should any one by accident arrive at the house, a wall, ten feet high, covered with iron spikes at top, must check further progress; while I have a dungeon under ground, where I can safely deposit any thing, and the way to which it is impossible to discover. The only servant that remains in the house is one man, so deaf, that I give him all his orders by signs and writing. The three fellows who brought you here are gone. Escape me then you cannot."

"Why all this on my account, Sir? How have I offended you? I was neither privy to my sister's flight, nor did I influence her—"

"Sweetest Fanny, I think not of your sister. Can it be possible my behaviour is a mystery to you? Beloved Fanny, 'tis you alone I care for. You, as a child, I loved—as a woman, I adore!" and he dropped on one knee, and seized her hand.

Fanny started away, and retreated to the door.—"What is it you say, Sir?—Me?—It cannot be."

"By all that's sacred I swear 'tis only you. Dearest, most lovely Fanny, turn not from me. You are the only woman for whom my heart was ever concerned. Without you I cannot live, and for you I will willingly die."

Calmly and deliberately Marauder spoke, and calmly and deliberately he swore to what he said.

Fanny felt a horror she dared not fully to express.—"Do you forget, Sir, my sister?—Is it possible I can ever think of the man who deceived and deserted her?"

"Yes, lovely Fanny, 'twas your bewitching charms that are answerable for my conduct there. How could I marry Emily when I knew there was a Fanny? Why did I get your sister into my power; but in hopes that my Fanny would have accompanied her? Why did I lament her loss, but that Fanny was lost too? All my thoughts, my wishes, ever turned to you. To have lived in your sight—to have seen your daily improvement—and, at a future day, to call you mine, has been the study of my life, from my earliest knowledge of you."

"Was it your love to me, Sir, that pledged the alliance with Alderman Barrow's daughter?"

"I swear the story you have heard is all false. I refused the alliance.—Why did I refuse it? because I remembered Fanny."

"Thinking so favourably of me, is it not strange you never discovered it till this day?"

"Dearest Fanny, you had taken an unnatural dislike against me, on account of your sister. Can you be ignorant why I so often sought your company?—You repulsed me;—you would not even give me an audience. I was forced to act in this violent manner. Love, the purest, the most true and fervent that ever glowed in a human breast, has from the first influenced my conduct. I may have erred, sweet girl; yet the love of you has been the motive.—Accept then my vows," and he took hold of her hand.

"It cannot be—I am betrothed to another."

"He cannot love you with half the ardour that I do. Every thing I will sacrifice for you—every thing I will venture on your account. Drive away this childish love from your thoughts, my dearest girl, and accept the heart of him who solemnly devotes his existence to your service."

"You talk in vain, Sir; I can never be yours. If you really love me, will you not oblige me?—Let me return to my friends. The person who carried me away shall never be known."

"You hate me!"

"No. I shall always esteem and respect you, if you will permit my departure."

"You will?"

"Indeed I will."

"And will you then accept my vows? Will you sacredly promise me yours in return?"

"It cannot be—they are already given."

"Love breaks every tie.—I have staked all for you. Most charming girl, say you will be mine!" and he endeavoured to catch her in his arms.

Fanny, in spite of her danger, could no longer conceal her disgust.—"No, no—never, never!"

Marauder's restrained anger burst through the contending passions of his bosom, and he swore, in the most strong and sacred terms—"You shall be mine—and only mine. All opposition is vain. I see it is of no avail for me to fawn and to flatter;—contempt is my sole reward. My rights I claim—possession—conquest. Let me exert the man."

Fanny had fled from him to a distant part of the room, and, dreadfully alarmed, sunk almost lifeless on a chair.

Marauder approached her.—"Hear me, Fanny—sweet Fanny—dearest Fanny—I would say!" softening his voice and smothering his violence. "Fatigued with your journey, and harassed with unknown fears, perhaps you may require rest.—Be it so.—I leave you till tomorrow;—let me not appear in my Fanny's eyes as a tyrant;—then I shall require your consent. Let me, as a fond lover, beg and entreat; I would not, as a master, force it from you."

Fanny endeavoured to exert herself. "My life is indeed at your disposal. You can take it;—but no earthly power shall ever constrain me to give you my hand."

"Ah, talk you so bold, Madam?—Beware!—Is my alliance to be despised? The day may come that you will throw your arms around me, and beg to be the wife of Marauder. *Then*, *I* may think otherwise. *Now* I am willing to take you on your own terms. I wait till tomorrow for your consent. Let me not again plead in vain.—Beware! my will is fixed.—Refreshments are prepared for you in the other room.—Shall I partake of them, or do you wish to be alone?"

The determined manner in which Marauder spoke, roused Fanny to a full sense of the danger she was in. She forbore saying any thing further that might irritate him, and, in a faint tone, replied—

"I am much fatigued and very weak. I shall take a bit of bread and a glass of water—I had rather be alone."

Marauder, ever suspicious, said—"Before I leave you, I must beg to see the contents of your pockets."

Fanny was necessitated to obey.

"On your honour, are these all?"

"Yes."

He took away with him a small knife and a pair of scissors—"Once more, Fanny, remember the cast is thrown. Mine you shall be!—willingly, or not, depends on yourself. If you accept the first—

marriage, love, and gratitude await you;—if you compel me to the last—Fanny, remember, ere it is too late. Think in time, and—beware!"

So saying, Marauder went out at the same door he entered, leaving the communication into the other room open.

CHAPTER XIII.

Fanny was so absorbed in thought at the wretchedness of her situation, that she sat for some time in her seat, like a second Niobe.[1] A seasonable flood of tears afforded her present relief.

Afterwards she walked into the other room. A table was spread with cold meat, red and white wines, water, biscuits, and fruit.

Fanny ate some fruit and a biscuit, and drank a glass of water.

The evening closed in. She rung a bell for a light. Nobody answered it. She repeated it again and again. It was all in vain.

She tried the doors of each room. Both were fastened. She examined if there was any fastening in the inside. In the room she had first entered, and in which was a bed, was none; but to the door which separated it from the other room, were two bolts, and a lock on that side. She next went to the windows. Iron bars made them sufficiently secure, both from within and without.

She determined to quit the room where the bed was. She drew the bed, which ran upon casters, easily against the outer door, and then secured the door of partition in the inside, with the bolts and lock. A small bell to the other she had also fastened, and endeavoured to hamper the locks by putting into them some pins. She looked around the room, and with difficulty drew a chest of drawers against the door. This took up some time, as she endeavoured to avoid noise. Tables and chairs, and every bit of furniture in the room, were sedulously placed for the same purpose.

In removing the drawers, she perceived a large piece of cord; one end of this she fastened to the lock of the chamber, and the other to the lock of the passage-door, which, as the latter opened from her, she conceived to be her best security. Fanny drew an arm-chair towards the window. The moon was rising. She perceived many trees before her, and fancied she saw the high wall Marauder had mentioned, beyond them.

---

1 In Greek mythology, Niobe embodies bereavement and grief, her hubris having motivated Apollo and Artemis to kill her twelve children. She continued to weep even after she had been turned into a rock.

Fanny remained in this station for some hours, till exhausted nature insensibly lulled her into an irregular slumber.

If fears and alarms of the most dreaded kind harassed during the still hours of night the mind of Fanny, and kept aloof the sweet soother of cares—gentle, mild, invigorating sleep; phantoms of another form passed before the eyes of Marauder, and the possession of the lovely enchantress who raised them, realized the same.

Restless, plotting, and abandoned to his passions, for two nights had Marauder been incessantly on the watch around the house where Fanny dwelt at Richmond; the occurrences of the foregoing day, therefore, his exhausted body felt, though his mind disdained to own it. It was this lassitude which had induced him to put on that shew of favour towards his captive, which no mental feeling could ever have induced him to grant. Marauder felt his corporeal frame unequal to that violence his daring soul had resolved on.

As soon as he left Fanny, he sat down to a repast, which he greatly needed. Imphell was at the time in the house, and had assisted in preparing it for his reception; this trusty confidant was to leave him in the evening. The two men who had been employed by him, had before departed with the carriage and horses.

About nine o'clock, Imphell set off. Marauder had before drank freely, and, as soon as he had made fast the outward door, and sent his deaf servant to his repose, he retired to the parlour. Completely tired, he dropped asleep in his chair. He was awoken, about one, by falling off it. His light was exhausted; he roused his servant to strike another, and proceeded to his chamber.

Rest now forsook him, and his disturbed thoughts kept him awake.

The scheme that he had before planned, of carrying Fanny off with him to America, was again revolved in his active brain. In the lone and distant spot where she was now in his power, far from the busy ken of men; impervious to pursuit, was he resolved to confine his lovely victim, till he had bent her stubborn heart to his will.

The obstacles which might oppose him, from hatred and anger, with his usual philosophical forecast he thus reasoned upon.

"The most savage of animals, by the attention of a watchful keeper, become tame, and the person against whom they first vent their rage, in the end is ever the dearest object of their love.—Is a woman's heart alone not to be subdued?—No. The experiment has for ages been repeated; and when, but through the foolish feelings of the master, has it failed?

"The rising state of Rome made not a *single* trial, but by *thousands* attempted it, and by thousands succeeded. Not one of all the Sabine Virgins, who were forcibly carried away and detained, but, when the choice came, gave the preference, before all others, to the ravisher.

"Is it to be supposed that none of these fair ones had, in their own neighbourhood, still dearer ties than fathers, mothers, kinsmen, and friends?

"Is it possible so many lovely and beautiful young females could have been without lovers, the objects of their own simple fancies?—Nay, in the war that followed, many of those chosen youths were doubtless destroyed by their present violent masters; yet, in defiance of every obstacle, possession once obtained, easily held its rights.

"Shall I forget the noble, the valiant, and, I doubt not, handsome,"—Marauder always prided himself on his own personal beauty,—"Richard the Third? Willingly did the Lady Ann marry him, though with his own hand he thought proper to take off her young husband, and her father-in-law. That he subdued the implacable hatred of the Queen mother, is universally allowed, whose sons, brothers, uncles, he had all destroyed; and the fair Elizabeth herself is generally supposed not to have been indifferent to the match: for, while historians own that the mother's favouring of Richard's suit, occasioned the enmity of Henry the Seventh, they do not deny that the knowledge of the same induced the King to dislike his spouse Elizabeth.[1]

"Have I any cause to doubt my success?—Not the smallest.—Do any simple feelings harbour in my breast, unworthy a rational man, to check the dictates of my will?—Am *I* a tame, weak, wavering fool?—What my mental faculties conceive to be right, do my animal powers fear to execute?—Irresolution is the curse of fortune.

"Success has as yet crowned my utmost hopes. *To-morrow* completes my glorious attempt. Why not *this night*? why not *this moment*?"

Marauder started up from his couch; the fumes of the wine animated him, and he proceeded to Fanny's chamber.

He tried the door. It was fastened. He had forgotten the key, but not at the moment recollecting the circumstance, he slightly knocked.

Fanny, in the adjoining room, heard him not.

He put down the light. The wind whistling under the door, it was instantly extinguished.

---

1 Marauder is referring to Shakespeare's version of *Richard III* in which the anti-hero murders his way to the crown, having already persuaded Lady Ann to marry him, despite his hand in the death of her father-in-law (Henry VI) and husband (Edward, Prince of Wales).

Marauder paused. He remembered the key;—as he returned to his room to renew his light, his promise of forbearance till the morning occurred.—The ardour of the moment was lost.—"Yet as I have promised till to-morrow, perhaps the breach of my word may create a needless hostility against me. To-morrow is already arrived to me— but a few hours, and it will be to her!" And he threw himself again on his bed.

Vague and wandering thoughts of Fanny, of Wilson, of his flight to America—schemes, plots, and contrivances, roved incoherently through his mind during the rest of the night.

CHAPTER XIV.

Early the next morning, for she lost not her recollection the whole night, Fanny clearly distinguished the high wall, and a wild dreary plain, as far as her eye could reach.

She took out her handkerchief, and, opening the window, would have waved it.—"Alas!" cried she, "the trees are too high!—Who is there to see it?—Should a shepherd look this way, would he understand the signal?"

Looking despondently round the room, she perceived a curtain-rod in a corner, to which the cord had belonged that she had fastened to the doors. To this she tied her handkerchief, and, lifting it as high as possible, forced it through one of the upper-panes of the window, and stuck it in the shutter.

For three long hours anxiously she looked over the plain—not a being was to be seen.

About nine o'clock Marauder came, and tried to open the door. Finding it was fastened on the inside, he requested it to be opened, and said he had brought her some breakfast.

Fanny was prepared with her answer. "You promised me to-day to myself. I wish not for any other nourishment than the food upon the table."

"No, Fanny," replied Marauder, in the mildest accents, "I promised you but *till* to-day. But, to oblige you, I wait for your determination till the evening. Let me not be trifled with."

He was not displeased of having made a merit of obliging her. He smiled to himself as he went down the stairs.

"How easy are women taken! In twelve hours she wavers. Let her have a little more reflection, and I am sure of my prize. Fool that I was to doubt for a moment my success!"

After deliberately breakfasting, Marauder walked into the garden.

The sun shone bright. The birds were singing. The lark, mounting into the air with his cheering note, seemed to animate the rest. All nature hailed the genial warmth of the coming spring. Even Marauder could not help admiring the scene around him.

"What a charming day!" exclaimed he. "England, thou has few such! but soon I leave thee for a more genial clime, where, in the arms of my Fanny, I shall taste perpetual spring and love. This day I shall for ever bear in my memory—Ah! 'tis the twenty-first of March—'tis the day of my birth, and again a day on which a second life depends!—What would an old Grecian, or Roman have given for so good an omen, at such a crisis!—It would have immortalized an Alexander or a Cæsar."

Visionary prospects of bliss, of a superior kind to any his soul had yet conceived, floated before his fancy.

In the course of his walk he came opposite the window of Fanny, and with the softened smile of success he looked up.

Her white flag expanded before the breeze; she herself was anxiously looking out at the window.

"Oh the sorceress!" exclaimed he, "she still hopes for assistance."

Fanny heard his exclamation, and timidly drew back.

In an instant he was in the house, and ran up stairs.—"Fanny," said he, in a sharp tone, "you infringe on the privilege I give you. You abuse my kindness. Take down your ensign directly, or I annul every agreement."

Fanny made no answer.

"Again," continued he, "I am going into the garden. If I see it is not removed—beware of a man, who will not be injured with impunity."

Quick as thought, he was again before the window.—Fanny had returned to it. She looked eagerly forward, as if she saw something. She regarded not the threatening gestures or words of Marauder;—she shook her white ensign;—she cried with her loudest voice—"Help! help! help!"

It was in vain. The objects passed at a great distance. They heard not her voice;—they could not distinguish her signal.

In the mean time Marauder had rushed into the house, and hastened to her room.

Fanny, still at the window, beheld distant objects passing. The noble stag bounded over the plain. In a few minutes came along hounds, horses, and hunters, now just in view of their game. Intent on the object of the chase, all eyes were directed towards the flying animal; while the sounding horn, the encouraging tally-ho, the enlivening notes of the hounds, more and more anxious as they approached nearer to their prey, left no hope to poor Fanny that the weak screams of a female could reach their ears.

Clearly could she discover the colours of the different sportsmen. Two dark-colour coats, on one of which a scarlet collar was evidently distinguished, passed with the foremost hounds.

Then first it was she shook the flag, and exerted her voice.—They see not—they hear not—and quickly are lost to her sight.

Now come on a troop, where the green and red coats were easily perceived. Again she exerts herself. In vain—they pass away as the former.

Marauder had violently assaulted the door. He found it was too well secured for a common exertion; he rushed into the kitchen for the cleaver.

As the scattered hunters behind passed, Fanny, in despair, continued shaking to them the flag, and crying out with her utmost might.—The whole are lost to her sight without the smallest notice. Nor dog, nor horse, nor rider is to be seen. The distant noise dies away—her hopes weaken—her spirits fail.

Marauder returns with the cleaver. He thunders against the frail wood.—Whither can Fanny fly?—In a few seconds he cuts the door to pieces. Enraged, he throws the other obstacles aside, and rushes to the window.

Fanny endeavours to defend her ensign—in vain!—Marauder tears it down.—Fanny screams more violently than ever.

"Mad, rash, foolish girl!" Marauder exclaiming, catches her hand, "what mean you by thus irritating me?"

A buzzing noise is heard through the trees. Again she exerts herself, breaks from his grasp, and screaming, flies to the window.

He pulls her hastily away to the other end of the room. The huntsman's horn re-echoes around the plain.

Marauder knows the note.—"The gallant deer is taken," exclaims he. "Sweet Fanny, it is an emblem of thee. Why then this useless opposition?—Your toils are not less certain than his." Marauder, as he speaks, seats himself in a chair, and holds her firmly by the hand. "Far, too far off are the sportsmen to hear your alarms. Their own noises drown a thousand female notes. Come, dearest girl, be pacified. Listen to the man who adores you, who wishes to be every thing to you, and is willing to own his bliss not to his own success, but to your kind consent.—Most charming Fanny, why should we wait for the morrow?—Say you will be mine, and let me kiss these pearly drops from your sweet face;" and with soft insinuating blandishments he endeavoured to pull her upon his knee.

"Never, never, never!" exclaims Fanny, struggling from his hold. "I am betrothed to another, and *his* alone I will ever be."

Marauder restrains himself no longer; he gives his passions full scope.—"Dam——on! is this the reward of my lenity?—Is the alliance of Marauder spurned for the cursed son of a base mechanic? *His* blood I have long vowed to my injured honour;—yet consent to be mine, and I forgive him."

"It cannot be.—Oh spare him, spare him!"

"Beware! I deign to intercede;—and here I call every power of Heaven, Earth, and Hell to witness," and he drops upon one knee, still holding her hand, and swears with that depravity he was accustomed to, "in spite of your future tears and supplications, when I have humbled you beneath my feet, his death shall complete my triumph."

Marauder rises up, and with affected calmness continues—"One moment yet remains to save him, and your own honour.—Will you accept me for a husband?"

"Never! whilst I have life!"

"Then I'll exert the rights of a conqueror. This instant I claim my own. Henceforth, not vows, nor tears, nor even a forced consent shall check the love that burns within me.—Now, even now, will I make sure of my lovely prize."—And, as he spoke, he seized her, with determined lust, in his arms.—"Nor man, nor devil, nor G-d shall hinder me!"

Her screams rend the air. Marauder pauses a moment. He holds her firm by the arm, while he unfastens the door that leads into her chamber.

In vain she struggles;—like as the lion the lamb, he grasps his prey.

Her screams are repeated—she holds by the door—he tears her violently away from it.

CHAPTER XV.

A noise is heard without, as some one violently assaulting the door which leads into the house.

Marauder stifles her cries, and listens. The door bursts open—a person rushes into the house.

He leaves his victim, and, with a hellish horror, glances his eyes around the room for the cleaver. She guesses his intention, catches up the deadly instrument, and flings it out of the window.

Marauder, with a curse, strikes her; puts his hand in his pocket, draws out a small pistol, and rushes to the head of the stairs.

Fanny, with dishevelled hair, a wild and alarmed, though resolute look, follows him.

A man, in a blue coat and scarlet collar, is seen flying up the stairs.

Marauder exclaims—"Ah! now I'll make sure of thee, though a legion of fiends—"

The behaviour of Fanny prevents further speech. She looks at her defender, and throws her arms around Marauder—around him whom, a few moments before, she had struggled to get free from.

Marauder now spurns the embrace he had just so eagerly solicited, and, desperate, flings her with violence from him.

The pistol goes off in the air. Fanny falls lifeless against the stairs.

The stranger has gained the landing-place.—'Tis Wilson!

Briefly shall I relate the circumstances which brought Wilson to her help, and exposed him alone, unarmed, to the fury of his rival, his implacable foe.

Early in the foregoing day, on which Fanny was so forcibly carried off, Wilson arrived in England. The house of his first patron and friend, Mr. Lockeridge, lay in his road to town; and here Fanny had agreed to direct a letter for him, that the lover, without loss of time, might know where to find his mistress; for, as yet, he was in doubt whether she was in town, at Richmond, or at her sister Rattle's in Wales.

On *Sunday*, about the hour of dinner, Wilson arrived at Wheatland.—The expected letter was not come. There is no mail on the Sunday from London, for it leaves not the metropolis till Monday evening; therefore all letters that go into the distant party of the country, cross-posts, &c. &c. are not received before the Tuesday.

This Mr. Lockeridge explained to the expectant lover, which induced him to accept the kind invitation of his friend to stay with him another day.

Mr. Lockeridge, in spite of some touches of the gout, was engaged to follow the hounds on the Monday morning. He lent Wilson one of his hunters; and a most noble animal had led them an excellent chace, when they had come in view of the spot, where Wilson had little idea his fair mistress was confined.

Her shrieks were lost in the air. Her white flag, the fair emblem of her mind, was unnoticed, as intently they followed their game.

Near the house of Marauder was a fine piece of water. To this the wearied animal turned, and, taking to the midst of it, kept his pursuers at bay.

The dogs launched into the flood; the attendants, with proper toils ready, endeavoured to save the object of their sport, while the loud horn of the huntsman called the scattered hounds together, and declared the pursuit at an end.

The first who had arrived were Mr. Lockeridge and his friend; as soon as the huntsman and some others came up, Mr. Lockeridge motioned to Wilson to follow him out of the group, and said, pointing to Marauder's house—"This is the strange place, which you heard mentioned yesterday, that all the neighbourhood believe to be haunted; and no one creature knows who lives in it, or who is the owner of the spot."

Wilson rode close to the wall.—"That there is an inhabitant of some kind or other, is evident, for I see through the trees something like a white flag suspending from an upper window.—Hark, Lockeridge! On my life I heard a shriek!—See, see, the flag is taking down! The trees prevent my full view of the window," and he changed his spot.

"Surely I discern people struggling," exclaimed Mr. Lockeridge. "Another shriek!" and they both, actuated by the same sentiment, leaped from their horses, and strove to force the door.

Now the full sound of the horn drowned every other noise.

They could not make the least impression on the door. Mr. Lockeridge proposed returning to their companions for further assistance; but Wilson, impelled by that heroism which fearless flies to the succour of the distressed, prepared to scale the wall.

In an instant he ungirted his horse, took the saddle in his hands, sprung upon his friend's horse, and threw the saddle on the spikes. Quickly he was upon it; and springing in safety over the spikes, he let himself down, with the assistance of the stirrup, on the contrary side. The depth was great, and, with the quickness of his exertion, and the strength of his efforts, he tore the saddle on one side, and left Mr. Lockeridge, who, forgetting his gouty impediments, was preparing to follow him, unable to give him any assistance.

Wilson rushed towards the house. The door was only closed by a springing latch. The shrieks were clearly heard, and demanded immediate aid. The voice vibrates to his heart. The quick blows of Wilson soon forced his way within; and, without the smallest weapon in his hand, he resolutely flew towards the sound.

CHAPTER XVI.

Is it possible to describe the agonizing pang which tore the heart of *Wilson*, when he beheld the lovely Fanny dashed lifeless by Marauder, as she attempted to turn aside from *him* the murderous weapon of that assassin.

Not less enraged was Marauder to be checked in the very moment of successful villainy by the man who had already overthrown his most flattering schemes of glory and ambition, and whose testimony now threatened his life.

Like famished tigers, they seize on each other. Each strikes at his enemy, and despises the defence of himself. Their strength is nearly equal; both have exerted themselves before. Their blows soon labour—they struggle—they pant for breath.

Marauder, skilled in every species of warfare, tries to free himself from the other's grasp. He succeeds. A moment's pause ensues.

Marauder feels in his pocket for a clasp-knife. Wilson observes him drawing it; and again grappling with his foe, strains every nerve, exerts his whole force to throw him.

Wilson lifts him from the ground; Marauder, at the instant, strikes him with his foot, they both stagger, and fall together with great violence against the railing of the stairs.

The frail wood cracks with the double weight. It gives way. Marauder and Wilson are sinking with the broken fragments into the stony abyss below. The former clasps both hands around the other, who catches hold on that part of the railing that remains firm. Each sees the imminent danger that threatens him.

Wilson tries to disentangle himself from the deadly hold of his adversary. Marauder strains to rise; big drops of sweat roll down his forehead;—his grasp begins to fail him;—one hand after the other looses its hold;—he fetches a deep groan, and tumbles headlong on the pavement below!

Wilson, exhausted, with his utmost effort rises upon the stairs.— A mental prayer ascends the throne of Heaven to that Almighty Power which had saved him!

In an instant he springs to Fanny, and raises her in his arms.

He bears her into the next room.

Among the fragments scattered upon the floor, he perceives a broken bottle of water. He sprinkles the remains upon her face, and kisses her pale cheek.

A noise of people is heard below. The name of Wilson is sounded. As he replies, they come up the stairs. He knows they are his friends.

Mr. Lockeridge enters the room, holding in his hand the pistol that Marauder had so lately attempted to fire at Wilson; others accompany him.

They find their friend covered in blood, supporting a lifeless female in his arms. Every face exhibits a scene of horror!

As soon as Mr. Lockeridge perceived the melancholy situation of Fanny, he hastened back again for a surgeon, whom they had left attending on the miserable Marauder.

The gentleman came without loss of time into the room, and opened a vein in the fair arm of Fanny. Wilson still held his lovely burden; he scarcely breathed as the surgeon performed his operation; his eyes were riveted to the fascinating object before him; her blood he feared had stopped, never to flow again.

Happily his alarms, in a few second subsided. The pure stream trickled forth, and Fanny opened her eyes.—Fixing them on the bloody countenance of him she had so long, so dearly loved, she had nearly swooned a second time; but the voice of her fond lover recovered her.—"Be not alarmed, dearest Fanny! These are all your friends."

"But you are hurt, dear Wilson?"

Wilson made light of it, though the strength and virulence of his enemy had left legible marks of his pugilistic skill. His friend Lockeridge came up, and wiped the blood from his face.

Not a word would Wilson hear of his own hurts; but, together with the surgeon, minutely enquired of Fanny if she felt any pain in her head. While the anxious lover supported her, the surgeon carefully examined her left-side, on which she had fallen; and then announced, to the great joy of the whole company, that he was certain no fracture had taken place, though a large swelling was very evident.

The medical gentleman now left them to attend on his wretched patient below, and all the spectators, except Wilson and his friend Lockeridge, accompanied him.

In the midst of a group below, stood the old deaf servant, who had been roused from his work at the other end of the garden. Some of the servants of the sportsmen had found him; they seize, and question him. He tells them of his malady, and professes total ignorance of the affair. They bring him into the house along with them.

Marauder was a dreadful spectacle: one thigh broke, his ankle dislocated, and a violent contusion on the upper part of his head. For some time the surgeon thought his skull was fractured, but his side had struck against a pillar; and when the surgeon returned to him, he discovered that three of his ribs were broke.

Though he shewed signs of life, he was a long time in recovering his senses.

It was nearly an hour before his recollection fully returned; the virulence of his passions was still evident, in defiance of his weak state, and the pain he experienced.

The first word Marauder spoke was with his usual haughtiness— "Let me be left with the surgeon, and my servant."

They all left the room.

"Am I the only victim?" said Marauder to the surgeon, in a surly tone.

The other replied—"No one besides is materially hurt."

He gnashed his teeth together, and muttered a curse of displeasure.—"I'll leave this infernal place directly!"

"It is impossible, Sir. You'll endanger your life."

"Impossible!—Endanger my life!—Think you my life is my first care?—Let a chaise be sent for directly. That deaf fellow," continued he, pointing to his man, "can receive orders in writing."

In the room were ink and paper. The surgeon gave the orders, as Marauder desired. He went out of the room to get other assistance, and, at the same time, desired one of the company to inform Wilson that the gentleman below, in spite of his hurts, had sent his servant off for a chaise.

Wilson was resolved not to let him escape him, and therefore made enquiries for the nearest Justice of the Peace.

The master of the hounds and Mr. Lockeridge were both in the commission.[1] As it was necessary to take Wilson's deposition on oath, a man was instantly sent to the next village for a Bible, pen, ink, and paper. The distance for a chaise was ten miles—to the village but four.

When every thing was ready, Wilson swore that he believed Mr. James Marauder to be the person who, under the name of M'Ginnis, headed some troops in open rebellion, in Ireland.—The assault upon Fanny was for the present omitted, as, among other reasons, it was an affair of not so serious a nature, and for which Wilson well knew the Magistrate could not refuse bail.

Fanny, who was rather alarmed at the detention of Marauder, had wished him to be suffered to depart wherever he thought proper, glad to be so easily rid of him; she was therefore greatly surprised when she found herself extricated from personal interference, by the deposition of Wilson.

---

1 To be in the commission was to be a magistrate, otherwise known as a Justice of the Peace.

It was necessary to inform Marauder of what had been done. The other Magistrate, Mr. Woodland, wrote upon a piece of paper the following:—

"To James Marauder, Esq.
"Wilson Wilson, Esq. a Captain in the Southford Fencibles, has made oath before me, Thomas Woodland, and another Justice of the Peace for this county, that he has every reason to believe that you, James Marauder, under the assumed name of M'Ginnis, commanded a body of rebels in arms against his Majesty's troops, in the late disturbances in Ireland."

The surgeon received it at the door.

"'Tis a note for you, Sir."

"Read it," said Marauder.

"Wilson Wilson, Esq. a Captain in the Southford Fencibles, has made oath before me—"

"Curse on their arts! Do they dare to think of detaining me, till I get bail, for this pretended assault."

"No assault is mentioned by the Magistrate," said the surgeon.

"Well, Sir," exclaimed Marauder, impatiently interrupting him, "go on."

The surgeon read the note.

Marauder seemed evidently confused. He paused a moment. His usual *hauteur* forsook him, and, assuming that fashionable suavity, in which he excelled, he sent his compliments to the Magistrate, and begged the favour of his company for a few moments.

Mr. Woodland came to him.

Marauder, in spite of all his pain, and the weakness he experienced from loss of blood, in the interim of the surgeon's going up to the Magistrate, had fully recovered the command of himself.

When that gentleman had arrived, therefore, he said, reclining on a couch, and holding the paper in his hand—"This falsity, Sir, I hope is not to be made the instrument for detaining my person."

"Captain Wilson," replied Mr. Woodland, "has taken his oath. We must do our duty, as Magistrates."

As yet Marauder knew not by what circumstance Wilson came so opportunely to the rescue of Fanny. Little did he think that he was one of the sportsmen; but supposed that he had broke his way through by the chance assistance of the others, or that he had been accidentally followed by them. He concluded that one of the fellows, whom he had employed, had betrayed him, and, having conducted him to the house, had perhaps afterwards left him. Believing any thing but what was really the case, he did not consider that Wilson was likely to be known by any of the company.

Thus reasoning, and swelling with hatred and revenge towards his enemy, with difficulty he stomached his passions to the Justice's remark, and replied calmly—"Beware, Sir, how you meddle in this affair. In another quarter of the globe was I at the time. I have thousands, ten thousand of witnesses to prove an *alibi*. A Magistrate is not obliged to proceed on so gross a falsehood as this, even where it is affirmed by an oath."

"True or false, Sir, we must detain your person. If you are injured by a perjury, the laws are open for redress."

"The villainy of my adversary's conduct—the high respectability of my own, is a sufficient excuse for you, Sir."

"How am I to know this?—I am not acquainted with either of you."

"*My* assertion, Sir. He does not deny my name. I am nephew to the late Duke of Silsbury, and by right am, at this moment, the present Duke; but by the chicanery, forgeries, and perjuries of this Wilson, I am for a while kept from the title. *I* tell you, Sir, the infamy of his character."

"He says the same of yours. Mr. Lockeridge, who is the other Magistrate, and a respectable Clergyman in this neighbourhood, is above, and is well acquainted with him."

Marauder was abashed.—"I am surrounded by a gang of designing and prejudiced people. My bodily hurts prevent my personal exertions. My friends are absent. From hence then I will not be removed. This gentleman," pointing to the surgeon, "will confirm the dangerous nature of my case. If I must be your prisoner for a few hours, while I send for my friends, let it be here."

"I understood you had ordered a chaise."

"No matter. I feel myself worse. Enquire of my surgeon."

The surgeon of course said, as he had before, that a removal would endanger his life. The Magistrate told him that he must appoint people to attend in the house, till he could be delivered up to more regular custody.

While this conversation was passing below stairs, another circumstance had occurred above, which furnished additional proof to Wilson that Marauder and M'Ginnis were the same.

Mr. Lockeridge, when he first came up, had picked up the pistol which Marauder fired off. In assisting Wilson to recover Fanny, he had put it in his pocket. He now drew it forth, and shewing it to Wilson, related where he had found it.

Instantly Wilson recognized it to be the fellow to the one O'Rourk had been employed with. He took it in his hand, and had not the smallest doubt. The maker's name was the same, a person well known, and upon whom he had purposed to call, as soon as he came to England, to see if he could make any discovery by that means.

This circumstance, in a few words, he did not fail to mention to Mr. Woodland as soon as he came to them, and Mr. Lockeridge delivered the pistol into his care.

A servant had been dispatched for Mr. Lockeridge's chaise for Fanny.

Mrs. Lockeridge, receiving a short note from her husband, that a young lady was in distress, had, instead of being over anxious to exhibit two puddings upon her board, thought proper to shew her hospitality in a far better way—by coming herself.

Mr. Lockeridge's Parsonage was about eight miles off;—the chaise had been sent for when the surgeon first left the room to attend on Marauder, and arrived a little after the Justice had settled his business.

Mr. Lockeridge was agreeably surprised when his servant informed him that his mistress was arrived. He welcomed her with a warm kiss, the ardour of which twenty winters of matrimony had not in the least damped.—"Dear Mary, you are always so kind and considerate. I shall fancy you are possessed of my thoughts, as well as my heart."

"If my actions are ever different from your wishes, it is solely occasioned, my dear, by my want of judgement."

I shall repeat no more of the short conversation that passed between the husband and wife, as they crossed the court-yard, with her arm in his, and ascended the stairs, lest that I should be supposed to have borrowed the conversation of a *honey-moon, "that had not yet filled her horns."*[1]

When Mrs. Lockeridge was introduced to Fanny, her bright eyes again thanked the wife of Wilson's friend for her kindness in coming herself; and, without loss of any further time, they immediately left the place.

Wilson was obliged to resign his wishes of accompanying them, to be a guard that Marauder was not clandestinely carried off, till proper people had arrived, whom the Magistrates had sent for.

---

1 The crescent-shaped new moon is said to have "horns," even, Lucas puns, if it is a honeymoon. These horns are "filled" when the moon becomes full, which must happen within the month.

The instant Marauder's man returned, he was again sent away for his favourite attorney, Imphell; neither pain nor remonstrance prevented his writing the following to his trusty instrument.

"I am much hurt. Come instantly, and bring a surgeon with you I can in all cases depend upon."

"J.M."

The common attendance of servants Marauder greatly needed; the man therefore was ordered to send a man and a woman from the first village he was to pass through; and the surgeon gave him a note to proper people for that purpose, who were approved of by the Magistrates.

CHAPTER XVII.

It was evening before the persons, appointed by Mr. Woodland to watch the prisoner, arrived. Wilson, with Mr. Lockeridge, then left the house; and, having detained the chaise which the deaf man had ordered for Marauder, and sent their horses home before, the happy lover soon clasped his beloved Fanny in his arms.

The next morning Imphell came with two surgeons. The gentleman, who had as yet attended Marauder, had staid with him the whole night. By the patient's earnest desire, he remained with him till his steward and his own surgeon arrived.

Marauder now dismissed him with a very handsome present, conceiving it the best way to ensure his good word, though he dispensed with his attendance any longer.

In a short private conversation with Imphell, Marauder soon understood that one of the persons, who he had brought, was engaged to stay with him as long as he thought proper; the other was a gentleman of great eminence in his profession, whose abilities and skill Imphell thought might be necessary. When this last, with the other two, had thoroughly examined the hurts he had suffered, and given directions to the one who was to stay, he took his leave, promising to call again in two days, to meet and consult with the surgeon who had first attended him. Skeibar was the name of the person who remained. His look was the true index of the man—an adventurer, equally needy in pocket, principles, and ability.

As soon as Marauder was alone with Imphell, he discovered the particulars of his ill fate.—"D—nation! I am a prisoner in my own house!—What is to be done?"

"The confinement," replied Imphell, "is scarcely legal; yet the very attempt to set it aside, will only involve you in worse circumstances. At present, Sir, your illness prevents your removal. This you may lengthen out to what time you think necessary, while you consult how you shall act, or to plan your escape, as you think best."

Imphell spoke in this manner, that he might sound Marauder, whether he were M'Ginnis, or not; but the hero was resolved not to expose himself to any person breathing, and replied—"A trial I should court concerning my kinsman, M'Ginnis, did I not know that when they fail here, I shall be indicted for the assault on that young vixen. Unluckily I have not witness on my side, and the girl and her paramour will out-swear me."

"Can we not *make* witnesses?"

"No one but my *deaf man* was on the premises."

"I wish, Sir, you had suffered those two fellows to have—but 'tis too late to reason now. Shall I question *him*?"

"Not at present, Imphell; that you may do at any time. The greatest service you can at present do me, is to endeavour to find out in what manner my enemies intend to proceed.—I can depend on your friend Skeibar?"

"Yes, Sir, most assuredly. I have him in every point."

"Know you any thing of those two fellows, whom I employed"

"I can find them, Sir."

"I wish to see them in a few days, when I feel myself better. But take care that they are sufficiently disguised not to be known.—Call Skeibar here;—I feel myself faint."

From the great exertion Marauder had undergone in this conversation with his trusty agent, he nearly swooned by the time his apothecary came. Salts and hartshorn recovered him; and, having rested a few hours, he dismissed Imphell on the search for intelligence of his enemies' intentions towards him, and took a composing draught, according to the orders of the medical men, who had departed.

Nor was Wilson idle in hastening to substantiate the charge he had advanced concerning his rival. To explain which more clearly, it will be proper to note some circumstances which had happened, since the day when M'Ginnis and his party had been attacked, as they endeavoured to enter a small town, in his way to join the French.

By the men, who were made prisoners, the name of their leader was discovered.

A diligent search was immediately set on foot to discover M'Ginnis; but owing to his very cautious behaviour, it proved to be fruitless.

A little after he had recovered of his wounds, and left the cabin, one of the men who had conducted him there was made a prisoner. In hopes to secure his own life, he betrayed the concealment of his General.—The pursuers came too late.

By a bribe to the lesser villain, his host, they partly discovered his disguise, and continued their search; but M'Ginnis, who trusted no man, and endeavoured to deceive every one, had neither exposed his real intentions, or his road, to this needy wretch.

Wilson, on account of his knowledge of the person whom the Government were so desirous to apprehend, was the principal employed in the search after him. Once or twice they gained some tidings, and, among other places, they came to the house where Duchesne, the Emigrant French Officer, the friend and second of the unfortunate Geutespiere, was.

With the owner of the mansion Wilson had some acquaintance, and dined in company with Duchesne. Wilson, mentioning the object of his search, said—"M'Ginnis's face I should instantly recognize in any disguise; he is so extremely like his cousin, Marauder, whose large property he has had the command of, and whose features I have known from my childhood."

"You said, Marauder, Sir?" said Duchesne, quickly; "Mr. James Marauder, the nephew of the Duke of Silsbury?"

"Yes, of the late Duke. Do you know him?"

"It has been my misfortune!" replied Duchesne, shrugging up his shoulders; and he told, with his usual volubility, the story of Geutespiere, Leonora, and the unfortunate double duel.

"Fahany has shot himself," said Wilson.

"Ah! ah!" replied the Frenchman, "then my countryman's grand ally has got one of them."

"Who, Sir?"

"The Devil.—No matter.—Captain Wilson, I was about to tell you that I saw the very spectre of Marauder, the other day, in the form of an old Italian Jew."

"Sir?" exclaimed Wilson, as asking a question that expressed surprise and doubt.

"No joke, upon my honour, Sir," answered Duchesne, assuming the utmost gravity, and clapping his hand upon his breast. "Mr. O'Leary, and Mr. Steele (an elderly gentleman, Mrs. O'Leary's father)," Duchesne continued calling each of the company by name, to corroborate his assertion, "will all assure you I told them so immediately after the Jew went away."

Wilson made many enquiries concerning the person of this

pretended Jew. The emigrant gave him a much more minute detail than he had any reason to expect.

Duchesne did not forget to mention that their conversation was in the Italian language, yet his features were neither of the Jewish nor Italian cast.—"I beg pardon of his Roman nose.—He could not speak decently to me in my native tongue; but since, I understand from my servant, that he spoke very good French to him."

This, in Wilson's mind, was a very strong circumstance that the person was otherwise than he seemed to be; and what is more likely than that Marauder recollected Duchesne?

He desired Duchesne's servant might be called into the room; and questioned him closely upon this circumstance, which the man fully confirmed.

Duchesne mentioned the strong scar on the left-side of his forehead, and was very nice in pointing out the spot; but concerning this wound which had so fully marked him, nothing had transpired to the knowledge of Wilson, and it neither favoured the supposition that the person was Marauder or M'Ginnis.

"Do you think, Sir," said Wilson, as a concluding question upon the subject, "that you should know this person again, if you were to see him in a very different garb?"

"Most assuredly," replied the Officer warmly. "Were he in the royal robes, if he had on the rags of the Witch of Endor, or were he in masquerade, like an English fox-hunter, I am sure he could not deceive my inspection."—The company smiled at the Frenchman's similes, which alluded to some pictures in the room, while he continued—"I narrowly observed the form of his teeth, the shape of his eyebrows, the very turn of his upper-lip; and I trod on his toe, for the purpose of seeing him raise it."

"But why the last, Sir?"

"It throws the features out of all disguise, Sir."

Wilson could not fail admiring how wonderfully deep the Emigrant Officer was in the science of Pathognomy and Physiognomy;[1] and Duchesne gave him many other curious and *systematic* remarks upon the former subject, but which are now totally *erratic* from mine.

A fortnight had passed since the Italian Jew had made his appearance at Mr. O'Leary's. No doubt remained in the mind of Wilson

---

1 Pathognomy is the science of emotions and passions, or the manifestation of them. Physiognomy is the art of judging character from the physical features of the face or body.

that this was M'Ginnis, and it seemed to him most probable that he was gone to England.

Wilson hastened from Mr. O'Leary's, and stated to the superior powers the particulars which had come to his knowledge; they thought it right that he should go over to England, and try if he could gain any intelligence of Marauder.

Duchesne also agreed to give him the meeting in London.

CHAPTER XVIII.

The scar across the forehead of Marauder had not escaped the observation of Wilson; and, soon after he arrived at Mr. Lockeridge's, he wrote a letter to Duchesne, to come down to him in the country.

In the morning after the rescue of Fanny, Wilson, with his friend Lockeridge, waited upon an attorney in that neighbourhood, with whom they were both acquainted.

Mr. Warwick was an honour to his profession. He was neither the haughty, proud, insulting demagogue of his district; nor the base, litigious, pettifogging scribe;—he was neither the fawning, sycophantic tool of the great; nor the ready, officious bully of the licentious vulgar. He was to the poor an adviser, to the great a peace-maker, and to all a friend. In three things particularly he had made himself beloved in the country: his attention to the poor laws; his compromising, in lieu of the payment of tithes in kind; and, the methods he had adopted to prevent the petty villainies of the country (*i.e.* poaching, robbing of gardens, orchards, &c. &c.), by allowing to the labourers a moderate quantity of land for the support of their families.

He was supposed to have saved more men from the gallows, than any Bow Street Officer ever sent; yet no man was more resolute against open idleness or profligacy.

He has been known to talk to a confirmed reprobate in this manner.—"My friend, I'm afraid you're *hardened* in these bad habits."

"Why, your Honour, none of the farmers like to employ me."

"And are you not fond of work.—Why don't you go for a soldier?"

"Better be hanged, your Honour, than flogged to death for deserting."

"Go to sea, then."

"There, your Honour, I can't even run away from the cat-a-nine-tails."

"Come, come, you don't want courage, and when you are out of the old way, perhaps you may mend. If you continue in the country, you'll very soon come to the gallows. Bad as you are, you cannot but believe you have got a *soul?*"

The fellow scratched his head, and, without speaking, looked affirmatively. *Happily he was no modern Philosopher!* Mr. Warwick continued—

"*That* is worth saving, if you don't think your body is. Have some respect for the service of God, if not for man. Try at least—take my advice—go to sea."

The man did, and went from his house, without going home, to the nearest sea-port, and entered immediately. In the late mutiny, this very fellow cut down, with his own hand, two of the chief mutineers in the ship in which he was stationed; with a few others who joined their Captain, he prevented the massacre of their Officers; and he is now the boatswain of a man of war, under the command of the same Captain whom he so gallantly defended.[1] He never comes into the country without paying his respects, with a most grateful heart, to Mr. Warwick, and was very earnest with that gentleman to accept *the medal*, which had been given him for his good conduct, and which Mr. Warwick, explaining its *individual* worth, of course refused.

Such was the man of law, on whom Mr. Lockeridge and his friend waited.

Wilson, in a few words, related the whole of the story, and dwelt on the corroborating circumstances that induced him to believe that Marauder and M'Ginnis were the same person.

Mr. Warwick told him that the method of proceeding was very simple and plain; that it would be necessary to inform the Government, that he might be taken into legal custody, and, as soon as his health would permit, be sent over to Ireland to take his trial. The attorney advised Wilson to go himself to town for that purpose; to see the maker of the pistol, and get his testimony properly authenticated, and to bring Duchesne back with him.

As Mr. Lockeridge and Wilson came out of Mr. Warwick's house, Imphell, who knew all the parties, and naturally guessed to whom they would apply, was riding down the street. Imphell, seeing them a little before him, turned his horse, and put up at a different house than he intended.

With great effrontery he went to Mr. Warwick's, though he knew he was held in abomination by him, and had ever and anon come under his lash.

---

1 A reference to the mutinies which took place amongst the ships of the Royal Navy stationed at Spithead and the Nore in 1797.

"Good morning to you, Sir," said Imphell.

Mr. Warwick, with unusual *hauteur*, slightly bowed his head.

"I understand," continued Imphell, "that you are employed by Mr. Wilson in the cause against *us*."

"Who is *us*?"

"Mr. Marauder, I mean; I am always his attorney, you know, and my Lord, his father, used to—"

"Pray, Sir, who could tell you so?"

"I of course concluded it, knowing your intimacy with the Reverend Mr. Lockeridge; and I just saw Mr. Wilson and his clerical patron come out of your house."

"On this business you can having nothing to say to me," and Mr. Warwick got up.

Imphell kept his seat.—"Oh, yes. I have a great deal. I know you are not fond of a losing cause, and I wish to forewarn you in this ridiculous case, which is all occasioned by a family likeness."

"So I have been informed."

"Yet there is a very great difference between Mr. Marauder and Captain M'Ginnis."

"You have seen Captain M'Ginnis?"

"No, I cannot positively say, *upon my honour*, that I have."

"Are you in doubt then?"

The biter began to be bit; though Mr. Warwick was mistaken, Imphell was not in the secret.

Imphell replied—"When Captain M'Ginnis was in London, before Mr. Marauder went to the West Indies, I called at his house; but Captain M'Ginnis was very ill, had been overturned in a carriage. But, Mr. Warwick, I was saying to you how very clear this business is. It is impossible Mr. Marauder can be Captain M'Ginnis, because he was in the West Indies at the time; and, besides, Mr. Marauder is a Papist."

"He *was*."

"We've ten thousand witnesses to prove an *alibi*."

"*You* are not one, I find; as you cannot say, *upon your honour*, that you ever saw the Captain."—Imphell looked confused. A thousand fancies crowded into his head: his friend, Marauder, might perhaps *wish him to be a witness*. Mr. Warwick checked all his ideas by enquiring—"Who are your witnesses?"

"The Captain and crew he went out with; the Captain and crew he came back with; all the people he met with there."

"What are the names of the two Captains, whom he went out and came back with?"

Imphell endeavoured to be more on his guard.—"Upon my word and honour I have forgot their names; but I am going to London on purpose to find them out."

"And then—you'll know their names?"

"I shall see Mr. Marauder again before I go to town."

"Your visit to-day was *purposely* to me?"

Imphell was rather confounded; but though he often lost himself, he never lost his assurance, but replied—"I had a little business besides in town;" and, endeavouring to turn the conversation to that point for which he came, said—"You see how sure an *alibi we've* got. Now *you* have no witness at all, but the *bare word*—I should say *fancy*—of Captain Wilson."

"Indeed!"

Imphell was obliged to ask the question—"Have you?"

"What?"

"Any body besides Captain Wilson, who fancies Mr. Marauder and his kinsman, M'Ginnis, the same?"

"I'll tell you something, Mr. Imphell," replied Mr. Warwick. The other was all attention;—now, thought he, I shall get all the particulars.—"I am not to be the attorney in this business."

"Sir!" exclaimed Imphell, with the utmost astonishment. "Who is?"

"The most honest attorney we can find in Ireland; for if Mr. Marauder is ever tried for being the rebel M'Ginnis, depend upon it the trial must be there. Neither, therefore, can you act, Mr. Imphell; and it's extremely unlucky you cannot be a witness."

Without any further ceremony, Mr. Warwick, who had been standing some time, rung the bell, and wished the other a good morning.

Not so wise, nor so able as when he entered, the pettifogger departed, having left a certain portion of his knowledge behind him, and lessened the means of his exertions for the service of his patron. From the foregoing conversation, Mr. Warwick began to be of Wilson's opinion, which he rather doubted before; that M'Ginnis and Marauder were more than cousins.

Imphell, thoroughly disappointed in his first attempt, was yet resolved to wait in the town till the two gentlemen left it, that he might know if they had another conversation with Mr. Warwick.

They dined with that gentleman, and Wilson took a place in the mail to go to town in the evening. This Imphell having discovered, as soon as it was dark, he, disguised in a horseman's large coat and a slouching hat, dodged them to the inn from which the mail-coach set off. As he hovered around them, listening to the conversation, among other things, he overheard the following.

Mr. Lockeridge.—"Do you think Duchesne is already in town?"

Wilson.—"I have reason to suppose, from what he said to me in Ireland, that he has been there a week."

"Have you any thing to say to Fanny, concerning your return?"

"I'll write the moment I get to London, and follow it as soon as possible."

With this, as the reward for his day's trouble, Imphell returned to his employer. He himself conceived it to be of very little consequence, but he knew not the secret mind of Marauder. But before he went to the house upon the Downs, it was necessary to see the two men, who had assisted in the carrying off of Fanny.

One he found was gone to Newmarket[1] to try the strength of his new pocket, at a famous race there; the other Imphell dressed in Marauder's livery, and took back with him as a servant.

His business detained the man of law over the night; but in the evening of the next day he returned to the expectant Marauder.

CHAPTER XIX.

Imphell found his noble employer somewhat better in health, and considerably better in spirits. When the attorney had been a few minutes with him alone, he mentioned the servant he had brought, and the man was called in.

He proved to be the one of the two whom Marauder most wished to see. After asking him if he had a mind to stay with him as a servant, and the other having willingly assented, Marauder was left alone with Imphell.

The attorney now told the fruitlessness of his attempt to discover the proofs Wilson might be able to produce.—"I could get no intelligence whatever of that sly fellow, Warwick; but I overhead a trifling conversation in the inn-yard, concerning Miss Fanny Bellaire, and one Duchesne."

"Who?" vociferated Marauder.

"One Duchesne, Wilson had met with in Ireland."

Marauder shook as he lay in the bed, with unusual agitation. Nothing but a few curses for some moments escaped him. Recovering himself—"Imphell," said he, "deliver me, as near as possible, the very words of the conversation."

---

1 A horse-racing course seventy miles north of London.

Imphell, who had taken it down, repeated it *verbatim*.

"Confusion on the Frenchman's tongue!—I see their cursed plots!—This damned scar!—Call Skeibar here."

Imphell hastened out, thinking that Marauder was worse. Skeibar returned with him.

"Examine this scar," said Marauder, as if nothing else was the matter with him.

Skeibar, noticing it, replied—"The wound is perfectly healed, Sir; you need not fear that it will open afresh."

"Fear!" exclaimed Marauder. "It must be opened afresh! Nay, what is more, it must be taken quite away."

"Impossible, Sir."

"I say it is, and shall be possible.—Yet, let me see—if I can get rid—Ah! it will do."—Marauder seemed on a sudden deeply in thought.—"Mr. Skeibar, I can dispense with your attendance for the present.—Send my servant here."

The man came in.

Marauder spoke to Imphell.—"You said my enemy promised to send a letter the instant he got to town?"

"Yes, Sir."

"I must have that letter."

"Sir!"

"I know it's a cross-post from the town Woolborough to the village where that Parson lives.—Dick, come nearer.—Are you not able, without assistance, to take a parcel from a little boy?"

Dick, whose taciturnity had caught the notice of Marauder, replied, with a sneer—"Yes."

"Imphell shall tell you when—shall completely disguise you, and shew you the place. Bring the bag to me.—I'll make your fortune, you dog;—you shall have its weight in gold."

Dick grinned, and went out.

Marauder now explained to Imphell his firm determination to get rid of Wilson.—"Yet while the Frenchman lives—" Marauder checked himself.

Imphell was greatly alarmed; he perceived himself involved deeper in Mr. Marauder's affairs than he had any intention of. He was almost necessitated to be a party in robbing the mail; he was made privy to an intended murder; and, if the fellow should turn informer, or they should by any means be discovered, he saw no loop-hole through which he could escape the gallows. The attorney was not much afraid of the devil, unless he came in an hanging form. Money could purchase any thing of him but a swing.

Too much in awe did he stand of Marauder to dare to dissent from him when Dick was present; but now they were alone, he was determined to use every argument to dissuade him both from the robbery and murder, at least for the present, till his own neck was out of the collar. From Marauder's conduct too, he had no doubt that he was the renowned M'Ginnis; and he was astonished at his want of confidence in this point, when he exposed himself so openly in the plans of murder and robbery.

The arguments of Imphell prevailed on Marauder to give up the idea of the robbery, chiefly on account of the improbability of any letter from Wilson leading to a discovery, when he himself was to follow it so soon after. Yet still more determined did Marauder seem in his resolution to destroy Wilson; but Imphell painted so very strongly what he felt, that the suspicions would immediately fall on them, that there were spies in the house, who watched their whole behaviour; and, what was a more forcible reason than any of the rest, that Marauder should first consult his own safety, while the delaying of the blow would occasion it to fall with double force.

"Neither," concluded the lawyer, "have we time to think of any thing but your escape. A different kind of guard, appointed by Government, will soon be set over you, which will make it much more hazardous."

Marauder was struck with his arguments, and began at once revolving the means of effecting his escape. This he would have considered no difficult matter, if he had been able to walk; but, as it was, it required the utmost circumspection and prudence.

At last, however, it was settled that a chaise and four was to be ready at some little distance from the house; that the surgeon, who was a strong muscular man, was to let him down from the window; that Imphell and Dick were to carry him to the chaise; that Skeibar was to join them, and all four leave the kingdom together. Imphell knew he could easily get the key of the garden-door, as, from Marauder's ill health, the people who were appointed to watch him, could have no idea of his attempting an escape.

But this scheme was obliged to be laid aside from the indisposition of the principal, whose weak state would not permit any exertion, and whose fever, from the agitation of his spirits, increased so considerably in the evening, that his medical attendant assured him that the very attempt would certainly cost him his life. This person, being let into his intentions, endeavoured to prevail upon him to wait with patience till his health was established; assuring him that he would so deceive his guards, or even any other medical man that might be called in, that no one should discover any amendment either in his health or personal hurts.

Thus totally prevented, at present, from making his escape, Marauder, ever restless and dissatisfied, insisted on Dick's robbing the mail. Imphell's arguments could not swerve him from the purpose; and the pettifogger having discovered that the lad who carried the letters, was no regular messenger of the King's, but solely employed by the inhabitants of Wheatland, took fresh courage upon the occasion, and agreed to equip Dick for the business.

The parcel of letters was but small; but among them was one for Fanny.

Eagerly Marauder tore it open.

"My Dearest Fanny,
"I have concluded every thing in town, but finding Duchesne. If I am so fortunate as to meet with him at Windsor, where I am going instantly for that purpose, I hope to anticipate this, by being my own messenger; if not, you may expect me every hour.—Dearest Fanny, beloved of my soul, every moment seems lost to me when absent from you.—Your most faithful friend and grateful lover,
"Wilson Wilson."

"Stuff!" exclaimed Marauder, throwing it contemptuously from him. "Is that fellow, Wilson, returned?"

Imphell told him he believed he was.

A little bustle without, and a violent ringing at the front-bell alarmed the group.

Marauder and his gang supposed the robbery had been traced, and he ordered his door to be fastened, and all the papers to be put in the fire.

The papers were quickly consumed, and soon after some one rapped at Mr. Marauder's door, and desired to be admitted.

The surgeon said—"In a few minutes. Any thing particular?"

The person who had the chief guard of the house, answered, that the Bow Street Officers were arrived to take the charge of Mr. Marauder's person, and required immediately to see him.

"Cover my forehead instantly with some plaister," exclaimed Marauder; "and to any question that may be asked, let me answer."

The surgeon covered his forehead with some salve, and, by his patient's order, also pricked it all over with a needle.

The new guards were now admitted.

They came up to the bed, and, in a very civil manner, told him their business. They asked the surgeon how his patient was, and where his hurts were.

Marauder, in a faint tone, answered them, that if they were not satisfied that the general state of his health was such as to confine him at present, they might send for any other medical advice; and he referred them for uninterested information concerning his situation, to the other two surgeons who had visited him on the foregoing evening. He added, that particular enquiries were troublesome, and that they had no concern with any thing belonging to him, but the guard of his person; and he concluded with saying, that so far from wishing to lengthen his illness, he had already witnesses sufficient to establish an *alibi*.

"It is necessary, Sir," said one of them, "that we should have a thorough knowledge of your person, as it is committed to our care; and I must beg leave to see your forehead, which is so strangely covered."

The surgeon spoke—"I have but just dressed it, and it will be highly improper to tear off the bandages."

"How came it hurt?" asked one of the Officers.

"A violent bruise, which we did not at first notice, by being neglected, has spread all over the forehead."

"I must desire you to leave me," spoke Marauder, as if in much pain; "if you have any desire to see the place, the surgeon shall inform you when it is next dressed."

The Officers of Justice spoke together, and civilly retired.

Imphell, who might have sat for the picture of Sir Trevisend, in the Cave of Despair,[1] began to breathe again, and Marauder now required of the surgeon, without loss of time, to apply a blister all over his forehead; resolved, in his own mind, that the cicatrice[2] of his wound should be covered, before it was exposed to the inspection of his guards.

Whatever suspicions, therefore, might be entertained on this account, on the morrow, when they attended with the surgeon, the whole forehead was completely covered with the effects of the blister.

But the scar was much too deep to be erased by these means; and

---

1 In bk. I, canto ix, of Edmund Spenser's *The Faerie Queene* (1589-96), the Red Cross Knight encounters Sir Trevisan fleeing, with a rope around his neck, from the Cave of Despair. They return to the cave together where Despair again tempts them to kill themselves. They only narrowly escape (stanzas 21-54).

2 The scar of a healed wound.

three weeks having elapsed since the Officers were in the house, and Marauder in no respects better, their suspicions began to be strengthened, and they positively required that another surgeon should be called in.

Marauder, who had always before opposed it, pretended also to wish for such advice, and agreed to receive any person they thought proper to send for. His real hurts were by this time nearly well, and, in defiance of the remonstrance of the surgeon, he was resolved in the night to attempt his escape.

CHAPTER XX.

The following was the plan Marauder adopted. A fortnight before, under the pretence of having fresh air, he had been carried to the upper story of the house. The windows were furnished with bars; but his intention was to mount up the chimney to the top of the house, and to let himself down by a long cord, prepared for the purpose.— The surgeon and Imphell were to be off early in the morning, before it could be discovered, and to take care of themselves.

Yet Marauder did not intend to leave the premises, as he doubted if he should be able to get over the spiked wall, and the outward door, he knew was sufficiently secured; but, by throwing a rope over, he intended to cause suspicion that he had escaped by that means.

In an out-house, where the garden tools were kept, was a secret opening, known only to himself; here he purposed to conceal himself, till his guards were supposed to be absent in pursuit of him, and the house deserted. At twelve at noon, Imphell and Dick were to return with some fresh horses, and they were to be provided with pistols, to shoot any one who might oppose them.

In vain Imphell used every argument to dissuade him from this desperate scheme. Imphell chiefly dwelt upon his innocence, earnestly entreated him to stand a trial, promising to get any kind of witnesses to assist, if it were necessary, to prove an *alibi*.

Marauder, still tenacious of his secret, was positive in his determination.

The attorney now began to be most grievously alarmed. He not only saw the dreadful danger his patron ran; and the utter improbability of his succeeding, but he knew that he himself was an accomplice in the attempt, and the violated laws of his country seemed ready to overwhelm him. His fears at last overpowered every other sensation; even interest crouched before them; and, under a promise of secrecy, he gave notice of the intended attempt to the Bow Street guards.

Most cunning was the game Imphell played on the occasion. By these means he gained their confidence; and, as they were not to betray him, Marauder was to suppose that they heard some one ascending the chimney, and had mounted, by the trap-door, upon the house top, ready to receive him.

This petty treason of the attorney's had not yet proceeded further than the before-mentioned circumstance; and the motive he alleged to the Bow Street people was, that he believed Marauder to be light-headed, which was partly confirmed by the surgeon, who had lately told Imphell that he feared the gentleman's brain was affected.

As soon, therefore, as Marauder had descended from the top of the chimney to the roof of the house, and began adjusting his cord, the Officers rushed from a door which opened upon the leads, and seized him.

In vain Marauder attempted any resistance; after one faint struggle, he quietly surrendered himself.

Without speaking a word, he was conducted down into his room. His guards searched him, took away some improper weapons, and two persons remained with him.

About one o'clock Imphell was admitted to him, who had invented a plausible story for the purpose.

Marauder heard him in silence.—"Where's Dick?" said he.

Imphell replied that he was at a little distance, with the horses.

Marauder faintly smiled, ordered him to be called, and mentioned the name of *Skeibar*. Imphell professed his total ignorance of him. The truth was, Imphell wished to get rid of both. Dick stuck close to him; but Skeibar, who was to wait at a certain place for the party, had been liberally supplied by the attorney with money, in hopes that he would abscond with it: and Skeibar perceiving the ticklish situation in which he had involved himself, had acted accordingly.

While these things were passing at the house upon the Downs, the less conspicuous persons in these memoirs were not idle on their part.

Wilson had discovered Captain Duchesne at Windsor; but the Frenchman, hearing the condition of Marauder, had given him the slip, and was gone for a short time with a friend to Scotland. In vain Wilson remonstrated; he alleged that his presence was not yet necessary, and faithfully promised to answer his first letter in person.

Miss Bellaire's friends had received an express of her safety, as soon as possible after her arrival at Mr. Lockeridge's. Mr. Townsend came himself for her, and she returned with him to Richmond.

As it was necessary for Wilson to attend the trial of M'Ginnis, *alias* Marauder, in Dublin, he was obliged to yield to the arguments of the friends of Fanny, and postpone his nuptials till his return. During the confinement of Marauder, most of his time was spent with the beloved object of his heart, at Richmond.

He now received notice of Marauder's being sufficiently recovered to attempt his escape, and was ordered to prepare to go to Ireland in eight days. He accordingly wrote to Duchesne, and only waited his arrival. They were to proceed to Holyhead, and cross in the same vessel that was appointed to carry Marauder.

Orders instantly followed the information of his intended escape, to the keepers of Marauder to set off with their charge. He heard of his removal with one of his contemptuous smiles.

The violence of the hero's temper was wonderfully subsided since the failure of his attempt; the *Stoical* principle seemed to have taken possession of his whole frame. Imphell, who had before resolved to confess every thing, now began to think his own neck was safe without any further discovery; and, with a full confession, he knew he must say—"farewell!"—not only to his greatness, his interest, but to the little portion that remained to him—of character. Alarmed with perplexities and doubts, one moment buoyed with hope, the next sinking with fear, was Imphell. Marauder, on the contrary, was unusually calm, even less communicative than before, and to all the solicitations and artful questions of his attorney, concerning the expected trial, kept the secret of M'Ginnis safe, and solely answered—"I defy them."

Every thing was now ready for Marauder's departure. Dick was not to be found; he had not been seen since the evening before.

Marauder heard of his absence without any remark. He dressed himself in the morning with unusual composure, and his faithful steward began to suppose that his melancholy silence was wearing off.

They were alone.—"Imphell," said Marauder, looking upon the ground, "will you also forsake me?"

The attorney's fidelity flowed trippingly from his tongue.

"Come here," continued Marauder, in a mild tone.

Imphell went up to him.

Marauder laughed; and lifting up his eyes, with a sly look, which appalled the very heart of the other, exclaimed—"Who drove them from me?—If I am mad, wretch, beware of my fangs! Would these were the infernal regions, that I might toss thee into the flames! Accursed rascal! thou has betrayed me."

As he spoke, he seized him by the collar. Imphell cried out. Now burst forth the restrained rage of Marauder. He shook the lawyer with a desperate violence; he struck him again and again with his fists; he pushed him against the wall; he threw him upon the ground with all the violence of revengeful rage.

Quickly had the base tool of his villainy met the fate he deserved from his employer's hands, but the attendants came to his rescue.

All reason had forsaken Marauder. He sprung upright upon the prostrate, senseless wretch; his eyeballs glared with fire, and he rushed, with very little appearance of thought, against the persons who entered the room, and endeavoured to force his way through them. With great exertion on their part was he at length overpowered, and he sunk to the ground exhausted. It was but for a moment—his rage returned with redoubled violence; he cried but on Imphell, and with the most shocking execrations swore he would destroy him.

By force only was he restrained; he seemed lost to every thing that was said to him, and still repeated his curses.

Every feature was distorted with madness; confined to the ground by cords, he tried to gnaw them asunder, and when all other means of offence failed, he venomously spat at his opponents.

At last, finding himself completely subdued, and entangled in the cords which were bound round him, he roared out with his utmost efforts; his screams pierced through the apartments, and he only paused to give vent to a torrent of oaths and blasphemies.

His attendants, who were not ignorant of scenes of horror in every form, stood aghast at the one before them, and looked at each other in a silent agony, unknowing how to dispose of their prisoner.

Imphell, dreadfully bruised and hurt, lay senseless on the ground.—Marauder, bound hand and foot, glared at his prey, against whom all his rage seemed directed.

Imphell, somewhat recovered, was led out of the room, Marauder even to the last straining to force the bonds that held him, that he might satiate his vengeance.

As soon as the lawyer was removed out of his sight, the fury of Marauder subsided; but the attendants, not willing to trust to appearances, lifted him upon the couch, and fastened him there till the surgeon should arrive, whom they had, at the appearance of their prisoner's insanity, sent for.

The gentleman, who had at the first attended him, arrived. When he felt his pulse, Marauder exclaimed—"Well, Doctor, if he's mad, there's reason in it."

He was bled without the least resistance. The surgeon next examined his forehead, and testified his surprise at finding any injury there. Marauder unwillingly suffered his interference in this case; but knowing all opposition useless, he at length silently acquiesced.

The surgeon discovered that a large sore, which covered his forehead, had been improperly healed over, and that the morbid substance had penetrated inward. To this corporeal ailment he partly attributed the deranged state of his patient's intellects; little did he know the far more grievous mental evils which racked the inmost soul of Marauder. The various medical men who had attended him, had found it no difficult matter to administer such remedies as his body required; but among the whole circle of his acquaintance, where was he to find one who could ease the agonizing pain of thought?

The dry scaly flesh being removed from Marauder's forehead, the malignant humours received a vent, and in a few hours the patient seemed easier, and fell into a repose. In the evening the fever had considerably abated; and, though Marauder spoke but little, the surgeon remarked that the deadly frenzy of his eye was much calmer, and his manner more consistent and composed.

CHAPTER XXI.

The amendment of Marauder on the following day was truly astonishing. He spoke rationally, even professed a readiness to set off immediately towards Ireland; and calmly desired that that infamous villain, Imphell, might not again be admitted into his presence. Imphell, indeed, had taken the opportunity of the chaise which had been ordered for Marauder, and, urged only by his present fears, returned to his own home.

In the evening of the same day, at his earnest entreaties, Marauder was released from the inconvenience of a strait-waistcoat, which, at the surgeon's first arrival, had been placed upon him.

On the third day, no appearance of insanity returning, and Marauder himself being extremely anxious to depart, the Bow Street Officers proceeded forward with their charge. To their enquiries—if he did not require a servant—he accepted the attendance of a man, who had come with them, and who had waited upon him for the last three days; thus removing every suspicion of his wishing to make his escape.

Before his departure, he ordered the deaf man to remain in the house till his return, of which he spoke with confidence; he made a handsome present to the surgeon, and wrote some letters. He received also, from his medical attendant, proper dressings for the hurt on his forehead, which was ordered to be kept open, and also some medicines.

They now proceeded slowly on their journey, with short stages; as the late frenzy, with which Marauder had been seized, had left a weakness and languor upon him. His mildness and civility were remarkable; and though for a while he would be wrapped in thought, he asked many questions, and spoke more than he had been accustomed to for some weeks. In the course of the journey he frequently got out of the carriage, and walked for a few miles, that he might enjoy the full breezes of the refreshing spring; but ever on these occasions his attendants were on their guard: one of the men, who rode in the chaise, always walked with him, while his new servant, and another man on horseback closely followed.

Without any interruption they continued their progress till the well known shores of Holyhead, and the adjacent view struck the notice of Marauder. He was now within a few miles of the place; and close on one side of the road was an entrance into the ever memorable wood, where the fatal double duel had taken place, and the unhappy Geutespiere had fallen by the pistol of Marauder.

Marauder desired the carriage to stop; he got out. He praised the genial warmth of the day, and taking off his great-coat, gave it to his servant. He slowly approached an opening in the wood—he paused—the attendants stopped at some little distance.

In an instant he rushed among the trees—more to the astonishment than the confusion of his attendants. Beyond the wood was the town, and rocky impassable cliffs; around it an open and level country. In such a situation they had no doubt of quickly recovering him. The two men, who had accompanied him in the chaise, hastened after him on foot, and the horsemen skirted the extremities of the wood.

Now alone and free, Marauder, with maddening fury, rushed desperately through the most arduous places. The brambles, the bushes yielded before him, and he was soon lost to the sight of his pursuers. Their shouts quickened his pace, as exulting he bounded along; and now he had gained the opening to the fatal lawn where Geutespiere fell.

One moment he paused. Recollection flashed across his mind. A guilty pang smote him; and, with incredible speed, he flew across the plain.

Now, almost arrived at the other end, sudden the sound of voices checked his career. With eyes intent, watchful ears, his breath scarce moving, observant he stood.—Who can conceive what thoughts, what ideas, strange, confused, unbounded, infinite, pressed upon his distempered brain?—Like the wary tiger, he crouched, as it were, on the watch, to fight or to fly.

Forth from the opening came a figure—such as had just marked itself in his mind in the vague form of Geutespiere; the military garb and uniform were like those the murdered Geutespiere had worn.

The soul of Marauder staggered. The figure stopped. Every deadly fiend of guilt, depravity, and madness urged Marauder forward. He was about to force his way against it, when, lo! another form sprung forward, in which his appalled heart recognized the features of Wilson.

Marauder trembled;—his eyes avoided a sight so dreaded. Every form but this, Marauder could have opposed; against every other he had been successful; here he had been again and again subdued and humbled.

Guided only by fear, away the conscious Marauder flew—no matter where—every thing dreaded was behind him.

Wilson was swift of foot—he closely followed his prey.

Each Fury aided the speed of Marauder—Despair goaded him forward to the edge of the yawning precipice that overhangs the town;—just tottering on the brink, one look he threw behind him—he saw—and leaped with his utmost exertion, into the deadly abyss.

Wilson, petrified at the ghastly act, instantly paused. The horsemen galloped up; from them he first learned of the frenzied virulence with which disappointed guilt had smote the soul of Marauder.

The horsemen hastened round the cliff. The haughty Marauder was no more. That turbulent and fiery spirit, which spurned the laws of God and man, had fled his harassed body;—dashed to pieces by the tremendous fall, it lay deformed, and scarcely to be known, upon the beach!

They bore it to the town.

Wilson and Duchesne came up.—Wilson turned from the shocking sight. Duchesne took one look at his old enemy, the murderer of his friend, but spoke not a word. Horror sat in the countenances of every person present.

Wilson and Duchesne instantly set off to town; they had been some days at Holyhead, waiting for the prisoner and his escort; and, without knowing the reason, had been surprised that they were not arrived. Duchesne, wishing to review the fatal spot where his countryman fell, had been accompanied by Wilson, when they, to the amazement of all parties, so strangely encountered the execrable cause of all.

The Officers of Justice, who had had the care of Marauder's person, prudently applied, by the advice of Wilson, to a respectable attorney in the place, and in his presence, searched the pockets of the deceased, for the purpose of finding either letters or papers, that might give them a reference to some friend or relation of his; but not the least clue could they find to direct them in this point. The Coroner's Inquest having determined the suicide insane, he was buried in the plainest manner on the third day.

The gay, the gallant Marauder, whose birth, fortune, and expectations made him *equal* with the first characters in the kingdom—whose pride, conceit, and ambition lifted him *above* them all—whose graceful person and manly strength were the praise of one sex, and the envy of the other—whose ardent and indefatigable soul never flinched at what his imperious will commanded;—Marauder—whom not to know was ignorance, to whom every circle in life had produced friends and followers by the dozen—Marauder, the active Chief wherever he appeared, untimely perishes a miserable suicide, the wretched victim of Despair!

Not a friend—not an acquaintance—not even a domestic is to be found to pay the last offices of his funeral.—A felon he dies;—fear and frenzy perform the part of the public executioner; and the servants of Justice close the scene, instead of the ever dear connections, of relation or friend.

What knowledge the departed spirit may possess of the things of this world, has nothing to do with our duty towards God or man; but it is one of those speculative reflections which a religious belief will be apt to raise in the mind.

Conceive the proud, tyrannic, and restless spirit of Marauder beholding his funereal obsequies!—Conceive it impotent and disabled, yet swelling with hatred and revenge—conscious that all it ever held dear was now become the property of its first supplanter—conscious that all its worldly art and cunning had not the common prudence to prevent this!—The young Duke of Silsbury, as heir at law, takes possession of the whole estate of his kinsman, Marauder, in lands and personals.

Reader, what are *thy* intentions in this life?—Inspect thy prospects—look boldly at the summit of them. Is it wealth, honours, or what does thou call it?—Cast thine eyes around—among the myriads before thee find out the favoured mortal, whose envied state thou hopest to resemble. Observe him narrowly—see him at home, abroad, in the moments of pleasure and of retirement. Now answer thyself.—Art thou willing to take his station for that uncertain period of existence which may happen to thee? Wilt thou sacrifice to this idol all hopes of a happy lot in the boundless unknown region beyond? or wilt thou check thy worldly career now, and turn thy feet, without loss of a moment, to the path of futurity?

What art thou, reader?—No matter.—Be thou ever so great in thine own eyes, thou must yield to the power of that Almighty fiat, which can say—"This night thy soul shall be required of thee!"[1]

CHAPTER XXII.

Wilson had many reasons for leaving the spot immediately upon the death of Marauder. He not only wished to inform the Government; but, as he was the head steward of the Duke of Silsbury, who was Marauder's heir at law, he avoided at present any interference into his affairs, till he was informed whether there was any will; and he thought, also, that his Grace ought to know, without loss of time, of his kinsman's fate.

Before he left Holyhead, he wrote to Imphell (though the Bow Street Officers told Wilson of the late chastisement that he had received from his principal), as the attorney was the only person he knew of, who had any trust in Marauder's affairs.

Imphell denied the least knowledge of a will; and, after the most minute enquiries of every person with whom Marauder was in the remotest degree connected, the Duke of Silsbury took possession of the whole of his property.

The history properly closes here;—but a page or two may not be amiss concerning the more prominent characters, which have appeared in these volumes.

Wilson's regiment soon returned to England; and the warmest wish of his heart, his union with Fanny, immediately took place. The Duke made him a present of the house at Hazleton, where he now resides, in the same village with his parents, and but a small distance from his patron.

Marauder had deeply mortgaged this property; but the Duke instantly cleared the whole, and keeping the manor in his own hands, gave the estate to Wilson.—His parents and Dr. Line, are all in high health and spirits, and are ever the most welcome guests to Mrs. Wilson and her husband.

The Rev. Mr. Lockeridge has changed his residence, to be near

---

1 Luke 12:20.

his young friend, having been appointed domestic chaplain to the Duke, and occupies a wing of the Castle; though the slanderous part of the neighbourhood says it is for the sake of hunting with his Grace's fox-hounds, that he has appointed a Curate at Wheatland, where he nevertheless spends the summer months.

The Duke of Silsbury's household is very large, as, exclusive of his brothers and sisters, he has thought proper to adopt a large family of orphans, his near relations by his mother's side.

Mr. and Mrs. Rattle seem exactly suited to each other, and frequently enliven the group at Hazleton.

Young Harrety is in orders, and is married to Nancy Evans. He lives with his mother; and, having learned moderation and the manners of the world, brandishes the scourge over the head of Vice with double success, no longer liable to the terms of madman and enthusiast.

The virtuous and reflective Hambden is now in the Senate, equally respected in public life, and beloved in private.

Imphell did not long survive his base employer. Dick, having been apprehended for a highway robbery, told, at the fatal tree, the whole of his transactions with the attorney; whose fears preyed so violently upon his miserable state of health, that he never rose from the sick couch, where the revengeful frenzy of Marauder had thrown him.

Cloudley remains among the incurables in Bedlam. His Messalina flew with the re-coated Philosopher to the soft Italian plains. Other Syrens warbled upon the young Ivory, and he basely fled from Maria. The dame had too much of the Roman in her soul to bear this insult to her virtues. She grasped the dagger of Justice, nor ceased to pursue the traitor to Love, till she had fixed it in his heart. How the violated laws of the place where the deed was perpetrated, might have treated the lady, cannot be said; for Reason, Liberty, and Equality then ruled the country; and the virtuous dispenser of justice, a gallant General in the French service, being tempted to see the fair heroine, was instantly smitten, and crowned the noble act by his peculiar favour and love.

Of the other characters, who have not appeared in the foreground of the picture, it will be useless to remark.—Mrs. Mountford, her daughters and son, and the Honourable Miss Berwicks might indeed come forward in an episode of some fourscore pages; or, with the assistance of the worthy Mr. Townsend, and the simple Vasaley and his trifling wife, be woven into a pretty little Novel. Then there is the reformed villain, O'Rourk; his brother Irishman, Wilson's servant, who had lived with his present master from a child;

Nelly, the former flame of O'Rourk; Alderman Barrow, his unmarried daughter, and I know not how many others, might be made most excellent use of.

To aid the plot, Emily's picture, which was given by Marauder to Fahany, might be given to some one else, or found among his papers, and brought forth for notable discoveries. The late habitation of Marauder, on the Berkshire Downs, if it were narrowly searched, who knows not what wonderful papers it may contain: and, above all, that secret place in the house, which has been so carefully kept from intrusion, that Marauder himself was never seen, in these pages, to enter it. Unlike the profound Godwin, who often sets *his* murderer to explore a wondrous iron chest, and *his* hero, at last, to break it open; then, giving other places to the implements, and all the things, directly or indirectly belonging to the murder, he leaves us to *guess* what can possibly be in the chest.*

For my part, I shall leave this recess of the DIABOLISTS in the same manner as I first spoke of it—unknown. Let some other find the place, send forth his searchers, and discover its contents.

FINIS.

---

* [CL] This circumstance is quoted by the admirers of that Philosopher, as an instance of the depth of his wisdom, his astonishing ingenuity, and the wonderful progress of his great mind; and, for that purpose is here alluded to. [In Godwin's novel *Caleb Williams; or, Things as They Are* (1794), Caleb breaks open a chest belonging to his employer, Falkland, and discovers evidence of a murder perpetrated by Falkland. The novel formed the basis of a play, by George Colman (1762-1836), entitled *The Iron Chest*, first performed on 12 March 1796. See William Godwin, *Caleb Williams*, eds. Arnold A. Markley and Gary Handwerk (1794; rpt. Peterborough, ON: Broadview Press, 2000), "Appendix E.1."]

Appendix A: From Charles Lucas, Gwelygordd; or, the Child of Sin. A Tale of Welsh Origin *(1820)*

[In the first chapter of his final novel, published at the Minerva Press in 1820, Lucas looked back over his career, explaining what he had attempted to achieve in each work, and why he thought the novel a useful tool in his didactic campaign.]

The author has published three novels before. The *first* was the CASTLE OF ST. DONAT'S, which aimed to shew the dangerous and destructive habits of fashionable dissipation, and the fallacious examples of many eminent novels, on suicide, seduction, sudden reformation, and some well-known affected virtues. One passage in this work, to expose the adage, that "reformed rakes make the best husbands," a lady, of rather formal manners, thought so strongly written, that she obliterated the same; while another lady, more skilled in human character, pointing out the passage, said to a clergyman—"If I had a dozen daughters, I would desire them to read and remember this." The last lady had two daughters, whose amiable lives have shewn, that a clear knowledge of evil is the best guard against vice. The writer and the preacher must speak plain, if they mean to be good.

The *second* novel was the INFERNAL QUIXOTE, avowedly written against the modern principles of atheism and licentiousness, disguised as philosophy and liberty: in this work the characters were almost all drawn from the etchings of real life, and their doctrines and sentiments most correctly taken, literally, and without straining the meaning, from the actual publications of these impostors; so that however great the names, and however ridiculous, infamous, and contemptible, the sentiments of the Jacobins of that day were, there is not a man that has been able to advance one word against the veracity of any part of it; and the political facts, as to the Irish Rebellion, &c. were taken from state-papers. The work was written to counteract the *revolutionary* mania among the community at large, and it has become much more known to the higher orders than the author could have conceived. It was twelve years after the publication of the Infernal Quixote, that he found it had been translated into French immediately upon its coming out, and circulated by our great booksellers in Paris, directly to advocate the cause of religion, morality and social order, when Buonaparte began to overthrow the Jacobins. It is extremely well translated, evidently by a French *gentleman*; the religious conversation is shortened, the satire against the French nation directly applied to the Jacobins, and the general ridicule of the pretended virtues of the modern infidels, and their pompous ignorance, amplified and fully exposed, with some explanatory and salving notes by the translator. The antichristian spirit which at that time contaminated all Europe, was nourished in the breasts of many pretended loyalists and royalists, courtiers, magistrates, the higher characters of the army and navy, and even the social and domestic citizen. The hero of this tale, therefore, was a sincere Jacobin, while he was a proud aristocrat; for thus, at the military mess, and the hospitable table of the wealthy merchant, had the author detected this evil spirit in disguise in the evening, which the hair-dresser and retail tradesman openly shewed in the morning. One point (the only one he will further add) in this publication was to give the answers to the arguments of infidelity, so that the Christian might instantly see the weakness of, and reply to, the insidious remarks of the atheistical plagiarist.

The third novel was the BIBLE AND SABRE, which endeavoured to portray the practical result of REAL liberty, independence, and Christianity, in the hero, warrior, reformer, and philosopher. As the satire of the Infernal Quixote partook very strongly of sarcasm, so that of the Bible and Sabre may be noticed for its ironical bearing.

It is a subject of self gratulation to the author, that his candour, impartiality, and conscientious intentions, have been never called in question, though unprotected by literary connexions, and unknown by advertisements, friendly and party critiques, and other means of publicity.

The present work takes a different field from either of the former. The author had not intended to write another novel, but the peculiar circumstances, and the very interesting characters that came to his knowledge, were an easy temptation; for among the many cants of the day, he knows none more contemptible than the cant of superior scholarship, in the general condemnation of novels. Our modern novels are particularly moral and religious, and the highest professors of divine attainments have recourse to a species of composition very similar, though a comparison may be drawn in favour of novels, if, to tell truth, under the veil of fiction, is more honourable than, exceeding the truth, "things wonderful to shew." And in the course of his life he does not know an instance of a person professing generally to condemn novels, but through ignorance, pedantry, or bigotry.

Appendix B: An Advertisement for the Minerva Press (1794)

[This advertisement for the Minerva Press, which published *The Infernal Quixote*, makes clear the political principles of the proprietor, William Lane, and shows why his Press was regarded as the leading purveyor of popular fiction (and particularly gothic novels) during the 1790s and early 1800s. All the novels listed here were published between 1791 and 1794. The advertisement ran in the first two numbers of the London *Morning Advertiser*, for Saturday 8 February and Monday 10 February 1794.]

PROSPECTUS of the MINERVA,
LITERARY REPOSITORY, &c.

IMPRESSED with a sense of the favours this undertaking has received from the Public, not only as a Library, but in all its various branches of Literature, the Proprietor embraces every opportunity to come forward with gratitude to his supporters, and assures them, regularity, attention, diligence, and propriety, shall mark every part of the concern.

The Printing department shall be open to such subjects as tend to the public good—the pages shall never be stained with what will injure the mind, or corrupt the heart—they shall neither be the Instrument of Private Defamation or Public Injury—conceiving in the first instance "That, he who robs me of my good name, robs me of that which not enriches him, and makes me poor indeed,"—And, in the latter, it shall never convey to the happy subjects of this kingdom false founded doctrines or opinions, but attached to the prosperity of the country, it shall be a barrier for its support.

In publishing, both at the Minerva and the West End of this Metropolis, by auxiliary friends, it shall introduce to the world Improvement and instruction, happily conceiving in this enlightened age, literary subjects should be for the amusement and advantage of mankind.

To the subject of the Subscription Library, it is presumed little may be said, as upwards of twenty years establishment by industrious application, and sanctioned by the reward of a generous and respectable list of patronizers, speaks its conduct.

From the number of Books in this selection, and the manner in which it is conducted, it can now boast being the first in London.

Under these recited particulars, the Proprietor concludes with his assurance that it shall be his ambition to secure his kind Friends and Subscribers favours, and also the general sanction, opinion, and approbation of the Public.

Leadenhall-street.
WILLIAM LANE

NEW PUBLICATIONS by WILLIAM LANE,
Minerva, Leadenhall-street, London,
(Sold by every Bookseller).

		s.	d.
Ellen and Julia, by Mrs. Parsons	.2 vols 12mo	7	0
Frederica Risberg	.2 vols 12mo	7	0
Errors of Sensibility	.3 vols 12mo	9	0
Romance of the Cavern	.2 vols 12mo	7	0
Orphan Sisters	.2 vols 12mo	6	0
Advantages of Education	.2 vols 12mo	7	0
Mortimore Castle	.2 vols 12mo	6	0
Henry	.2 vols 12mo	7	0
Marianne, or Irish Anecdotes	.2 vols 12mo	6	0
Woman as she would be, by Mrs. Parsons	.4 vols 12mo	14	0
Castle of Wolsenbach	.2 vols 12mo	7	0
Rosina	.5 vols 12mo	17	6
Stellius, or the New Werter	.2 vols 12mo	6	0
Fille de Chambre	.3 vols 12mo	10	6
Theodore	.2 vols 12mo	6	0

Matilda and Aubin	.2 vols 12mo	7	0
Emily	.3 vols 12mo	10	6
Moggy; or Female Philosopher	.2 vols 12mo	7	0
Child of Providence	.4 vols 12mo	14	0
Frederic and Louisa	.4 vols 12mo	14	0
Errors of Education	.3 vols 12mo	10	6
Lake of Windermere	.2 vols 12mo	7	0
Man as he is	.4 vols 12mo	14	6

IN THE PRESS
Haunted Castle, 2 vols 12mo.
Pauline, 2 vols 12mo
Lucy, by Mrs. Parsons, 3 vols 12mo
Ellen, Countess of Castle Howell, by Mrs. Bennett, 4 vols., 12mo

Lane has also a catalogue of quire books, to sell to the trade cheap, which he will frank to any part of the kingdom.

His new songs, jests, &c. are also in circulation, and may be had by his Correspondents in every town.

Appendix C: From William Godwin, Enquiry Concerning Political Justice, and its Influence on Morals and Happiness (1796)

[Godwin's opinions on cohabitation, marriage and sexual relations, and their place in the utopian, rational society for which he hoped, quickly proved one of the most controversial parts of his *magnum opus*, first published in 1793. He modified his thinking in each successive edition of the *Enquiry*. Lucas quotes from the second edition, published by G.G. and J. Robinson in 1796 (but actually appearing in late 1795), from which this extract comes (Vol. 2, bk. VIII, Chap. viii, 497-503).]

Another article which belongs to the subject of cooperation is cohabitation. The evils attendant on this practice are obvious. We have already shown,* that, in order to the human understanding's being successfully cultivated, it is necessary that the intellectual operations of men should be independent of each other, and that we should avoid those practices as are calculated to melt our opinions into a common mould. Cohabitation is also inimical to that fortitude which should accustom a man, in his actions as well as in his opinions, to judge for himself, and feel competent to the discharge of his own duties. Add to this, that it is absurd to expect the inclinations and wishes of two human beings to coincide through any long period of time. To oblige them to act and to live together, is to subject them to some inevitable portion of thwarting, bickering and unhappiness. This cannot be otherwise, so long as men shall continue to vary in their habits, their preferences and their views. No man is always cheerful and kind; and it is better that his fits of irritation should subside of themselves, since the mischief in that case is more limited, and since the jarring of opposite tempers, and the suggestions of a wounded pride, tend inexpressibly to increase the irritation. When I seek to correct the defects of a stranger, it is with urbanity and good humour. I have no idea of convincing him through the medium of surliness and invective. But something of this kind inevitably obtains, where the intercourse is too unremitted.

---

* [WG] Vol. I, bk. IV, chap. III, 290.

The subject of cohabitation is particularly interesting, as it includes in it the subject of marriage. It will therefore be proper to pursue the enquiry in greater detail. The evil of marriage, as it is practised in European countries, extends farther than we have yet described. The method is, for a thoughtless and romantic youth of each sex to come together, to see each other for a few times and under circumstances full of delusion, and then to vow eternal attachment. What is the consequence of this? In almost every instance they find themselves deceived. They are reduced to make the best of an irretrievable mistake. They are led to conceive it their wisest policy to shut their eyes upon realities, happy, if, by any perversion of intelligence they can persuade themselves that they were right in their first crude opinion of their companion. The institution of marriage is made a system of fraud; and men who carefully mislead their judgements in the daily affair of their life must always have a crippled judgement in every other concern. We ought to dismiss our mistake as soon as it is detected; but we are taught to cherish it. We ought to be incessant in our search after virtue and worth; but we are taught to check our enquiry, and shut our eyes upon the plainest facts. Whatever our understandings may tell us of the person whose connection we ought to seek or to avoid, of the worth of one woman and the demerits of another, we are obliged to consider what the contract into which we have entered, and not what justice or reason, prescribes.

Add to this that marriage, as now understood, is a monopoly, and the worst of monopolies. So long as two human beings are forbidden by positive institution to follow the dictates of their own mind, prejudice will ever be alive and vigorous. So long as I seek by despotic and artificial means, to engross a woman to myself, and to prohibit my neighbour from proving his superior claim, I am guilty of the most odious selfishness. Over this imaginary prize men watch with perpetual jealousy; and one man finds his desire and his capacity to circumvent as much excited, as the other is excited to traverse his projects and frustrate his hopes. As long as this state of society continues, philanthropy will be crossed and checked in a thousand ways, and the still augmenting stream of abuse will continue to flow.

The abolition of marriage in the form now practised, will be attended with no evils. We are apt to represent it to ourselves as the harbinger of brutal lust and depravity. But it really happens in this, as in other cases, that the positive laws which are made to restrain our vices, irritate and multiply them. Not to say, that the same sentiments of justice and happiness, which in a state of equality would destroy our relish for expensive gratifications, would decrease our inordinate appetites of every kind, and to lead us universally to prefer the pleasures of intellect to the pleasures of sense.

It is a question of some moment whether the intercourse of the sexes, in a reasonable state of society, will be promiscuous, or whether each man will select for himself a partner, to whom he will adhere, as long as that adherence shall continue to be the choice of both parties. The general probability seems to be greatly in favour of the latter. Perhaps this side of the alternative is most favourable to population. Perhaps it would suggest itself in preference, to the man who would wish to maintain the several propensities of his frame in the order due to their relative importance, and to prevent a merely sensual appetite from engrossing excessive attention. It is scarcely to be imagined that this commerce in any state of society will be stripped of all its adjuncts, and that men will as willingly hold it with a woman whose personal and mental qualities they disapprove, as with one of a different description. But it is the nature of the human mind to persist for a certain length of time in its opinion or choice. The parties therefore, having acted upon selection, are not likely to forget this selection when the interview is over. Friendship, if by friendship we understand that affection for an individual which is measured singly by what we know of his worth, is one of the most exquisite gratifications, perhaps one of the most improving exercises of a rational mind. Friendship therefore may be expected to come in aid of the sexual intercourse, to refine its grossness and increase its delight. A friendship of this sort has no necessary connection with the cowardice which so notoriously characterises the present system of marriage, where each party desires to find in the other that flattering indulgence, that overlooks every frailty, and carefully removes the occasions of fortitude. This consequence is best prevented by preserving the commerce, and abolishing the pernicious practice of cohabitation.

Admitting these principles therefore as the basis of the sexual commerce, what opinion ought we to form respecting infidelity to this attachment? Certainly no ties ought to be imposed upon either party, preventing them from quitting the attachment, whenever their judgement directs them to quit it. With respect to such infidelities as are compatible with an intention to adhere to it, the point of principal importance is a determination to have recourse to no species of disguise. In ordinary cases, and where the periods of absence are of no long duration, it would seem, that any instance of inconstancy would reflect some portion of discredit on the person that practised it. It would argue that the person's propensities were not under that kind of subordination, which virtue and self-government appear absolutely to prescribe. But inconstancy, like any other temporary dereliction, would not be found incompatible with a character of uncommon excellence. What at present renders it in many instances peculiarly loathsome, is its being practised in a clandestine manner. It leads to a train of falsehood and a concerted hypocrisy, than which there is scarcely any thing that more eminently depraves and degrades the human mind.—It seems material to observe that, when just notions upon this subject shall be formed, the inconstancy of either sex would be estimated at precisely the same value.

The mutual kindness of persons of an opposite sex will, in such a state, fall under the same system as any other species of friendship. Exclusively of groundless and obstinate attachments, it will be impossible for me to live in the world, without finding in one man a worth superior to that of another. To this man I shall feel kindness in exact proportion to my apprehension of his worth. The case will be the same with respect to the female sex. I shall assiduously cultivate the intercourse of that woman whose accomplishments strike me in the most powerful manner. But "it may happen that other men will feel for her the same preference that I do." This will create no difficulty. We may all enjoy her conversation; and we shall all be wise enough to consider the sexual commerce a comparatively trivial object. This, like every other affair in which two persons are concerned, must be regulated by the unforced consent of the parties. It is a mark of the extreme depravity of our present habits, that we are inclined to suppose the sexual commerce any way material to the advantages arising from the purest affection. It is by no means necessary, that the female with whom each man has commerce, should appear to each the most deserving and excellent of her sex.

Appendix D: A Contemporary Review

[*The Infernal Quixote* received just one, anonymous, review. This appeared in *The Critical Review; or, Annals of Literature* 33 (September 1801): 113.]

The Infernal Quixote, whose story is here related, is a young man of quality, who, after living the life of a villain, dies the death of a madman, by a sudden leap from a precipice. Many of the events are described in such a manner as clearly to prove the author well acquainted with the actions and passions of men: but he is at times intolerably prolix. The last one hundred and twenty pages contain no more matter than might have been comprised in a dozen; it is little else than the examination of a delinquent before a magistrate. Doctor Line's astrological hobby-horse is very pleasantly laughed at, in the event of two young men who were born at the same period. But here our author has puzzled us exceedingly. He is, at times, so violent against democracy, that we can hardly doubt his wish to exercise the charity of bishop Bonner[1] towards all who differ from him in opinion; and yet he has made a carpenter's son to turn out a credit, and the lord's son a disgrace, to society. As Mr. Lucas is a master of arts, and uses Latin in his novel, perhaps he will not object to our quoting Ovid, that he may ask himself how far the world may say of him—

"Nec duo sunt, at forma duplex, nec fœmina dici,
Nec puer ut possint, neutrumque et utrumque videntur."[2]

---

1 Edmund Bonner, bishop of London (1500?-1569), was often accused of harshness in executing heretics against the Protestant regime which he had helped to introduce into England. He is reported to have coerced one fifteen year old boy to "speeke muche good, of the Bishop of London, and of the greate Charitee, that he shewed hym" before having him burned at the stake. See *Hall's Chronicle; containing the History of England, during the Reign of Henry the Fourth, and the Succeeding Monarchs to the End of the Reign of Henry the Eighth* (1548; rpt. London: J. Johnson *et al.*, 1809), 841.
2 Ovid, *Metamorphoses*, bk. 4, ll.378-89: "Both bodies in a single body mix, / A single body with a double sex."

Appendix E: A London Corresponding Society handbill (1795)

[The London Corresponding Society (LCS) quickly became the most important radical group in Britain after its foundation in January 1792. This manifesto was printed on one large sheet of paper in late 1795 in the aftermath of several LCS-led mass reform meetings, and a spate of physical attacks on King George III, and just before the consequent introduction into Parliament of the bills which would become the repressive "Two Acts." This handbill sets out the Society's aims, but also strikes a markedly conciliatory note.]

TO THE
Parliament and People of Great Britain.
An explicit Declaration of the Principles and Views of the
LONDON CORRESPONDING SOCIETY.

The London Corresponding Society feeling the aweful importance of the situation in which their own efforts in behalf of liberty, and the arbitrary measures of an encroaching administration have conspired to place them—feeling also that the affairs of this long harassed and distracted nation have arrived at a most momentous crisis—that the people and their oppressors are at issue, and that there is now but one alternative, Liberty and Reform, or Encroachment and absolute Despotism, conceive themselves called upon, once more, to appeal to that public so frequently warned by them, and deluded by their calumniators; and to state in the most clear and explicit terms the following Declaration of their Principles.

I. This Society is, and ever has been, most firmly attached to the principles of Equality, accurately defined and properly understood; but at the same time they regard with the utmost abhorrence, the base misrepresentations to which, for interested purposes, these principles have been subjected.

Social equality, according to its just definition, appears to them to consist in the following things:

1. The acknowledgment of equal rights.
2. The existence of equal laws for the security of those rights.
3. Equal and actual representation, by which, and which alone, the

invasion of those laws can be prevented; and such an administration of those laws insured, as will alike preserve the poor from the insults and oppressions of the rich, and the rich from the insults and invasions of the poor.

In their ideas of equality, they have never included (nor, till the associations of alarmists broached the frantic notion, could they ever have conceived that so wild and detestable a sentiment could have entered the brain of man) as the equalization of property, or the invasion of personal rights and possessions. This levelling system they know, and all rational men must immediately perceive, to be equally unjust and impracticable; and they are ready to a man, not only to protest against, but to oppose, with their lives, every attempt of that description—attempts which they are well aware, instead of equalizing the condition of mankind, could only transfer property from its present possessors to plunderers and assassins of the most profligate description, and subject the nation to the brutal and ferocious tyranny of the most ignorant and most worthless of mankind.

II. With respect to particular forms and modifications of Government, this Society conceive, and ever have conceived, that the disputes and contentions about these, which have so often distracted the universe (like bigoted attachments to peculiar forms of worship) are marks only of weak and inconsiderate minds, and in the pursuit of fleeting shadows forget the substance. Their attention has been uniformly addressed to more essential objects—to the peace—the social order—and the happiness of mankind; and these they have always been ready to acknowledge and believe might be sufficiently secured by the *genuine spirit* of the British Constitution. They have laboured therefore, with incessant application, not to *overthrow*, but to *restore* and *realize* that Constitution; to give practical effect to those excellencies which have been theoretically acknowledged; and to reform those corruptions and abuses which, though some have attempted to justify, no one has had the hardihood to deny.

Peaceful reform, and not tumultuary revolt, is their object; and they trust to the good sense and candour of the Nation that something more that *vague accusation* and *interested calumny* will be expected to discredit their protestations, that *They abhor alike the* FANATICAL ENTHUSIASM *that would plunge into a sea of anarchy in quest of speculative theories,* and the VILLANOUS HYPOCRISY *that would destroy the very essence of existing institutions, under the pretence of preserving them from destruction!!!*

III. This Society have always cherished, and will ever be desirous to inculcate, the most decided abhorrence of all tumult and violence. Anxious to promote the *happiness*, and therefore jealous of the *rights* of Man, they have never failed to propagate, nor to practice, the constitutional doctrine of opposing, by every peaceful and rational exertion, the encroachments of power and corruption. But they have never countenanced, nor ever will, any motion, measure or sentiment tending to excite commotion—to inflame the mind with sanguinary enthusiasm—or to extinguish the emotions of tenderness and humanity which ought particularly to characterise a free and enlightened nation.

At the same time, they do not wish to be understood as giving, by this declaration, any sort of countenance to the *detestable* and *delusive doctrines of Passive Obedience and Non-resistance.* This is a system which none but *hypocrites* will *profess*, and none but *slaves* will *practice*. THE LONDON CORRESPONDING SOCIETY are neither the former, nor the latter; and on the altar of their own hearts they have sworn—That *no insolent encroachments of a corrupt and tyrannical administrations—no dread of the last fatal arbitriment, shall ever compel them to be either!* They know that they have rights—they know that it is their duty to defend them—they know also, that to profess implicit submission is to invite oppression; and that to practice it is treason to posterity, and sacrilege against nature.

To resist oppression (when no other means are left) ever with the same arms with which it is enforced is, they are aware, not only a natural right, but a constitutional duty: and if their ancestors had not so resisted, the HOUSE OF BRUNSWICK never would have swayed the British Sceptre, the exiled family of the STUART would have been still upon the throne, and Britain never could have boasted of her GLORIOUS REVOLUTION of 1688.[1]

But resistance of oppression, and promotion of tumult, are, in their minds, distinct propositions. The former they *profess* as solemnly as they *abjure* the latter: and they trust that the Nation at large is equally sensible of the distinction; and that *if the dire necessity ever should arrive, when the liberties of Britain must be asserted not by the voice*

---

1 Having alienated the nation by his Catholicism and his perceived tyrannical tendencies, King James VII and II, of the royal House of Stuart, was deposed by the "Glorious Revolution" of 1688. James's two daughters, Mary II (with her husband William III) and Anne, successively occupied the throne until 1714 when the crown passed to the nearest Protestant heir, George I of the House of Brunswick.

and the pen, but by the sword, Britons will rally round the standard of Liberty, not like a band of depredators and assassins, but like a Spartan Phalanx; prepared and resolved, to a man, rather to die at their posts, than to abandon their principles, and betray the Liberties of their Country!!!

J. ASHLEY, Secretary.
Committee Room, Beaufort Buildings, Nov. 23rd. 1795.

Appendix F: From Augustin Barruel's Memoirs, Illustrating the History of Jacobinism (1797-98)

[Barruel's massive work, over 2000 octavo pages in all, was published in Britain during 1797 and 1798. In this prefacing material, Barruel outlined his ideas of the vast conspiracy against church, state, and society which accounted, he thought, for Jacobinism and the French Revolution. Many Britons apparently accepted Barruel's conspiracy theory at face value, though some writers may simply have decided to promote his ideas as a useful tool in the anti-Jacobin campaign. Lucas certainly drew heavily on Barruel's *Memoirs* in *The Infernal Quixote*, but diluted its paranoia and earnestness with a certain whimsicality. Barruel's identification of a long pre-meditated plot also contrasts with Lucas's insistence on the opportunism of his Jacobin anti-hero, Marauder. At the end of Barruel's *Memoirs*, the translator added a "Note" containing a "more circumstantial application" of Barruel's ideas to Ireland. This drew upon a United Irishmen pamphlet from 1791 (see Appendix G.1) to "prove" that the Irish Rebellion was another manifestation of the Athiest-Jacobin-Illuminati-Masonic conspiracy Barruel purported to have uncovered.]

PRELIMINARY DISCOURSE.

At an early period of the French Revolution, there appeared a sect calling itself Jacobin, and teaching *that all men were equal and free!* In the name of their equality and disorganizing liberty, they trampled under foot the altar and the throne; they stimulated all nations to rebellion, and aimed at plunging them ultimately into the horrors of anarchy.

At its first appearance, this sect counted 300,000 adepts; and it was supported by two millions of men, scattered through France, armed with torches and pikes, and all the fire-brands of revolution.

It was under the auspices of this sect, by their intrigues, their influence, and their impulse, that France beheld itself a prey to every crime; that its soil was stained with blood of its pontiffs and priests, of its rich men and nobles; with the blood of every class of its citizens, without regard to rank, age or sex! These were the men who, after having made the unfortunate Lewis XVI, his Queen and Sister, drink to the very dregs the cup of outrage and ignominy during a long confinement, solemnly murdered them on a scaffold, proudly menacing the sovereigns of the earth with a similar fate! These are the men who have made the French Revolution a scourge to all Europe, a terror to its Powers, who vainly combine to stop the progress of their revolutionary armies, more numerous and destructive than the inundations of the Vandals.[1]

Whence originated these men, who seem to arise from the bowels of the earth, who start into existence with their plans and their prospects, their tenets and their thunders, their means and ferocious resolves; whence, I say, this devouring sect? Whence this swarm of adepts, these systems, this frantic rage against the altar and the throne, against every institution, whether civil or religious, so much respected by our ancestors? Can their primogeniture in the order of the revolution give them this tremendous power, or were they not anterior? is it not their own work? where then was their hiding place? Their schools, their masters, where shall we find them, and who will dive into their future projects? This French Revolution ended, will they cease to desolate the earth, to murder its kings, to fanaticise its people?

These certainly are questions that cannot be indifferent to nations or their rulers, or to those who watch for the happiness and preservation of society; and these are the questions which I will attempt to answer. I will seek their solution in the very annals of the sect, whence I will shew their plans and systems, their plots and means. Such, Reader, will be the object of the following Memoirs. [...]

We shall shew that with which it is incumbent on all nations and their chiefs to be acquainted: we shall demonstrate that, even to the most horrid deeds perpetrated during the French Revolution, every thing was foreseen and resolved on, was combined and premeditated: that they were the offspring of deep-thought villainy, since they had been prepared and were produced by men, who alone held the clue of those plots and conspiracies, lurking in the secret meetings where they had been conceived, and only watching the favourable moment of bursting forth. Though the events of each day may not appear to have been combined, there nevertheless existed a secret

---

1 A Germanic people who sacked Rome in AD 455, destroying and looting many of the city's treasures.

agent and a secret cause, giving rise to each event, and turning each circumstance to the long-sought-for end. Though circumstances may often have afforded the pretence or the occasion, yet the grand cause of the revolution, its leading features, its atrocious crimes, will still remain one continued chain of deep-laid and premeditated villainy. [...]

There are men who make no difficulty in owning that the French Revolution was premeditated, but that the intention of the first authors was pure, and that they only sought the happiness and regeneration of empires; that if great misfortunes have since happened, they arose from the obstacles thrown in their way; that a great people cannot be regenerated without commotion, but that the tempests will subside, and a calm succeed the swelling billows. Then nations, astonished at the fear they had conceived of the French Revolution, and true only to its principles, will be happy in imitation.

This error is the favourite theme of the Jacobin missionaries; it was this that gained them their first instruments of rebellion; that cohort of constitutionalists, who still look on their decrees of the RIGHTS OF MAN as the summit of legislative perfection, and still impatiently wait the fatal day when the world shall impetuously move in the sphere of their political rhapsody. It was this that gained them that prodigious number of votaries more blind than wicked, and who might have been mistaken for honest, if virtue could have combined with ferocity in search of happier days. It was this that gained them those men whose well-meant, though stupid credulity, misled them to believe in the necessity of the carnage of the 10th of August, and of the horrid butcheries of the 2d of September;[1] in a word, all those men who, in the murders of 3 or 400,000 fellow-creatures, in the extermination of millions of victims by famine, the sword, or the guillotine, seek consolation, in spite of this depopulating scourge, in the empty hope that this dreadful chain of horrors may be productive of happier days.

In answer to these fallacious hopes, to these pretended good intentions, I will oppose the real views of this revolutionary sect, their true projects, their conspiracies, and their means of execution.

---

1 On 10 August 1792 in Paris a huge crowd stormed the royal palace, overcoming the garrison and forcing the Legislative Assembly to arrest the King. A month later, believing that imprisoned royalists might rise up in their gaols, ordinary Parisians massacred more than 1,200 detainees over the period from 2 to 6 September.

I will show them, for they must be divulged, the proofs being acquired. The French Revolution has been a true child to its parent sect; its crimes have been its filial duty; and those black deeds and atrocious acts, the natural sequel of the principles and systems that gave it birth. I will show more; so far from seeking future prosperity, the French Revolution is but a sportive essay of its strength, while the whole universe is its aim. If elsewhere the same crimes are necessary, they will be committed; if equal ferocity is necessary they will be equally ferocious; and it will extend wheresoever its errors are received.

The reflecting reader must then conclude, that either this Jacobin sect must be crushed or society overthrown: that all governments must give place to those massacres, those convulsive disorders, and that infernal anarchy which rages in France: 'tis true there is no other alternative, universal destruction or extinction of the sect. But let it be remembered, that to crush a sect is not to imitate the fury of its apostles, intoxicated with its sanguinary rage to propense to enthusiastic murder. It is not to massacre and immolate its adepts, or retort on them the thunders they had hurled. To crush a sect, is to attack it in its schools, to reveal its imposture, and show to the world the absurdity of its principles, the atrocity of its means, and above all the profound wickedness of its teachers. Yes; strike the Jacobin, but spare the man; the sect is a sect of opinion, and its destruction will be doubly complete on the day when it is deserted by its disciples, to return to the true principles of reason and society. [...]

The result of our research, corroborated by proofs drawn from the records of the Jacobins, and of their first masters, had been, that this sect with its conspiracies is in itself no other than the coalition of a triple sect, of a triple conspiracy, in which, long before the revolution, the overthrow of the altar, the ruin of the throne, and the dissolution of all civil society had been debated and resolved on.

1st. Many years before the French Revolution, men who styled themselves Philosophers conspired against the God of the Gospel, against Christianity, without distinction of worship, whether Protestant or Catholic, Anglican or Presbyterian. The grand object of this conspiracy was to overturn every altar where Christ was adored. It was the conspiracy of the *Sophisters of Impiety*, or the ANTICHRISTIAN CONSPIRACY.

2dly. This school of impiety soon formed the *Sophisters of Rebellion*: these latter, combining their conspiracy against kings with that of the Sophisters of Impiety, coalesce with that ancient sect whose tenets constituted the whole secret of the *Occult Lodges* of Free-masonry, which long since, imposing on the credulity of its most distinguished adepts, only initiated the chosen of the elect into the secret of their unrelenting hatred for Christ and kings.

3dly. From the Sophisters of Impiety and Rebellion, arose the *Sophisters of Impiety and Anarchy*. These latter conspire not only against Christ and his altars, but against every religion natural or revealed: not only against kings, but against every government, against all civil society, even against all property whatsoever.

This third sect, known by the name of *Illuminés*, coalesced with the Sophisters conspiring against Christ, coalesced with the Sophisters who, with the Occult Masons, conspired against both Christ and kings. It was the coalition of the adepts of *impiety*, of the adepts of *rebellion*, and the adepts of *anarchy*, which *formed the* CLUB *of the* JACOBINS. Under this name, common to the triple sect (originating from the name of the order, whose convent they had seized upon to hold their sittings), we shall see the adepts following up their triple conspiracy against God, the King, and Society. Such was the origin, such the progress of that sect, since become so dreadfully famous under the name of JACOBIN.

Appendix G: Publications of the United Irishmen

[Many United Irishmen documents, including the two reproduced here, were reprinted as appendices in *The Report from the Committee of Secrecy, of the House of Commons in Ireland, as reported by the Right Honourable Lord Viscount Castlereagh, August 21, 1798* (London: J. Debrett, and J. Wright, 1798). Given that these documents were reproduced to support the government's case, their complete authenticity cannot be guaranteed, but there is no *prima facie* evidence to suggest that they were doctored.]

1. A United Irishmen pamphlet from 1791, providing an early "manifesto-statement." Reprinted in *The Report from the Committee of Secrecy*, appendix IV

IDEM SENTIRE, DIVERE, AGERE[1]

IT is proposed, that at this conjecture a SOCIETY shall be instituted in this city, having much of the secrecy, and somewhat of the ceremonial attached to Free-masonry; with so much secrecy as may communicate curiosity, uncertainty, and expectation, to the minds of surrounding men; with so much impressive and affecting ceremony in all its internal economy, as without impeding real business, may strike the soul through the senses, and addressing the *whole* Man, may animate his philosophy by the energy of his passions.

Secrecy is expedient and necessary; it will make the bond of union more cohesive, and the spirit of this union more ardent and more condensed; it will envelope this dense flame with a cloud of gloomy ambiguity, that will not only facilitate its own agency, but will at the same time confound and terrify its enemies by their ignorance of the design, the extent, the direction, or the consequences. It will throw a veil over those individuals whose professional prudence might make them wish to lye concealed, until a manifestation of themselves become absolutely necessary. And lastly, secrecy is necessary, because it is by no means certain that a country so great a stranger to itself as Ireland, where the North and the South, and the

---

1 To think, to speak, to act are the same.

East and the West, meet to wonder at each other, is yet *prepared* for the adoption of one profession of Political Faith, while there may be individuals from each of these quarters ready to adopt such a profession, and to propagate it with their best abilities, when necessary—with their Blood.

Our Provinces are perfectly ignorant of one each other;—our Island is connected; we ourselves are insulated; and the distinctions of rank, of property, and of religious persuasion, have hitherto been not merely lines of difference, but brazen walls of separation. We are separate nations met and settled together, not mingled, but *convened*; an incoherent mass of dissimilar materials, uncemented, unconsolidated, like the image which Nebuchadnezar saw with a head of fine gold, legs of iron, and feet of clay, parts that do not cleave to one another.

In the midst of an island, where Manhood has met and continues to meet with such severe humiliation, where selfish men, or classes of men, have formed such malignant conspiracy against Public Good, let one benevolent, beneficent conspiracy arise, one Plot of Patriots pledged by solemn abjuration to each other in the service of the People—the PEOPLE, in the largest sense of that momentous word. Let the cement of this Constitutional Compact be a principle of such strong attraction, as completely to overpower all accidental and temporary repulsions that take place between real Irishmen, and thus to consolidate the scattered and shifting sand of Society into an adhesive and immoveable Caisson,[1] sunk beneath the dark and troubled waters. It is by wandering from the few plain and simple principles of Political Faith that our Politics, like our Religion, has become Preaching, not Practice, Words, not Works.

A Society, such as this, will disclaim those party appellations which seem to pale the human heart into petty compartments and parcel out into Sects and Sections, Common Sense, Common Honesty, and Common Weal. As little will it affect any speculative unimpassioned, quiescent benevolence. It will not call itself a Whig Club, or a Revolution Society. It will not ground itself on a name indicative of a party, or an event well enough in the circumstances and in the season. It will not be an Aristocracy affecting the language of Patriotism, the rival of Despotism, for its own sake, not its irreconcilable enemy, for the sake of *us all*.

---

1 A watertight chamber, open at the bottom and from which the water is kept by atmospheric pressure, used in the construction of underwater foundations.

It will not, by views merely retrospective, stop the march of mankind, or force them back into the lanes and alleys of their ancestors. It will have an eye provident and prospective, a reach and amplitude of conception commensurate to the progressive diffusion of knowledge, and at the same time a promptitude in execution requisite in a life like this, so short and so fragile, in a nation like this, so passive and so procrastinating. Let its name be the IRISH BROTHERHOOD. Let its general aim be to make the light of philanthropy, a pale and ineffectual light, *converge*, and by converging kindle into ardent, energetic, enthusiastic love for Ireland: that genuine unadulterated enthusiasm which descends from a luminous head to a burning heart, and impels the spirit of man to exertions greatly good, or unequivocally great. For this Society is not to rest satisfied in drawing speculative plans of reform and improvement, but to be practically busied about the *means* of accomplishment. Were the hand of Locke[1] to hold from Heaven a scheme of government most perfectly adapted to the nature and capabilities of the Irish nation, it would drop to the ground a mere sounding scroll, were there no other means of giving it effect than its intrinsic excellence. All true Irishmen agree in *what* ought to be done, but how to get it done is the question. This Society is likely to be a means the most powerful for the promotion of a great end—what END?

THE RIGHTS OF MEN IN IRELAND, the greatest happiness of the greatest number in *this island*, the inherent and indefeasible claims of every free nation, to rest in this nation—the *will* and the *power* to be happy—to pursue the Common Weal as an individual pursues his private welfare, and to stand in insulated independence, an imperatorial People. To gain a knowledge of the real state of this heterogeneous country, to form a summary of the national will and pleasure in points most interesting to national happiness, and when such a summary is formed, to put this *Doctrine* as speedily as may be into *Practice*, will be the purpose of this central society, or lodge, from which other lodges in the different towns will radiate.

THE GREATEST HAPPINESS OF THE GREATEST NUMBER—On the rock of this principle let this Society rest; by this let it judge and determine every political question, and whatever is necessary for this end, let it not be accounted hazardous, but rather our interest, our

---

1 John Locke (1632-1704), political theorist and philosopher, whose *Two Treatises of Government* based government on the consent of the governed and argued that rulers who became tyrants ought to be actively resisted.

duty, our glory, and our common religion. The rights of Men are the rights of God, and to vindicate the one is to maintain the other. We must be free in order to serve him whose service is perfect freedom.

Let every Member wear, day and night, an Amulet round his neck, containing the great principle which unites the Brotherhood. In letters of gold, on a ribbon, striped with all the original colours, and inclosed in a sheath of white silk, to represent the pure union of the mingled rays, and the abolition of all superficial distinctions, all colours and shades of difference, for the sake of one illustrious end. Let this Amulet of Union, faith and honour, depend from the neck, and be bound about the body next to the skin and close to the heart.

This is enthusiasm.—It is so; and who that has a spark of Hibernicism in his nature, would not feel it kindle into a flame of generous enthusiasm? Who, that has a drop of sympathy in his heart, when he looks around him, and sees how happiness is heaped up in mounds, and how misery is diffused and divided among the million, does not exclaim, Alas! for the suffering, and Oh! for the power to redress it? and who is there that has enthusiasm sufficient to make an exclamation, would not combine with others as honest as himself to make the will live in the act, and to swear,—WE WILL REDRESS IT—Who is there? Who?

The first business of the Brotherhood will be to form a transcript, or digest of the doctrine which they mean to subscribe, to uphold, to propagate, and reduce to practice. It is time for Ireland to look her fortune in her face, not with turbulent ostentation, but with fixed resolution to live and die Freemen. Let then those questions be agitated and answered fully and fairly which have been wilfully concealed from us by interested persons and parties, and which appear terrible only by being kept in the dark. Always armed with this principle, that it is the duty of the people to establish their rights, this Society will carry it along with them in their course, as the Sybil did the branch of gold,[1] to avert or to disperse every vain fear and every unreal terror.

What are the *means* of procuring such a reform in the constitution as may secure to the people their rights most effectually and most speedily?

What is the plan of reform most suited to this country?

---

1   Seeking to gain entry to the Underworld, Aeneas was advised by the Cumaen Sybil (a prophetess of classical legend) to seek out and carry with him a golden bough. The bough acted as his talisman and he was carried safely across the River Styx by Charon.

Can the renovation in the constitution, which we all deem necessary, be accomplished by the *ways* of the constitution? "The evil," says Junius, "lies too deep to be cured by any remedy, less than some great convulsion which may bring back the constitution to its original principles, or utterly destroy it."[1] Is this opinion still truer when applied to *this* country? or is it false?

Who are the people?

Can the right of changing the constitution rest any where but in the original constitutive power—the People?

Can the will of the People be known but by full and fair convention, to be constituted on the plan which will come recommended on the most popular authority?

What are the rights of Roman Catholics, and what are the immediate duties of Protestants respecting these rights?

Are the Roman Catholics generally or partially *capaces Libertatis?*[2] and if not, What are the speediest means of making them so?

Is the independence of Ireland nominal or real, a barren right, or a fact regulative of national conduct and influencing national character?

Has it had any other effect than raising the value of a house, and making it more self-sufficient, at the expense of the People?

Is there any middle state between the extremes of union with Britain and total separation, in which the rights of the People can be fully established and rest in security?

What is the form of government that will secure to us our rights with the least expense and the greatest benefit?

By the BROTHERHOOD are these questions, and such as these, to be determined. On this determination, which with honour and good faith they are to subscribe, and which is to regulate their course.—Let the Society at large meet four times in the year, and an acting Committee once a month, to which all Members shall be invited. Let these meetings be *convivial*, but not the transitory patriotism of deep potation; *confidential*, the heart open and the door locked; *conversational*, not a debating society. There is too much haranguing in this country already: a very great redundance of sound. Would that we spoke a little more laconically, and acted a little more emphatically; and we shall do so, when our aim is at

---

1   Presumably the still unidentified author of many letters published in
    English newspapers between 1769 and 1772 which attacked the political
    influence of George III and the ministry of the Duke of Grafton.
2   A legal term meaning "free to inherit property."

something nobler and fairer than even the sublime and beautiful of Mr. Burke:[1] —the sublimity of Common-sense—the beauty of Common-weal.

Our society should at first be very chaste and cautious in the selection of Members, shunning equally the giddiness of the boy, and the sullen indifference about the public good which comes on with decline of years, looking around for those that are competent, and with respect to themselves content, yet zealous and persevering; not venal, not voracious, not confined in their manners and their morality to the pale of a profession, not idle philanthropists, who fidget round the globe with their favourite adage; not those who are bound down by obedience to that wizard word *Empire*, to the sovereignty of two sounding syllables; but honest, honourable *Irishmen*, of whatever rank, of whatever religion, who know Liberty, who love it, who wish to have it, and who will have it.—Members should be admitted only by an unanimous ballot, and perhaps once a year there should be a general re-election.

The *external* business of this Society will be, 1st, Publication, in order to propagate their principles and effectuate their ends. All papers for this purpose are to be sanctioned by the Committee, and published with no other designation of character than—ONE OF THE BROTHERHOOD. 2dly, Communication with the different towns to be assiduously kept up, and every exertion used to accomplish a *National Convention* of the People of Ireland, who may profit by past errors, and by many unexpected circumstances which have happened since the last meeting. 3rdly, Communication with similar societies abroad, as the Jacobin Club in Paris, the Revolution Society in England, the Committee for Reform in Scotland. Let the nations go abreast. Let the interchange of sentiment among mankind concerning the rights of man be as immediate as possible. A correspondence with distinguished men in Britain, or on the Continent, will be necessary to enlighten us, and ought to be cherished. Eulogies on such men as have deserved well of the country *until death*, should be from time to time delivered by one of the Brotherhood, their works should live in a Library to be formed by this Society, and dedicated to Liberty, and the Portraits of such men should adorn it. Let the shades of the mighty dead look down and consecrate our meetings. The Athenians were accustomed to fasten their edicts to

---

1 Edmund Burke (1729-97), an Irishman who became a Whig politician in London, published *An Philosophical Enquiry into the Origin of Our Ideas of the Sublime and the Beautiful* in 1757.

the statues of their ancestors. Let our Laws and Liberties have a similar attachment, taking heed always to remember what has been always too much forgotten—that *We* are to be ancestors ourselves; and as our bodies moulder down after sepulture, merely to pass into new forms of life, let our spirits preserve a principle of animation to posterity, and germinate from the very grave.

What is the time most applicable for the establishment of this Institution? Even NOW. "Le grand art est dans l'apropos."[1] Why is Administration so imperious? Because the nation does not act. The Whig Club is not a transfusion of the People.[2] We do not thoroughly *understand* that Club, and they do not *feel* for us. When the Aristocracy come forward, the People fall backward; when the People come forward, the Aristocracy, fearful of being left behind, insinuate themselves into our ranks, and rise into timid leaders, or treacherous auxiliaries. They mean to make us their instruments. Let us rather make them *our* instruments. One of the two must happen. The People must serve the purposes of Party, or the party must emerge in the mightiness of the People, and Hercules will then lean upon his club.

On the 14th of July, the day which shall ever commemorate the French Revolution, let this Society pour out their first libation to European Liberty, eventually the Liberty of the World, and with their hands joined in each other, and their eyes raised to Heaven, in his presence who breathed into them an ever-lasting soul, let them swear to maintain their rights and prerogatives of their nature as men, and the right and prerogative of Ireland as an Independent People.—"Dieu et *mon* Droit!" is the motto of kings. "Dieu et la Liberte!" exclaimed Voltaire, when he first beheld Franklin his Fellow-Citizen of the World. "Dieu et *nos* Droits!"—Let Irishmen cry aloud to each other. The cry of Mercy—of Justice—and of Victory.

June 1791.

---

1 "Great works are always opportune." From the essay "Esprit" in Voltaire's *Dictionnaire Philosophique* (1744).
2 Though the Whig party's political ideology was based on financial reform and a reduction of the power of the crown, in both in Britain and Ireland its support was largely drawn from the social élite.

2. A United Irishmen handbill distributed in 1798. Reprinted in *The Report from the Committee of Secrecy*, appendix XXV

IRISHMEN!

The period is fast approaching, which must fix our destiny. The present rulers of Ireland have extended the system of tyranny and extermination, as far as can be executed, without depriving them of worshippers, and slaves; not satisfied with fleecing the people, and mercilessly exposing them to penury and want, they glut themselves with blood.—

> "See with what heat these dogs of Hell advance,
> To waste and havoc yonder world, so fair
> And good created."[1]

Ah! whence that noise? Cometh it from the spirits of murdered friends, the groans of imprisoned patriots? No; your groans shall not be heard in vain, you shall be revenged—soon shall we hail that auspicious day, ushered in by a bright and cloudless sky, which shall set you free, accompanied by a general shout of *Ireland as it should be.*— Tremble then, thou minister of death; ere that day arrives, fly from a soil which you have cursed by your counsels, which you have polluted by your crimes.

Countrymen,

Be firm: trust in your strength: be united. Before one month passes, you shall be free. Honoured patriots become more respectable by captivity. And you, ye virtuous fugitives, with hearts of sterling worth, be not appalled at the gorgeous show of power exhibited—a few declining suns, and it passeth away, never more to sully our horizon. Be of good comfort, the hearts of the people are with you, and soon shall you receive the marked gratitude of a free people.

We are accused of a predilection for French principles—supposing the fact, who forced them on us? Men who have taken from us that which not enriches them, and makes us poor indeed; usurpers, who exceed in persecution the human sacrifices of former ages. But they mistake; we contend only for Irish rights; and whatever coincidence there be between the rights of Ireland and France, has been

---

1 Slightly misquoted from Milton's *Paradise Lost*, bk. 10, ll.615-17.

established by the God of nature; and who shall impiously disjoin them?

Friends,
Liberty, like the great orb of nature, has its periods of darkness and effulgence; but let us not vainly imagine that what is only contingent, can interrupt the great plan of the Deity, in perfecting the happiness of mankind. We, as a portion of intelligent beings, want not the moral freedom to will, nor the physical power to act. The first is confirmed by our union; and to support our claim to both, half a million of heroes are ready—yes, they only wait the second coming, to commence the millennium of freedom.

And thou, noble-minded youth, whose princely virtues acquire new splendour, from a fervent zeal for your country's rights: oh! may the genius of liberty, ever faithful to its votaries, guard your steps—may the new harp of Erin vibrate its thrilling sounds through the land, to call you forth, and hail you with the angelic cry of the deliverer of our country.

March 27, 1798   A CITIZEN

Select Bibliography and Works Cited

Anon. *Report from the Committee of Secrecy, of the House of Commons in Ireland, as reported by the Right Honourable Lord Viscount Castlereagh, August 21, 1798.* London: J. Debrett and J. Wright, 1798.

Anon. *The Soldier of Pennaflor: or, A Season in Ireland. A Tale of the Eighteenth Century.* 5 vols. Cork: John Connor, and London: A.K. Newman and Co., 1810.

Barrow, Andrew. *The Flesh is Weak: An Intimate History of the Church of England.* London: Hamish Hamilton, 1980.

Barruel, Augustin. *Memoirs, Illustrating the History of Jacobinism. A Translation from the French of the Abbé Barruel.* With a "Note" appended to vol.4. 4 vols. London: Printed for the Author by T. Burton, 1797-98.

Belanger, J. "Some Preliminary Remarks on the Production and Reception of Fiction Relating to Ireland, 1800-1829," *Cardiff Corvey: Reading the Romantic Text* 4 (May 2000). Accessed 10 January 2003, <http://www.cf.ac.uk/encap/corvey/articles/cc04_n02.html>.

Blakey, Dorothy. *The Minerva Press, 1790-1820.* London: Bibliographical Society, 1939.

Brown, Stephen J. *Ireland in Fiction: A Guide to Irish Novels, Tales, Romances and Folklore.* Vol.1. New York: Burt Franklin, 1919.

Brown, Stephen J., and Desmond Clarke. *Ireland in Fiction.* Vol.2. Cork: Royal Carbery Books, 1985.

Butler, Marilyn. *Jane Austen and the War of Ideas.* Oxford: Clarendon, 1975, rpt. 1987.

Carlyle, Thomas. *The French Revolution.* 3 vols. London: James Fraser, 1837; rpt. 2 vols. London: Macmillan, 1900.

Clery, E.J. *The Rise of Supernatural Fiction, 1762-1800.* Cambridge: Cambridge UP, 1995.

Curtin, Nancy J. *The United Irishmen: Popular Politics in Ulster and Dublin 1791-1798.* Oxford: Clarendon Press, 1994.

Dickson, David, Daire Keogh, and Kevin Whelan, eds. *The United Irishmen: Republicanism, Radicalism and Rebellion.* Dublin: Lilliput Press, 1993.

Elliott, Marianne. *Partners in Revolution. The United Irishmen and France.* New Haven and London: Yale UP, 1982.

———. *Wolfe Tone: Prophet of Irish Independence.* New Haven and London: Yale UP, 1989.

Gahan, Daniel J. *People's Rising, 1798.* Dublin: Gill and Macmillan, 1995.

Gallaway, W.F., Jr. "The Conservative Attitude Toward Fiction, 1770-1830," *PMLA* 55 (1940): 1041-59.

Garside, Peter, with Jacqueline Belanger and Anthony Mandal. "Update 1 (April 2000-May 2001)," *The English Novel, 1800-1829.* Accessed 9 January 2003, <http://www.cf.ac.uk.encap/corvey/articles.engnov1.html>.

Garside, Peter. "Popular Fiction and National Tale: The Hidden Origins of Scott's *Waverley*," *Nineteenth-Century Literature* 46 (1991): 30-53.

Godwin, William. *Caleb Williams*, 1794; rpt. Arnold A. Markley and Gary Handwerk, eds. Peterborough, ON: Broadview Press, 2000.

———. *Enquiry Concerning Political Justice, and its influence on Morals and happiness*. 2 vols. London: G.G. and J. Robinson, 1793; 1796 and 1798; and ed. Isaac Kramnick, 1 vol., Harmondsworth: Penguin, 1985.

———. *Memoirs of the Author of A Vindication of the Rights of Woman*. London: J. Johnson and G.G. and J. Robinson, 1798; rpt. Pamela Clemit and Gina Luria Walker, eds. Peterborough, ON: Broadview Press, 2001.

Grafton, Anthony. *Forgers and Critics: Creativity and Duplicity in Western Scholarship*. Princeton: Princeton UP, 1990.

Grenby, M.O. *The Anti-Jacobin Novel: British Conservatism and the French Revolution*. Cambridge: Cambridge UP, 2001.

Hall-Stevenson, John. *The Works of John Hall-Stevenson, Esq.* 3 vols. London: J. Debrett and T. Beckett, 1795.

Hamilton, Elizabeth. *Memoirs of Modern Philosophers*. 3 vols. London: G.G. and J. Robinson, 1800; rpt. Claire Grogan, ed. Peterborough, ON: Broadview Press, 2000.

Hayes, William J. *Tipperary in the Year of Rebellion 1798*. Roscrea: Lisheen Publications, 1998.

Heidler, Joseph Bunn. *The History, from 1700 to 1800, of English Criticism of Prose Fiction*. Urbana, IL: University of Illinois Studies in Language and Literature, 13, 1928.

Hume, David. *Essays and Treatises on Several Subjects. […] Containing Essays, Moral, Political, and Literary. A New Edition. To which are added, Dialogues Concerning Natural Religion*. 2 vols. Edinburgh: Bell and Bradfute, and T. Duncan; and London: T. Cadell, 1793.

Kelly, Gary. *The English Jacobin Novel 1780–1805*. Oxford: Clarendon Press, 1976.

Kelsall, Malcolm. "The Byronic Hero and Revolution in Ireland: The Politics of *Glenarvon*," *The Byron Journal* 9 (1981): 4-19.

Keogh, Daire and Nicholas Furlong, eds. *The Mighty Wave: The 1798 Rebellion in Wexford*. Blackrock, Co. Dublin: Fourcourts Press, 1996.

Lamb, Caroline. *Glenarvon*. 3 vols. London: Henry Colburn, 1816.

Lucas, Charles. *The Castle of St. Donats; or, the History of Jack Smith*. 3 vols. London: Minerva, 1798.

[Maxwell, William Hamilton], *O'Hara; or, 1798*. 2 vols. London: J. Andrews, 1825.

More, Hannah. *Strictures on the Modern System of Female*. 2 vols. London: T. Cadell Jr. and W. Davies, 1799.

O'Dwyer, Martin. *A Biographical Dictionary of Tipperary*. Folk Village, Cashel, Co. Tipperary, 1999.

Pakenham, Thomas. *The Year of Liberty: The History of the Great Irish Rebellion of 1798*. London: Hodder and Stoughton, 1969; rpt. London: Orion, 1992.

Philp, Mark, with Austin Gee. *The Political and Philosophical Writings of William Godwin.* 7 vols. London: William Pickering, 1993.

Playfair, William. *The History of Jacobinism, Its Crimes, Cruelties and Perfidies.* London: John Stockdale, 1795.

Power, Thomas P. *Land, Politics and Society in Eighteenth-Century Tipperary.* Oxford: Clarendon Press, 1993.

Radcliffe, Ann. *The Mysteries of Udolpho.* 4 vols. London: G.G. and J. Robinson, 1794; rpt. Bonamy Dobrée, ed. Oxford: Oxford UP, 1990.

Roberts, J.M. *The Mythology of Secret Societies.* London: Secker and Warburg, 1972.

Robison, John. *Proofs of a Conspiracy against all the Religions and Governments of Europe, carried on in the secret meetings of Free Masons, Illuminati, and Reading Societies.* Edinburgh: William Creech, and London: T. Cadell and W. Davies, 1797.

Rousseau, Jean-Jacques. *The Confessions of J.J. Rousseau: with the Reveries of the Solitary Walker. Translated from the French.* 2 vols. London: J. Bew, 1783.

Taylor, John Tinnon. *Early Opposition to the English Novel. The Popular Reaction from 1760 to 1830.* Morningside Heights, NY: King's Crown Press, 1943.

Thrale, Mary, ed. *Selections from the Papers of the London Corresponding Society 1792-1799.* Cambridge: Cambridge UP, 1983.

Tillyard, Stella. *Citizen Lord. Edward Fitzgerald, 1763-1798.* London: Chatto and Windus, 1997.

Trumpener, Katie. *Bardic Nationalism: The Romantic Novel and the British Empire.* New Jersey: Princeton UP, 1997.

Walker, George. *The Vagabond. A Novel.* 3rd ed. 2 vols. London: G. Walker, 1799.

Watson, Nicola J. *Revolution and the Form of the British Novel 1790-1825: Intercepted Letters, Interrupted Seductions.* Oxford: Clarendon Press, 1994.

Watt, James. *Contesting the Gothic: Fiction, Genre and Cultural Conflict, 1764-1832.* Cambridge: Cambridge UP, 1999.

Watt, Robert. *Bibliotheca Britannica; or A General Index to British and Foreign Literature.* 4 vols. Edinburgh: Archibald Constable and Company, 1824.

Whelan, Kevin. *The Tree of Liberty: Radicalism, Catholicism and the Construction of the Irish Identity, 1760-1830.* Cork: U of Cork P, 1996.